Clementine Camille

Clementine Camille

Volume One
An American Romance

By
Ronald John Vierling

Advantage™

Published by Advantage, Charleston, South Carolina.
Member of Advantage Media Group.

ADVANTAGE is a registered trademark and the
Advantage colophon is a trademark of Advantage Media Group, Inc.

Printed in the United States of America

ISBN: 1-59932-004-5

Cover Design and Interior Layout by Carla Holzer
Cover Photo supplied by Lisa Surles

For Lisa Surles

Part One

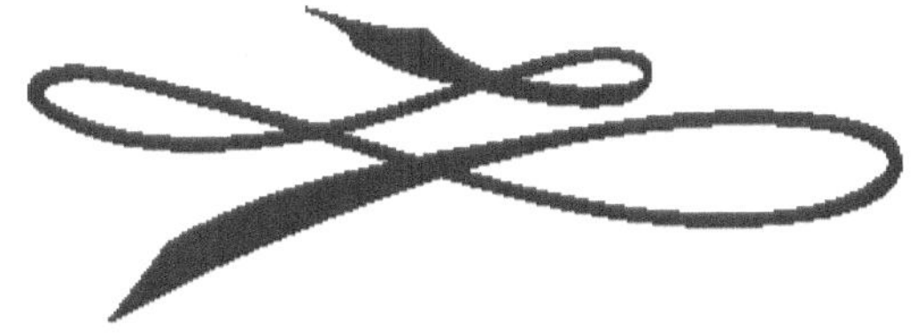

She is beautiful, whole and free.

Alice Walker
"Beauty"

1

I did not intend to write a memoir. I had no reason to ever think that I would ever do so. I teach history. I've never been concerned about writing anything personal. I've been too busy living with Clementine, loving Clementine, raising our two wonderful daughters to ever consider writing anything even remotely like a memoir. Then something happened during Hurricane Max in 2002 that made me realize once again that there is more to my life with Clementine than how much I love her tenderness and respect her strength and admire her generosity.

I don't mean anything tragic happened. No one was injured during the storm. No one died. At least, not any of the four of us. But something important did happen during the two days and one night when the four of us took refuge in a middle school just outside of Columbia, South Carolina, for that was when we met Arnold and his wife Marie, who are from Australia. Please don't jump to the wrong conclusion. Both Arnold and Marie were very kind to Clementine and me and our six year old twin daughters, Josephine and Abigail, when we very much needed someone to be kind to us just as I hope we were kind to them. No, what is important is what happened when Arnold and I began to talk.

As people do under those kinds of worrisome circumstances, Arnold and I started to talk to pass the time even as the hurricane howled past the gymnasium to which we and hundreds of other people had fled for shelter. I explained that we had spent the weekend in Charleston but had left when we were told the Hurricane, which at first had been predicted to make landfall just north of Jacksonville, Florida, would now come ashore somewhere along the South Carolina coast between Beaufort and Georgetown. So we drove to Columbia, from where we intended to drive home to Augusta on Interstate 20. Then we were warned that the hurricane was moving inland faster than the authorities had expected and that we should seek immediate shelter. So we did.

Over cups of coffee, Arnold and I talked about a variety of things, from politics to travel experiences, during which I mentioned that I taught history at Augusta State University. At that point, Arnold asked if I had ever heard of what the Australians term the Stolen Generation of Aborigine Children. I said I had heard the term, but I didn't know anything specific about what it meant. That prompted an abbreviated description of the social policy the Australian government forced on the Aboriginal people, which led to Arnold saying, "You might want to find out more about the topic, Professor, because it was much more than just a terrible cultural injustice." When I asked him what he meant, he said that the policy resulted in the forced removal of thousands of Aborigine children from their homes between 1900 and 1972. "The politicians said the objective of the policy was to re-educate the students so they might more easily make their ways in Caucasian society."

Then Arnold looked at me and then at Clementine and then at our daughters—he said all three were very handsome—and added with a private sort of smile, "Perhaps you should investigate the policy yourself. You might find it particularly interesting in view of your own personal life."

I asked Arnold what he meant, but the only thing he would say was, "There was something much more sinister at the heart of the policy than just education, Professor Raymond." Just as I was about to ask him to tell me more, the storm suddenly grew louder, so

Arnold turned back to his wife Marie in the same way I turned back to Clementine and our daughters who were trying to go to sleep on the blankets the Red Cross had provided.

As I now look back on that conversation, I still do not think Arnold intended to draw a parallel between the Australian racial policy and my life with Clementine and our daughters. But later that night, with the wind howling too loudly for us to sleep, Clementine let me know in her own way that she was offended not only by his references to the Australian racial policy—and she knew far more about it than I did—but by what she considered Arnold's telling glances.

As we lay together under our blankets, I asked what she meant. Clementine said she knew about Australia's Aboriginal population and its continuing struggle for civil rights. Then she rolled over and pressed her face against my shoulder and said in a whisper, "I did not marry you, Tyler, because you are a white man, and I did not marry you so our daughters could be more white than black." I replied that I knew that.

"We've had this conversation before, Clementine," I said. "We don't need to have it again," I said.

Clementine raised her head and looked at me in the dark. "But you know that's what Arnold was thinking. He looked at Josephine and Abigail, and he looked at my light skin, and you know that's what he was thinking."

"It doesn't matter what he was thinking. You and I have been through all of this since the beginning. Since we first fell in love. It doesn't matter what he meant," I whispered. "Besides," I said, "I don't see how the Australian policy has any reference to us."

Clementine put her left arm around my waist. "Then you should go look it up," she said. "Because he was right about one thing. The policy wasn't just about taking Aboriginal children out of their culture and turning them into imitation white people. It was much worse than that." Then she pressed her face against my shoulder again. "So go find out about it," she said. "Then come tell me what you think." At that point, I could tell from her tone of voice that she was finished talking.

The storm cleared the next day so we were able to drive back to Augusta and our home. The next morning, I went to the University library as soon as it opened and started what turned into six weeks of reading. And while this memoir is not the story of Australia's policies—that is a task other historians must complete—I now understand that talking with Arnold, and seeing the degree to which my wife was offended by what she still maintains were inferences about our daughters, was the beginning of what I am now intent on trying to achieve in this manuscript. So if my very good friends in the English Department are right—that every story has a once upon a time, and every once upon a time has a *because*—then Clementine's and my meeting Arnold and Marie Howell is the *because* for this memoir. However, all of that is getting ahead of my story. You will have to bear with me as I go back and tell you the whole story from the beginning.

2

I met Clementine the second day of class in the fall of our ninth grade year. We were both enrolled in Mrs. Justine's biology class. On the second day, we were told to choose lab partners. While a number of the students apparently knew each other from middle school, my family had only moved to Tampa from Cleveland that previous summer, so I didn't know anyone. After a moment, it was obvious that the girl sitting next to me didn't know anyone either. When she turned to me and said, "Should we be partners?" I certainly wasn't going to say no. When she held out her hand to shake mine and said, "My name is Clementine. What's yours?" and I replied, "Tyler," I knew I didn't want to refuse. Besides, I wouldn't have refused anyway. That's not the way my mother and grandfather had raised me. After all, Clementine had been gracious enough to ask me to be her lab partner, and she had been courteous enough to introduce herself. It was only right that I shake her hand in return and become her partner. It certainly didn't matter to me what other students might have thought. It was biology, after all, a class in which I had little interest and even less innate skill, so my hope was that Clementine was a good science student.

Now, I realize that my comment "It certainly didn't matter to me what other students might have thought" needs an explanation. I don't want to leave anything important unsaid or unexplained.

Tampa Coast High School was then and is now racially mixed. In the fall of 1980, perhaps thirty percent of the student body was black, twenty percent Hispanic, and fifty percent white. Even then, that was somewhat unusual, especially in Tampa, because it meant that the area the school served was also racially mixed. Coming from Cleveland, that did not seem odd to me. Looking back years later after I learned more about Tampa, I can now see that the racial makeup of the school, while it was not the city wide norm at the time, was a precursor of what was to come.

More to the point, in the case of Mrs. Justine's biology class, Clementine was only one of five black students in the section. Two other black girls were obviously friends, so they immediately became partners. One black boy, William, seemed to know everyone, so he was picked immediately by the white boy sitting next to him. Another black girl was sitting across the room, but she was picked by one of the three Hispanic girls in the class. The rest of us were white. All of which left Clementine, who was sitting next to me, with no other black student close by, so in her own shy way she chose me, a decision we have talked about over the years, a decision for which I am most thankful, for it is not an exaggeration to say her shy question—"Should we be partners?"—changed my life.

I am not suggesting that there was anything dramatic about her question. At the time, I assumed it was prompted by necessity. I mean, we were not only sitting in the last row of lab tables closest to the classroom door, we were sitting in the last two seats facing the front of the room. Unless she got up and moved around as some of the other students did, she had no option but to ask me to become her partner. In any case, that was the beginning.

Jump ahead to the cafeteria two days later. I am beginning to make friends because I have signed up for junior varsity football, which logically means that when I go to lunch I will see guys with whom I had started practicing. But that was not the case. First, the cafeteria at Tampa Coast is a very large room; second, while I could see three of the other members of the junior varsity team across the room, I had to get into the lunch line as quickly as possible if I wanted to eat at all. So I certainly wasn't going to be eating with them.

After a few minutes as I began moving through the line and selecting what I wanted to eat, I heard Clementine selecting her food. When I turned and made some comment about how hard it was to buy a lunch and actually have time to eat because the cafeteria was crowded with sophomores in line ahead of us, she agreed. Then as we each paid for our food and stepped back out into the lunch room and looked around for places to sit, she nodded towards a table where two people were getting up and said, "There're two places," which meant we ended up sitting across from each other as we ate, which also meant that we began to talk.

I would really like to say that our conversation the first time we ate together was profound and memorable, but that would not be the truth. We were fifteen, after all. I don't think many fifteen-year-olds have many profound things to say. Yes, we had sat next to each other in biology class for two days, but like all of the other students, we had not dared to speak to each other or anyone else about anything not related to biology, for Mrs. Justine's reputation for being strict had been passed on by sophomores to freshmen the first day of school. So this was the first time we had spoken to each other about anything other than what pages to read in the text and what information to prepare for the first quiz, which was coming on Friday. What I remember is that as we ate our hurried lunches, we talked about our families and how both of us had just moved to Tampa that summer. I think the fact we were both new to the school made each of us feel more comfortable with the other. If you've ever been the new student at a school you will know what I mean.

Clementine's mother, who was a social history professor, had joined the faculty at the University of South Florida after having taught at Rutgers University, in New Jersey, for six years. I said that was ironic because my grandfather, with whom my mother and I lived, was a retired history professor from Cleveland State University, and my mother taught fifth grade social studies at the Robert Roripaugh Elementary School, which was only five blocks away from Tampa Coast High School. Given the length of the lunch period, I don't think we had a chance to say much more except to exchange information about which English teacher we each had and what books we had to read and which World History section we were in, because we were not in any classes together except biology.

3

It is important that I say something here about my family. When we moved to Tampa, my mother was a widow. My father, Robert Raymond, an army captain and a pilot, had died in Viet Nam in 1970 when his helicopter was shot down, leaving my mother to raise me by herself. A month after his military funeral, which I do not remember, of course, because I was only three, my mother moved us into the house my grandfather owned near the Cleveland State University campus where we lived while she went back to school to earn her master's degree so she could earn more money. When my grandfather retired and said he wanted to move to Tampa, Florida, he invited my mother and me to come along.

My mother had some social life in Cleveland, because I remember two men who took her to movies, one of whom proposed marriage, but she turned him down, saying that she was still too much in love with my father to marry at that time. It was a subject I heard her discussing with my grandfather one night very late when I was feverish and could not sleep and came into the kitchen when they did not think I was awake. My grandfather urged my mother to not bury herself in the past, which was odd advice coming from him since, as my mother retorted, "You never expressed any interest in getting married after mother died, Dad, and you were only fifty at the time." From what I remember, that both ended the conversation and closed the topic.

I do not mean to suggest that either my grandfather or my mother were morose or melancholy or in any way hostile towards each other or each other's situation. They were not. Both had wonderful senses of humor, both were realistic about life, both were very good to me in every way a mother and grandfather can and should be good to a son and grandson. It was simply that each had loved, each had married an adored partner, each partner had died. Life went on. The move to Tampa was as dramatic a change as either was prepared to make at the time.

So there I was, newly turned fifteen years old, new to Tampa Coast High School, a new member of the junior varsity football team. After tryouts and a week of practices, I was given a playbook and told I would be the second string right split end. When I brought the book home that first evening, my grandfather, who had been a very good athlete in his own right—he played left guard and linebacker at his high school in Omaha, Nebraska, decades before—sat down with me and started helping me memorize my assignments. Both of us enjoyed our times together at the kitchen table; both of us enjoyed going to the park on Saturday mornings so I could run the routes I was told I must learn while he threw the football.

The reason I am telling you about my first year on the junior varsity football team is not because I was a particularly good player, at least not that year, but because of something that happened during and after our first game.

I was not in the starting line-up, so after the initial excitement of being on the sidelines while others played, at least for the first quarter, I had time to turn around and look at who had come to the game. As you might expect, the crowd was sparse. A few parents. A few school friends. I even remember two teachers sitting in the top row of the bleachers. Because my mother was still at school, she had not been able to come, but my grandfather was there, and so was Clementine. I saw him first. Then I saw her. She didn't wave to me, and I didn't wave to her, but I could tell she was watching me.

After half time, with Tampa Coast winning by two touchdowns, the offensive coach put me in for a series of plays. One of my routes was called on the second play. I lined up the way I was supposed to line up. When the ball was snapped, I ran down field fifteen yards and turned back to face the quarterback, only to see the ball sail high over my head and go out of bounds.

When I returned to the huddle no one said anything. All of us were too excited to blame anyone or praise anyone. We punted two downs later. But I was sent in again when we got the ball back, and this time, when I ran my route fifteen yards straight down the sidelines, the ball arrived just as I turned my head. More a matter of reaction than intent, I caught the ball and ran another five yards before two players tackled me.

Like most American boys, I had grown up watching football on television, and I had played tackle football in the yard with friends, but I have to admit the first real tackle by two boys my own age who had been very well trained was a shock. The only reason I didn't drop the ball is because when they tackled me I went to the ground and landed on the ball at the same time they landed on me. Lying there under them, I wondered if I was ever going to breathe again. Then a teammate reached down and pulled me to my feet, and I trotted back to the huddle, trying very hard to act as if being tackled had not hurt.

I caught one more ball that afternoon but dropped one that might have led to a touchdown. When it was all over, as I cheered along with my teammates, I was glad I was there. Tampa had become home. Tampa Coast was my high school. What happened next was even more important.

Because we had played on our own campus, we players and our coaches walked back towards the gym and the locker room together. As we did, we were joined by family members and friends. I was walking with my grandfather, who was as excited as I was, although as we walked together he said very little except that I had run good routes, when I realized that Clementine was also walking next to me. When I turned to say something, she smiled and said, “You played very well, Tyler.” I was startled. Not because I was unhappy or embarrassed. I was very proud she was there. “I remember you said you had a game today, so I asked my mother if I could stay,” she said as the three of us stopped walking for a moment. Then my grandfather smiled and said, “Are you going to introduce me to your friend, Tyler?” So I turned to my grandfather and said, “Yes, Grandpa. This is Clementine Brown. She’s my lab partner in biology.”

Always gracious and sincere, my grandfather replied that he was very happy to make Clementine’s acquaintance, to which Clementine responded in the same way she had when we first met in class, and the two of them shook hands. Then they walked with me to the locker room entrance, and I went in. When I came out a few minutes later, having hurried through my shower as quickly as I could in the hope that Clementine would still be there, I saw she was gone. My grandfather said he had offered to drive her home, but she’d arranged that her mother would come get her.

That was Thursday afternoon. My grandfather and I talked about the game as we drove home, and he told my mother how well I had played when she got home, and even though he exaggerated some, what he said made me feel very good. He did not say anything about Clementine except to mention that a number of students had come to support the team and that I seemed to be making nice friends.

On Friday, as I hurried to biology class, I was very much aware that my eagerness had nothing to do with the subject and everything to do with my lab partner. Clementine was simply the most polite person I had ever met. She was more intelligent than me, at least in biology, and she was pretty. I had seen that the first day when she asked me to be her lab partner, and I had seen it even more when we had eaten lunch together, but as the days went by, and particularly when she had walked next to me after the football game, I became very aware of how pretty she was, how delicate her features were, of how smooth and pale her skin was, of how her long hair seemed to curl down around her shoulders in a way the hair of the other black girls in class did not. I could not help but wonder why, although, naturally, it was not something I was going to ask about, at least, not right then. However, the subject did come up later, indirectly at least, when we sat together and ate hamburgers after having gone to a movie together.

4

I have never been very good at making new friends. That is not to say that I did not have friends in Cleveland, because I did. After all, we lived in the same neighborhood for years. It was only natural that I would have friends from school. But that had happened over a number of years. In Tampa, it was a different matter. Most of the other students seemed to know each other from middle school. Other students who were new seemed to fit in rather quickly. I found that harder to do. I'm not sure why. Maybe because I'm so close to my mother and grandfather. Maybe because I tend to be somewhat shy. I don't know. I never did know for sure. I was just never very good at speaking up, I suppose. In any case, during class on Friday, I told Clementine that I was going to go to a movie on Saturday night. I think I surprised myself when I said that, because it wasn't something that I had planned to do. But sitting next to Clementine as we gathered up our books and backpacks to leave, I knew I wanted to go to a movie with her. When I asked if she would like to go with me, she asked me which movie I was going to see. That startled me because I had no idea. I remember saying quickly, "Any one you would like to see."

That made Clementine smile, and I knew that she knew I had not even planned to go to a movie until I saw how pretty she was that day. When she replied and told me that she wanted to see "All that Jazz," the movie about the Broadway choreographer Bob Fosse, I said that sounded great, although I wasn't sure that I had heard of Bob Fosse. Then she added that she would have to ask her mother, and I said I understood, not explaining that I would have to do the same. As we walked into the hallway and then to the lunch room, where we ate together again, the first time we had done so since that first time weeks before, she said she should give me her telephone number so I could call to see if her mother had given her permission to go. With that she wrote down her number, and we left each other to go to our afternoon classes.

I would like to say that everything went smoothly at Tampa Coast High School, that the fact Clementine was a black girl and I was a white boy did not ever cause any comments, but that would not be true. Although it did not happen very often, there were times when it was obvious our relationship was not looked on favorably. The first time was that afternoon at football practice.

Because the varsity team was going to play that evening, the junior varsity had a short practice. As we were dressing out, Timmy O'Brien, who played on the defensive line, and who was probably twenty pounds heavier than me and inclined to talk too much all of the time, said something about my *dark* girlfriend. We were dressing in the locker room, which was noisy, and I didn't hear him at first. That only provoked him, so he made his comment even louder. When he did, the locker room became very quiet. For a moment, I didn't have the slightest idea of what to say or what to do. I certainly didn't want to get into a fight, not only because I might get into trouble, but because I assumed Timmy O'Brien was probably a better fighter than me. So when I turned and looked at him but did not say anything, he just smiled in a really snotty way and brushed passed me. Because he was already in his uniform, his shoulder pads pushed me back a step until I fell against the locker. Regaining my balance, I was just about ready to say something, although for the life of me I cannot imagine today what it might have been, when another player, Edward Crooms, who was black, turned to me and said, "Don't worry about it, Tyler. Timmy's a real fat jerk." Edward raised his voice loud enough to be sure that Timmy heard him say, "Timmy's a real fat jerk." When Timmy turned back to see who had spoken, I could see that he thought he would have a chance to fight someone, but he was surprised it was Edward who had spoken. It was also obvious he was afraid. So he turned and went on out onto the field.

That day at practice, I had to line up opposite Timmy once, and I thought I heard him say something about "dark meat," but I could not be sure. I decided that Timmy O'Brien was not worth getting into trouble for. Besides, I did not want Clementine to ever hear that someone had said something like that. If I responded and got into a fight, the coaches would find out why, and then so would everyone in ninth grade. I had never felt that way before because I had not ever faced that kind of an insult. My face felt red not just because of what Timmy O'Brien had said but because I had not known what to do in response. It was the first lesson in what has proven to be a lifetime of learning about such things.

5

When I got home that night, I asked my mother if I could go to a movie on Saturday night with a friend. When she wanted to know with whom, I told her Clementine Brown. She smiled in the way that mothers smile when a fifteen year old son wants to go to a movie for the first time with a girl and said something about my having to pay for both of us. I said I had enough money. Then my grandfather, who was reading the newspaper at the kitchen table, spoke up and said he had met Clementine at the football game that she seemed like a very nice girl. "She even shook hands with me, Elizabeth. And she was the one who made the gesture."

My mother has always been impressed with people who are polite if she also senses that they are sincere. I told her that I had to call Clementine to see if her mother would give her permission. I think that impressed her as well. I saw my mother glance at my grandfather, and I saw that he smiled and then looked away, which was his way of giving my mother permission to give me permission without him seeming to interfere. With that, I called Clementine, and she said, yes, she had been given permission. Of course, the next matter to settle was getting to the shopping mall, which was too far away for us to walk. When I asked my grandfather if he would drive us to and from the movie, my mother very quickly said she would do so. I returned to the telephone and told Clementine what my mother had said. Then a very odd thing happened; at least, it seemed odd to me at the time. Now that I have two daughters of my own, it does not seem out of the ordinary.

In any case, Clementine said it was fine for my mother to bring me to her house, but that her mother would then drive us to the movie and then drive me home afterwards. I said that was fine. When I told my mother what Clementine's mother had said, my mother seemed puzzled but appreciative. "I'm sure Clementine's mother is just being cautious," she said. "And that way we can meet each other," she went on.

I am not sure why, but for a moment my heart sank, which is not the truth, of course. I did know why. I knew exactly why.

Now please understand, I had never heard either my mother or my grandfather ever make a racially derogatory remark about anyone. Why should I be afraid of what my mother might think when she saw that I was going to a movie with a black girl? Perhaps I sensed that what people say and what they think are sometimes two different things. Certainly there must have been students and maybe even some teachers who had seen me with Clementine in the lunch room at Tampa Coast who did not approve of us keeping company in that way, but no one other than fat Timmy O'Brien had ever said anything. In fact, on that one occasion when Timmy had said something, it was a black teammate who had told me not to worry. But I did worry. I should not have, but I did.

6

The United States is a racially diverse nation. That is not particularly unusual today. Many nations are racially diverse, although I dare say none quite so much as America. The issue is how did this country become so racially diverse? That is the factor that shapes the American consciousness. For our history of racial diversity did not come about without ethnic pain, without moral violations, without suffering and death. It follows, therefore, that at present there are conflicting points of view that dominate race relations.

First, and most reprehensible, are those who measure an individual's worth as emblematic of the negative stereotype of that person's race. For those folks, diversity means division. Second, there are those who acknowledge that what they perceive as racial differences are simply always going to be a part of the common culture of the United States, even if they are too polite to say so. For those folks, diversity frequently equates to unstated resentment masquerading as tolerance. Third, there are those who understand that race cannot be ignored—talking face to face with a person of a different skin color cannot *not* be acknowledged; however, they make every effort to fend off the negative stereotypes in an effort to accord every racial group its just due. For those folks, diversity lies at the heart of the nation's collective consciousness and conscience. Acknowledging the precarious nature of race relations in America is, for those people, very much a part of our strength of moral character and moral purpose. Of course, those are all things I decided later, when I was more grown up. They are not definitions I could have said when I was fifteen.

When I walked to Clementine's front door with my mother, I felt as if my heart was in my throat. I cared about Clementine. She was witty and graceful, even if at that point in my life I might not have used those terms. I would probably have said she was pretty and nice and let that be enough. At the same time, I knew my mother was a political liberal; I did not have to fear she would somehow disapprove of the fact that Clementine was a black girl. Perhaps what I feared was simply a fifteen year old boy's hesitation to have his mother meet the first girl to whom he felt attracted. Perhaps what I feared most was Clementine's mother. What would she think of white me? What would she think of my white mother? Clementine had never once mentioned her race or my race. From all she had said in class and at lunch and after the football game, she liked me. She was certainly easy to talk to, and for me that mattered a great deal, not just because I was new to the school but because I am, I feared even then, too introspective for my own good, too sensitive for my own ease, too inclined to silence when I probably should be more assertive. Clementine's shy smile and easy humor had put me more at my ease than I had ever been in my life. Yet standing on that porch as my mother rang the doorbell, completely unprepared for the fact that no matter if Clementine or her mother answered the door, my mother was going to be looking at a black person, did little to give me any sense of confidence. Ironically, I should have had more faith in my mother. For both my grandfather and my mother were people of their word. They believed in the liberal political and social and cultural ideal of a racially diverse nation. They believed in the notion that each group makes its own important contribution to the common mix, and that each of us grows in relation to our relations with people who are not just like ourselves. But I was still fifteen, and I could not have articulated those sentiments. As aware as I was of my mother's ideals, ideals she had passed along to me, when I sat with Clementine at lunch talking and laughing, I knew perfectly well that I was looking at a beautiful young black girl just as, I assumed, she knew perfectly well, no matter her obvious pleasure in talking with me, that she was talking to a nice looking and polite white boy.

The doorbell rang. I heard music being turned down. Then the door opened. It was Clementine. She was dressed like me—casual but nice. Her slacks were tailored, her blouse maroon silk with small white flowers, her hair drawn back and accented with a white ribbon that complemented her blouse and dark blue slacks. For a moment, I could think of nothing but how pretty she looked. In fact, all I could think of was that she was the most beautiful girl I had ever seen in my life. Next, of course, I glanced at my mother. What was she thinking? Clementine wasn't surprised my mother was white. I mean, it stood to reason. But my mother . . . what was she thinking? Praise be. Her face said nothing about surprise. She simply smiled her very best smile as Clementine opened the door, and I stepped back as I had been taught and let my mother enter first. Then I followed.

Before I had a chance to introduce my mother to Clementine and vice versa, they had taken care of the honors, Clementine doing as she had with me and my grandfather—extending her hand and shaking my mother's hand as they each said how happy they were to meet the other. My mother added that I had told her many good things about Clementine, which was not true, save to say she was my biology lab partner and that she was smart, which I had said. Clementine said the same thing to my mother, which was more accurate, for I had explained that my father had been killed in Viet Nam and that my grandfather was a retired professor and that my mother was a sixth grade teacher. But not much more. Certainly not anything about personal feelings or how we got along or why my mother had never remarried.

Then Clementine's mother came into the room. I must admit I was thunderstruck. First, she was a tall and slim woman, every bit as beautiful as Clementine but in a more mature way. Second, she smiled broadly and stepped toward my mother and offered her hand in the same way my mother offered hers. As she spoke to my mother, saying, "Clementine has told me about Tyler. She says he's both a good student and good athlete," I stepped toward Clementine's mother and extended my hand, which she accepted. My mother then thanked Clementine's mother, who had introduced herself as Ruth Ann Brown, and added that I had told her how thankful I was to have Clementine as a biology lab partner since science was not my strongest subject, which was absolutely true—I had said I was glad Clementine was my lab partner. However, I had told her almost nothing else. In fact, I suddenly wondered if my mother had talked to my grandfather. Perhaps that is why she did not seem surprised that Clementine and her mother were black. Of course, it was also a subject I knew I was never going to bring up. I had learned that as a very small boy when I saw my mother sitting alone in her room and crying; sometimes, it is best to just let things be what they will be.

Then as we should have expected from our mothers, who I could see were really very much alike, they agreed we could see "All that Jazz" because Clementine had grown up going to Broadway musicals. My mother agreed it would be a good cultural experience. "Better than some action film," she said.

Ruth Ann Brown added that she would be happy to pick us up and bring me home. When she said that, my mother offered to take us to the shopping mall. At that point, what I had thought was going to be the transportation arrangement was now changed, and it was agreed that my mother would take us to the mall, and Clementine's mother would pick us up. I am pretty sure my face must have said to Clementine, well, so far so good, because that's what I swear I saw in her expression.

The ride to the shopping mall movie complex was quiet. I remember very little that was said. I opened the door for Clementine so she could sit in front with my mother. Then I got in the back. I remember that my mother and Clementine spoke to one another. Neither of them seemed particularly interested in me, which was another thing I decided I would not tempt by interjecting anything into the conversation.

Because we had agreed to call Clementine's mother when we got out of the movie, my mother let us out in the full confidence that we knew what we were doing. In that regard, she was correct. In every other matter, she could not have been more wrong. There was no way I was not aware of Clementine's race as we went into the shopping mall. From the way more than one black person glanced at us, Clementine must have been just as self conscious. But I swore to myself that nothing was going to get in our way. I really liked Clementine. This was the first time I had ever gone anywhere like this with a girl on my own. In fact, I couldn't even remember if I had ever gone anyplace socially with even a girl in a group. More than anything in the world that evening, I wanted Clementine to know that I cared about her. I mean, I knew full well by then as we walked through the mall past department stores and smaller shops and through the crowd that was gathering in the ticket line in front of the theatre that this girl was very special. I wanted her to think of me in the same way.

7

In the years since that first time we went to our first movie together, we have gone to hundreds of more films, dozens of operas and plays, and more art museums than I can remember. But this was the first time we had ever been with one another away from school. Because of my grandfather's taste in music, I had been raised listening to Mozart and Verdi at home. Clementine said she had grown up listening to the Saturday afternoon radio broadcasts from the Metropolitan Opera from New York City. What we realized as we walked toward the movie theatre was that our musical upbringings would be hard to explain at school. Neither of us felt as if we were weird, but we were not at all confident that our classmates, with a few exceptions, perhaps, would have understood why we liked that kind of music. I commented that I didn't think many of my football teammates would know much about Mozart. Clementine added that she also listened to jazz because her mother had worked her way through college singing with a small combo. As you might expect, each of us was encouraged by the other's response.

While we were waiting in line, we saw a number of our school friends. Most of them were in groups of four or five. A few were paired off into couples. I was not sure how Clementine might feel about being seen with me. I didn't say anything because I was very proud to be with her. I mean, who would not want to be with an attractive, intelligent, funny girl who knew how to talk about serious things without sounding as if she was trying to impress anyone. I decided Clementine was the most natural person I'd ever known.

Once we sat down and began watching the film, and I don't think any of our friends were in the same theatre, I waited until we finished the box of popcorn that I bought and we each were part way finished with our soft drinks before I very tentatively reached over and took her hand. Of course, I half suspected she would gently pull her hand away, but she did not. I felt encouraged.

When the movie was over, I asked Clementine if she would like something to eat. She said she didn't need anything, but she would like to sit someplace and have another soft drink. So we went to the McDonald's restaurant on the outside of the mall where we each ordered another drink and sat together talking, this time about our families.

Clementine said that her mother and father had gotten a divorce when she was six. I did not ask, but she said that her father's father was a black man and her father's mother was a white woman. She said she did not know them very well. She had not visited with her father since she was seven. He had moved away and remarried and had other children, but she didn't know them either. She said she was very close to her mother's parents. "They're wonderful and kind and fun to be with," she said. "I think I get my hair from my father's mother," she said. "I know some of the other black girls don't like it that my hair is long and wavy, and their hair tends to break when they try to grow it out, but it's just my hair, so there's nothing I can do about it."

"I think your hair is pretty," I said, at a loss for anything else to say.

Then she asked about my family. I told her how my grandmother had died not long after I was born. That I was being raised by my mother and grandfather. That both of them expected me to be a good student and go to college. That I never thought about not going to college. Clementine said that because her mother had raised her alone while she was going to college, there was never any question about her going on to a university once she graduated from high school.

At that point, we both found ourselves at a loss for more to discuss. I tried to say something about Cleveland, and Clementine said that living in New Jersey was very different from living in Florida, but she thought she was going to like the change. "We won't be so cold this winter," I said. She agreed, and we both laughed. She told me how her mother took her on the train to New York City to the Metropolitan Museum of Art once every two months and how they went to the Museum of Modern Art every time a new exhibit opened. Clementine said that her mother had wished she could have gone to New York City when she was a girl to see the museums but that her parents had not been interested. "They were too busy trying to raise five children," Clementine said. "My mother isn't critical of them. She understands. It can be hard raising children. She just wanted me to see things that she had read about in school but never seen until she was grown up."

Then I told Clementine about how my mother and grandfather had taken turns driving me to the Cleveland Art Museum for exhibitions. "My grandfather knows a lot about painting," I said. "He wants me to enjoy paintings as much as he does. He even took two of my school friends when I was in sixth grade to a classical music concert at the University where he taught, but afterwards we agreed the friends hadn't enjoyed the music, which he thought was a shame." Clementine and I talked that way for maybe ten more minutes, laughing some, each of us recognizing some of the names of artists that the other knew, when I noticed a woman sitting in a booth across the restaurant with a man her same age. I tried not to look at her, but I could see she was looking at us.

At first, after I realized she was saying something to the man in a way that made me think she was talking about Clementine and me, I tried to look away. I'd never had anyone look at me that way before. It was as if she was angry at something Clementine and I had done, and I knew we hadn't done anything. There were other students in the restaurant, and some of them were being noisy, but we weren't. We were just two fifteen year old high school students talking quietly and drinking cokes and laughing some at funny things. Then I saw the man turn and look over his shoulder at us for a moment. When he turned back to the woman he shook his head. Suddenly, I felt the anger rising in me just as it had when Timmy O'Brien had made his remark in the locker room. I knew what the man was saying. I mean, I didn't really know, but I knew. The woman's face told me what both of them were saying. I decided they must be really stupid people. I didn't look at them again, but I could feel them all the time we sat in the booth. I didn't think Clementine had seen them, and I didn't say anything because I didn't want her to know. I wanted to protect her. It was at that moment that I realized something I had not seen before. I have always been told that I looked older than I am. At least, that was true all through middle school and high school and even in my first years in college. I don't know why. I look in the mirror, and I just see me. But people have been telling me and telling my mother that I looked mature for my age since I was twelve. That is not true of Clementine. When I sat looking at her after I was angry that the two people were sitting across the room scowling at us, I realized that Clementine looked like she was maybe thirteen years old. When I saw that, I mean really saw it for the first time, I was even angrier at the two people. I wanted to protect Clementine from . . . everything. From them. From Timmy O'Brien. From the whole world. Clementine was beautiful and kind and smart and fun to be with. What was wrong with those people? What in the world was wrong with those two stupid people?

I tried not to think about it. I listened to what Clementine was saying about moving to Tampa and how lonely she had been during those first weeks because she didn't know anyone in their neighborhood and school hadn't started yet. "I've always liked school," she said. "But last summer. Last July. I was more ready to be back in school than I have ever been before." I said I understood. It had been the same for me. Then Clementine smiled at me in a way that took my breath away. I could tell she was happy she had met me and happy that we had gone to a movie together and happy that we were sitting together and talking. I could feel my heart beating.

Then it was time to call Clementine's mother so she could pick us up and drive me home. I telephoned from a pay phone next to Sears. We waited inside the mall entrance. When her mother came, we went out to the car and got in, this time both of us sitting in the back seat. As we drove to my house, I wanted so much to hold her hand, but I was afraid she might not want me to, especially with her mother driving and talking to us and looking in the rearview mirror as she did. Then Clementine took my hand. I was surprised, but it was wonderful.

Once we got to my house, I got out of the car and held the front passenger's side door open so Clementine could get in the front seat next to her mother. Then I said goodnight to both of them. After I watched them drive away, I walked to my front porch where my mother was waiting with the door open. Then I went back to my mother, who was waiting for me. "She seems like a very nice girl, Tyler," my mother said as I went in.

I said she was. Then I said, "She likes opera. And jazz. And she's been to the Metropolitan Opera in New York and art museums just like you and Grandpa used to take me to the museum in Cleveland," I said.

"Well, she seems like a very nice girl," my mother said again. "And her mother seems very nice, as well," she said.

"She is," I said quickly. "I mean Clementine. She's very nice. And her mother is nice, too," I said. Then I didn't say anything more, and my mother didn't say anything more, so I went to my room and went to bed without saying any more because I remember

I was afraid to ask my mother the question I really wanted to ask. I would ask it later in the next week, but not that night. I did not want to talk any more about Clementine or her mother or me or anyone else.

8

It's interesting how those first days with Clementine are so clear in my memory. I say that because later, as I try to remember things that happened when we were older, often times the days seem to run together. Yes, some things stand out. Some moments changed my life and her life and our life together. Those incidents certainly stand out. But those first days are as clear as a movie. The next day, for instance, the Sunday after we had gone to the movie together and held hands was a very long day. I watched a football game with my grandfather. The three of us ate dinner. My mother did school work, and I did my homework. I thought Monday would never come. When it did, I hurried to school more excited than I had ever been about going to school before. I didn't see Clementine in the hallway that morning. I worried that she might be home sick or something. Then it was time for biology. When I went into the lab room, she was already at our table. She did not look at me for a moment when I sat down on my lab table stool. Mrs. Justine had started talking. We both took notes. Then Mrs. Justine started explaining what we were going to be doing next. When she paused for a moment, Clementine whispered, "I had a wonderful time at the movie, Tyler."

My heart leaped into my throat. I wanted to tell her that going to the movie with her was the most wonderful thing I had ever done, but I couldn't speak because Mrs. Justine had started explaining the experiment again. As she was handing out our assignment sheets, I turned and whispered under my breath, "I missed you on Sunday."

"You should have telephoned me," Clementine said very quietly.

"I didn't know you wanted me to do that," I said under my breath.

"You should have telephoned me," she said again.

Mrs. Justine passed our desk, looking at us as she did. Oh, God, she knows, I thought to myself. She can see everything I feel about Clementine. But Mrs. Justine just smiled and said, "I assume you two are fine today."

"Yes, Mrs. Justine," I said, almost choking on my words. "We're just fine."

"That's nice," Mrs. Justine said, and I could see everything in her eyes. The whole school knew. The whole world knew. I caught my breath. Well, let them, I thought. Just let them. I don't care who knows what. I just want to be with . . . . Then I felt Clementine pushing my arm with hers. "We have to write things down," she said, pointing at our lab worksheet.

I looked at her and then at the other students, who were bent over the lab tables talking quietly to each other filling in the blanks on their worksheets. So Clementine and I went to work. We had to hurry because before I knew what had happened, the period was over and it was time for lunch.

9

From that day on, for the rest of our high school years together, Clementine and I ate lunch together. The only days we missed were when one of us was not in school or one of us had some sort of activity obligation, because during her sophomore year, Clementine joined the school newspaper staff, and I was elected by my homeroom to the student council so we had meetings maybe three or four times each month that kept us apart. But that day, that first day after our first movie, I remember exactly. I can even remember what each of us ate. More important, I remember what we talked about: our mothers.

Clementine and I have had many really important conversations. We have made decisions that defined the direction of our life together. But that day, that lunch period, what we said mattered more than anything else we ever said afterwards because what we said during what amounted to no more than twenty minutes determined everything that would happen to us for the rest of our lives.

Clementine said she had expected her mother to want to have a conversation about me, she just had not expected it would happen when she got home on Saturday night. She said her mother asked her what she felt for me. She said her mother said that she liked me because I seemed polite, and she liked my mother, because she was obviously a well educated person. When Clementine responded that I was the nicest person she knew, that she liked the fact I was intelligent and serious about school but that I also had a sense of humor, her mother said that was very nice. Then her mother said, "I assume, Clementine, that you are not overlooking the fact that he is white." Clementine said she knew perfectly well that I was white, but because her mother had always told her to judge a person by how that person treats other people and not by race, she did not think it should matter. Her mother then said, as Clementine expected she would, "But the world may not feel that way," which caused Clementine to say, "We are not asking the world to approve of us, mother. We are just trying to be friends."

Her mother then asked if she thought my mother would be concerned that Clementine was black. Clementine said she replied that she did not know what my mother thought because "Tyler has not told me about any conversations he has had with his mother about us."

It was obvious that Clementine wanted to know anything my mother had said to me about her being black and me being white. I was embarrassed because here Clementine and her mother had at least talked about the subject while I had been afraid to talk to my mother. I didn't want to admit that to Clementine so I said, "My mother just said that she thought you were a very nice person, Clementine," which was true. But that wasn't the point. Clementine wanted to know, for the same reason her mother had wanted to know, what my mother thought. I had to admit that my mother and I had not talked about the subject. "I want to ask her, Clementine. I really do want to know what she thinks."

"But you are afraid, aren't you?" Clementine said quickly. "You are afraid of what she might say."

We were trying to finish our lunches. We didn't have much time. "I don't think afraid is the right word," I remember saying. "My mother and my grandfather have never once ever said anything bad about anyone's race. That's the way I was raised."

"But that doesn't answer my question," Clementine said.

"I know it doesn't," I said just as the bell rang ending the lunch period. "But I will. I promise," I said.

"Talk to her?" Clementine asked.

"Yes, talk to her," which I did that night. That is, I talked to my grandfather. I thought that was the best way to approach the subject.

10

You have to understand that my grandfather is a really great man. I know some of my friends think their grandparents are nice and kind and all of that, but I mean more than that. My grandfather taught history at Cleveland State University for the last twenty years of his career. During those years, he saw American society change. He talked about those changes in his classes. He was the first white professor at Cleveland State to talk about black history. The only thing he ever admitted hating was injustice. It was as simple as that. He used to say he was only prejudiced against prejudiced people. From what my mother said, in the 1960s, he upset a number of administrators at Cleveland State who thought his lectures were too extreme. In response, he said he thought their concerns were ludicrous. He said there is never anything extreme about facing up to the truth, and America was and is, he said, a racist nation. "Until we come to grips with that fact, we will never be what we purport to be." My mother said she was very proud of her father. So I thought it would be best to start with him.

I had a hard time figuring out where to begin, but I finally found what I thought was a good moment when I got home from football practice and my grandfather was sitting in the living room reading and my mother was not home from school yet. I know I must have looked a little silly, standing in the doorway that led to the hall, trying to look relaxed, but just standing there for maybe five minutes before my grandfather looked up and said, in that voice of his that tells me he understands what is on my mind even before I say anything, "Is there something you want to say, Tyler?"

I tried to act mature, but at that moment, I knew it was an act. "Well, yes, Grandpa, there is."

"Would you like to sit down and tell me about it?"

"I would. Yes, I would," I said as I came into the room and sat down on the couch across the room from where my grandfather was sitting in his reading chair.

He waited.

"It's about last Saturday night."

"All right."

"Did you say anything to mother about Clementine?"

"Like what, Tyler?"

"Did you tell her that you'd met Clementine after the football game?"

"Yes."

"Did you tell her that before she drove to be Clementine's house or after?"

My grandfather lowered his book to his lap, which was a good sign because it meant he was going to be very candid with me. "Before."

I nodded. "Mother said she thought Clementine was a very nice girl," I said.

"Yes. She told me the same thing when she got back from taking you to Clementine's house. She said she liked Clementine's mother, as well."

I did not go on immediately, so my grandfather did. "But that isn't all you want to know, is it, Tyler?"

"No, sir, it isn't."

"Then why don't you ask me the question you want to ask me."

I swear I could feel my heart pounding in my chest. Then I said, "Did you tell mother that Clementine is black before she took me to Clementine's house?"

"I did not."

"Really?"

"Yes, really."

"Why not?"

"Why should I?"

That stopped me cold. He was right. Given who he was, what he believed, why should he?

"I assumed your mother would notice, Tyler."

"So you didn't warn her?"

"Warn her? Warn her about what?"

"Grandpa . . . "

"Tyler, are you trying to ask me if I think the fact Clementine is black and you are white is a problem?"

"No, sir. Yes, sir." I stumbled over my own words. "I don't know."

"Tyler, which is it? Do you think it is a problem? Or do you think it is not a problem?"

I sat back and took a very long breath. "For us. For Clementine and me . . . we know she's black and I am white. It would be silly to think we didn't know that ourselves. But we don't care. I sure don't care. I know that for sure. I just like her. She is smart and funny. And we can talk about all kinds of things."

"All right."

"All right, what?"

"All right. Just . . . all right. She is smart and funny and you can talk about all kinds of things."

I was silent again, which is something I probably do too much.

"But there is something else on your mind, isn't there."

"Yes, sir."

"You want to know if you should care that the world may not care that she is smart and funny and that you two can talk about all sorts of things."

"Yes, sir," said quickly. Then I stopped again and tried to think of exactly what I wanted to ask him. "I don't want to *not* be friends with Clementine because she is black, Grandpa. That would be terrible. But I also don't want to be friends with her *because* she's black, either."

"Ah," my grandfather said, nodding slowly.

"What does 'Ah' mean, Grandpa?"

"It means you are a very honest young man, and I am proud of you."

"I haven't done anything, yet."

"Yes, you have."

I was puzzled. I didn't understand what he meant. "What am I doing? I'm asking questions, that's all."

"Yes, Tyler. You're asking questions. But the ability to ask the question means you are well on your way to arriving at the answer."

"I'm not sure you're right, Grandpa."

"Well, I am. I think you are well on your way to arriving at the answer."

"If that's true, then why don't I know the answer?"

"Well, why do you care so much?"

"Care so much about what?"

"Care so much about the question. Care so much about the answer. Remember what you said. You don't want to not be friends with Clementine because she is black just as you do not want to be friends with her because she is black."

"Yes. Because either one would be wrong."

"In what way?"

"You know what I mean."

"Yes, I do. But I want you to explain."

I sat back in the chair and tried to think. Then I said, "You and mother taught me to never judge a person by the color of that person's skin. So if I liked Clementine but then didn't let myself be friends with her because she is black, then that would not be right. On the other hand, if I let myself be friends with her because she is black, then that is just as wrong. Both things would insult her."

"That's right. Both things would insult her because both would be racist."

"And I don't want to be racist. Ever."

"Fine. But can you ignore race?"

"Do you mean, can I ever not know she is black?"

"Yes. Can you pretend she is not black? Can she pretend you are not white?"

"I don't see how."

"Then that is your answer."

"What is my answer?"

Grandpa smiled. "Tyler, are there other boys and girls at your school who are couples who are of different races?"

I stopped and thought. "Yes. I've seen some."

"And does it matter?"

"I don't know what you mean."

"Does it seem to matter to the people around them?"

"I don't know. I don't know any of the couples personally, and I don't know the people around them who are their friends."

"All right. Answer this question. Should it matter to their friends?"

"I don't see why. If two people want to be friends, they should be able to be friends."

"What if they fall in love?"

"It's still the same, isn't it?"

"What do you think?"

"I think it should still be the same. It's their business."

"Fine. It's their business. Which means it should only be your business and Clementine's business if you like each other or not. Is that a fair statement?"

"I think so."

"But you have other questions, don't you, Tyler?"

"Yes, I do."

Grandpa waited.

"I have three questions."

"Ask them."

"What does mother think?" I said.

"You'd have to ask her."

That was not what I had wanted to hear although it was what I thought he would say.

"Next question, Tyler," he said.

"What does Clementine's mother think?"

"You can only find that out by talking with her," he said.

"Yes, sir," I said, my tone expressing my hesitation to ask Clementine's mother the question for fear of what she might say. Then I waited. My grandfather did not.

"That's only two questions, Tyler. So there's something else, isn't there? Something has happened."

"Yes. At McDonald's after the movie."

Grandfather waited.

"I saw a woman looking at us. We were sitting in a booth and talking and laughing and drinking cokes and not being loud, but she looked at us, and I could feel her anger."

"Ah," my grandfather said slowly.

"And so did the man sitting with her. She looked at us and said something to him, and then he turned and looked at us and then said something to her."

Grandpa waited.

"I didn't tell Clementine. I didn't want her to know. I didn't want her feelings to be hurt."

Grandpa nodded again. "And you haven't said anything to her about the man and the woman."

"No, sir."

"Are you going to?"

"I don't think so. I don't think she needs to know about things like that. The people are probably stupid anyway."

"Yes, they probably are. At least, when it comes to race they are probably very stupid. Or you and I would think they're stupid. But there is a lesson in what happened, isn't there?"

"A lesson? I don't know what you mean."

"Tyler, if you and Clementine continue to be friends, and it sounds as if you want to, then you will have to accept that you will run into people like the man and the woman again. Maybe many times. What you have to ask yourself is . . . is the friendship worth it?"

"Worth it? Of course it's worth it. Clementine is wonderful. She is fun to be with. She is smart and funny and . . . "

"Yes, she's smart and funny and you can talk about all kinds of things," Grandfather said, interrupting. "You said that. And that's fine. But are you prepared to always . . . and I mean always . . . have to be aware that some people who look at the two of you when you are together may not like it? Because it will always be there, Tyler. Unless society changes a lot more than I think it will change, it will always be there. What you will have to decide . . . what both of you will have to decide is . . . is the friendship worth it?"

I wanted to say, yes, Grandpa, it is. I can't explain why yet, but her friendship is worth everything to me. But I wasn't ready to say that yet.

I leaned forward on the couch and looked at my hands. My fists were clenched. I was thinking about the man and the woman, and my fists were clenched. "I think . . . " I started to say then stopped.

"You think what?" my grandfather asked.

I was ready. "I think Clementine is pretty and smart and funny, and I can talk to her about all kinds of things, and . . . I think that is very important."

My grandfather smiled and picked up his book and went back to his reading. That night, because I just could not make myself wait any longer, I talked with my mother.

11

My mother is a very talented and intelligent woman. She survived the grief of losing a husband she loved profoundly in a war she opposed. What made it even worse was that he had also opposed the war, but he thought it was his duty to serve. After he was killed, she went back to school to earn her master's degree in education. That she was close to her father was fortunate, in that he made everything easier for the two of us as I was growing up, and a tribute to both of them, for together they taught me not just how to use my intellect but how to use my moral compass as I made my way into the complex and often times frustratingly contradictory world. All of that was important to me, especially later when I began to evaluate the way I had been raised. It was not so important to me that evening, however, because at that point in my life I needed to talk to her about what were increasingly intense feelings, increasingly difficult emotions.

I know that many fifteen year olds think they have fallen in love. Most of them would probably reject any suggestion that their feelings would not last through the following school year. I know that at that point I would have done the same. I also understood that there was an even more important issue at stake in my relationship with Clementine, because at that moment, as I went into the kitchen to talk with my mother after dinner, I found myself for the first time thinking the word *relationship* in reference to my feelings for my biology lab partner. I also knew that I was not very good at getting really personal conversations started with my mother. Having watched her battle her own emotions—her lingering grief over my father's death—I did not have a very clear notion as to how I might now start a conversation with my mother about Clementine the person and Clementine the black girl and Clementine my friend. Prompted by my grandfather, I felt I had no choice but to simply plunge in. So after I went into the kitchen and sat down as she was finishing putting dishes in the dish washer, I simply jumped in with a question, "Mother, did Grandpa tell you that Clementine was black before you took me to her house so we could go to the movies, or did you find out when you met her?"

My mother is a cautious woman. She very rarely reacts immediately no matter the circumstances. It is a characteristic I must have inherited from her, because I was told many times growing up that my father was a man of both quick wit and ready passion. It did not surprise me, therefore, that she did not answer the question immediately but turned slowly and smiled, more to herself I thought than at me, and walked to the table and sat down in the opposite chair. "What do you think, Tyler?" she said slowly.

"I don't know. That's why I'm asking you."

"Did you ask your grandfather?"

"I did."

"And he said . . . what?"

"He said to ask you."

"Which you are now doing."

"Yes."

"Well, which do you think?"

"Mom, that's not fair."

"I just thought you might have an opinion. You saw my reaction. What do you think?"

"I . . . I don't think grandpa told you."

"Because of the way I reacted?"

"No. Because that's the way he is."

"Well, you are right. The only thing that he said when he told me he had met her was that she was very polite and seemed very intelligent and that she obviously liked you very much."

"Really?"

"Yes."

I was quiet for a moment.

"Did I conduct myself in a way of which you approve, Tyler, when I met Clementine and her mother?"

"Mother . . . " I started to say, almost laughing.

"No. I mean it. It's important to me. Did I do okay?"

"Mom, you always do okay. You know how to talk to anyone. I know that."

"Well, I liked Clementine. And I liked her mother. She seems very responsible. And since she wasn't wearing a wedding ring, but there was a picture of her with what must have been a husband and I assume Clementine as a little girl, I assume she is either a widow or divorced, so it cannot be easy raising a daughter on her own, which I can understand."

"She is divorced. Clementine told me."

My mother waited.

"What I want to know . . . to ask you . . . ." I stopped. My mother waited. "What both Clementine and I are wondering is . . . does it matter to you that Clementine is black and I am white?"

"Well, first, you are white, my son, because your father and I . . . because you were born of white parents."

"Oh, mom . . . ."

"Second, Clementine is black because her parents are black."

"C'mon, Mom, you know what I mean."

"Well, then third, as you apparently like her and as she apparently likes you, I assume that you two will continue to see each other from time to time until one or both of you wants to stop seeing the other."

"Mom, that's not what I am asking."

"Then what are you asking?"

"Does the black-white thing matter to you?"

"No."

"No?"

"No. What did you think I would say?"

"I don't know."

"Is there something you want me to say?"

"No."

"Then why . . . "

"When we were in McDonald's after the movie," I said, interrupting for fear I would never have the courage to say what followed if I waited, "When we were in McDonald's, there was a woman and a man who kept looking at us and scowling as if they disapproved."

"And?"

"I didn't tell Clementine. I don't think she saw them. I didn't want her feelings to be hurt by people we didn't even know."

"So you are asking me . . . what, Tyler?"

"Should I be concerned? About people like that. Should I be concerned about what people at school might say?"

My mother looked away for several moments.

"I told Grandpa that I didn't want to not be friends with Clementine because she is black, but at the same time I don't want to be friends because she is black."

"Are you asking me if you two . . . Clementine and you . . . can you ever be free of the issue of race? Of your differences?"

"Yes. What people think. What we think."

She was quiet again. "I'll bet I know what your grandfather said. And I'll bet that I'm going to say very much the same thing." She leaned forward and took my right hand and held it in both of hers. "Tyler, affection, individual affection for individual people . . . is what matters more than anything else in the world. You must never let anyone else dictate to you who should matter to you. Never. Only you can know who you care about. Only you must decide." She took my hands in hers. "As for race . . . as for the black-white thing—you two will never be able to act like it is not there. Your skins will tell you different if you do. That would be pretending. But your skin colors are just that . . . skin colors. That is not who a person is. That is not what makes a person grow up and become whatever that person grows up and becomes. I know that some people would argue with me on that, but they are talking about society, about sociology, about something else. I am saying that who you are . . . your talents and your interests and your qualities . . . intelligence and kindness and sympathy . . . that is you. It is not your race. It's you. And those are the things that matter. Intelligence and talents and interests and sympathy."

With that she let go of my hands and sat back and waited.

"Clementine is the most intelligent, funniest, nicest person I've ever met in school, Mom. I told Grandpa that I can talk to her about anything. About all of the things you two have taught me. Music and museums and. . . everything."

My mother smiled. "Well, then it sounds as if you have made a very special friend, Tyler."

I nodded and smiled and said, "I have," which not only ended our conversation about the subject that evening, it ended it forever. In a matter of weeks, my mother would learn to love Clementine the way a mother loves a daughter just as I learned to love her the way a boy learns to love the girl who eventually became his wife, which is not the same as saying that from that day forward Clementine and I never experienced any opposition to or conflicts within our relationship, because that would simply not be the truth. And it certainly is not the same as saying everyone with whom we had contact approved of our relationship, because that was also not true.

12

I don't know what kind of conversation Clementine had with her mother at the same time I was talking with mine. The next day at school she told me that she told her mother that I was going to talk to my mother about the black-white thing. She said her mother had said that she assumed that I would. But Clementine didn't tell me anything more than that. Just that her mother had said, "I assume they will talk about it, Clementine. And I assume you will know eventually what they said." But that is all Clementine would say. And it isn't that I didn't ask her to tell me more, because I did even if I also felt that we were beginning to go ring around the rosy—having conversations and then having conversations about our conversations. I began to fear that it would be very easy to get lost. Of course, that didn't keep me from asking Clementine. But even then, at fifteen, Clementine had the ability to look me straight in the eye, smile her shy smile, and then tell me exactly what she wanted me to know and nothing more. Often times over the years, I have sensed that I was finally getting my question answered, only to figure out later that Clementine had once again said only as much as she was prepared to say and nothing more. It was skill she would perfect during the next twenty years. At the same time, sitting with her in the lunch room at Tampa Coast High School, because her smile was and still is so wonderful, I found it impossible to become angry or frustrated. I suppose that means I was in love with her even at fifteen; certainly it means I have been in love with her ever since.

In any case, my charming Clementine would only say that yes, she had talked to her mother again in more detail, and that, yes, the subject of her being black and me being white had come up, but no, her mother was not going to object to us going to movies or her coming to my football games, and that, yes, both she and her mother liked my mother very much. Then Clementine said that her mother remembered reading one of my grandfather's books when she was in undergraduate school and two more when she was in graduate school, and that she would like to meet him because she had found his writing not only informing but, particularly at the time, courageous in the way it faced up to the history of racism in America. I told Clementine that I would tell my grandfather what her mother had said. I was sure he would be pleased and that he would want to meet her mother.

What mattered as much to both of us, at least at fifteen, was that Clementine's mother had agreed to bring her to the junior varsity football game that following Thursday even though the game was being played at another school. I was very glad about that, of course. I also assumed that my grandfather would come to the game so I hoped that might be a time for him to meet Clementine's mother. That proved to be true.

The game itself was a rather easy victory for Tampa Coast. I played the whole second half. I very quickly saw that the defensive back assigned to me when I split wide could not back up and run and then turn as quickly as I could run at him and then make the cuts I was supposed to make. In addition, because it had rained the day before, the field near the sidelines was slippery, which is always in the favor of the offensive player. That meant that I was able to get open four times. Three times our quarterback got passes to me. I caught three of them, the last one for a touchdown. And even if my score didn't mean anything in terms of our winning the game, because that had already been determined, it meant a great deal to me. After all, by that time I had found my grandfather in the stands, he was sitting with Clementine and her mother. As I stood on the sidelines during the fourth quarter, I could see that my grandfather and Clementine's mother were talking and that she was smiling. I thought that was very promising.

After the game, when the Tampa Coast family members and fans came down onto the track to walk with us back to our bus, the four of us—Clementine and her mother and my grandfather and I—all walked together. As we did, I felt Clementine take my right hand. My hand was pretty dirty, so I quickly pulled it away, but before she could be offended, I wiped it off on my jersey and then took her hand again. So there we were, right out in public, with her mother and my grandfather, walking toward the team school bus, surrounded by teammates and other people, holding hands. I knew it was important. That is, I knew other people were going to see us. But I didn't care. I mean, I cared because I wanted to hold her hand, and I was glad she wanted to hold mine, and I was glad she wanted to do so in front of her mother and my grandfather. Other players were holding their girlfriends' hands. What I didn't care about was if other people approved or not. At that moment, walking with Clementine and not talking because her mother and my grandfather were still talking about some historical thing, but feeling her shoulder touching my arm as we walked side by side, I felt happier than I could ever remember feeling in my whole life. I decided that I not only didn't care if people saw us, I wanted them to see us. What was even more wonderful was that as we got to the bus, my grandfather said that he and Clementine's mother had agreed to meet at Chili's for dinner and that he would telephone my mother so she could join them and that, he assumed, Clementine and I would like to join them as well.

I laughed because that's the way my grandfather always talked. He could make the most ordinary thing seem like a great surprise that you would not dream of missing. Clementine squeezed my hand as she let go and smiled, and I laughed and said, "Yes, Grandpa, we would like that very much." Then I got on the bus and the three of them turned back toward the parking lot.

The bus was noisy on the ride home. Not real noisy, because our coaches didn't ever want us to be rowdy or be too cocky about winning a game. As we rode, I sat next to Marty Markham, a really nice guy. He had played in the first half because he was a very good running back. He didn't say much because that's the way he is, but when we got near the school and players were starting to gather up their gear so they could get off the bus, he turned to me and said, "You'll be a starter very soon, Tyler. You're really good." For me that meant everything. A really nice and really good sixteen year old sophomore starter on the team had just told me, a fifteen year old freshman, that I would be in the starting line up soon. I thanked him, of course, and told him he had played a good game, which was true. In fact, I was so happy about what Marty had said that it didn't even matter to me that as we got off the bus, I saw Timmy O'Brien looking at me and smirking. Of course, smirking was Timmy's usual expression, so I certainly wasn't going to let that bother me. Not at the time, at least. It would be a different matter in just a few days.

13

An hour later, the five of us were sitting at a round table at Chili's Restaurant. Clementine was sitting next to her mother; I was next to Clementine; my mother sat next to me, and my grandfather sat in between my mother and Clementine's mother.

Now, I certainly understand that most fifteen year olds would rather do anything other than have a boy friend or girl friend with them and eat with the couple's parents. That's why, as I sat in the middle of the group, I found myself thinking about why neither Clementine nor I were embarrassed by the situation. First, Clementine had been raised by her mother without her father around, and Clementine had no siblings. That meant she spent most of her time with her mother. When adults spend time talking with children, the children become comfortable being with them. Second, while my grandfather had at that point always been a part of my life, I was fully aware that my mother was raising me without benefit of a husband. And while I spent more time with my grandfather than my mother, because he was retired from teaching, I still spent most of my time with the two of them because, like Clementine, I also don't have any siblings. In fact, while Clementine and her mother spent most of their time together traveling and talking about what they had seen or about other things that mattered to both of them, I spent most of my childhood with my grandfather and mother listening to their adult conversations. What it meant was that Clementine was comfortable with the adults in her life in the same way I was at ease with the adults in my life. Perhaps that was why she seemed so comfortable talking with my grandfather, because that evening—and for the rest of his life—it was the two of them who talked as much as any of us when we gathered as what very quickly became a family.

The meal itself was just a meal. The getting to know each other was what mattered. When I looked at Clementine's mother, I could see Clementine. Yes, her mother was grown up and very striking, as you would expect from a mature woman, and Clementine was only fifteen, and a young looking fifteen year old at that, but no matter; Clementine looked like her mother, and I could see that her mother was a beautiful woman. Of course, Ruth Ann was also a little intimidating, I will admit, partially because she was Clementine's mother and could end our relationship if she wanted, but mostly because she was a strong person, a strong personality. I don't mean she was outspoken or pushy. I just mean that she knew who she was and what she was doing, and she had gotten where she had gotten because she had set goals and worked hard and was very intelligent. Clementine had said that of her when we talked at lunch at school. I could certainly see it was true as we sat at Chili's and ate. I decided Clementine's mother must be really fun to be with. Then, as if to say she agreed with me, before the meal was over, my mother invited Clementine and her mother to our house the following Sunday for dinner. So the whole going out for dinner after the football game idea, even on a school night, was both a good idea and a good experience. Unfortunately, that wasn't the case the following Wednesday at football practice.

14

There are probably lots of foolish people in the world who have foolish notions come into their minds. Even smart people sometimes have really foolish thoughts. But most people, even the foolish ones, also know that it is sometimes best to simply not say what they are thinking. That wasn't the case with Timmy O'Brien.

Please understand that in a racially mixed school, where the students for the most part get along rather well, more so from racial group to racial group than within some racial groups, it just isn't wise to make remarks that insult another person's race. In my four years at Tampa Coast, I saw three fights, and all of them started because some one of one race said something insulting to some one of another race, and whether or not the remark was intended to be racist, the fight always turned into a racial incident.

Timmy O'Brien is white. He was bigger than me. He was also probably stronger than me. But he wasn't smarter than me. I don't think anyone who knew the two of us would argue with that statement.

The problem had come up before, of course. Twice he had made stupid remarks to me about Clementine being black. When we got to the practice field on Wednesday and were running drills, he made a third. For me, that was one too many.

I found myself that day playing with the first string offense just as Marty Markham had predicted. On one particular play, I was put in the tight end's place on the line of scrimmage. And who did I line up against? Timmy O'Brien, a defensive tackle. That's how it started.

The first two times we ran the play, I was able to do what I was supposed to do—block Timmy quickly then release and go out into the flat where I was the second receiver option for the quarterback.

From the expression on his face, Timmy must have been surprised that I was able to block him and then get loose the first time we ran the play, because when we ran it a second time, he tried to grab my jersey, but I got free because Coach Fiorini had shown me how to lower my shoulder and then use my elbow to push his arm away. When I did that, Timmy swore under his breath.

Twenty minutes later, we lined up and got ready to run the same play. This time, Timmy got down in his stance and whispered, "You won't beat me this time, you asshole."

I was a little surprised because our coaches didn't allow swearing on the field, but considering who had said it, I also wasn't surprised. What did surprise me was that when the ball was snapped, and I collided with Timmy, he didn't just grab at my jersey, he grabbed at my pants waist and then pushed me over backwards. As I fell, I knew what was coming next. I had seen it happen in our first game, and I certainly didn't want to be on the ground under Timmy O'Brien. But it was too late. He pushed me down and then landed on me, driving an elbow into my stomach, which knocked out my breath. If that wasn't bad enough, as he got up, he pushed a knee into my groin. Then he leaned down and laughed and whispered, "Tell your dark meat about that, pretty boy."

I lay on the ground for a moment trying to figure out what was worse, having my breath knocked out or being kneed in the groin or having Timmy say dark meat again. I decided it was a toss up. So all I could do was roll over on my side and wait a minute as the pain came because I knew the groin pain was going to come. I was not wrong.

Coach Hicks and Coach Craft came over to see if I was okay. At first, they had me lie back, and Coach Craft pulled on my pants waist so I could get air and relieve the pain in my groin. After a few minutes, they helped me to my feet. I was sent to the sidelines where I watched the rest of practice. After everything was finished for the day, we all started walking toward the locker room. Of course, what Timmy O'Brien could not know was that by then I had both regained my breath and strength, and Eddie Crooms, a defensive back, who also sat next to me in English class, so we had talked some, had come and stood by me and said, "You know why he did that, don't you?" To which I replied, "Besides the fact that he's a stupid idiot, you mean?"

"Ya. Besides the fact that he's a stupid idiot. You know why he did that, don't you?"

"I think so," I said.

"You think so?" Eddie said, as if he couldn't believe I was that naïve. "You know it's because of Clementine."

I didn't respond immediately. I didn't know what to say.

"Look, Tyler, Clementine is a nice girl. She's not one of the real lookers at school, but she's a nice girl. And you're a nice guy. So no one cares if you two want to be boy friend and girl friend, except idiots like Timmy O'Brien and some of his stupid friends."

"I know," I said quietly, as the coaches whistled all of us into line for our wind sprints, which was the way they tortured us at the end of every practice. But Eddie's and my conversation didn't end just because we had to run wind sprints. In fact, Eddie, who was certainly faster than me, ran next to me, talking all the time. "So what are you going to do, Tyler?" he said during the first sprint. Then he said, "You can't just let him get away with something like that" during the second sprint. The topper was when he said, "You know he's going to say something at school when Clementine is around."

With that the sprint groups divided, and Eddie ran with the defensive backs and I ran with the ends. Then we all started back toward the locker room. That was when it happened: I felt a hard push from behind in the middle of my back which made me stagger against another player. When he turned to see what had happened, and I turned to see Timmy O'Brien standing behind me, I heard Timmy say under his breath, "Dark meat is good," which was his big mistake, because for the first time in my life I doubled up my right fist and turned and planted my feet at the same time I punched him right in the middle of his face.

For a moment he looked surprised. Then he realized that his nose was bleeding. He stepped back and looked at me and mumbled something about how I was really going to get it, but I sure wasn't going to let that happen, so before anyone could intervene, I hit him again, this time on his left cheek. It hurt my hand but it also felt really good. That knocked him down, but before I could do anything more or he could stand up, I felt hands pulling me back and heard Coach Craft shouting and Coach Hicks shouting, and I knew I was in very big trouble. The only consolation I had in the moment was that as I was being led away to Coach McClure's office, I saw Timmy O'Brien trying to stand up. Besides a bloody nose, he was going to have a very black eye, which made my hand feel better even if it still hurt from my having hit him twice.

15

What happened next taught me more than one lesson. In fact, it taught me three lessons. The first is about friends because you can never know who will stand up on your behalf. The second is that sometimes the people you think will understand don't understand right away, but if you are patient they will come around. The third is that sometimes, no matter what others think, you just have to take a stand and hope for the best.

The first lesson started in Coach McClure's office, because he was really mad that I had started a fight. At least, that's what he said he had been told. "You hit Timmy because he out played you today, Tyler. You hit him because he knocked you down in practice."

By then, Timmy was sitting in a chair with a towel under his nose and an ice pack on his left cheek. I looked at him and then turned back to Coach McClure. "That's not why I hit him, Coach."

"Then why did you hit him?" Coach McClure said, still as angry as I'd ever seen him. "You know we don't allow fighting on this team, and we don't allow fighting in this school. So why did you hit him?"

I stood silent for a moment. I didn't want Clementine to be embarrassed. I didn't want what Timmy said to get around school. I didn't see how I could stop it now, but I didn't want it to because I knew Clementine would say it only called attention to us. I felt terrible. Not for hitting Timmy. I felt terrible about everything else. My grandfather . . . my mother. I just wanted to die.

"You hit me with a sucker punch," Timmy said. "You could never beat me in real fight."

"Be quiet, O'Brien," Coach McClure said. Then he turned back to me. "I'm surprised you did something like this, Tyler. I didn't think you were the trouble making kind."

"I'm not, Coach. It's just that . . . what Timmy said. Twice," I replied, fumbling for words, confused about my own emotions, about my own anger. "Three times."

"All right. What did he say, Tyler? What was so awful?"

Coach McClure was an intelligent man. I could see that he had figured out something had happened that had provoked me. I didn't want to tell him, but I did want to tell him. "He said 'Dark meat' to me, Coach."

"Dark meat? Dark meat? What does that mean?"

"It's because . . . ." I hesitated.

"Dark meat. It's because . . . what, Tyler?"

"It's because I am friends with Clementine Brown."

"Who is Clementine Brown? I don't know any Clementine Brown. Is she Timmy's girl friend or something."

Timmy snorted from behind me. I turned around and said, "I'm glad I hit you, O'Brien. I'd do it again."

"Hold it, Tyler," Coach McClure said. "Hold it just a minute."

I turned back to the coach.

"You're in here because you started a fight. You are in serious trouble. And now you're shouting how you'd do it again."

Coach Craft had gone out of the room when someone had knocked on the door. I had heard the knock but not seen him go. Then I heard him behind me. "Two players want to talk to you, Coach."

"What two players? I'm trying to deal with our brawler, here," he said, gesturing at me with his thumb.

"I think it's about the fight, Coach," Coach Craft said.

"Tell 'em to wait. I'm still trying to get Tyler to tell me why he hit Timmy."

I took a deep breath. "Clementine Brown is my friend, Coach," I said.

"You've already said that," Coach McClure replied.

"Clementine is black, sir. She is black, and I am white."

"I can see you are white, Tyler. But I don't know Clementine Brown so I couldn't know that she is black."

"Well, that's what Timmy was saying, sir. 'Dark meat.' It's insulting."

"So you think that every time someone insults you or insults your friend Clementine Brown you should get into a fight?"

"No, sir. But Timmy . . . he wasn't going to quit saying things."

"I never said anything like that," I heard Timmy say through the towel under his nose.

I turned and looked at Timmy, but before I could say anything, Coach Craft spoke up. "I think you need to talk with Eddie and Ramon, Coach."

"Eddie and Ramon? Good grief, how many people does this involve?" Coach McClure asked.

"I think you need to talk to Eddie and Ramon, that's all," Coach Craft said.

Coach McClure sighed and looked at me. "All right. Coach, you take O'Brien to the training room and get him some more ice. Tyler, you go out into the hallway and wait. I'll talk with Eddie and Ramon. Maybe they can help me figure out what's going on here."

With that, Timmy stood up and followed Coach Craft out of the room. I followed and went out into the hallway. As I did, Eddie and Ramon Ruiz went into the room, and I heard Coach McClure tell them to close the door, which they did. So there I was, standing in the hallway with my back against the wall, afraid of what was going to happen next, afraid of who was going to find out what I had done, and most afraid that Clementine was going to hate me or something. What made it even worse was that I could almost hear what Eddie and Ramon were saying, but not well enough to really hear, if you know what I mean. So I waited, with my heart pounding, picturing the Principal, Mr. Ballard, throwing me out of school and my mother crying or something and my grandfather shaking his head in disappointment. Then the door opened and Eddie and Ramon came out, and Coach McClure called to me, "Come back in, Tyler," which I did, although frankly I'm not sure how I managed to stand up.

"Okay, Tyler, apparently you have good friends."

"I do?" I said too quickly.

Coach McClure did not look pleased at my interruption. "Yes, Tyler, apparently you have friends. And your friends tell me that Timmy O'Brien has said some pretty horrible things before today, some of them to you, others when you and this Clementine what's-her-name weren't around. So I'm going to refer that to the Dean of Students so he can talk to both Eddie and Ramon as well as to you and Timmy."

"Yes, sir," I said quietly.

"And apparently, according to Eddie, who plays on the defensive team, Timmy told the players on the defensive team that he was going to get you, which apparently he did, because I saw you on the ground during practice."

This time I did not reply.

"So I will have to deal with that in a separate way because that's a violation of team policy."

"Yes, sir," I said.

"But you also started a fight. And no matter how justified you might feel you were, it is still against the school rules and the team rules. So I'm going to send you to the Dean of Students tomorrow. He'll decide what to do on the school's behalf. I'll talk to my own coaches and decide what we should do about you and Timmy as far as the team is concerned. Does that seem fair to you?"

I waited before replying. "Yes, sir. It's fair. I know I will be punished. I just don't want to be kicked out of school or off the team," I said.

"Whether or not you're kicked out of school is not my decision. The matter of the team is. But I will talk to other coaches before I decide. Now, you need to take a shower and go home. If I were you, I would explain what happened to my parents and then ask them to come to school tomorrow with you. Can they do that?"

"My mother teaches sixth grade, sir. She'll probably want to come anyway. But my grandfather can come. We live with him. He'll want to be here," I said.

With that the conversation ended, and I went to the locker room and took my shower. Luckily, everyone else was gone by the time I got there, so I could hurry but not have to explain anything to anyone. I knew I faced a whole lot of explaining at home that night, which was going to be more than enough.

16

When I said I learned three lessons that afternoon, I meant three things. I said that sometimes you don't know who is going to stand up for you. That was the case with Eddie Crooms and Ramon Ruiz. As I said, I knew Eddie from English class and from being on the team with him, but I certainly didn't think he would come and speak up for me, which he apparently had, because I learned later that he had even complained the day before about what Timmy had promised he was going to do to me. As for Ramon—I don't think I'd ever had occasion to speak to him, but apparently that didn't matter, because he was the one who said he had heard Timmy O'Brien making terrible comments about Clementine being black and me being white, and he'd been brave enough to tell Coach McClure exactly what he had heard.

All of that had certainly helped me with Coach McClure, but what I still dreaded as I walked home from school was that I was going to have to tell my mother and my grandfather. I decided that it would be best if I waited until after dinner, and I decided I wanted to talk to both of them at once. My hope was that if they could talk to me and talk to each other at the same time, they might better understand the problem I faced and why I reacted the way I did. Who I didn't want to talk to was Clementine. I certainly didn't want to tell her what Timmy O'Brien had said any more than I had wanted her to know about the man and the woman in the McDonald's Restaurant who had sat scowling at us. At the same time, I didn't want her to hear it from someone else who might get it all wrong and embarrass her even more.

Yes, I know that some people think a fifteen year old girl would be flattered that her boy friend had fought because he believed she was being insulted by a stupid jerk's stupid remark, but I didn't think that applied to Clementine. Because even then—even at fifteen—Clementine was the most refined person I'd ever met. I wouldn't have used that term at the time, but it's the term I began to use later as we grew up together. For all of her strength of person and strength of purpose, she was and still is the most refined person, the most refined mind I have ever known. I didn't think that punching Timmy O'Brien in the nose and then in the cheek was necessarily going to be high on her list of things she wanted to have happen on her behalf. However, I knew that I had to talk to my mother and grandfather first. Talking with Clementine would have to wait. So that night, after dinner, I took the bit in my mouth, so to speak, and addressed the issue as we sat at the table finishing our desert. Wisely, I thought I would start with a question rather than an admission. As I look back from my vantage point today, all these years later, especially after years of raising two daughters, I confess I continue to be impressed with my wisdom in doing so.

17

From the outset, I thought that my mother would be angry because I had violated a school rule and put my education at risk and that my grandfather would be disappointed but understand why I did what I did. My hope was that my mother would be influenced by my grandfather and at least be sympathetic. My instincts were pretty close to being on the mark.

Of course, given my anxiety, it did not take long for my grandfather to notice and to say something after dinner. So while I lingered over my ice cream and he lingered over his and my mother lingered over hers, he asked me if everything was okay at school. "I only ask because you've been more quiet than usual tonight, Tyler."

A very long silence followed. Neither my mother nor my grandfather was going to press me to speak before I was ready. They didn't need to. I knew this was the opening for which I had prayed, even though we were not church going people. "Well, yes, Grandpa, something has happened at school, and I think I need to tell both of you about it."

"You aren't in trouble, are you?" my mother asked before I could say anything more.

I glanced at my mother.

"Let the boy explain, Elizabeth," my grandfather said quietly.

I don't think my mother liked my grandfather's comment very much, but she did sit back then and wait for me. So I told them about the first time Timmy O'Brien had said "Dark meat," and how I hadn't done anything, mostly because I hadn't known what to do and because a teammate named Eddie Crooms who is black had told me to forget about it because Timmy was stupid. I could tell that both my mother and my grandfather were relieved, but I could also tell that they understood perfectly well what Timmy had meant. Then my grandfather said quietly, "But there's more to the story, isn't there, Tyler?"

"Yes, sir," I said.

"Oh, dear," my mother said.

After another very long silence, I finally went on and explained what had happened during practice. I could tell from their expressions that my mother was becoming alarmed and my grandfather was becoming angry. My hope was that he was angry at Timmy and not at me.

Then I explained how, after Timmy had kneed me, he bent down and told me to tell my dark meat about what he'd done. As I did, I looked at my grandfather. When I used the term *dark meat* a second time, his face became hard and angry in a way I had never seen it before. Yet all he said was, "There's still more, isn't there, Tyler?"

"Yes, sir," I said.

"Oh, Tyler, you didn't get into a fight, did you?" my mother said.

"Elizabeth!" was all my grandfather said, but it was enough. My worried mother sat back again, but I could tell she knew what was coming. So I told how I hit Timmy twice as quickly as I could. Then before they could ask any questions, I explained how I was taken to Coach McClure's office and what he said and how Eddie and Ramon Ruiz and come to my rescue by telling the coaches what Timmy had been saying about Clementine and how I was supposed to come to school in the morning and go to the Dean of Students' office. I said it would probably be best if one of them could come along. When I finished what proved to be a very long nearly breathless statement, I looked down at my ice cream and decided that it was now time to be very quiet. I was right about that, too.

After what seemed like minutes, my mother said, "Certainly we will come with you, Tyler," to which my grandfather said, "Elizabeth, you have to teach. I will go with Tyler. He doesn't need both of us there."

"But he's my son," my mother said. "I think I should be there."

"I agree you should if I wasn't available. But I am. You'd have to call tonight and get a substitute. Then you'd have to get plans to the school. That's very complicated. So you go to school and teach, and I will go with Tyler, and as soon as you get your break after lunch, call here and I will tell you what was decided."

Reluctantly, my mother agreed to let my grandfather take me to school to meet with the Dean of Students. I would never have said so at the time—perhaps I would not even have thought it—but frankly, I was relieved. I thought it was best that my grandfather come with me. After all, I assumed this was going to be a whole big thing among boys and men and that Timmy was probably going to have his father at school whining about how he was such a good boy that he would never have said such things. As much as I loved my mother, I thought it would be best to have a man on my side. My next problem was telling Clementine, because out of everyone involved, she was the one whose opinion mattered most to me. The problem was, I didn't want to talk about it on the telephone. Once again, as he had all of my life, as he would continue to all of the rest of his life, my grandfather was one step ahead of everyone.

"C'mon, Tyler," he said. "Get your coat. I'll drive you."

"Where are you taking him, Dad?" my mother asked.

"Well, since I assume he hasn't had time to talk to Clementine or her mother yet he needs to go talk to them now. He sure doesn't want to wait until tomorrow at school."

"Why does he need to see Clementine and her mother?" my mother asked.

"Because this is all about Clementine and Tyler, Elizabeth. You must see that. This is about black and white. And I think it's only fair that Tyler get to explain to both Clementine and her mother before anyone else tries to and gets the facts wrong."

With that, I stood and went to my room and got my jacket, and in fifteen minutes was standing on Clementine and her mother's porch waiting for one of them to come to the door. When the door opened, it was Clementine's mother, who looked about as surprised as a person can be to see both me and my grandfather. Recovering, she invited us in, and I quickly explained that I needed to talk to Clementine. A tad confused but nonetheless poised as always, she disappeared down the hallway, coming back in a minute with Clementine, who smiled as she always smiled, but who also said, "Teresa called me, Tyler. So I already know what happened."

"You may not know everything, Clementine," I said.

"And I don't know anything," Clementine's mother said. "But from what you two are saying, I think maybe I need to."

My grandfather smiled and said, "Why don't we let them talk together first, then the four of us can talk."

"Really?" Clementine's mother said. "Are you sure about that, Professor Thomas? If this involves my daughter, I think I need to know."

"And you will, Mrs. Brown. I promise. Tyler wants to talk to you. I just think it might be easier if they went out and sat on the porch and talked, and you and I waited in the kitchen."

"All right. I'm not sure about any of this, but I'll trust your judgment," she said. Then she turned to Clementine and me. "You two go talk, but then you'd better come into the kitchen and tell me what's going on."

With that, Clementine and I stepped out onto the porch and sat down. We both heard my grandfather and her mother going toward the kitchen. Then Clementine turned to me and smiled. "Just tell me what happened, Tyler," she said. And she took hold of my hand, which was exactly what I needed her to do.

It took a while to explain, but I did. I told her about the first time Timmy O'Brien had said anything. Then I told her about practice and what he did and what he said and then, finally, what I did. She didn't react at all as I spoke. She just continued to hold my hand. I hadn't thought I would say anything about the man and the woman in MacDonald's, but with everything that had happened, it just came out as part of the story. After I finished, I waited for Clementine to respond.

For a moment she put her head down. Then she grasped my hand even harder. Without looking at me she said, "People are horrible sometimes, Tyler. Just horrible."

"I know," I said. "I'm learning."

"And I knew about the man and the woman in the restaurant."

"You did?"

"I saw them in the mirror over your shoulder. I was hoping you hadn't noticed them."

I almost smiled. "So we were trying to protect each other."

"I guess so."

I laughed quietly. "You're so smart, Clementine. You're so much smarter than me."

"No, I'm not, Tyler. It's just that I've seen people like that before. And I'll see them again. And if we're going to keep on being friends, you're going to see them too. I just don't know if you want to do that."

"Do what?" I asked.

"Keep on being friends. Like we are. With all of this."

I was afraid. "Clementine, I don't want to lose you."

Clementine looked at me.

"Please, I don't want to lose you. Ever," I said.

Clementine smiled. "You aren't going to lose me, Tyler. I promise. And people like Timmy O'Brien . . . he just doesn't matter." Then she shook her head. "But the Dean of Students. That's another matter."

"Yeah, that sure is. But my grandfather is going with me. He'll know what to say."

"Tyler, you know what to say. Just tell the truth. Just tell him what happened."

"I'm going to."

"And no matter what, we're still friends, aren't we?"

"Yes. We're still friends."

We sat together for a moment more without speaking.

"Then we need to tell my mother. She's going to imagine all sorts of terrible things," Clementine said, starting to stand. But I held on to her hand and kept her in place.

"I need to tell you something," I said.

Clementine waited.

"I don't know if it's the right thing to say or if this is the best time to say it," I went on.

Clementine turned to me. I knew right then she knew exactly what I was going to say, but I went ahead. "I don't think of you that way," I said.
"The way . . . that was said."

Clementine looked at me for a very long time. Then she said, "I know that."

Then we stood up and went inside where Clementine's mother and my grandfather were waiting in the kitchen.

I had only been in Clementine's house once before, and that was with my mother when she brought me to Clementine's house so we could go to a movie. Now I followed her through the living room and down a hallway past what I assumed were two bedrooms and a bathroom into the kitchen where her mother and my grandfather were sitting at the kitchen table over cups of tea. For a moment, the two of us stood, not sure what we should do next. Clementine's mother spoke first.

"You two sit down. Let's hear what you've been up to."

"It's me, Mrs. Brown. Not Clementine. She hasn't been up to anything," I said quickly.

"All right. But it apparently involves her. So you two need to sit down and tell me what's going on," Mrs. Brown said.

We sat, me next to my grandfather, Clementine next to her mother. Because I assumed my grandfather had said nothing, and because I knew it fell to me to begin, I started.

"A few days ago, a boy on the football team with me said a horrible thing to me that was an insult to Clementine."

"What did he say?" Clementine's mother asked.

I hesitated.

"Tyler, don't be afraid. I've heard a lot of horrible things in my lifetime. I'm afraid Clementine has too," she said.

"He said 'dark meat.'"

Clementine's mother nodded. "Well, that's not as bad as I've heard, and it isn't as bad as she's likely to hear, but it's certainly not a good thing." She waited for a moment. "What did you do when you heard the comment?"

"I wasn't sure what to do. I know what my coaches say about fighting, and I know the school rule about fighting. And another player, a friend of mine, he told me to not pay any attention to Timmy . . . that's the player who said 'Dark meat' . . . he said I shouldn't pay any attention because Timmy's a jerk anyway."

"Your friend is probably right. It isn't likely that you'll change this Timmy person. But something else has happened, hasn't it?" she went on.

"It wasn't Tyler's fault," Clementine said quickly.

The three of us looked at her for a moment.

"I didn't say it was his fault, Clementine. Besides, I don't even know what happened," Clementine's mother said slowly. "But I still want to know."

"Sorry," Clementine said. She sat back in her chair.

"Today, when I had to line up opposite him on the line of scrimmage, Timmy deliberately knocked my wind out and then kneed me in the groin."

I saw Clementine's mother grimace.

"Then, when I was lying on the ground before the coaches came to help me, he leaned down and said I should tell my dark meat about what he'd done."

A very long silence passed.

"And you want to go to the school to complain?" Clementine's mother said.

"No," I said. "I have to go to the school to meet with the Dean of Students."

"Ah," Clementine's mother said, the look of concern on her face in contrast with the subtle smile that played across her mouth.

"Yes, ah," my grandfather said, trying to remain expressionless but smiling at Clementine's mother instead.

"So why do you have to report to the Dean of Students, Tyler?" Clementine's mother asked, looking at my grandfather as she did as if she knew the answer already.

"My grandfather is going with me."

"Fine. But why do the two of you have to report to the Dean of Students?" Clementine's mother said, turning and looking at her daughter before she turned and looked at me.

"Because I hit Timmy in the face."

"Really?"

"Twice."

"Really?"

"I may have broken his nose. I think he's going to have a black eye," I said.

"Two other players went to see the head coach, Coach McClure. Apparently they told him what Timmy has said on other occasions and what he said he was going to do today," my grandfather added.

"So we'll all have to wait until tomorrow to see what the Dean of Students decides, is that it?" Clementine's mother said.

"Yes, ma'am," I said.

"And you are telling me this because . . . " she said, letting words hang in the air so I would supply the response.

"Because I did not want Clementine to hear about it from someone else. Because I am sorry she might be the subject of gossip at school tomorrow. Because I don't want anyone to blame her for anything. And because I don't want you to tell her she can't be my friend anymore."

I hadn't expected to make the last statement, but having done so, I was very glad, but I also knew that I'd had my say, so it was time to sit quietly and wait.

"What does your mother think about all of this?" Clementine's mother asked.

"She's disappointed. But I think she understands. Or at least I hope she will understand."

"And your grandfather?" she asked, turning to him.

"I think it is unfortunate it came to this, but I also think there are times when I man has to stand up for the people who matter to him, and I suppose at fifteen this was about the best way Tyler thought he could respond," my grandfather said.

I watched as my grandfather spoke. I know he meant what he said about wishing it had not become a fight. I also sensed that he was pleased I had handled myself the way I had. Certainly he had no more reason to think I would be good in a fight than I did, because I'd never had to fight ever before. I decided I was going to hang onto the last sentence come what may.

Then Clementine's mother did something and said something I had not expected. She turned to Clementine and asked, "Do you still want to be friends with Tyler, even if he gets into trouble at school?"

"Yes, mother," Clementine said quickly.

Then she turned to me and said, "As much as I hope you don't get into too much trouble for what you've done, and as much as I hope you will never have to do anything like it again in Clementine's defense, I must also tell you that I am pleased she has a friend who cares enough to think about her before he thinks about himself."

"Nicely said, Mrs. Brown," my grandfather said. "My sentiment exactly."

I took a deep breath and looked at Mrs. Brown and then at Clementine. "I hope I never have to again either, Mrs. Brown." Then, as I looked at Clementine looking at me, I could not keep myself from adding, "But I will if I have to, no matter what happens to me."

Then all four of us were silent. My grandfather took a sip of his tea but didn't say anything more. Mrs. Brown said, "I will serve you and Clementine her favorite tea, Tyler. It's mint. I hope you will like it."

"Yes, ma'am," I said. "If it's Clementine's favorite, I'm sure I'll like it too." Then I was quiet, because there wasn't anything more to be said.

The next day, as instructed, I showed up at the Dean of Students' office at 8 A.M. My grandfather was with me. Part of what took place in the office in the next hour was pretty much what I expected to happen. Part of what happened was a complete surprise.

Most fifteen year old boys assume that they know everything that is important to know. They learn otherwise during the next ten years, of course, but that does not keep them from thinking they know everything that is important to know when they are fifteen. I may have been an exception. I had been raised by two caring adults without a sibling. Therefore, I had been very much a part of the adults' intellectual and moral world without the distraction of having a brother or sister to make me believe children were being put upon or that children deserved special treatment or that children did not need adults in their lives. I was, in short, I suppose, a bit of an odd duck in that way, although I managed to cover it up at school by keeping my mouth shut most of the time while I waited to find a companion or companions who might share my interests. Having found one in Clementine, with the added benefit that she was a lovely girl, I was not about to let either her or me be insulted because of our relationship.

At the same time, as my grandfather and I arrived at the school that fateful Thursday morning, I knew that my justification was not going to sit well with the Dean of Students; I had, after all, not only been in a fight, it had been with one of my junior varsity football teammates. No matter that he was stupid and mean, I had still hit him first.

When my grandfather and I were shown into the Dean's office and the Dean greeted me and shook my grandfather's hand, he started by saying he was sorry that I had taken the course of action I did in the face of what was clearly a very insulting moment. He agreed, according to reports he had received from coaching staff, that I had been provoked by another student whose behavior and whose words had been intended to both injure me and to insult me and my friend, Clementine Brown. However, that did not mitigate the seriousness of my attack on Timmy O'Brien, who suffered a broken nose and a black eye as a consequence. By the time he finished, I must admit that I was impressed by the Dean's official sounding vocabulary. I wondered if I had been an outsider if I would have had the slightest idea of what he was talking about.

In any case, by the time he finished his summary of what had happened, he then asked if I had anything I would like to add. For instance, was I planning on seeking out Timmy O'Brien and fighting him again? I said I was not. Did I feel badly that the situation had come to blows? I said I did, which was not necessarily true, but I knew it was what I needed to say. Did Clementine Brown feel she needed to come to the office to discuss the matter with him? I said he would need to ask her, but I did not believe she wished to do so. Did my grandfather wish to say anything in my defense?

Now, my grandfather is a man of words. Ideas and words. Yet in this situation, I did not expect him to come to my defense. I was somewhat surprised when he said, "Well, Dean, it seems to me that Tyler did not see he had any other recourse but to do what he did." Then he hesitated for a moment. Then he went on: "Yes, his mother and I wish he had not been in a fight, although it sounds like it was pretty one sided, come to that . . . yet I am not sure if I would have done much differently at his age in the same circumstances."

The second sentence surprised the Dean. I could see that from his expression. I mean, my grandfather was not saying he approved of my punching Timmy O'Brien, but he also wasn't saying that he disapproved. I thought my grandfather really was grand. I'm not sure the Dean would have agreed. For the Dean then said, "Yes. I understand. However, you will also understand that the school must punish Tyler."

My grandfather said he understood, which was when he reached over and put a hand on my shoulder.

"Coach McClure has informed me that he is suspending Tyler from the team for one week, which means he may not practice with the junior varsity team starting today until next Wednesday. It also means he will not play in the game today. Coach McClure says he will talk with Tyler himself when he reports back to practice next week, and that he will urge Tyler to come to him personally if any thing untoward happens again."

I waited. What about Timmy O'Brien I wondered?

"I cannot, of course, discuss how Coach McClure intends to punish Timmy O'Brien, but rest assured that punishment will follow."

My grandfather said he understood. I just wanted Timmy punished at least as much as me.

"Now, as for the school. We cannot condone fighting between or among students, no matter the cause. Tyler may not have known it at the time, but he could have come to this office and complained, and I would have intervened myself." He looked at me as if I was now supposed to be a wiser person.

Then the Dean went on: "Here is what I believe I am required to do. Tyler's record in middle school shows no discipline problems. His teachers this year say he is polite and cooperative. I am aware that his relationship with Clementine Brown may be part of what provoked this situation, but I am not in any way critical of that relationship."

Not in any way critical of that relationship? I thought. Who was he to be or not be critical of my relationship with Clementine. Boy, what a jerk, I thought. Why didn't he just say it? If a white boy and a black girl are going to be boyfriend and girlfriend, they should probably expect trouble. I wished Mrs. Brown had been there right then. She would have taken care of this dummy.

"The school believes that Tyler must be suspended from classes for three days. That means Friday, Monday, and Tuesday. However, this is not going to be a holiday. Tyler is to report to this office with his books. He will sit in a room by himself, where he is expected to study. He will have no contact with any students during the day. He will not go to lunch with other students. What he must do now is go home, organize his books, and report back to school tomorrow to begin his suspension."

My grandfather hesitated. "But if you send him home today, he will not be able to get his assignments from his teachers. That means he will not have anything to study on Friday, Monday, and Tuesday. It also means his suspension is not three days. It's four."

The Dean looked at my grandfather. That's telling him, I thought.

"His assignments will be sent to this office. They will be waiting for him. Consider it this way: he is suspended for one day at home for fighting. He is then given three days at school to serve an in-house suspension, during which time I trust he will consider how much it means to him to be a student at Tampa Coast High School. Does that make sense?"

"Yes, sir," I said before my grandfather could be brilliant. "I will report here in the morning."

"Fine. Now. You are to go to your locker and pick up your books. But you are not to make any contact with any other students. Then you are to go home. Is that understood?" the Dean asked.

"Yes, sir," I said.

With that the Dean stood as did my grandfather and I. As we turned to the door to leave, a woman suddenly appeared. That was when I got my surprise.

"Mrs. O'Brien," the Dean said. "I'm just finishing with Tyler and his grandfather. I will see you and Timmy in just a moment."

"I know that, Dean. I just wanted a moment to say something to Tyler," she said, turning to me. "I assume you are Tyler, young man?"

I thought, oh, God, here it comes. She's going to jump all over me, and then my grandfather is going to get mad and jump all over her, and then everything is going to be worse. My heart was pounding.

"My husband wanted to come this morning, but I told him I would handle the situation," she said.

God, she's as fat and ugly as Timmy, I thought. This is going to be a mess.

"But I told him to stay home," she went on. "He's just as stupid as his son, sometimes. And I didn't want him shooting off his big mouth."

What did she say? Did I hear her right?

"My son is a bully, Tyler. I am sorry about that. But it is true. He is a bully. He's been a bully since he was in grade school, and I have hated it every day," she said.

I couldn't believe what I was hearing.

"I know what he said. Coach McClure called us at home last night and told us. My husband doesn't believe it, of course. But I do. I know my son, and I believe he would say something just that stupid and mean."

This woman was beautiful. She was absolutely beautiful. My mother would have loved her.

"I just want you to know that I am glad someone finally stood up to him. What he said was horrible. I am ashamed. So I am glad you stood up to him."

I loved her!

"Maybe now he'll think twice before he shoots off his big mouth," she said. Then she looked at me. "He probably won't, of course. I fear he's a slow learner. But I also suspect he won't come around bothering you or your girlfriend . . . whatever her name is."

"Clementine Brown," I said very quickly, surprising even myself.

Mrs. O'Brien hesitated for a moment. "Yes. Clementine Brown. I suspect he won't come around and bother either one of you."

The Dean of Students was still standing. My grandfather and I were still standing. Mrs. O'Brien was still standing in the doorway. "Well," she said, "that's all I wanted to say." Then she turned to the Dean. "I'll go back out and wait with Timmy until you call us, Dean."

"Yes. Thank you. Please do that," the Dean said, looking as surprised as I have ever seen a person look. "Thank you." Then he turned to my grandfather and thanked him and thanked me and told me to go get my books and go home and report to school the next morning. I said I would, and we left, passing through the office where Timmy O'Brien and his wonderful mother sat waiting. I didn't want to look at Timmy, but I couldn't help myself. Wow! His mother was right. His nose was broken, and his left eye was black and swollen shut, which made the pain in my right had feel a whole lot better as my grandfather and I went on into the hallway to retrieve my books, with me hoping all the while that I would come on Clementine. But she was in class, as was everyone one else who knew me or who might have heard what had happened at football practice. I was very disappointed.

20

It would undoubtedly help this book if I could follow up on the drama of my fight with Timmy O'Brien with another traumatic moment, but that wouldn't be the truth. Yes, I certainly talked with Clementine that evening on the telephone. And as planned, she and her mother came to our house for dinner on Sunday afternoon, which turned into a wonderful occasion. My grandfather and Mrs. Brown had read so many of the same books that it was hard to keep up with which one they were discussing. My mother was her usual gracious hostess. Clementine and I went for a walk in the park near my house where we sat in the swings and talked about all sorts of things, mostly about her New Jersey cousins. What we didn't say much about was my fight with Timmy O'Brien. That subject had been exhausted. And sitting at school in a room alone studying was not any fun at all. I missed being with Clementine, I missed my classes, I missed talking to other students, I missed football practice. By the next week, as promised, I was able to rejoin the team. No one said anything about the incident. Obviously, my teammates must have been told that was the rule because I can't believe they wouldn't have wanted to say something if they'd been left on their own. Timmy was suspended for two weeks, so by the time he got back it was all pretty much forgotten anyway.

By late October, everything had settled into the routine that school is supposed to be. Clementine and I were accepted as a ninth grade couple, which I am sure tenth graders thought was stupid, eleventh graders thought was cute, and twelfth graders didn't notice. But that was fine with us. We just wanted to go to school and be friends. She came to all of my football games, either with her mother or my grandfather or with both. The only thing of particular note and out of which came an unusual incident was the school homecoming dance.

Tampa Coast holds its homecoming football game and homecoming dance the first weekend in November. It began doing that the first year the school opened; it's been doing the same ever since. I told Clementine that I wanted to take her to the dance if it was the usual practice for ninth graders to attend. My only question was—were freshmen encouraged to go to the dance, or are they not encouraged? Clementine asked some of her friends, but they didn't know any more than mine. We decided that better than asking an older student, and by then we knew several, we would ask a teacher. Since Mrs. Justine had been at the school for several years, we assumed she would know, and because we had biology together the last period before lunch, we thought we might get a chance to ask her when no one else was around. We decided to ask her on the Tuesday one week ahead of homecoming week.

The biology class ended that day as it always did, with students gathering up books and backpacks while Mrs. Justine was trying to make herself heard so we would know our homework reading. Once all of the other students were gone, and we were still at our lab table, Mrs. Justine turned to us and asked if we needed something.

"Yes we do, Mrs. Justine," I said. "Clementine and I have a question."

"Okay. What it is?"

"You've been a teacher here at Tampa Coast for several years, haven't you?" I said.

"Is that your question, Tyler?"

"No, ma'am."

"Then what is your question?"

"I need to know something about the homecoming dance. I thought since you've been a teacher at Tampa Coast for several years, you'd know the answer. That's why I asked about you're being here for several years."

"Well, to answer your first question: yes, I've been a teacher here for several years. Ten years, in fact. And yes, I do know something about the homecoming dance. I was the sponsor for a number of years."

"Good," I said. "Good. Then you can answer our question."

"Which is?"

"Which is . . . do ninth graders usually go to the dance? Or do the seniors not want them to come?"

Mrs. Justine smiled. "Well, first, it doesn't matter what the seniors may or may not want. It isn't just a senior dance. That comes later in the year. Second, most ninth grade students don't come, but that doesn't mean they're not welcome. I think it's more a matter of asking for a date or arranging for transportation."

"So we could come if we wanted to?" Clementine said.

Mrs. Justine looked at both of us for a moment. "So what I've heard is true. You two are a couple."

I glanced at Clementine. I didn't know how to answer the question. I knew how I wanted to answer the question, but I wasn't sure what Clementine would want me to say. As she has done many times since, she relieved me of the decision by answer the question herself: "Yes, we are, Mrs. Justine. And we'd like to come to the dance if ninth graders are welcome."

I had never before heard Clementine's voice sound exactly like it did right then. I've heard it since, but I hadn't heard it sound like that up to that point. It was obvious she wasn't angry, but there was an edge in her tone of voice that was new to me.

"Yes," Mrs. Justine said. "I'd heard that." She paused for a moment. "But to answer your question, yes, ninth graders are welcome at the dance."

"Thank you," Clementine said before I could thank her myself. Then Clementine began gathering her notebook and backpack so I did the same, following her out of the room and going to our lockers where we left our backpacks before we went to lunch.

After not talking all the time we were in line, because Clementine did not look at me in a way that made me think she wanted to talk, I finally couldn't stand it anymore. Sitting over our meal, I said, "Okay. What is it? What's wrong?"

Clementine looked at me. She was not smiling. "You heard her," she said very quietly.

"I heard who? Mrs. Justine?"

"Yes."

"And?"

"You heard her."

"You said that, Clementine. But what do you mean that I heard her?"

"You heard how she said it."

"I heard how she said what?"

"Tyler!"

"Wait. Clementine. What are you talking about?"

"You really don't know?"

"If I knew, I wouldn't be asking."

Clementine took a deep breath and looked away and then looked back at me. "I shouldn't let it bother me. She's a good teacher. That's all that matters."

"Yes, Clementine, Mrs. Justine is a good teacher. She seems like a nice person. Students respect her. So I don't know what you mean."

"The way she answered our question."

"Which one?"

"Tyler . . . good God."

"Clementine, this isn't working. If I've missed something, then help me understand."

"The way she said we would be welcome."

"She said ninth graders would be welcome."

"That's just it."

"What's just it?" I said, raising my voice slightly.

Clementine took a drink of her milk. "Tyler, think about it. If you were a teacher and two ninth grade students came to you and asked if ninth grade students would be welcome at the homecoming dance, and they obviously wanted to go to the dance together, and you knew ninth grade students were welcome, even if they didn't go to the dance very often, wouldn't you have said to your students that *they* were welcome?"

"What?"

"Wouldn't you have said to the couple, 'Yes, you *two* would be welcome?'"

"I don't know."

"Tyler, if the couple was the one couple who had asked—and she didn't say anyone else had—then wouldn't you have replied to that one couple?"

"Clementine, what are you getting at?"

"What did she say? We told her that, yes, we were interested in going to the dance. What did she say?"

"She said ninth graders were welcome."

"After that. What did she say?"

I had no answer. I was trying to remember.

"She said, 'So what I've heard is true. You two are a couple.'"

"Okay."

"Didn't you see her face? Was she smiling? Did she act like she thought we were a cute couple? Did she act like she was pleased? C'mon, Tyler, this is important."

"I know it's important. You're upset. That makes it important. To you and to me. I'm just trying to understand what you're saying. Because if you are saying what I think you're saying, then . . . I don't know what to do."

"Tyler, I think it is very clear. She is too polite to say it right out. But she does not care for the idea that we are a couple and that we want to go to the homecoming dance."

"Because . . . "

"Yes, Tyler. Because."

I sat silent over my lunch.

"Because . . . Tyler," she said again.

"All right. All right. I get it. Because . . . . But what are we supposed to do? She gave us the information we wanted. She said ninth graders are welcome. That's it. She didn't say anything else that we could quote. So there isn't anything we can do about it."

Clementine waited for a very long several minutes without eating and without speaking. Then she looked at me. "Am I your girlfriend even though I am black, Tyler, and you are white, or am I your girlfriend *because* I am black?"

I was stunned. I shouldn't have been. I knew the subject would have to come up one day. But I didn't know what to say. I wanted to be honest with Clementine as well as with myself. I didn't want to try to be clever or not answer her question. I took a deep breath and looked away. Then I turned back to her. "Clementine, am I your boyfriend even though I am white and you are black, or am I your boyfriend because I am white?"

"That's not a fair question."

"Why not? You asked me the same question."

"Yes, but I asked you first."

I smiled. She smiled. I shook my head slowly and looked away and then looked back at her. She was just about ready to laugh.

"Clementine, I am not going to argue with you about what Mrs. Justine might or might not have meant when she told us that we could go to the homecoming dance."

"But you do see what I mean?"

"I see what you think you saw."

"What I *think* I saw?"

"Yes. I see what you think you saw. And I'm not saying you are wrong. I'm saying that there is nothing we can do about what you think you saw, and that it's not worth us getting into an argument with each other, and that I still want to go to the homecoming dance, even if we are the only ninth graders who have ever gone, because I want to dance with you even though I am not a great dancer, because if I dance with you, especially slow dances, I will get to put my arms around you, which is something I have wanted to do for a very long time."

Clementine was very quiet. She looked away. "You're changing the subject."

"Yes, I am."

"Why?"

"Because there isn't anything else we can do."

Clementine was quiet again. She took a bite of her sandwich. Then she drank more of her milk. Then she said, "You put your arms around me in the park that Sunday when my mother and I came to your house for dinner."

"Yes, but I did not kiss you because I thought you would not like for me to kiss you, but if we go to the dance and we end up in the middle of a whole crowd of older students, and we are dancing a very slow dance, you just might let me kiss you," I said.

"Tyler, you have now made one very long statement about dancing and one long statement about dancing and kissing."

"Yes, I have," I said emphatically.

"You've never made a long statement about dancing and kissing before. Not up to now, at least," she said.

I did not think I knew what to say so I said nothing.

"Tyler, you could have kissed me any time."

I definitely knew I did not know what to say.

"You could have kissed me after your first football game."

Now I had something to say. "I was all muddy."

Clementine smiled. "Tyler, do you think I would have cared that you were all muddy?"

"My grandfather was there."

This time she laughed. "Do you think I would have cared that your grandfather was there?"

Once again, I had nothing to say. Clementine was very slim, so slim that she looked like she was maybe twelve or thirteen. I looked like I was already sixteen. I'm not sure what that meant, but I remember thinking it and remember wondering if it meant anything. Did I want to protect her from a mean world because she looked as if she was frail? Did I want to protect her from whites because she was black and I was afraid that she was going to be hurt by the mean white world? Because that would suggest that I didn't think she could take care of herself. And if I thought that, wouldn't that also be some sort of insult? It was so confusing. I wanted to shake my head and stand up and say out loud, "This is all so confusing, Clementine. It's all so confusing." But I didn't, which wasn't the first time that had happened since I'd known Clementine, and it certainly wouldn't be the last.

Anyway, after a moment of my silence, Clementine said, "Tyler, eat your lunch. We have to go to class. We will buy our tickets tomorrow when they go on sale. I will bring money for mine," Clementine said.

"No, you won't," I said quickly.

"No, I won't what?"

"You will not bring money and buy your own ticket. I have money. I've been saving it. I will buy both tickets."

"That isn't fair. You bought the movie tickets."

"No, my grandfather bought the movie tickets. He wouldn't let me use my money."

"He did?"

"He likes you. He likes that I like you. He likes it even more that you like me. But I will buy the tickets to the homecoming dance."

She smiled one of those wonderful smiles of hers and said, "Or you'll do what?"

I looked at Clementine for a very long time. She was simply the prettiest girl I had ever seen. Every time she talked to me, I felt as if the whole world just plain disappeared. I had already told my grandfather what I felt. He said it sounded to him like I was learning something about love. He was quick to add that he wasn't saying I was *in* love—just that it sounded to him like I was learning something about what it *feels like* to be in love. I thought that was very nice of him to say that and not make fun of me, even if I didn't understand the difference. So I looked at Clementine. "Don't mess with me, Miss Clementine Camille Brown," I said very slowly, smiling as much to myself as at her.

"Oh. All right, Mr. Tyler Thomas Raymond . . . the man with three first names," she said, which made both of us laugh just as the bell rang signaling the end of the lunch period.

21

The discussion Clementine and I had at lunch that day about our earlier conversation with Mrs. Justine was the first part of our homecoming game dance experience. The second was my grandfather taking me to buy a blue suit and Clementine's mother taking her to buy a dress for the dance.

I already owned a pair of gray slacks and a blue blazer. My grandfather had said as I grew up that every boy and man always had to have gray slacks and a blue blazer in his wardrobe. I kept that in mind over the years as I grew up. The blue suit experience was another matter. I don't know who got more pleasure out of the two of us going to J. C. Penney's, him or me. After all, my grandfather had only raised one child, my mother, so he had not had a blue suit experience since he was a young man. I could tell as he stood behind me watching the salesman fit first the pants and then the coat that he was remembering his own father. As I looked at myself and then looked at my grandfather in the mirror, I also knew he was very much aware that it should have been my own father doing the honors. It was something that we talked about over lunch that day in the food court.

I have to admit that I really do like food courts. I always pictured myself growing up and traveling all over the world. I had not yet been able to do that when I went to high school—I would later when I went to college and then married and Clementine and I traveled together and then with our daughters—but sitting in the food court surrounded by all of the ethnic foods gave me pleasure even though I was fully aware that all of the menu items had been Americanized to please our tastes. In any case, that is not as important as what my grandfather said that day over our Chinese lunch.

"Your father was a very brave man, Tyler," he said as if he had been thinking of a way of saying that for a long time..

"Grandpa?" I replied.

"I said, your father was a very brave man. Not just because of Viet Nam," he went on. "He had a whole lot of very serious questions about what we were trying to accomplish. But that didn't matter finally. He accepted a commission in the army. He became a pilot. He did his duty."

"Yes, sir," I said, unsure as to how I should respond or what I should say. After all, I'd grown up with the picture of my father in his flying uniform standing next to his helicopter at the base where he trained. I grew up with the picture of him in his football uniform at the University of Maryland. I'd grown up with the picture of my mother and him the day they were married and the one picture we had of my mother and him holding me when I was just a year old. I knew he was handsome. I knew he must have been brave. And I knew that he should have been there that day to buy me my first blue suit so I could go to my first real school dance with my first girlfriend. But he wasn't. That was the hard truth. It is still a hard truth even all of these years later. It was a hard truth when Clementine and I walked the Viet Nam Wall in Washington, D.C., together, when we were in college, and I found his name, but that is another story that I will tell later.

What mattered that day was the way in which my grandfather handled his emotions when he bought me my first blue suit.

"Did your father take you to buy your first blue suit?" I asked him, trying to change the subject because I really didn't want to talk about how my father was not there that day.

"Oh, yes," my grandfather said, smiling. "He sure did. It was in Omaha. It was a fall day, just like today, only a little cooler. But yes, he took time on a Saturday morning just like today and took me downtown to Wildsmith's Men's Store. That was where he got all of his clothes. Wildsmith's." He smiled. "I always thought that was a really unusual name for a store. Wildsmith's. But he said Don Wildsmith was the funniest man he'd ever met. And he trusted him. So did almost all of the other men who worked downtown in the business district, which is where my father had his surgical office."

I nodded. "Mother said he was a doctor," I said.

"He was. He was a surgeon. He was very good," my grandfather went on.

"How come you didn't become a doctor, then, Grandpa?" I asked.

"Oh, a lot of reasons. Didn't like science class much. But I loved history. My mother was a history teacher. I started reading her books when I was very young. It just seemed natural for me."

"I don't know what I want to be when I go to college," I said.

He smiled at me. "That's all right. You're a very intelligent young man, Tyler. You will decide. And you'll do very well," he said.

"Sometimes I think I want to be a history professor like you, Grandpa," I said. "Or an English teacher. I like both subjects. But I think history is more interesting."

My grandfather smiled. "There are a whole lot of worse things you could do with your life, Tyler," he said. "I know I loved every minute of teaching history."

"And writing," I said quickly. "Writing your books."

He nodded and looked away for a moment then looked back at me. "Yes, and the writing too. Which I did for your grandmother, you know."

I said I didn't understand what he meant.

"Well, it's a pretty complicated subject. And you and I will have to talk about it some time at great length. Right now, I'll just say that as you grow up, and when you fall in love for the last time, the time that will really count, if you're like me and if you're like most men who give it any thought, you're going to find out that everything thing you do you do so you can show off for the woman you marry."

I smiled. "Really?" I said. "Is that true?"

My grandfather laughed quietly. "It sure is, Tyler. I promise, it sure is true. It almost won't matter what other people think of you. You'll care a lot about what your children think of you, but most of all, I promise, you're going to find out that you spend your whole life showing off for your wife in the hope she'll think you're a really good man."

I waited for a minute. I wanted to tell him that I understood what he meant. At least, I thought I understood what he meant. "I think maybe that's what I already do, Grandpa," I said.

He waited.

"For Clementine. I think about what she will think of me all of the time," I said.

He smiled and nodded. "Well, that's okay, son. She's a very nice girl. She'd be a good one to show off for, that's for sure."

I felt a whole lot better, not just because he'd said what he had said, which explained a very important thing to me, but because I'd told him what I told him. It felt good to have said what I did about Clementine. And of course, it was true. It had been true since the first day I met her. It still is.

What's interesting is that when Clementine and I went to another movie that night—and this time I don't remember what it was—she told me about going with her mother and buying a really nice dress for the dance. When I told her about the conversation I had had with my grandfather, she said she'd had almost the same conversation with her mother.

Of course, she and her mother didn't talk about Clementine's father. He wasn't at all like my father. But she did say her mother had told her the same thing about falling in love with a man and then spending your time with him hoping he would love you and think you were doing the right things. Her mother had said that was what had made it hard for her—that she had hoped her husband would understand why she wanted to go to college and earn a degree and become a professor. Instead, he had resented her ambitions, which she assumed was at least part of why he had left and gone and married a Mexican woman he had met in Houston, Texas, where he still lived with his wife and three sons. From everything she had heard, he did not feel challenged by his new wife.

I've never been sure if Clementine had planned on telling me those things as we sat in the Burger King after the movie and ate hamburgers. Maybe what I had said prompted her to do so. Maybe what I said my grandfather had said made her feel she could talk to me. I do know for sure that she looked down and smiled, which is what she does when things are really important to her, when I told her that I had said to my grandfather that I cared so much about what Clementine thought of me that I thought maybe I'd been showing off for her since that first day in class when she asked me to be her lab partner. I know for sure that made her happy, because as soon as she looked up, and I could see tears in her eyes when she did, she reached over and started eating my French fries without even asking if she could, which from that evening to this day is a sure sign she is happy with me.

22

The homecoming dance, itself, was very nice. My mother drove me to Clementine's house, and then her mother drove us to the school for the dance. When Clementine came into the front room where I was waiting, she was so beautiful I thought I was going to have to sit down. Her dress was a very dark blue velvet. I probably won't describe it very well, but it was dark blue velvet; it went down just below her knees. It had a full skirt, which would kind of whirl around when we danced that night. It was long sleeved. Well, it was almost long sleeved. It came down over her elbows, I remember. Because Clementine is very fair skinned for a black woman—that's not being racist, it's simply making an observation—the blue was a wonderful contrast to her complexion. She had her hair pulled back over her shoulders and tied in a ribbon that was the same color. Her mother took a picture of us, of course, and so did my mother. We must have posed for five minutes before both of us protested that we couldn't stand any more flashbulbs.

Clementine's mother was going to drive us to the dance, and we were going to walk across the street from the school afterwards to eat at a nice neighborhood restaurant that always stayed open late on Saturday nights. What I remember is that as Clementine and I walked out the front door with my mother, who was going back to her car, and so we could meet Clementine's mother who was going to meet us in the drive way with her car, my mother turned to both of us and said, "You two are so very handsome. You are just so very handsome together."

Yes, my mother had told me many times as I grew up that I was handsome—her "handsome boy," she used to say. "You look so much like your father," she would say, which I knew was true because I could see so from the pictures we had. But that night, standing with Clementine, as my mother looked at me and then at Clementine, she wasn't just talking about me. She was talking about both of us. That was very important to me. It turned out that it was very important to Clementine. She told me years later that was the night she decided she loved my mother as much as she loved her own.

23

When we got to the dance, we very quickly saw that Mrs. Justine had been correct. There were other ninth grade students who had come, but not nearly as many as juniors and seniors. That didn't bother us, of course, because we had already decided that we wanted to go no matter who else came. Anyway, it was a very nice dance. We danced to almost every song the five piece rock band played. And yes, during the second slow dance of the evening, even though Clementine is shorter than me—her eyes are even with my mouth—she did turn her face up to me, and we kissed each other. No, we didn't make a big public display. Not like some of the seniors were doing. But we did kiss. And it was wonderful. I mean, her lips were so soft. I could feel her nose touching my cheek. I knew I wasn't breathing. I couldn't. I had never felt anything like that in my life.

When we stopped our kiss and went back to dancing, Clementine put her head on my left shoulder, and I swear I knew right then that no matter what happened to me or to her for the rest of our lives, I was just never ever going to not be with her. I didn't care what we had to do or where we had to go to make it come true, but I just knew I did not want to grow up and be an adult and make a life unless Clementine was with me. After a moment, I knew I had to say something. I was just about to try when Clementine turned her face up toward my ear and said, "You are the only man I will ever love, Tyler."

Oh, my God. *You are the only man I will ever love, Tyler.* That's what she said. Really. That's what she said. Now I couldn't breathe for sure. I don't know how I even managed to stand up. But I did. And I said, "And you, Clementine, you are the only woman I will ever love."

We did not talk much after that. And I know what you are thinking. Two kids. Two teenagers. Puppy love. How many others have said the same things, right? But we both meant it. We really did mean it. And it's what we have done every day since we said that at the 1980 Tampa Coast High School homecoming dance.

The other important thing happened later, when we went to the restaurant. Neither of us has ever figured out what it meant, exactly. We don't think anyone meant any harm. But truthfully, we have never really figured out what it meant, and we still talk about it sometimes even today.

24

The Greek Flame Restaurant sat in the corner of a strip mall across Hillsborough Avenue from Tampa Coast High School. I think it still does. It was family run at the time. My mother and grandfather used to take me there at least once a month. We knew the owners by name, and they knew my mother's and my grandfather's names. Clementine's mother and my mother gave us permission to go there for dinner after the dance. We would walk to the restaurant and then call my grandfather when we were finished, and he would pick us up and drive Clementine home.

When the dance was over and the students who drove were leaving, Clementine and I walked across the street to the restaurant. I assumed that not many other students would want to eat after the dance at a restaurant so close to school. I had heard that others, juniors and seniors mainly, were all going to parties. The Greek Flame was the perfect place for Clementine and me to eat dinner without being around other people from school. We hadn't planned on two teachers and their wives being there, but they simply smiled as we passed by their table and didn't try to strike up a conversation. That left Clementine and me to eat dinner as we had wanted to eat dinner, alone together, if you know what I mean.

Up to that point in our relationship, Clementine and I had always had a great deal to talk about. Yes we talked about school, but both of us really preferred to talk about other things. After all, the three adults in our lives were well read, well informed, intellectually curious people. Neither of us had ever been excluded from any conversations about important topics, no matter if the issues were historical or literary or political or social. For that both Clementine and I were grateful. We would be even more appreciative as we grew up and went to college.

However, sitting that night across from one another in a dimly lit restaurant at that point populated by adults, we both felt unusually grown up, more grown up than we actually were. That may have been the reason why we didn't talk as much. It also may have been because we had kissed each other for the first time, and because each of us had said what we had said to the other.

Years later, Clementine could remember exactly what she said to me once we were seated in the restaurant and had ordered. Prompted by her memory, I found I could also recall. Clementine started by saying in a whisper, "I meant what I said, Tyler."

I waited for some time before replying, not because I did not know what I wanted to say, but because I hoped she would understand I was going to mean what I said. Finally I said, "I meant what I said, Clementine. Every word."

"Which means we are being very serious, doesn't it," she said.

"Which means we are being very serious," I said.

Clementine looked away. There was a very nice looking older man and woman seated three tables away. Both had white hair. Both were well dressed. The woman was looking at us and smiling. Clementine looked at her in return. Because Clementine had turned to do so, I turned and looked at the woman for a moment. As I did, the man turned and looked at us over his left shoulder. Then he smiled. The woman nodded, and Clementine nodded in return. "Do you know them?" I asked.

Clementine turned back to me. "No. I've never seen them before."

"They act like they know you."

"Do you know them?" she asked me.

"No. I've never seen them," I said. "Maybe they think you are very beautiful."

Clementine looked at me and gave me one of her mock-frowns. "Tyler . . . "

"Well, it could be. You are beautiful."

"Tyler, I don't know them. And you don't know them," she said.

"So maybe they're just smiling," I said. "Maybe they're happy."

"Maybe," Clementine said.

Then our meals came, and we ate.

After our meals were over and I paid, I stood and helped Clementine get up. As we turned to leave, we passed next to the table where the two older white haired people were sitting. Clementine was next to her when the woman looked up and said, "We just think you look lovely."

Clementine stopped and looked at the woman and smiled in return. "Thank you," she said.

"And you, young man," the man said. "You are very handsome. You two look very nice together," he said.

Then the woman said, "I think it is so encouraging."

I was standing next to Clementine. "What is so encouraging?" I asked as politely as I could.

"The two of you. It's so encouraging to us. There's so much strife in the world."

Clementine glanced at me for a moment.

"Obviously you two care about each other very much," the woman said.

"That's true, ma'am," I said. "We do care about each other."

That made the woman turn to the man, who was probably her husband. "See what I mean, dear," she said. "They're proof, aren't they?" she said, turning and looking at the two of us.

The man turned and looked at us. "Yes. You two are certainly proof. You make us feel very glad," he added.

Clementine turned to me. Her body was rigid. I looked at her and then turned to the woman and the man. "Thank you," I said. "Thank you for the compliment." Then I touched Clementine's arm and turned her away from the couple, and we walked to the door, thanking the owner who thanked us for coming in, and left.

Once we were outside and had walked maybe fifty feet, Clementine stopped and turned to me. We stood looking at each other. "I swear, Tyler, I swear . . . " she started to say.

"I know," I said. "I know. I know."

Clementine turned to the traffic on Hillsborough Avenue. "What are we going to do, Tyler?" She turned back to me. "What are we going to do?"

I knew what she was feeling. At least, I thought I knew what she was feeling. I stepped next to her and took her right hand in my left and like her looked at the traffic on Hillsborough Avenue. "I am going to accept their compliment that we look good together."

"Is that all?" Clementine said.

"Yes," I said. "That's all. I am going to accept their compliment."

"But you know what they meant."

"I know what they meant. And I'll bet they didn't mean any harm."

"Tyler . . . " Clementine started to say.

"No. Listen," I said, turning to her. "I'll bet they didn't mean any harm. Maybe they worked for civil rights when they were younger. They're about the right age. Maybe they even knew Martin Luther King or Medgar Evers or people like that. Maybe they're very brave people. I don't know. I just don't think they meant any harm."

Clementine looked at me and then turned back to the traffic.

"We can't change the world, Clementine. We can't. And I am not going to let anyone change how I feel about you," I said.

Clementine turned and looked at me and gripped my hand harder.

"I do not want to be with you because you are black, Clementine. I just want to be with you. That's all."

"But I am black."

"Yeah. I noticed that."

"And you are white."

"And I assumed you'd finally notice that, too, Clementine."

"So there are always going to be . . . "

"People like that," I said, interrupting, finishing her sentence for her. "And there are always going to be people like the man and the woman in the McDonald's that first time we went to a movie. But we are not the people in McDonald's who acted like they hated us. And we are not the people in the restaurant who probably believe they made us feel better by what they said."

Clementine sighed very deeply. "I know," she said. "I know."

"Then let me go back inside and call my grandfather."

"Wait. Can't we just stand here for a while and hold hands?" she asked.

"Sure. Yes. We can do that," I said. I smiled. "I would like to do that."

"Good," she said.

So that is what we did.

25

The next morning, I was restless. I wanted to talk with my grandfather. I needed his advice. But I wanted Clementine to be with me. I waited until we had eaten lunch and my mother was grading papers, which she almost always had to do on Sunday afternoons, and my grandfather had decided that the professional football games were so uninteresting that he had gone back to reading the newspaper. Then I went to him and said, "Grandpa, would you take me to the Tampa Art Museum?"

My grandfather was surprised, not that I wanted to go to the museum. We had gone before. But that I had waited until 12:15 P.M. to ask him. He said he would be glad to take me.

"I want to call Clementine," I said.

He smiled. "Ah," he said.

"It's not just that, Grandpa. I really do need to talk to you."

He said fine. So I telephoned Clementine. "I have an idea," I said. "My grandfather is going to take me to the Tampa Art Museum. Ask your mother if you can come."

"I was trying to finish my algebra, Tyler," she said.

"Ask your mother anyway. Because I think we need to talk to my grandfather, and this is the only way you and I can get to talk to him."

I heard Clementine tell her mother who was on the telephone. I heard her ask if it was all right for her to go with my grandfather and me to the museum. I heard her mother say yes. When she came back to the telephone I told her I was wearing blue jeans and a long sleeved shirt. She said she would do the same. Twenty minutes later the three of us were in my grandfather's car driving to the museum. I wasn't sure exactly what I wanted to say or how I would say it, but I knew this was a good way.

When we got to the museum, my grandfather paid for all three of us. Inside, we started walking through the exhibits. My grandfather has always been smart enough to know that when I need to talk to him, it sometimes takes me a while to work up to the subject. So he doesn't ask me what's on my mind. He waits. It was one of the many things about him that I loved.

After maybe an hour of looking at paintings, my grandfather suggested that we all go to the cafeteria for something to drink. "It's going to close in a little more than an hour," he said.

The three of us went in and sat down. My grandfather asked what we wanted. We told him Cokes. I told him I'd get in line to get whatever he wanted, but he said we should just sit and he would get everything. While he was standing in the drinks line, Clementine turned to me and said, "What is this about, Tyler?"

"I think we need to ask him a question."

"About what?"

"About us, Clementine."

"What about us?"

Just then my grandfather came back to our table. He gave each of us our drinks and sat down and put sugar in his iced tea. After a moment, he looked at Clementine and then at me and said, "All right. Talk to me, Tyler."

I looked at Clementine. Then I turned to him. "Grandpa, I want to be with Clementine more than anyone else in the whole world."

He waited.

"I think she feels the same about me."

He waited. Clementine was looking at her drink.

"But we've been friends for only two months, and already four things have happened," I said.

"Four things?" he said.

"Yes." I glanced at Clementine. She looked very serious. "There were the two people in the McDonald's that I told you about. And then there was Timmy O'Brien at school." I hesitated. "I didn't tell you about Mrs. Justine at school." He looked at me quizzically. "It wasn't a terrible thing, but Clementine felt as if Mrs. Justine didn't approve of our being a couple."

"Did she say something to you two?" my grandfather asked.

"Not in so many words, Grandpa," I said. "Clementine and I asked her if ninth graders were welcome at the homecoming dance." Before my grandfather could ask us what she said, I went on. "She told us yes. But Clementine thought that her comment about how she had heard we were a couple made it sound like she didn't think it was right that we were."

My grandfather nodded. "You hadn't mentioned that before," he said.

"We didn't want to make a big deal out of it, Grandpa. We wanted to go to the dance no matter what anyone thought."

"So you did."

"So we did."

"And was everything all right?" he said.

"Yes. At the dance. Everything was fine. It was afterwards that I want to ask you about."

"Afterwards? After the dance?" he asked.

"Yes. At the Greek Flame."

"Did something bad happen? Weren't you welcome there?" he said quickly.

"Nothing like that, Grandpa," I said. "Everything was fine. It was after we finished eating," I said, turning to Clementine before going on. "Something happened that I suppose the people thought was a good thing, but it made Clementine uncomfortable," I said. "And I understand why," I said.

"Clementine?" my grandfather said, turning to her. "Is that true?"

Clementine looked at me and then at my grandfather. "Yes, sir," she said very quietly.

"It sounds like Tyler wants to tell me about it. Do you want to say something too?" he asked her.

Obviously, Clementine did not know my grandfather as well as I did. And I had just sprung this on her without any warning, which was probably unfair. But I thought it mattered. "You can tell him anything, Clementine," I said. "Really. You can tell him," I said.

"It was after we had eaten," Clementine said. "A couple—an older couple had looked at us during dinner and smiled."

My grandfather nodded and waited.

"When we were leaving, they stopped us and told us we looked very nice," she said.

"They said Clementine was very beautiful," I said.

My grandfather smiled. "Well, they were right," he said.

Clementine smiled. "They said that Tyler looked very handsome," she went on.

"Which, of course, he did," my grandfather added.

"Yes," Clementine went on. "But then they said seeing us together gave them such hope."

"Such hope for what?" my grandfather said quickly.

"That's what I wanted to tell you about, Grandpa," I said. "What they said."

My grandfather took a sip of his tea and looked at Clementine and waited. Clementine was obviously reluctant to say anything more. I turned to her and said, "You should go ahead and tell him what they meant."

Clementine sighed very deeply. Then she turned to my grandfather and said, "They said that it was obvious we cared about each other very much, which, I think, they saw as proof that the races could get along."

"Oh," my grandfather said, nodding.

"They said that seeing us gave them hope," Clementine said.

The three of us were silent for a while. Then my grandfather said, "So now you've seen the other side," he said.

"The other side . . . " I started to say.

"Yes. The other side, Tyler. Which I am sure Clementine has seen before."

Clementine nodded but did not speak.

"And that has made you uncomfortable?" he said to her.

She nodded and looked at him. "Tyler said he thought they probably thought they were paying us a compliment."

"They probably did think that, Clementine," my grandfather said.

Clementine waited.

"But it's still the 'other side' isn't it?" my grandfather said to her.

"Yes, sir," she replied.

"And you," he said, turning to me, "want to know what, Tyler?"

I sat back in my chair. Clementine was sitting with both of her hands around her paper cup of Coke. I reached over and took her left hand in my right hand and held it right there on top of the table. "I want to know if we are going to run into things like that . . . or things like the couple in McDonald's . . . all of the time. That's what I want to know," I said.

"Ah," my grandfather said, nodding and sitting back. "And is that what you want to know, Clementine?'

Clementine looked at me. "No, sir," she said.

"No?" my grandfather said.

"No, sir. Because I know it's what we are going to run into all of the time," she said. "It's just that it's new for Tyler."

"And how does that make you feel?" my grandfather said. "That it's new for Tyler."

Clementine looked at my grandfather. She had tears in her eyes. "It makes me sad," she said. "Because I just wanted to . . . " she started to say. Then she stopped speaking.

My grandfather waited. "Tyler, do you want to say something?"

"Yes, sir. I just want to know if we are going to run into things like this all of the time."

My grandfather thought for a moment. I held Clementine's hand. I could feel her hand pulling away, but I held on tighter. "And what will you do if I tell you that, yes, it is likely you two will run into things like this in the future?"

I looked at Clementine. "Nothing," I said.

"Nothing?" my grandfather asked.

"About us, I mean," I said. "I want to be with Clementine, no matter what happens," I said. "I just want to know so I can get ready."

Clementine turned and looked at me. I turned to say something to her, but she was crying without making a sound. The three of us were quiet for a very long time. Then my grandfather said, "Clementine, how do you feel about all of this?"

Clementine looked at my grandfather. "I am sorry Tyler has to go through any of it," she said in a whisper. "It isn't what I wanted to have happen."

"But what about you?" my grandfather asked.

Clementine looked at me and then at my grandfather. "I don't understand the question," Clementine said.

"I mean, is 'all of this' worth it to you? Being with Tyler, I mean," he said.

Clementine almost started to laugh. "It is if it's worth it to him," she said.

I turned and looked away. Then I turned back to my grandfather. "I know what you're going to say, Grandpa. That we're only fifteen, and that fifteen year olds don't always know what they're talking about."

"I wasn't going to say that," my grandfather replied.

I looked at Clementine again. Then I turned back to my grandfather. "Clementine is the most wonderful friend I've ever had, Grandpa. I will do anything to be with her," I said.

My grandfather nodded.

"I didn't ask the question so I could decide if I want to be with her or not," I said.

"Ah," my grandfather said.

"I asked the question so I would know how to get ready,"

Clementine looked at me.

"I asked the question so I could tell my mother and her mother . . . if either of them ever says anything . . . . I asked the question so I could tell them that I don't care what other people think," I said. "I mean, I don't want the fact Clementine and I go someplace public to make Clementine uncomfortable. And I know that so far it's only been white people who have looked at us or said anything, but I know that some day we are going to run into black people who are not going to like it that she's going to a movie or a football game or something with me. But I just don't care what any of them think. Because I know how it feels when I am with Clementine," I said. "I know how it feels," I said again.

The three of us were quiet again for some time. My grandfather looked around the room at the other people who were eating. There were adults and children all talking and busy with their own affairs. Then my grandfather turned to me and asked, "And how does it make you feel to be with Clementine, Tyler?" Before I could answer, he turned to Clementine. "How does it make you feel, Clementine, to be friends with my grandson?"

I turned and looked at Clementine. She looked at me. One of us was going to have to be the first to speak. Maybe I should have let her go first. But I didn't. I wasn't trying to be polite. I was trying to take care of her. "Last night, Grandpa . . . last night when we were dancing, I told Clementine that she was the only woman I would ever love," I said.

My grandfather nodded. He turned to Clementine. "Last night at the dance I told Tyler that he was the only man I would ever love," she said.

My grandfather nodded again. Then he sat and took another drink of his iced tea. Then he looked at both of us. "Well, I guess that just about settles things between you two, doesn't it?"

"Sir?" I said.

"I said, that just about settles things, doesn't it. What you feel and what you know you feel."

"Yes, sir," I said.

Clementine laughed and wiped her eyes and picked up her Coke and took a drink and said, "Yes, sir." Then she laughed again. Then she looked at me. Then we laughed together.

26

At that point in our relationship and that point in the school year, all Clementine and I wanted was for everything to be routine. We wanted to go to school, eat lunch with each other, and participate in both our studies and the activities that we liked. We wanted to go to varsity football games and movies and have time to go for walks. Fortunately, that's what unfolded. The five of us shared our Thanksgiving meal when Clementine and her mother came to our house. Ruth Ann Brown and my grandfather spent most of the afternoon sitting on our front porch while Clementine and I persuaded my mother to come with us for a walk. My mother and Clementine were obviously becoming closer all the time, which on one hand made me feel very good but on the other hand sometimes made me feel as if my mother would rather spend time talking with Clementine than with me. Frankly, that hasn't changed over the years, although I no longer have any mixed feelings about their closeness.

I was able to play in the last two junior varsity football games. I caught two passes in the first of the games and four in the last game of the season. I even scored a touchdown in the middle of the fourth quarter of the last game. What I remember most was trotting to the sidelines and seeing Clementine and her mother and my mother and grandfather all standing up and cheering. I could not have described the feeling to anyone at the time. I'm not sure I could do so even today. All I know is that it felt wonderful to see all of them together and to know they were excited because of what I had done.

When Christmas came, Clementine told me she and her mother were going to New Jersey to visit with her mother's parents and her two aunts and two uncles and their children. She said they would fly from Tampa two days before the holiday and not be back until New Year's Eve afternoon. That was just about the worst news I could have imagined. To be on holiday from school was wonderful; to have Clementine be out of town was awful. What in the world was I going to do with myself? My mother would be home so she would want to have me around. That wouldn't have been so difficult if Clementine had been in town. And I just knew my grandfather was going to know full well that I was sad so he was going to do what he always did when I was at loose ends—he would try to cheer me up by wanting to take me places. As it turned out, he surprised both my mother and me when he said he had arranged for us to stay in a cottage on the Gulf of Mexico on Fort Walton Beach, which is a barrier island just off the Florida panhandle coast. When I saw how happy my mother was, I knew that I had to shake off my melancholy and try to be nice. After all, she worked very hard at being a teacher. She envisioned eight days of sitting on the beach and reading. It was the least I could do to be as cheerful as possible.

As it turned out, even though I missed Clementine, the trip to Fort Walton Beach was really fine. First, my grandfather brought almost twenty dollars in quarters and dimes so I could telephone Clementine for a few minutes every afternoon from the pay phone at the end of the row of cottages where we stayed. Second, he decided that it was time I really learned how to play chess. As you might expect, he was a very good player. Our morning sitting at the table on the patio outside or cottage facing the Gulf turned into a very special time. I'm not sure that my game improved much, but I did get to talk to him about more things than I even knew were on my mind. Clementine was a frequent subject. Interestingly enough, as I recall our long conversations, what most strikes me now was that race was never a topic. We just talked about her talents and her personality. Things like that. It made me feel very good.

Besides reading, my mother wanted to walk along the sand every afternoon. I went with her. It was during those times that she told me stories about my family that I had never known. By the time the eight days were over, I felt more connected to my personal history than I ever had before. Couple the experience of feeling as if I had been allowed to walk through a door into a family story all the way back to the early 1800s with my grandfather, and it doesn't take much imagination to understand why I grew up and became an historian.

Of course, the highlight of my days was talking with Clementine. I only missed talking to her one day when she was out shopping with her cousins. However, I did talk to her mother that day, who assured me that Clementine spent so much time talking about me that her grandparents did not know for sure if they wanted to meet me or if they were sick and tired of hearing about her perfect boyfriend. That was the day that I told Mrs. Brown that my grandfather had promised me that I could meet the two of them when they arrived at the Tampa airport on New Year's Eve afternoon. I said that they were invited to come to our house to celebrate if they had no other plans. Mrs. Brown accepted the invitation. At that point, I think I started counting minutes instead of just days and hours.

Having grown up in Cleveland, it was very strange on Christmas morning to wake up and to sit outside in the sunshine looking at the water. And even though I was not raised in a church, the idea of giving gifts to each other because we loved one another was still important to us. I had given a gift for Clementine to her mother and asked that she give it to Clementine on Christmas morning, which she agreed to do. Shopping for that gift was the most confusing thing I had ever done. Fortunately, my mother helped not just with the money but with the selection, because I was determined to buy Clementine a pair of earrings. My mother said we could buy imitation pearls that would be nice, which is what we did. What I didn't know was that Clementine had done the same for me, giving my mother a gift to keep in secret until Christmas morning. When I opened the package, I found that Clementine had bought a leather bound journal in which she said, in her inscription, that I needed to start writing down my most important thoughts. Inside the journal, which I still have today, she put one of the pictures her mother had taken of us before the homecoming dance. The picture was a 5 x 7 enlargement. When I sat and looked at the picture, I wanted to cry, and I probably would have except my grandfather looked at the picture and said, "That may be the most handsome couple I have ever seen. I think it will need a frame." I knew he meant what he said. I still have the picture, and it's still in the frame he bought two days later in town.

The three of us drove back to Tampa the day before Clementine and her mother were to return. I tried to sleep, but the idea of seeing her again kept me awake until well past 2 A.M. As I lay in bed, I tried to picture her lying in bed in her grandparents' home thinking about me. That was the last thought I had before I slept. It was very comforting.

27

Have you ever gone through a day when you were so excited about what was coming that you could hardly contain yourself? If you have, then you understand what I felt that New Year's Eve day. Because even as I sat and ate breakfast, I knew that Clementine and her mother were driving to the airport in Newark to get on their flight. By the time my mother said it was time for lunch, I said I couldn't eat. I said that wasn't it time for us to go the the airport. My grandfather smiled and said I should not worry. He was going to drive me there in plenty of time. Then we would take Clementine and Ruth Ann to their home. Then they would drive to our house for dinner.

I sat at the table with my mother and tried to be calm. "Why didn't you go play basketball with your friends this morning?" my mother asked. "You played with them for three days before we went to Fort Walton Beach."

I told her that two of them were out of town now. "And besides, it's raining, mom. The courts at the park would be slick."

"That's never stopped you before, Tyler," she said. Then she smiled and glanced at my grandfather. "It must be something else, Dad. Maybe Tyler is getting sick. Maybe we should put him to bed, and you and I can go to the airport to meet Clementine and Ruth Ann."

The look of exasperation on my face made my grandfather laugh, although he did try to muffle the sound. Then my mother sat down and started eating her soup very slowly. I couldn't stand it anymore so I got up and went out onto the back porch. I knew what they were doing, of course, and how they were only trying to help me, so I wasn't mad. Not really. But that didn't make the time pass any faster. I know, because I sat on the porch in the drizzle and looked at my watch. I know that was a silly thing to do, but I did it anyway.

When I went back inside, my grandfather and mother were not in the kitchen. Then I heard my grandfather calling to me. "You'd better change if you're coming with us, Tyler."

I caught my breath. He was right. I rushed to my room and changed my clothes and rubbed a towel over my wet hair and then combed it as best I could and got my billfold and a jacket and went out into the front room where both of them were waiting. "We started to think you weren't coming, Tyler," my mother said.

Oh, yeah, right, I thought, following them out of the door across the yard to where my grandfather's car was waiting. Twenty minutes later, we were inside the airport looking for the Newark to Tampa flights. Five minutes after that and we were at the gate. Then the really hard waiting began. I looked at my watch. I swore to God that time was slowing down right there in front of my eyes. Einstein was right! It was slowing down. The second hand had gone a whole lot faster when I was sitting on the back yard porch in the rain. My mother tried very hard to not look at me because every time she did she smiled one of those *mother knows* sympathetic smiles that drive a son crazy. Of course, as usual, my grandfather sat very calmly reading a book.

Then the flight was announced. It was arriving. It was on the ground. It was taxiing to the gate. The doors opened. An attendant stood waiting as people began to file off the plane and into the airport. I started counting, and I don't even like math. Five. Six. Ten, eleven, twelve. When? When? Twenty. Twenty-five. Did they miss their flight? Oh, God, please don't tell me they missed their flight. Then twenty-six and then Clementine. I couldn't breathe. And her mother. Smiling. Both of them were smiling. I hurried to the aisle the waiting people had created. Then Clementine was right in front of me. Smiling. I saw her mother. Ruth Ann reached out and shook my grandfather's hand. She embraced my mother. I stood in front of Clementine. She took my hand. I had tears in my eyes. I hadn't expected that. I didn't know what to do. I knew what I wanted to do. I wanted to shout and pick her up and kiss her and swing her around. But then her mother was saying how it was nice to see me and see my grandfather and my mother and how she was glad to be back home and something about that evening and I just couldn't stand it so I threw my arms around Clementine who hugged me back and we just stood that way for a very long time until we both knew the adults were tired of waiting so we very slowly, I mean very, very slowly let go of each other and then, as we stood looking at each other I just leaned over and gave her a very light kiss on the lips. When I stood up straight I could hear my grandfather saying something to Clementine's mother but I sure couldn't understand what he was saying, which didn't matter anyway because Clementine was holding my hands very tightly and saying, "I missed you, Tyler. I missed you," and I was saying, "I missed you, Clementine. I missed you. I missed you." And then she said, "I love the earrings," which she pointed to because she was wearing them. And I said "I have started writing in the journal" and "The picture is in a frame." And so she was home. Clementine was finally back home.

28

That evening the five of us celebrated New Year's Eve together. Clementine told me about her cousins and how they went into New York and saw two musicals, 42nd Street, which she said was fun but not very serious, and Chicago, which she said she wished I could have seen, and how they had shopped on Fifth Avenue and how she bought me a really good wool scarf because the next time she went to visit her grandparents during the winter she wanted me to come along.

Then we all stood in front of the television set as the mirrored ball that counts down the last minute in Times Square slowly slid down the pole. When it reached the bottom and everyone in the crowd was shouting and making all kinds of noise the five of us turned to each other and wished each other Happy New Year. Then Clementine's mother and my mother kissed each other on their cheeks, and then each of them kissed my grandfather on his cheeks, my mother saying, "Happy New Year, Dad. I don't know what Tyler and I would do without you." Then Clementine's mother shook my grandfather's hand and they wished each other happy new year. Then all three of them turned to the two of us and all three of them kissed both of us and told us they hoped we would have a very happy new year. Then I turned to Clementine and said, "This is the best New Year's Eve I've ever had," which made the three adults laugh and make those adult sounds that tell you they know that even if they are laughing they understand what you are saying. Then Clementine turned to me and said, "We are going to have the best year of our lives this year, aren't we, Tyler?" I said we were. Then she reached up and kissed me on the lips the same way we had kissed in the airport, and her mother and my mother made those mother knows sounds again.

Then my grandfather did what he always did. He surprised us by saying, "Let's go eat Chinese food."

"What?" my mother said.

"Let's go eat Chinese food. The place we go to all of the time, over on Dale Mabry. It's open. I saw the sign two days ago."

"Are you really hungry?" my mother said.

"Elizabeth, it's New Year's Eve. Let's go," he said, laughing.

So all of us got into his car, and we drove to Alice Lung's Chinese Restaurant and sat together surrounded by other people doing the very same thing and celebrated and ate Chinese food until almost 2:30 A.M., and I decided that life just could not get any better than that. I was wrong, of course, because life got a lot better in the next few years, which is not the same as saying nothing bad or sad ever happened, it is just saying that as I look back on my life, that New Year's Eve, sitting with Clementine and her mother and my mother and my grandfather, who was still witty and charming and fun to be with, was a memory that I will treasure. When we've talked about our life together since then, Clementine says the same thing.

29

The rest of the winter passed, although in Tampa it is hard sometimes to tell the winter from the rest of the year. Clementine and I went to the St. Petersburg beach with four of our friends, one of whose father had a camper van and was willing to drive us there and then pick us up later in the day, even though on that particular day in February, by the late afternoon, it was windy and too cool to stay in our bathing suits so everyone who had them pulled on sweatshirts or jackets. What Clementine and I liked best about that afternoon was walking together along the beach away from the others, our feet cold because of the water, our bodies warm because of the sweatshirts. We talked about how we always wanted to live someplace where a person could go to the beach in the winter. "I liked visiting my family in New Jersey," she said, "But I don't ever want to live anyplace where it's cold." Then she stopped and turned to me and said, "Is that all right with you? That we live where it's warm enough for us to walk on the beach in the winter."

I looked at Clementine for a very long time. I understood what she was saying just as I had understood what she had said at the homecoming dance when she had told me I was the only man she would ever love. Because I knew that Clementine meant exactly what she was saying. This was not just a fifteen year old girl telling her fifteen year old boyfriend that she thinks he is cute and that she just knows that somehow they are going to be together forever. This was a serious young woman saying a serious thing.

"That is fine with me," I said. "I never want to live where it's cold in the winter ever again."

Clementine was quiet for a moment. I understood why she was quiet in the same way I understood what she had said. "Yes, Clementine, I would like to live someplace where the two of us will always be able to walk on the beach in the winter just like this," I said, which made her smile. Then we started walking again. And I know that very few of the adults in our lives would have believed it if we told them what we had decided that afternoon, but it was true. We had decided. But we never told anyone what had happened that day, not for many years, at least. By the time we did tell her mother and my mother what we had said that day, it was also obvious we had meant every word.

30

I got a big surprise that spring. Clementine told me she was going to try out for the track team. In Florida, most high schools have spring football practice. I asked Clementine if she was going out for track because she knew I would be on campus every afternoon until almost 5 P.M. Her tone of voice when she told me that no, that was not the reason, also told me that I had said the wrong thing. "I love running," she said. "This isn't about you, Tyler."

I decided to be quiet. I have done so many times since when her tone of voice was the same.

"I am trying out to be a middle distance runner," she said.

"Wow. I am impressed," I said. "I don't know much about track, but I know enough to know that middle distance races are the hardest of all."

"That's why I want to try out to be a middle distance runner," she said. And so she did. And so this time, when Clementine took part in track meets, because she was, in fact, not just a good runner, she was an exceptional runner, it was my turn to sit in the stands and cheer for her. My grandfather even joined me, and he and I joined Ruth Ann Brown. That was when Clementine's mother told us that she had been a sprinter in college and had run the 100 yard low hurdles. She had been so good that she had earned a scholarship, which she said was the only reason she was able to afford to stay in school long enough to earn her undergraduate degree. From that point on, track became yet another subject about which my grandfather and Mrs. Brown talked endlessly. Me—I just sat and watched Clementine and shook my head in amazement. My lovely, thin, young-looking fifteen-year- old girl friend could fly. I mean, she could flat out fly. And she was tough. I saw her come around the last turn many times a stride or two behind older, bigger runners, only to not just catch them but sometimes go flying past them like they were standing still. So Clementine Brown proved she was every bit as good an athlete as Tyler Raymond. In fact, the truth be told, she was a whole lot better. The fact she earned a varsity letter in her ninth grade year proves that. After all, there I was laboring all spring just so I might have a chance to make the starting lineup on the junior varsity football team the following fall while Clementine got her picture in the *Tampa Tribune* that spring when a sports writer came to Tampa Coast High School and wrote an article about the area's most promising younger runners. She was so good that after her first race, when she came in second to a senior from Hillsborough High School, against whom she later ran again at the conference championship, and a runner from Palmetto High School, who was just too good for anyone in Tampa to beat, she won four races in a row. But even on that day, my Clementine showed everyone what she was made of.

31

By the end of the school year, it is hot in Florida. I know that people from other parts of the country think it is hot where they live, but unless they live in Arizona, they're just kidding themselves. And if you've ever gone to a track meet, unless it was held at night, you know that sitting in the sun for anywhere from three to four to even five hours can simply drain you of not just your energy, you'd swear you've lost all of your brain power.

The conference championships were not held at Tampa Coast. That year, the spring of 1981, they were held at Northcrest High School, which is some distance from Tampa Coast.

Driving there, the four of us knew we were in for a long day. That's why both my mother and Clementine's mother brought umbrellas, as did my grandfather. We sure didn't want to sit in the sun all afternoon without them.

When we got to Northcrest, the meet was just about to start, so we missed a chance to see Clementine warming up with the team. However, her mother did get a chance to check if Clementine had enough water, because that was a necessity. When Mrs. Brown came back to us she said everything was fine. However, as I sat next to her, I could feel the tension. It wasn't that Clementine's mother ever expected Clementine to do anything but her best. She was simply concerned about her daughter's well being. "I've seen a lot of runners go down on the last turn," she said. "And the track doesn't look like it's in good shape. And it's too hot for a track meet anyway."

I understood what she meant. Because by the time we got to the 440 yard sprint, it was about as hot a day as it was going to be. When the runners lined up for the second heat, which was Clementine's race, all of us could see she was at least three inches shorter than the next tallest girl and at least twenty pounds lighter. We knew without even saying anything to each other that if she didn't get out of the pack very early, she just might get run over. As has been the case so many times since that day, we shouldn't have worried.

Before Clementine tried out for the track team at Tampa Coast, I knew very little about track and even less about track meets. What I learned I learned by going to her meets and watching her and her teammates compete in pretty much the same way she said she learned about football from going to my games.

In the case of the conference championship, I had read in the newspaper that the two favorites, one senior girl from Northcrest, the other a senior from Palmetto High School, had both already signed letters of intent to run on college teams, the Northcrest runner with the University of Florida, the Palmetto runner with Clemson. It was not at all realistic, therefore, for anyone to expect that Clementine was going to win the race. She was not a fool. She knew who she was running against.

When I played in football games, I never gave much thought to how Clementine or my mother or grandfather must have felt when they saw me lining up and then running a pattern. I suppose I didn't give much thought to how they must have felt when I caught a pass and then was tackled. I knew they were on my side no matter what happened. That had been enough. But watching Clementine when she got ready to begin a race, I think I learned a lesson, because if at football games they felt anything like I felt at Clementine's track meets, I don't know how they stood it. I know that for me, seeing her preparing, my heart felt like it had stopped beating. She was so wonderful a person, so important to me, that I wanted to be there with her, running with her. I even imagined pushing other runners out of the way. Of course, that's assuming I could have kept up with her or them. I don't think I could have.

In the case of this, her first championship meet, I thought she was amazingly calm. I could see it in her face, in the way she held her shoulders. She really was ready. That's why, when the race began, I watched her stride. She told me I must always watch her stride and tell her after the race if it had stayed the same all through the race until the last turn. On that day, it did. She was in fifth place as the group made the first turn. By the time the pack came out of the turn, she had moved to the outside, which meant she would run farther, but it also meant she wasn't going to be caught on the inside and not be free to move up when the time was right. When the runners started down the back stretch, she moved into fourth and then third place. The only runners ahead of her were the two to whom she had lost earlier in the year—the two seniors. Then it began.

As the runners started into the last turn, the runner from Northcrest looked over her left shoulder, as if she thought someone was coming up on her inside. When she did that, Clementine moved to her outside shoulder. By the time the girl turned to find her, Clementine had moved into second place. Mid way through the turn, Clementine opened up a three yard lead on her. The only runner left was the senior from Palmetto. I could see Clementine starting to lengthen her stride. As she moved to the final turn, I could see she was going to make a run at the lead. She pushed up to within one yard of the leader.

The girl from Palmetto must have felt her coming, because in the space of one stride she sped up. Two strides later, Clementine did the same. Three strides later, the runner from Palmetto pulled up next to Clementine, so that coming around the corner, as they flattened out, there they were: Palmetto in the lead, Clementine on her shoulder but slightly behind, Northcrest even with Clementine.

As they started their final sprint, with the crowd screaming, I could not believe what Clementine was doing. She was shorter, lighter, but she was holding her own against stronger, more experienced runners. She was doing exactly what she had told me was why she went out for track: "She just loved to run."

Then more yards and nothing changed. Twenty more yards and nothing changed. Then with thirty yards to go, the Northcrest runner moved ahead of Clementine. Then she was even with the runner from Palmetto. And that is how they finished, with Palmetto getting the lean for first place, Northcrest second, and Clementine finishing within one stride of both of them.

Everyone was cheering. Clementine's mother had been on her feet screaming the last half of the race. My grandfather had joined her. My mother cheered all during the final straight away. I didn't shout. I held my breath. When Clementine crossed the finish line, I had to sit down. I had tears in my eyes. I couldn't believe how well she had run. She had taken on two muscle runners and almost beaten them both.

When I looked down on the track, the two senior runners were embracing Clementine. I could see them telling her how well she had run. She was thanking them. I could see it the way all three were smiling.

Then I was at the rail. Clementine came to me. I handed her the towel she had asked me to keep for her and the water her mother had brought. She had regained enough of her breath by that time to look at me and smile. “God, you were so wonderful,” I said. “You were so wonderful,” was all I could say.

“They’re really good, Tyler,” she said.

“Yeah. They’re really good. But you’re wonderful, Clementine. You’re wonderful.”

Clementine leaned toward me and put her hands on my shoulders. “I was running for you, Tyler Raymond,” she said, smiling. “I always run for you.”

Then her mother was there, and they embraced.

32

The next Monday, I finally realized why I had been so quiet when the five of us, who were rapidly becoming a family, sat at Olive Garden Restaurant eating. The conference championship track meet was the last sports event of the year. The last sports event of the year meant that in one more week, final examinations would start. Final examinations meant that the school year was almost finished. And what was I going to do if I couldn’t see Clementine every day? What was I going to do if I couldn’t eat lunch with her? I sometimes wondered if I was becoming too dependent. I wondered if I was closing out other friendships to be with her. But when I thought about the questions for any length of time, I concluded that it wasn’t a matter of being dependent or closing out other people. It was a matter of having met someone with whom I could share every part of my life, personal, school, outside of school. That’s not being dependent; that’s being very, very fortunate.

Sitting next to Clementine at dinner that night, I decided that somehow, in some way, we had to have a summer together. I just didn’t know how. My grandfather did. He told us about it that night. It came as a complete surprise—at least, to Clementine and me. It also turned out that my mother and Clementine’s mother had known what my grandfather was up to for some time.

33

I have spent so much time telling the story Clementine’s and my ninth grade year in high school because that was when we first met and that was when we shared experiences that have played such a significant part in shaping who we are individually and who we are together. That does not argue that other years in our lives and life have not been important or that other experiences have also not played profound parts in our journeys. It is simply that the 1980-1981 academic year was our first together. However, even with the close of the school year, what we shared that year was not over. My grandfather and Clementine’s mother had arranged for the biggest surprise of all. They told us about it after Clementine’s conference track meet when we all ate together.

As I have already said more than once, my grandfather loves to surprise people, and his surprises are always wonderful. That night was no exception. In fact, that night may have been the best ever.

It did not take long for all three adults to figure out why Clementine and I were being so quiet that evening. High school romances that bloom during the school year are often times put to the test during the summer in much the same way that summer romances often go south when the new school year begins. And while I don't think either Clementine or I feared that our relationship would start to fade during the summer if we were not together each day, I do know that both of us knew it was going to be hard to share as much time as we had during the school year. It only stood to reason. It might have been different had we been sixteen. Then maybe we could have gotten summer jobs in the same place, but neither of us would be sixteen until well into the summer—Clementine on July 8th, me on August 1st. So there we sat, happy but sad, celebrating but gloomy, pleased but getting ready for disappointment. That is, there we sat with our mixed feelings showing until my grandfather started one of those half-questions, half statements that he just loves to make.

Looking away from the two of us for a moment, he said, "Well, the school year's just about over. Do you two have any summer plans?"

I shook my head and looked at Clementine. My grandfather knew full well that I didn't. And Clementine hadn't mentioned any. I turned back and looked at him. "He's up to something," I whispered out of the corner of my mouth for Clementine to hear.

"Did you say I'm up to something, Tyler?" my grandfather said, leaning back towards the four of us.

I smiled. "Yes, sir, I did. I said you're up to something."

"Now why would you say that?" he asked.

"Because that's just the kind of thing you say when you already know the answer and when you're up to something," I replied.

My grandfather shook his head. "I don't know where this young man comes up with these notions, Ruth Ann," he said, turning to Clementine's mother.

"For the life of me, I don't either," she said.

My mother sat smiling. I could tell she already knew what was going on.

"Well," my grandfather began, "I don't know if it's such a big deal or not. But here's the thing. I know your mother has to be in a certification class at the University of South Florida during June because her teacher's certification right now is only temporary. And I got a letter from the University of Edinburgh six weeks ago asking if I would like to come deliver five lectures on the history of American chattel slavery as a moral violation of black culture, which probably wouldn't interest the two of you very much, but it did interest Professor Brown," he said, gesturing toward Clementine's mother. "But when I told the folks at the University that I thought I knew someone who could lecture on the subject just as well as I could—and maybe even better—they wrote back and said they had enough money in their lecture series budget to hire both of us."

Clementine and I looked at each other. I turned back to the two of them. "That's great, Grandpa. It's great, Mrs. Brown," I said. I looked at Clementine, who said, "Yes. That's wonderful, mother. Sir," she said.

"Yes, but there's a problem," my grandfather said.

Clementine and I waited.

"You see, neither Professor Brown nor I are married, as you two know. And we wouldn't want people to get the wrong idea," he said.

"That we're traveling together," Clementine's mother said quickly, smiling.

"But your mother can't come along and chaperone, Tyler, because of her class," he said.

"Yes," my mother said. "I'd love to go, but I can't."

"So it looks like neither Professor Thomas nor I will be able to accept the invitation," Clementine's mother said. "Which is really too bad, because when we talked about it, we realized that as long as we had to travel all the way to Edinburgh, it would be a shame if we didn't spend at least a few days in London on our way back."

Clementine pushed her elbow against my elbow.

I looked at my grandfather. "So the two of you can't go. That's too bad," I said, nodding and glancing at Clementine and then turning back to the two smiling adults.

"Ah," my grandfather began, "unless the two of you might have time in June to go with us . . . as chaperones," he said.

I heard Clementine take a quick deep breath. My grandfather waited. Mrs. Brown waited. I turned to Clementine. My heart was racing. But the two adults had set the tone. "Well," I said. "What do you think, Clementine? Should we go with them?"

Clementine was bursting. "Well, Tyler," she began, nodding slowly, "I think . . . I think that . . . if they promise to behave and not cause us any problems, I think that . . ." She sighed again and then turned to her mother and stood up and walked around the table very slowly and then put her arms around her mother's neck and said, "I think Tyler and I would like nothing more than to go with the two of you to . . . wherever you are going." Then she turned and looked at me and shouted, "Tyler! Tyler!" And she came back around the table as I stood up, and she threw her arms around me, and I threw my arms around her, and we just stood there hugging for a very long time while other people in the Olive Garden Restaurant looked at us and smiled and laughed and a few even applauded although I cannot imagine that they knew what had made us so very happy.

Then my grandfather said, "I don't know, Ruth Ann. Maybe we'll have to chaperone them."

Then all three of our adults laughed. And Clementine and I just stood and looked at each other and laughed with them.

We all had passport photos taken the next day. That afternoon Clementine and I went to Westshore shopping mall to buy new suitcases.

34

If it sounds as if Clementine's mother and my mother and grandfather are exceptional people, you are right. They are. Clementine and I know perfectly well that we experienced very important opportunities while we grew up. What is interesting, of course, is that those opportunities were not the product of money. Yes, both Mrs. Brown and my mother and my grandfather earned good livings, but that is not what made having them as the adults in our lives so important. It was the way in which each of them had gone to college; it was what each of them did with their educations; it was what each of them gave to us in our relationships with them. The trip to Edinburgh and then London is an example. It was my grandfather's life long devotion to justice that led him to the civil rights movement. It was his academic expertise that made his contribution important even beyond his teaching at Cleveland State University. For he was willing to spend hours reading and researching and then writing about facets of American history that many professors would rather just leave unexamined and unsaid.

The same was true of Clementine's mother. She had not only faced down personal challenges in her life that might well have discouraged another young black woman, she discovered as she made her way through the academic world that she could do more than just lecture. Her own essays began to call attention to her insights into the roles of black women in black American culture and in the civil rights movement. It was that latter subject that caused her studies to intersect with my grandfather's, and it was their individual articulations, intersecting in Edinburgh, that began a professional relationship that produced an extraordinary book of lectures, which I have used in my own teaching.

However, for Clementine and me, what mattered most during that wonderful June when we flew with her mother and my grandfather to London and then took the train to Edinburgh was that we got to be together for extended periods of time. Flying over the Atlantic, for instance, in a plane that featured two seats on the aisle, five seats in the middle, and then three seats on the other aisle, we sat together in two of the seats that were side by side. That not only meant we could talk as much as we wished, it also meant that when we slept during our night flight to London, Clementine leaned her head on my shoulder. You cannot imagine how much pleasure that gave me. She fell asleep holding my left hand, with her head on my left shoulder. What more could a young man in love want, even though it meant that after four hours or so my shoulder began to go numb, and her breathing next to my face kept me from sleeping as well as she was. But who cared? Not me, that was for sure. When she awoke just before the attendants began moving around and preparing us for our landing, I turned and there she was, her lovely brown eyes looking into my blue eyes. She even said, "You have beautiful eyes, Tyler. I've been meaning to tell you that." Do you know what that feels like? To have the young woman you just know deep in your heart that you will love forever say you have beautiful eyes. I swear I could have sat there all day and just looked at her.

But, of course, that is not the way life works. So in less than two hours, there we were, standing with Mrs. Brown and my grandfather in the customs line, our passports in hand, passing through the gate and into the airport, where we retrieved the one suitcase we had each allowed ourselves, then going to the train station below the airport, where we immediately boarded the train to Edinburgh.

Settling down in the train was more of the same. As tired as all of us were, we still managed to stay awake for another two hours looking out of the windows first at the city and then at the landscape as we sped north. I had seen a food counter in one of the cars when we got on, so taking some of the English money that my grandfather had obtained at the currency exchange counter in the airport, Clementine and I had the adventure of ordering both familiar and unfamiliar food from the attendant, who I believe was as taken with our American accents as we were with his. After we ate, as you might expect, all four of us could not stay awake much longer. By the time we awoke, we were passing through England's lake country. "The land of the romantic poets," my grandfather said. Speaking to Clementine and me he said, "You two will study Wordsworth and Keats and Shelly some day in school. Well, look outside and you will understand why they wrote what they wrote."

As we traveled, as he always does, my grandfather began talking to people sitting around us. Now I know that could be embarrassing for some young people, but it wasn't for Clementine or me. In fact, we listened carefully as both my grandfather and Mrs. Brown began talking about politics in Great Britain. I think all four of us learned a great deal from the man and the woman sitting across the aisle from us. Even the conductor stopped and talked with them for a while. He was particularly interested in telling us about places we needed to visit in Edinburgh. At the same time, I don't think he could figure out the relationships that the four of us shared. Clementine caught him looking at her and then her mother and then at my grandfather as if he could not quite define why we were all together. What I found most particularly interesting, however, was that unlike earlier experiences when Clementine had deeply resented what she assumed were people trying to decide what kind of relationship she and I shared when we went someplace in public, on this occasion she was obviously if discreetly amused as people sitting nearby tried to disguise their questions about how a young black woman and a young white man, who were holding hands, were related to an older but still vigorous white man and a strikingly handsome black woman in her late thirties who had apparently traveled together all the way from America.

Then we were in Edinburgh, and the first part of what Clementine still today calls our Great Youthful June Adventure began for real.

35

Edinburgh is a beautiful city. The Princess Hotel on Princes Street faces Edinburgh Castle, which sits at the top of a bluff overlooking the city on one side and the Firth of Forth on the other. The Castle is lit up at night so you can see it from every room facing the street. It is a stunning sight.

The University is not far away. The first day after the four of us arrived, as tired as we were, we took a cab to the campus, and my grandfather and Clementine's mother met with the people who had arranged for their lectures. While they were gone, Clementine and I sat on a low brick wall outside of what looked like a classroom building and watched students going in every direction.

"Do you know where you want to go to college?" Clementine asked me.

I turned to her. She had never asked me that before. As ninth graders, even though there was no question that we would go on to college after high school, we hadn't been very specific in our thinking. "Well, when I lived in Cleveland, I always thought I'd go to a school in Ohio or maybe Michigan. But then we moved to Tampa. Now I'm not sure. Someplace closer to home, I suppose. What about you?"

"I'm like you. My mother went to Rutgers. Then she earned her master's degree and doctorate at New York University. I assumed I would go to school somewhere near to where we lived in Queens. Then we moved to Tampa, and now she is talking about smaller schools in Georgia."

"Which ones?" I asked.

"In Atlanta. There are some traditionally black colleges in Atlanta. Several. She's talking about some of them. The women's colleges."

"Women's colleges? Really?" I said.

"Yes."

I looked away. A group of five students walked by talking. Three of them looked at us sitting on the wall. One of them said hello. I replied. He smiled and said something to the others. I assumed it was about my accent.

"I always wanted to go to a big school," I said. "That's what I've grown up with, of course. Maybe if I visited a smaller school, I'd feel different."

"Maybe," Clementine said.

I looked away but spoke to Clementine from over my right shoulder. "No matter where I go, though, even if we aren't at the same school, I want to be close by. I want to be able to be with you," I said.

Clementine did not respond. Then she said, "It's a long time from now."

"Right. It's a long time from now," I replied, because, in fact, it was a long time. Three whole school years. That seemed like a lifetime sitting on a low brick wall on the campus of the Edinburgh University in June, 1981.

Then we saw my grandfather and Clementine's mother coming towards us. They waved, and we waved in return.

36

Two days later Clementine and I sat in a very large lecture hall with maybe two hundred students and faculty members as first, Clementine's mother, and then second, my grandfather began their partnership lectures.

Clementine's mother spoke about the West African kingdoms from which blacks had been taken and sold into slavery. She began by describing the sophisticated and creative tribal cultures that populated West Africa. Then she detailed conditions on the slave ships and how some African men and women committed suicide rather than be taken to the new world. Her lecture focused on the way in which slavery destroyed not just families but village societies. She ended the first of her five lectures by describing the conditions the slaves faced as those who survived were taken from the ships and prepared to be sold in the slave markets in the Caribbean islands.

My grandfather's first lecture complemented Ruth Ann's by focusing on the justification Christian Europe used for chattel slavery. His analysis began by citing prominent church fathers who had spoken extensively on the subject of the inferiority of African culture. His lecture then focused on the intersection of religious rationalization and economic exploitation. He ended by outlining the early boom economy that the discovery and colonization of the new world brought to Europe and how that new economy was, in fact, supported in large part by both the slave trade and slave labor.

Both Clementine and I sat silently and listened. Both of us had heard both of them speak about the subjects in conversation. Both of us had heard both of them talk about some of the facts they laid out that day. But neither of us had ever heard either of them lecture on the subject before. When they both ended, Clementine and I turned to each other and sat without talking for some time. Being in the presence of brilliant minds, I learned as I grew up, is always a privilege. When those brilliant minds are two of the three most important adults in your lives, it is a humbling experience. Not only were we moved by the topic and the analysis, we were moved by knowing who the lecturers were. Because as they spoke, they were not Clementine's mother and my grandfather; they were both extraordinary people who richly deserved the very sincere applause they received. Of course, we also knew that by the time we went to dinner that night, they would have to be Clementine's mother and my grandfather again. Not only did we need for that to happen, they would want it to happen.

During the lunch that was given in their honor, to which Clementine and I were invited, a very nice professor asked the two of us what we wanted to do in Edinburgh. Clementine said we wanted to visit the art museums. He advised that the best museum in the city was the Scottish National Portrait Gallery. We decided that we would take his advice and make that our first destination.

After the lunch was finished, Clementine's mother and my grandfather said they needed to go to the University library to complete the editing of the lectures they were to deliver tomorrow. They asked if there was something we wanted to do besides wait for them. I said that yes, we had been told we should go to the Scottish National Portrait Gallery. Clementine said that the gallery was not far away and that we could take a bus there and back to our hotel on Princes Street for dinner. Once they were assured that we had enough money for whatever we might need and that we knew how to reach them in case of an emergency, they agreed we could go. So we said goodbye and set off.

37

As we walked to where we were told we could get a bus and then rode it to within walking distance of the museum, we did not say anything to each other. Both of us were too busy looking at everything. As you would expect, what was ordinary for people who lived in Edinburgh was extraordinary for us. There were advertisements for food brands we'd never heard of, for clothes that looked like ours but did not look like ours, both at once. There were advertisements for the Scottish Premier Football league teams. There were placards on the sides of the buses for beers I had never heard of and cosmetics Clementine had never heard of. But it wasn't just signs and stores and buildings that made it interesting; even more it was listening to people talk, and not just their accents. We knew full well that in Edinburgh, we were the ones with the accents. But listening to people talk about whatever people talk about when they are walking on the sidewalk or sitting on a bus was fascinating for us. So by the time we arrived where we had been advised to get off the bus and began walking, holding hands, of course, I knew exactly what Clementine was thinking, and she knew exactly what I was thinking: here we were, two fifteen-year-old American students who had become boyfriend and girlfriend because Clementine had asked me to be her biology lab partner, and I had asked her to go to a movie, holding hands and walking down a street in Edinburgh, Scotland, just ten months later, on our way to a Scots museum of art, paying no attention whatsoever to the way people looked at us, for we both realized without speaking about it that in Edinburgh the black-white thing didn't mean nearly as much as the fact we were visiting Americans. For a moment, as we stood on a street corner waiting for the light to change, looking the wrong way at first, of course, then the correct way for any oncoming traffic, I wondered how it had all happened. I don't mean I wondered about Clementine's mother and my grandfather giving lectures. That's what they did for a living. And they were good so they deserved to be invited to lecture. It was us I was thinking about. How did our relationship lead to us being in Scotland? How did our relationship lead to their relationship and my mother's friendship with Ruth Ann? For a moment, it seemed so wonderful and so exciting that I wanted to shout or laugh or say something to the man standing next to us or the woman and the child standing next to Clementine. I didn't, of course, because most folks, including me, don't say things like that no matter how they feel. Then Clementine smiled and pulled at my arm, because the light had changed and it was our turn to cross the street.

38

I remember two things about the Scots National Portrait Museum. First, after we had looked at a number of paintings of people who were apparently important in Scots history, Clementine smiled and said, "You know, Tyler, you look just like some of these people."

I scowled and turned to her, because I had just been looking at a portrait of Sir Charles Grant Robertson, a man with a very long nose that made him look a little like a bird. "You mean, that guy?" I said, pointing at the painting.

Clementine laughed. "No. Not him. Him," she said, pointing at a portrait of Jane, the Duchess of Gordon, and her son, George, the Marquess of Huntley that we had just passed. "I'll bet you looked like that four or five years ago," she said. I was relieved because the young Marquess of Huntley had been a handsome boy. Then, as we walked further, she said, "But your eyes, Tyler. Your eyes look more like his." She pointed at a portrait of Sir Walter Scott, the novelist, painted by Sir Henry Raeburn in 1822. I moved closer and looked. "Maybe, Clementine. But it looks even more like my father." I turned to her. "You've seen the photograph of him with my mother and the three of us together. I think it looks like him."

Clementine stepped up and looked at the painting. "You're right," she said. "He does look like your father. Your father had darker hair, but it does look like him. She smiled. "So Raymond is a Scots name?" she said.

"Yes. It is. And my grandfather's name, Thomas, is a Welsh name."

"I wonder if we'll find anyone in here who looks like me," Clementine said.

I didn't know what to say. Unless some important Scot was shown with a slave or a house servant or a horse handler, which wasn't very likely, it wasn't going to happen. And I didn't want that to be the case. That would have been worse than not seeing a black face at all. So after a moment I turned to Clementine and said not just the only thing I could think of to say, I said what I really meant: "Clementine, if we did find someone who you looked like, she'd have to be a whole lot more beautiful than any woman we've seen so far."

Clementine stopped walking and looked at me. She smiled, not just with her mouth but with her brown eyes. That was enough. She didn't have to say anything, and she knew she didn't have to say anything. And rather than me say anything more, all I had to do was walk back to where she had stopped and take her hand as we started walking again so we could see the rest of the paintings.

39

Although both my grandfather and Clementine's mother did not expect that Clementine and I would attend all five of their lectures, we said that we wanted to. After all, we had gotten to come because of the two of them. And we thought the lectures were important. When they said they didn't think we'd find the lectures very much fun, Clementine said that she knew that. "What you do is important, mom. And I want to know about it." I told my grandfather the same thing. So we attended all of the lectures for the rest of the week. Clementine's mother continued her lectures by outlining the devastation visited on the Africans brought to America as slaves by not only detailing what their daily lives were like but by demonstrating that every aspect of their culture was devastated—tribal associations, family life, individual dignity. She documented the pattern of abuses. At the same time, she also began to develop a second theme: the way in which African slaves began to create a new culture, a new society even in the face of the destruction of the old. In the end, the moral wrongs that threatened to destroy black slaves in America in every way human beings can be destroyed stirred in them a new capacity for endurance in the face of social cruelty and perseverance in the face of politically outrageous laws meant to protect the rights of slave owners while ignoring the fundamental humanity of the black victims. "That a race, a people, a culture could emerge from that unrighteous visitation is not only extraordinary historically," she said, "it is testimony to the human capacity to face down evil and to triumph over ignorance." When she finished her last lecture, she received a standing ovation, which Clementine and I joined.

My grandfather's lectures were parallel to Clementine's mother's lectures. His focus was on the complex ways justifying slavery had corrupted every aspect of early American life. His lectures did not try to invoke any sympathy for white America. Rather, his lectures outlined the process by which the moral potential of white Christian culture in America had corrupted itself in the process of rationalizing the institution of chattel slavery. "The ultimate and tragic irony is," he said, "that while the agony of the War Between the States, with all of its horrors, should have acted as both punishment and exorcism for the sins of American society, it did not. It may have freed the slaves legally, but it did not free blacks culturally, socially, or psychologically of their wounds, nor did it free whites culturally, socially, or psychologically of the burden of their crimes." He concluded with a statement that I can still remember verbatim: "America is still a nation caught in the throes of its criminal past. Until it acknowledges that fact and then acts to root out the root cause, racism will continue to infect every aspect of civil life, no matter the face the nation puts on its past." My grandfather also received a standing ovation. I was very proud. I only wished my mother could have heard him. I was even more proud of what he did in response, because he did not simply accept the applause and then leave the stage. Instead, he stepped forward and called Ruth Ann to come join him, which she did.

So there they stood, hand in hand, accepting the gratitude of an audience that, as Clementine heard one professor sitting next to her say, had never heard anything like their lectures. And there we stood, Clementine and me, in the audience, applauding both of them. What more could two fifteen year olds ask for? Yet when we joined them for lunch, as much as the two of us wanted to hold on to the feelings we had had when they each had lectured and each been applauded, they by contrast wanted to go back to being Clementine's mother and my grandfather, which made for a very interesting atmosphere during the conversations over the meal. Both Clementine and I were glad beyond words that we had been able to travel with them to Scotland and then attend the lectures.

At the same time, attending the lectures still left Clementine and me free to go places in the afternoons. Her mother and my grandfather joined us two times. All four of us went to Edinburgh Castle and took the tour and saw the Crown Jewels, which were beautiful. We had tea that afternoon in a pub part way down the hill from the Castle. It was the first time either Clementine or I had been in a place like that. It was wonderful because it wasn't just about serving beer. It had very good food. In fact, my grandfather said that when he had studied in Ireland for a semester when he was in graduate school, it was the pub food that had kept him alive. It was a lesson that Clementine and I would remember and put to use years later when we traveled in Ireland after we were married.

What impressed me the most about Edinburgh was that from the Castle you can see the water on three sides of the city. Starting with that experience in Edinburgh, I learned that almost all of my favorite places in the world have high elevations. From most of them you can see the water. What Clementine said she liked the most was how green the city was. We especially enjoyed that when we went for walks. Edinburgh is not a city of skyscrapers. No building is more than seven stories tall. You can walk and not feel overwhelmed. And the streets are wide. Clementine said she liked that almost as much as she liked all of the trees. However, every moment in Edinburgh was not a highlight. At least not for me. There was one night when I not only made a fool of myself, I came very close to insulting both my grandfather and Ruth Ann. It happened after my grandfather and Clementine's mother had delivered their last lectures.

Two very well-known history professors and their wives invited my grandfather and Clementine's mother to join them for dinner. While neither of the men would have been so impolite as to say they couldn't bring the two of us—and by then it was widely known that we had come with them—it seemed to the four of us that maybe this was a time when Clementine and I should fend for ourselves. After all, we were comfortable with our hotel and with the streets around it. And we knew there were places to eat nearby. So we told them to go and have a good time and we would walk someplace and eat and then come back to the hotel and read because both of us had three novels we were supposed to have read by the time we started back to school in the fall. Clementine had already started one of the novels; I hadn't started any of them.

After my grandfather and Ruth Ann left for their dinner, I knocked on Clementine's door and said we should go find something to eat. Dressing in nice clothes, but certainly not dressed up, we walked to a Wimpie's Hamburger Place on Princes Street five blocks away.

I have to say that as nice as the Scots are, they do not know how to cook hamburgers. Clementine said it's because the meat is too lean. She is right. I thought we were eating hockey pucks. As for the rest of the hamburger: who in America could get away with serving a hamburger without tomatoes or pickles? Or even lettuce. It was the one time that we were not taken with things in Edinburgh. We even came very close to laughing out loud at the way the young people who were in the restaurant were eating the hamburgers as if they thought that was the way they were supposed to be served. It took all of our self control to not say something. What happened when we got back to our hotel wasn't as funny. At least, it wasn't as funny to me. Not at the time at least. I have to admit that it has become funnier since it happened.

40

Clementine and I went back to our hotel. I got the novel I was going to start reading, *To Kill a Mockingbird*, by Harper Lee, and we went to Clementine and her mother's room. Clementine got out the novel she was reading, *The Awakening*, by Kate Chopin, and sat down in one of the two chairs that stood on opposite sides of a reading table. I slipped off my shoes and sat down on Clementine's bed with my back against the headboard. What didn't seem very important at the time but what proved to be important in a short time was the fact that the headboard was against the wall that adjoined the two rooms. Then both of us settled down and started reading. We sat that way for an hour, maybe a little more, when I heard through the wall the door open to the room I shared with my grandfather. The sound was muffled, of course, but I could still hear it, and I could hear the sound of what I assumed was my grandfather and Clementine's mother's voices. I couldn't understand what they were saying, and I wasn't particularly interested. I was too engrossed in the novel to pay much attention. Then I heard it. It sounded like a squeak. A bed spring squeak. Then I heard it again. Then I heard a laugh. It sounded like a woman's laugh. Like Ruth Ann Brown's laugh. And a man's laugh. I stopped reading and listened. I heard the squeak again. Then again. Oh, God, I thought. Clementine. Clementine!

I jumped up from the bed. Clementine hadn't looked up. "Get your jacket," I said.

"What?"

"C'mon," I said.

"Why?"

"I want to go for a walk," I said.

"A walk? Why do you want to go for a walk?"

"I just do. Put on your jacket. Put on something. C'mon."

Clementine looked like she was going to object, but she didn't. I pulled on my sweatshirt. "Bring your key," I said. Then we left. I didn't want to go past my grandfather's and my room. So we turned the other way and went to the stairs at the end of the hallway and went down them.

"Why aren't we taking the elevator, Tyler?" Clementine asked.

"I need the exercise," I said. "I've been sitting too long. So have you."

It was hard to argue with that. If we'd been at home, we'd have run every day together.

In a moment we came through the double doors at the bottom of the stairs and went through the lobby and then went out onto Princes Street and started walking. After half a block, Clementine stopped and said, "I'll walk with you, Tyler. But slow down. Let's at least look in some of the store windows."

That sounded like a good plan to me. So that's what we did. We walked for almost an hour before Clementine said she was getting tired and that we should probably go back to the hotel because when her mother and my grandfather got back to the hotel they would wonder where we'd gone. When we got to Clementine and her mother's room and she used her key and opened the door, they were waiting.

"Where have you been?" Mrs. Brown said.

Before either of us could answer, my grandfather said, "Tyler, why didn't you tell us you were going out?"

I hesitated. What was I supposed to say? How could I possibly explain? "Well," I said, "I heard you next door. It sounded like you were busy."

"When was that?" Ruth Ann asked.

"About an hour ago," said. "Maybe a little less. We were both reading, and I heard you talking."

"I didn't hear them," Clementine said.

"I did," I said.

"You heard us? What were we doing?" my grandfather asked.

"Talking," I answered. "I heard you in my room. In Grandpa's room," I said.

"You didn't stop in and say anything about hearing us," my grandfather said.

"I didn't want to disturb you," I replied.

"But where did you go?" Clementine's mother asked.

"We went for a walk, mom," Clementine said. "Tyler said he wanted to go for a walk, so we went for a walk."

"It was okay," I said. "The street is safe."

"It was nice. There were all sorts of people out walking," Clementine said. "We looked in store windows."

"Yes. It was nice. We looked in store windows," I said.

"Tyler, We don't mind you two going for a walk. And I know the streets are supposed to be safe," my grandfather said. "I just wish you'd told us you were going."

"I didn't want to interrupt," I said.

"Interrupt?" my grandfather said. "Interrupt what?"

"You were laughing. I couldn't hear what you were saying. I didn't want to interrupt anything you were doing," I said. God, I wish I hadn't said that, I thought immediately.

Everyone was quiet for a moment. "Tyler, what did you hear us doing?" Clementine's mother said.

I looked at her. Oh, God. What now? "I heard you and grandpa. It sounded like . . . you were laughing," I said.

"You said that before, Tyler, but it doesn't answer the question," my grandfather said.

I had to retreat very fast. "I didn't want to bother you," I said. "Either of you. I didn't think we should bother you."

"You've said that," my grandfather replied slowly.

"And I heard you," I said.

"You said that too. But you still haven't answered Ruth Ann's question," my grandfather said. He turned to Clementine's mother. "I don't remember doing anything that couldn't have been interrupted," he said.

I did not answer. I turned and looked at Clementine. She did not answer.

Mrs. Brown smiled. "I think I understand, Tyler," she said very slowly. She turned to my grandfather. "I think maybe I understand, Edward," she said.

"Really?" my grandfather replied. "Well, I don't."

"I think it must have been when I was sitting on your bed and we were talking. I thought I heard a door close. But I didn't know it was next door," she said.

"When you were . . . ," my grandfather started to say. Then he stopped. "Really?" my grandfather said again.

"Yes, really," Clementine's mother said.

Then my grandfather turned to me. "So you heard us and then you took Clementine for a walk?"

"Yes, sir. I did that, sir," I said. "I did do that."

My grandfather turned to Clementine. "Did he tell you why he wanted to take you for a walk, Clementine?"

Clementine looked at me. She did not want to get me into trouble. I could see that in her eyes. "He just said he wanted to go for a walk. All of a sudden when we were reading. And he got up and pulled on his sweatshirt and said we should go for a walk. He said we'd been sitting too long." She looked at me again as if she were asking me if she'd said the right thing.

"And so he took you for a walk on Princes Street?" my grandfather said.

"Yes, sir," Clementine replied.

"And you looked in windows?" he said.

"And you talked?" Ruth Ann said.

"We always talk," Clementine replied.

"When you talked, did he tell you then why he'd taken you for a walk," my grandfather said.

"He didn't say anything about why. We just walked and looked in windows," Clementine said.

My grandfather turned to Clementine's mother. "I think you're right," he said.

She nodded. "I think I am," she said. Then she turned to me. "You are a very noble young man, Tyler. You have a vivid imagination. Perhaps too much in this instance. But you are a very noble young man, Tyler."

"What do you mean, mom? I still don't understand," Clementine started to say.

At the same time, my grandfather turned and walked to one of the two chairs that sat on each side of the reading table that stood under the window overlooking the street. No one spoke for a moment. He sat down and smiled and turned to me. "I am flattered, Tyler, that you would think that of me . . . I think. Of course, maybe I should be insulted. But I think that I'm going to let myself be flattered. I'm not sure how Ruth Ann must feel."

Clementine's mother smiled. "Well, I am flattered too, Edward. A little surprised, I suppose, but I think, like you, I will let myself be flattered"

"Mom, what are you two talking about?" Clementine said. "I don't understand what you're talking about." Then she looked at me. "You don't mean that you thought . . ." She did not finish her sentence.

"It's my fault," I said quietly. "I heard . . . what I heard. And I thought that maybe . . . I thought it was . . . ."

"So you thought . . . " Clementine started to say. Then she stopped.

"I didn't want you to hear," I said quickly. "I didn't want you to hear or to think that . . . ." I stopped. I wanted to die. Right there. Then I added, "I didn't want you to hear."

My grandfather smiled. “Clementine, I think our young man thought you might be embarrassed, and he was trying to protect you,” he said very quietly.

Ruth Ann Brown was just about ready to laugh. She sat down on the edge of my bed. It made a squeaking sound. She bounced once, and it made another.

Clementine did not speak. Instead, she turned and looked at me.

“Don’t be mad, Clementine,” I said.

“I’m not mad. How can I be mad? You were trying to do what you always do,” she said, her smile, like her mother’s, about ready to become a laugh.

“Okay, okay,” I said. “I was very foolish. I know,” I said. “What can I say now?” I wanted to sit down. Somewhere. Anywhere. Preferably outside in the hallway or out in the middle of the traffic on Princes Street. “But I was sitting on the bed reading, and you were sitting where grandpa is sitting now, reading. And I could hear them through the wall talking and laughing and . . . . You know. The springs on the bed. But I couldn’t hear what they were saying, and I wasn’t trying to, but I could hear,” I said.

“And so,” Clementine’s mother said very slowly, turning to Clementine, “when Tyler heard me laughing and talking and sitting on Edward’s bed, he took you out for a walk, my dear.”

I sat down on the straight back chair that sat next to the bathroom door.

A very long silence passed. At least, it seemed like a very long silence to me.

Then my grandfather turned to Clementine and said, “Well, did you and Tyler enjoy your walk?” he said, smiling. Then he laughed.

Then Clementine’s mother laughed. Then Clementine laughed and moved to the bed and sat down next to her mother, and all three of them looked at me.

And I blushed. I mean, I really blushed. I know that because Clementine told me at least once a year for the next ten years whenever the subject of someone blushing due to some embarrassing incident came up that she had never seen anyone blush the way I had blushed that night in Edinburgh.

I don’t have much choice but to agree.

41

On Friday afternoon, the four of us took the train back to London where my grandfather had arranged for us to spend four nights in a small hotel. He said that as long as we had to go through London, we might as well stay and enjoy ourselves. On Saturday, because all four of us enjoy theatre, he took us to see a matinee performance of “Nicholas Nickleby,” a big play adapted from a Charles Dickens novel. He surprised us even more when that night he rushed us to see Sean O’Casey’s play “Juno and the Paycock.” It’s one of those Irish plays that’s both funny and touching at the same time. Seeing the play introduced both Clementine and me to O’Casey’s writing. Then we spent Sunday walking from place to place, so much so that all four of us could barely eat any dinner that night. On Monday, we took the tour boat from London to Greenwich and back again. Clementine and I agreed that was the best way to see the city.

On Tuesday morning, we spent the day at the National Portrait Gallery, which was very interesting. But I think both Clementine and I most enjoyed sitting in a small restaurant overlooking Trafalgar Square. We took photographs of each other in various combinations in front of the British Lion statue. That night, we saw the musical "Cats," which had just opened. All four of us agreed it was spellbinding.

On Wednesday morning at breakfast, Ruth Ann and my grandfather announced that we were not flying back to Florida that day, even though that's what Clementine and I had been told. My grandfather said we had one more very important thing to do. So we took the train from London to Cardiff, Wales, where we stayed in a hotel near the railway station. At dinner that night my grandfather explained what he had in mind.

My father's family is Scots. That is why my grandfather thought I would enjoy visiting Edinburgh. My mother's family is Welsh. My grandfather told the three of us that when he was a boy, he'd grown up hearing stories of how his father had come to the United States from South Wales and how, because he'd been a coal miner in Wales, he'd settled in Pennsylvania, where he could get a job in the pits. My grandfather said that because his own undergraduate studies had focused on politics, he had become very interested in the conflicts that animated life in the coal mines in South Wales. As he'd grown up, he'd done enough genealogical research to know where his father's people had lived and worked and from where his father finally left. "It's a village named Maerdy," my grandfather said. "It's the last village in one of the two Rhondda Valleys. When I was studying the history of the South Wales Miners' Federation, I kept coming across my grandfather's and my father's names because both of them had been important union organizers. Over the years he was in the middle of a number of very dangerous conflicts with the mine owners and with the government. That's why he finally had to leave. He couldn't work in the pits anymore. His name was Evan Thomas. That was my grandfather's name as well and my father's. It's where your uncle Evan gets his name."

We waited because we knew there was more to come. "Anyway," he went on, "years ago, when I was studying the way the miners had fought against the owners and the government and even the British army when it was called in to stop one of the early strikes, I promised that one day I would come back to Maerdy and bring my son." He smiled. "Well, as all of you know, I don't have a son. I have a lovely daughter. But she gave birth to a son. And the first time I held you in my arms, Tyler, I promised myself that one day I would bring you here and that we would go to Maerdy." He looked at me in a way that told me this was very important to him. "So here we are, Tyler. And if you will all indulge me, that's where I want to take you tomorrow."

We all said we would be happy to go.

42

The next morning, bright and early, we took the train to Pontypridd, a town at the south end of the Rhondda Valleys. From there we took a bus up the narrow valley road to Maerdy. Once we got there, we got off the bus. What I remember is how quiet my grandfather had gotten as we rode. When we got off the bus, I watched him more than I looked at the village.

My grandfather was a man of very sincere sentiment. I mean by that that he felt things deeply, especially family things. He said more than once during the years when I was growing up and my mother and I were living with him that, in the end, all that really mattered in life was family. Fame and money were not important. Blood relationships were. I could see all of that as we started walking. I always knew my grandfather liked watching people in public places. It is a characteristic I inherited from him. But in Maerdy he did not just watch the people who lived and worked there, he memorized them. Years later, he could still describe some of the people we passed and all of the people to whom we spoke. There was nothing about them that he did not recall. More important, his sense of what the village was began showing up in his essay writing years later. Not just the facts of the village. I mean, the sense of a caste of miner warriors who had braved the dangers of the pits, and who had achieved, he claimed, a kind of camaraderie that most people do not understand. I think as he looked at his own life, he felt as if he had missed something. He never said as much, but the way in which he spoke about life in the villages that line the valleys suggests that he almost wished his father had never left South Wales. Then he did something that it had never occurred to me he would do but which was obviously important to him.

After we stopped in a very small restaurant and ate, and my grandfather talked to the owner and then to two older men who were sitting at the counter, he came to me and said, "Tyler, we have to go for a walk." He turned to Ruth Ann and Clementine and said, "You are welcome to come along, but it will involve a very long climb."

Both Clementine's mother and Clementine were puzzled, but they said as they had come that far, they sure were not going to miss whatever it was my grandfather had in mind. So the four of us set out, turning to the hillside that rose up above the village, and the row after row of what I would learn were called terrace houses because they'd been built on a network of terraced streets carved out of the side of the mountain, each street running parallel to the only two lane roadway that traced the valley floor all the way from Pontypridd.

It took a good twenty-five minutes to climb to the top because the street that goes straight up the hillside is steeper than any street I have ever seen. But when we got to the top we realized it had been worth it because we could see all the way to the pits farther north. We could see the top of the mountain on the opposite side of the valley. We could see at least four of the villages that edged the two lane roadway as it snaked back down the valley.

Clouds were rolling in from the ocean to the south. The wind was stronger than it had been in the village. My grandfather moved away from us for a moment and stood quietly looking at the very top of the valley to the north. Then he let his vision trace the pathways from the houses as they networked toward where the highway ended and the pit works began. He turned and motioned that I should join him, which I did. So there we were, standing where his family had stood so long ago, standing where his great-great grandfather had most probably stood when he'd gone for walks or taken the young woman he would marry and bring with him to America when they were courting. Then my grandfather put an arm around my shoulder and touched my head and whispered words I had never heard him say before, words I would never have thought he would say. "I have brought this boy here, Grandfather, for you to see." He was quiet for a moment, and I did not move. I could feel his hand shaking slightly. "Bless him Grandfather Thomas. He is brave and kind. He has a good mind. He has a true heart, Grandfather. He cares about justice. So please bless him, and bless his life, Grandfather. Bless his soul."

Then he was quiet again. We stood quietly for a moment more. Then he turned and we went to where Clementine and her mother were waiting. He smiled at them, but he did not say anything more as we walked back down the hill and got the bus and rode back to Pontypridd where we caught the train back to Cardiff. Once we were on the train, my grandfather quietly explained what he had done when he sat next to Ruth Ann and Clementine, although he did not try to repeat what he had said.

"I thought it must be something like that, Edward," Clementine's mother said.

Clementine did not speak, and I did not speak. But I could feel her looking at me as we rode back south, and she held my hand. However, she did say something to me the next day when we rode the train back to London, something very important. So important that I made her a solemn promise that I was able to keep years later.

When you travel by train from London to Cardiff or from Cardiff to London, you have to change trains in Redding. Standing on the platform in Redding, Clementine turned to me and said, "I am very glad you got to have your moment on the hill in Maerdy, yesterday, Tyler."

I nodded but did not speak.

"But you know, don't you, that I can't do anything like that," she said. "Ever."

I turned to her. "Why not?" I said.

"Because I have no idea where my ancestors came from," she said.

"They came from Africa," I said.

"Yes, some of them did. My mother's ancestors. Some of my father's ancestors. But I can't go to a hill like you did and look at a valley like you did and say that was where they came from."

I waited a long time before I spoke. "They came from West Africa, Clementine. Some of your ancestors. Most of your ancestors. They came from West Africa," I said.

Clementine looked at me. I could feel her sorrow. I could feel her hurt.

"And we will go there someday, Clementine," I said in a whisper.

She turned and looked at me again. The most beautiful girl in the whole world stood there and looked at me.

"We will go there, Clementine. To West Africa. And we will find a hill just for you. I promise," I said. "We will find a hill just for you."

Clementine looked away from me and did not speak, but as we started walking toward the train we were to board for our return to London, she did not let go of my hand. She held on as hard as she has ever held on. I have come to believe over the years when I've thought back about that moment that it was her way of accepting my promise.

43

The flight back to the United States was both happy and sad. Going to Edinburgh and then London had been a rich experience for all four of us. Except for my overly hasty reaction in Edinburgh when my instinctive desire to protect Clementine had turned into an embarrassing moment, every part of our time in Scotland and then in London and, for me, especially in Wales, had been more than I ever could have anticipated. Leaving all of that behind made each of us a little sad. At the same time, each of us was happy to be going home. We had good lives in Tampa, after all. And I missed my mother. I wanted to tell her about everything that had happened. Among all of us, we had ten rolls of film to develop. That was a good start, it seemed to me. Yet mixed into all of that was the knowledge that when we got home, Clementine and I would not be able to spend virtually every waking moment with each other in the way we had when traveling. I knew I needed to try to record every moment of the flight back in my mind: the look of her slim, delicate hand holding mine as she leaned towards me; the small sound of her breathing as she slept; the touch of her hair against my cheek when she shifted in her seat; the book that she had opened and then left on her lap when she napped; the very soft sound of her voice when she woke up and without moving whispered, "I do love you, Tyler Thomas Raymond, the man with three first names," without my having said anything; the way she then shifted in her seat again and continued holding my hand as she went back to sleep for another hour; the way she finally woke up but continued to sit with her head on my shoulder for some time before I knew she was awake and how she said, "I love sitting with you when you read," before she sat up slowly and turned to me and smiled and said, "I have to go to the restroom," and smiled as I stood up and moved out into the aisle so she could go to the lavatory; the way she came back, her hair combed, smiling, climbing over me in a way that let her push her left hand against my shoulder and for a moment sit on my lap as she climbed back into her seat, laughing quietly all the while. I wanted to remember each moment, each sound, each feeling.

After we arrived in New York, we flew to Tampa. My grandfather got his station wagon from long term parking and drove Clementine and her mother home. When we arrived, we got Clementine and her mother's suitcases out of the trunk and carried them to their doorstep. Then all four of us said goodbye to one another and thank you for such a lovely trip and we will call you tomorrow and we'll see each other soon. Clementine's mother went in, and my grandfather walked back to his car, and I stood facing Clementine. For a moment neither of us said anything. Then she smiled, as much with her eyes as with her lips, and she said, "We'll have to do that again, won't we?" And I said, "Yes. We should. And we will." And she said, "I know." Then she put a hand on my face and then turned and went up the steps onto her porch and then went inside, and I stood on the sidewalk for a moment not believing the trip was over but knowing I had no choice but to believe it was. So I turned and walked back to my grandfather's car and got in, and he was quiet all the way to our house where we knew my mother was waiting to hear all about our adventures.

44

As you can imagine, my mother was excited about seeing both of us. We talked well past midnight before we finally went to bed. The next morning the conversation continued, with my grandfather briefly summarizing both Ruth Ann's and his lectures and the response from the University audiences. He told her about what we did in London. I told her about the shows we saw and about the boat ride on the Thames. Each time I brought up something new she wanted to know how Clementine had liked it. I could tell her in all honesty that Clementine had been as excited about everything as I had been.

Then my grandfather told my mother about going to Cardiff and then on to Maerdy. He told her about taking me to the top of the valley from where we looked down on the village and the valley and about what he had said. He did not repeat what he had said. He just said that he had finally gotten to do something he had wanted to do all of his life.

Later, when my mother and I were together in the kitchen and my grandfather was sleeping, she asked me what my grandfather had said. I told her it was a very important moment, not just for him but for me as well. I told her that I had thought about it coming home on the plane and that I decided it was something that was going to mean more and more to me as the years went by.

When she asked me again what he had said, I told her I would describe the moment, but that as they were my grandfather's words it would be better if he told her. I told her that it wasn't a matter of remembering the words. I remembered every one. I remembered how I had felt when he had spoken them. I said that I believed that because the moment had obviously been very special for him that he should be the one who decided how much he would repeat.

Then it was July, and Clementine and I started counting the days until she was sixteen. The five of us and another woman with whom Ruth Ann taught at the University and two of Clementine's girl friends from school celebrated at Clementine's house. All of us brought presents. I got her a copy of the novel *Cry, the Beloved Country*, by Alan Paton. My grandfather said it was a very important novel portraying the agony of Apartheid in South Africa. He told me I should read it as well. I also surprised her with a double frame of two enlargements of pictures taken on our trip: one of the two of us at Edinburgh Castle with the water behind us, the other in Trafalgar Square standing at the base of the British lion monument. My grandfather took the picture in Edinburgh, her mother in London. In both cases, we had our arms around each other and we were smiling at the camera. I made copies for myself as well. Then, two days later, Clementine surprised me in return.

45

It was late in the afternoon. I had spent the day mowing six lawns in my neighborhood so I could earn money. It was hard, sweaty work, and I hated every minute of it, but until I turned sixteen, I could not get a regular part time job. After I finished, I came home and took a shower and lay down before dinner. Clementine and I were supposed to go to a movie. Then the telephone rang. My mother said it was Clementine calling. When I got on the telephone, Clementine said I needed to be dressed and ready and out on my porch in ten minutes. I asked her why. She said it was a surprise. I told her I hadn't eaten. She said she had not eaten either, but that didn't matter. I was supposed to be on the porch in ten minutes ready to go.

I told my mother what Clementine had said and what she wanted me to do. My mother acted surprised, but not in a way that said she was really surprised. It was one of those mother reactions when you know she knows what's going on but she isn't going to tell. As I went through the living room, my grandfather was reading. He looked and me and smiled one of those grandfather smiles that said he knew as well what was going on but that he sure wasn't going to be the one to tell me anything. I would have been upset were it not for the fact that like my grandfather I also love surprises. It was certainly obvious that both my mother and my grandfather were in on whatever Clementine had planned. As far as I knew, her mother probably was as well.

So I went out onto the porch and sat down on the steps and waited. I did not have to wait long. Because in no more than five minutes, Clementine's mother's car came to a slow stop in front of our house. When I stood up and looked through the windows, expecting to see both Clementine and Ruth Ann, the only person in the car was Clementine, and she was driving.

I stopped walking and looked at her as she leaned over to the passenger's side and rolled down the window and called to me, "Hey, you there, wanna go to a movie with a pretty girl?"

I started laughing. "Sure. Do you know one?" I called back.

"Okay, smart guy, just for that, I may go pick up someone else," she called back. "So you better hurry if you're going to ride with me."

When I got to the curb, she reached over and opened the passenger's side door and smiled. "Well, what do you think?" she said.

"I don't know what to think. I didn't know you could drive," I said.

"I took lessons. All of those Saturday mornings when I couldn't come study with you."

I shook my head. "That's awesome, Clementine," I said, getting in and closing the door.

"You don't mind?" she asked.

"Mind? Why should I mind?"

"Because I got my license before you."

I looked at her. "You're older than me. Not by much, but you're still older than me."

"Good. I thought maybe you'd think you should have gotten your license first," she said.

"Clementine, you turned sixteen two days ago. I turn sixteen on August 1st. My grandfather has been teaching me to drive. You even came along twice. But I want to know about the test. The driving part."

Clementine nodded and turned back to the street and looked over her shoulder at the street behind her. Then she pulled out into the street and we started driving toward the shopping mall. "This is my first solo, Tyler. You're my first passenger, besides my mother. I had to drive her all over town yesterday before she would let me drive the car on my own. She was a lot tougher than the man from the motor vehicle department I drove with when I took my test." She glanced at me and smiled. "I'm glad you're not one of those ego guys who always has to be first to do things."

I shrugged my shoulders. "That kind of stuff doesn't matter to me, Clementine. You know that. I just want to be with you. I'll be driving soon. Then we can take turns as far as I'm concerned."

So we entered another phase in our relationship. It meant it was going to be easier for us to be together and to go places, but it also meant we were taking on a very big responsibility. Both of us knew that. Our mothers made sure we understood. The lesson served us well years later, when our own daughters started to drive. But that afternoon, all we cared about was that we were now on our own, just the two of us, heading for the shopping mall, where we would eat together and then go to a movie. I sat back and relaxed. I trusted Clementine in every way. I had no reason not to. Besides, if her mother said she was ready to drive in the streets, she was truly ready.

46

On August 12th, I also passed my driving test, which meant Clementine and I could now drive ourselves places and take turns when we went places together. Clementine even got a part time job at a Burger King Restaurant close to her house. I wanted to do the same, but football practice began before the school year started, so I was not able to join her.

Our tenth grade year was similar to our ninth grade year in many ways. We both did well in classes. We were accepted by our friends as a couple. One of my friends said that because Clementine and I were dating, and because we each had several friends, our individual friends had become friends. What it meant in social terms was that a few white students and a few black students who might not have had occasion to get to know one another began to do so.

I became a starter on the junior varsity football team. As they had the year before, Clementine and my grandfather came to all of the games. My mother and Clementine's mother came to several. No matter who had been able to come, when the game was over we all went out to eat. It was my grandfather's treat each time. At the end of the junior varsity season, twelve players were invited to practice with the varsity. Three of us were actually added to the varsity roster. I was one of the three. In the middle of the fourth quarter of the last game of the season, I was put in and caught a pass. However, I have to admit that, first, I was very nervous when I looked across the line of scrimmage and saw the defensive end I was supposed to block before I ran out into the flat. I had grown up from a 140 pound freshman to a 160 pound sophomore, but he was a senior and must have outweighed me by forty pounds. When I made my block, he pushed me aside like I wasn't even there. I started to fall but recovered my balance quickly enough to still run my pattern. I caught the ball when it was thrown to me, but it was as much a surprise to me as it was to everyone else. I was only in that game for two more plays, neither of which involved me, which is probably a good thing because both times the defensive end from Brandon High School ran over me like a truck. By the time I left the field, I knew I had a whole lot of growing up to do before I was ready for varsity football. However, I was invited to join the varsity team for spring practice, which I took as a good sign.

Students at Tampa Coast did not get to create their own class schedules, so it was coincidental that Clementine and I ended up in the same English class. That turned out to be a very good experience, not only because the teacher was excited about the subject matter, but because the two of us could spend time together talking about the books we read. As we had the year before, we ate lunch together almost every day. Otherwise, the year at school was without any issues of concern. We went to two dances without any unpleasant incidents, went to movies almost every week, went to all of the varsity football and junior varsity and varsity girls volleyball games. By the time basketball season began, both of us were working part time at the Burger King Restaurant. Our manager put us on the same shifts so we could drive each other to work and back home.

At home, things were very interesting. As my mother and Clementine's mother got to know each other, they became very close friends. I was happy to see that because I sensed that both had felt rather isolated before, the kind of thing that can happen when a person is new in a city and new in a school. When my mother invited two women teachers from her school to our house for dinner, she also invited Ruth Ann. When Ruth Ann began to develop friends at the University, she included my mother. Clementine and my grandfather and I were very glad that was happening.

The most exciting news of the year came when, in November, Edinburgh University Press asked Ruth Ann and my grandfather to sign contracts to publish the lectures they had delivered in Edinburgh the summer before. After they got the news and told Clementine and my mother and me, the three of us organized a dinner at our house to celebrate. We invited Ruth Ann's and my mother's new friends and three people my grandfather had come to know. The highlight of the evening was having them sign the publishing contracts right there in front of all of us. We toasted them with champagne as they did. What I remember most clearly was Ruth Ann's personal toast of my grandfather. My grandfather had already published three books. This was Ruth Ann's first. She thanked my grandfather for making it possible. In fact, she said that the lectures would not have been written and the trip to Edinburgh University would not have happened had it not been for my grandfather's support. "So while Edward and I have decided to dedicate the book to the thousands of unknown African and American blacks who suffered the outrages of slavery, I want all of you to know that if I had my way, my lectures would have been dedicated to Professor Thomas." My grandfather was very touched by Ruth Ann's sentiment.

All of that would seem to say that the year went without any major problems. Mostly, I suppose, that's true. However, there was one thing that happened in February which was very difficult. I am only thankful that I was there because I am sure it would have been much more painful for Clementine had I not been with her. Clementine said as much at the time. Her mother said the same afterwards.

47

When Clementine and I were students at Tampa Coast, we knew a number of students whose parents were divorced. Some of those divorces had gone relatively well. Others had been very difficult. In every case, the children had been caught in between. More than one talked about it over the four years of high school. Only two ever said it had been for the best. I bring that up because suddenly, in February, without any warning, Clementine's father wrote and said he was bringing his wife and three sons to Orlando to spend a weekend at Disney World and that he would like to have her come and spend the day with them in the Magic Kingdom.

Clementine was stunned. Her mother was angry. Clementine drove to my house, and we drove to the shopping mall to eat lunch in the food court so she could talk without her mother present. What she told me was both interesting and troubling.

Clementine's father is named Jefferson Julius Hayden III. His grandfather, Jefferson Julius Hayden, was only one generation removed from the slavery his family had endured in Georgia. Jefferson's father, Jefferson Julius Hayden II, took over Jefferson Julius I's small grocery store, renamed it Hayden's Grocery Haven, and worked hard to establish himself in business, even though he was trying to do so during a time when Jim Crow laws flourished in Georgia and South Carolina, where he managed to open stores. By the time Jefferson II was living in Wilmington, Delaware, he married a white woman.

Their son, Jefferson Julius III, grew up in Wilmington. Unfortunately, the fact his father was black and his mother was white was a great discomfort for him. He constantly heard his own father deriding blacks who were not industrious, who could not face up to the everyday facts of American racism, who could not make it in the same way he had made it. So young Jefferson was conflicted from childhood. His school experience did not help. Was he black or white? Should he be proud of his black father's accomplishments or embarrassed at his father's prejudice against people of his own race, even members of his own extended family? He could not identify with his mother's family, because they had turned their back on their daughter when she married a black man even if he was far more successful than her own father. So who was Jefferson Julius Hayden supposed to be?

In an effort to escape, he enrolled in New York University. There he met Ruth Ann. When they married, Jefferson's father was outraged. How dare he marry a black woman? Especially since her family was of no particular importance. Just working people. The kind of people Jefferson II wanted to avoid.

Ruth Ann said that on one hand, Jefferson was handsome and charming. Certainly he was intelligent and well read. On the other hand, he was angry, as angry a young man as she had ever met. He looked Negro enough to not be accepted by whites; he was too light skinned to be accepted by blacks. Marriage was supposed to give him a place to be, a person to be. But it did not. He wanted a subservient black woman. Ruth Ann was not about to be subservient to anyone. She was intelligent, creative, ambitious. She was going to earn degrees and become a college professor.

After Clementine was born, the conflict both within Julius and between Julius and Ruth Ann became worse. The day Julius shouted at Ruth Ann and then struck her was the end. Ruth Ann took Clementine and went back to her parents' home. Within a month, she had a small studio apartment. She continued her part time job. She kept up her grades so she maintained her scholarship. Julius moved away. Ruth Ann did not pursue child support. She would raise her own daughter in her own way. Clementine would be respected, educated, accomplished.

Years passed. Julius made no effort to contact Ruth Ann to inquire after her or after his daughter. For Ruth Ann, that was just fine. She had heard through her family that he had married a Mexican-American woman he met in Houston when he moved there to open yet another Hayden's Grocery Haven. She heard he had three sons. None of it mattered to her. She was raising Clementine. Clementine was lovely. Then Ruth Ann moved to the University of South Florida, in Tampa, to teach history. Her focus would be on African-American history.

When Clementine first talked about me and then brought me home, you can well imagine that Ruth Ann felt some trepidations. However, she also knew Clementine knew her own mind. How could she quarrel with a daughter who wanted to date a boy who happened to be white when Clementine described him as the most accepting person she'd ever met? When she found out the boy was the grandson of Professor Edward Thomas, she withdrew even her unstated objections. Then she met me and met my mother and met my grandfather, and any questions about our relationship disappeared. When I responded to insults directed at Clementine the way I did, Ruth Ann was more pleased than uneasy. Her comments to me after the Timmy O'Brien incident made that clear.

Then came the letter from Clementine's father. At first, Ruth Ann said no: "Your father has not wanted to see you in all these years. There is no reason for him to see you now." That was when Clementine called me, and we went to lunch, and we talked.

"What am I supposed to do, Tyler?" she wanted to know.

I waited for her to say more because it was obvious there was much more to be said.

"He didn't want to be my father," Clementine said. "He left my mother and got a divorce and just ran away."

"But now he wants to know you," I said.

"Yes. But why? Why now?"

Then she told me the story of her father's family. She trusted her mother. She did not think her mother had distorted the facts. It was very complex. She knew that. "Nothing is ever just one thing," she said. "I know enough to know that. But why now? All of a sudden? Out of the blue?"

"Clementine, I can't answer that question. You can't answer that question. All you know is that he wrote and said he was bringing his wife and sons to Disney World. And he wants you to come for the day and join them."

"But what am I supposed to do? Do I just go and meet him and meet my three half-brothers like nothing happened? Like nothing he did years ago matters?"

I waited again. I had grown up without a father. But my situation was entirely different. I knew that. Clementine knew that.

"Look, you can't know what he's like now. You can't know if he feels guilty. You don't know what kind of relationship he has with his wife. Or with his sons. All you can do is decide do you want to accept his invitation or not accept his invitation."

Clementine looked away.

"What does your mother say? What does she think you should do?" I asked her.

Clementine turned back to face me. "She says she doesn't want to see him."

"That's not what I mean."

"I know what you mean. What does she think about me going?"

"Yes."

"She will drive me to Disney if I want to go. She said that. But that would mean she'd have to wait around all day because I wouldn't want her to drive back to Tampa and then back to Orlando to pick me up."

"Does he want you to stay the night?"

"He didn't say that. And I wouldn't anyway. That wouldn't be fair to my mother. It would seem as if I want to be with him. And I don't."

"But you're curious."

She smiled her shy smile and looked at me. "Sure, I'm curious. I think that's natural."

"Then maybe you should go."

"But I'm angry, too. Because of what happened."

"That's natural, too," I said. Then I looked at her. "But do you know what happened?'

"What do you mean?"

"I mean, do you really know what happened?" Before she could respond, I went on: "I'm not saying your mother hasn't told the truth. I'm sure she has. But what've we learned this year in English class? Point of view. Everything is point of view."

"It's not just point of view that he hit my mother."

"No, it isn't."

"And it isn't just point of view that he didn't want her to become educated."

"From what you've said, it isn't just point of view."

"So then what do you mean?"

"I mean that from your mother's point of view, he failed in several ways. I mean that from her point of view, she has had to be strong for both of you."

"So?"

"So . . . maybe he has a point of view, too."

Clementine looked away for a moment.

"I'm not justifying anything that he did, Clementine. I can't. I don't know what went on between your mother and your father. And that's the point. I don't know what went on. And you don't know what went on."

"I know what people have told me. How can you take his side?"

"I'm not taking his side. I'm not taking your mother's side. I'm on your side, Clementine."

"What does that mean?"

"It means what matters to me is how you feel. What happens to you. I respect your mother. It must have been hard. It must be hard now. But most of all I care about you. I can't tell you what to do. I can just tell you that I am on your side."

She bit her lower lip for a moment. Then she looked at me. "Then will you go with me, Tyler?" she said.

I looked back at Clementine. I could see it in her eyes. She trusted me. She was ready to rely on me. There was nothing more I wanted to be in the whole world than the person she trusted. The person she relied on.

"Clementine, I will go with you where ever you want to go when ever you want to go for the rest of your life."

Clementine sat up straight. "Thank you, Tyler."

"You're welcome," I said.

"And I'll do that for you, too," she said.

"I know," I replied.

"I'll tell my mother that you'll go with me. That we can take turns driving. She'll like that. She already thinks you're special. If you come with me, she'll know you're wonderful."

I did not smile. I was far too happy to smile. She knew that.

"The darling man with three first names," she said in a whisper.

I looked away and started to hum the song "My Darling Clementine" under my breath. She started to laugh.

"You know I hate that song, don't you," she said.

"Right," I said.

She laughed harder. I continued singing until I started to laugh along with her.

48

The next Saturday, I awoke early, ate breakfast with my mother and grandfather, and then taking my grandfather's car, drove to Clementine's house and picked her up. Her mother was quiet when I arrived. I could see the tension in her face. But as we were leaving, she turned to Clementine and whispered, 'I love you."

Clementine stood away from her mother for a moment. Then she said, "And I love you, mother."

An awkward moment passed. Then Ruth Ann turned to me. "Take care of her, Tyler."

"I will always take care of her, Mrs. Brown."

She looked at me for a moment. "You must take care of her, Tyler."

"I will," I said. "I promise."

She started to look away.

"I love her, Mrs. Brown," I said in a whisper.

Clementine's mother turned back to me. "I know that, Tyler. I know."

Then we left.

Once we were in the car, Clementine was very quiet. I could feel the conflict she was feeling. "She said I should go," she said.

"To see your father?"

"Yes. At breakfast. Last night at dinner, she said she didn't want to see me get hurt. But this morning, she said I should go. She said she understood why I would want to find out for myself."

I drove for another five minutes before I responded. "Find out what?" I finally said.

Clementine turned and looked at me. "What kind of man he is."

I did not reply. We drove on. In a few minutes, we were out of town. A few more minutes, and we passed Lakeland and then we came to the rest stop. I pulled in and found a parking place. It was still very early so very few cars were in the parking lot. We both went inside and used the restrooms. I waited outside for Clementine. When she came out of the restroom, she smiled. As we walked back to the car, she took my hand. As always, I opened the door for her. Then I went around and got into the car. We started again. Another thirty minutes passed. Clementine was silent. I could feel her thinking, mulling over all of the things that attended the morning, her decision.

"Your mother loves you," I said. I was surprised at myself. Why had I said such a thing? Clementine knows her mother loves her.

"I know," Clementine said. Then she turned and looked at me. "How did we get here?" she asked.

"Get where? Driving to Disney World?"

"Yes. No. Yes."

I smiled. "Which. Yes or no or yes?"

She laughed quietly. "I mean here. You and me. How did we get here?"

I smiled. "Big picture or little picture?"

"What?"

"The big picture is: how did we become boyfriend and girlfriend? The little picture is: how did we end up driving to Disney World on a February morning?"

"Both."

I drove for another two or three minutes before responding. "Well, the big picture is that you asked me to be your lab partner in biology, and I said yes, because even if I didn't know it for sure at the time, I fell in love with you the first time you spoke to me."

Clementine smiled. "That's a very nice thing to say, Tyler."

"It's true," I said. "The little picture is more complicated."

"How so?"

"Because the little picture for you and me . . . driving to Disney World this morning . . . is really the really big picture for you."

"Ah."

"Your whole life. Your mother fighting for her education. Your father."

"Yes," she said. "Another black man who ran away."

I did not reply immediately. Clementine had never said anything like that before.

She turned to the interstate highway. "You won't run away, will you, Tyler?"

"Big picture or little picture?" I said.

"Both."

"Little picture. Today. I'm going to Disney World. I promised your mother to take care of you. Not that you probably need me to take care of you, but I promised her anyway."

Clementine remained quiet for a moment. Then she said, "Big picture."

"Big picture," I said. I turned to her for a moment and then turned back to the highway. "The only way you are going to get me to go away, Clementine, is to send me away. And I swear if you ever do that . . . ." I did not finish my sentence. Then I did, "I swear . . . I still wouldn't go."

Clementine smiled. Then she whispered, "Tyler Thomas Raymond, the man with three first names, swears he would not go." She turned to me. "And Clementine Camille Brown believes him."

We drove on. Then we saw the signs on the Interstate for Disney World. We were almost there.

49

Clementine was visibly tense as we pulled into the parking lot of the Swan Hotel. I could almost hear her breathing as it changed, as it became more shallow, more labored. I did not blame her, of course. This was a very difficult moment for her. What was she supposed to say? How should she greet the man who had run away? How should any child or young person act in a moment such as this?

I got out and went around the car and opened the door for her. "Does he know you're bringing me?" I asked her.

Clementine looked at me. She hesitated for a moment as if she didn't want to get out of the car. When she looked at me, I wanted to cry. Why should she have to feel conflicted? She hadn't done anything wrong.

"I wrote him and said I was bringing a friend," she said.

I reached for her hand and helped her out of the car. Her hand was shaking. I stopped. "Come here," I said as she stood up. Then I put my arms around her and held her face against mine. "I'm here, Clementine. I'll be here all day."

She did not reply but stayed there in my arms for a moment. Then she said, "Let's go inside." So we did.

Once we were in the lobby she stopped and looked around. Then she saw him. He was coming towards her. A pale skinned man, smiling nervously and holding out his right hand. She stepped toward him and took his hand and shook it. I could see he wanted to hug her, but he knew better. Nothing in her body posture said she wanted to be hugged. Then the man turned to me. "I'm Tyler," I said. "Clementine's friend."

The man looked surprised, but he covered well. "Yes. Fine. I'm Jefferson, Clementine's father." And he held out a hand, which I accepted. Then he turned to Clementine. "You're so grown up, Clementine. You're a beautiful young woman."

"Thank you," Clementine said.

I noticed she had not addressed him as father or dad or even sir.

"Please, both of you, come meet Rita. She is eager to meet you, Clementine. And the boys. They want to meet their sister."

We crossed the lobby to a sitting area where an attractive woman in her middle thirties was sitting. She stood and smiled, extending a hand to Clementine. "This is Rita," Jefferson said. "Rita, this is Clementine." Clementine accepted Rita's hand.

"I'm so pleased to meet you," Rita said.

"And these are your brothers, Clementine," Jefferson said.

Three handsome boys stood up and came to their father.

"This is Carlos," Jefferson said, gesturing toward the oldest. Carlos shook Clementine's hand.

"And this is Jorge," Jefferson went on. Jorge shook Clementine's hand.

"And the youngest is Perez," Jefferson said, turning to a three year old boy who like his older brothers held out a hand to Clementine.

I wondered if any moment in life could be more awkward, more tense, more unnatural?

"Have the two of you eaten?" Jefferson asked.

"I had breakfast with my mother before we left," Clementine said.

"I've had breakfast," I said when Jefferson turned to me.

Then Jefferson said very quickly, "I'm sorry. Tyler is it?"

I said yes, that was my name.

Jefferson quickly introduced me to Rita and Carlos and Jorge and Perez. Rita said she was happy to meet me. I didn't think she was. All three of the boys extended their hands for me to shake. I told them I was happy to meet them. I am nothing if I am not polite.

Then Jefferson said, "Well, please, let's sit down and talk about what we want to do today."

Rita sat on the couch with all three boys crowded in close to her. Jefferson sat in a single chair. Clementine sat on a love seat facing all of them. I stood behind her until she turned and glanced at me, her eyes asking me to sit next to her, which I did.

"The boys are very eager to go to the Magic Kingdom. I said that in my letter, didn't I, Clementine?" Jefferson said.

"Yes. You did," Clementine replied.

"Is that all right? With the two of you," he asked.

"Yes. That's fine," I said quickly, relieving Clementine, I hoped.

"Would either of you like something to drink before we go?" Jefferson said, trying harder than anyone I've ever seen before to be at ease.

"I'd like a Coke," Clementine said. "We didn't stop for anything on the way here."

"Tyler?" Jefferson said.

"That would be fine," I answered.

Jefferson turned to Carlos. "Would you like something, Rita?"

Rita said she did not want anything. I looked at her for a moment. She looked miserable. She was trying to smile, but she looked like she would rather be any place else in the world than sitting there with Clementine and me.

"Should the boys have anything?" Jefferson asked his wife.

Rita turned to her sons. They all smiled. Then she turned back to Jefferson. "Yes. Three Cokes," she said.

Jefferson turned to Carlos. "Carlos, go ask the waiter to please bring five Cokes."

Carlos stood up. Jorge stood up with him. Both boys walked across the lobby to the counter where a waiter stood talking to a young woman.

Then Jefferson turned to Clementine. "So, you and Tyler. You go to school together?"

"Yes," Clementine replied.

"And you're both in . . . what grade?"

"We're in tenth grade, sir," I said.

Jefferson smiled.

"Do you like school?" Rita said, her voice edgy and thin, reflecting her extreme discomfort.

"Yes," Clementine said.

"Yes, we both like school," I said.

"Are you thinking about college after you graduate?" Jefferson said, adding hurriedly, "I know it's what . . . two, three years away. But are you both making plans?"

"We'll both go," I said, holding Clementine's hand as we sat next to each other, pressing her left hand down into the love seat cushion with my right hand. "Clementine is an excellent student," I added.

Jefferson nodded. "How did you two meet?" he said, which I could tell was the question he had wanted to ask the moment he saw me.

"In biology class," Clementine said, pushing my hand up from below but not taking her hand out from under mine. "I asked Tyler to be my lab partner," she said.

"For which I was very glad," I said. "She's a better science student than I am."

Jefferson smiled. "Is that your interest?" he asked. "Science."

"Yes," Clementine said, leaning towards me, her left shoulder touching my right. "I want to be a doctor."

Jefferson smiled broadly. I turned and looked at Clementine. I hadn't known that. She'd never said that before. What in the world was she . . . . I felt her hand turn over and grasp mine hard.

"And what about you, Tyler?" Rita said. "What do you want to do with your life?"

I hadn't ever been asked that question before in exactly that same way. Certainly not in circumstances like this. I pressed Clementine's hand back down on the couch, as if the two of us were now playing a game. "My grandfather was a history professor," I said. "I've always wanted to do the same."

"Ah, an academic," Jefferson said. "Like Clementine's mother."

Rita winced. So did Clementine, but for a different reason.

Carlos and Jorge returned. The waiter followed. The boys sat down next to their mother. The waiter served the five of us. Jefferson signed the bill. All five of us started sipping our drinks. Rita leaned forward to make sure her youngest son did not spill anything. I could feel Clementine looking at me. "A professor?" she said in her wry voice.

I glanced at her. "A doctor?" I said in a whisper.

She grasped my hand harder then released it so she could hold her Coke with both hands.

I turned to Rita. "What grades are the boys in?" I asked.

Rita smiled. "Carlos is in fifth grade. Jorge is in third. Perez is just three so he's in preschool."

I nodded. "They're very handsome boys," I said.

Clementine pressed her left knee against my right knee.

"Thank you," Rita said.

"How did you and . . . " I began, hesitating, then going on, "Jefferson meet?" I asked Rita.

"When he moved to Houston and opened another family grocery store, I went to work for him as a manager."

I nodded and smiled my most polite nod and smile.

"Tyler and I traveled in England and Scotland and Wales this past summer," Clementine said quickly.

I pressed my right knee against her left knee.

"Really?" Jefferson said in a voice that told me he did not know what to say next. But he recovered. "How did that happen? Was it a school trip?"

I knew exactly where Clementine was going. God, the girl was so tough sometimes. I held my breath and waited for the next thing she was going to say. I could feel the warmth of her body next to mine. Here it comes, I thought.

"Tyler's grandfather was invited to lecture at Edinburgh University," she said. "In Scotland," she said, as if implying the two of them would not know where Edinburgh was. "He arranged for my mother to give a series of lectures with him."

The silence was audible. I glanced at Rita. She was trying very hard not to look at me.

"So Tyler's grandfather and my mother invited us to go with them." Clementine said.

One silent beat. Two silent beats. "That's very nice," Jefferson said. "I imagine you had a wonderful time." He turned to me as if asking me to say something.

"Yes, we did, sir," I said. "The lectures were very well received. And we got to spend four days in London and two in Wales."

I could see that at that moment Jefferson was very sorry he had invited Clementine. He wanted to see her, of course. But this? This was simply too hard. But he smiled. The man did know how to smile. It was a skill I sensed he had honed over a lifetime of having to know how to smooth the way no matter what was happening around him. I also sensed that Rita was going to have a lot to say to him that night no matter how the rest of the day went. I mean, a white guy? I could see it in her eyes. Clementine had brought a white guy.

"Well, are you ready to go see the Magic Kingdom?" he said, turning to his sons.

They all three said they were ready. All three were smiling. Jefferson was smiling. Rita was not. I was just trying to breathe. I didn't know what Clementine was trying to do.

50

When you live in Tampa for a number of years, as I did, you hear mixed reviews about Disney World. There are some people, but only a few, I confess, who think Disney is part of a conspiracy to take over the world. They hate the corporation. By contrast, there are others who have loved taking their children to Disney. Others love the hotels or the golf courses or both. Most of the people I've met who live in the Orlando area believe that Disney has proven to be a good neighbor. In any case, no matter how I might have felt about Disney before Clementine and I joined her father and his wife and their three sons that day in February, by the time the day was over I thanked God Disney had developed the Magic Kingdom. Because it was the boys' excitement that saved the day. For it did not take long before all three of them were laughing and jumping up and down and taking turns holding Clementine's hands as they went on rides together. It was just that simple. The boys didn't care anything about their father and Clementine's mother or even how their mother might have felt about the day—and I assume she did not ever tell them how she felt about meeting Clementine—they just knew that they had a sister who was very pretty and very nice and who, once she began to smile and laugh with them, was fun to be with.

I watched as the child in Clementine who had never had siblings and who, up to that day, had never been to Disney World, let herself go, let herself enjoy, let herself laugh at the three handsome boys who just could not get enough of her. I walked with Rita most of the time and watched, sensing that she was as conflicted as Clementine had been about coming: who was this girl? Why did she have to be so charming? Why did her three sons like her husband's daughter so much? What was she supposed to feel about Clementine or Clementine's mother or this Tyler boy who was walking beside her and being polite? What had she gotten herself into?

No matter, thank God for Disney World. Because every minute the boys kept her busy was another minute when Clementine did not have to talk to her father or walk with her father or answer his questions. I could see that in her face. Unfortunately, it did not last all day. We stopped for lunch. Jefferson seated everyone so Clementine was sitting next to him. He tried to talk to her. I give him credit for that. It couldn't have been easy seeing her under these circumstances for the first time since he'd walked out on Ruth Ann and Clementine—with his wife watching every move and hearing every comment and his daughter's white boyfriend standing guard over his daughter. It couldn't have been easy. But he soldiered on, trying to say the right things and ask the right questions and respond in the way a father should respond. And Clementine did the same. She smiled and answered questions and was generous and kind and as graceful as ever, even though I could see the strain around the edges and hear the tension in her voice at times when she just couldn't keep up the pretense. Because I knew what she was thinking. She had never told me in so many words, but I knew her sensibilities and sensitivities well enough to know that somewhere buried under all of her training to be polite there beat a heart that was angry, that was offended, that did not know if she should hate this Jefferson stranger or give him a chance to have his say.

So we got through lunch and having to talk directly to one another. Then we got through the afternoon, during which I could see that not only were the boys getting tired of the rides and maybe even a bit tired of this new sister of theirs, but Clementine was beginning to wear down. I could see it in her body language. Even more evident, I could hear it in Rita's voice. She kept glancing at her wristwatch because she wanted the day to be over. Jefferson tried not to notice she was looking at her wristwatch, but he could not help it. I even felt him turning to me for help, as if he was asking with his eyes, how do I talk to my daughter, young man? Will you help me? Do you know what I should do next? Then it was time to go back to the hotel and have dinner.

Dinner was a disaster. I don't mean the food wasn't good, because it was. And I don't mean that the boys were impolite, because they weren't. I don't even mean that Rita's weariness with the whole situation was evident, because it wasn't. After all, she knew it was about over. What I mean is that Jefferson could not ask Clementine the questions he really wanted to ask with Rita there. He couldn't ask about Ruth Ann. And with me there, he couldn't ask about me. As we were nearing the end of what by then was a ceremony the likes of which I had never seen before and hoped that I would never see again, Jefferson asked the question that being polite required he ask—"Do you two want to stay here tonight rather than drive back to Tampa so late?"—my answer to which, as he had hoped, was "Thank you, very much, but we didn't bring any thing that we would need to stay over, and my mother and Clementine's mother are expecting us back tonight." I could see the relief on his face, and he knew I could see the relief on his face, and I knew he knew I could see the relief on his face. So having gotten that cleared up, it did not take long for us to finish our desserts and say our goodbyes and for Clementine to bend down and hug the boys and then hug her father awkwardly and for me to shake Rita's hand and the boys' hands and Jefferson's hand and tell them it was a pleasure meeting them and for Rita to say how she hoped that Clementine would come visit them in Houston some day, which her glance at me as she said it told me that it was about the last thing she ever wanted to have happen, and my expression said to her that she could rest easy, because that was for sure one trip Clementine was never going to make, not if I had anything to say about it, anyway.

Then it was over, and we were back in my grandfather's car, and we were driving on Interstate 4 back towards Tampa. Clementine was silent for at least thirty minutes until she saw the two mile marker saying that the rest area was up ahead. "I need to stop," she said.

It didn't take long before we reached the rest stop on Interstate 4, during which neither of us said anything. I didn't because it wasn't my place. Clementine didn't because she was obviously mulling over what had happened. When we had stopped at the rest stop in the morning on our way to Disney World, it had been so early that very few cars were parked. Now it was so late that once again very few cars had stopped. We both got out and walked to the restrooms. When we were finished, we walked back to the car. As I opened the door for Clementine, she stopped and looked at me. Turning away, she walked across the drive and stood on the grass looking into the trees that lined the pasture to the north. I watched for a moment. Then I followed her.

The wind was blowing, and it promised to be a cold night. Clementine was wearing a jacket that had been fine for the day, but it was not heavy enough to keep her warm now that the temperature had dropped. I walked up behind her and put my hands on her shoulders. She did not say anything. Instead, she reached with each of her hands up to her shoulders and took mine. I felt her shudder. I heard her sob once. Then she was silent again.

What am I supposed to do now? I wondered. I don't want to say anything. She needs to speak first. She needs to let me know in some way what she needs. Then she turned and looked at me. The moon was up so I could see her face. I could see her eyes. She was crying. Then she stepped back for a moment and suddenly said in a bitter, angry whisper, "Don't run out on me! Don't run out on me!" And without warning she doubled up her fists and struck me with the sides of her hands like hammers, once, twice, three times, until I reached up and grabbed her wrists. She struggled for a moment against my strength. Then she cried again, "Don't you ever leave me! Don't you ever leave me!" bursting into tears, into sobs that tore at her chest, that twisted her face up into a mask, everything she had felt for five years, for ten years, for all of her life bursting loose in one hail storm of anger, of fear, of desperation. "Don't run away from me! Don't run away from me!" And I held on and stood strong against her anger and pressed my face against her and said, "I won't. I won't. I promise. I won't. I won't."

With one surge she pulled her hands free and stood looking at me, her body rigid, shaking, trembling. And I stepped to her and reached and pulled her close even as she struggled to get loose. Even as she tried to free herself, I held on. I fought back. I did not let her go.

After a moment, she stopped fighting and let herself dissolve against my shoulder. And that is where we stood for five minutes, for ten minutes, maybe more, until she finally had cried the last, sobbed the last, given over to her weary sorrow, her bitter joy. And she whispered one last time, "Don't ever leave me, Tyler." And I said, "I will never leave you, Clementine. Never. I promise. I will never leave you." And I meant what I said. I meant exactly what I said.

51

Clementine was quiet as we traveled, but she was not silent. "The little boys are nice," she said.

I agreed they were very nice.

"They seemed to like me," she said.

"They were crazy about you," I said.

After another period of quiet she said, "It feels strange."

"What feels strange?"

"Knowing I have three brothers," she said. Then she added, "Half brothers."

I kept on driving.

"But it feels nice, too," she said.

"Well, they sure liked you."

We were just about to Tampa when she asked, "What did you think of Rita?"

I laughed under my breath.

"Why did you laugh?" Clementine asked.

"Because I almost felt sorry for Rita."

"Really? Why?"

"Because she was about as uncomfortable as a person can get."

"Because of me?"
"Yes. And me."
"Oh."
"That's all. I almost felt sorry for her."
"But you didn't."
"Not quite."
"And my father?"
"That's your business."
"But I'm asking you."
"Well, he was relieved we didn't want to stay longer."

She smiled. I could hear it in her voice. "Yes, I think you rescued him when you said we had to drive back to Tampa."

"Which was true," I said.

"Yes. But you still rescued him."

I drove without speaking. We crossed over into the city limits.

"Thank you for coming with me, Tyler."

"I didn't want you to face him alone."

"And I didn't want to face him alone. Thank you for coming with me."

52

When we pulled up in front of Clementine's house shortly after midnight, the porch light was on. So were the living room lights and her mother's bedroom lights. When we got inside, Clementine's mother was sitting in an overstuffed chair drinking tea. She had obviously stopped reading as we came in through the front door, for she was standing as Clementine entered the room.

"It's late," she said.

"We stayed and ate dinner with them," Clementine said.

"With your father?"

"Yes. And with his wife and three sons."

"So you met them all?"

"Yes."

Her mother was quiet for a moment. "Are you all right?" she asked Clementine.

"Yes."

"Did it go well?"

"As well as can be expected."

"What does that mean?" she asked.

Clementine stood and looked at her mother. "It means that I love you. It means he is a stranger. It means he means nothing to me."

Ruth Ann nodded. "You met his wife and sons?"

"Yes. Rita. The boys are named Carlos, Jorge, and Perez."

"So he's become Hispanic?"

"She's Hispanic," Clementine said. "The boys look like her."

"I didn't know his sons' names," Ruth Ann said.

"They're very nice. They had fun."

"You went . . . where? The Magic Kingdom?"

"Yes."

She turned to me. "And you, Tyler, did you have fun?"

"I took care of Clementine."

"That doesn't tell me much," Ruth Ann said, smiling.

"It means I was there to take care that Clementine was okay. The fun part for me was being with her. Watching her with the three boys."

Ruth Ann turned back to Clementine. "You had fun with the boys?"

"Yes. They were nice."

"But how do you feel about them? They're your half brothers."

"How am I supposed to feel? I just met them. I don't know them, and they don't know me. We just rode the rides and laughed. That's all."

"And your father?" Ruth Ann said. "How was he?"

"Having great difficulty," Clementine said.

"Difficulty? Why difficultly?"

"Because it was obvious he wished he'd not invited me to come."

"Really?" Ruth Ann said. "But he did invite you."

"I know. And part of him meant it. But another part said what in the world are you doing, Jefferson?"

"He said that?"

"No. But you could see it on his face. Tyler saw it. We both did."

"Ah." Ruth Ann turned back to me. "Is that true? Did you see it, Tyler?"

"Yes, ma'am."

"Tyler, you've got that 'There's more' expression on your face," Ruth Ann said.

"I suppose that's because there is more."

"Which is?"

"Me."

"You?" she said.

Clementine interrupted. "Can we sit down? It's been a long day."

"Oh, yes. Certainly," her mother replied. "Would you like tea? Either of you?"

"No, I have to go home. My mother will be worried."

"Yes, she telephoned an hour ago to see if I had heard from you."

"We're fine. We left Disney just after 10."

Clementine sat. I sat next to her. Ruth Ann sat opposite us. "You were going to say something else," Ruth Ann said.

I smiled. "Yes. I was."

"About Jefferson. About you."

"Yes, about Jefferson. And about Rita."

"His wife?"

"Yes."

Ruth Ann waited.

"They were surprised. Her as much as him."

"By you?"

"Yes."

"Dare I guess why?"

Clementine poked me in the ribs.

"I don't imagine you have to guess, Mrs. Brown."

Ruth Ann nodded and smiled. Then she turned to Clementine. "And Tyler took care of you?" she said.

"Mother, Tyler always takes care of me," Clementine answered.

Ruth Ann turned back and faced me. "Tyler, you must stop calling me Mrs. Brown."

"Ma'am?"

"From now on you must call me Ruth Ann."

Clementine leaned back and punched my shoulder. I winced as if she had hurt me. Then Clementine turned to her mother. "He will," she said. "From now on. He will, right Tyler?" she said, turning back to me.

"Of course," I said to Clementine. Then turning to Ruth Ann, I said. "Ruth Ann it is. Ruth Ann it will be."

"Fine," Ruth Ann said. Then she stood. "Now, go home, Tyler. It's late."

"Yes, ma'am," said, standing.

Then Ruth Ann turned to Clementine. "Well, see him out," she said, turning and starting towards the kitchen.

"Yes, mother," Clementine said.

So she saw me out. We kissed. And I left and drove home where I knew my mother and grandfather would be waiting for a report.

Clementine and I went for a walk in the park near her house on Sunday afternoon. At first, we didn't talk about what had happened at Disney World. I assumed she was still mulling it over and that she would have something to say when she was ready. We sat on the teeter totter for a while, each of us playing at suspending the other in the air even while the other protested. I was better at that, of course. Then we walked to the lake and followed the footpath around to the other side where the city had built a gazebo. We sat down. Clementine had brought dried bread crusts to feed the ducks so she did that for a while. When she was finished she sat next to me, curling her left arm inside my right arm, putting her head on my shoulder.

"Have you finished the reading assignment in English?" she asked.

"Yes."

"So what do you think?"

I thought for a moment. We had been assigned Jack London's short story, "To Build a Fire," which is about a man in Alaska who tries to get from one camp to another by himself in weather that is more than sixty degrees below zero, with only a dog for his companion, against the advice of more experienced trappers. When he gets wet, he builds a fire, but he makes the mistake of building his fire under a spruce tree. When the snow on the tree becomes heated, it falls into the fire. From that point on, the man is fated to die, which in the end, he does by freezing to death. "I think that the protagonist was guilty of ignoring the wisdom that told him he should never travel alone in that kind of cold."

Clementine was quiet for a while. "I agree," she said. "He thought he knew more than he really knew."

I waited, for I sensed it was coming.

"I suppose I shouldn't have gone to see my father," she said. "But now that I have, I am glad because I know I won't do it again."

"Are you sure about that?" I said. "Maybe someday things will change, and you will feel more comfortable seeing him."

"I don't think so. Maybe. I don't know," she said. "I don't think so."

"What did your mother say after I left?" I asked.

"Not much. I told her I loved her. Which is true. That ended the conversation. I think she knows what I learned."

I sat and looked at the sun starting to set behind the bank of gray clouds.

"She's glad you were with me," she said.

"So am I," I said.

Then Clementine stood, and holding hands, we walked back around the lake and then back to her house where I joined Ruth Ann and Clementine for dinner.

At dinner, Ruth Ann said Clementine had told her that when her father had asked me what I wanted to study in college, that I had said I wanted to teach history. "Is that right, Tyler? Is that what you think you'd like to do?"

I nodded. "Yes, ma'am." Then I smiled. "It's funny though, because until he asked me, I don't think I'd really decided. Maybe that's because no one has ever asked me the question in the same way. But when he asked, and I answered, it seemed perfectly natural to say that."

Ruth Ann smiled. "Is it because of your grandfather? Is it because you admire him?" she asked.

"Probably," I said. "I do admire him. In many ways. Or maybe it's because I'm his grandson. Maybe it's just the way I think."

"Genetic?" Ruth Ann said.

"Genetic?" I said. "Maybe. Probably. I mean, my mother teaches fifth grade social science. That's very close to history. And my father was going to teach English at the University level. Maybe it's destiny."

"Well, I'm certainly not going to discourage you, Tyler. I'd be the last one to do that," Ruth Ann said. "Just don't be surprised if you have doubts someday or if you change your mind. That can happen as well."

I told her that I knew that was certainly possible.

Then she turned to Clementine. "And Clementine says she told her father she wants to be a doctor." She smiled. "I didn't know you'd made that decision," she said.

Clementine smiled. "I think I'm like Tyler. I'd thought about it before. And I know I liked biology. And this year I like anatomy. Maybe I just wanted to say something definite."

"That can happen," Ruth Ann said.

"Or maybe I felt like I had to defend myself. As if he was challenging me. If I hadn't made up my mind, then I wasn't very smart. I think I felt that maybe he was challenging me. And you, too," she said.

Ruth Ann took a sip of her wine. She turned to Clementine. "How was he challenging me?" she said.

"I'm not saying he was, mother. I just mean, for a moment, I felt like he was saying that if I didn't know what I wanted to do with my life that you'd been a poor mother. As if you hadn't raised me right. I didn't want him to think that."

Ruth Ann turned to me. "You were there. Do you think he was saying that or inferring that?"

I hesitated before answering. "It was very awkward being with him," I said. "I could see Clementine felt that. And yes, I suppose there was something like that in his tone of voice. But when we walked through the Magic Kingdom and talked with his wife, and watched him as she and I talked, I could see he was very defensive."

"Really?"

"Not in what he said so much. More in his expression. He was very uneasy."

"About . . . what?"

"I don't know. About everything. About what he did when Clementine was a little girl. I can't say anything for sure. But I think Clementine is right. Maybe he didn't even realize it, but I think he was trying to catch her out or catch you out."

Ruth Ann nodded. "You two are pretty smart," she said.

Clementine smiled at me. I smiled at her. Ruth Ann smiled at both of us. "Just so neither of you does something you don't want to do because you think someone else expects it," Ruth Ann added.

"We won't," Clementine said. "We won't," she said again.

54

The rest of the school year was perfectly ordinary. We had friends. We went to games with them and movies with them sometimes, although more often than not, we just went together. Ruth Ann and my mother and grandfather continued to be very close. In addition, the people each of them had brought to our houses continued to be friends. Some of them who had not known each other before became friends in their own right.

In the spring, I was invited to join the varsity football team, which made me very happy if a tad nervous at the same time. Given the chance, I had to measure up. I knew it was going to be a challenge. More important was Clementine's track season.

Clementine began the season by winning the 440 in four meets in a row. When the first big meet came, which was staged at Berkeley Prep, a private school, in which twenty teams from all over Central Florida and Tampa and St. Petersburg took part, she finished second. Since the girl from Edgewater High School in Orlando had run the second best time in the state up to that point, everyone at Tampa Coast was excited. Then Clementine won another five meets in a row before the big conference meet took place.

At the conference meet, she ran her best time ever, winning the event by almost a full second. That put her in the regional meet. She won that as well. Ruth Ann and my mother and grandfather and I were beside ourselves in the stands. We had a big celebration that night at Clementine's house. There must have been at least twenty of her and my and our mothers' and my grandfather's friends there to congratulate her. One of the men Ruth Ann knew said he was friends with one of the track coaches at Georgia Tech, in Atlanta, and that he'd telephoned his friend and told her about Clementine, and so the coach said she wanted to hear how she did at the regional meet.

Two days before the regional event Clementine stopped talking. I don't mean she didn't say a word. I just mean that she stopped talking about the normal things that we usually talked about. I thought I knew what was going on. I hated talking to anyone on football game days. So I let her sit when she wanted to. I brought her lunch to her. I didn't say anything unless she brought something up.

On the morning of the regional meet, which was going to be held at Brandon High School, east of Tampa, I got up early as I always did on meet days and drove Clementine to school so she could travel with the team to the stadium. Then I went home and got my mother and grandfather, and then all three of us picked up Ruth Ann, and we drove together to the meet.

It was a very warm day. That meant that by the time Clementine's event was scheduled to start, it was going to be hot. But that didn't matter, not to Clementine, at least. I could see it when I'd driven her to school. She slouched against the door and didn't say anything. When we got to Tampa Coast where the team bus was waiting, I went around and opened the door for her as I always did. When she got out she didn't say anything. She just looked me in the eyes and then punched me in the stomach. I wasn't surprised, of course, because that's what she always did before a meet. But this time it was harder than usual. So hard that I winced, which made her smile just a little bit. Then she leaned close to me and said, "Just watch me, Tyler Thomas Raymond." Then she turned and walked away. And I knew it was going to be her day. It was going to be Clementine Camille Brown's day. And I was right. She won the race by three seconds. The two other runners who challenged her at the top of the final turn wilted because she didn't just pick up the pace as she got to the middle of the turn, she started sprinting. Oh, God, I remember thinking, she's started her kick too soon. But I was wrong. She missed breaking the regional record by 1.5 seconds. It was time for another celebration because she was going to the state championship meet in Gainesville the next Saturday. And as wonderful as that was, there was more to come. Much more than just a state race.

55

During the next week, I did what I could to keep Clementine focused on school and not on anticipating the upcoming race. She had done the same thing for me during football season, and it had helped. I went to her house two nights where we did our studies sitting at her dining room table. The two other nights, she came to my house, and we did the same. The local television stations did a short feature on all of the runners from Tampa high schools who were going to compete. Clementine did not want to watch any of the coverage. So we didn't. Instead, we talked about everything under the sun except the race.

Then it was Thursday night, and we went to an early movie. I don't even remember which one. I'm sure she didn't either. I made sure she was home by 8 P.M. Then I went home and read and tried to sleep but with very little success. I wasn't worried about her running a good race. I knew she would do that. I just didn't want her to be disappointed with the outcome, whatever it might be. I had learned by then what it was like for family members to sit and watch other family members take part in athletic contests. It is much easier to be a competitor than to be an observer. At least when you are competing, you can try to do something. But just try to hold onto your emotions when someone you love is on the field or on the track getting ready for competition.

On Friday, I got up early and drove Clementine to Tampa Coast High School so she could ride the bus with the team to Gainesville and stay overnight. As always, while she rode to school, she slouched down in the front seat and didn't say a word. When I went around and opened the door for her, I got ready. She was going to punch me just like she always did. It was her comment that would be different.

So I opened the door and stepped back so she could get out, bringing her track equipment bag with her. Then she stood up and looked at me. I flexed my stomach muscles as much as possible and got ready. But she just looked at me. Then she leaned toward me and kissed me very tenderly on the lips. I started to relax. Then she hit me. Hard. I caught my breath and stepped back and felt my knees buckle slightly. She smiled and looked at me. "You'd better be ready, Tyler Thomas Raymond. You'd better be ready for a big surprise."

I tried to catch my breath. "Apparently," I said, half gasping.

Then she started to turn away. But she stopped and turned back to me and pursed her lips and made a kissing gesture and turned and walked away, and I went around to the car and got back in where I sat for a while with the door open and my feet on the ground, because the girl is strong, and the girl can hit. And I mean hit hard.

Then I drove home where my mother and grandfather were eating breakfast, and I got ready for school. The next morning, my mother and grandfather and Ruth Ann and I drove to Gainesville together.

56

As you might well expect, track coaches are obsessed with time: times of races, times of what they call splits, which are laps in a multi-lap race; times of parts of a race—the turns, the back stretch, the last turn, etc. I didn't know anything about track until I started going to Clementine's meets. I learned about times from her. What both she and her track coach, Coach Lawton, knew was that there were two girls from the Miami area who had run faster times than Clementine, and one from Orlando. What that meant, of course, was that if each of those girls ran their best times and Clementine ran her best time, she would finish fourth. All I wanted to have happen, therefore, was for Clementine to run her best race and then see what happened. That's all any of us wanted when we entered the stadium and took seats and got ready for a very long state championship meet. We were not disappointed. There were a number of truly exciting races as well as a number of excellent field event performances. None of which really mattered to us in the end, because we had come to see Clementine run in the state championship 440 yard race.

I am not going to detail all of the races Clementine ran as a junior and senior. She became a stronger runner, after all, so strong in fact that she eventually received a partial scholarship to run for Georgia Tech, in Atlanta. But on that day, during her sophomore year, she taught me more about who she really was than I had learned during the two years we had already dated. And from what I've told you thus far, I would assume that you understand I had already learned a great deal about her character, about her person.

As for the race that day, here's how it unfolded. First, she won her heat, which put her in the finals along with the other heat winners. As the evening approached when the finals were to begin, the weather cooled some, for which we were all very thankful. We had been drained by the long hot day. All four of us agreed we couldn't imagine what the heat must have done to the runners. Clementine had waved at us when we'd first come in, and I'd spoken to her for a moment after she won her heat, but it was obvious she didn't want to spend any time with any of us so I went back to my seat and left her alone. Then it was late afternoon; then it was evening. Then it was time for the 440 finals.

When the runners prepared for the gun, I found Clementine positioned among the outside third of the runners, but the closest to the middle of that group. Then the fun and games began.

The first thing Clementine did was jump the gun. That, of course, not only concerned us, because if she did it a second time she would be disqualified, it to some degree distracted the other runners. They had gotten ready and then set, and then she had jumped. As they all walked back to their places, you could see some of them scowling at her. Others looked as if they were struggling to regain their concentration. Clementine was expressionless. Or at least I could not interpret her facial expression. So I didn't know what to think. Neither did Ruth Ann.

Then the runners prepared themselves again. When the gun went off, they broke out and began. Before they reached the first turn, Clementine had moved into second place. I was stunned. By the time they entered the first turn, she was in front. I thought for sure she had gone out too fast. She could never hold that pace. What was she thinking? Was it nerves? Was it bad coaching? Who in the world decided she should do that? The best runners were all older than Clementine. They were all heavier, more muscular, probably stronger, I thought.

As they finished the first turn, my fears were realized. The other runners, including the favorite three, all passed her, and she slipped into fifth place down the back stretch. I wanted to cry. I loved her so much. I was so proud of all she had accomplished. But I kept my binoculars on her. It seemed odd. She should have been laboring. She'd gone out too fast, I thought. She was going to fade. So she should have been laboring because that's what runners do when they've spent too much energy at the wrong time. But she wasn't. She was running as smoothly as ever. More smoothly than ever. As if she was floating.

Then the front runners started around the last turn. Nothing had changed. A runner from Miami, followed by the runner from Orlando, followed the other runner from Miami. Then Clementine was in fourth place. Fourth place? How had she gotten from fifth to fourth? I hadn't even seen it happen.

"What's she doing?" Ruth Ann said sitting next to me.

"Moving up?" I said, asking the question more than stating the fact.

"Good grief," Ruth Ann said.

The runners were in mid turn. Clementine was even with the third place runner. Shoulder to shoulder. But Clementine was on the outside. She would have to run farther.

Then the runners came around the final turn. Clementine pushed ahead of the third place runner. She pushed up even with the second place runner. I saw the Orlando runner glance at Clementine. Bingo! That was her mistake. Because Clementine wasn't there. She was now in second place. Then they entered the home stretch. The runner from Miami was the favorite. She should have been. She had the best time in the state. She was strong. But she had not seen or heard Clementine coming up behind her. Then they had forty yards to run. And before she knew what was happening, Clementine had gone wide and turned on all of her sprinter's speed and was even with the leader. With twenty yards to go, she reached down someplace and found another gear. The Miami runner saw her. She tried to push harder. But it was too late. She was too heavy. Too muscular. She'd spent too much too early when Clementine had set the pace. And thin, lithe, splendid Clementine left her. Passed her and left her behind. Clementine won the race. The crowd was screaming. Ruth Ann and I were hugging. My mother and my grandfather were hugging. My grandfather was standing on the bleacher ahead of us jumping up and down. Clementine had won the state championship 440 yard race. She was on the track with the other runners, walking back slowly toward the finish line. The favored runners were all three together. They could not believe what had happened. You could see it in their faces. Who was this skinny Tampa girl? What had happened?

Then the two Miami runners walked to Clementine. One of them put her arm around Clementine's shoulders. The other shook her hand. Clementine thanked them. I could read her lips from the stands. The Orlando runner walked away. Clementine turned to the stands and turned to us and waved.

I vaulted down the steps of the stadium. When I got to the bottom, Clementine was climbing over the railing and leaping into my arms and wrapping her legs around my waist and the audience all around her was applauding. I stood and held her up off of the ground as she buried her face in my neck. And I heard her say, "That will show him. That will show him."

When I pulled my face away from hers so I could see her but before I could respond, she said, "It's over, Tyler. It's finally over."

I let her down very carefully, and she stood and looked at me, but she didn't have to say anything more because I understood who he was and what was over, and I didn't have to tell her that I understood, because she knew I did.

Then Ruth Ann was with us with her arms around both of us. And Clementine's coach was calling to her to come back down on the track. So she turned and climbed back down over the railing, and Coach Lawton hugged her, and Clementine hugged her in return. And it was over.

The meet ended that night at 11:35 P.M. But by then, Clementine had pulled on her track warm up suit, received her first place metal; Tampa Coast athletes who were not going to ride the team bus home had joined their families.

The five of us climbed into my grandfather's station wagon and started the drive home, talking and laughing until I realized that Clementine had rested her head on my shoulder and dozed off, so we all became very quiet and let her sleep. What I remember so clearly that it seems like it happened yesterday is that just after we passed Ocala going south, Clementine stirred and shifted her position and pressed her lips against my neck and kissed me and then whispered into my ear, "I told you to be ready, didn't I? I told you to be ready."

I smiled in the dark, but I did not reply, because her breathing told me she was already asleep again.

57

Then it was summer. With no trips planned, Clementine and I got jobs working thirty hours a week on the same shifts at the Home Depot lumber and tools and nursery warehouse on Tampa Avenue near the airport. To drive there for our shifts we had to borrow Ruth Ann's car or my mother's car or my grandfather's car. After a week of that, while sitting in a Burger King having a cold drink on our way home, I said I needed to get a car so we wouldn't have to borrow from our families all of the time. I said that besides driving Clementine during the summer, when school began, the two of us would have our own transportation. She said she had been thinking the same thing, only she had thought about buying a car for herself so she could transport me. For a moment we sat and looked at each other. Then we laughed because suddenly we realized had the same idea. We'd buy a car together.

"Louis, the guy in the plumbing department . . . he gave us a ride home one night. He said he's trying to sell his car," I said.

"The one he drove us in?" Clementine asked.

"Yes."

"Do you think that's a good car? I thought it made a lot of noise."

"I don't think it's a good car. It just came to mind because he said he wants to sell it. I don't think we should buy it. But the woman in payroll. Maggie. I think that's her name. She's got a sign on her office window saying she wants to sell a Chevy," I said.

"But it's almost new," Clementine said. "I think it's an '80. We couldn't afford a car like that, could we?"

"Probably not. I wonder if we could finance a car?" I said.

"No one is going to finance us. We don't work all year. We'll have to save up and buy a car for cash. Because we can't make payments. Not during the school year. But maybe," she said. Maybe together . . . . "

She didn't have to finish her sentence. I understood, and I agreed with her.

"How much can we pay?" Clementine said.

"I don't know. How much can you come up with?"

"I'm not sure. Maybe a thousand dollars by the end of July. I'm trying to save money. So are you. That's why we took these jobs."

I nodded. "Okay. If you can raise a thousand, so can I. But that's only two thousand dollars. I don't know what we can buy that's worth buying for two thousand dollars."

"Do we need to look in the newspaper?" Clementine askeds.

"We can start with that," I said.

I got up and went outside to the newspaper rack and bought a copy of the *Tampa Tribune*, and we sat down and took the paper apart and I sat next to Clementine as we began to read though the ads. "No dealer's going to have a car for $2000," she said. "At least, not one worth having."

"So we'll have to buy a car from some person. An individual. Someone who's advertising," I said.

We opened the advertising section to the cars for sale. I still remember sitting there over our Cokes reading down the columns of cars for sale. We must have looked very serious. At the same time, it was very discouraging. The good cars cost too much. Every car in our price range sounded suspect. We wanted a car, but we certainly didn't want to buy a problem. We both leaned forward and sipped our Cokes. Then we were looking at each other. And thinking. I could see she was thinking. I knew she knew I was thinking.

"My grandfather," I said very slowly at exactly the same time Clementine said, "Your grandfather."

We each were silent for a moment.

"He has been talking about getting a new car for the last six months," I said.

Clementine smiled. She did not say anything. She did not have to say anything. I could read her mind.

I sat back. "I think you need to come to our house for dinner. I will take you home. You clean up and change. And then we will drive to my house, and you will eat dinner with us," I said.

"Will your mother . . . " Clementine started to say.

"My mother's asked me every day for the last week when you were coming over for dinner. I'll telephone her right now and ask if you can come tonight. She'll say yes."

So that was that. Clementine came for dinner. We explained our problem to my grandfather. We told him how much money we could put together as a couple. We were not trying to take advantage of his good nature. He loved doing things like this. Besides, as he said, it finally gave him good reason to go buy the new car that he'd been thinking about all winter.

But he was no push over. He was far too smart for that. Even after he had agreed to sell us his car, he was wise enough to say, "You realize this is a business partnership. You'll need to have everything in writing."

"In writing? Grandpa, Clementine is my girlfriend. We don't need to make it that formal, do we?"

"Tyler, you two are talking about spending two thousand dollars. You are talking about owning something together. Yes, you need to have everything in writing. Who's going to pay the insurance? What about repairs? Who's responsible? If one of you is driving and something happens, do you both split the cost?"

"Tyler, your grandfather is right. We need to be sure we understand what we're getting into," Clementine said.

"I suppose you're right. It's just that what you're saying makes it sound so formal," I said.

"It is formal. A formal agreement to divide the cost of buying a car. Of insuring a car. Of maintaining a car and repairing it. And what about using it? How are you going to decide who drives the car from day to day?" my grandfather said.

"All right. I get the point," I said, not at all pleased by what my grandfather was saying. But I understood what he was saying. My grandfather was too clever by half.

Clementine put the icing on the cake when she said, "Did you see this coming, Professor Thomas?"

"See what coming?" he said, as if he did not understand what she meant.

"That Tyler was going to want a car of his own. That the two of us needed transportation."

He smiled. "I assumed that the two of you were going to get pretty tired of having to borrow from one of us," he said, referring to Ruth Ann and my mother and him.

So it was settled. Clementine and I agreed to buy my grandfather's car. My only question was could two people like us, who weren't related buy a car together? My grandfather assured me that anyone can buy a car with anyone from anyone. Two weeks later, my mother and Ruth Ann went with my grandfather and the two of us went to the Florida Department of Motor Vehicles to sign over the title of his 1978 Dodge station wagon to Clementine Camille Brown or Tyler Thomas Raymond for $1500 because he refused to take the $2000 we offered. Fortunately for us, our mothers agreed to split the cost of the insurance the first year even as they warned us that if we broke up, as so many high school students do, they didn't want us coming to them for help. The two of us would have to decide what to do about the car. They weren't going to baby sit us through any confusions or animosities that might crop up. It was our deal. We would have to live with the consequences. So with those motherly warnings ringing in our ears, we began our junior year in high school.

Of course, besides driving to school every day and to one another's homes almost every evening to study together and to movies on Saturday nights, we also took to driving the Courtney Campbell Causeway Bridge to Clearwater Beach every Sunday afternoon because one of the benefits of having a station wagon was that it was perfect for transporting umbrellas and beach chairs and a cooler to Clearwater or St. Petersburg or where ever we decided to go. Unfortunately, on the third of our nice Sundays in September, we suddenly faced an experience that might have undone all that we felt about each other. One that required we muster all of our intelligence and moral strength. One that required we cling almost desperately to Ruth Ann's wisdom lest we be shattered. At the same time, when we now look back on our lives from the vantage point of where we are today, as unsettling as the experience was at the time, we also recognize that it was one of the defining moments in our relationship. Life is like that sometimes, isn't it? A horrible thing can teach really important lessons even while it remains really horrible.

58

I am the first to admit, especially now as I look back on our ninth and tenth grade years together, that when Clementine's and my relationship began to develop, we were naïve. Yes, we had some unpleasant experiences with people who either did not approve or who did not understand that we simply loved each other. I mean, we liked many of the same things: opera, jazz, Broadway musicals, plays, movies, art museums. We both read the newspaper and could talk about politics not just with each other but with our mothers and with my grandfather. We both wanted to travel because we had been raised to be interested in the world. Our personalities were compatible: she was warm and humane. She had a subtle sense of humor. She was developing a very clear and steadfast core of values that did not waiver in the face of our friends' opinions or during classroom discussions. In short, I admired her person. I don't know how else to say it. I admired who she was. I very much wanted to be the same: worthy of her admiration and friendship. She said I was. She said all of the things about her that I admired she admired about me.

Yes, we were both very young. We heard that from more than one person during our high school years. We would change. We would grow apart. Our relationship would change. We would go our separate ways. We heard those comments. We understood why people said them. But we did not agree. Yes, we certainly understood that the racial issue was a part of why people said what they did. No, none of our friends ever said anything about race. However, both Clementine and I knew that it was on their minds. Not that they wanted us to have any bad experiences. It was just that they felt that one day, when we were living beyond the protected environment of Tampa Coast High School, a less sympathetic society would throw up obstacles that we could not overcome. Naturally, as you would expect, we disagreed. So we simply continued on as we were. Then it happened.

We drove to Clearwater Beach. As always, we went into the water after we set up our umbrella and folding chairs. After we came out of the water, we settled back and talked some. Finally, we got out our books and started studying.

I didn't pay any attention to him the first time he passed by and stopped for a moment to look at us. I noticed when he came back a few minutes later and walked past us again, but he moved on so I continued reading. Then he came back a third time. This time I had no choice but to look up because he was standing in front of us looking at us and smiling.

He said his name was Blessed Billy. He was carrying a black *Bible*. He was of no more than average height and weight, and he was wearing jeans and no shoes and a white shirt open at the collar and a scruffy black dress coat that had seen better days, probably before Billy had gotten it from some Mission Church, I assumed. He looked at me first. Then he looked at Clementine. He smiled again. His face was shaven, but his hair was uncombed. Then he said, "You look like nice young people," to which I replied, "Who are trying to study." That was probably my mistake. I should have told him to go away immediately, although looking back that probably wouldn't have helped. Blessed Billy was going to have his say.

"Yes. Study. Enrich your minds," he said. "Study."

I glanced at him but did not reply.

"And you, young lady. Are you also trying to enrich your mind?" he said to Clementine.

Clementine looked at him for a moment. "Yes," she said, glancing at me and then turning back to her book.

"Are you two saved?" Blessed Billy asked.

Oh, God, I thought. Not that.

Clementine looked at me, her expression saying, make him go away.

"We are studying. We don't want to talk about being saved," I said quietly but firmly.

Billy smiled. "The unsaved never want to talk about being saved," he replied.

"Then go away," I said. "Thank you for your concern, but please just go away."

"If you do not listen today, you will have to listen someday," Billy said.

"Fine. I will listen someday. But not today," I said.

"Ah, yes. But someday never comes," Billy said. "Sin comes. Death comes," Billy said. "But someday never comes."

I looked at Blessed Billy. This guy is crazy, I thought.

Blessed Billy smiled again. "The white lad does not understand the danger he is in."

That got my attention. White lad? Next he'll say . . . .

"But the black girl knows, doesn't she?" Billy said.

Clementine looked up.

"The *Bible* forbids what you two are doing," Billy whispered.

"What we are doing?" I said, lowering my book, my voice growing tense.

Billy opened his *Bible* and acted as if he was reading a passage. "And the black woman shall tempt the white man into lust and sin."

I started to stand. "Get away from us," I said as I did.

"Oh, yes, oh, yes. Drive Blessed Billy away," Billy said, taking a step backwards. "But you cannot deny God's word, white lad."

Clementine stood up.

"The word of Holy God forbids the fruit of your womb, black woman," he said.

"Get out of here!" I snapped. I could hear Clementine starting to gather up her books.

Billy stepped towards me. I was startled, but I did not give ground. "You have lain with a sister of darkness, white lad. You have enjoyed the cream of her sweet loins," he said in a sing-song voice. "You must be saved. You must be saved!" he suddenly said as if he was angry.

"You go to hell, mister. Get away from us!" I said, almost shouting, glancing around us at the older couple sitting not far away from us who had turned to watch and listen. "Get away from us," I said again, turning back on Billy.

"Listen," he said urgently, moving toward me, as if he were going to grab my shoulder. "You must flee, white lad. You must flee from her," he said.

"You're crazy!" I shouted. "We're leaving. Leave us alone."

Billy stopped and looked at me. "I know her," he said.

I folded up our beach chairs. Clementine brought down the umbrella.

"I have seen her with other men," Billy said, almost laughing.

"Go to hell!" I snarled, picking up the beach chairs and turning to Clementine. "Let's go. This bastard's crazy."

Clementine looked afraid. Her hands were shaking. She dropped her beach bag of books. Scrambling, she knelt down and started picking them up.

Billy rushed towards her. "There. See. She kneels at your feet, white lad. She kneels. She craves you. I know. But it's a trick. A vile trick!"

I threw down the beach chairs and started towards him. He stumbled backwards and fell. I was between Clementine and him. "You lie with her! I know you lie with her!" he screamed, trying to get to his feet.

"Get out of here!" I said, standing rigid. "You get out of here!"

"Or what?" Billy said, on his feet again, facing me. "Or what? You will beat a messenger of the Lord? Is that it? You will beat a messenger of the Lord God Almighty?"

"No, you stupid bastard. I will beat you. So help me God, I will beat you!"

"Leave her!" Billy shouted, pointing at Clementine. "She is vile! They are all vile!"

People were moving towards us.

Then Billy snarled, "Leave her to me," and he held his *Bible* over his head and turned to the people who were now closing in around us. "The black woman is sin! The white lad must be saved!" Billy shouted, laughing and turning to face the people who were now within ten feet of us.

I turned to Clementine. She had regained her beach bag and was holding one of the beach chairs and the top half of the umbrella. "I've got your books," she said, her voice unsteady.

I saw her legs trembling. I reached down and picked up the beach chair and the bottom half of the umbrella standard. I heard Billy ranting. Someone told him to shut up. Another voice shouted he was crazy. I turned back and saw him moving towards us. I stepped back towards Clementine and brandished the umbrella standard. "Don't you come near us!" I screamed. "Get away! Just get away!"

Billy stopped. He looked startled. He looked at Clementine. "You have beautiful skin, girl. Beautiful skin. You are not all black. I can tell. I know your kind. Mixed race. You are a curse. I know your kind. I know your kind."

I turned to Clementine. "Let's go. Let's go," I said, trying to move her away.

But she stood still and looked at the smiling Billy. "You will hide your seed in the white lad's child," he said, smiling and pointing at Clementine. "You will hide your evil seed, black woman," he snarled.

That was enough. I turned to Billy and held up the umbrella standard like a baseball bat, advancing on him. "Get out of here!" I shouted. "I'll kill you! I swear I'll kill you!" I screamed.

The people started to fall back. Billy stumbled away from me, laughing as I followed. "You're crazy!" I raged. "I'll kill you!"

"I know, white lad," Billy laughed hysterically. "I know, white lad. But it is too late. You have lain with her! I can tell! You have lain with her! She had hidden her seed in your child!" And he fell to his knees and began to shout as if he were reading from his *Bible*, "And the black vixen shall hide her sin in the loins of the white . . . "

I moved toward him, raising the umbrella standard above my head.

He looked up and screamed. "Look at her! Look at her! Her thighs! Her breasts! Look at her lips!"

I stepped toward him and started to swing the standard when I felt three hands grabbing me, one on each arm, one on the back of my neck. Clementine screamed. I felt myself falling backwards. Then I saw them. Two police officers. "Don't!" one was saying. "Drop it!" the other was saying.

Billy was back on his feet, stumbling away, laughing.

"Drop it!" the officer said again. And I was on my back. I could not move. Clementine was crying. People were shouting: "It's not his fault!" and "The crazy guy! He started it!" and "Let him go! The kid didn't do anything!"

"We know! We know!" one of the officers shouted back and the crowd.

Another officer had Billy by the coat collar. One of Billy's arms was being held behind his back. He had dropped his *Bible*.

Then I was being lifted to my feet. "Hold on, kid," an officer was saying. "Stand still."

I stood still. Clementine was there, her arms around my body, her face pressed against my neck. She was crying.

"We know who he is," the officer who was holding my arms said as he let go of me. "We know who he is," he said again. "We'll take him away."

I saw Billy being led away. He was laughing. "She will hide her seed in your child!" he was shouting.

The officer leading him away told him to shut up.

Billy laughed and stumbled and then went with the officer.

The crowd was telling one of the officers how Billy had started it, how we had simply been sitting and reading and how Billy had come after us and begun shouting and that I had been defending us from him. The officer was nodding and saying he understood. They knew Billy. He understood.

The officer who had been holding me said, "I'm sorry this happened, kid." He turned to Clementine. "I'm sorry this happened, miss. We try to keep an eye on him, but sometimes we lose track of where he's gone."

Clementine was crying softly.

"He's crazy," I said quietly.

"You're right. He's crazy. And we've locked him up before. But he always gets out after serving his time. And then he does it again."

I was shaking.

"We had to stop you," the officer said. "For your sake as well as his,"

"I know," I said. "I know," I said, trying to calm Clementine.

"It's just . . . seeing you two together . . . " the officer started to say. But he didn't finish his sentence. "He always goes after black women," the officer said. "I'm sorry we didn't see him before he got to you."

I tried to regain control. Clementine had stopped crying.

"We'll take him in," the officer said. "You two can press charges if you wish."

I held on to Clementine.

"Of course, I've gotta warn you. The fact you were about to brain him with your umbrella pole . . . that won't sit well with the judge on duty."

"He wouldn't stop," I said. "I told him to leave us alone, but he wouldn't stop."

"I know, I know," the officer said. "But he wasn't attacking you. Physically I mean. But you were just about to attack him."

"I was ready to kill him," I said.

"And I don't blame you. I don't. Really. But the judge? He wasn't here. He didn't see Billy. I'm not sure what he'll think."

I took a deep breath and exhaled slowly.

"Let's go home," Clementine said in a whisper, holding me for a moment longer, then stepping away and looking at me as if she wanted me to decide.

"All right," I said to her. Then I turned to the officer. "Thank you for your help," I said.

"I'll need to get your names for our report. Then you can go. But I think that's what I'd do. I'd just go home and try to forget what happened."

I nodded that we would, which does not mean I agreed.

"I'm just thankful no one got hurt," the officer said, turning to his partner who was preparing to write down the information he needed on his notepad. So we gave him our names and our addresses and the names of our mothers. And I told him very briefly what had happened. He said what I had said was the same as what the other people had told him.

I turned to Clementine. I didn't need to ask her if she was all right. She wasn't. I could see it in her face. She had been afraid of the man who confronted us. I was afraid for her. I was still seething. I was trying to control my anger for her sake. But she was shaken. Her hands were still trembling. For a moment I held her in my arms. I could feel her legs against mine. They were cold. I could feel her body against mine. She was shaking. She buried her face in my neck. She was trying hard not to cry. I said, "It's over, Clementine. It's over." But I knew I was wrong. Even as I tried to reassure her, I knew I was wrong. She stepped back and looked at me and nodded, but I knew she did not believe me. And she knew that I knew that she did not believe me. It was a terrible feeling. An awful feeling.

Then we gathered up our beach umbrella and beach chairs and cooler of food, which we had not even had a chance to open, and our books, and we went back to our station wagon and put everything in the back and drove home. But it was not over. What happened to us that day on Clearwater Beach was definitely not over.

59

As we drove back over the Campbell Causeway and turned north toward Clementine's house, Clementine sat away from me, slumped down into the seat, leaning against the door. She had done that when I took her to track meets, but on those occasions I knew she was trying to get her mind wrapped around what was coming. Now I could see she was withdrawing not to get her mind focused on what was coming but on what had happened. Her hands were still shaking when we pulled into her driveway and stopped and got out. I went around to the passenger's side door and opened it. She did not look at me but went to the back and waited as I lifted the rear door and got out the food cooler. She got her book bag. She took my books out of her bag and went around to the passenger's side door and put them on the seat. "Let's just leave everything else," I said.

Clementine nodded and turned to her house. Her mother was on the porch smiling. As Clementine started towards the house, Ruth Ann stopped smiling. She waited for a moment before speaking. Clementine was not looking at Ruth Ann. As I walked behind Clementine, I was. So she spoke to me. "What's wrong, Tyler?" Then she turned to Clementine. "What's wrong, Clementine?"

Clementine didn't reply. She stopped and looked at her mother. Her face said all Ruth Ann needed to know. Ruth Ann stepped down from the porch and put her arms around Clementine. As she did, she looked at me. "Something happened on the beach," I said.

Ruth Ann's face said she was frightened.

"We're all right. We didn't get hurt. But Clementine's upset," I said.

"I can see that," Ruth Ann said, turning to Clementine.

Clementine stepped away from her mother.

"What happened, honey?" Ruth Ann asked her.

Clementine looked at her mother. Then she turned to me. "Tyler took care of me, mother," she said, turning back to Ruth Ann as she spoke. "Tyler always takes care of me." Then she fled, pushing past her mother and going into the house.

Ruth Ann turned to me. "Tyler?" she said.

I took a deep breath. "There was a crazy man. He had a *Bible*. The police know him."

"The police?"

"They came. They took him away."

"Tyler? What happened? What man? Who was he? What happened?"

My legs were shaking. I was surprised they were shaking. They had not been shaking before. Not when I was protecting Clementine. But they were shaking now.

"Tyler, sit down," Ruth Ann said, moving back towards the porch. "Come sit down. I want to know what happened. But I need to go in and see about Clementine."

I moved to the porch as she climbed the steps.

"Wait for me, Tyler," Ruth Ann said. "Wait right here."

"Yes, ma'am," I said. And I sat down.

A long silence passed. I could not hear Ruth Ann or Clementine from inside the house. Clementine must have gone to her bedroom. I waited. A car passed. Then a second and a third. I looked at my hands. Now they were shaking just like my legs. I took a deep breath and put my hands on my knees and tried to steady them.

I'd wanted to kill the man. I remember thinking that as I sat on the porch. I'd wanted to kill him. I don't know what I would have done if the police hadn't stopped me. Would I really have hit him with the umbrella standard? That's what I intended when he fell to his knees and kept on screaming at Clementine. I wanted to hit him and hit him and hit him until he was dead.

I looked at my hands. They were rigid. My face was covered with sweat. It was still a hot day, but it didn't feel like that kind of sweat. It was anger sweat. And fear sweat. It was I-wanted-to-protect-Clementine sweat. And I-wanted-to-kill-Blessed-Billy sweat.

I put my head in my hands and my elbows on my knees. Then the tears came. Hot and salty and hard and bitter. Swearing mad tears. Fear tears. My mother. I thought of my mother and my grandfather. What was I going to tell them? How could I ever explain? What was all of this going to mean? Would our mothers say that's the end of it? Clementine and me. Was this going to be the end of Clementine and me?

"No," I said under my breath. "That's not fair," I whispered. "That's not fair," I whispered again. Then Ruth Ann was sitting next to me. She put an arm around my shoulder and held me against her shoulder.

"Clementine told me," she said quietly.

"Is she all right?" I whispered.

"She's afraid," Ruth Ann said. "Of what you might think," she said.

I stopped breathing and turned to Ruth Ann. "Of what I might think? What does that mean?" I asked.

Ruth Ann could see the tears in my eyes. "I telephoned your mother. She's coming with your grandfather. I told them you were all right. That Clementine was all right."

I nodded and slumped forward again.

"Clementine is afraid for you, Tyler," Ruth Ann said.

I sat up straight. "Afraid for me?" I said, turning to her.

"Yes."

"Why would she be afraid for me? I was afraid for her. Of what the man might do. That what he said would hurt her."

"That's why she's afraid for you. She thinks you will not want to be with her anymore."

I turned to Ruth Ann. "I don't understand. The man was horrible. He was vile. Crazy. Nothing he could ever say would change how I feel about Clementine."

Ruth Ann nodded. Then she sat back, lowering her arm from my shoulder but taking my hand in hers at the same time. "Tyler, I need to tell you something very important. You are too young for all of this to be happening, and it is not fair that I have to tell you what I'm going to say when you are so young."

My heart was in my mouth.

"But there are things you need to know. Things about black women in America," she said.

I had no idea what she was going to say. All I knew was that I loved Clementine Camille Brown.

"Black women are victims, Tyler. The white world thinks we are only three things."

I waited.

"We are Aunt Jemimas who smile and cook and care for children, usually white people's children. Or we are super moms who must protect our children when our black men run away. Or we are whores. Sexual predators," she said.

I turned to her. I was listening.

"Some black women have to become the bread winners because white society has tossed so many black men in jail. And the welfare system tells black women they won't get help if the men come back home."

I'd heard her say this before. In the lectures in Edinburgh.

"But that isn't the worst of it. Because being super moms at least gives black women credit. It's not credit they want because it isn't a burden they want to inherit. It's the sexual predator that hurts black women the most."

I waited. I could feel my hands shaking, but I waited.

Ruth Ann looked away for a moment. Then she turned back to me. "It all goes back to slave row, Tyler. When white slave owners came looking for sex from black women. The same black women who weren't good enough to live in the big house. And the black women had no choice. Black men couldn't protect them. So the white slave owners had their way."

I wanted to cry. I wanted to swear and cry and scream all at once.

"Of course, when that happened, white women didn't like it. Some of them accepted it because they didn't have any right to protest either, but they sure didn't like it. Which is when black women, according to whites, became whores. Women who lured white men into their beds. Women who were over sexed. Women that whites had to be afraid of. Black women were evil."

There were tears in my eyes. My stomach hurt. "But I don't think about Clementine that way. I could never think of her that way," I said.

"I know that, Tyler. I know that. But you're a part of white society. And to defend itself, white society had to create a justification. If black women were so sexually powerful, then it must be because black men were sexually powerful."

Now I knew what was coming.

"And if black men were sexually powerful, but black women were busy luring good white men into their beds, then black men must be lusting after white women," Ruth Ann said. "So a part of the racial and racist equation in America is sexual. Maybe most of it is sexual. Black women as vixens. Whites visiting slave row. Black women as whores.

White men wanting black women because white women are frigid. It is complex and confusing and confounding and crippling."

I waited. I felt Ruth Ann sitting next to me. I could hear the pain in her voice.

"Then this crazy man comes to the beach and says horrible things. That black women want to have babies with white men so their babies won't have to be black. So they will be protected. None of which makes any sense because mixed race babies probably have a harder time than babies that aren't from mixed race parents. But things don't have to make sense and things don't have to be true to get themselves believed and then be buried deep in the psychological history of a nation. In fact, sometimes I think that the more unreasonable a notion is the more likely it is to enter the common consciousness and get itself believed."

Ruth Ann stopped. I turned to her. "But why is Clementine afraid, Ruth Ann? I love her. I love your daughter. For who she is. Because she is smart and cares about the kinds of things that matter to me," I said.

"I know that, Tyler. I know that. But what that crazy man said. She is afraid you believe it without even knowing you believe it. That she's using you so she won't have to be black."

I put my head in my hands and started to cry. I could feel the anger boiling up in me. I hated Blessed Billy. I hated all of them. Every one who had made Clementine hurt or be afraid.

"She's afraid you will have to spend the rest of your life trying not to believe that you believe it," Ruth Ann said.

I turned her. "What am I supposed to do?" I said. "All I want is to be with Clementine. Everyday. All I want to do is to laugh with her and hold her hand and sit and talk about things that matter and read to each other. What am I supposed to do? I don't know what I'd do if I couldn't hear her voice. I wouldn't know where I was or what the world was about. How do I tell her that? The crazy man. Billy. I would have killed him! I swear! I would do anything for her."

"Yes. And she's afraid about that too. She doesn't want you to think she wants to be with you so she can be white, and she doesn't want you to kill someone someday and be in trouble because some crazy person thinks a black girl and a white boy shouldn't be together."

"But Ruth Ann, I can't stop people from being crazy. Or prejudiced," I said.

"I know that. Clementine knows that."

"So what was I supposed to do? I couldn't let him say what he was saying. He wouldn't stop. We tried to leave. But he wouldn't leave us alone. And I could see Clementine's face. It hurt her. What he said . . . it hurt her. She was afraid. I couldn't let him just keep on saying those things." I was crying, sobbing, my voice hard and hateful.

I turned away from Ruth Ann. She put a hand on my back. "I would do anything for Clementine," I said, my voice breaking. "Anything. I love her. I love her," I said.

Then I felt two more hands on my back. Then I couldn't feel Ruth Ann's hand. Then I felt Clementine's face against my neck. I didn't turn around because Clementine had put her arms around my shoulders and pressed her hands against my face from behind. I felt her touch my tears. I turned slowly in her arms as she sat down next to me. I put my arms around her shoulders and pressed her face against mine. And I whispered, "Don't send me away, Clementine. Please don't send me away."

And she said, "I will never send you away. Ever. Just don't run away from me, Tyler. Please don't run away," she whispered. "Please don't run away."

I turned and held her face in my hands. She pulled back enough so she could see me. She was crying. "None of this is fair, Tyler. I don't want things to be unfair for you."

"I know," I said, trying to smile. "But I don't care about fair. I care about you."

Then I knew my mother and my grandfather had arrived and were standing on the sidewalk halfway between the street and the porch where Ruth Ann had met them. I could hear the three of them were talking. I could hear Ruth Ann say, "They're all right. They had a bad experience, but they'll be fine."

60

We returned to school on Monday and coped with our emotions as well as we could, which is not the same as saying we were fine and dandy. We were not. Both of us were more quiet, not only around other people but around each other. Certainly we didn't want to tell anyone what had happened. And as far as we ever knew, no one at school ever found out. At the same time, we found ourselves increasingly sensitive to one another. I am not suggesting that our respect or affection for one another changed. It did not. In fact, it deepened. At least, that was what both of us concluded months later when we talked about what happened on Clearwater Beach that Sunday. No, I mean that each of us was more measured in our responses to the other. We had been forced to visit a very difficult place in our relationship, and while we certainly rejected everything that crazy Blessed Billy had said about us and about black women in general as well as white men in general, we both found ourselves being more inclined to listen not just to what the other was saying but to any sign of hurt or indication of injury that might have remained.

Of course, our everyday life at Tampa Coast continued to be our everyday life, which was a good thing. We did not have time for too much introspection. Both of us were in Advanced Placement English and American history classes. Clementine was in Advanced Placement chemistry. My humanities class required more reading than either my Advanced Placement English or history classes, and they required more than I sometimes thought I could accomplish. And while it was to our advantage that both of us were enrolled in Spanish III class, which meant we could drill each other every day and try to practice having conversations, the study load was challenging for both of us. As you might expect, Clementine remained a straight A student. I managed A's in English and history, but it was another thing in humanities and in Spanish. I just wanted to earn B's. In addition, Clementine became an editor on the school newspaper, which demanded more of her time than just being a writer, and I continued to serve on the student council, although I had no ambition to run for school wide office. Being a junior class representative was work enough.

As for playing football: the spring before, I had been given every opportunity to show the coaches that I could play tight end on the varsity team. But by the end of the two weeks of practice, I sensed that my days in that position were numbered. I was not wrong. When the fall practice season began, I was called into Coach Golstyn's office and told the other coaches all agreed I should be moved from offense to defense. Their reasoning was that I still wasn't big enough to play tight end, which required that I block either the defensive ends, who were bigger than me, or the outside linebackers, who were very often quicker than me. I knew myself that I wasn't fast enough to be an outside receiver, and no one on the coaching staff envisioned me as a running back. They did say, however, that they thought I would make an excellent defensive safety. Coach Badger said they all agreed I was smart, that I would learn to read offenses quickly, that I would know how to anticipate the cuts that receivers made when they were trying to catch passes since I had been a receiver for two years. Their only question had to do with tackling. Was I physical enough to come up on running plays and tackle running backs who had already built up their speed by the time they got into the defensive backfield? Was I strong enough to bring down some of the wide receivers that we would face in the coming season? All I could do was accept their decision and show as much enthusiasm as possible even if I was disappointed. Besides, none of them expected me to be the first string strong side safety. I would have the advantage of playing behind a very good senior from whom I could learn the position as well as Coach Dickson, who had played safety in college.

So the practice season began, and I came home more sore than I ever had when I was a tight end, even with all of the times I'd been tackled hard. I quickly found out that running backwards and then changing direction took its toll on my legs, that tackling running backs and receivers took its toll on the rest of my body. But I was determined, and I knew I was learning, which is all my coaches asked of me.

When the season began, true to their words, I was not the first string strong safety. I played on the kick off team, so I learned how to find the ball and tackle the player returning the ball, and I actually did make a few tackles. Of course, I also found out what it feels like to be blocked by some offensive lineman who outweighed me by twenty or even thirty pounds. It is a very quick way to get upended and find out what pain means.

By the second game of the season, I got to play in four series of defensive plays during the second half. I knocked down two passes, made one tackle, got burned on one pass play and had to get help from the weak side safety to prevent a touchdown against us. By the third game, I played late in the first half and during the fourth quarter. Of course, we were losing that game badly, so I didn't perform any better than any of the other Tampa Coast players. By the fifth game, when the first string strong safety was injured early in the first half, I found myself playing the rest of the game. I intercepted one pass, which had actually been tipped by our defensive back, but I got the credit. I returned it twenty yards before being tackled. I knocked away four passes that night, one in the end zone. And I remember making five tackles, one of which hurt more than I'd ever been hurt before because the running back was both fast and strong and outweighed me. I remember thinking after he ran into me and I managed to hang on that now I knew what it felt to be hit by a small pickup truck. The fact he smiled at me when we both got up told me that either he admired my tenacity or he thought he could run over me the next time. Fortunately, the game ended so I did not have to find out what his smile meant. I was glad for that.

After every game, my mother and grandfather and Ruth Ann and Clementine and I went out to eat. Early in the season I enjoyed our meals together. Later, when I was playing more, I found sitting up more difficult.

Tampa Coast was a good but not outstanding football team. By the time we got to our homecoming game, we had four wins and three losses, but we had scheduled Tarpon High School, from Pinellas county, and Tarpon High had only won two games that year, so we felt as if we had both a chance to win the game and to make our fans happy in preparation for the dance on Saturday night. We were confident about both notions; maybe too confident. However, Clementine and I did not get to go to the dance, even though we had looked forward to the evening. Because during the game, I was hurt very seriously. So seriously that not only did we not go to the dance, I came very close to dying on the field and then on the operating table. Since it was Clementine more than anyone else who helped me fight my way back, I need to tell you the whole story.

Just as I had always driven Clementine to school for her track meets, Clementine drove me to school before football games. Just as she always sat in the front seat trying to focus on her running event, I sat in the front seat trying to focus on the upcoming game.

When we arrived at school, she always came around and opened the door for me and gave me a hug and told me to play well and be well. I always hugged her in return and said I'd look for her in the stands and see her after the game for dinner.

Then she would whisper in my ear, "I love Tyler Thomas Raymond, the man with three first names," and I would smile and say, "And I love Clementine Camille Brown, the most beautiful young woman in the world."

Then I would disappear into the locker room, and she would go home and prepare to come to the game. But the night of the homecoming game, I did not see her for dinner after the game. In fact, I didn't see her until almost 5 A.M. the next morning when I was moved from the operating room to the recovery room. And I will never be able to explain how happy I was to see her that morning. As I told her later, when I saw her I not only thought she was the most beautiful person I would ever see in my life, I also knew I was still alive. At that moment, that was more than enough to make me glad.

61

The homecoming game was going our way. Tarpon High School was better than we had thought, but we were still leading 21-10 going into the fourth quarter. Half way through the period, Tarpon started a long drive. By the time we could get ourselves organized, they had reeled off two long runs and two good short passes and were on the Tampa Coast thirty yard line. That is when it happened.

I knew enough about the Tarpon quarterback to know that on first down he was going to go long and try to pass into the end zone. I knew his favorite target was Tarpon's best receiver, a very quick wide out who was three inches taller than me. And I knew from our scouting reports that he was going to be coming my way. I was correct.

What I remember now as I try to recall what happened—and I admit that my memory of some of the moments is not clear—is that Tarpon stacked two receivers on their left side. Our defensive back picked up the short route. I took the longer of the two. That meant I drew their best receiver, because he was the one they went to on long passes.

I back peddled as much as I dared, then I began moving towards the middle, which was his favorite route. Then the ball was in the air. He was coming towards the center of the field looking over his left shoulder. I cut my angle so I came to him just as the ball was arriving. At that point, I was still facing him but my back was coming around so the ball was over my right shoulder. Then it happened. He went up for the ball. I went up for the ball. But the ball was just beyond his grasp. So he started to fall backwards towards the end zone. Because he was already falling when I leaped, I was able to reach up into the ball's path. My right hand, coming over my body, was above him as he fell. When he came down, he landed on his back. His left leg was stretched long. His right leg was folded under him. His foot was pinned as he landed, so his knee was up.

He was one of those really good but skinny wide receivers who did not wear knee pads, so his knee was exposed when he fell. I saw the ball. I saw my right hand flick it away. Then my head started to come around as I fell. For a fleeting instant, I saw his knee. Then I landed on him. I heard his right ankle snap under me. I heard him scream at the same time I felt the pain. I had fallen on his bent knee, which had driven into my abdomen. I felt something break. I felt the wind go out of me. I saw black and stars for an instant. Then I saw nothing. I must have rolled on over him. I saw the lights for one more instant. Then I could not breathe. It felt hot and burning in my stomach, in my chest. I gasped. I wanted to scream but I could not make a sound. Then I don't remember anything. I didn't see the lights. I didn't see the emergency medical crew. I felt hands. I felt my helmet being removed and my uniform top being cut away. I knew I wasn't wearing my shoulder pads. I felt a needle prick somewhere in my body. I don't know where. Then I felt pain. Something in my throat. Something in my side. Hands were lifting me, but I could not see the people. I could not hear their voices. I could not breathe. I was afraid. I remember that. I could see blue light, but I don't know if my eyes were open or not. Then I didn't see anything or hear anything or feel anything because it was dark and quiet and nothing mattered.

When I awoke I was in a hospital recovery room. I didn't know that right away. I only knew that I could see gray light and hear voices and feel pressure. Something was hot in my right side. My throat hurt. I could not move my legs. I could not move my arms. I could not turn my head. Then I did. I tried with all of my might to turn my head. Then I heard a man's voice. It wasn't a voice I recognized. Then I heard my grandfather's voice. He was far away. So far away I couldn't hear what he was saying, but I knew it was him. I heard my mother. She was crying. I remember wondering how I had managed to die on a football field. Then a woman was touching my head and looking into my eyes as I looked into hers. I had no idea who she was. I learned later she was the recovery room nurse. That I had been in surgery for five hours.

I tried to move my arms. They would move but they were too heavy to lift. I tried to move my legs. I wanted to pee. I felt my feet move. The sheet on top of me was cold. It felt good. My body felt hot. My chest was heavy. I didn't know what that meant. I tried to open my eyes, but I couldn't. Then I felt my mother next to me. She was pressing her face against mine. She was saying she loved me. I tried to tell her that I loved her, but I don't think I made any words. Then I felt my grandfather's hand on my forehead. I would know that hand anywhere. It was strong and gentle. I heard his voice saying something. I don't remember what. But I heard his voice. That was a good sign, I decided. He was near by. I could hear him. That was a very good sign.

I turned to him. I tried to say "Clementine" but I don't think I did. I could smell him next to me. His skin. I tried to say "Clementine." It was very hard to do. I had to fight through the haze. I felt like I was lying down in smoke. I knew it wasn't smoke, but it looked like smoke. My eyes burned. My head hurt. I tried to move my right hand, but my mother was holding it. I moved my left hand. "Grandpa," I whispered.

I know he heard me because I felt his face against mine. I heard him say something. I don't know what it was, but it must have been "I'm here." So I said "Clementine" again. And he said, "She's here." I heard that. "Clementine," I said again. "She's here," my grandfather said.

I was trying so hard. I couldn't understand why they didn't understand. "Clementine" I tried to say. "Clementine," I said again.

It hurt my throat. The woman was leaning over me again and saying "Don't talk. Don't try to talk." But I wanted to tell my grandfather. I reached towards where I had heard his voice. I felt him move closer. I felt his face against mine. "Get Clementine," I must have said, because that is what I wanted to say.

Then I could hear him tell the woman that I wanted Clementine. The woman said she couldn't come in. Only family. I heard my grandfather's voice. He was not happy. "She is family," I heard him say. But the woman said, "She still can't come in."

I reached for my grandfather. I felt him holding my hand. I knew my mother was standing over me. I could almost see her. I pressed my grandfather's hand. "Clementine," I said. And he leaned down and whispered, "I'll get her," he said. Then he let go of my hand.

I still don't know for sure what he did or what he said. I didn't know anything for a while. I couldn't feel time passing. And I knew that I didn't know anything, but I knew that time must have passed. Time always passes I tried to tell myself. Then I smelled her skin against mine. It was a sweet smell. Then I felt her skin against mine. It was so soft and warm. She must have been crying because I could feel tears. I didn't think they were mine. They must have been hers. Then I felt her lips against my left ear. I could feel her words more than hear them when she said, "I love you, Tyler. I love you, Tyler." And I formed words with my lips even though I don't think any sound came out when I said, "'My Darling, Clementine.'" And I heard her almost laugh. Then I felt her hand in my hand and felt her lips on my cheek and felt her hair brushing against my brow. Then it was too hard to hear and feel and speak. Then I was asleep again. All of that happened at 5 A.M. Then I slept for three more hours, if you can call it sleeping. When I finally woke up at 8 A.M., I could see Clementine sleeping in a chair next to my bed and my mother sitting in a chair next to the window, and I could hear my grandfather standing in the doorway. And I could smell coffee. It smelled wonderful. But I hurt all over. And I said, "Did we win?"

Everyone in the room looked at me. It was as if they were surprised I was back from wherever I'd been.

62

It wasn't until almost noon that I was conscious enough for my grandfather and the doctor who had headed the surgical team to explain what had happened. While they talked, Clementine sat next to me holding my hand. I wanted that as much as I wanted to know how I had been injured.

My grandfather explained that when I had leaped to knock down the pass, I had come down on the bent knee of the receiver. Either my weight or his own had broken his right ankle. I said that I thought I remembered hearing him scream. My grandfather said he certainly had screamed. "We could hear the snap and the scream all the way up in the stands."

He then said that when I came down and landed on the receiver, at first people assumed that I had simply had the wind knocked out of me. Players from Tampa Coast ran to me, but then one of them yelled to the coaches that I was hurt.

To their credit, the emergency medical team came running on the field immediately. They found me gasping for breath and my lips starting to turn blue. They reported that my skin was ashen. While the Tarpon coaches moved their injured player away so they could both attend to him and make way for the paramedics people, a Tampa Coast teammate took off my helmet. What happened next had never happened in a high school football game in Tampa before.

The paramedics cut off my uniform top. They could see I was struggling for breath. While the coaches were removing my shoulder pads, the two paramedics started feeling my ribs. Two were broken on my right side, one on my left. It looked as if all three had punctured both of my lungs, which had collapsed. Unless they got air back into my lungs, I could die right there on the field. I was obviously bleeding internally, but at that point the bleeding was secondary.

Then the two attending paramedics did two things. First, one drove their ambulance onto the field. Then they lifted me onto a stretcher. The attending doctor inserted a tube into my chest to drain the fluid that was pressing on my lungs. Then with a paramedic's assistance, the doctor performed a tracheotomy and inserted a tube into my air pipe so my lungs would re-inflate, even though what he was doing was not standard protocol. "It's do it now or let him die in the ambulance," the doctor said.

I was bleeding from the mouth, and I was unconscious. A paramedic called the nearest hospital to alert a trauma team that a player with collapsed lungs and possible damage to his heart and liver was on his way. A surgical team had to be ready the moment they arrived with me.

I have a vague memory of the ride to the hospital. I could see flashes of lights on the ceiling as if we were driving along a street with shops or something on each side. For a moment I could hear the ambulance siren. I heard one of the paramedics men say something about a police car clearing the way ahead of the ambulance. Then I don't remember anything.

As you can imagine, my mother was almost hysterical. My grandfather told me that she fought her way through several men who were trying to hold her back as I was being taken to the ambulance on the stretcher but that when she saw me she stopped dead in her tracks and stood without moving until my grandfather took her to the police car that had already come onto the track to escort the ambulance. When my grandfather shouted to the officer that she was my mother, the officer grabbed her and put her in the back seat. Then my grandfather asked which hospital I would be taken to. When he was told, he ran into the stands and got Clementine and together they ran to his car. Because Ruth Ann had come to the game with my mother and my grandfather, she shouted she would follow in Clementine's and my car.

My grandfather and Clementine arrived at the emergency entrance just after the police car and the ambulance. By the time they were inside, Ruth Ann came running in to find them. My mother was already down the hall standing outside the emergency room into which I had been taken. Clementine told me that my mother's whole body was shaking. Clementine rushed into her arms and started crying. Clementine said that my mother never cried. She just stood still. But her body would not stop shaking. Clementine told me that the only thing my mother said was "Not him too. Not him too" over and over again.

Then my grandfather got to both my mother and Clementine and led them to the small waiting room just a few feet away off of the hallway.

My grandfather had a very hard time describing what happened next. He was trying to be brave, but he was also overwhelmed by fear. I could tell as he sat next to me and held my hand that he had thought I was going to die. I know that's what my mother thought. It was hard seeing them like that, sitting with me, trying to be calm, but at the same time being reminded of what they had felt and feared just hours before.

My grandfather then explained that after a few minutes in the emergency room, I was brought back out into the hallway and wheeled immediately into an operating room. I was in surgery for five hours. Three surgeons worked on me.

First, my broken ribs had to be removed from my lungs. Then the tears in both of my lungs had to be stitched and the sack that covers the lungs repaired. There was a great deal of blood in my chest cavity that made the work very difficult. As it turned out my liver had not been pierced, which was good news. The problem the surgeons had, however, was that with so much bleeding they could not tell if my heart had been damaged. They could tell there was no major rupture, but they were not sure if there was not a small wound someplace that would keep bleeding. So even as they tried to set my ribs and put me back together, they were not sure if they might have to go back in again or not. Only time would tell them that.

Meanwhile, my mother and grandfather and Clementine and Ruth Ann had all moved to the waiting room outside near the surgical wing of the hospital to wait for the doctors to tell them something. They said a nurse named Blakey came twice to tell them that my vital signs were holding steady, which she said was a very good sign. A doctor named Shokoohi came out of the surgery after three hours and said my lungs had been repaired and that now they were trying to see if any other damage had been done, but that was going to be very hard to do because of the bleeding.

My grandfather said that my mother turned to Ruth Ann and buried her head in Ruth Ann's arms at that point and finally started to cry softly. He said that Clementine got up and walked away and stood at the end of the hallway at a window looking out into the darkness. He said that at first he thought maybe he should leave Clementine alone, but then he could tell from her shoulders from the back that she was crying, so he went to her and stood behind her and then put his arms around her. He said that when she turned to look at him he knew he had never, ever seen more pain in a person's face than he did at that moment in Clementine's. When he told me all of this, he leaned very close to me and said, "All Clementine said was 'He's my whole life, Grandpa. He's my whole life.'" Then my grandfather had to sit up and turn away because by then he was crying himself.

I lay in my bed until almost 1 P.M. not at all sure of where I was or what had really happened. Ruth Ann had gone out of the room. When she came back she said the whole team and all of the coaches were in the waiting room downstairs but the nurses weren't going to let them come up to see me. She said she had promised them that my grandfather would go tell them how I was. So my grandfather stood up and left, but I could see that he was not walking very well. I looked at my mother. "Go with him," I whispered.

My mother moved to my side. "What did you say, Tyler. I couldn't hear you."

"I said, go with him."

She hesitated for a moment. Then she nodded as if she understood and turned and left.

I lay still. Then I felt Clementine standing next to me. I knew Ruth Ann was in the room. I had heard them speaking to one another for a moment. Then Clementine put a hand on my brow. She didn't say anything. She didn't need to. Her fingers touching me as she traced the shape of my face said all that needed to be said. I remember reaching up with my right hand and trying to touch her face in return, but I couldn't reach her. So she bent down and with her other hand guided my hand so it was touching her. Then I closed my eyes, and I think I smiled, because I could hear her smiling. She didn't say anything, but I could hear it anyway. Then she sat down next to my bed and we just touched each other's faces for a very long time. I think we were trying to commit each other to memory. Something more profound than just seeing. I knew that I wanted to make her face a part of my body. It was a strange feeling. It was almost as if I was telling myself, well, if you are going to die, the very last thing you want to remember is how Clementine's skin and face felt when you touched them and memorized them so you could take them with you. Then I felt tears on my fingers, and I knew she was crying. I tried to open my eyes, but I couldn't. Not really. And I knew I was about to go back to sleep again—at least I hoped it was sleep—so I gathered up as much strength as I could muster and whispered, "Clementine Camille Brown is my reason . . . ." Then I was asleep.

63

Then I was awake. I could see the clock. It was 8 P.M. I didn't know if it was night or day. But I felt afraid. "The dance," I said out loud.

I heard them coming to me. My mother at the foot of my bed. My grandfather standing up from the chair near the door. Ruth Ann at the window. Clementine standing up from the chair next to my bed.

"What did you say?" my mother asked.

"The dance," I said again. "Is it too late to go to the dance?" I said.

Clementine leaned down and pressed her face into my hand and started to laugh.

My grandfather was standing next to me. "I think you and Clementine are going to miss this one, Tyler."

"But she bought a new dress," I said.

My mother laughed. Clementine leaned down and kissed my cheek and whispered, "I'll put it on and wear it just so you can see it when you feel better."

"When?" I said.

"When what?" she asked.

"When will you put it on so I can see you wearing it?"

Clementine sat down next to my bed and said, "Well, how about tomorrow? I could wear it tomorrow."

"Promise?" I whispered.

"I promise," she said.

Then Ruth Ann was standing next to Clementine. "Clementine, you need to sleep," she said.

"I will," Clementine replied.

"How long have you been here?" I said to Clementine.

"I don't know. Since last night," Clementine said.

"Last night when? After the game?"

"We've all been here since after the game," my mother said.

I nodded. "What day is it now?"

"Saturday," my grandfather said. "Saturday night."

"Then we have to get to the dance, Clementine," I said again.

Ruth Ann stepped closer to the bed. "Tyler, I think Edward is right. You two are going to have to miss the dance this year."

I was quiet again. "Did we win?" I said, turning to my grandfather.

He stepped close to my bed. "Well, you were winning when you knocked down the pass in the end zone."

I tried to smile.

He did not say anything for a moment more.

"Did we win?" I asked again.

My grandfather stood over my bed. "The coaches agreed that because of your injury the game should just end."

I was stunned. "They shouldn't have done that," I said. "That wasn't fair to the Tarpon team."

"Tyler, Tarpon's player was taken to the hospital too. His team didn't want to finish the game any more than your teammates wanted to finish the game," my mother said.

"The referees agreed that the game should just end," my grandfather said. "None of the players wanted to go on. So it ended with Tampa Coast winning. But from the newspaper story, it doesn't sound like anyone on either side cared about who won or lost. So everyone just went home."

Then he smiled and said, "Did you know that the whole Tampa Coast team and all of your coaches were here at the hospital to see how you were doing?"

I said I didn't know that.

"Well, they were," he said.

I nodded. "Yes. I do remember. And you talked to them."

"I talked to them. They all said they want you to get better very fast," he said.

I nodded again and felt Clementine's hand in mine. "I'm hungry," I said very quietly. But before anyone could respond, I was asleep again, which was just as well, because I was told later that ten minutes later, a nurse came into the room and said they had to start preparing me for surgery again, because the doctors believed I was bleeding from a small wound in my heart and they didn't think it was going to heal on its own. My grandfather said that my mother turned away and left the room and that Ruth Ann went to be with her. He said that Clementine sat down in the chair next to my bed and started to cry. He didn't tell me what he did, but he didn't have to, because I know that he must have sighed a very deep sigh and come to my bed and decided that he would have to be strong for me one more time.

64

I know that when I started this memoir, you undoubtedly assumed it would focus on Clementine. And I know that the whole football injury story may make it seem as if I've changed my intention. But that isn't the case. Because I don't know if I would have had the will power to make the life I've made had Clementine not been there with me every step of the way. So even if I now have to finish telling you about the injury and my surgery and my getting better and returning to school to complete my junior year, I want you to keep in mind that Clementine was there every step along the way. She was the reason I was able to recover not just my health but my life. Because Clementine was and still is my reason for everything.

So there I was being prepared for surgery again just hours after I had come out of the first operation to restore my lungs and repair my ribs. Now it was my heart.

The doctor who came to us and explained what was going to happen, Dr. Jahagirdar, said he would be honest with us. "Tyler is strong. That is in his favor. He has just been through a major operation. That is not in his favor."

My mother wanted to know what the doctors believed they had to do. Dr. Jahagridar said, "We have to open up his chest, this time slightly higher than before, and look at his heart."

My grandfather told me later that my mother gasped. He held her in his arms as she listened to what Dr. Jahagridar explained.

"The repair to Tyler's heart is relatively minor. There's no evidence at this point that the bleeding is severe. But any bleeding is a problem. At the same time, even if the tear is small, going in and working around the heart is always a concern."

Dr. Jahagridar paused and looked at my grandfather and my mother and Clementine and Ruth Ann. "He's strong. He has great will power. We've already seen that. When he was on the table for the first surgery, when he should have been completely under, he was still saying 'Clementine, Clementine, Clementine' in a whisper. So whoever this Clementine is, she must mean everything to him."

My grandfather smiled. He nodded toward Clementine. "That's Clementine," he said.

Dr. Jahagridar smiled. "He must care about you a great deal, young lady."

Nurse Blakey smiled as she finished changing my I.V. medications. "That was the first thing he said in the recovery room as well. I got the impression that he must have been thinking your name even when he was under," she said. Then she turned to Dr. Jahagridar. "I think we need to let her come with him as far as the surgery," she said.

Dr. Jahagridar smiled. "Of course. It's a little unusual, but given the circumstances, it makes sense."

Then the doctor was gone. I had heard and not heard all that had been said, if you know what I mean. I could see the light going gray again. I felt my mother kiss my cheek. I felt my grandfather do the same. The last thing I saw dimly was Ruth Ann standing over me. "You come back now, young man. You be sure to come back."

I don't know if I smiled or not, but I wanted to because I wanted to tell her that I would. Then I could feel the bed moving and Clementine's hand in mine. I knew we were in the hallway. I swear I heard Coach Dickson, who was in charge of the defensive backs on the Tampa Coast football team, yelling from down the hallway somewhere, "Ball! Ball! Ball!" But I know now it wasn't true. My grandfather told me later that Coach Dickson and a number of other players had called and found out from him that I was going back into surgery, so they were all together in the surgery waiting room. It was only my imagination that made me think I heard him calling to me. But it mattered. His voice mattered. It told me what I had to do. Then I wasn't seeing anything. I could feel Clementine's hand, but I couldn't see anything. The next day, when I was awake again, Clementine told me that I had whispered to her as she had walked next to me while one orderly and two nurses moved me along the hallway to the surgery, which I'm sure I did, but I don't remember doing so.

65

I was back in my hospital room. I was awake. I don't remember waking up. I was simply not awake. Then I was awake. I remembered seeing bright light at one point as I was placed on the surgical table. But nothing more. Then I was awake in my room.

My mother was standing next to me. My grandfather was sitting in a chair next to the window. I did not see Ruth Ann. Clementine was sitting in a chair opposite my mother. I could feel her head against my leg. I could hear her sleeping.

"Tyler," my mother whispered.

Clementine was awake. She moved closer to me.

I looked at my mother. I wanted to speak, but I could not. I was not in pain. I could not feel anything. I wasn't floating exactly, but I didn't feel the bed either.

Clementine leaned out over me and looked into my eyes. "Can you see me?" she said.

"Yes," I whispered. "You are Clementine Camille Brown. I remember you won the state 440 yard dash championship last spring," I said slowly.

She smiled.

My mother spoke again. "Are you thirsty? Can I get you anything?"

I sighed. "I'd love to pee," I said quietly.

"You are," my mother said. "They put a catheter in you. Just like before."

I groaned.

Clementine touched my face. She didn't say anything. She didn't need to.

"What day is it?" I asked.

"Sunday," my mother said.

"What time is it?" I asked.

"Five o'clock," Clementine said. "P.M."

"How long have all of you been here?" I said.

My grandfather was next to my bed. "Hey, Tyler. Son. How are you feeling?" he asked.

"How long have all of you been here?" I asked them again.

"Since Friday night. When you were brought here," my mother said.

"Have any of you slept?" I asked.

"Some," Clementine said. "Here in the room. Outside in the surgery waiting room. There's a couch. That's where my mother is right now."

I was quiet for a moment. "I'm sorry," I said in a whisper.

"Sorry? Why are you sorry?" my mother said, smiling through her fear.

"Because of this. Because of what happened. What I put you through."

"Tyler, you were in a football game. It was an injury. An accident. You don't need to be sorry," my grandfather said.

I was quiet for a moment. "We missed the dance," I said, turning my head so I could see Clementine.

She smiled. I could see she had been crying. "We'll go next year," she said. "And we'll go to the prom." Then she laughed softly. "If you'll be my date, I mean," she said.

I nodded. Then I said, "Yeah. I'll be your date."

She pressed her face next to mine.

"You're my favorite, you know," I said.

She pulled her face back and looked at me. "Your favorite what?" she said smiling.

I sighed. "Oh, my favorite runner. My favorite study partner."

"He's feeling better," my grandfather said, standing up straight and smiling.

"And travel partner. You are my favorite travel partner. And dance partner. And art gallery partner," I said.

"Ah," Clementine said. "And movie partner?"

"Yeah. And movie partner. And I love you," I whispered. "But right now, I'm going to puke."

My mother grabbed for the basin on the table next to my bed. I tried to roll towards her. Clementine helped me roll towards where my mother was holding the basin. I retched mostly water. Very little food. It was horrible and embarrassing. Then I was finished and rolled back so I could see my grandfather and Clementine. "That was certainly graceful," I muttered.

The three of them looked at each other and smiled.

"You need to sleep," I said to them. "All of you must need to sleep."

"We're all right. We'll sleep when it's time to sleep," my mother said.

I knew that's what she would say. "I'm hungry," I said. "My stomach feels like it's empty."

"It probably is," my grandfather said. "I'll ask the nurse, but my guess is it will be some time before you get to eat."

"That's great," I moaned. "I try to intercept a pass, and I end up stopping the game, missing the dance, and missing I don't even know how many meals."

Clementine and my mother smiled. Then Ruth Ann was in the room at my side, touching my brow. "Good," she said, smiling in a serious way. "You're back."

I looked at her. "Yes, ma'am."

"We were worried," she said. "But I knew you'd be back.

"Yes, ma'am. I'm back," I said.

Ruth Ann smiled at me. Clementine touched my hand. My mother straightened the sheets across my chest. I winced, which made her hurry to loosen them again. My grandfather stood up straight and nodded. I was back.

66

I was in the hospital for five more days. My grandfather came every morning to sit and read the newspaper to me. Clementine came in the afternoons because she was organizing my schoolwork so I wouldn't fall too far behind. My mother came every evening and helped me with my studies. By the third day, I was well enough to stand up and go to the bathroom on my own, which meant no more urinary catheter.

When I was brought home, I found cards from teammates and school friends and flowers from the parent boosters club, all of which was very encouraging. What helped me at home the most, though, was my grandfather discussing my history and English class studies with me in the mornings and Clementine sitting with me after school to keep up my other classes. After one week at home, my grandfather took me out on the porch one afternoon to sit and talk. It felt good just to be out in the sunlight.

I always loved talking with my grandfather, not just because he was wise and patient but because he always encouraged me to think issues through and then try to talk about my ideas. The first afternoon that we sat outside, after we'd discussed a whole range of issues, he turned and looked at me for a long time without speaking. I could tell there was something very personal he wanted to say. So I waited. Then he turned away and said very quietly, "You know, Tyler, we were very afraid we were going to lose you."

I didn't know how to respond.

"I'm not sure your mother could have stood it," he said. "I remember when we got the news about your father. It took all of her will power to just go on every day after that." He paused. "But she had to." He turned and looked at me. I looked at him. "She had you." Then he turned away again.

I still didn't know what to say.

"You've been her great joy, Tyler. You're a very fine young man."

After a moment I said, "Thank you, Grandpa, for saying that."

"As for me. Well, frankly, I think that if anything were to happen to you, I'd just want to pack it in and have it be over."

I was stunned. I knew my mother loved me. I knew my grandfather loved me. But he'd never said anything like that before. I thought of him as indomitable, as steadfast, as always there, alert, witty, wise. But then I'd never been injured as seriously as I had been, so the issue of me maybe dying had never come up.

I turned to him. I could see his profile. His strong nose. His strong chin. I liked the way his gray hair curled around his ears and over his collar. To me he looked like what a professor was supposed to look like. What I wanted to look like some day.

"I love you, Grandpa," I said quietly. "You and mom. I love both of you."

He cleared his throat and touched the cover of my history textbook, which was sitting in his lap. Then he turned to me and smiled his very special, quiet smile and said, "Tyler, let's talk about how the compromise between the New England culture and Old Southern Planters culture became the Middle Atlantic States culture that then went west all the way to the Pacific Coast. Because if you understand the layers of compromise and contradiction that make it up you will understand everything else that happened in the American 19th century experience," which told me it was time to get back to our studies.

At the end of that week, he and my mother took me back to the hospital to have a scan made of my torso. Dr. Jahagirdar said I was healing very well. He showed me the place where the paramedic had inserted the tube into my chest, which drained the fluid around my lungs and, in his words, saved my life. He showed me the long incision where the surgeons had opened my abdomen so they could get inside my chest cavity and the incision they made when they went back in and repaired my heart. I knew that I was very fortunate to have had such good medical care available. I was fortunate to be alive.

On Tuesday of my second week at home, Clementine took me for a very slow walk around the block. For the first twenty minutes or so I felt as if I had never walked with her or held her hand before. I was weak, but I was very happy. When we stopped for a moment under a canopy of trees and we kissed each other, I thought I would never breathe again.

Now, I need to say something here about Clementine's and my kisses. I know what you're thinking. But you're wrong. We did not kiss each other with the same kind of exaggerated passion that we saw among our school friends. They were all over each other. Both Clementine and I thought that they looked silly because for us they were missing the point. Kissing is not supposed to be a contest. It is a gesture of profound affection. We understood that the first time we kissed. I'm not trying to give a lecture here, I just want you to know that when Clementine and I kissed, we touched lips ever so slightly, lightly, carefully because we wanted to feel the anticipation, the feel of our lips coming together, of our breath becoming one, of the long, sustaining emotion that we could feel. Our friend, Eddie Crooms, said that the first time he saw us kiss when we were dancing, he thought we had turned into one person. That is what we wanted to feel. That we were one person embracing the self. I know that sounds very philosophical, but I promise you, it was not philosophical for us. It was the moment when we knew we were most and truly alive. We talked about it. We agreed. To touch the other's lips with our own was to feel the breathless electricity of being a person. I cannot describe it any other way. It was tender and electric.

So we stood under the canopy of trees and kissed as we had not kissed since before I was injured. Both of our bodies vibrated with the other's touch. Then Clementine drew back and looked at me as seriously as she had ever looked at me and said, "Tyler, I swear, if you'd died . . . if you hadn't come back to love me . . . I swear I'd never have spoken to you again."

For a moment I stood looking into her deep and dark brown eyes. I heard what she said. Then I *really* heard what she had really said. And I began to laugh. I stepped back and still holding both of her hands began to laugh.

"I guess that's right," I said. "I guess you wouldn't have spoken to me ever again. Which would have made me very sad."

And Clementine laughed at what she had said.

Then we started walking again very slowly, with Clementine holding my hand and trying to stay in step with me so I would not become too tired.

67

The more I think back about those days, the more I realize how crucial Clementine was to my recovery. I played football for her. I held on when I went into surgery for her. I knew I had to get well for her. I don't know how else to explain it.

My grandfather took me to see Dr. Shokoohi at the end of the second week. The doctor told me I could go back to school the next Monday. I know some students might think it is odd that I was overjoyed, but the fact is, I missed my friends. You have to understand that Clementine and I shared friends who were not just intelligent and serious about their studies, some of them were wonderfully funny. There were times at lunch at school or on a weekend night we'd all sit together and talk and laugh so hard my sides hurt. I missed talking to them between classes, and I missed hearing them during discussions in class. I realized I even missed my teachers. Most of all, I missed eating lunch with Clementine.

When Monday finally came, my grandfather helped me dress for school. Then Clementine picked me up in our car and drove me to Tampa Coast. I remember walking into the school and knowing that I had better stay very close to her. Not just to steady me as I walked, but to steady my emotions as well. Because for a moment I felt as if I had never been in the school before. Everything seemed new and strange. But before we had gone very far a number of our friends saw us and came to say hello. For the rest of the day when I saw them my football teammates were particularly friendly. The season had ended the weekend I was sent home from the hospital, but they said they had postponed the team awards banquet until I could attend. I thought that was the nicest thing they could ever have done for me.

When I went to my classes, my teachers greeted me warmly, and I was made to feel that I had been missed. That might have been an exaggeration on their parts, at least in the case of my anatomy teacher, because I was not a very good student in the class even if I was interested in the subject. My passions were history and English. Nonetheless, they all made me feel good. But it was Coach Badger who had the biggest surprise when he went out of his way to find me at school and to make sure I was going to attend the awards banquet and that my mother and grandfather should come with me. I knew that the parents were invited, but he said it was important that they come. I said I knew they were planning to attend. He said that was good. But he didn't explain why it was so important.

What helped me the most, of course, when I went back to school was knowing that Clementine was in both my English and history classes and that everyone seemed to understand that for a while at least she was going to escort me everywhere I had to go.

Because only the football coaches and players and the players' parents are invited to the football awards banquet, Clementine was not able to go with us that evening in the same way that I had not been able to attend the track team's awards banquet the previous spring when she had received the Most Valuable Runner Award as voted by the team members.

At the football banquet, after a number of other really outstanding players on both offense and defense were given awards for their individual achievements, including four who made the all conference team, Coach Dickson, the defensive backs coach, called me to the podium. I had no idea what he was going to say. When I got there I got the biggest surprise in my life, because Coach Dickson read a letter written to me by Coach Vince Dooley, the head coach of the University of Georgia football team.

Vince Dooley was a nationally important football coach. What I didn't know was that he had been an All-Conference defensive back at Auburn University and had played against my father when my father was a running back at the University of Maryland. In his letter, Coach Dooley said he had heard from Coach Dickson, whom he'd known for many years, about what I had gone through. Then he said, "What I want you to know, Tyler, is that if you are truly the son of your father, a man I respected both on and off of the football field, then you will not only recover from your very serious injury, you will continue on in your life and grow up to be a man worthy of his name." I assume that you will understand why, at that very moment, I decided that not only was I going to play football at Tampa Coast High School the next year, I was going to attend the University of Georgia, and come hell or high water, I was going to play football for Vince Dooley.

68

I am not going to tell you everything that happened the rest of our junior year. It isn't necessary. School is school, after all. I became stronger although it was a very slow process. Clementine was with me every day. By the end of my first week back at Tampa Coast, we went to a movie. She drove because it would be another month before the doctors said I was strong enough to do so. But we had always taken turns driving even before I was injured, so neither of us minded.

There were three important things that happened during the rest of the school year that I remember as being important in shaping who we became individually and who we became together. The first came after both of us read the introduction to the essay "Nature," by the American religious philosopher Ralph Waldo Emerson.

What I found interesting about the essay was the way Emerson redefined the meaning of the term *divine*. His thinking about how one truly experiences the divine was a radical departure from Christian thought when the essay was written in the middle of the 19th century. It remains a radical rejection of monotheistic theology even today, particularly his proposition that revelation is on going, that all truth has not been revealed and codified in what are called sacred texts by a number of religious traditions, that each person must engage his spiritual person in his own way in his own time. And while I decided Emerson's thinking made sense to me, I found it interesting that my classmates, many of whom said they were professing Christians and observant Jews, sat and listened to the classroom discussion without any indication that they really understood that Emerson was rejecting the foundation of their systems of belief. If they understood, I kept telling myself, they would have objected, unless, of course, their acceptance of their religious discipline was done by rote, which as far as I was concerned meant it was meaningless. Or they really weren't listening. And all they could do when the teacher, Miss Brody, tried to explain what Emerson meant when he said we must all become transparent eye-balls was snicker. But I understood. I told Clementine that he meant the same thing that the poet William Carlos Williams meant in his poem "The Red Wheelbarrow."

"'The Red Wheelbarrow'?" Clementine said. "Do you mean the poem she put on the board last week. The one we haven't talked about."

"Yes. That one. 'so much depends/upon/a red wheelbarrow/glazed with rain/water/beside the white chickens.'"

Clementine waited.

I leaned toward her. "Clementine, what's the so much that depends upon a red wheelbarrow glazed with rain water against the white chickens?"

"I don't know. You tell me," she said.

I smiled. "Everything depends upon the red wheelbarrow glazed with rain water. Because we aren't looking at the red wheelbarrow ourselves. We can't. It isn't a picture. It's a poem. In words."

Clementine loved it when I became passionate about poetry.

"We're watching the poet watch the red wheelbarrow . . . glazed with rain water against the white chickens. We're watching the poet. So it's about point of view. It's about distancing ourselves so we can observe. Be outside of ourselves looking at ourselves watching the world. It's what Emerson is saying. We become an eyeball. Our minds become an eyeball. We see and we see ourselves seeing. Both at once."

Clementine smiled. "Ah," she said.

We talked about the essay over lunch for almost a week. We sat with my grandfather after school and talked about it even more. Then I read in the biographical information that Emerson had been a Unitarian minister, and I asked Clementine if I might go with her and Ruth Ann to the Tampa Unitarian church they attended. She said she had wondered how long it would take me to want to come with her. That is how I became a Unitarian-Universalist. Yes, some of our friends think it was only because of Clementine, but that isn't the case. Slowly but surely, I finally found a religious home where reason was at the heart of the theological considerations. And while my grandfather had not gone to church since he was a child and my mother had not been raised in a church at all, neither of them objected to my doing so. "As religious organizations go, the Unitarians make the most sense," my grandfather said. "So if you've decided you want to attend some sort of worship services, I suppose the Unitarians are the best place for you. Certainly it seems to serve Ruth Ann and Clementine very well."

At the same time I was finding my way into both Emerson and Unitarian theological thought, Clementine bought a book for me about the history of the Celtic peoples of Europe. I had a vague sense that both my Scots and my Welsh background made me a Celt, but I knew very little about Celtic European history. Even my grandfather admitted that he didn't know nearly enough about what the text called the ancient cultural and racial history of the Scots, the Irish, the Welsh. "Most of my interest in history starts with the Magna Carta," he said. "The first real step in the process that leads finally to the Enlightenment notion of democracy."

In any case, when I opened the book, I realized I was entering a whole new world. I found a people whose racial and cultural characteristics explained my passions, whose eye for story detail manifested itself in my own attempts to write for my teachers, whose sense of egalitarian justice was apparently as native to me as it was to my mother and her father. I certainly could not have said it that way at the time, because I still had years and years ahead of me during which my intellectual life would find its focus, but that book about the Celts expressed what eventually became my sense of what history means. I believe I would be safe to say it was the *beginning of the beginning* of what would become my passion and my career.

The third thing was Clementine's track season. Yes, we went to the junior-senior prom, and yes, Clementine was beautiful, and yes, both of our mothers took photographs of us that they still have, and yes, we had the usual formal portrait taken at the dance, which both of us still have in frames, and yes, most of all, we had a wonderful time with each other and with our friends. But it was Clementine's track season more than any other event that junior year that determined what our lives individually and together were going to be for the four years of our undergraduate studies. Because it was her achievements in track that first attracted the attention of university coaches. I would be a senior before any coaches noticed me.

69

When Clementine started running as a ninth grader, she was 5'2" and weighed 105 pounds. As a tenth grader, she had grown to 5'4" and gained five pounds. She knew without anyone telling her that if she wanted to continue to compete at the best levels of track she would have to become stronger by adding muscle weight. By the time the track season started when she was a junior, she had grown to 5'6" and 120 pounds mostly by lifting weights with me after school in the training room at Tampa Coast as I tried to regain my strength. What lifting weights, combined with running sprints four days a week did for her was not only to increase her speed, it enhanced her endurance, which is why, when the season began, Coach Lawton told her she needed to start training for both the 440 and the 880, the two most grueling events in every meet. She said if Clementine could continue to win competitions while running those events she would definitely begin to attract college coaches.

Clementine won her first four dual meets in both events. When the first large regional meet was run, she won the 440 handily and finished a very close second in the 880 to a girl from Hillsborough High School who was a specialist and headed for the University of Texas on a track scholarship.

By the time Tampa Coast took part in the conference championships, there was no one close to Clementine's times in both events. When she then won the state championship for the second year in a row in the 440 and finished a very close second in the 880, she began to receive letters. Ironically, sitting with her mother for hours as they looked at college and university catalogs wasn't necessary. Clementine knew she wanted to attend Georgia Tech so she could study biology because by then she had decided she wanted to attend the University of Georgia Medical School in Augusta.

At the same time she was winning races and receiving letters trying to interest her in the several colleges and universities in the southeast that were keeping tabs on her success, I was running and jumping and lifting weights so I could be stronger and heavier. It was obvious I was never going to be taller than six feet. In fact, I had to stretch to make that height. I knew that if I tried to put on too much weight, I would lose speed, and since I didn't think I had much to spare, because I certainly wasn't a sprinter, Coach Dickson and I decided that I should not try to go above 180 pounds for my senior year. It took several long talks to convince him that I would be okay to play football again. By the time I showed him letters from two doctors saying that my injuries were healed and that my playing football was no more dangerous for me then than it had been when I had first begun, he said that if I had a good season while gaining no more than five more pounds, I might well get some college coaches interested. When I told him the only place I wanted to go was the University of Georgia, and the only coach I wanted to play for was Vince Dooley, he said he would write a letter and let Coach Dooley know what I had said and then keep him posted as the season progressed.

That was all I could ask him to do. Just like Clementine, it was up to me to perform in both the classroom and on the field. During the summer, both of us reviewed for the SAT exams. Both of us did our assigned summer reading for our Advanced Placement English class. I tried to prepare for chemistry class by sitting with her and reviewing what she knew, which was far more than I would ever learn. We were, in short, two very serious students even if we went to the beach at least twice a week in the evenings and worked at Home Depot again. In fact, even our part time jobs were part of our training. Clementine got a job in which she had to walk all over the store during her entire shift. I asked for and was given a job in the lumber yard. It was hot and horrible work, but it also meant I spent my shifts unloading lumber from the trucks that came to the warehouse and then putting lumber on trucks for contractors.

At the same time, we were also aware that if our plans developed as we hoped, we would not be on the same campus. Georgia Tech is in Atlanta. The University of Georgia is in Athens. That means we'd be going to universities that were not only seventy miles apart, they were intense rivals. We talked about what it would be like for each of us to not have the other on the same campus, to not be able to walk together every day or eat meals together regularly. We talked about it, and we avoided talking about it. It didn't ever occur to either of us that our relationship would change. We just knew we'd have to work harder at seeing each other. I think the day we had that talk while sitting in the park close to Clementine's house we also started counting the days until we would move to our two campuses. It was not a happy thought. The only consolation we took at the time was that maybe she wouldn't get into Georgia Tech and maybe I wouldn't get into the University of Georgia so our trepidations would be for naught. Of course, we also knew that we both had the grades to get into our respective universities so our sense of impending dread mixed with anticipation was not lessened appreciably. Then something completely unexpected happened in August.

One evening when Clementine and I were eating dinner with Ruth Ann and my mother and my grandfather, Ruth Ann handed Clementine an envelope and me an envelope, saying that all three of them were very proud of the way we had worked at our studies and at our sports and our studies all summer. So they decided to reward us with a trip.

"It's not elaborate," Ruth Ann said. "But it took some arranging."

"We know the two of you received your Advanced Placement examination scores," my grandfather said. "We know that Clementine earned the highest possible grade on all four of her Advanced Placement courses. And we know that you, Tyler, earned the highest possible scores on your two Advanced Placement examinations."

"So we think you two deserve to be rewarded," my mother said.

With that, Clementine opened her envelope first and found two tickets to the Broadway musical "A Chorus Line," which Clementine had wanted to see since it opened in New York in 1975, and a new musical that my grandfather said he believed we would find moving, "Miss Saigon."

After shouting her surprise for a moment and then showing them to me, she wanted to know what they'd given me. So I opened my envelope in which I found two round trip tickets to New York for the following Tuesday morning. We would then return on Friday.

We didn't know what to say. Then Clementine asked, "Where will we stay? With Grandma and Grandpa in New Jersey?"

"No. That's too far away," Ruth Ann said. "You'll need to telephone them, of course, and telephone your cousins, but you aren't to feel any obligation to go see them. This trip is for you two. That's why I've made arrangements for you to stay with one of my best friends when I was a student at New York University, Betsy Winter. She's a lawyer with a big firm in Manhattan. That's where she lives. Her husband owns his own business. Something to do with cargo containers for ships. Their daughter is away for the summer studying in France. Betsy assured me that they have room for you. They're looking forward to meeting both of you."

Clementine and I just sat and looked at each other. The tickets to the musicals were expensive. The flights were the same.

"You're going to need money for cab fare from the airport and for subway fare in the city," my grandfather said. "Ruth Ann worked out getting the tickets and making arrangements for you two to stay with her friend and her husband. And your mother paid for the air fare. So I am giving you a check so the two of you won't have to spend any of your own money while you're in New York." With that he handed me a check for $300. I was flabbergasted. I don't think any other word will do. "I assumed you two would want to visit the Metropolitan Museum of Art and the Museum of Modern Art. Probably other places as well," he said.

At that point, Clementine and I and looked at each other for a breathless moment. Then we got up and went around the room and kissed all three of them. We were going to travel again together, this time just the two of us, to New York for a two day stay. What more could two high school students who were in love want for their summer vacation? What awaited us, however, was another surprise, one that even Ruth Ann and my mother and my grandfather could not have predicted and one that, quite frankly, had they known was coming, might have given them serious pause. It certainly would have the two of us.

70

We flew from Tampa to New York City on Tuesday morning. When we arrived, we followed Ruth Ann's instructions and took a train into the city. Once we arrived, we took a cab to the address Ruth Ann had given us. It was almost three in the afternoon. The building was ten stories high, one of several blocks of apartment houses that all looked very much the same. We told the doorman who we were. After he found our names on a list, he opened the door, and we went in.

We crossed a small lobby and took the elevator to the sixth floor. Carrying our suitcases, we went down the hallway to the end where we found the Winters' apartment. Clementine rang the doorbell. We could hear music from inside. A jazz group of some sort. The door was opened by a very tall, very handsome black man. He was dressed in suit pants and dress shirt. He was in the process of tying what even I knew was a very expensive silk tie. He smiled and told us to come in. "I'm Martin," he said. "Betsy's husband. She's sorry she isn't here, but she got a telephone call this morning and had to take a flight to Boston. Something about one of her cases." Then he extended a hand. "You must be Clementine," he said. "You look like your mother's pictures."

Clementine returned his greeting.

"And you're Tyler. Ruth Ann thinks you're a prince. That's the word she used." He smiled and extended hand to me, which I accepted.

"Look, I've got an appointment across town. So I'm going to have to leave the two of you on your own. Betsy said you're a couple. That you go to college together."

Clementine started to explain that we were high school students, but by then Martin had turned and was directing us to follow him through the living room and into a hallway. "Your room is here," he said. "Second door on the right. Make yourselves at home." He smiled and said, "I know you've got tickets for 'A Chorus Line' tonight. And I think Betsy said you're going to see 'Miss Saigon.'" He was hurrying. "Betsy won't be home tonight until you've gone to the theatre. She may not even be home when you get back. And I won't be home until after her because I've got to go to the docks to meet with clients. Sometimes that takes almost all night."

He nodded towards the room that was going to be ours. Then he said, "I've left a key on the dining room table. Take it. It's for you two. And the doorman knows you'll be coming and going for the next two days. So don't worry if you forget the key. He can let you in." He turned and went back down the hall and called out as he crossed the living room, "There's food in the refrigerator. Help yourselves. Relax. Make yourselves at home." Then he had his suit jacket on. He picked up a brief case. "It's a big double bed. You'll find towels in the bathroom." Then he was gone.

Clementine and I stood in the hallway not knowing what to do or to say. She looked at me and then turned and opened the door to the bedroom and went in, turning on a light as she did.

The room was large. The window had a view of what we assumed was the other side of the building across the enclosed courtyard. Clementine walked across the room and into the bathroom. I stood in the doorway. There were two overstuffed chairs facing each other that formed a conversation area. A television set sat on top of the waist high wall length bookshelf on the wall between the two chairs. A stereo was on one of the shelves. The shelves were packed with books and framed photos of the family posing together on a ski slope, near the ocean, on a boat. All three were smiling. All three were very handsome. Betsy was as dark as Ruth Ann but not as dark as Martin. Their daughter looked like her father but her skin was the same complexion as her mother's. There were travel posters on the walls of New York City, London, Paris, Madrid. The family obviously liked to take trips. I envied them.

Clementine came back into the room. "So what do we do now?" she said. "I don't think this is what my mother or your mother expected."

"I think you're safe in saying that."

"Do we tell someone?" Clementine said.

"Who do we tell? And what do we say? Your mother and my mother are in Tampa. Your mother's friend is in Boston. She won't be back until late tonight. Her husband is on his way to the docks and won't be back until even later."

Clementine looked at me. "Are we going to share the bed?" she asked.

I moved to the window and looked out at the street below. It was a very sunny afternoon. "Clementine, this is a misunderstanding. I don't think it's an invitation," I said.

"Are we going to share the bed?" she asked me again.

"Are you asking me if I want to sleep with you?" I said.

Clementine sat down on the edge of the bed. "I don't know what I'm asking, Tyler."

I sat down in one of the overstuffed chairs and looked at her. "Clementine, this is not what was planned for us. This is not what you and I expected."

"You're right about that," Clementine said.

I drew a deep breath and exhaled slowly. "We certainly don't want to embarrass your mother's friends. And we don't want to disappoint your mother," I said. "Or upset mine."

"Yes, but we have to sleep somewhere," Clementine said.

"Fine. You're right. You'll sleep in here in the bed. But that's later. I think right now we're much safer just going ahead and getting cleaned up and then going out to get something to eat. Does that make sense?"

Clementine has several expressions that I'd learned to read by then. One was her look that said I'm determined; I'm going to finish what I set out to accomplish. Another says I'm through with talking. Another says Tyler, you are wrong even if I'm not going to argue with you. I assume she learned to read my expressions as well. This time, her expression said, all right, Tyler, I'm going to trust you right now, but I'm going to have more to say later. So I thought it wisest to not say much more but to simply suggest we go ahead and do what we had planned to do when we arrived: clean up and get something to eat. "Then we're going to go see 'A Chorus Line,'" I said. "What your mother and my mother want us to do."

Clementine waited. She looked worried.

"Clementine, the one thing I know for sure is that your mother trusts me. She expects me to take care of you. And that's okay. I want to do that." Then I looked away. "And my grandfather. You have to understand what he's been telling me all of my life. That's it's the gentleman's responsibility. That's his term for moments like this. 'The gentleman's responsibility.'"

I looked at Clementine.

"Yes, Tyler," she said. "And that's you, isn't it?"

I didn't answer. Then I said, "I don't know, Clementine. I hope I am."

"So what are we going to do?" she said again.

"Clementine, please. Can't we discuss this later? Doesn't that make more sense?"

Clementine was quiet for a moment.

"Clementine, you're supposed to call your mother to tell her we got here safely. She asked me to remind you. She said she'd call my mother," I said. "Let's start with that. Please call your mother."

Clementine stood up and moved to the telephone on the desk. "What do I tell her about this?" she said.

"Clementine . . . " I started to protest.

"I'm asking because you're supposed to be the prince," she said, smiling.

I shook my head. Clementine could be so exasperating sometimes. "Yeah, well, if I'm a prince then you're a princess," I said. "Which also means your mother is the queen. I'll let you figure out what that means."

"I know what it means," Clementine said as she laughed as she sat down at the desk and began to dial.

After a moment, I went to my suitcase and opened it up and got out my toilet kit. Then I went into the bathroom. "I'll start getting ready," I said. "I suppose we'll laugh about this some day, won't we," I called to her as I closed the bathroom door.

"I hope so," Clementine called back to me as she began dialing the operator so she could place her collect call. "Let's just hope our mothers will laugh with us."

71

Although Martin Winters had said we should help ourselves to the food in the refrigerator, because we had only talked to him as he had hurried out the door and because we had not even met Betsy Winters yet, we decided we were more comfortable trying to find a small neighborhood restaurant. With the help of the doorman, we found a small Italian café within walking distance. Then we took a cab to the theatre where we would see "A Chorus Line."

If you know anything about musicals, you'll know why "A Chorus Line" became my favorite that night. Clementine and I discussed it at length several times both that evening right after we'd seen the show and later, when we thought back on our New York experience. The stories of the several dancers, each of whom spent years training so they might one day dance in a Broadway musical, was fascinating if for no other reason than each of them has endured hardship and heartbreak, disappointment and disillusionment. When they line up on the stage and talk with Zack, the director, who asks them questions they had never been asked before at any other audition, each of them responds in an individual way. The cumulative impact is profoundly moving, for in the end the tales are psychologically honest and painfully touching. Yes, both Clementine and I left the theatre singing several of the songs, but not the same way we've left theatres singing the songs before or since. This time each song was laced with melancholy, a disposition that is more natural to me than to Clementine, but a disposition that on this occasion she shared. The songs remain my favorites.

After the show we took a cab back to the Winters' apartment. As we expected, neither of them had yet returned. Clementine said she would make two cups of tea.

I went to the double glass doors in the dining room and discovered the apartment had a very nice small terrace balcony. Opening the doors, I went outside. The night was still warm, but it was obviously going to be cooler very soon. I called Clementine to come join me. So we sat for some time on their small balcony talking about how we had come to that moment in our lives individually and our life together. After a while, Clementine moved her chair next to mine and took my hand. Then she said, "Do I have to ask again, Tyler?"

I turned to her. It was dark on the balcony. Light from the open sliding glass door lit the left side of her face, but the right side, which was closest to me, was in the shadow I cast from the small balcony light behind me. After some time, I responded to her question. "No, Clementine, you don't have to ask again."

She waited because by then, just as I had learned to read the tone of her voice as a code when she had no more to say, she had learned to read my tone of voice when I was preparing to say more but in my own good time.

"Clementine, I can't think of anything I would like more than to make love with you. It is something I want to think about. And it is something I try not to think about."

She continued to wait.

"You are a wonderful young woman. I believe in all of my heart that you are going to be a most wonderful woman in the future. I want to be a part of your life now. I can't imagine who I would be if you hadn't asked me to be your lab partner in biology." I hesitated. "But even more I want to be a part of your life in the future. I can't imagine what my life could possibly be ten years from now or twenty years from now if you aren't in it." I waited. "Does that make sense?" I asked.

Clementine smiled and turned away for a moment. For a moment the wind gusted between the buildings. Clementine gathered her sweater up around her shoulders. Then she turned back to me. "You are my whole life, Tyler. Everything I do is because of you."

I waited again. I wanted to find the right words. I wanted to be whatever Clementine wanted me to be.

"But if we make love tonight . . . here, in this place," I said, "under these circumstances . . . we won't be alone. I think the three people we love the most in the whole world will be in the room with us. And I don't think they'll be comfortable."

Clementine nodded. Then she turned in her seat and swung her legs up over my thighs.

I wanted to pass out. I wanted to be somewhere else. I sure didn't want to not make love to this woman. All I could do was speak very slowly. "Clementine, one of these days . . . I don't know when. But one of these days, there will just be the two of us in a room someplace. But until then . . . I can't turn to you and say what I want to say because when we fly back to Tampa and you talk to your mother about this trip and I talk to my mother and grandfather about this trip both of us will have to leave out the part about us sleeping together."

Clementine reached over and took my hand in hers. She pressed my hand to her lips and kissed it very slowly. "I would make love with you, Tyler. I would. I have wanted to show you how much I love you. But I have also wanted to wait. And I know the right time will come. I don't know when. But I know it will come."

I nodded and looked at her and with my hands grasped hers and lifted them to my face where I held them against my lips.

"I've talked with your mother, Clementine, after that horrible day at the beach. We talked about black women in America. I don't want any of that to matter to us," I said. "I just want it to be us. But I'm conscious of what she said. Of what I learned. I don't want what she said to intrude on us. But it's hard to do that."

Clementine swung her legs down to the floor and stood up. I was suddenly afraid. What had I done wrong? She's going to be angry. Why hadn't I just kept my big mouth shut? But she wasn't angry. She turned and sat down on my lap and put her arms about my shoulders and lay her head against my chest. I could feel her tears. She wasn't crying. Not the kind of crying you can hear. But I could feel her tears.

My voice was shaking. "I suppose any man worth his salt wants to protect the woman he loves from harm. It's part of who we are. Men and women together. Even if the world is changing. I want to protect you from hurt." I waited for a moment. How much could I say? How much should I probe our relationship, the dangers to our relationship. I didn't know. It was confusing. "I am not some white man come to slave row . . . to find a black woman for the night," I finally said. "I . . . I will never be that man," I stuttered. Then my voice was more fierce. "I am Tyler Thomas Raymond, and I am in love with Clementine Camille Brown, who is the most honorable woman I will ever know."

Clementine was quiet. She did not have to say anything. And I did not have to say anything more. She kissed me. That was enough.

An hour later, as Clementine prepared for bed, I gathered up the bed spread and took a pillow and made myself as comfortable as I could on the front room couch. I told Clementine I would explain everything to both Martin and Betsy when we saw them the next morning. Clementine said we should both explain. I accepted her decision.

72

But the story isn't over. Because sometime during the night, I really don't know when, but after I must have been asleep for an hour or more, when I felt Clementine kneeling next to the couch where I was sleeping. "Tyler," she whispered. "Tyler."

I tried to wake up. "Clementine, what's wrong?"

"The sirens," she said.

"The what?"

"The sirens. Outside in the street. They woke me up."

I tried to see her in the light that was coming from the kitchen, because I had left the light on over the stove so I could see even if just a little.

"What do you want me to do?" I said.

"Let me sleep here. I hate sirens. They scare me. Ever since I was a little girl."

I sat up. "You don't want to go back to the bed?"

"No. I want to be close to you."

"All right," I said and stood up. You take the couch. Wrap yourself up in whatever it is you've brought with you."

"A sheet," she said quickly.

"What?"

"It's a sheet."

"Fine. It's a sheet. Wrap yourself in the sheet. I'll use the bed spread on the floor."

So she wrapped herself up in the sheet and lay down on the couch. I did the same with the bed spread.

"Turn your back to the couch," Clementine said.

"What?" I said, trying to lie down on the carpeted floor.

"Turn your back to the couch so you can lie close to it."

"Clementine, what are you talking about?" I said. God, I loved this woman. But it must have been 2 A.M.

"I want to lie on my stomach and be able to touch your shoulder. If you lie close to the couch, I will be able to reach you."

So that is what we did. Wrapped in the sheet she had brought from the bedroom, Clementine slept on the couch with her left hand dangling down and resting on my left shoulder as I lay backed up against the couch wrapped in the bed spread that I'd taken off of the bed. And that is where Betsy Winters found us at whatever ungodly hour she came home, which must have been a considerable surprise to her because I know she stood in the light from the kitchen for a moment and looked at us. And when she saw me open my eyes I remember her whispering, "You must be Tyler," to which I replied in a whisper, "Yes. And that's Clementine on the couch." But before she could ask the obvious question, I said, "We'll explain in the morning." To which she said, "Okay. Goodnight." And then she was gone.

Clementine, of course, had not stirred at all during the exchange, and I fell back asleep with the "A Chorus Line" anthem in my head, "What I Did for Love." If you know that song, you will know why it was wonderfully appropriate.

73

In the morning, after we both got up and showered and prepared ourselves for the day, we found Betsy in the kitchen making breakfast for the three of us. She explained that her husband had come in at 4 A.M. but then had to go out again at 7. He would join us for an early dinner that evening before the two of us went to see "Miss Saigon." When Betsy asked why we hadn't slept in the bedroom, we tried to explain in a way that would embarrass her husband as little as possible. Betsy found the whole thing wonderfully funny. "It's something I can hold over him for a long time," she said. "He's always in such a hurry that he doesn't listen to all of the details. I know I told him you were both in high school." She poured coffee for both of us and served us our meal and then sat down to eat. "No wonder Ruth Ann said you were a prince, Tyler," she said. "And no wonder she thinks you are a princess, Clementine."

I was properly red faced. We wanted to change the subject, but Betsy said she found it very interesting that we would be as close as we obviously were, which is what Ruth Ann had told her, but that we would then behave as we had. Then she wanted to know why Clementine hadn't stayed in the bedroom even if I was going to sleep on the couch. Clementine explained how the sirens had awakened her and how it reminded her of when she'd been a little girl and she and her mother had lived in Hackensack before her mother began teaching at Rutgers and they moved closer to the campus. "I could hear sirens almost every night," Clementine said. "They would wake me up. When I heard them last night, I wanted to be where Tyler was sleeping."

Betsy said she understood.

We finished our meals and dressed for the day, insuring Betsy that we would be back in time to eat with her and with Martin. Then we left for the Metropolitan Museum of Art.

To understand what our day was like you have to remember that both of us had been raised in museums. So for us going to museums was not just seeing artifacts. It was returning to what our mothers and my grandfather had all said by their behavior were cultural cathedrals. When we went to a museum, not only in New York that day but any museum any place in the world where we've traveled, we feel as if we are stepping out of the mundane and into a profound *other* sort of experience in which we get to savor the best humanity has to offer for consideration. I know that sounds like a mouthful of aesthetic philosophy, but it's true. We wouldn't have said it in those same words at the time, but I promise when we entered the Metropolitan Museum we felt as if we had walked into a holy shrine. What meant the most to me, however, was that as we started into the first great hall, Clementine was confident enough in our relationship to say, "This isn't want I want to do, Tyler." When I asked her what she meant, she said, "I have come here to see the African artifacts."

I understood. I was glad she had said it. I was glad that was what we did. I let her lead. She walked very slowly, reading each explanatory sign, looking at each object. As she did, I felt as if I was watching her pick up each item and turn it over in her hands and feel its texture and smell what she could smell of its original odor. What became clear to me in a very short time was that Clementine was not looking at artifacts. She was trying to enter her past. That is one of the reasons why I contend Clementine is the bravest person I will ever know. It is not just her intellect that has been educated; her sensibilities have been educated as well.

At the same time, as wonderful as the experience in the Metropolitan was that first day, the second day when we went to the Museum of Modern Art was equally important, albeit in a different way. But if I tell you about that here then I will be getting ahead of my story.

74

We ate a late afternoon meal with both Betsy and Martin Winters in their apartment. Martin took some ribbing from his wife about his hasty assumptions about the two of us, which he accepted with good grace, responding to his embarrassment by saying that when he met us we seemed so mature that he contended it was a natural mistake. We accepted that as a compliment. Then we got ready and took a cab to see "Miss Saigon."

When my grandfather said that he was the one who suggested Clementine and I should see "Miss Saigon," I did not know why he would be so adamant. After we saw the production, I understood.

I knew from what Clementine told me that "Miss Saigon" was based on the opera "Madame Butterfly," by Giacomo Puccini. "Madame Butterfly" is the story of an American naval officer, Lieutenant Pinkerston, who purchases a young Japanese bride while stationed with the United States navy in Tokyo. However, it becomes obvious as the opera unfolds that it was never Pinkerton's intention to take his bride and the son, to whom she has given birth, back to the United States with him when his tour is completed. In the end, shamed by her American husband's desertion, the beautiful but heartbroken Butterfly commits suicide.

"Miss Saigon" told a similar story. Set in Viet Nam, the tragedy repeats itself when the city of Saigon falls, forcing the American army to leave thousands of South Vietnamese who had been loyal to the United States behind. Thus, when the American, Chris, flees, he leaves his lover, Kim, behind.

For me, as I sat in the hall, stirred emotionally more than I thought I could ever be by a musical, it was not the racial differences and the racial tragedy that results, it was the sound of helicopter blades whirling in the air, that incessant beating that films about Viet Nam have made so familiar. When Clementine realized I was crying late in the second act, she took my hand and held it in her lap. Then later, when we left the theatre, she began to express her own emotional reaction to the story and the music. Assuming that it was the dilemma that Kim faced, for she would be left alone in Viet Nam to raise their mixed race son, Clementine very delicately and for the first time spoke about her own racial consciousness. "I know that you know my father is both white and black," she said. "I know that you know his mother is white and his father is black."

I said that I did know that.

Then she asked a question she had never asked before. "So what does that make me. A mulatto? Or does it mean, because as far as I know I am three fourths black and one fourth white, that in the eyes of the world I am black and so I should identify with black culture?"

I said I couldn't answer that question for her. I said that as far as I was concerned, I didn't care about her race.

"Oh, don't you? What about what you said last night?"

"What did I say last night?" I asked as we walked along Broadway looking for a cab.

"That you'd talked to my mother about what black women in American have to face. Which I assume was her black-women-as temptresses or black-women-as-whores speech."

"That's what I meant."

"And what about what you said about not wanting to be a white man come to slave row to have a black woman for the night?"

"I did say that. Because I don't want to be that."

"Fine. But it also means you are aware of race, Tyler."

"Okay. Okay. I am aware of race. And so are you. How can we not be aware of race? But that doesn't have to be what we are about, does it? Aren't we just two people who love each other?"

Clementine was quiet for some time. "It's what I want," she finally said.

"Good. It's what I want as well," I said. "But that isn't what made me cry," I said.

Clementine stopped and looked at me. I stopped and looked at her. "It was the helicopter blades," I said.

"The helicopter blades? You mean that beating sound?"

"Yes. And no."

She waited. Then she spoke. "Which?"

"Both. The sound of them beating. The sound of them not beating."

"Why would that make you cry?"

"Because of my father."

"Who you said died in Viet Nam."

"Yes, who died in Viet Nam."

Clementine said she understood.

"No, you don't," I said. "Because I've never told you how he died or why he died."

"You said he was a pilot."

"An army pilot. He flew helicopters."

"Oh," Clementine said in a whisper. Then she took both of my hands in hers and faced me. "I'm sorry."

"That's not the whole story."

"It isn't?"

"No. The whole story is why he died."

Clementine turned away. As she did, the neon lights flashed across her face, part of which was now clearly visible and colored blue and red, part of which was in shadows. Then she turned back to me.

"Do you want to tell me?" she asked.

I turned and still holding her hand started walking again. "He flew a gun ship. He took soldiers into combat areas. Then he picked them up."

"Which must have been very dangerous."

"It was. He had a co-pilot on board and a door gunner. They were fired on a lot."

Clementine was listening.

"But one day one of the medical evacuation helicopters went down. Which meant the medics were short of transport. There was a unit that had taken fire and had wounded on a ridge a few miles away. My mother says my father volunteered to fly his helicopter into the combat zone even though it wasn't his responsibility and even though he'd just come in from making his fourth trip that day."

I could tell from Clementine's expression that she knew what was coming.

"That's when his helicopter was hit. He picked up the wounded and was on his way out. That's when it went down. When it was coming out. And everyone was killed. He was killed and his co-pilot and the door gunner and the medic who had gone with him and the five wounded soldiers they had picked up. All of them died in the crash."

Clementine stopped and put her head on my shoulder. "Tyler," she whispered. "Oh, Tyler."

"So it isn't just the sound of helicopter blades that upsets me," I said. "It's the silence that comes when they stop turning. It was the sound at the end of "Miss Saigon" when you still think you can hear the beating but you know you really can't because it's gone because the Americans have gone."

Clementine was silent.

"That's what must have happened that day. First the propeller blades were beating. Then they weren't. Then the helicopter crashed. Then the men died."

75

The next day we went to the Museum of Modern Art where two things happened that both of us still remember today as being signal events in our life together. The first was seeing Pablo Picasso's painting "The Three Musicians." The second was seeing Robert Motherwell's painting "Spanish Elegy."

I need to start by telling you that Clementine says she has admired Picasso's painting for as long as she remembers admiring any kind of art. I assume it is the African influence that is so evident in the painting, but she has never said that in so many words, and I certainly never pressed her to do so. She just talks about the multiple ways in which

Picasso asks his viewers to see the subjects of his work. So it was particularly wonderful when we got to that painting. However, for me, it was not seeing the painting that mattered most. It was watching Clementine see the painting. Yes, she said she had seen it before when she was younger. But this time was different, she said. "I was a child the first time I saw it," she said. "Then I saw it again when I was maybe twelve or thirteen. Now I know that every time I see it I bring something else with me. Who I am at that point in my life." Then she turned to me and said, "This time I get to share it with you, Tyler. Which means I am seeing it for myself, and I am trying to see it for you." She smiled. "Does that make sense?" she asked. I said it did. What I could not say because I didn't have suitable words at the time, and I still don't, was what looking at her as she looked at the painting meant to me. If she was joyful, I was almost overjoyed. It felt as if I could feel her body reacting, as if I was inside of her as she let the painting move through her. It was a truly remarkable moment. Unfortunately, that changed far too quickly when we came to my favorite painting.

Of all of the abstract expressionist painters who exploded onto the American art scene in the late 1940s and during the 1950s and even into the 1960s, my favorite has been Robert Motherwell for as long as I can remember looking at art with my mother and grandfather. I would be hard pressed even today to explain why. Maybe I was reacting to what psychoanalyst Karl Jung termed my innate recognition of the archetypal dream images that are encoded into my brain simply because I am a human being. Of course, that's language I acquired long after Clementine and I went to New York together. Nonetheless, maybe that was what had happened to me the several times that I saw Motherwell's work as I grew up. What is most important, though, is what happened when Clementine and I arrived at Motherwell's "Spanish Elegy" painting in the Museum of Modern Art that day.

I know the Museum of Modern Art has changed since our visit, but when we were there "Spanish Elegy" was exhibited on a wall by itself. We came around the corner from having seen other works, and there it was.

I'm not so silly as to not admit that it took my breath away. This was the painting I had most wanted to see. From the moment Ruth Ann and my mother and grandmother gave us the airplane tickets, I knew that if did nothing else in New York, I was going to be sure see that particular painting. But my anticipated joy was almost shattered when we came around the corner, and there it was.

I had learned something about the Spanish Civil War from reading books my grandfather gave me and from reading Frederico Garcia Lorca's plays. As a result, I was sympathetic to the Republic and opposed to the Franco-led fascists who destroyed democracy in Spain. As a result of conversations with my grandfather, I knew about Picasso's painting "Guernica," which portrays the bombing of the village Guernica by the fascists during the Spanish Civil War. So it seemed to me that what Motherwell had done was go even deeper into the human contradiction in his work. Maybe it was only the title that connected it to the Spanish Civil war. Nonetheless, at least for me, it connected politics and art and something profoundly painful in me.

So there we were, standing in front of the one painting I most wanted to see the night after we had seen "Miss Saigon," and I was confronted by the sound of helicopter blades beating the air and then not beating the air, leaving the echo of death in the air in the *after* silence. And so instead of just being moved aesthetically, which would have been enough, or even politically, which would have been more than enough, before either Clementine or I knew it, I was crying from someplace so deep in whoever I am that I did not know it was going to happen and did not know what to do to stop it. And when that happened, before I could turn to her and say anything or make a sound or fumble to explain, Clementine stepped up next to me and without speaking rested her left hand on my back and crossed her right hand over her body so she could hold my right hand. And right there—right then and there—I knew in a way I had not ever known before that I was not alone. I was not alone in my life. And yes, I know that by telling about my Motherwell moment it sounds as if I've shifted the subject from the way "Miss Saigon" spoke to Clementine's intelligent sensitivity to the differences in our races and how the musical addresses that subject to talking about my sudden cathartic grieving for my father, but that isn't all that I intend. Because what I want you to keep upper most in mind is that I could not have stood the surge of pain that threatened to overwhelm me had Clementine not been there with me. It is as simple and complex and profound as that. I could not have stood the unanticipated juxtaposing of joy and fear and pain that I felt as I stood looking at my favorite painting had Clementine Camille not been right there with me. And that, in a nutshell, is the story of our life together. We are who we are because we are those people together.

Then it was Thursday night.

76

We found both Betsy and Martin Winters waiting for us when we returned from the Museum of Modern Art. And while they were eager to know all about our experience, we both avoided talking about my reaction when we stood in front of Robert Motherwell's "Spanish Elegy." It was far too personal and painful. Neither Betsy nor Martin needed to know, which was fine, because they both preferred to talk about Clementine's and my sleeping arrangement. We simply explained that Clementine didn't want to sleep alone with sirens going off during the night. I said I didn't think either of our mothers would be comfortable with the two of us sleeping in the same bed. "Even if I slept on the floor in the bedroom, there's a element of privacy about it that neither mother expected to have happen."

Clementine added that yes, we knew we were both sleeping in the same room, but the fact either of you, referring to Betsy and Martin, might well walk through the living room at any time served as a chaperone. With that the subject was dropped. Clementine intended to sleep on the couch; I would continue to sleep on the floor next to the couch so that she could touch me during her sleep if she wished. It wasn't an ideal situation, but it was the best solution we could manage.

That morning over breakfast, Betsy had told us that they wanted to take us to one of their favorite places in the city. We had no idea what it was or where it was, and she wouldn't explain. She simply said, "Martin found it three years ago. We go at least once every two weeks. More when we can manage. But he wants to surprise you." So after our light supper, we took turns in the bedroom putting on what Martin said should be casual but dressy clothes. Then the four of us went down into the garage below the building, and Martin drove us to another part of New York City. When we got there, he parked in a nearby garage, and we walked two blocks to Andre's Argentine Club. Once we went inside, we realized it was more than just a restaurant and bar. The most important feature of the narrow but long room was a circular dance floor situated between the restaurant section, which was towards the front, and the bar section, which was towards the back.

We sat down in the restaurant section, and Martin ordered a number of dishes that he and Betsy obviously liked. Martin ordered four glasses of Argentina red wine. When the wine and food came, Martin proposed a toast: "To the two nicest young people, besides our daughter, who have ever stayed with us." Clementine and I thanked both Martin and Betsy and took small sips. Then we turned to the food, all of which was new to us but wonderful.

It took another thirty minutes or so for Andrea's to begin to fill up, but by 8 P.M. it was packed. Then the musicians began setting up on the band stand that sat against one wall facing the dance floor.

If you had told either Clementine or me that morning that by evening we would be sitting in a New York Argentinean club absolutely mesmerized by music played live by three men playing accordions, one playing the bass, one playing a cello, and one rhythm guitar, I don't think we would have believed you. Especially the accordion part. But you would have been right, and we would have been wrong. It took less than eight bars of extraordinarily dramatic and theatrical music for Clementine to turn to me and say, "Listen, Tyler. Just listen."

Then, to compound our surprise, with no further ado, Betsy and Martin got up and took the floor along with four other couples who were just as eager to begin dancing the tango. Because that was what Betsy and Martin had discovered almost a year before: the tango.

Admittedly, neither Clementine nor I knew anything about the tango except that it came from Europe to Argentina and was something akin to the national dance in the way that nothing is in America.

What was most interesting was the mix of couples. There were two couples who must have been in their 60s if not their 70s. There was one couple who appeared to be a little older than Betsy and Martin, one couple that looked like the same age, and one couple who were younger. The fifth couple was what appeared to be a grandfather dancing with his granddaughter, because she accomplished the very complicated steps he led her through by standing on the toes of his shoes in her stocking feet.

As we sat watching and by then holding hands, Clementine and I realized we were not only hearing what for us was a new kind of music and seeing a new kind of community dancing, we were seeing a part of New York that we never would have visited on our own.

Of course, it didn't take long for both of us to become impatient with just watching. Clementine and I love to dance, especially with each other. No, we don't pretend to be *dancers*. We are just people who love to dance. And at exactly the same time we were both beginning to wonder if we dared to go out on the dance floor ourselves among what had become at least twenty couples, Betsy and Martin came back to the table and said they would show us enough steps to get us started. So there we were a moment later, Clementine dancing with Martin, me dancing with Betsy, being guided through basic steps, being advised as to how to catch both the beat of the music and the off beat, the slide, so to speak, between beats, that makes all the difference. I don't know what Martin told Clementine, but Besty told me that it was very much an attitude, a sense of freedom, and willingness to respond to the music. When I told her the music was the most sensual music I had ever heard, she said, "That's the point, Tyler. Why do you think people love the tango? It's all about sensuality."

Well, to make a long story short, that made sense to me. Which is why, five minutes later, there Clementine and I were, dancing our first tango together, at least, our version of a tango. And Betsy was right. Holding Clementine close, then having her move away, than having her wrap her body around mine in ways she never had before, certainly not on a dance floor, was about as much sensuality as I could stand. At last, when the music slowed and we could move even more closely for a much longer period of time, I know I was having as much problem as I had ever had trying to constrain my emotions. Finally, all I could do was whisper in Clementine's ear, "There is no woman in the world with a body like yours, Clementine." When I said that, I felt her hand grasping mine more firmly. I felt her torso pressing against my torso more assertively; I felt her breasts reaching to touch my chest. And so we held on to each other in a way that suggested a declaration had been made, a line between what we once were and what we would become had been crossed, a melding of hesitations and desires that, in the moment, became us dancing somewhere else, free and giving and loving.

Three hours later, when Betsy and Martin said they needed to go home so they could get up and go to work in the morning and we could get up and go to the airport for our flight back to Tampa, Clementine and I had not only fallen in love with the tango and with dancing the tango together, we knew without saying anything on the ride back to their apartment that we now understood each other in a way we had never understood each other before that night, even with all that we had experienced together, even with all we had said and done together, even with all that we had faced and overcome together. And if that isn't love, I don't know what is.

That night we slept in the same bed. No, we did not have sex. Neither of us was ready to use the tango to induce that. But we did sleep in the same bed, with her left arm draped over my left shoulder from behind. For the moment, that was enough.

The next morning, Betsy and Martin Winters drove us to the airport for our flight back to Tampa and for our senior year at Tampa Coast High School.

Part Two

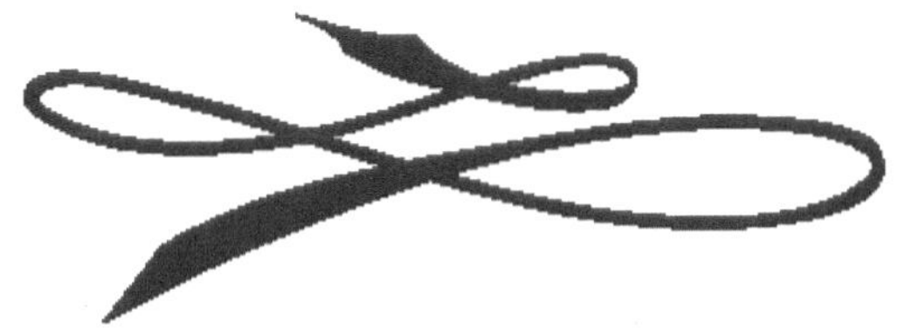

"When the snow falls the flakes spin upon the long axis that concerns them most intimately two and two to make a dance."

William Carlos Williams
"The Dance"

When I decided to write a memoir about Clementine and our life together, I assumed that I would divide it into three parts: our high school years when our relationship formed, our university years when our relationship matured, and our marriage and professional years when our relationship fulfilled itself. However, as I retold the story of those first years together at Tampa Coast and all of the attending experiences that turned us into who we are individually and who we are together, I decided that I would end Part One as we flew back from New York City to Tampa to begin our senior years in school. I've thought about why I found the end of the New York summer trip the right time to end Part One, and I have concluded it's because our senior year was more about what we were going to do than what we had done or even what we were doing.

I do not mean to infer that we did not have a good senior year. We did. Yes, there were some difficult moments, two of which might well have significantly unsettled our lives. But in the end, as we have talked about our 1983-1984 school year, we realized that like many other senior year students our last year was as much if not more a transition into the next stage of our lives as it was a culmination of the work we had begun during the three previous years. So I will start with football, because once we were back in school that was the first shaping and sharing experience that unfolded.

I'd love to say that my determination to become a quality football player paid off immediately. It would have been fun to be a star and even more fun to talk about it in this manuscript. But that is not the case. I had learned a great deal as a junior about playing safety. I had far more to learn that year. Not only did I have to deal with my initial fear of contact, especially when I was covering passes, a fear I did not initially either recognize or acknowledge, but a fear that my grandfather saw from the stands when he came to watch practice, but I had to deal with convincing my coaches and my teammates that it was safe for me to play. So initially Coach Dickson was reluctant to put me into contact drills, and my teammates on the offense were hesitant during practices to throw passes that I would have to cover. I finally convinced them that I was fully recovered when I asked Coach Dickson to put me on the kickoff coverage team, which would mean I would either try to make tackles or I could expect to be blocked very hard, sometimes by players you don't see coming at you until it is too late. Their doubts were ended when, during a coverage drill the third day of special teams practice, I came down the right sideline, avoided being blocked twice, and made a hard tackle, stopping the ball carrier before he could cross the twenty yard line. When I got up after making the play and realized I was still in one piece, I decided that it was time to forget about what had happened the year before and to get on with playing. I remember my grandfather saying that he had known that day everything was going to be all right. From that day on, I played first string on the kick off coverage unit and first string safety.

During the season itself, I know my mother and grandfather and Clementine and Ruth Ann sometimes had problems when they saw me drop into deep coverage and then move to cut off the receiver. But during the first game of the season, maybe because I was trying to prove something to myself as much as to them, I knocked down three passes and intercepted two.

After the game, as Clementine and I held hands and walked to our car so we could join my mother and grandfather and Ruth Ann for our post-game dinner, I could tell she was both relieved and happy. "You had a big night, Tyler," she said.

I smiled. "I was showing off," I said.

She laughed. "I know," she said.

She didn't have to say anything more, and I didn't have to explain. We both understood.

The rest of the season went very well. No, we didn't win all of our games. But we did manage to win seven and only lose three, one of which was against a non-conference team from Lakeland. I was beaten in coverage for two touchdowns in that game, which was a hard lesson because my lack of sprinter speed cost us that night, but I also ended the season with six interceptions. More important than those statistics and even the first team all conference honors at the end of the year, I was learning to read what Coach Dickson emphasized every day—the opposing quarterbacks' eyes.

When I talked to my grandfather about the drills Coach Dickson put all of the defensive backfield players through each day, he said I was learning to anticipate tendencies. He said he could see it from the stands. I was going to the places where I knew the receivers were going even before they made changes in their routes. Clementine even asked me one night after a game how I knew to go where I went until the ball was thrown. I told her what I was being taught. Beyond that it was instinct.

Clementine and I got to attend the homecoming dance that year. She had kept the dress she was going to wear the year before when I'd been injured. I don't have to tell you that she was beautiful. I've said it so many times up to now in this memoir that you may be getting tired of hearing it. So you will have to forgive me if I say it again. But she was beautiful that night just as she is beautiful every day. I never get tired of saying so because I never get tired of looking at her.

By the end of the season, Coach Dickson was true to his word. He contacted Coach Dooley at the University of Georgia and sent him films of our team, asking that Coach Dooley look at how I was learning to both cover receivers and to come up close to the line of scrimmage to attack running backs before they could get into the secondary. Yes, I received a letter showing interest in my play from Tulane University, in New Orleans, and from Wake Forest, in Winston-Salem, North Carolina. I even got an invitation to visit the University of Florida, in Gainesville, although I don't think the coaches there were really seriously interested. They liked taller players in my position. But none of that mattered because the only person I wanted to play for was Coach Dooley, and the only place I wanted to play was the University of Georgia. When he ended up being the key note speaker at a dinner honoring all of the all-conference players from the Tampa Bay area, I got to meet him in person. He said he remembered writing the letter to me the year before and that he was impressed by the films he had seen of my play. He said he wanted me to visit the University in the spring before I decided to go to any other school. By the time I got home that evening from the dinner, which my mother and my grandfather had attended with me, they knew that as far as I was concerned the matter was settled.

I should add here that the same question came up for Clementine during the spring semester, even if in her case the issue had more to do with academics than with athletics. In fact, what she should do about the other very fine schools that were interested in her was the first real question that came up that year, and it was a question that was not easily answered. In fact, for two weeks, it caused some consternation for both of us. It caused even more for Ruth Ann, who like any good mother had ambitions for her daughter. However, I don't want to get too far ahead in my story. I want to talk about our winter vacation first because thanks to my grandfather as well as to our mothers, it turned into a very special ten days not just for Clementine and me but for all five of us.

2

I have never figured out how over the years that I grew up with him my grandfather came up with the places that he took us to visit, because they are sometimes so far out of the way that it's hard to know how he ever heard of them. Yet somehow he did hear of them, and when he did, he very often decided that it was a place we should go visit or a place where we should all go stay. Winter vacation of 1983 was no exception. Because that year at Thanksgiving he announced that he was inviting all of us, my mother and me and Clementine and Ruth Ann to come with him for ten days to North Carolina where he had found a remote, three bedroom house sitting on a cliff side looking down into a valley that he believed we should rent so we could all relax and read and walk and talk and eat and sleep. When he added that he'd been assured it would snow by Christmas day, there was no way the four of us were not going to agree to go with him. Besides, he said, he'd already paid for the house, and he couldn't get his money back, so we had to go. Before the Thanksgiving meal was even over that day, we were all gathered around what became our long list of things we had to bring to make our ten days the best ten days possible. So that's what I want to tell you about at this point in my memoir: our winter vacation, 1983, in the North Carolina mountains.

First, it started the day after all of our schools closed for vacation. Second, it started at 4 A.M. I mean that. All of us were up at 4 A.M., because my grandfather said we were going to be on the road by 5:30. And we were. He and my mother and I picked up Clementine and Ruth Ann at exactly 5:30 in the seven passenger van my grandfather rented for the trip.

I am not saying that either Clementine or Ruth Ann were smiling when we got to their house. But no matter. We packed their things in the van, and we were off. My mother brought a thermos of coffee, which everyone wanted, and which made the van smell wonderful. We would eat breakfast in an hour, my grandfather said, once we were well along the road toward Atlanta. And that is how our winter adventure began, with my grandfather driving, with me sitting in front next to him, with my mother and Ruth Ann sitting in the bucket seats behind us, and with Clementine sitting in one of the two bucket seats in back, surrounded by small suitcases of clothes and boxes of things like chess and Trivial Pursuit and other board games and playing cards and poker chips and sleeping bags.

I have always loved driving very early in the morning when it's still dark. It makes me feel as if I am stealing away and that no one knows where I am. I like the way headlights throw their light out on the road in the morning before the sun comes up and the way car headlights look coming in the opposite direction. I always wonder why those people are up as early as I'm up. Most of all, I love drinking coffee and driving so early in the morning that it isn't even time for breakfast yet. For me, sitting in the van listening to my mother and Ruth Ann talk very quietly about all sorts of things, sitting next to my grandfather as he leaned forward into the darkness, and knowing that my beloved Clementine was probably dozing off as we drove was about as good a feeling as I ever thought I'd ever have again.

3

We were all sitting together in a booth at a Waffle House Restaurant at an exit road on Interstate 75. My mother was sitting on the inside of one of the booth seats. Clementine was next to her, squeezed into the middle. I was sitting on the end. My grandfather and Ruth Ann were sitting together on the other booth seat

"You all brought warm clothes?" my grandfather said.

All of us said we had, reminding him that we'd had this conversation before.

"I've arranged for a horse drawn sleigh ride on New Year's Eve afternoon," he said. "The owner of the houses that sit on the ridge said it's a favorite with folks who rent from him."

The four of us agreed that sounded wonderful.

"And there's no televison. I know I said that before, but I just wanted to remind you. Which I think is a good thing. Of course, I've got my radio with me. The one that gets shortwave. The fellow who rented me the house said the radio reception is fantastic on the mountain. He said he listens to the BBC World Service every night and every morning. I told him we try to listen in Tampa, but the reception isn't always very good."

Clementine said she'd brought her favorite game with her: Score Four. Her mother said we had to watch out for Clementine because she was a killer at board games. My grandfather wanted to know if Clementine played chess. She said she didn't but that she knew he was teaching me. She said she wanted to learn. "Now you've done it, Clementine," I said, laughing. "That's all he'll want to do now. Teach you how to play."

"Elizabeth and I have been talking," Ruth Ann said. "We think this is our chance to show the three of you how to really play poker."

The three of us laughed and said we were up for the challenge. Our conversation continued the same way even as our meals came. We knew there were serious conversations coming because all five of us were serious people and readers with things we wanted to talk about, but my grandfather had set the tone when he said people traveling together should never talk about serious things until they arrived where they were going. "Gossip is okay," he said, laughing. "But nothing serious. Then he demonstated what he meant, telling us two outrageous stories about President Andrew Jackson, whom my grandfather did not like, one about President Woodrow Wilson, whose intellectual arrogance was legendary—my grandfather's words—and one about President Lyndon Johnson, about whom my grandfather was terribly conflicted: loved his social policies, hated Viet Nam.

When my mother said that it sounded to her as if his version of gossip was just stories from history that don't usually get into history books, he asked her if she wanted to hear some old gossip from Cleveland.

"What do you mean?" my mother asked.

"Well, do you remember Sylvester Stillman, who owned the dry cleaning store we used to use, 'Sylvester's Stupendous Cleaners'?"

"I think so. A short man," my mother said.

"And do you remember the tall, red headed woman who ran the coffee shop next door? 'Maggie's Magnificent Coffee'?"

My mother said she did.

"Do you remember that Sylvester was a widower, and Maggie was a divorcee?"

"No. I was very young then."

"Well, should I tell all of you what happened when lonely Sylvester took a shine to Maggie?"

All four of us waited.

"Well, he did. And despite the fact that more than one of us in the neighborhood warned him about working without a net, so to speak, Sylvester went ahead and made his feelings known to Maggie."

My grandfather was quiet for a moment.

"And . . . " my mother said.

My grandfather looked at my mother. He looked at Clementine and me. Then he turned to Ruth Ann and, holding up his hand as if he wanted to guard his mouth but speaking to her in a whisper that he knew we could hear, he said, "I don't know how she did it, but within a month Sylvester's Stupendous Cleaners became Maggie's Marvelous Cleaners. Which was fitting, because that's sure what she did to him."

Ruth Ann grinned and glanced at us as if we should be listening to such a story.

"And Sylvester was working the counter at Maggie's Magnificent Coffee." He paused for a moment. "Now, how does a thing like that happen?" he said, his expression professing his innocent ignorance. Then he looked away from my mother and Clementine and me and said to Ruth Ann, "Maybe I shouldn't be telling stories like that, Ruth Ann. I think the children are listening."

My mother grimaced, and I booed under my breath, and Ruth Ann and my grandfather smiled and looked at us as if she were shocked that we'd been listening. Clementine just shook her head and whispered to me, "Is he going to be like this for the whole vacation?"

I spoke to Clementine from behind my hand in imitation of what my grandfather had done. "Probably," I said. "He gets this way sometimes."

Clementine smiled and put her head on my shoulder for a moment.

"This is a side of you I didn't know anything about, Edward," Ruth Ann said. "I thought you were a serious scholar. I didn't know you were a gossip as well."

My grandfather turned to Ruth Ann and smiled and said, "Ruth Ann, all historians are gossips. That's what history is. Gossip. We just like to use five dollar words, that's all. But it's still just gossip."

Ruth Ann raised her eye brows and made her favorite mock disbelief face, laughing as she did.

Twenty minutes later we were back on the road. My mother and Ruth Ann and my grandfather took turns driving. After lunch just outside of Atlanta, my grandfather, who by then had moved to the back seat, said he thought I should take a turn. I said we should let Clementine drive. So I sat in the front passenger's seat while Clementine drove on Interstate 85 to Greenville, South Carolina. As she buckled in and got ready to start the engine, looking a tad apprehensive about driving a van, I leaned over and told her she should just relax and enjoy herself. She smiled a rather uneasy smile, but she said she would. Then we started again, our mothers sitting in the two bucket seats talking, as always, about school and school administrators. I remember leaning over to Clementine at one point and whispering that I was going to tell both her mother and mine that when we got to where we were staying, they were not to talk about school anymore. To which Clementine said, "Please do." After all, Clementine and I were on vacation from our school. The last thing we wanted to hear about was theirs.

I took my turn driving when we reached Greenville where we turned north again and headed for Asheville, North Carolina. By then we had the radio playing softly and Clementine was sitting in the passenger's seat next to me. I'm telling you these things not because they're in any way extraordinary, because they aren't. And that's the point. I just want you to understand how the five of us, people from two different places, people of two different races, created a family, a *real* family, which was something all of us very much needed.

4

Sometimes life unfolds in ways no one would have predicted before it all came clear. Certainly that is what happened those first days in the three bedroom house my grandfather had found for the five of us. I suppose I should have expected something like what happened would take place. Clementine said she not only wasn't surprised, she had waited for two years for it to happen.

As I've already explained, my mother, Elizabeth Thomas Raymond, grew up under the influence of her father enough to become a social science major as well as a sixth grade teacher. I grew up under both her and my grandfather's influence. It isn't surprising, therefore, that I would decide to become a history teacher. I suppose you could argue it was in my genes. But there was another side to my genetic inheritance, of course—my father, who had intended to become a professor of English, which is why he earned his bachelor's and master's degrees in English at the University of Maryland and started teaching at Cleveland State before going into the army and being commissioned second lieutenant and trained to fly helicopters.

There have been many nights in my life when I've lain awake and wondered what it might have been like had he lived and I been raised by him and my mother instead of my mother and my grandfather. I probably wouldn't have moved to Tampa, of course, which means I wouldn't have met Clementine. When that thought crossed my mind, I felt very conflicted. I've talked to Clementine about my confusion. Should I be glad my father died so I could meet her? Should I wish he'd lived, which would most likely have deprived me of my life with her. To her credit, when I began to wonder about such things she didn't try to answer my question or resolve my sense of conflict. She simply held me in her arms and told me that she loved me and that all we can do is live the lives we have been given. She's right, of course. After all, what if her father had not left her mother. Would Ruth Ann have finished her doctorate and then moved with him to some city other than Tampa where he opened another family grocery store? If that had happened, there certainly wouldn't have been a Clementine asking me to be her ninth grade biology lab partner, and there wouldn't have been a me saying yes and then falling in love with her.

I must admit that today, even after being married for almost fifteen years, the parents of two very lively six year old twin daughters, whenever I get that far into my speculation, I become very afraid. I realize how very intricate our lives are, how very much the odds were against Clementine and me meeting let alone falling in love. When that emotion surges through me, I sometimes lie in a cold sweat wondering who in the world I would have become without my darling Clementine in my life. When I tell her what I'm feeling, she says she sometimes feels the same sense of fear and dread. But she also says that when that emotion comes in the night, she simply rolls over and puts her arms around me and whispers, "Tyler Thomas Raymond, I am here." When she does that, I understand what is happening. So I roll over in return and face her and say, "Clementine Camille Brown, I am here." Then we hold each other and are glad and safe. That's part of the *unfolding* that I want to talk about, but only part. The other more immediate part is what suddenly made itself clear to me when Clementine and I stood together at the edge of the cliff overlooking the valley that swept south and east that first morning after we arrived at our vacation house. Because that's when, as I was holding her in my arms against the chilly wind, and both of us were marveling at the view, I said, "I think I'm going to become a poet," and Clementine said, "I've been waiting for you to say that for two years."

I drew back and looked at her. "Really?"

"Yes."

"For two years?"

"Yes. Maybe longer."

"Why? What makes you say that?"

Clementine looked at me. "Because of the way you see life and feel life. Because of the way you love words."

I was quiet for a moment. "You know everything about me, don't you," I said. "Usually before I know things myself."

"Don't you do the same with me?"

"Do I?"

She looked at me and didn't answer. She turned to the distance. She moved closer to me and put her arms around my waist and pressed her head against my shoulder. "Yes, Tyler. You do. You don't always know that you know, but I know that you know."

"That's very complicated," I whispered.

She laughed her pleasure as she always does, in a whisper. "No. It's very simple. You know me in ways I do not know myself, and I know you in ways you do not know yourself. But I know I know you in those ways. You haven't yet admitted that you know me those ways yet. But you will. Probably on this trip."

After a moment, "You're a witch, Clementine. Did you know that?"

"A *shaman*, Tyler. A witch *shaman*," she said. Then she looked up at me. "Your own personal black African witch. It doesn't get better than that, does it?"

I chuckled this time. She hugged me tighter against my chest shaking. "No, Clementine, it doesn't get any better than that."

Then she looked at the distance. "Of course, you're going to be my own personal Celtic bard, aren't you?"

"If that's what you say I'm going to be, Clementine, then that's what I'm going to be."

Then we heard Ruth Ann on the porch that encircled the house calling to us that it was time for breakfast. We could already smell the fire that my grandfather had going in the stone fireplace.

"Write me a poem about this moment, Tyler," Clementine said as she released me and started walking back towards the house.

"That's exactly what I intend to do," I said. "That's exactly what I'm going to do."

5

After breakfast, we all sat for a while in flannel shirts and mountain jackets on the porch drinking coffee and tea. The air was cool and crisp, too cool for us to sit out very long. It was December, after all. Then my mother suggested we go for a walk along the trail that followed the ridge on which the house sat. So we trooped off together, walking single file at times and two side by side when the trail allowed for perhaps a mile or so before we came to the vista my grandfather had been told about.

It was a breathtaking view. The trees seemed to cling to the mountain side. Winter birds spiraled up towards us on wind currents that came all the way from the bottom of the valley. There were traces of snow among the rocks below us, the obvious remnants of a storm that had come through the mountains a week before. The five of us laughed some, but mostly we simply admired the view, the distance, the sense that we could see for miles, which was undoubtedly true. In the distance, we could even see three small towns edging a road that snaked its way down the valley until it disappeared into the blue haze that cloaked the other end of the valley.

As we walked back, Clementine took my hand. More than once before when Clementine and I had done something together I had thought that I could not possibly feel more happy to be alive. This was not just one of those occasions. This was *the* occasion, I told myself. In fact, I moved us aside on the trail as our mothers passed, following my grandfather, who loved to hike out ahead of the group, so we could walk behind all of them. At one point in a bend in the trail, we were behind them enough that I could stop and say, "This is how I want to spend my life with you, Clementine. Some place as beautiful as you."

Clementine looked at me for a moment. Then she touched my face and reached up and kissed my cheek. "Write me a poem, Tyler," she said.

I said I would.

Then we all went back to the house and took showers and changed clothes and got out our stock of board games. By 10:30 A.M., Clementine had beaten me at Score Four enough times that I said I wanted to pull on my heavy coat and go for another walk in the opposite direction. Clementine said she wanted to come with me. So we left the three adults talking and laughing and went for a long walk, climbing this time because the trail veered off from the ridge and ascended to a plateau three miles from where the collection of houses for rent clung to the mountain side. Once we reached the top, we found we were looking westward rather then south and east.

From where we sat on a great outcropping of boulders perched high above a fall into a narrow valley, we could see other mountains in the distance in a succession of shades of blue, until the most distant mountains almost faded into the color of the sky. We sat there for perhaps an hour, snuggled together against the chilly wind but basking in the dry warmth of the sun on our faces. We did not talk because there was no need. At one point, Clementine reached for my right hand and removed my glove, exposing my fingers to the cold. Then she pressed my hand against her lips where she held my hand for some time. Then still without speaking, she put my glove back on my hand. Then she took off her glove and pressed it against my lips. So I kissed her hand in return. After a very long moment, I put her glove back on her hand. Then we stood up and started walking along the trail that flattened out at that point before it descended into a stand of pine.

Once we were well into the pine, Clementine stopped again. When I stopped with her, she took my hand and removed one of my gloves. Then she unzipped her parka and pressed my hand against her breast. We stood that way for some time before I took my hand away and raised her face to mine and kissed her very gently, my lips just barely touching hers, for as long as I could.

That was enough. We had said all that we needed to say. We were as much a part of one another as we would ever be, even in the years to come. So we turned and began walking back along the same trail, this time pointing out things to each other that we had missed previously.

As we neared the house, we could see my mother and Ruth Ann sitting in their heavy jackets on what during the summer would have been lawn chairs, their feet propped up on the rail that edged the porch, laughing as only women can laugh who have finally realized that this is a vacation, and they are not going to talk about work or worry or anything else that might interfere with their friendship. When they saw us coming, they both waved, and we waved back. As we walked the final distance to the house, Clementine said for the second time that day, “Write me a poem, Tyler.” To which I once again said I would. And of course, I knew I had to. After all, I was in love with a black African witch. I didn’t have a choice.

6

My grandfather spent the afternoon reading. My mother and Ruth Ann sorted out their plans for meals. Clementine took a nap. I sat out on the porch. It was cold, but I did not mind. I walked some by myself, taking time to look at pine cones, to listen to the wind as its voice changed. I knelt down and picked up small stones and rolled them over in my hands. I found one that was gray and blue, flecked with what looked like gold shale. I rubbed it against my jacket until it was clean. I decided that I would give it to Clementine when I wrote the poem for her that I had promised.

That evening, we played poker. My grandfather drank wine, as did Ruth Ann and my mother. Clementine and I were allowed to divide a beer between us. I don’t remember how well any of us played, but I do remember we all laughed until our sides hurt. That is what I took away from that vacation, in the end—the sound of all of us laughing.

As we prepared for bed, Clementine came to me and gave me a kiss on the cheek. I returned the gesture. Then the five of us went into our three bedrooms. But I did not sleep well. I had expected that I would. We’d come a long way to a beautiful setting for me to be restless. Nevertheless, by 4 A.M., I knew I had to get up. So I gathered up my clothes and went into the bathroom and dressed. Then I went out into the living room. The fire had burned down to embers so the room was chilly. I pulled on my parka and stepped out into the night.

I had never been anywhere before where the sky was so clear. It was a cold night. There were no clouds. The moon had banked behind the mountain north and west of the ridge. I stood and looked up at the stars shimmering in the darkness. It took my breath away. Then I sat down on the porch step and looked out toward the valley. Lights from the town below were blinking in the wind. I heard the wind moving among the trees. And I knew that I would write a series of poems about the mountain. I knew I would begin that night. I could hear the words in my head.

I had heard words like that before over the years when I was falling asleep or waking up, but I had never written them down. I did not think of myself as a poet. By the time morning light was creeping ever so slowly over the crest of the mountains to the east, I knew what I would write. So I went into the silent house, found paper and a pencil in my backpack, and went back outdoors. For a moment I stood listening again. Then I turned and began walking along the trail the five of us had walked together. When I found a place from which I could see the valley falling away and see the towns below and hear the wind all around me, I sat down again and waited. I wondered if that was what all poets did. Wait. Then I began to write.

Sweet smoke on sweet wind
Trailing through the pine forest,
Following the path that marks the crest.

Sweet smoke on sweet wind
Climbing from the valley floor,
Kissing the morning mountain sun.

Sweet smoke on sweet wind
Drifting on snow clouds,
Moving from hard north to soft south.

Sweet smoke on sweet wind
Dancing as only you can dance,
Disappearing into my dearest dreams.

I sat and said the words out loud. I squinted into the dim darkness and tried to read the words. Then I copied them out again, printing as I imagined they would look when typed. Then I stood and started back towards the house, the stone I had chosen the day before nestled in my parka pocket. By the time I got back to the house, my mother and Ruth Ann were in the kitchen preparing breakfast. I accepted the cup of coffee Ruth Ann offered and answered my mother's question about where I had been by saying I'd gotten up while it was still dark and gone out and waited for the sunrise. She did not ask me anything more.

I went back into my grandfather's and my bedroom and shaved and showered and dressed in a new flannel shirt and jeans and came back out into the kitchen where Clementine was sitting at the table with my mother and her mother. She looked at me for a moment. Then she turned back to her cup of coffee, but she did not say anything. I took up my own cup of coffee, which my mother refilled for me. Then I lay the poem in front of Clementine, placing the stone in the center so she had to look at the stone first before she read the poem. My mother watched. Ruth Ann watched. Clementine picked up the stone, looked at it very carefully, and put it down. Then she picked up the poem and read it, moving her lips as she did. When she finished, she read it again. Then she read it a third time.

"What is it?" Ruth Ann said.

"A poem," Clementine said.

"Really?" my mother said.

"Yes."

"That you wrote or Tyler wrote?" my mother asked.

"That Tyler wrote," Clementine answered.

Ruth Ann waited. "Well," she said, letting her voice say her question.

"Well, what?" Clementine said.

"Well, are you going to read it to us?" Ruth Ann asked.

"I think Tyler should read it," Clementine said, turning to me.

"No," I replied. "I wrote it because you asked me to write it. You read it," I said. Then I waited, sipping my coffee as I sat.

Clementine leaned forward over the poem. She looked at her mother and at Ruth Ann. Then she turned back to the poem and read it out loud in her best, most gentle voice.

When she finished, Ruth Ann turned to me. "A poet, too," she said very seriously. "My, my," she said quietly.

My mother looked at me for some time. I did not know what she wanted to say, but it was obvious she was trying to find words, form words. Then she said, "You are your father's son, Tyler. You truly are your father's son."

With that she stood and walked to the front door and went out on the porch. After a moment, I followed her. We stood together for some time without speaking. Then she put a hand on my shoulder. Then she turned back to the house, and we returned to the breakfast table. By then, my grandfather had joined us.

"Tyler's written a poem," Ruth Ann said.

My grandfather put down his cup of coffee. "We've been waiting for that to happen for some time." Then he smiled because if anyone in the world knew who I was or what I was going to become, it was he.

Later that day, Clementine came to me and said the poem was more than she ever could have dreamed it would be. She said she would keep the rock. She still has it even today.

7

The next day was December 24th. Of course, neither Clementine nor her mother or my mother and my grandfather and I had ever celebrated Christmas in the usual way; observing the Winter Solstice was then and continues to be today a very important part of my family's life. At least, it has been as long as I can remember. For that reason, we have a very special dinner on the 21st, which that year we'd had to put off because we'd driven to the mountain that day. By the time we arrived that night, it was too late for a Solstice dinner. Instead we decided to put it off until the 24th, allowing us to make all of the necessary preparations.

However, that morning I asked my grandfather if I could borrow the van. I said I wanted to drive back down the mountain to Linville Falls. I told him I'd already bought a present for my mother and for him and for Ruth Ann, but I hadn't bought what I wanted to give Clementine. He said he trusted that I would be very careful. It was supposed to snow that night. If it started earlier than predicted it would be a very tricky drive back to the house. I assured him that I would be very careful. So in the middle of the morning, Clementine and I left. Of course, when Clementine asked why we were going back to town, I told her it was a surprise and that she should just come along and not ask any more questions. Reluctantly, she agreed to do so.

The drive was truly extraordinary. The sun was high over the mountains. The trees were bare so the shape of the terrain was clearly visible. Rock formations lined the highway. Snow left over from a week before was still white in the shadows thrown every which way by the trees.

When we got to Linville, we parked the van and walked up and down the main street. Clementine asked me what I was looking for. I told her I was looking for a shop that I'd seen when we came through together on our way to the house. After a few minutes, I found it: Jack and Mary's Fine Guitars Shop.

When I stopped in front of the store and looked in the window at the display, Clementine edged up close to me. "What are you doing, Tyler?" she said.

"Looking."

"At guitars?"

"Yes."

"But you don't play the guitar," she said.

"I know."

"And neither your mother nor your grandfather plays the guitar."

"That's right," I said.

"And my mother doesn't play the guitar. She plays the piano now and then, but not the guitar."

"I didn't know she played the piano."

"It was years ago, Tyler."

"But she sings."

"At home. Not in public."

"But she did. When she was younger," I said.

I moved away from her and bent over and looked more closely at a guitar. It was dark wood. I tried to see the price tag, but it was turned over.

"I want to go in," I said.

Clementine looked at me. "Can I come with you?" she said.

"I wish you would," I said. So we went in.

The shop was narrow but deep. Guitars lined the walls. Two glass cases contained guitars that I could see were very expensive. A very nice man, who introduced himself as Jack, came from the back. "Can I help you two?" he said, smiling.

"Yes," I said. "I'd like to see one of the guitars in the window. The dark one," I said, pointing towards the display.

Jack got the guitar and brought it back to where Clementine and I waited. "Is it for you?" he said, "Or for your wife?"

I took the guitar. "We're not married," I said, holding the instrument as if I knew what I was doing.

"Oh, sorry," Jack said. "I just thought . . . "

"That's okay," I said. "I'm sorry too. But someday. If she'll agree," I said.

Clementine poked me under my ribs.

"From the looks of that punch, I think she'll probably agree," Jack said.

I smiled and handed the guitar to Clementine.

"What am I supposed to do, Tyler?" she asked.

"Hold it," I said.

Jack stepped toward Clementine and helped her wrap her left hand around the fret board. "It's a little big," he said.

"My hand?" Clementine said.

"No. The neck. You'll need a slightly more narrow neck so you can finger the frets," Jack said. "If it's for her, I assume," he said, turning to me.

"It's for her," I said.

"Tyler," Clementine exclaimed.

"Have you got one in the same price range that would be better?" I asked.

"Tyler, I don't play the guitar," Clementine protested.

"But you sing. And I love it when you sing," I said.

"That's very nice. But I don't play the guitar."

"You could learn," I said.

"What?"

"I'm sure Jack, here, has books that will teach you how to play."

"We've got all kinds of books," Jack said. "For beginners. All the way up through advanced classical." He smiled. "Miss, if you can sing, then you need to be playin' the guitar. If for no other reason than it'll be fun."

"For who?" Clementine said.

"For you, Clementine," I said. "And for me. Because I'd sing along with you."

"Then why don't you learn to play, and I'll sing along with you?" Clementine said.

"Because you have beautiful hands. Beautiful fingers. And I've been dreaming for the last month about you playing the guitar and singing to our children."

"What?"

"I said, I've been dreaming for the last month . . . " I started to say.

"I heard that, Tyler. It's the children part I haven't heard before."

I looked at her in my best mock surprise. "We are going to have children, aren't we?"

"Tyler, we aren't married. I want to go to medical school," she said.

"I know we aren't married. But we're going to get married some day, aren't we?"

"You've never asked me to marry you."

Jack laughed. "Do you two need to be alone for a moment?"

"No. That's okay," I said. Then I turned back to Clementine. "I know I haven't asked you. But we've talked about our life together. We've talked about that many times. And I've been dreaming of our children."

Clementine looked at me for a very long moment. "Our children," she said.

"Yes."

She turned her attention to the guitar for a moment. Then she looked at me and said, "What were they?"

"What were who?"

"The children. What were they? Boys or girls?"

I looked at Jack. Then I looked back at Clementine. "Girls."

"Really?"

"Yes."

"Girls is plural. How many were there?"

"Two."

"Two?"

"Yes. Two. Twins."

"Twins?"

"Yes."

"Tyler . . . " Clementine began.

"It was a dream. And there were two girls. Twins. And they were as beautiful as you. So don't ask me how I know. Because I can't explain."

Clementine looked at Jack for a moment. Then she turned back to me. "Okay, Tyler. Twins it is. Girl twins," she said. "But what does that have to do with me learning how to play the guitar?" she asked.

"Ah," I said. "Yes. The guitar." I paused for a moment. "Because you were sitting with them and with me, and you were singing their favorite songs, and you were playing the guitar."

"I see. And so you think I should buy a guitar because you had a dream that we are going to have twin daughters and that I will play the guitar and sing to them?" she said.

"Yes. That's it. That's it. Except, I don't want you to buy a guitar."

"Really? Then why are we here?"

"Because I want to buy a guitar for you."

Clementine looked at me for a long moment. At first, I couldn't tell what she was thinking. Then I could see a smile playing across her lips. The smile she sometimes shows me when she has gone from being surprised to being pleased. Then she turned to Jack. She handed him back the guitar he had given her to try. "Do you have a guitar that will fit my hand better than this one?" she said.

"In the same price range?" Jack said, turning to me.

"Yes. In the same price range," I said. Which is not only the story of how I bought a guitar for Clementine, which she learned to play very well so we were singing together in two months, but it is also the story of the day when I told her that I had dreamed we were going to get married and that we would be the parents of twin daughters, which I swear is absolutely true. Every word. I really did have the dream, and the dream really did come true. Just don't ask me how I knew any of that because that I have never been able to explain.

8

With me carrying Clementine's guitar in a new case, we walked a block to a small coffee shop where we ate lunch. Clementine did not say very much until we were almost finished with our meal. I knew something was coming, of course, but I knew enough to wait. Finally, the wait was over when she said, "You've never told me about your dreams, Tyler."

"I know."

"Was there some reason why?"

"The moment never seemed right."

"Not until today."

"Not until today," I said.

Clementine took a sip of her hot tea. "Girl twins?"

"Yes."

"You're sure?"

"That's what I saw."

"So you're a shaman as well as a bard?"

I smiled. I loved her so much. "I suspect I am more shaman than bard," I said.

"You do realize that you've never really said you wanted to marry me. Not in those exact words, at least," Clementine said.

"I know. But we've each said we couldn't imagine lives without the other one. I don't think what I said today was much different."

"You do realize that we are high school seniors?" she said.

"Yes. And I also remember what we've been through together. How many high school senior couples have had our experiences?"

"Not many, I suppose," Clementine said.

"Right. Not many."

"Which means . . . what?"

"Which means our relationship . . . who we are together, doesn't have anything to do with being high school seniors or not being high school seniors," I said. "I think it has to do with us. Who we are. How we've been raised. How we met. What we've shared."

Clementine looked at me but did not reply.

"Clementine, one of these days, when it is closer to the time when we can do something about it, I am going to come to you and get down on my knees and ask you to marry me."

"Tyler, you won't have to get down on your knees."

"I know. But I think I want to anyway."

"Tyler, one of these days, when we are closer to being able to do something about it, I may come to you and get down on my knees and ask you to marry me," Clementine said.

I smiled. "You won't have to get down on your knees either, Clementine."

"I know," she said, smiling her wonderful now we both know what we both know smile.

"Then perhaps what we'll do someday . . . when we're closer to being able to do something about it . . . is you will get down on your knees and I will get down on my knees, and each of us will ask the other to get married."

"That would mean we both come to the same conclusion about the time being right at exactly the same time," Clementine said.

I nodded. "Yes, it will."

"And you think we'll both know that at exactly the same time?"

"I can't think of any two people in the whole world who are more likely to do that, can you?"

Clementine didn't answer. Not in words, that is. She took a sip of her tea and then looked at the guitar case. "I suppose I'd better get to work learning how to play my guitar," she said. "What with twins coming someday."

9

During our drive back up the mountain, it began to snow. That wasn't a surprise, of course, because it had been predicted. However, it was supposed to start after the sun went down. But it had started early. Within five miles of town, we found ourselves facing a very precarious road. I could feel the tires slipping at times as the van passed over patches of road that were freezing. Before long, both of us were leaning forward and trying to see through what was becoming swirling snow. It didn't help that the van didn't have snow tires. All we could do was take it slowly and carefully, trying to use the steering wheel and the gears for braking rather than the brakes and trying to be as smooth as I could be on the gas pedal. In the end, what had been a twenty five minute drive down the mountain became a forty-five minute drive back up.

At one point, I pulled off the road and had to get out and scrape snow off of the window because it was too wet for the windshield wipers to get it all. Then we started again. I could see Clementine was tense. I didn't say anything foolish like don't worry. I knew that talking was not going to make any difference. I just focused on the road and on my driving.

As we came around another bend, we found ourselves behind an older black couple whose car was having a terrible time staying on the road. When their car slid off the pavement and into a long bank of old snow that had been plowed off the road the week before and were obviously not able to get back on the road on their own, we had no choice but to stop behind them. I got out and went around to the driver's side and asked the man if he needed help. He said they couldn't seem to get out of the deep snow that was edging the road. And with the snow coming so hard, he didn't know exactly what to do.

I signaled Clementine that she should come help. When Clementine came up next to the passenger's side of the car, the woman rolled down her window. "We need help," the woman said. "Cars have passed us going the other way, but no one stopped. And my husband, he's had heart trouble. I won't let him get out and push."

Clementine agreed he should stay in the car. Then she said we'd do our best. So she and I pushed as hard as we could, and while it took more than one try, we finally got their car back out onto the road. Once they were safely back on the pavement, the man got out to thank us. "Not many of the white folks from around here are willing to stop and help on the road like you did, young man," he said.

I told him it was no trouble. We were just glad we could help. Then the man looked over the top of the car and saw Clementine. "Well, you young people have been very nice. Can we get you something as a reward?"

"No, sir," I said quickly. "We just did what we hope people might do for us if we were stuck like you were."

"We're just glad the two of you are all right," Clementine said, coming around the car and standing next to me.

"That's very nice of you," he said. Then he leaned into his car. "They don't want any reward, Clara. But I offered. I surely did offer, Clara," he said.

"That's very kind of them," she said. "Very kind indeed." Then she turned to Clementine and said, "You sure are a pretty young thing."

Clementine thanked her.

"You make sure your young man treats you right," she said.

"Oh, he does," Clementine said. "He always takes care of me."

With that I shook the man's hand, and he got back into his car, and we went back and got into the van. Then we followed them until we knew they were safe, watching as they disappeared into the distance as they drove on and we turned into the road leading to the house. But when we got to the house, the last thirty yards from the roadway to the house were far too steep to try to drive. So we got out and very carefully walked up the incline. I brought the guitar in its case. Clementine went ahead of me, reaching back and pulling at my arm as much as she could. We slipped and fell twice, but by then we were laughing. I helped Clementine up. When I fell, she helped me get up. So it was our laughter that my grandfather and Ruth Ann heard as we came over the last part of the ridge, looking like abominable snowmen as we climbed up onto the porch and joined them, for they'd been worried about us getting back safely in what by then had become a severe snow storm.

As we climbed up onto the porch to their greetings, Clementine and I held each other's hands very tightly. To them, what we had been through was a worry. For us, it was simply another experience that we would put in our book of memories. We've also often wondered if the older couple made it to their destination. We've never found out, just as they will never know what became of the young couple who stopped one late afternoon and helped them get back on the road during a snow storm.

10

That evening, the five of us celebrated the Winter Solstice with a wonderful dinner of both ham and turkey and curried rice and sliced tomatoes, which my mother and Ruth Ann prepared together. By this time, the two of them were becoming fast friends. In fact, for a while the two of them were talking and laughing and telling each other so many stories about Clementine and me when we were elementary school students, that the three of us were not sure dinner was ever really going to be served. But when it was, it was worth the wait. To this day I'm not at all certain as to how they brought so much food with us in the van, but they had managed to do so, much to our delight.

Before we began the meal, though, Ruth Ann and Clementine introduced us to a litany of Unitarian Winter Solstice prayers that called up the spirits of the four great Grandmothers—North, South, East, and West—and on the passing of hope through the darkest night of the year by using candles to light the spiritual way, all of which would change in due course by morning, when the process of moving from the darkest night of the year would begin, ending on June 21st with the shortest night of the year, which would then, in turn, start the cycle all over again. Then they recited an exchange of meditations on the gods that once walked the hills of Africa, connecting all of us to a profound sense of the great continuum of human life. This year, Clementine took it upon herself to add the same kind of meditations about the gods that once walked the hills of Scotland and Wales, an addition that further re-enforced both the closeness that my mother and grandfather and I felt to Clementine and Ruth Ann and further said to me how much my darling Clementine loved me and my family. Then as she and Ruth Ann spoke of their spiritual one-ness with their African ancestors, each lit one candle. When they then spoke similar words that invoked my family's Scots and Welsh heritage, Clementine asked each of us to light a candle, so in the end there were five candles in a circle in the middle of the table all burning together. By the time we sat down to eat, I knew with whom I would spend the rest of my life. When we then toasted each other with red wine, I found myself very close to tears, a sentiment I am not at all embarrassed to confess, for when I looked at my mother and my grandfather, they were both unashamedly crying very quietly. Small wonder then that before we sat down to eat, we each got up and went around the table in what almost became a dance, embracing one another until each of us had been kissed and wished a safe and joyous solstice by each of the others. When we finished and began to pass the food, accompanied I can assure you by my laughter, I found myself looking very often at Clementine. The problem for me as I now try to write this memoir is that I have no words to express what I was feeling. If ever a heart was overflowing, it was in that moment.

After dinner was over, we gathered in front of the fireplace and exchanged our gifts. Clementine, to my delight, showed off her new guitar. Each of us had a chance to show the others what we had been given. But as we neared the end of the gift exchange, I realized that Clementine had not given me anything. When Ruth Ann asked what she was going to give me, Clementine got up and went into the bedroom she shared with her mother. When she came back, because I was by then sitting on the floor leaning back against the davenport, she got down on her knees in front of me and handed me a flat package, which I opened very slowly. What I found took my breath away. For Clementine had gone through elaborate pains to come up with two 8 x 10 photographs, both in color, of the two of us together, both of which were taken with telephoto lenses so we had not known they were being taken at the time. The left hand side of the fold out double frame was a photo of Clementine and me walking together off of a football field after a game. I was in my uniform, muddy and sweaty and carrying my helmet in my left hand. Clementine was walking with me, holding my right hand, wearing her usual jeans and school polo shirt. She was looking up at me and smiling while I was obviously responding to something she had said or asked. The other photo was taken after the state championship track meet in the spring of our junior year. We were in almost identical poses, except Clementine was in her track top and shorts, with a towel draped over her right shoulder, carrying a water bottle in her right hand, holding my right hand with her left just as she was in the football photograph. In the photograph, I was turned to her and obviously asking her a question, and she was turned to me and obviously answering.

I sat over the photo for a moment before I turned them around for the others to see. "Where in the world did you get these?" I asked.

"From Bobby Miller's sister, Teresa."

"Bobby Miller. The kicker on the football team?"

"Yes. Bobby Miller the kicker on the foothball team. Teresa's majoring in photography at the University. I saw her at a football game when we were juniors. I asked her to take the pictures at the state championship track meet," Clementine said, "and then in the fall. Her only stipulation was that she could keep copies to display for her senior photography show."

"Which means you've been working on this for how long? Since our junior year?"

"Yes."

I shook my head slowly. I didn't know what to say. I realized that Clementine had not just kept a secret for months but she had wanted to capture what were two of the defining moments in our relationship that portrayed who we were individually and, even more important, who we were together. I have never ever received a gift I prized more highly or treasured more dearly. I took the photos with me to the University of Georgia. I kept them with me in graduate school. Today, they sit in our family room on the fireplace mantle. Our daughters say they love them as much as we do.

In any case, the evening ended with the five of us pulling on our parkas and going out doors into the new snow and standing away from the house and looking up into what was by then a crystal clear night. Have five people ever been so filled with happiness as they stood looking up at the canopy of stars? I don't know. Probably. But not many. I am confident about that. Not many.

11

The rest of our stay after we celebrated the Winter Solstice was very much like the days before. We read books. We played board games. We played poker. My grandfather taught Clementine the fundamentals of chess. We kept the radio on sometimes and listened to music from the BBC. We drank tea. We ate. We went for walks as a group. We went for walks in couples, each of us having some time alone with each of the others.

Most important to me, my conversation with my mother confirmed that she understood my relationship with Clementine was not simply a case of a high school romance. My conversation with my grandfather focused more on his delight that I had decided to major in history when I got to college. My conversation with Ruth Ann was more veiled, but certainly she implied very clearly that she understood how much her daughter loved me and how I held more of her daughter's future happiness in my hands than even I understood.

Up to that point in our relationship, my notion of Clementine was that she was extraordinarily strong. Very cautiously her mother let me know that while Clementine appeared to everyone else to be able to withstand any disappointment, any pain, the truth was she was a very sensitive young woman whose well being was far more precarious. Ruth and I were walking when she said that. And when she did, she stopped and faced me and put her hands on my shoulders and said, "Tyler, I know the two of you are young. And I know that as a parent I should warn both of you that what you feel about each other today may not be what you will feel in a year or two years or more. But I'm not going to say that to you, because I believe you know my daughter has given her heart to you in a way I never thought she would give it to anyone."

She paused for a moment, turning away and looking into the cloudy distance. Then she turned back to me. "What I am saying, Tyler, is that I am trusting you with my daughter's life. Because that is what you are to her. Her life. Her father hurt her more than she knows. Certainly more than she can say. He hurt her even more than I know. It will take her a lifetime to sort it out. But that's okay. She has a lifetime to do it. Because you are the man in her life now. You are the only person in the world who could have seen her through her seeing him. I know it's probably unfair for me to say this to you, but I will anyway. Tyler, you have her life in your hands. I know her well enough to know she will only love once in her life. And she has chosen you. So please, love her, Tyler Raymond. Just love her. God knows she loves you."

I didn't know what to say. That was the longest statement Ruth Ann had ever made to me. It was the most open she had ever been with me.

I turned to her and looked at her and then took her hands in mine and said, "Ruth Ann, I promise you, right here on this mountain . . . I promise you . . . I swear by this mountain and this sky . . . that I will love Clementine for the rest of my life. I promise you, I will guard her and protect her and honor her until the day I die."

Ruth Ann nodded and slowly drew back and looked at me and then looked at the mountain. "Good," she said. "Good. I believe you."

Then we walked back to the house through the snowy clouds. As we approached we could hear my mother and Clementine laughing at something my grandfather had said. For a moment we stood on the porch together and listened to them from inside. Then we went in and joined them.

12

That night, as I lay awake listening to the wind through the pine trees, I thought I could hear the snow falling. I thought I could feel the earth turning and the stars moving and the planets turning ever so gracefully in their orbits. I lay awake and listened to the fire crackling from the other room. Then I must have fallen asleep. But it did not last long. Because just as I must have fallen asleep without knowing I had, I was awake without knowing when I had awakened.

I listened to the house. It was silent. I got up and pulled off my pajamas and pulled on my jeans and heavy socks and a sweatshirt. Then I went out into the living room. It was still dark. The fire had almost burned away. But there was enough light for me to find my way to the front door and my parka and scarf and hat hanging on the coat rack. So I pulled them on and went out of the door as quietly as I could.

It was still dark, but I could see a faint outline of light coming over the mountains to the east. I stood and looked into the valley to the south. It was still night down in the town. But up on the crest, the light was beginning to draw a pencil line across the mountains. I stepped down off the porch and stood in the snow looking. I held my breath. I could feel my heart beating. I could feel the earth turning. I swear, everything was so still, I could feel the earth turning. I don't know how long I stood that way. Long enough for the light to begin to define the trees to my right and to my left. Long enough for the light to define the rocks that fell away into the valley. Long enough to begin to define the horizon sixty miles away.

Then I felt her. Clementine was behind me as she stepped forward and put her arms around my shoulders and I reached back and caught her legs as she mounted me from behind. I felt her press her face against my face. I felt her lips touching my cheek. And so I held her that way. She pressed her face against mine, and I held her and held her and held her, and the sun came up over the crest, and the snow was white and blue all around us, and the wind moved through the trees, and I held her and held her and held her until she said, "Like this, Tyler. Like this. Like this." And I said, "Yes. Just like this. Just like this."

And then it was dawn. And then it was light. And then it began to snow. And the wind began to move all around us. And then I let her down very, very slowly. And she stood behind me with her arms around me. And then we could smell coffee from inside the house. And then it was another new day.

13

I very much wish that I could say that every moment we spent in the North Carolina mountains was equally wonderful, but that would not be true. Not that the five of us had any problems with each other. I can't recall us ever having problems with one another. No, what happened took place in town on December 27th. And if I'm going to try to write an honest memoir of my life with Clementine, I believe I have to include that incident along with all of the good things that happened.

We had managed to bring enough food with us to see us through December 26th. But as we planned to stay until January 2nd, someone needed to drive to town to get groceries. I could see that my mother was deep into a novel she had been trying to get time to read since October. Ruth Ann was sitting with a legal pad making notes for an upcoming seminar she was supposed to conduct. My grandfather was taking a nap. So Clementine and I said we would be glad to do so.

We bundled up and went out and got in the van and drove very carefully down the mountain to Linville Falls where I had bought Clementine's guitar. It didn't take long to find the supermarket on the highway. So we pulled in and parked and went inside and started our shopping. Because the list was fairly long, it took maybe twenty minutes to fill the shopping cart. When we finally finished we pushed the cart up to the check out stand. There was a woman ahead of us who bought her groceries. As we waited, a man came from behind us and took his place in line. When it was our turn, Clementine and I unloaded the cart and waited as the young woman working the cash register began checking our items through. My mother had given me the money, which I took out of my pocket as the young woman turned to me and said, "That'll be $42.31." I said fine, and started to count out the money, when the young woman said, "You two must not be from around here."

Now, before I tell you what happened next, I want you to remember how the older black couple acted when Clementine and I pushed their car out of the snow along the side of the highway. They had ample opportunity to notice that Clementine is black and I am white. But all they did was thank us for stopping to help them.

All right. Back to the grocery store and the incident with the cashier, who told me that I owed $42.31 and then commented, "You two must not be from around here," which is why I stopped counting and looked at her and said, "No. We're not."

The young woman looked at Clementine. "I thought so. I didn't think I'd ever seen you before."

"We're from Tampa."

The young woman had her hand out ready to take my money. But just then she said, "We don't get many couples like you two here in Linville Falls."

I stopped moving my hand towards the young woman's. "What did you say?" I asked her.

She looked surprised. "I just said, we don't get many couples like you two here in town," she replied, looking at me and then looking at Clementine and then back at me again.

Still holding the money, I withdrew my hand and turned to Clementine. "She says they don't get many couples like us here in Linville Falls."

"Yes, I heard her say that," Clementine said.

"What do you think she means?" I said, turning to the young woman and then back to Clementine. "Do you think she means I'm taller than you?" I stepped closer to Clementine and looked at her as if I was measuring her height against mine.

"Maybe she knows you play football and I run track," Clementine said, her voice tense and growing harder with each syllable.

"That must be it. Somehow she knows I'm a just a pretty good football player but that you're the state of Florida 440 and 880 yard track champion."

Clementine looked at me. Even though it was obvious the girl was just plain stupid, the moment hurt her, which meant it was hurting me. I wasn't sure what to do next. This wasn't Tampa, after all. This was the girl's hometown, not ours. Then I decided I was not going to just pay and then go away. I knew perfectly well what she had meant when she said they didn't get many couples like us in Linville. I decided that I was going to prove her right, even if it wasn't going to be in the way she thought she understood. Which is why I went on and said in my best and most sarcastic voice, "Or maybe, somehow, Clementine, she knows that your grade point average is higher than mine."

I could see the tension in Clementine's face. What must this be like for her, I wondered? No, it wasn't Timmy O'Brien and his stupid insults or Blessed Billy on the beach and his threats. But damn it to hell, this was supposed to be our vacation. The countryside was beautiful. All we wanted to do was buy groceries. Then this fat, pimply faced, scraggly girl had to open her big mouth and say something stupid and screw it up royally.

I turned back to the young woman. "I don't think we'll buy groceries from you, miss. I think we'll just leave quietly."

"What?" she asked as much startled as offended.

"I said, I don't think we'll buy our groceries from you, miss." And with that I very slowly folded up the bills my mother had given me and put them back in my pocket. Then I turned to Clementine, who was looking at me with that expressionless expression that I'd seen before that says, "Get me out of here, Tyler. Just get me out of here."

I reached for her arm and turned her around so she was facing the front doors, and we started to walk away. Then from behind me I heard the young woman say, "What am I supposed to do with these groceries, mister?"

I stopped walking and turned back and looked at her and at the man who had been waiting in line behind us and said, "Any number of things come to mind, miss, but I believe it would be best if I just left them unsaid." With that we walked out through the front doors and went back to the van and got in and just sat in silence for some time before Clementine turned to me and said in a whisper, "I think you handled that rather well, Tyler Raymond."

I turned to Clementine and said, "Why, thank you, Clementine Brown. I think I did too, if I say so myself."

Then I started the van. "Of course, what I wanted to say was . . . ." I let my sentence hang in the air.

"I know," Clementine said. She looked away. "I know."

So we drove on into town and found another grocery store where we got a cart and gathered the items we wanted and were checked through by a very friendly young woman, and because the store was not busy, had our groceries bagged by the store manager who thanked us for shopping with them that morning.

14

As my grandfather had promised when we drove to North Carolina, late in the afternoon on New Year's Eve day, he told us to bundle up in our warmest clothes. Then we drove to a farm several miles off the paved road that led up to our side of the mountain. There we met Sam Jarrett, who not only owned a farm, he took people on hay rides during the summer and fall months and on sleigh rides during the winter.

Sam maintained two magnificent workhorses. "I fell in love with these big boys when I was a boy myself," he said. "They belonged to the farmer who owned the land next to my father's. When I retired from the air force, I came back here and took over my family's farm and bought them off a neighbor when he was selling his farm. I've kept them here ever since. Jimmy is nearly twenty five," Sam said. "And Sidney is nearly twenty. But they're good horses. Couldn't stand the thought of them being sent to the glue factory."

With that he finished hitching the horses to the sleigh, which Sam explained he'd found one day in a warehouse in Asheville. "No one who worked for the storage tank company had any idea how the sled had gotten there, and no one seemed to care about keeping it or letting it go. So I offered them $100, which the manager took. Then I had a friend of mine with a real big flat bed truck come pick it up." He smiled his satisfaction. "It took me three years to get it back into shape, but I loved doing it."

When Sam finished telling his story and finished showing us the framework that he'd rebuilt and the seat upholstery that he'd had redone by a man in Charlotte, and my grandfather was finished walking around the sleigh and admiring the work that Sam obviously loved describing, the five of us got in, my grandfather and mother and Ruth Ann in the front seat, Clementine and me in the back. Sam gave all of us blankets to sit on and to wrap around ourselves. As I was wrapping a blanket around Clementine, she whispered, "Does your grandfather know anything about rebuilding sleighs?"

"No," I said in as quiet a voice as I could manage. "But he loves to talk to people who are proud of what they've done."

Clementine smiled her delight and hugged me and grabbed one of my gloved hands with both of hers.

Then Sam climbed up in the driver's seat and turned around and said, "We don't go very far up into the hills. Not in the winter. It's a little too steep even for these big fellows. And sometimes the snow is too deep. But there's a real pretty road that goes up a little to a rise and then follows it around to the other side where you'll get a really good view of the lake and the valley that goes all the way to Tennessee." With that, we began.

My mother had brought along a thermos of coffee. Ruth Ann turned around and gave Clementine and me two mugs. "When we get cold, we'll have some," Ruth Ann said. Then she turned around and with my grandfather in the middle the three adults started talking about the landscape that fell away around us. In the back seat, Clementine took hold of my left arm and pulled herself up as close to me as she could. Then we turned our attention to the stands of forest and the crop lands that sloped away from the road and the mountain range in the distance.

The ride took almost two hours. And Sam Jarrett was certainly right about the view. No, we didn't climb to the top of the mountain. But we didn't need to. The shifting landscape was all we needed. After an hour, when we came to the ridge and followed it, the views were especially wonderful. We stopped at one point so Sam could point out how we could see part of the Great Smoky Mountains in Tennessee. As we moved on, Sam told us all about the history of the region—how it had been settled by Scots-Irish, how fiercely they had defended their lands against intruders, how protective they still were of their culture. "You can hear it in our music most of all," he said. "Blue Grass is really Scots music without bag pipes. Listen the next time you hear a really good Blue Grass band. You'll hear the violins playing as if they were pipes. I promise."

As we started our slow descent to the road that would take us back to the farm, we passed through a lovely stand of dark trees bent over the road. Cloaked by shadows, Clementine leaned toward me and kissed my cheek. I turned and looked at her. Then we kissed each other. And wouldn't you know that was exactly the moment when Ruth Ann turned around and said, "Do either of you want any more coffee?"

We separated. Clementine looked at Ruth Ann and smiled her displeasure and said, "Yes, mother."

"And you, Tyler?" Ruth Ann said, ignoring her daughter's humor.

"Yes, ma'am," I said.

"Unless, of course, you'd rather go back to kissing my daughter," Ruth Ann said, smiling broadly.

My mother turned around quickly and did her best mock surprised look. "Is my boy kissing your daughter again, Ruth Ann?"

"It would appear so, Elizabeth," Ruth Ann said.

I tried to interrupt their exchange. "Coffee would be fine," I said.

"Better give that boy some coffee," my grandfather said over his shoulder. "Give him something to do."

"Apparently, Edward, he's found something to do," Ruth Ann laughed.

"Mother, just pour Tyler some coffee, please," Clementine said.

"My, my, Elizabeth, my daughter is certainly bossy sometimes," Ruth Ann said.

My mother laughed, and Ruth Ann took my mug and poured it full of coffee and handed it to me and then turned around and faced forward again.

"I swear, sometimes . . . ." Clementine said. She did not finish her sentence.

I laughed with her. "Yes. Sometimes mothers are just . . . ," I said in a voice loud enough so all three adults could hear, which of course only provoked all of them to laugh.

"Yes, Tyler," my mother said. "Mothers are just . . . ." And she laughed again.

15

By the time we got back to our house, it was 7:30. We then spent two hours preparing the food for our New Year's Eve celebration. By 9:30 we were playing Trivial Pursuit. I teamed with Ruth Ann, and Clementine teamed with my mother. My grandfather took charge of the questions, assuming the right to correct the answers when he knew they were wrong.

As it neared midnight, we stopped playing, and my grandfather turned on his radio so we could listen to the celebration from Times Square. When the count down started, my grandfather turned the radio up very loudly, and we all trooped out onto the porch and counted along with the crowd. Then it was midnight, and we kissed each other and wished each other Happy New Year. At the same time, from down in the valley, we could see fireworks being shot up into the air. We could hear voices from other houses set back in the woods yelling "Happy New Year." So we all shouted back, "Happy New Year!"

Then more fireworks flared in the sky. And we stood together in the snow and in the cold as we watched the valley towns below celebrate. After maybe fifteen minutes or so, we went back inside and drank hot tea and then sat in front of the fire talking about what the next year would bring all of us. For Clementine and me, of course, it would be graduation from Tampa Coast and college. For our mothers, it would be a chance to share in the next stage of our lives. For my grandfather, it would be the new book he was trying to finish and his chance to go visiting the two of us when we went away. "That's going to be very hard for all of us," he said, speaking for both my mother and for Ruth Ann. "We're going to miss you two," he said, looking at Clementine and me. "But lord only knows, I envy you two what comes next. I surely do envy you what comes next."

We didn't respond except to thank him for what he'd said because we knew any more conversation would be very hard for him.

16

Two days later, we packed up our belongings and started the drive back home. As we passed through town, my grandfather saw the grocery store where Clementine and I had tried to buy groceries. When he asked if we wanted to stop and buy anything, Clementine said no, that wouldn't be a good place. When Ruth Ann said that Clementine's comment was a bit strange, Clementine told her what had happened.

"But you two didn't say anything when you got back to the cabin," Ruth Ann said.

"That's all right. We handled the situation," Clementine said, smiling at me.

Then Clementine told her mother and my mother and my grandfather what the girl had said and what I had said and then what the two of us had said and how we left very quietly but that we did not pay for the groceries but left them on the check out counter for the store manager to put back.

"It sounds like the two of you took care of things then," Ruth Ann said.

Clementine smiled and leaned against my shoulder. "I think we did."

"I think we did," I said, echoing Clementine's sentiment.

Nothing more has ever been said about the incident. By 11 P.M. that night, we were back in Tampa and back home. Clementine and I went to the Westshore shopping mall the next day and ate lunch together and talked about everything that had happened. We agreed that life was good. The next day, Ruth Ann and my mother both went back to teaching, and Clementine and I went back to Tampa Coast.

17

Like juniors all over the United States enrolled in secondary schools, eleventh graders at Tampa Coast High School sit the Preliminary Scholastic Aptitude Test in the fall of the year. The scores are then used to determine National Merit Scholar honors and National Merit scholarships, which can be worth a great deal of money as well as open the doors to excellent colleges and universities for high scoring students. Clementine was a stronger scholar than me. I don't have any trouble admitting that. We were both good students, but she was better. There was no reason why I wouldn't get into a good school, but she'd be able to go anywhere she wanted.

When PSAT scores were published during spring of our junior years, we were both informed we were in the running for National Merit Scholarships. By the fall of our senior year, I was listed as a National Merit Semi Finalist, which might not give me much direct money, but it would certainly help in my college admissions. The big news, however, was that Clementine was a National Merit Finalist. While we both received letters and brochures from a number of colleges and universities across the country, she received them from the most competitive schools in the country, including the Ivy League schools and the Seven Sisters schools.

That fall we sat the Scholastic Aptitude Tests. Out of 1600 possible points, I earned 1524, which I knew would more than qualify me for the University of Georgia. When Clementine's score came in as a 1587, the best schools in the country came courting, and I do mean courting. Aggresively courting. That was when our very long and very sensitive conversations began. The first happened the first Sunday in February. It was gray and cold. We were walking in the park close to Clementine's house because that's where we went to be alone. A number of our most important conversations had taken place in the park. This wasn't going to be any different. We both knew that.

"My mother is starting to talk to me," Clementine said.

I waited.

"She says she knows that places like Princeton and Harvard and Yale are going to come after me now. Even more than before."

"They probably will," I said. "And they should," I added.

"Let's sit on the teeter-totter," she said.

I smiled. "We always do."

"What do you mean?"

"When we talk about things like this. Important things. We always sit on the teeter-totter."

Clementine smiled. We walked to the teeter-totter and each took our places opposite each other.

"You're decided on Georgia," she said.

"Yes."

"You could go other places," she said.

"I know. Duke University called. So did Clemson."

"Admissions or football?"

"Duke was admissions. Then two days later the football coach called. Clemson was football then admissions."

"What did you say?"

"I thanked them. That's all."

"Have you heard from Coach Dooley?"

"A letter came Saturday. I opened it after I got home from the movie last night."

"What did it say?"

"He wants me to come visit next weekend."

"And you're going?"

"If you'll go with me."

"Me? Really?"

"Yes, you. And my mother. And my grandfather."

Clementine said she would be glad to go. Then she asked, "Do you think you can get a scholarship?"

"I don't know. Maybe not for football. But I don't care about that. I'll walk on if I have to."

Clementine was quiet. "Can you make the team if you walk on?"

"I don't know. Players do every year. No big school has enough scholarships for everyone on a football team."

"And you know your grades and SAT scores will get you in."

"They should. But what about you? You're the one who has a bigger decision to make."

"Why is my decision bigger?" Clementine asked.

"C'mon," I said, "you know why it's bigger. You can go anywhere in the country. I can go to Georgia. And there are probably a number of good schools where I could go. But I can go to Georgia. So I'm not facing any pressing problem."

"You could go to Duke," Clementine said quickly.

"I know that. And Duke's a really good school. I know that, too. But I want to go to Georgia. I don't care who else is interested. You know why."

"I know," Clementine said quietly.

"That was a really hard time for me, Clementine. You were there. I tried to be very calm about things, but you know better than anyone else how hard it was."

"I know," she said again.

"But when Coach Dooley wrote that letter. And what he said about my father. I knew I had to go there. I want to play for a man like that. I want to know him," I said.

Clementine nodded. "Then I want you to go there. And I want to go to Georgia Tech."

"But you could go to an even more prestigious school," I said. "Your scores are fantastic. And you run track. Just look at how many schools have written to you because of your track. The University of Texas. The University of Michigan. You even heard from the University of Arizona. And now, with your scores, you could write your own ticket."

Clementine was quiet for some time. "Do you want me to go farther away?" she said.

"What?"

"Do you want me to go father away than Georgia Tech? Haven't we talked about this before? How we'll only be sixty miles apart. We've talked about how even that will be hard, but it won't be impossible. Have you changed your mind now, Tyler?"

"Clementine. Stop. You know that isn't what I'm saying. I wish we could be on the same campus. That would be the best thing in the whole world. But that isn't what is best for us. You want to go to Georgia Tech for biology. And they want you to run. I want to go to Georgia to study history and play football for Vince Dooley. My grandfather has looked at the Georgia catalog with me. He says the history department is very good. He says he knows some of the people by reputation. He's even met two of the men and one of the women. So it's really a good place for me."

"So that's what we're going to do," Clementine said. "We've made up our minds."

"I know we made up our minds. But what if you could get into Princeton or Yale or someplace like that? Or Harvard? The Harvard medical school. Is there anyplace better than that?"

"I don't know. Maybe. Maybe not. That's not the point."

"Then what is the point?"

"Do you want me to go far away?" she said.

"Clementine, that's not fair."

"Do you want me to go far away?" she said again.

I sat quietly for a moment. "Clementine, I want you to do what is best for you. That's how much I love you."

It was Clementine's turn to be quiet. "I know," she said.

"I'm here today because of you. I'm alive today because of you. I'm who I am because of you."

"Then don't send me away."

"What?"

"Don't send me away."

"I'm not sending you away."

"My mother wants to."

"What?"

"My mother wants me to go to Harvard if they want me. She says it's what's she's always wanted for me."

How could I respond to that? I wasn't about ready to start opposing Ruth Ann. I respected her too much. I also feared her. Had she decided it was all right for Clementine to have me for a boyfriend in high school but not when Clementine went to college? All of a sudden what I had always sensed was now something to fear. "Is this about me?" I said.

"What do you mean?"

"You know what I mean. Is this about me?"

"It's not about you, Tyler," she said.

I did not respond.

"But I do think it's about her," Clementine said. "There were battles she tried to fight when she was my age, but there was no way she was going to win. Not then. She says it's different now."

"Wait. I'm confused. Who are we talking about? You or your mother?"

"Both," she said.

"You're going to have to explain that, Clementine."

Clementine put her weight on her end of the teeter-totter and held me in the air for a moment. Then I slowly descended, and she was up in the air.

"My mother wanted to go to one of the Ivy League universities. But she didn't have the background. She knew that. So she worked hard in undergraduate school and got the grades. So she thought she'd go to one of them for her master's degree. Yale turned her down. Harvard said she needed more background. Brown acted like they were interested, but then she didn't get a big enough scholarship. So she stayed on at New York University instead. By the time she was working on her doctorate at Rutgers, she had to take care of me by herself because my father was gone."

Clementine was quiet for a moment. Then she went on. "She's not unhappy about her education. She says she had wonderful professors. But I think she feels that if she'd had a different kind of background more doors would have opened up for her."

I said that I understood. I said I could see why she might feel the way she did about Clementine's education.

"But I've told her this can't be about her. I remind her that she's been telling me that all of my life. That my education was for me. Now she sounds like she's just about ready to change her tune. I told her to not even go there. I don't think she was very happy with me for saying that, but I told her I could feel her priorities shifting, and I didn't want that to happen."

I was listening. I didn't face Clementine's problem. But I could understand what she was facing.

"Besides, there's another reason as well."

"All right," I said, waiting for her to explain.

"It's about race."

"How so?"

Clementine looked away for some time. Then she turned back to me. "Tyler, there must be a whole lot of high school seniors with SAT scores as high as mine. There must be a whole lot with higher SAT scores."

"But not many," I said quickly.

"All right. Not many. But enough. So why is a school like Harvard or Yale or someplace like that going to come looking for me?"

I didn't want to hear the answer.

"Because I'm black. Okay. Because I'm a black female. That's why."

"Clementine, that's not all of it," I said. "You are a superior student. You are a superior athlete."

"I am a superior black student and a superior black athlete. And I am a superior black woman student and black woman athlete," she said sharply.

"What's wrong with that?" I said.

"Because I don't want to be a black student or black athlete or black woman," Clementine said.

"Wait. I'm confused. You're not ashamed of being black. Good God, we've talked about that a hundred times."

"I don't mean I don't want to be black. I am black. That's a fact. That's fine. That's who I am. A black. A student. An athlete. A woman. That's all well and good. But I don't want to be *their* black student and *their* black athlete and *their* black woman. I don't want to be paraded around so they can feel good about helping black people advance."

I was stunned at her anger.

"I don't want to be a token," she said. "I just want to be me. Just me. Whatever that means. I just want to be Clementine Camille Brown. A student and maybe an athlete and always a black and always a woman."

I sat quietly. This was new territory. At least, it was a new kind of sentiment, a new kind of statement and anger. I sat quietly.

"Tyler, listen to me. My mother fought a really hard battle. Two battles. Being a black student and being a black woman with a child. And she fought it for herself, which was right, and she fought it for me, which I appreciate more than I can say. And she won. And that's just the point."

"Wait. I'm confused. What's just the point? And what does that have to do with you not going to a Harvard or a Yale or someplace like that?"

Clementine looked away for a moment. Then she looked back at me. "Tyler, are you proud of being white?"

"What?"

"Are you proud of being white? Are you self-conscious about being white?"

I knew she was serious. I was trying to understand. "I don't know how to answer that, Clementine. I'm me. I'm just me. No one has ever asked me to be proud or not be proud of being white."

"Yes. And that's the point."

"What's the point?"

"You're white. American society is mostly white. So you get to be just you. No one asks you to think about it. You just get to be you. But it's not like that for black people. For people of color. Any color. Not in America. People of color have to fight for their places. Do you see that? I know you understand that."

I nodded. "Yes. I understand that. I understand that it's different. That you are self-conscious. That people of color have to fight for their places. But your mother made sure you had great opportunities, Clementine. Where you live. Where you go to school."

"Yes. And that's just the point. I've had opportunities. For which I am grateful."

"Which has what to do with you not wanting to go to Harvard or Yale or one of the other Ivies?"

Clementine was quiet again for a long time. I did not question her silence. I waited.

"Tyler, there are thousands of black students my age who haven't lived the way I've lived. Who haven't had my advantages."

"Okay," I said slowly.

"So I don't think it would be fair for me to take a place at one of those really prestigious schools that should go to someone who needs it more than I do."

I sat silent. Did she mean that? Was she really that generous? Did she really think in those terms?

"That's very noble, Clementine. But is it fair to you? Don't you deserve a chance to go to a Harvard or a Yale as much as a black student who hasn't lived like you've lived?"

"Tyler, I love you so much. You have the most wonderful heart. Better than anyone else in the world that I will ever know."

"Clementine, you're changing the subject."

"No, I'm not. You are the subject. I am the subject. My mother thinks she's still fighting the battles she fought when she was my age. When she was in college. But the battles are different now. So I don't need to fight the battles she fought. I need to fight my own battles. And I'm not going to take a place at one of those schools that everyone thinks is so wonderful that some black woman coming from a whole different background really needs. I'm past that."

"Clementine, the world is still racist. America is still racist. You and I know that. We've seen it. We've seen it together."

"I know. But I'm equipped to deal with it. I've been given a chance to learn how to deal with it. Some girl my age from some really bad neighborhood or really bad school or both is still trying to figure out how to deal with it," Clementine said. "And I don't want to take up her place in a school that might help her sort it out. I don't need that place."

I took a deep breath and looked at her. "How did I get so lucky to have you come into my life?" I said. "I don't understand why I'm the guy."

Clementine smiled. "You weren't lucky," she said. "I picked you."

"I know you picked me. But why did you pick me? You're wonderful, Clementine. You are the most . . . noble person I will ever meet. So how come you picked me?"

Clementine was quiet for a moment. "I don't know. You were looking around for a biology lab partner, and you looked lost. I thought maybe I could help."

I laughed. "Well, yeah, I was lost, all right. But you did more than that. You know you did more than that."

"And you did more than just accept my invitation to be my lab partner, Tyler. You know you did more than that."

I was quiet. I waited. I knew there was even more. My grandfather always told me that if a person waited there would always be more.

"Tyler Thomas Raymond, I just want to go to school at Georgia Tech so I can get ready for medical school. And I just want to be as close to you as I can."

"And I want to be as close to you as I can," I said in a whisper, pushing down so I could hold her up in the air.

"And no matter what my mother thinks or thinks she thinks, I want to be close to her. She doesn't have anyone else. Not really."

"Ah," I said.

"What does 'Ah' mean?" Clementine said.

"That being close to your mother . . . Tampa to Atlanta . . . that that's the *more* my grandfather always talks about."

"The *more*?"

"Wait long enough, he says, and a person telling you a story will always have even more to say."

Clementine smiled. "I guess he's right."

"He usually is," I said.

"So then let me make my own decision. I told you once that I didn't want you to ever go away. Well, I don't want to go away from you, either. So don't send me away," she said.

I sat but did not smile even though I was overjoyed because this was such a serious thing she was saying. "Clementine, I will never send you away. And I will never go away," I said.

"Good. Fine. Then it's settled," she said. Then she smiled in that very special way she has of smiling when she knows that she's not only gotten her way right then, she's going to get her way for a very long time. Then she said, "Now, let me down."

I smiled. "And what's the magic word?"

Clementine shook her head as only she can shake her head at me. Then she said, "Tyler Thomas Raymond . . . please let me down."

I let her down slowly and carefully because I did not then nor have I ever wanted to do her any hurt or harm.

18

I know that at this point in my memoir, it may well sound like everything in Clementine's and my life together was wonderful—that no more upsets happened—that we just waltzed on through high school without a care in the world. But that isn't quite true. You know what I mean. Just when you think you've handled every possible situation that might come down the pike, along comes something that you never in your wildest dreams ever expected. That's what happened next.

I have not said anything up to this point about my father's parents or my father's family because at that point in my life I knew very little about them. All my mother had said over the years was that he had a falling out with his parents and his older brother. I suppose that satisfied me as I grew up. After all, two factors were at work. First, from my child's point of view, my father had died a hero in a war, even if it was a war, I was told, that he did not believe should have happened. Second, I was loved by my mother and her father, my grandfather. I did not feel deprived. There were pictures of my father in the house, and it was obvious to me as I grew up that my mother had loved him very much. My grandfather assured me that my father had loved my mother. My grandfather went on to say my father was at the beginning of what promised to be a brilliant career as an English instructor at Cleveland State University, which is how he met my grandfather and, because my grandfather had liked him, how he met my mother.

Then one day a letter came for me from Mildred and Preston Raymond, II. At first I did not know who they were. When I read the letter I understood. My grandparents were going to be in Miami for six days in the middle of February. They were inviting me to come join them at their hotel so I might have dinner with them. Not only did they wish to get to know me, there were legal details that their Miami lawyer, a Mitchell Barrows, wish to explain to me about my trust fund.

I was reading the letter in the kitchen when my mother came home. After she got herself a cup of tea, she joined me. I didn't say anything, I just showed her the letter. "Who are they?" I said.

My mother read the letter a second time. Then she looked at me. "They are your father's parents," she said.

"Have I ever met them?"

"They saw you at your father's funeral. They came to Cleveland to attend."

"Other than that?"

"Other than that, no. They've never seen you."

"Or wanted to?" I said.

"I don't know about that. I can't answer for them."

I sat back. "Should I be offended?" I said.

"That they didn't want to see you until now?"

"Yes."

My mother looked at her cup of tea. "It had more to do with your father than with you. More to do with me."

I waited. "What does that mean?" I said.

"It means, your father made decisions with which they disagreed."

"So they . . . what? Cut him off? Cut you off?"

"Yes."

"Then why should I want to see them now?"

My mother sighed. "You are eighteen. You'll be going to college in the fall. There are things you need to know."

"About what?"

"About your trust fund."

"I have a trust fund?"

"Yes."

"A trust fund . . . as in money?"

"Yes."

"How much?"

"I don't know. They can tell you how much. I don't have anything to do with it."

"Mom, do you know how strange that sounds. I'm your only child, and I have a trust fund, and you're the adult who's been responsible for me since my father was killed. So why don't you know anything about my trust fund or whatever it is?"

"Because I didn't want anything to do with your father's parents, Tyler. Not with the way they treated him. Not with the way they treated us when we got married."

My grandfather was in the doorway. "Tell him the whole story, Elizabeth."

"Dad . . . " my mother started to say.

"No, Elizabeth. Obviously something has happened. And if it's going to involve Tyler, he deserves to know the whole story."

I turned to my grandfather. "Did you know them, Grandpa?" I asked.

"I met them. But I sure didn't want to know them."

I had never heard my grandfather speak in that tone of voice before. "I don't understand. What do you mean?"

"Elizabeth, tell Tyler the whole story. He's a young man now. He deserves to know," my grandfather said.

My mother looked away. "All right. I will tell what I know. I will tell what I remember."

I turned to my grandfather. "Grandpa, would you come sit with us?"

My grandfather sat next to me without speaking. He put a hand on mine for a moment. Then he took it away and waited for my mother.

My mother turned back to me. "Your father's people come from a very old Virginia family. The Raymonds. They have owned land in Virginia since it was a crown colony."

I waited.

"Your grandfather Preston Raymond is a very wealthy man. Farms. Real Estate. Mills. Even shipping. Big ships. Cargo ships."

My grandfather looked away. I could feel the rigidity in his body.

"Preston Raymond expected his sons to follow him into the family business. The Raymond Holding and Investment Company. He didn't care what his daughter, Jessica, did, but he expected his two sons to follow him into the family business."

"I have an aunt?"

"She's dead."

"What?"

"She's dead."

"How did that happen?"

My mother turned on me. "Tyler, I can only tell you one story at a time," she snapped.

I was silent.

"Elizabeth, be patient. He's going to have questions," my grandfather said quietly.

"I know," my mother said. "I'm sorry, Tyler."

"That's okay. Just tell me about the family. Please."

My mother got up and poured herself a second cup of tea. She poured one for my grandfather. "Do you want anything, Tyler?" she asked.

"No. I'm fine. Just sit down and talk to me," I replied.

My mother sat. She took a sip of her tea. "Your father was the second son. The oldest son is your uncle Preston III. He was eager to follow his father into the business. As far as I know, he's still in it. But your father had problems. Ethical problems. He was a good student. He studied the history of Virginia and the history of the family. And he didn't like what he found."

I was beginning to get a glimmer of what was coming.

"The family had made its initial fortune from three plantations. Colonial land grants. That was before the Civil War, of course. So they owned slaves. After the war, with the slaves freed, the family fell on hard times. Then the men who were in charge of the Raymond money discovered overseas trading. Wars came. They bought mills and supplied armies and became rich again. I don't remember all of the details. Your father knew. He knew every single detail. And he was ashamed."

"They were war profiteers?"

"Yes. During the war with Spain. And World War I. When World War II came, Preston II, your grandfather, took charge of the business. They contracted with munitions factories up and down the eastern sea board. There were scandals about . . . influence. With people in Washington. It was a pretty sordid affair. At least, that's what your father believed. So when he went to the University of Maryland, he made it clear that he didn't want anything to do with the family money. He played football and worked in the student cafeteria. He wouldn't take anything from his parents. Which they resented, of course.

After he earned his master's degree at Maryland, he accepted a teaching position at Cleveland State. The Raymonds were outraged. How could he desert them? It was bad enough that he hadn't wanted to go to school in Virginia for his undergraduate studies. When it became obvious that he wasn't ever going to come home, they refused to even talk to him anymore. When he wanted to marry me, they were so angry they wouldn't even come to the wedding."

"Which had to do with me, Tyler," my grandfather said, interrupting my mother.

I turned to him. "With you? Why with you?"

My grandfather smiled. "You know my politics, Tyler. You know what I care about: racial injustice. Racial equality. Real left wing stuff, according to the Raymonds."

I smiled. "But I'm proud of your left wing stuff, Grandpa," I said.

"That's good. That makes me very happy, Tyler. But to the Raymonds—Civil Rights, the Democratic Party . . . those were dangers. And John Kennedy getting elected. A Catholic. That was just too much for them to bear."

"So what did they do?"

"What could they do? Your father had cut off the relationship. He knew his own mind. He knew what he believed was right," my grandfather said.

"The war was the end for them," my mother said.

"The Viet Nam war?" I said.

"Yes," my mother replied. Then she waited to collect her thoughts. "It was very complicated, Tyler. Your father didn't believe America should become involved in the Viet Nam war. But he saw how young black men were being drafted and sent away to fight and die while lots and lots of young white men got draft deferments because they could afford to go to college. He didn't think that was fair. So he accepted a commission in the army and was trained on helicopters and went to serve. The rest you know," she said quietly.

"It was a very hard time for the whole country, Tyler," my grandfather said. "It was confusing. I opposed the war. So did your mother. Yet we loved your father. Both of us. An intelligent, sensitive white man who could have avoided serving because he came from a privileged background. A background of which he was ashamed." My grandfather turned to me. "Tyler, your father despised the way his family had become wealthy."

"We talked about it long into the night for weeks, Tyler, before he decided he had to go," my mother said, her voice strained by the tension and the pain. "I tried to get him to see that he wasn't just trying to serve his country, which I could understand. He was trying to atone for his family's sins. Which he finally admitted was true." She hesitated. "Those were his words, Tyler, not mine. Atone. When he said that, I told him it was futile. That he could never undo what his family was. But he said he had to try."

I sat silent. What did all of this mean?

"Your Raymond grandparents have sent $1000 to you for every one of your birthdays and every Christmas. I told them years ago, after your father died, that I didn't want the money. But they sent it anyway. So your grandfather and I have put it in a savings account. It will be yours when you start college next fall. That's the way we set it up."

I was stunned. $1000 twice a year for how long? For sixteen years? Good grief. That was . . . what? $32,000? I didn't know what to say.

"Why didn't you use the money to raise me?" I asked my mother. "That would have made your life easier, wouldn't it? I wouldn't have cared," I said.

"Because it isn't our money, Tyler. It's yours," my grandfather said.

I sat dumbfounded. What was I supposed to think now? I had money in the bank. I had a rich family that my father had rejected. I had grandparents I did not know and an uncle I did not know and an aunt who had died. I turned to my mother. Then I turned to my grandfather. "What about my aunt? What about . . . what was her name? Jessica? You said she died. How did she die?"

My grandfather looked at me. I had never seen his eyes like that before. I had never seen him in such pain. "In South Africa," he said. "She went there with a group of teachers. She was teaching in a rural community. A black township. The white Afrikaaner government found her. Storm troopers. Soldiers. She was teaching children to read. They killed her, along with the other young women."

"My God," I said.

"They denied it, of course. They said blacks had killed the women. But the blacks had loved them. They were white women and black women. All from America. Who just wanted to teach," my grandfather said. "I've given lectures about them. About her. I've just never told you who she was. That she was your aunt."

I looked out of the window.

"Ruth Ann knows," my grandfather said. "I don't think she's ever said anything to Clementine, but she wondered about your name. About the name Raymond. She said she read an article about your Aunt Jessica in the *New York Times* years ago. She said she thought she remembered that Jessica had a brother named Robert Raymond. She asked me about it when we were in Edinburgh. I told her she was right. That Jessica Raymond was your aunt."

I sat without speaking for some time. "I don't know what to say," I finally said.

"I know Ruth Ann loves you, Tyler, for who you are," my mother said. "For how you treat Clementine. I know she trusts you. And she knows quite a bit about the Raymond family. About the Virginia Raymonds. And about your father. And your aunt. And that means a great deal to her. That Jessica Raymond was your aunt."

I sat silent. My grandfather reached out and touched my hand.

"But what do I do about Miami?" I said. "What do you want me to do?" I said to my mother.

"I can't answer that, Tyler. They're your grandparents. No matter what, they're your father's parents. And they want to see you," she said. "What you choose to do will have to be your decision."

"It's about money, isn't it?" I said. I turned to my grandfather. "But do I want their money?" I said. "Apparently my father didn't want it. Am I suppose to want it?"

"I'm like your mother, Tyler. I can't answer that for you. Apparently, it's your money whether you want it or not. It sounds like all they want to do is tell you how much."

"But God, Grandpa, after all of these years," I said.

"That's not entirely their fault," my mother said. "Yes, I know they didn't want your father to marry me. And yes, I know your father turned them away after they acted so horribly. But over the years, I've also kept them away. I didn't think you needed to know about any of this until you were old enough to sort it out."

I understood what she was saying. My life with her and with my grandfather had been good. Was very good. Could I have managed to sort out the Virginia Raymonds if

I'd known about them when I was ten or fifteen or sixteen? I don't know. To this day, I don't know. Which didn't matter, finally, because now was when I was learning about them. And now was when they wanted to see me.

"If I go, I don't want to go alone," I said.

My mother looked at my grandfather.

"I don't think it would be good if your mother went, Tyler," he said. "And I know they wouldn't want to see me." He hesitated. "Of course, one of us could drive with you and stay with you. But neither of us should be with you when you see them."

I was silent. Then I said, "I don't want to go alone."

"Who do you want to go with you, Tyler?" my grandfather said.

"Clementine," I said. "I went with her. I won't go if she can't go with me."

My mother hesitated.

"I think Ruth Ann will understand," my grandfather said.

"I won't go without Clementine," I said quickly, my voice threatening to break. "I won't," I said. "I can't."

"I know," my grandfather said. "I understand. I understand."

Which was why, eight days later, on a Saturday, I drove to Clementine's house at 5 A.M., and picked her up, and we drove south on Interstate 75 to highway 41, known affectionately in Florida as Alligator Alley, to Miami, arriving at the Miami Beach Hilton at 5 P.M., where we checked into a room overlooking the water that had been reserved for me by my grandparents. Then we changed our clothes and sat from 6 P.M. to 7 P.M., which was when I was supposed to appear in the dining room where Preston II and Mildred Raymond and their Miami attorney would be waiting for me. What they didn't know, of course, was that I was bringing a guest.

Before I tell what happened at the conversation I had with my paternal grandparents when I met them and their Miami-based lawyer in the dining room of the Miami Beach Hilton Hotel, I need to tell you about two conversations that took place earlier. I was not a part of either of the two conversations. I didn't even know the first had taken place until after Clementine and I were driving home from Miami Beach after she and I met Preston II and Mildred Raymond. I knew the second conversation had taken place just days before Clementine and I drove to Miami, but I didn't know what had been said.

The first conversation was between Clementine and Ruth Ann. It took place just after she and I had returned from New York City the previous fall. Clementine told her mother what had happened when we'd stayed with the Winters. She explained about the misunderstanding and about the bedroom and about how I had slept on the floor the first two nights and how Clementine had slept on the couch next to me because the sirens had made her afraid. She explained how I had reacted to seeing "Miss Saigon" and then how I had reacted to seeing Robert Motherwell's painting Spanish Elegy. Then she told her mother that the two of us had slept in the same bed but that we had not had sex.

From what Clementine told me, Ruth Ann had remained very calm. She said she not only appreciated knowing what had happened in New York but she respected the way both Clementine and I had responded to a very awkward situation. When she asked Clementine if she and I had ever had sex at any time before or since we went to New York, Clementine told her that we had not. She told her mother that we had discussed how we felt about each other, but that neither of us wanted to disappoint her or my mother or my grandfather. From what Clementine said, Ruth Ann was very moved by the respect we had shown each other and the three adults who cared so deeply about the two of us.

Clementine said she could see her mother's mind working. Because then Ruth Ann had said, "I'm not trying to change the way you two feel about each other, Clementine, or the way you have demonstrated your respect for each other. But I also know both of you are getting older. And I don't want either of you to ever find yourselves faced with a situation that could interfere with your plans."

Clementine said she asked her mother what she meant. Ruth Ann replied that she wanted Clementine to come with her to see her doctor. When Clementine protested that it sounded as if her mother did not believe her—that we hadn't had sexual intercourse—Ruth Ann said no, that wasn't the case. "I want you to go on the pill," she said.

Clementine said she had been shocked.

"I'm not telling you to have sex with Tyler. I'm just trying to be realistic, Clementine."

Clementine told me that at first she had objected. But then her mother had said, "Listen, Clementine, I know you are a good girl. And you know how much I respect Tyler. But one of these days, you two are going to want to express yourselves sexually. It happens. I don't know when it will happen, but it will happen."

Clementine said she was sad for a while after the conversation. But she also knew her mother was right. That it would happen one day when the two of us knew it should happen. So she went with her mother to a doctor and accepted a prescription for birth control pills.

I was stunned when Clementine told me about the conversation. I didn't know if I should feel embarrassed that my sexual restraint or my possible sexual conduct had been discussed by Clementine and her mother. "How am I going to look your mother in the eye, Clementine? How can I know what she's thinking from now on?"

"Tyler, you just go on with your life. We just go on with our lives. That's all," Clementine said.

The second conversation took place before Clementine and I drove to Miami. My grandfather met Ruth Ann on the University of South Florida campus for lunch. He explained the situation with the Raymonds to her. Ruth Ann said she had been expecting that someday something like this might happen. When my grandfather told Ruth Ann that I had said I would not go to Miami without Clementine, at first Ruth Ann had looked apprehensive. "I don't know if I want to put Clementine in that kind of situation," she said.

"I know," my grandfather said. "I know it's a lot to ask. But remember, Tyler went with Clementine to meet her father. That was hard for him. Not because it hurt him, but because he saw how much it hurt Clementine."

From what my grandfather told me, Ruth Ann had looked concerned but she also looked as if she understood.

"Ruth Ann, Tyler and I talked about Clementine after they got back from Disney that time. I asked him if it was hard for him. He said that he'd walk on hot rocks for Clementine," my grandfather said. "And I don't think that was a metaphor, Ruth Ann. And I don't think it was hyperbole. I think he really meant it."

Ruth Ann said she agreed. "He probably would walk on hot rocks to protect Clementine." Then she said, "I won't even ask about the hotel, Edward, or where they're going to stay."

"Good," my grandfather said. "Because neither Elizabeth nor I are going to ask either."

So there we were, sitting on the edge of the bed in a room overlooking the ocean at the Miami Beach Hilton hotel, with Clementine wearing a back blazer jacket and gray slacks and a gray silk blouse and loafers that I know she bought especially for the trip, and with me sitting in my blue blazer and gray slacks and a blue oxford cloth dress shirt and a very subtle silk tie that my grandfather had helped me pick out and black loafers holding hands and looking at the clock and counting down the minutes until it was time for us to leave the room and take the elevator to the lobby and then walk to the dining room where Preston and Mildred Raymond and their Miami lawyer would be waiting. And right then I think for a moment that I knew exactly what the hero of Charles Dickens's novel *The Tale of Two Cities* must have felt like when he accompanied a young, perfectly nice and perfectly innocent young woman to the guillotine, except as I recall he had wanted to make the sacrifice, while I would have preferred to be almost anywhere else in the world with Clementine except right there waiting and waiting and waiting until finally—oh God, spare us—it was exactly 7 P.M. So we stood up at the same time and walked to the door, which I opened, and we went out into the hallway and walked to the elevator and pressed the down button and waited until the elevator stopped at our floor. Then we stepped in and started what I feared was going to be a descent very much akin to the poet- narrator's descent into Dante's infernal inferno. And as fate would have it, I was more right than I could have foreseen even in my most dreaded nightmare.

20

When the elevator arrived in the lobby, we stepped out and looked for the dining room. Seeing it across the room, we walked through the double doors where we were met by a man in a tuxedo who asked us if we had a reservation. I said we were with the Raymond party, which caused him to smile one of those, "Oh-I-am-so-smart-and-know-so-many-important-people" kind of smiles that you sometimes get from people in his position. Then we were ushered across a room that was so heavily carpeted that it didn't feel as if we were walking on solid ground, although that may have had as much to do with my emotions as it did the decor.

Then I saw them: three people sitting at a table set for four. I recognized Preston Raymond immediately because he looked like an older version of the photos of my father on display in my home. He was golf course tanned, had a full head of gray wavy hair, and was dressed and groomed perfectly in an obviously very expensive, custom tailored blue blazer, a white oxford cloth shirt, and one of those regimental stripped school ties, and light gray slacks. He was speaking to a man I assumed was Mitchell Burrows, the family's Miami lawyer, who was slightly balding but just as well dressed in a dark gray suit and white dress shirt and tie. Both of them were ignoring the woman sitting with them, my grandmother, Mildred, whose tan looked artificial. She was not as attractive a woman as her husband was handsome, an unfortunate fact both her expensive dress and jewelry were supposed to disguise. When Preston and Mitchell saw us approaching, both of them stood, although I could see on their faces that Clementine was a surprise.

Coming around the table to greet us, Preston extended a hand, which I accepted. "You must be Tyler. I would know you anywhere, young man," he said.

"Yes, sir. I am. It's an honor to meet you, sir."

"And for me as well, Tyler," he said.

Then I stepped back so Clementine could step next to me. "This is my friend, Clementine Brown. She's been kind enough to come with me from Tampa."

Without missing a grace beat, Preston extended his hand to Clementine, who accepted it with equal poise.

Then Mildred stood and came around the table. "Tyler, I've so looked forward to meeting you," she said, leaning toward me and kissing my cheek, although I don't think her lips actually touched my skin.

I then introduced Clementine to her. And while she did not and would not ever have said the words, I could almost see them burning on her lips: "Oh, my, are you a *negress*, young woman?" and "Are you and my grandson really friends?" Of course, she would rather have died than have said such crude things. She would express her sentiments in more subtle ways.

Then Preston introduced both of us to Mitchell Burrows, who extended a hand across the table to me but who did not do so to Clementine even if his "Pleased to meet you, miss" directed at her was as perfunctory as his greeting was to me.

Of course, as you would expect, Preston realized immediately that the table was set for four but now there were five of us. So he signaled the waiter, who quickly brought a fifth chair. Then we all sat, with me pulling out the chair for Clementine. I moved to Mildred and did the same, which caused her to say how I was certainly a well trained gentleman. That was followed by five minutes of meaningless conversation about the weather in Miami and how was our drive from Tampa. After that, Preston and Mitchell began moving in on more serious and what was for Preston quite obviously uncomfortable personal matters.

First, Preston asked after my mother's health, which I said was fine. He asked if she was still teaching, to which I said yes, she was. Then he asked if Edward Thomas was still alive. I said he was, and that my mother and I lived with him in Tampa as we had lived with him in Cleveland before he retired from teaching. Preston then turned to Mitchell Burrows and said that my grandfather on my mother's side was Edward Thomas, the historian, although from his reaction I could tell Mr. Burrows had never heard of him even if it was obvious from the way Preston said *the noted historian* that he meant noted *left winger* and noted *socialist* historian, of whom he certainly disapproved.

In an effort to take part in the conversation, Mildred turned to Clementine and said, "I trust you will allow me to say that you are a very pretty young woman."

Clementine smiled her very best smile and thanked Mildred for saying so.

Then Mildred went ahead and asked the question I knew she wanted to ask: "Are you, perhaps, Puerto Rican or Cuban?"

Clementine must have known the question was coming, because without missing a beat she sat up straight and said, "No, ma'am. I'm not, although I do speak Spanish rather well."

That stopped Mildred for a moment, but only for a moment. "I only asked because you have a lovely complexion."

Clementine said, "My father's father is a black American, ma'am. My father's mother is white."

Mildred smiled one of those, oh-God-that's-what-I-was-afraid-of smiles. But before she could say whatever she was going to say, Clementine went on. "My father's family owns grocery stores in several states, although I have no contact with them."

A deadly silence followed. I could hear myself thinking, "You tell her, Clementine."

Preston smiled and dropped the big question on the table: "And what about your mother's family?" which both of us knew was a question about race not about profession.

One step ahead of both of the Raymonds, Clementine turned to Preston and said very politely, "My mother's parents are American blacks, sir. Both of them. My mother's father is a plumber. In Newark, New Jersey. He owns his own shop." Then Clementine said that her parents were divorced, that she lived with her mother, that her mother was a history professor at the University of South Florida.

Mildred replied that was very nice, as if she had not expected Clementine to have an educated mother, even if to her teaching history at a regional state university in Florida was not to her a particularly impressive achievement.

Fortunately, the waiter then appeared with menus. He asked what people might wish to drink. Preston and Mildred and Mitchell Burrows all ordered martinis. Clementine and I said we would prefer water. When the waiter asked if we might like glasses of wine, I said yes. Without asking for identifications, he said he had a very nice house white that we might enjoy. We both accepted his suggestion.

As the five of us sat studying the menu, listening politely as Preston made suggestions because he and Mildred stayed in this particular hotel quite often, Clementine leaned over to me and asked a question about something on the menu, which to this day I don't remember but for which I was thankful she did because it gave me an excuse to lean close to her, something I very much wanted to do at that exact moment.

Preston then took charge of ordering salads, and each of us ordered our main courses. With that accomplished, Preston turned to me and asked if I had made up my mind about a university in the fall. "Yes, sir," I said. "I very much want to attend the University of Georgia."

I could tell from both his and Mildred's expressions that they found that a great disappointment. "Are there any schools further north in which you might be interested?" he asked.

"No, sir. I'm hoping to play football at Georgia for Coach Vince Dooley," I said, quickly adding, "I want to study history, sir. My grandfather knows a number of the professors by reputation. He says he believes it is a strong department."

"So you wish to become an academic?" Preston said.

"I do, sir. Very much. Like my father and mother. I would like to teach history at a college like my grandfather," I said.

I could tell that at that point he wanted to say something about more selective schools, but before he could, and not to be out done, Mildred turned to Clementine and asked if she had plans to go to a university. Clementine said she did. "I have applied to Georgia Tech, ma'am," she said. "I want to study biology then go to medical school. I'm very interested in pediatrics."

Mildred nodded. "That's very interesting," she said, "very commendable," as if she admired in her own patronizing way the fact that by going to medical school Clementine might be able to improve the general condition of her race. Fortunately for everyone in the dining room, before I could stand up and scream at her, "You bitch! You insufferable bitch!" which I could almost hear myself doing, Mildred went on and said, "Of course, medical schools are very difficult, very challenging," adding, "I have a brother who's a doctor in Richmond. He says medical school is as much an endurance contest as anything else."

That was my opening. So I very proudly pointed out that Clementine had earned all A's at our high school and that her SAT score was 1587, which was actually higher than mine. As I watched their faces, I am certain both Preston and Mildred realized what I was doing, which took a bit of the victory out of my statement. But I am also just as certain that they did not appreciate my defense of Clementine, which I decided made it a draw.

Mildred asked if Clementine and I had been friends for very long. "Since we were in ninth grade," Clementine said. "I asked Tyler to be my lab partner in biology."

"We've dated ever since," I said, directing my comment to Mildred without saying her name, because at that point I didn't know what to call either her or Preston except ma'am and sir. I mean, I certainly wasn't going to call them grandmother and grandfather.

Then I went on and said, "Clementine's mother and my mother have become great friends," trying to make certain they understood that this was not just a matter of two high school students having crushes on each other.

The waiter appeared with our drinks. Preston was clearly uncomfortable with my comments. To change the subject he proposed a toast: "To your educational futures," he said, looking at both of us, without any particular evidence of enthusiasm.

Then it was Mitchell Burrows's turn. "Tyler, I don't know if you are aware, but the Raymonds created a trust fund for you when you were just a child."

I said that I knew a trust fund existed but that I did not know any of the details.

"Well, first let me say there are no strings attached, which is very generous of them, as most trust funds under circumstances like this come with a number of conditions."

I waited.

"The point is, Mr. and Mrs. Raymond want very much to provide for your education. They have provided funds to insure that you be able to study whatever you wish wherever you wish.

"That's very kind of them," I said, turning to Preston and then Mildred. "I don't know what else to say. I didn't know about the trust fund until my mother explained that it had been established, although she said she didn't know any of the details."

Mr. Burrows smiled. "The only proviso is that the money is yours at nineteen as long as you are in school. Whatever is not used for that purpose becomes yours at thirty. But from nineteen on, if you are attending a college or university, you will receive money at the beginning of each academic year."

"Yes, sir." I waited for a moment. "How is that arranged?" I asked.

"The Raymonds have arranged with the Bank of America to handle the details. They have documents for you to take to whatever branch you wish to use. The money will come to you when you present verification of your registration to whoever at the bank is handling your account."

"We just want to be sure that you can afford a quality education, Tyler," Preston said. "Are you sure that you want to attend the University of Georgia? With the funds available to you, you could afford to go anywhere you wish."

"I appreciate your generosity, sir. And I know that I'm academically qualified to go to other schools. So is Clementine. The reason I want to attend the University of Georgia, beyond the academics, is that during my junior year, when I was injured very seriously, it was a letter from Coach Dooley that encouraged me to not become discouraged." Then I knew I had come to my moment. "Apparently, Coach Dooley knew my father. I think he competed against him. Against your son. He spoke of him in the letter as a man he admired both on and off the football field."

The subject of my father made both Preston and Mildred terribly uncomfortable. I could see that. But I wasn't going to back down. "As I've grown up, especially in the last four or five years, I've learned a great deal about what my father believed. I have come to admire him very much," I said.

Our food came. But I could see Preston was not finished with the subject. As we began to eat, he turned to me and said, "I don't know if you realize it, Tyler, but your father, as fine a man as he was, and as much as we loved him, made a number of decisions with which we disagreed very strongly."

"I understand that's the case, sir. But I can't address those disagreements. It would not be fair. They were between you two and him. I can only try to understand what I have been told he believed. And I can only be responsible for what I have come to believe. I am pleased that they are very close to being the same things."

Mildred was not pleased. "Your father made decisions that changed his life in ways that we believe were unfortunate, Tyler."

Yeah, right, I thought, like marrying my mother and fathering me. Damn it, how was I supposed to respond to that? Was I supposed to apologize because my parents fell in love? Did they expect me to apologize for being born? I could feel Clementine next to me. I could feel her warmth. I took a bite of food and waited until I knew how to respond. After several moments of very awkward silence, I turned to her and said, "Ma'am, I do not wish to be disrespectful in any way. And I certainly don't know what decisions he made that caused you to be unhappy. I only know what I have learned about him," I said.

"From your mother," Preston said, almost interrupting me.

I hesitated. Clementine put a hand on my left leg for a moment. Then she took it away.

"Yes, sir," I said very slowly, very politely. "From my mother. And from my grandfather."

"Yes. Edward Thomas," Preston replied, his voice edged with his remarkably controlled distain.

"I am very close to my grandfather, sir," I said. "Much of what I believe about life I have learned from his example."

"Which may not be an entirely good thing, Tyler," Mildred said curtly.

I took a deep breath. I looked at Clementine for a moment. Then I turned to Mildred. "Ma'am, I'm not sure my relationship with the two of you will be helped by discussing either my mother or my grandfather. I came here at your request to discuss a trust fund that you have very generously set up for me. I promise you I will use those funds for their intended purpose. But what I believe about the life I want to lead and what I believe about the people who are important in my life is very personal."

"As it should be, Tyler," Mitchell Burrows said quickly, obviously tying to quell the rising tension.

"And we don't mean to interfere in any way," Preston said just as quickly.

I nodded. "Thank you, sir. And I do appreciate your support. Very much. But if this conversation is going focus on my grandfather, Edward Thomas, in some negative way, then I cannot stay. I would rather not have the trust fund, if that's the case."

A very long and difficult silence hung over the table. I was amazed I had said such a thing. But I couldn't just sit there and let either my mother or my grandfather be insulted. I was going to go to the University of Georgia. I had enough money to do so. I was confident I'd get some kind of academic or athletic scholarship. I didn't need the Raymonds' money.

It was Mr. Burrows's turn to try to cover for them. "Tyler, I believe I speak for the Raymonds when I say that their relationship with their son and their own personal opinion of Edward Thomas, whom I've never met, of course, has nothing to do with their desire to be of service to you."

I turned to Mr. Burrows, but Preston spoke before I could reply.

"And we want you to know that from everything we know about you, Tyler, we are very proud of the fine young man you've become," Preston said quickly.

Was I really supposed to believe that?

"Tyler, you are still our grandson. We care about you a great deal," Mildred added, reaching over and placing a hand on mine, a gesture which I found very insincere and unsettling.

"All we wish to do at this dinner is give you a number of important documents," Mr. Burrows said, "which the Raymonds will sign in your presence. The documents instruct the Bank of America to begin preparing your trust fund for next fall when you enter the university you finally choose."

"Thank you, sir," I said very politely.

With that, Mr. Burrows reached down next to his seat, where he apparently had a briefcase, and brought four pieces of paper up onto the table. He moved aside his plate of food and spread them out. "The Raymonds must sign all four documents," he said. "You must do the same. I will witness their and your signatures. Do you mind if we do that in the presence of your friend?" he said, turning to Clementine.

"No, sir. That's fine. There isn't anything I don't share with Clementine," I said.

I saw Mildred wince, which made me very glad.

"Just get on with it," Preston said.

With that, Mr. Burrows slid all four sheets of paper to Preston, who signed them. Then Mr. Burrows gave the papers to Mildred, who signed them. Then he gave all four to me. "You need to sign on the line above your name, Tyler."

I looked at the papers. I read them. The annual figure they had provided for my education was $20,000. I was stunned. "Is this right, sir," I said, turning to Preston. "Am I reading this correctly? I am to receive this amount each year?" I said, turning the top paper toward Preston, who leaned over and looked at the figure.

"Yes, Tyler, you will receive that amount each year," Preston said.

"Sir, I don't know what to say. You and your wife are very generous." Then I turned the paper toward Clementine so she could see.

"Good God," she said in a whisper, looking at me.

"We just want to insure that you have every opportunity to make a good life, Tyler," Preston said. "You are our only grandchild. Our oldest son has never married. It does not appear that he ever will."

"Yes, sir," I said, noting to myself that at no point in the conversation had they mentioned my Aunt Jessica. For a moment I wondered if they knew I knew about her. Then I realized they couldn't have known that I knew and probably wouldn't have cared if they had.

Mildred looked at Clementine. "Do you plan to qualify for scholarships of some kind?" she said to Clementine.

I could not believe Mildred said that. "She's been offered a track scholarship to Georgia Tech, ma'am," I said before Clementine could reply, bristling at the implication. "And she's a National Merit Scholarship Finalist. She can write her own ticket."

Mildred was silent for a moment. Recovering, she said, "That's very nice. I wish you the best of luck."

I had to get out of there. But it was too soon. We had to finish our meals. But damn it, I wanted to get away from these people who say everything they need to say or want to say without any regard for what it might do to other people.

I turned to Clementine, who was looking at me. Then she turned back to her meal and began to eat again. If she wasn't going to give them any satisfaction by displaying her offense, I had to do the same. No one spoke. I signed the four pages of paper. Then I handed all four back to Mr. Burrows, who signed all of them.

"I have copies of all four pages for you to take with you, Tyler," Mr. Burrows said, producing four more sheets. "You will receive a letter from me within a week detailing what your bank will do for you."

Preston looked at the signed copies I was to take with me, which he then put into an envelope that Mr. Burrows had taken from his suit coat pocket. Then we ate in silence for five minutes. When the waiter approached to see if we wanted any desert, both Clementine and I said we did not. The Raymonds each ordered a piece of cake. Mr. Burrows wanted nothing more.

After a moment, Mildred Raymond turned to me and said, "I hope that your room is satisfactory."

"Yes, ma'am. It's very nice. We can see the ocean."

"Ah," she said, as if it just then occurred to her that because they had only invited me and therefore only provided one room, but I had brought Clementine, that we would be staying together.

"It has a lovely view," Clementine said.

"Good," Preston said, glancing at his wife as he did.

I could not resist any longer. "Clementine's mother and my mother know we are traveling together," I said.

"Ah," Preston said, unsure of what to make of my remark and even more unsure of what to say in response.

Mildred remained silent. I could see by his expression that Mr. Burrows was smart enough to know he didn't want to get involved.

Then the meal was over. So with as much good grace as I could manage, I thanked the Raymonds for inviting us to Miami. I thanked them for the lovely hotel room. I thanked them again for their remarkable generosity. They, of course, responded by telling me it was a pleasure meeting me and that I was certainly a handsome and intelligent young man and that they were certain my education would serve me well. With that, I stood and helped Clementine with her chair. Preston came around the table and shook my hand.

"You come from a long line of noble people, Tyler," Preston said. "I don't want you to ever forget that."

"A very long line of people, to be sure, sir," I said very deliberately.

At that point, Preston looked at me in a way that said very clearly, "Well, we understand each other now, don't we, boy? We don't like each other, but we certainly understand each other. Now take the money and get out of our lives." However, I also knew that men like Preston Raymond are not going to be undone by me or by the moment. Ever the gentlemen, he turned to Clementine and shook her hand and told her he was pleased to have had the opportunity to meet her, which I had to admit I think was remarkably constrained behavior given what he must have really been feeling.

Then I turned to Mildred. She had traces of tears in her eyes. "You look very much like your father, Tyler," she said.

"Yes, ma'am. I've been told that before. I appreciate the compliment," I said.

Then Mildred came to me and put her arms around my shoulders and pressed her face against mine. This time her lips did kiss my cheek. When I started to step back, I could feel her holding on for a moment longer. When she released her grip on me, she turned to Clementine. "I trust you will find medical school to your liking," she said.

"Thank you," Clementine said. "I trust I will."

Then I turned to Mr. Burrows. "It was a pleasure meeting you, sir," I said. Clementine said the same.

He said it had been a pleasure for him to meet the two of us as well.

Then I stepped back and opened a path for Clementine, and we left the three of them standing at the table and crossed the dining room and went out into the lobby and walked without saying anything to each other to the elevator, where we pressed the up button. As we waited, Clementine took my right arm, but she did not say anything.

In a moment, the elevator doors opened, and we got in. I pressed the button for the eighth floor, and we began ascending. Clementine moved next to me and took my hand in hers. When the elevator arrived at our floor, we got off and walked towards our room, but when we got there, I did not stop. Instead, I walked to the end of the hall to a window that looked south from which I could see both the beach and the city. Clementine followed. I could feel her standing next to me. After a moment, from deep in my anger, in my hurt, I found words that came in a whisper: "Those self righteous, mean minded . . . ." I choked on my words.

Clementine touched my tears.

"My God, Clementine," I whispered. "Do you understand? Do you understand? My father . . . . My good father, Clementine. My aunt. Who they do not even acknowledge. They died for their parents' sins." My body shook for a moment. Then I was silent. Hard and silent.

Clementine was silent for a moment. I could feel her turning to look at me. "Tyler, you can't say that," she whispered. "I know you want to. I know you think you need to . . . ." Her voice hung in the air.

"How they died," I said, barely able to speak. "Where and why they died," I said, my voice a painful whisper. "It matters. Damn it, it matters, Clementine."

Clementine breathed deeply and waited. Still standing next to me, she pressed her body against mine. "They died, Tyler. People die. They died," she said. After which we stood that way for some time. I had no more words. I remembered standing with Clementine at the rest stop on Interstate 4 after she had met her father and his new wife and their three sons. I had wanted to take care of her. To take away the pain. Now here we were in Miami standing at the end of the hallway on the eighth floor of the Miami Beach Hilton Hotel, and she was holding onto me. What in God's name were we doing to each other? What in God's name were we doing to each other?

Clementine took my hand and slowly but deliberately turned me back towards the hallway. Then we walked back to our room where I unlocked the door, and we went in. Clementine found the light on the wall and turned it on. I was inside the room, but just barely. She turned and looked at me. Weeks later she would tell me that she knew I was more angry and more hurt than she thought possible because my face suddenly showed no expression whatsoever. Meeting the Raymonds had buried itself so deeply in me that she was afraid it would never surface, that my anger and grief would never be resolved. So in the moment, as I stood rigid just inside the room, she said she knew she could not change that. She said all she knew for sure was how much she loved me, which is why, in the silence, she came to me and reached up and pressed her lips against mine. She said she wanted to take the pain away. To take it into her own body. To guard me. And that is how we stood for some time, with her in my arms and me in her arms. Then, without speaking, she turned out the light. Then very slowly she undressed until she stood naked in front of me. Then she came to me and slowly removed all of my clothes until I stood naked in front of her. Then she led me into the bathroom and turned on the shower. After a moment, she stepped into the shower and, reaching back and taking my hand, brought me in with her.

There were tears in my eyes. I could see that. Anger and love and fear and desire. And she washed my body with soap and water, and then I washed her body with soap and water. Then she turned to me and kissed me as the water rinsed away every thing that had ever conspired against us loving one another.

When she turned off the shower and stepped out onto the bath mat, I followed. Then she toweled me dry, and I toweled her dry. When we finished, she led me back into the bedroom where she went to the bed and drew back the covers and gestured I should get in and lie down. Then she got into the bed and lay down next to me. For a moment, neither of us moved. Neither of us spoke. "It must be you, Tyler," she whispered.

"It must be you, Clementine," I whispered in return.

She rolled over on her side and put her arms around me. And we lay like that for some time until she lifted her body up and lay on top of my body, her face against mine, her breasts pressing against my chest, her legs stretching along my legs. Then she rose up on her elbows and looked at me. Then she moved, and I knew. And we made love for the first time. And it was good. We were patient with one another, cautious with one another, gentle with one another. And it was tender and good. It was tender and very, very good. And when she lay next to me afterwards, she whispered that it was more than she ever thought it could be. And I whispered that it was more than I ever thought it could be. And she said she loved me. And she said she would always take care of me. And I said I loved her and that I would always take care of her. And I knew that Clementine Camille would be the only woman I would ever hold in my arms, the only woman I would ever caress, the only woman I would ever want to love. Then we slept until it was morning.

21

The next morning we awoke early. When I rolled over, there she was lying wide awake watching me. "So now we are lovers, Tyler," Clementine said.

"Now we are lovers," I said.

"Which is more than just being in love, isn't it?" she said.

I looked at her for a very long time. I touched her face. Traced her nose with my fingers. Traced the curve of her upper lip. Touched her cheeks and forehead. Then I smiled from as deep a place in my happiness as I had ever felt. "Yes. It is much more than just being in love," I whispered.

She got up out of bed and went into the bathroom. I heard what sounded like her brushing her teeth and using the toilet. Then she came back and got back into bed. "Your turn," she said.

I got up and took my turn. When I came back to bed, she was lying with the sheets thrown back. "I love you, Tyler Thomas Raymond," she said, smiling.

I said I loved her. Then she took me in her arms, and we were lovers for the second time.

Afterwards, we lay next to each other for some time without speaking. Then I said, "We need to get ready and check out and leave."

"Do you want to eat here before we start driving?"

"No. I don't want to run into the Raymonds in the lobby. I don't ever want to see them again," I said. "Ever."

Clementine did not reply. Instead, she got up and went into the bathroom and showered. While she did, I got up and packed my clothes. When she finished, I went into the bathroom and shaved and showered and then came out and got dressed. By the time I was ready, Clementine was packed and dressed. So we left, went down to the lobby, checked out of the room the Raymonds had paid for in advance for me. The manager on duty said nothing about my having a second person in the room, so either he did not care or the Raymonds had adjusted their payment to the hotel. I didn't inquire as to which it was because I didn't care. I just wanted us to leave.

Then we walked to the parking lot and got into our car and left. We crossed over the causeway between Miami Beach and the mainland. We stopped to eat at a Burger King before we left the Miami area. Twenty minutes more and we were back on the highway leading west toward the Gulf coast.

22

The day was sunny. Very little wind blew across the highway. So the drive was without incident, which does not mean we did not talk. An hour into the journey Clementine summarized the conversation she'd had with her mother the previous fall about Clementine going on birth control pills. I have to confess that I was surprised at what had taken place. At the same time, given what had just happened in Clementine's and my relationship, I felt obliged to say, "We aren't going to sneak around so we can be together, Clementine. I won't do that to you."

"I understand," Clementine said. "I don't want to sneak around either."

"Should we get married after we graduate?" I said.

"Before we start college?"

"Yes. I have found out that I have $36,000 of Raymond money in the bank right now. Birthday and Christmas gifts. My mother never said anything until after the letter came inviting me to come to Miami. She says it's mine."

"Really?" Clementine said. "They're just full of surprises."

"Apparently. And I'll have the trust fund when the fall begins."

Clementine was quiet for some time. "We'll be at different schools. Both of us have plans," she said.

"I know."

She was quiet again. "Do you think we're ready to get married?" she asked.

I waited a long time to answer. Then I said, "I want to marry you, Clementine, because I want to spend my life with you. But no, I don't think we're ready for that yet. I don't think our mothers are ready for that either."

Clementine smiled.

"But I can't imagine a life without you," I said.

"And I can't imagine a life without you, Tyler," Clementine said. "But I think you're right. The time isn't right for us yet. And I don't think our mothers would be happy. And I know both of us want them to be happy," she said.

It was my turn to be quiet for a while. "They will be," I said after a few moments. "When the time is right. You know they will be."

Clementine said she agreed. So it was settled. We both would know when the time came. We didn't even question that notion. We both would know. And we did. One day, we both knew. But that was several years in the future. And there is much more story to tell between our ride back to Tampa after my painfully conflicted meeting with the Raymonds and their attorney and when, after yet another extraordinary challenge, we knew it was time to marry. But that is getting ahead of my story.

The trip back to Tampa was uneventful. The traffic was light. We took turns driving. We listened to the radio. When we arrived at Clementine's house, we found a note saying her mother was eating dinner at my house with my mother and grandfather.

When we arrived, the three of them greeted us with a mixture of happiness that we were safely back and an obvious curiosity about what had happened. As much as I did not want to say anything about the Raymonds as individuals, my mother's obvious discomfort that I had felt obligated to drive to Miami Beach to meet them meant I owed her as much explanation as I could manage. Fortunately, Clementine was there to help. So I could assure my mother and my grandmother that the Raymonds did not expect and had not earned any of my loyalty and that I had no plans to see them again.

When I explained how I had resented their distain for both my mother and for my grandfather, Clementine very quickly said that I had stood my ground by making it clear I would not stay if they pursued that sort of conversation. I am sure that knowing the Raymonds still resented her made my mother uncomfortable, but the fact I had proven myself the faithful son helped salve the hurt to some degree.

When my mother then wanted to know what the trust fund was going to mean, I showed them the papers that authorized the Bank of America to begin transferring funds into my account as soon as I enrolled in college. All three of them were stunned by the amount. "What it tells me," I said, "is that they must feel a burden of guilt for how they treated both my father and you, mother."

My grandfather wasn't so sure that the Raymonds had ever felt guilt over anything that the rest of us might believe they had done wrong. "I'm not convinced that the Preston Raymonds of the world ever think they've done anything for which they should be sorry."

I told my grandfather that I agreed. But in the end, I didn't care about them. I knew who mattered to me in my life. "You're all in this room. All of you," I said, gesturing toward both my mother and grandfather and Clementine and Ruth Ann. "That's all I care about. So yes, I'll take their money. And I'll go to the University of Georgia, I hope, and then to graduate school if I'm smart enough, and then become a professor if I can. And I'll end up teaching the things that you and Ruth Ann teach, Grandpa, and I think by the time Clementine and I left, they knew that was the case. So they're probably just as happy to have me out of their life as I am to be gone."

Ruth Ann, of course, was taken aback by the whole situation. Clementine explained that the Raymonds had been very polite to her. "But it was the kind of politeness that you've seen before, mother. They were appalled that Tyler would bring someone like me. Once I got over the hurt, I realized that both Tyler and I were really in control. We didn't need to be there. But I think Tyler is right. They needed to see him at least once." Then she smiled. "But Tyler didn't play their game or play by their rules."

Ruth Ann said she was proud. Then she asked about where we stayed. Without missing a beat or hesitating in any way, Clementine said the Raymonds had arranged for a lovely room for Tyler overlooking the water. "So we stayed there."

I could feel Ruth Ann looking first at Clementine and then at me and wanting to ask the obvious question, but Clementine's tone of voice said that part of the conversation was over. When Clementine turned to my mother and grandfather and said, "You would have been very proud of Tyler. Both of you. He was not impolite. But he did not give any ground, either. When they said how their son had made decisions that had hurt them, Tyler said he would not discuss those matters. He said he only knew what he had learned about what his father believed, and that he had come to believe the same things."

My mother looked away for a moment. My grandfather nodded. "Professor Thomas," Clementine went on, her voice softening for a moment, "I think you should know that you are your grandson's hero, and no amount of trust fund money from people like the Raymonds is ever going to change that."

My grandfather did not know what to say. Then he looked at Clementine and said very slowly, "My dear Clementine, I trust my grandson will always treat you with the respect you so very much deserve."

"He always does, sir," Clementine replied. "You can count on that. He always does, sir."

With that my mother and Ruth Ann both got up and went into the kitchen where they prepared the chocolate cake that Ruth Ann had brought in honor of Clementine's and my safe return. With that we all celebrated, even if Clementine and I both thought the idea of a celebration was a bit overdone. After all, we'd driven to Miami Beach and met my paternal grandparents. What was obvious to me was that neither the Raymonds nor I wanted to cultivate a relationship. Perhaps that's what my mother really wanted to celebrate. That was Clementine's opinion at any rate. And after the two of us had a chance to discuss both my mother's restraint while I described Clementine's and my dinner with the Raymonds, as well as her obvious although unstated pleasure when Clementine described the way I had refused to let the conversation with the Raymonds become a litany of complaints about her or my grandfather, I concluded that Clementine was right. My mother was celebrating her relief that I was not going to turn her and my lives upside down with new loyalties.

What Ruth Ann was feeling when Clementine inferred but did not explain the change in her and my relationship was not as clear. Even Clementine could not put a label on it. Was Ruth Ann relieved that the waiting was over? I certainly could not answer that question. Yes, Clementine and I were now lovers. It was clear she understood that. Yet we had not come back to Tampa with any wild-eyed schemes that said we were going to disrupt the normal tenor of our lives or start conducting ourselves in some radically different way. We were still us. We still loved our mothers. My grandfather was still the chieftain of our small two family clan. We were going to go on with our plans to attend the universities of our choice if we were accepted. Clementine was convinced all of that must have gone through Ruth Ann's mind as she sat across the table from the two of us while we summarized our conversation with the Raymonds, and Clementine had matter-of-factly acknowledged that we had stayed in the same room. However, any lingering concerns my mother or Ruth Ann might have felt were never articulated, at least to us. Then, the next day, Monday, as fate would have it, Clementine's letter came from Georgia Tech, and mine came from the University of Georgia. We were both accepted. Equally important to the two of us, Clementine received a letter on Tuesday that invited her to come to Atlanta to visit with the Georgia Tech track coaches. On Wednesday, I received a letter inviting me to come to Athens to talk about playing football for the University of Georgia.

24

You may well have heard of parents who take their children out of school during their junior of senior years in high school so they can make what the families call "college trips." Well, you can bet that neither my mother nor Ruth Ann were about to approve that sort of nonsense. Yes, they were pleased we both had been accepted to our respective universities, and yes, they were pleased the track coaches wanted to meet with Clementine, and the football coaches wanted to meet with me. But if we were going to make trips to our universities, we would do so during spring vacation.

Needless to say, neither Clementine nor I were very happy about their reactions. Other students sometimes took off whole weeks from school to go visiting campuses. Both of us argued that we had done so well in school up to that point that two or three days away from classes would not damage our grades. We pointed out that we wanted to visit the campuses when classes were in session so we could see how the students lived day to day. We argued that it would help both of us if we were able to meet athletes who competed for Georgia Tech and the University of Georgia. And while both of our mothers agreed our arguments made sense, they still said no. And they said it in ways that told us the discussion was over. So both of us sat down and wrote letters in response to our invitations and made arrangements to visit in keeping with our mothers' dictates. Fortunately, the coaches understood our requests. Which was why, on the first Monday of our spring vacation, the Raymond-Thomas-Brown clan set out, all five of us in the van my grandfather rented for the occasion, because as he said, he wanted to see as much as did our mothers. To top it all off, as we left for Atlanta and Georgia Tech, our mothers, sitting as usual in the middle seat together, my mother turned around and looking straight at both of us, said in that mother- will-not-be-disobeyed tone of voice that both of them " . . . would be sitting in on both of our meetings."

When Clementine and I asked did that mean that my mother would be with Ruth Ann when Ruth Ann was with Clementine as she met with the admissions people and the track coaches at Georgia Tech, my mother said yes, she would. When I then asked if Ruth Ann would be with my mother when I met with the admissions people and the football coaches at the University of Georgia, they both said, in one simultaneous voice—as if they had rehearsed the moment—"You'd better believe it."

Clementine protested that she couldn't believe it. I protested that I couldn't believe it. They said we had better believe it. "If your grandfather is not about to let his two favorite students in the whole world go off and visit their universities without him in attendance, do you really think that your mothers aren't going to do the same?"

Clementine and I realized we were now in highly sensitive territory. That her mother wanted to go with her was understandable. That my mother wanted to with me was understandable. But that both of them were going to attend both meetings . . . like a pair of sisters bent on whatever they were bent on . . . that seemed to us to be beyond the pale.

As we sped toward Atlanta and our motel and the first stop, Clementine turned to me and mouthed the words, "What are we going to do?" I looked at her and mouthed the words, "I don't know." Then she whispered, "Well, you need to do something." To which I replied, "Why me?" in my own whisper. "Because I can't tell your mother that I don't want her to come with me." To which I whispered, "What do you want me to do? Challenge your mother?"

Clementine grimaced. Neither of us wanted to sail into those dangerous and uncharted waters. So we sat back and held hands and decided that maybe this family bond idea was more than it was cracked up to be. But as we drove on, listening to the two of them as they started talking about their own university experiences, some of which neither of us had ever heard before, we slowly but ever so surely realized that they were not trying to interfere; they were simply proud mothers, each of whom not only loved her child, she loved her friend's child as well. So we settled back and began to appreciate how fortunate we were, even if mixed into that sense of good fortune there was a small dose of what we feared might be some pending embarrassment. By the time we crossed the border from Florida into Georgia, their stories had both of us laughing so hard that we decided to give up any hope of resisting their plans and just enjoy the experience of seeing them have fun together.

25

So there we were that first morning, an odd looking troop walking across the Tech campus toward the Admissions Office, my grandfather in the lead because somehow he had managed to find a map of the campus and knew exactly where we needed to go, followed by my mother and Ruth Ann, who were still talking, followed by Clementine and me. As I watched from the rear for a fleeting moment I thought perhaps my grandfather was being just a tad presumptuous until Clementine commented quietly that he must have been waiting all of my life for this day to come. When I replied that might well apply to me but it shouldn't necessarily apply to her, she squeezed my hand and said, "Maybe he loves me as much as he loves you, Tyler."

That set me straight, of course. A widower, he became my father when my father died. He had guided and supported me every day since. Now not only was I going to begin my university studies, so was the young woman I loved. For my grandfather, retired from his own teaching, this was his moment of glory. "He looks like a Major in an English movie," Clementine said, "leading his troops into the breach."

I laughed quietly and agreed.

"Just let him be," Clementine said. "I'm loving every minute. He's my grandfather, too, you know."

I hadn't known that, of course. I mean, I did know it—that she felt that way—but I hadn't acknowledged that I knew it, if you understand what I mean.

In any case, before long we were there. When Ruth Ann and Clementine presented themselves, they were greeted warmly, and they and my mother were ushered into an office. My grandfather and I waited. After twenty minutes or so, during which my grandfather walked around the office chatting with secretaries as if he was one of the Georgia Tech faculty—a homing pigeon come home to roost, I thought to myself—Clementine and Ruth Ann and my mother emerged, all three of them smiling as broadly as I had ever seen them smile. When Clementine came to me she said in as subdued a voice as she could manage, "Everything, Tyler. Everything. Room, board, and tuition."

"The National Merit Scholarship?" I said.

"Yes. Everything," Clementine said.

Ruth Ann was beaming. "My grown up girl," she said. "Praise be," she said.

Then my grandfather was there. For the first time ever, he kissed Clementine on her lips. Then he stepped back and smiled and looked at her. "Congratulations, young lady. You deserve everything you can get."

Clementine smiled and thank him. Then all five of us took deep breaths and smiled. In a moment, our smiles turned into laughter. At the same time, the admissions officer who had spoken to Clementine emerged from her office, stopping for a moment to congratulate Clementine again for her achievements. Without missing a beat, Clementine turned to her and said, "I want you to meet my boyfriend, Ms. Street. He's going to go to the University of Georgia."

The young woman turned to our group. I stepped forward and extended my hand. "I'm Tyler Raymond," I said.

I could see the surprise in her face as she accepted my gesture but she was too poised to let it show for more than an instant.

"This is Kate Street, Tyler," Clementine said.

Kate Street said she was pleased to meet me. Smiling, she added that she was sorry I was going to Georgia but that she'd be interested in how our relationship would fair when the two universities competed. "Especially in football," she said. "It's pretty intense around here that weekend."

When Clementine said that I intended to play football for Georgia, Ms. Street smiled even more broadly. "Well, that really will be interesting."

Then Ruth Ann introduced my grandfather to Ms. Street.

"We're proud to have Clementine join our student body," Kate Street said. "And I understand she's also going to run for the University."

Ruth Ann said that our next appointment was with Quincey Davidsen, the women's track coach. With that we said goodbye to Kate Street and left the admissions office, Clementine loaded down with folders and brochures and forms, and started for the athletic department. My grandfather suggested that since we had almost forty minutes that we stop in the student union for a cup of coffee. "After all, we drove almost all day yesterday. And that wasn't much of a breakfast the motel fed us this morning." Following him again, we walked to the student union building where we all ordered coffee and rolls and donuts.

As you might expect, both my mother and I wanted to know about Clementine's conversation with Kate Street. So Clementine repeated Georgia Tech's offer of what amounted to a full ride scholarship based on Clementine's PSAT score, her SAT scores, and her grades at Tampa Coast. It was Clementine's triumph. I could not have been more proud. At that moment, whatever happened to me the next day at the University of Georgia seemed of secondary importance. The day belonged to Clementine.

Ruth Ann sat quietly looking at her daughter. I could feel what she must have been thinking. What an extraordinary journey she had taken. What an extraordinary achievement for her as well as for Clementine. Then we all got up and walked back to our van and drove to the Athletic Department, which was some distance away.

Accompanied by Ruth Ann and my mother, Clementine met with Coach Davidsen, who was well aware of the National Merit Scholarship that was bringing Clementine to Georgia Tech. Clementine told me after the meeting that because the athletic department did not have to use a track scholarship on Clementine, arrangements had been made to pay for her books and all standardized examinations she would be required to take in order to get into the pre-med program. The University would even pay for the examinations she would have to sit to get into medical school, provided that she was interested in the Medical College of Georgia in Augusta. In short, Clementine was going to attend Georgia Tech for free. "Coach Davidsen said she'd never had a woman come to run for Georgia Tech with grades like mine," Clementine said. "She said that when I got to be a junior, I could become an Athletic Department tutor. It's a paying job, but even more important, it would be really good on my application to medical school."

Then Clementine came out and said Coach Davidsen wanted to meet both me and my grandfather. And while Coach Davidsen did not show as much surprise at my grandfather and me being white as we thought she might, she did go on to say that it was too bad I'd chosen to play football for Georgia instead of Georgia Tech, which provoked the same kind of response that Kate Street's comment had caused: "It will be interesting to see how you two fare when Tech plays Georgia in football."

Then the five of us went to visit the dormitory in which Clementine would live the next fall. We spent the afternoon touring the rest of the campus as well.

26

Four years at a university is a considerable period of time. So I have no intentions or any need to detail everything that happened to Clementine and me during our undergraduate years. However, the day we spent in Atlanta and then the day we spent in Athens are vivid memories for both of us. After all, they signaled the beginning about which each of us had dreamed since our ninth grade years at Tampa Coast. And while I remember everything that took place on the Georgia Tech campus with great pleasure, I recall everything that happened the next day in Athens on the University of Georgia campus just as well.

My day was similar to Clementine's in that the five of us walked across the Athens campus in formation, save that this time Clementine and I followed my grandfather, my mother and Ruth Ann following us. When we got to the Admissions Office, my mother and grandfather and Ruth Ann all went with me to meet with Ms. Dixie Caskey, an Assistant Dean of Admissions. I didn't expect a full-ride scholarship such as Clementine had earned at Georgia Tech. I hadn't been a National Merit Scholarship finalist, after all. However, my PSAT and SAT scores and grades at Tampa Coast not only had gotten me into the University, they had also earned what Ms. Caskey called a University Presidental Scholarship, which covered half of my tuition and half of my dormitory room costs. She said that while she was not at liberty to explain what the Athletic Department was offering, she did know that Coach Dooley's staff had informed her that I was to receive a partial scholarship for playing football. In the end, I was not only pleased at how encouraging Ms. Caskey had been during our visit, I was pleased to know that the Athletic Department was also interested. After all, I was perfectly aware that I was not a first pick recruit for the football team. I was going to have to prove myself in a number of ways to make the team.

Before we left Ms. Caskey's office, I told her I wanted to introduce her to Clementine, who I explained was my girlfriend and who was going to attend and run track at Georgia Tech starting next fall. With that I brought Clementine into the office, where Dixie Caskey's comment echoed Kate Street's at Georgia Tech: "I'll be interested in how the two of you get along when it's football season. Especially with you playing for the Bulldogs, Tyler." When I told her that her counterpart at Tech, Kate Street, had said very much the same thing, she said she wasn't surprised. "In state rivalries are as intense as it can get, Tyler. You and Clementine will find that out when football season rolls around."

Everyone laughed, and I said that Clementine and I had been discussing that very thing for weeks. We decided that the rivalry between the two universities might turn into a very interesting part of our relationship.

Then the five of us left for my visit with Coach Lundin in the Athletic Department. I will admit that I was very nervous. I really wasn't sure how much the University of Georgia wanted me to come play football. As it turned out, I should have had more confidence in myself. For Coach Lundin was both cordial and encouraging. He said more than once that Coach Dooley had looked forward to seeing me again, which told me that he actually remembered meeting me the previous fall when we had met in Tampa. I thought that was a good sign. At the same time, I was realistic enough to know what else was coming.

"We aren't offering you a full scholarship, Tyler, at this point. It isn't that we don't think you're going to make the team. Coach Dooley has said that you're just the kind of young man we want in our program. It's just that we've been fortunate in our recruiting this year. And there's a senior ahead of you who's been a starting safety for two years."

I said that I understood. I said that I was prepared to play on special teams if that was what the coaches decided.

Coach Lundin smiled his very generous smile. "That's exactly what Coach Dooley said you'd say. He told me he knew your father. Said he competed against him in college. So he definitely wants you to come to Athens."

"And I'm prepared to come, sir," I said. Then I told him about my conversation with Dixie Caskey in the Admissions Office. He said that he knew about the details. "That's why I'm so happy to be able to tell you that the Athletic Department is going to offer a half scholarship to you. We're also going to pay for your books. And since we're counting on you to make the team, you'll live with other football players in the dormitory. If you put that together with the University's scholarship, you'll see that you're going to come to Georgia on what amounts to a full ride."

I was really surprised. I knew I didn't need the scholarships. I had Raymond money, after all, money that was mine once I verified that I was duly enrolled at the University. Even as I sat in Coach Lundin's office, I was already calculating how much of the Trust Fund money I could save towards graduate school, because I knew full well that my education, just like Clementine's was going to take more than four years. Like Clementine, I was in for a very long haul. After all, if I was going to be a college professor like my grandfather, I would have to earn my doctorate. I was looking at seven years as a minimum. What I wanted to do was get through undergraduate school, then use my Trust Fund money to support Clementine and me when she was in medical school and I was in graduate school. She and I had talked about it. And while she protested it was my money not hers, I stopped her in mid argument when I said, "Are you telling me that you don't want to get married for another seven years?" When her answer was no, that she did not want to wait that long, I replied, "Then it doesn't matter where the money comes from, does it?"

"No, Tyler, I suppose it doesn't," she said.

However, before I left Coach Lundin's office, I returned Clementine's favor by having her come into Coach Lundin's office so he could meet her. And while I don't want to say that both Clementine and I were playing a game with the people at Georgia Tech and the University of Georgia, I must admit that maybe we were. If that sounds manipulative on our part, keep in mind what we had gone through a number of times while we were high school students. Is it any wonder, then, that we decided rather than wait to see how folks might react to us, we chose to be in as much control as we could? We were who we were, after all. It was as simple as that. We didn't need anyone's approval. But we did rather enjoy watching their reactions, especially when really nice people who harbored no ill intentions towards us at all demonstrated in their body language or the expressions on their faces that we had caught them by surprise. It was especially satisfying to watch them as they watched us as we simply went on about our business as if there was nothing unusual about our relationship. In fact, by the time Clementine interviewed at Georgia Tech and I interviewed at Georgia, we were so good at the game that even my grandfather commented over lunch that he had enjoyed watching.

"Is that what those two are up to, Edward?" Ruth Ann said.

"I think so," my grandfather replied.

"I thought maybe they were doing something. But then I decided they weren't that devious," Ruth Ann commented.

My grandfather laughed. "I think they're a whole lot more devious than any of thought," he said.

"Which means the three of us had better start watching them a whole lot more closely," she said.

My mother agreed. "You two," she said in her best mock critical tone of voice, "you two are too clever by half."

Clementine and I protested our innocence, which none of the three said they were prepared to believe.

27

Even before spring vacation and our trip to both Georgia Tech and the University of Georgia, Clementine had started training for the spring track season. I tried to run with her, and I had some success in improving my own speed, but what I noticed was something new in Clementine's stride. She had always been physically slight, which was, of course, not an indication of her strength. More than once, as far back as her ninth grade season, I saw her run past stronger, more experienced runners. When she had won state championships, she did so against girls who were older and who looked more impressive. It had been her determination that had produced victories. She was a smooth runner. She often looked as if running races was almost an afterthought. Even in races when she had come from behind with a sprint down the home stretch, she had always made it look almost effortless. Perhaps that is why she had surprised so many runners who should have beaten her.

Given her times and performances for three years, it is logical that Georgia Tech assumed it was getting a runner who could compete with some success in the Atlantic Coast Conference. And while I am not in any way trying to suggest that the ACC does not sponsor top quality athletic competition, when the whole of American track and field is considered, the truth is there are other, tougher conferences that produce more nationally recognized runners. What happened to Clementine during her senior year at Tampa Coast, however, told me that Georgia Tech was getting more than just a good conference runner. The Georgia Tech Yellow Jackets were getting a runner who potentially might well do more than just win conference meets.

Once we were back home, the Tampa Coast track season began with team workouts. I usually went in the afternoon and sat in the stands and did my studies. Sometimes, as Clementine had done for me during the football season, I even organized Clementine's homework assignments so she would be ready in the evening. I was so focused on both her and my studies that it took a few days of sitting in the stands for me to look up one day and pay enough attention to her practice sprints to start seeing what had happened. I even remember the first time I really noticed. It was a cloudy day, and I was watching her and probably thinking about other things when it dawned on me that her feet didn't look like they were touching the ground. She had always been a smooth runner. But all of a sudden it appeared to me that she was floating.

I didn't understand. Was she stronger? She didn't look heavier. Her muscle tone looked the same—smooth and lithe. But her legs, especially her thighs, had changed. The big muscles were more defined. Her calf muscles were more evident. I looked at her through my binoculars, which I always had with me when she was running, even at practice. I swear I couldn't see her feet touching the ground. There was no evidence that I could see of her muscles contracting when her feet came down or evidence of push when her feet came up. She was gliding. I looked again. I was sure I could see two inches between the bottoms of her feet and the track. How was that possible? I certainly didn't know. Yet her speed had not lessened. In fact, even though I didn't have a stop watch with me as I did when I came to her meets, she looked faster than ever.

After the practice when I first became aware of the change, I asked her what was going on. Did she feel different? What had she done with her stride?

Clementine was delighted that I was impressed. Then she told me that Coach Lawton had given her both stretching and strength exercises to do every morning at home and every evening before she went to sleep. She said they had made her muscles feel both longer and stronger. One of the exercises was for ankle conditioning. I told her whatever she was doing, it was certainly working. The next day I brought my stop watch. And yes, while I know sitting in the stands and trying to start a stop watch when her coach fired the practice gun and then trying to click the watch off when it looked to me like she was crossing the finish line is certainly not as accurate as the timing devices at a track meet, the first time I clocked her I swear she was a second below her best time the previous spring when she won the state 440 yard championship. Coach Lawton must have been pleased too, because down on the track I saw her smiling and hugging Clementine as Clementine finished her sprints.

When we drove home that afternoon, I told her that I'd timed her and that it looked to me as if she was faster than ever. She said Coach Lawton had her running almost two seconds better than her best time at the state championship meet. Four days later, I had a chance to test my observations. As always, my grandfather went with me to the dual meet. I didn't tell him anything special, just that he should watch her very closely.

He replied that he always watched her closely. So when it was her race, we both trained our binoculars on her. As she crossed the finish line, winning easily, he turned to me and said, "What's going on, Tyler?"

"So you saw something different?"

"I sure did. She never touches the ground."

"Well, obviously, she has to touch the ground, Grandpa. But you're right. It doesn't look like it, does it?"

"She was wonderful last spring. But God . . . she's spectacular now. How in the world is she doing that?"

I explained what Clementine had told me. He agreed that whatever it was, it was certainly working. And it kept on working all through the dual meet and conference meet season: Clementine won every 440 and 880 race. In fact, it wasn't until the Tampa Coast team traveled to the regional meet that there was a runner within three seconds of her 440 and four seconds of her 880 times. By then, Coach Lawton had contacted Coach Davidsen at Georgia Tech and invited her to come to see Clementine at the state meet in Orlando, which she was able to do.

Coach Davidsen sat with Ruth Ann during the state meet in Orlando, which was hosted by Winter Park High School. While the two of them spent most of the meet talking about Clementine's academic ambition to go to medical school, when it came time for Clementine to run the finals in the 440, both stopped talking and watched through their binoculars. When it was over, as always, I ran down the stands so I could be near the track when she finished. As always, she came to me, and I leaned out over the guard rail and we hugged. Then she whispered, "Wait until you see the 880, Tyler."

I went back up to my seat with my mother and grandfather and Ruth Ann and Coach Davidsen, all of whom were delighted she had not only won the race, she had broken the state championship meet record by almost three seconds. "It's her turns," Coach Davidsen said. "In the films Coach Lawton sent me last year, which I looked at again before I drove here, I could see she handles the turns very well. But tonight. That was really something. She looked like she was running a straight away. Somebody's been teaching her some really good technique."

Other final events took place, of course, before Clementine and the other 880 runners were called to the starting line. I remember feeling butterflies in my stomach. This was going to be her very last race ever for Tampa Coast and her very last race ever in Florida. I wanted this to be her triumph. I wanted the whole world to know that Clementine Camille Brown was simply the best runner ever.

As the runners lined up, Clementine did something she had never done before: she looked up in the stands and put both her hands over her heart. I saw her mouth the words, "I love you" and point at the six of us sitting together. I heard Ruth Ann say, "That was for you, Tyler." And my heart swelled.

Then the runners were given the vocal commands, "Ready. Set." Then bang! They were off.

By the end of the first turn, Clementine had established that this was going to be her race. And it was. She ran away from everyone. She might just as well have been on the track by herself. I could see her joy. When we'd been in ninth grade and she'd said she wanted to go out for the track team, I'd asked her why, and she had said, "Because I love running, Tyler." Well, the splendid sprinter who loved running was running that night like I had never seen any woman run before. She was off the ground. She was running smoothly. She was beautiful. My God, I loved that girl. I loved her. I loved her. I loved her.

When she crossed the finish line and threw up her arms in a gesture of victory and then turned back to where the crowd in the stands was applauding, she turned and pointed at me as I vaulted down the stairs. And just as she had the first time she'd won a state championship, she climbed up into the stands and leaped into my arms, and there we stood, with her legs wrapped around my waist, with my arms wrapped around her thighs, and she kissed me. She really kissed me. Right there in front of the cheering crowd. She kissed me and held on and held on and held on until I finally began to put her down very carefully. When she drew back her head, I could see tears in her eyes. There were tears in my eyes. But she was smiling. She was laughing and saying, "You! You! You!" And I said, "Yes! Yes! Yes!" And then Coach Lawton was calling her to come back onto the track. So I helped her climb back over the guard rail. But as she walked away, she turned back and pointed at me. And I pointed at her. And that was that. I turned slowly and started walking up the steps. And would you believe it, the fans in the stands, many of whom were parents of Tampa Coast runners, many of whom were from other schools, were still standing and applauding. When I realized they were looking at me and applauding me, I stopped and raised my hands over my head in the same way Clementine had raised her hands when she'd crossed the finish line.

Then I went on up to where Ruth Ann and Coach Davidsen and my mother and grandfather were waiting. After hugs all around and as I sat down next to her, Coach Davidsen turned to me and smiled and said, "You've got quite a girl there, Tyler."

I turned to her and smiled and said, "Yes, ma'am. You're right. I've got quite a girl there."

28

The senior prom was held one week after the state track championships. Clementine and I decided that as much as we would have preferred to be alone together, that because this would be our last major social event as part of the Tampa Coast student body, we would join our friends and be a part of a group at both the dance and at a restaurant afterwards.

I know that up to this point I haven't said much about the friends we made in high school, but that isn't because we didn't have any. We had a number of very close friends with whom we've maintained contact over the years. One of my closest friends, a teammate on the football team, became a psychologist who now has a private practice in Washington, D.C. Another friend from English classes became an Episcopal priest, although I don't think any one who knew him in high school would have predicted that would become his calling. The friend with whom I talked a great deal about school as well as about personal issues always knew what he wanted to be: a railroad engineer. He's been making the run between Jacksonville, Florida, and Los Angeles for the last ten years. Of all of my friends, I think his job must be the most romantic.

Another works for the City of San Francisco Transportation Authority. He's in charge of the crew that paints the Golden Gate Bridge. When I last talked to him, he said he spends about half of his working day high up on the spires to which the cables that hold the bridge in place are connected. He says he never gets tired of the view of the ocean to the west and the city to the east.

There are female friends with whom I am still in contact, although Clementine is closer to several we know in common. Two of her closest companions in high school now own an art gallery in New York City that specializes in women artists. Another is an assistant director at the Women's History Museum in Washington, D.C. Two are married and raising children. Two are school teachers. One of those two now coaches the girls lacrosse team at Tampa Coast.

Of course, there have also been two divorces, one of which was a couple who like Clementine and me dated in high school. One of Clementine's closest girl friends died six years ago after a three year battle with cancer, which was hard for all of us who knew her because we all remember her as the most cheerful person at Tampa Coast. Another friend whom I first met in humanities class died of AIDS. That was devastating not just because he died but because he had never felt confident enough in any of his friendships to talk about his homosexuality in high school or to the two high school friends to whom he stayed close when they all three attended the University of Florida.

Clementine and I attended both of those funerals. The first took place in Tampa during the summer after Clementine's first year of medical school and my first year of master's degree studies. The second took place years later in San Francisco. Unfortunately, we didn't learn about it until two days before it was scheduled to take place. By then Clementine was in her second year of her residency and I was finishing my doctorate. But we went anyway, as did six of our high school friends. And while it was good that we could be together again, the fact it took a death to do so told us something very unsettling about life and love and relationships. We've done a better job since then of keeping track of each other.

In any case, Clementine and I went to the senior prom with five other couples. Clementine was, as always, radiant and beautiful. Her off the shoulder, beige, floor length dress clung to her body and moved gracefully as she moved. I remember that as we danced, and my hand touched her back, the perfume rising up from her body was more intoxicating than any liquor I've ever drunk since. And that hasn't changed for me over the years. When I am lying next to her at night in bed, I am at the center of the universe.

At the same time, most of the evening was spent laughing, because while I tend to be a melancholy sort, perhaps too much for my own good some times, a number of Clementine's and my friends have wonderful, wry senses of humor. Their comments on anything of interest were and continue to be wonderfully funny.

The only complication was that three of the couples had worked out an elaborate plan so they could all end up in a beach house south of Sarasota for the weekend. Neither Clementine nor I wanted to take part, not because we didn't think we would enjoy being together and being with them, but because Clementine had already made plans for us. So we ended up after the dance driving until almost 3 A.M. to a small hotel facing the water just north of Horseshoe Beach.

I am fully prepared to admit that I have no idea how she dealt with Ruth Ann or what she said, because I know Clementine would not lie to her mother, and so I assume that Ruth Ann was aware we were going away together. I also remember that when I was leaving for the dance, with my suitcase in hand, my mother had simply said drive carefully. Then she added that even though seniors were not expected back in school on Monday, she and my grandfather expected that Clementine and I would be back on time to go to school on Tuesday. With finals only one week away, I assured her that we would be back by Monday evening.

As we were driving north at about midnight on Saturday night, I came very close to asking Clementine what she had said to her mother and to my mother, but then I decided that there are some things I didn't need to know, and that this was one of those occasions.

What I do remember is arriving at the hotel and waking up the night manager, who was sleeping sitting up behind the check in counter, and then going to our room where both of us promptly fell asleep the moment we lay down after undressing and showering. I remember how the next day was beautiful and that we walked along the beach after our late breakfast, holding hands, but not talking much because we also knew that once finals and graduation were over, we would have to start counting down the days until she would enroll at Georgia Tech and I would enroll at the University of Georgia, and that it would undoubtedly be four years before we would be together every single day. I also very clearly remember at one point as we were walking how Clementine stopped, which meant that I stopped, and how she looked when she faced me and said, “Four years is not a lifetime, Tyler.”

I said I agreed. I said it would be hard, but yes, it was not a life time.

“It is just part of us. Of who we are. Of what we have to do to be together.”

I said I agreed.

“And we will have weekends and holidays and summers,” she said.

I said I agreed.

“But nothing is ever going to change for me. Not how I feel about you. You know that, don’t you?” she said. “You are the man who has stayed. You are the man who has loved me enough to stay when enough happened to drive another kind of man away.”

I remember waiting for a moment before responding. I wanted to get the words right. Then I said, “Clementine, if I died this afternoon, I would die happy because I have loved you.”

“But you’re not going to die this afternoon, Tyler,” she said, pushing a hip against mine.

“No, I am not. But when I do die, even if it’s when I’m eighty or ninety, I will still love you. So I will die happy.”

Clementine embraced me for a moment. Then we turned and continued walking.

That night we were lovers again. Then on Monday we walked on the beach in the morning, and as we had Sunday afternoon, but like Sunday, we said very little. We checked out of the hotel shortly after noon and drove back to Tampa.

By the end of the week, we had met with friends and reviewed all we could possibly review for our final examinations. The following Monday, the testing began. By Thursday at noon, everyone was finished. And so it was over. Four years of high school. Gone.

Of course, it wasn’t *gone* for Ruth Ann or my mother or my grandfather. No, they had one more dinner to organize, one more Raymond-Brown clan celebration to arrange.

29

Graduation day at Tampa Coast High School was just like graduation day at every high school in America. Most of us were smart enough to realize we weren’t the first nor would we be the last seniors to cross a school auditorium stage and be handed a diploma by a high school principal. So as much as we would have liked to see it as a big deal, I think most of us kept it in perspective, especially those of us going on to colleges or universities. After all, what we faced was more school.

Yes, it was exciting. Wearing graduation robes is exciting. Moving the tassel at the appropriate time to signal one has graduated is exciting. It’s a ritual, a rite of passage, a signing by the community. Teachers had talked to us about it in those terms. And the class valedictorian spoke. So did the salutatorian, a young woman Clementine and I both knew whose grade point average was only .12 higher than Clementine’s. And while I felt badly because I thought that with her accomplishments in track, Clementine’s achievement was extraordinary, she said she really didn't care because, mostly, she didn't want to have to write and then deliver a speech.

Of course, a guest speaker gave the commencement address, which was probably like every other commencement address that has ever been delivered. What can one say to a senior class except you are the future and you can achieve your dreams? Certainly no one is going to get up and talk about how some of you will fail, and some of you will die untimely deaths, and some of you will have failed marriages and children who suffer as a consequence. In any case, none of us knew who the speaker was before he delivered his address, and none of us ever heard from him again after it was over.

On the other hand, for the parents, it was that moment they have waited for. Pride. Pleasure. Some sense of relief for not a few. Now get on with your life, son. Now get serious, daughter. But that day, at least, it was hugs and photographs and promises to never forget each other. We'll always be best friends. I couldn't have made it without you. You were always there for me.

I'm not making light of those sentiments. They're important. The people who say them mean it. We had entered Tampa Coast four years before as intimidated, insecure ninth graders. We were leaving as seniors who really had learned a few things, but who, if we were smart, would keep in mind we had much more to learn in the future. Certainly that's what I felt as I crossed the stage. Certainly that's what Clementine said she felt as she crossed the stage. But I didn't say what I really wanted to say when first my mother and then my grandfather embraced Clementine and me and told us they loved us, and we told them we loved them, and Ruth Ann embraced Clementine and then me and said she loved us. I couldn't say what I really wanted to say: "I wish my father could have been here." That would have been too hard for my mother to hear, and too hard for me to hear myself say. So I did the next best thing. As I walked away from Tampa Coast High School for the last time, I turned around and looked at the building and said in a whisper that Clementine heard, because by then she was at my side hand holding my hand, "Be proud of me, dad. Please, be proud of me," which was followed, to my surprise, by Clementine saying, "He would be, Tyler. He is." It wasn't until later that I realized why, when I turned to Clementine to thank her, that she turned away for a moment before turning back to me with tears in her eyes. For she could not then and would not ever say that of her father, because she didn't want him to be proud of her. She didn't want anything to do with him while I had no choice, which I realized years later must have been harder for her to accept than for me. After all, my father couldn't be with me. Her father could. He chose not to. My father would always be my hero. Hers would always be her villain.

The two of us then followed my mother and grandfather and Ruth Ann to my grandfather's car, and after one more round of hugs and kisses, we said, yes, we'll follow you. So we drove to a restaurant overlooking Tampa Bay where we were met by three of my mother's teacher friends from her school, two of the retired academics with whom my grandfather had become friends, and five of Ruth Ann's closest friends from the University of South Florida, and four people from the Tampa Unitarian Church that I had also come to know, all of whom were there to congratulate us and tell us how proud my mother and grandfather and Ruth Ann were of both of us. Then we sat down to eat, and my mother got out photographs of me as I was growing up and passed them around, and Ruth Ann got out photographs of Clementine as she was growing up and passed them around, and Clementine and I sat at the two chairs placed at the head of the table, caught in that odd divide between being profoundly grateful that three wonderful people loved us and embarrassed almost to tears at how we had looked as we'd grown up and how much everyone in the room kept laughing affectionately and telling us how we had become such a handsome couple over the years.

30

Then it was summer, and Clementine and I went to work for Home Depot again. No, I didn't really need the money. But there was no way I was going to let Raymond money change the way I conducted myself. However, in late June, Clementine and I got a very big surprise.

My mother planned to fly to Boston for the National Social Studies Teachers Conference, because by then she had become one of six board members of the Hillsborough Public Schools Social Studies Teachers Association. The conference was to take place at Emerson University. The conference featured speakers who were both educators and public figures. My grandfather and I were delighted for her because it would give her an opportunity to interact with elementary and middle and high school teachers from all across the country.

Five days before my mother was scheduled to leave, as we did very often, my mother and grandfather and Clementine and Ruth Ann and I were having dinner. When my mother and Ruth Ann were discussing the speakers who were to appear at the conference, my grandfather turned to Clementine and me and said, "By the way, I haven't told you. But while your mother is in Boston, I'm leaving for San Diego."

"San Diego?" I said. "Why are you going to San Diego?"

"To visit friends. Professor Ross, who I taught with at Cleveland State for a number of years. He and his wife are retired and living just north of San Diego," my grandfather replied.

I nodded. "That's great. That's very nice, Grandpa."

"I thought I'd drive."

"Really? Drive. That's a long way," I said.

"I've got other people to see. A professor with whom I've corresponded for years. He lives in Austin, Texas. That's where he teaches. At the University of Texas."

I could see in his face something more was coming. I didn't know why I felt that way, but something in his eyes said more was coming.

"And I'm going to stay a few days in Albuquerque." he went on.

"Albuquerque?" I said.

"Yes. You may or may not remember Molly Wilson. She was a student of mine years ago. She came to our house when she was finishing her doctorate. I was her advisor."

"Grandpa, a lot of your students came to our house. I'm not sure if I'd remember one in particular by name," I said.

"She was studying race relations in Chicago. That was her dissertation subject. The immigration of blacks to Chicago between the World Wars. The impact on Chicago social and economic life."

"All right. But I still don't remember her," I said.

"It doesn't matter. In any case, she and her husband live in Albuquerque. She teaches at the University of New Mexico."

"That sounds great, Grandpa. It sounds like you'll have a very nice trip. But that's still a very long drive," I said. "Especially alone."

My grandfather took another sip of wine. I felt Clementine's leg pressing against mine. "I'm not going to be alone," he said. I felt Clementine's leg pressing against mine even harder. "Ruth Ann is going with me."

I did not reply. "Oh," I said very quietly after a moment.

"Edward asked me if I'd like to come meet his historian friends," Ruth Ann said, looking at Clementine first and then at me. "I said yes, that sounded very nice. And I've never seen the Grand Canyon," she said.

I could hear Clementine exhaling very slowly. I hadn't heard her take a deep breath, but I could hear her exhaling very slowly. "That's nice, mom," I heard her say. "Don't you think that's nice, Tyler," Clementine said, her leg pressing against mine again, her left hand gripping my right thigh very firmly just above the knee cap, which usually makes me laugh, but which I did not do this time because I could tell that for Clementine this was no laughing matter any more than it was a laughing matter for me. But what was I supposed to say?

"We know you two are leaving in August," my mother said. "But the three of us feel like these are interesting chances for us to travel."

I turned to my mother. "You don't need to apologize, mom," I said. "I think it's great." I turned to Clementine. "Right?" I said. "It's great that they all get to travel."

Clementine looked at me for a moment. Then she said, "Yes. It's fine," she said. "I think all of you will have wonderful trips."

"And since you're all going to be gone," I said, recovering my creative wits for a moment, "Clementine and I will have a chance to take the golf trip we've been talking about for two years," I said.

"What golf trip?" my mother said quickly.

"The golf trip Clementine and I have been talking about," I said, pressing my leg against Clementine's. "To the east coast. The Florida east coast. Where it's cooler on the Atlantic."

"You two want to take a golf trip?" Ruth Ann said.

"Yes. I read about it in the newspaper," I said. "It's a package deal. For two people. We'd start in St. Augustine. Then we'd play six other courses all the way to Miami."

I have to explain at this point that after my surgery during the football season of my junior year, the doctors wanted me to take up some sort of recreation that would get me outdoors, get me walking, but not require physical impact on my legs or torso. Tennis was out because it requires running and stopping. One of the physical therapists who met with me twice to make certain my equilibrium had not been affected by the long recovery period said golf would be good for me. It required walking and concentration and would continually test my hand-eye coordination and dexterity. So Clementine and I had taken up golf. As soon as I was able, she drove me to a golf store where each of us bought a recommended set of clubs. We took a series of five lessons from a professional who ran a driving range not far from where we lived. Neither of us became exceptional golfers, but that wasn't important. We were doing what the doctor wanted me to do, and we were doing it together, which meant I would follow through. Before long, we realized that we had chanced onto a game we could share the rest of our lives. My mother and grandfather and Ruth Ann had all been pleased that we'd done so. Now all three of them looked a little uneasy. That part was easy to understand. But what they didn't seem to understand was where their travel plans put Clementine and me. What were we supposed to think? What were we supposed to do?

"Look, the three of you are going to be gone," I said. "Mom for a week, which I assume really means two weekends. And Grandpa, you and Ruth Ann are going to be gone for . . . how long? Two weeks. Maybe more. If I was driving all the way to San Diego and back, I'd make it a month."

"But you have jobs," Ruth Ann said.

"We don't need to work there all summer," I said.

"We're both over it," Clementine said. "We really want to quit. I've saved money. So has Tyler. We'll be fine."

I knew we had caught the three of them off guard. And I'd caught Clementine off guard. Yes, I'd known my mother was interested in the Boston conference. But neither Clementine nor I had known about my grandfather's and Ruth Ann's plans to travel together, which means they'd caught us off guard.

"I think it would be nice for Clementine and me to play different courses," I said. "Every day will be a new challenge," I said. "We'll stay at Holiday Inns. That's part of the package."

My mother looked unconvinced. Ruth Ann looked as if she understood but wasn't particularly pleased. My grandfather was quiet.

A very long five person silence hung in the air.

Then Clementine leaned her head against my shoulder. "There's not much point in the two of us hanging around Tampa while all three of you are gone," Clementine said. When none of them replied or agreed with her logic or even objected, Clementine said, "I think Tyler and I are going to take a walk, if all of you don't mind," she said.

The three of them mumbled sure and that's fine and okay and be back for dessert, with which Clementine pulled me to my feet with no further comment, and we left and went for a walk.

As we started walking, we didn't have much to say at first. We had been surprised. We'd responded by surprising them. It had been an interesting exchange.

We must have gone two blocks before Clementine stopped and turned to me and said, "Did you know anything about their plans?"

I started to laugh because I didn't know what else to do. Then I didn't. "You mean my grandfather and your mother?" I said.

"Yes, your grandfather and my mother," she said sharply.

I wasn't going to respond in kind. So I said, "No," very politely.

For a very long several moments Clementine was quiet in her I'm-thinking-Tyler and you'd-better-be-thinking-as-well way, so I stayed quiet.

"Golf?" she finally said.

"I had to think of something."

"But golf?"

"Do you have a better idea?"

She looked at me. "No," she said after a moment.

I was quiet for several more moments. I suspected there was going to be a lot of quiet in this conversation. So I turned and started walking. Clementine followed. We came to the front lawn retaining wall where we'd sat after my surgery and where we'd sat many times since. I sat down. Clementine sat down next to me.

"Do you think it's been going on for some time?" she asked.

"I don't know," I said.

"What am I supposed to think about it, Tyler?"

I was quiet for some time. "I don't know what you're supposed to think about it, Clementine. But I think it's nice," I said.

"Nice?"

"Yes, it's nice. They're friends. They've been friends because of us for four years."

Clementine looked at me. "It's my *mother*, Tyler," she said.

I turned to her. "Yes. And it's my grandfather, Clementine."

"What's that supposed to mean?"

"I don't know. What's 'It's my mother' supposed to mean?"

"I don't know. It's just . . . ," she started to say then didn't. Then she said, "Why didn't you see this coming?"

"Why didn't I see it coming?"

"Yes, why didn't you see this coming?"

"Why didn't you see it coming?" I said.

Clementine turned away from me. She'd never turned away from me that way before.

"They're adults, Clementine. They're grown ups."

"Your grandfather's certainly grown up," Clementine said.

"Wait a minute. What about your mother? She's an adult woman," I said quickly. "And as for my grandfather . . . ," I began.

"I know. I know. And I love him, Tyler. My mother and I both . . . ." This time she did stop. "We love Edward."

"And I love your mother, Clementine. She's a great woman."

"And your grandfather's a great man. But that isn't what we're talking about."

"Then what are we talking about, Clementine?"

She didn't answer. I looked at her. She didn't look like she was going to answer. We sat quietly for several minutes. Finally I turned to Clementine and said, "Look, Clementine, no one is forcing either one of them to travel with the other. And we don't know anything about their plans. We don't know anything about anything . . . except that they're going to drive to San Diego and back."

Clementine turned very slowly and looked at me. "Tyler, get real," she said.

"All right, Clementine, what do you want me to say. My grandfather is still a vigorous man? That he's been a widower for a very long time? Is that it? And your mother. She's been divorced for how long? Good grief, only a blind man wouldn't see your mother's a beautiful woman. Am I supposed to not tell you that I see men look at your mother in the way men look at beautiful women when we all go places together?"

"No."

"No . . . which? That my grandfather is a vigorous man? Or that your mother is a beautiful women or that men look at your mother?"

"No, you don't have to say any of those things. I know those things are true."

"Then what do you want me to say? I love my grandfather. He's not frail. He's not dying. But good God, how many years does he have left? What kind of a personal life does he lead?"

Clementine did not respond.

"And your mother. What about her? She's in the prime of her life. What kind of personal life does she have?" Before Clementine could respond, I went on. "They've both given their lives to us, Clementine. Almost all of their energy . . . their personal energy, at least, has gone into raising the two of us. And we owe them, Clementine. We owe them everything."

I stopped speaking and waited. Then I said very quietly, "I love them, Clementine. And you love them. And maybe now it's their turn to love each other . . . or whatever they have in mind."

Clementine was silent.

"Clementine, my grandfather is a great man. And your mother is a great woman. Intellectually. They're both great historians," I said. "And both of us, you and me, we've been spoiled. Two great people love us," I said. Then I said very quietly, "Maybe that's why we lost sight of the most important facts."

Clementine turned to me very slowly and said, "Lost sight of what important fact?"

"That my grandfather is a man. That your mother is a woman."

Clementine nodded. "And they respect each other," she said.

"Yes. They do."

"And they're grown ups," she said.

"And the rest of it just isn't our business."

"You're right," Clementine said.

"And if they want to travel together . . . well, they don't need our permission," I said.

"So it's not something we need to worry about," she said quickly.

"Or something we want to think about," I said.

"Or need to think about," she said as much to reassure herself as to reassure me.

"Or should think about," I said quickly for the same reason.

"Yes," Clementine said.

Then we sat without talking for some time. Then I turned to her and said, "But did your mother ever say . . . " I started to ask, but Clementine cut me off: "Tyler!" she said.

I did not go on. We sat for some time without speaking.

"We need to go back," Clementine finally said, standing.

I stood, and we started walking.

"So when do we leave and where do we go?" Clementine asked.

I smiled because . . . well, just because.

31

My mother left for Boston on a Friday morning. My grandfather and I drove his car and Clementine's and my station wagon to Clementine's and Ruth Ann's very early the next morning. Clementine and I let them leave first. We stood on the porch and waved goodbye as they drove away. Then we went back inside and started putting her suitcases and golf clubs in the station wagon. We went back into the house and made sure all of the windows were locked. Then we sat down and had a last cup of coffee and a donut. It felt strange. Clementine and I had never been in this kind of circumstance before. My mother would be staying in a hotel in Boston. My grandfather and Ruth Ann were going to stay in motels, but they didn't know which ones or in what towns. It all depended on the driving conditions. At least the three of them would know we were starting at the St. Augustine Holiday Inn where we would buy our package tickets for the golf courses.

As we sat at the table I felt Clementine looking at me. When I turned to her I asked her what she was thinking, she smiled and said, "Sometimes I wonder what would have happened had you said no when I asked you to be my lab partner."

I shook my head. "Clementine, there was no way that was going to happen."

"Why not? You could have known someone else in class. Lots of other people knew each other. That's what I was afraid of. That you'd know someone else and want to be that person's lab partner."

"Clementine, you don't get it, do you?" I said.

"I don't get what?"

'What I've been trying to tell you for years."

"What've you been trying to tell me for years?"

I smiled and reached out and took both of her hands in mine. "That I fell in love with you the first time I turned and looked at you, and you hadn't even spoken to me yet."

"Really?"

"Really."

"And you knew right then?"

"Clementine, I knew even before I met you. I swear. I dreamed you. Then I walked into the room, and there you were sitting right next to me."

"Tyler . . . " she started to say.

"I dreamed you," I said again.

She smiled again and held onto my hands. "If that's true then I was right when I said you're a shaman, Tyler. A Celtic shaman."

"And I was right when I said you're an African witch, Clementine."

"Which means we belong together," she said.

"I think we do. I think we belong together," I replied.

We sat like that for a moment more. Then she said, "All right. Then let's go play golf."

32

At this point in the story I am trying to tell, I need to try to recreate two conversations that took place the evening my mother said she was going to Boston and Ruth Ann and my grandfather said they were going to travel together to California and when, in response, I conjured up a golf trip for Clementine and me to take.

The first of the two conversations was between my mother and me, the other between Clementine and Ruth Ann. I can, of course, report my conversation with my mother almost verbatim, for I remember what we said to each other in some detail. What I will record of Clementine's conversation with her mother is my attempt to assign statements to both of them based on what Clementine summarized for me as we drove across Florida on our way to St. Augustine and the first stop in our golf vacation. What is important to keep in mind is that neither my mother nor Ruth Ann was trying to restrict Clementine's and my relationship. At the same time, both were concerned that if ever Clementine or I changed our minds about the commitment we had obviously made to one another the consequences might be devastating. In short, neither wanted either of us to be hurt if the future brought changes that we did not expect.

My mother came to me that evening after Clementine and Ruth Ann had gone home. She said she wanted to talk. I could tell from her tone of voice that she was not angry or upset. But I could also tell she was serious and concerned. I knew of course what was on her mind even before she said, "I need to have a serious talk with you."

"All right."

"I assume you know what I'm going to say."

"It's about Clementine and me going away together."

"Yes. That's right," my mother said.

"Are you going to object?" I asked.

"To the two of you traveling together?"

"Yes."

"No. I suppose many mothers would. But at this point in your relationship with Clementine, that's not what I want to say."

I waited.

"I loved your father very much, Tyler," my mother said.

"I'm sure that's true."

"I miss him every day."

I did not respond,

"So I know what it is to love someone so much that he becomes more a part of your person than you feel like you are yourself," she said.

"Grandfather has told me how much it hurt you when he died."

My mother hesitated for a moment. "Tyler, I'm not the same person I was when he was alive. I'm sorry about that because it means I haven't been a whole person since he died. Which means I've cheated you in the process."

"Mother, you haven't cheated me. You've loved me. I've always known that," I replied.

"Yes, I do love you. But not as much as I would have had he not died."

I wasn't sure how to respond to what she had just said. "We can't go back, mother. We can only be who we are," was the best I could do.

"I know. And I've tried. Your grandfather has been more helpful than you can ever know. More than I can ever say. I don't think I would have survived had he not been with us."

"I know that. I understand," I said.

"But that's not what I want to say to you."

"All right."

"Sometimes . . . Tyler, sometimes . . . some people . . . maybe people like me. Maybe people like you. We love so completely that if anything happens . . . anything terrible. It hurts so much that life just stops being worth living."

I waited again.

"That's the way it was with me, Tyler. When your father died."

"It must have been awful."

She looked away for a moment. Then she looked back at me. "The night the telegram came. In the afternoon. That night. I went to bed and cried. And I decided I didn't want to wake up. I knew you were in the next room. So a part of me knew I had to wake up. But me. Just me. I didn't want to wake up. I could not imagine I could live even the next day knowing he was never coming home," she said, her voice nearing the breaking point.

I found it hard to look at her. It was even more difficult listening.

"Your father was so brilliant. He thought such profound thoughts. He saw things that most people just don't see. Things . . . connections between things . . . among things . . . that most people can't even imagine."

"That's what Grandpa has said."

"But even more, Tyler. Even more. His heart was so big. Grand. Noble. It used to frighten me. That I wouldn't be a good enough person or care enough about what was important or understand what he felt. Because he felt pain, Tyler. Other people's pain. He wanted to do something. To cure pain. I would lie next to him in bed at night, and he would talk, and I found myself trailing after him, trying to follow his mind, follow his sentiment, his feelings."

I wanted to say something to help her, but I could not.

"When he held me in his arms, I was the world, Tyler. I was the center of the universe. He took me to the very center of being alive. So when he died, I died. Part of me died. The center of me died. Does that make any sense?"

"Yes. It does."

"I don't want you to not love Clementine. I know why you love her. I can see it when you are together. It's almost as if you are one person. I can see it in her eyes when she looks at you. And in your eyes when you sit and listen to her talk. I've never seen a man do that before. Not that way, Tyler. Maybe your father did. When I talked. I don't know. I think he did. I think he listened to what I said. Truly listened. But you. You hang on Clementine's every thought. It's as if you are only truly alive when you are with her. And she is only truly alive when she is with you."

"It's how I feel," I said very slowly. "I think it's how she feels as well."

"That's what concerns me, Tyler. Not the loving each other part. Not that. That's good. It's beautiful to see. It makes me happy to see you so in love. But it concerns me at the same time."

"Because we're so young?"

"No. Not because you're young. Not the way most people would say it. As if you didn't know your own minds."

"Then what do you mean?" I said.

"Because you are so young, which means there are so many years ahead."

"I don't understand."

"I mean . . . I think I mean . . . that yes, you are both mature. Very mature. More mature than anyone else I've ever known who was your age. But that also means there are so many years ahead of you. It isn't like you met when you were thirty. You met when you were fifteen. You've gone through so much together. You've grown up together. Now you're going to be away from each other."

"Do you think we'll stop loving each other? That we'll change our minds?" I asked.

"No. That's not it."

"Then I'm really puzzled. We believe that just because we aren't on the same campus or seeing each other every day . . . we know that will be hard, but we believe we can manage. We know what comes next."

"When you get married?"

"Yes. I mean, with the Raymond money, we could get married now. But we knew you and Ruth Ann would not be comfortable with that. And we both think we might be uncomfortable as well. So we're not going to run off and get married."

"That's not my worry. I mean, I thought you might want to do that, but then I knew both of you were too level-headed to run away like that. What I mean is something else. I'm trying to warn you about loving each other."

"Warn us . . . about loving each other?" I said, my voice pitching slightly.

My mother waited a moment before replying. Then she said, "When a person loves as I loved your father, and then when something happens . . . when something awful happens . . . life becomes empty . . . or less full than it was before. And what fills up the void is pain."

"I know that. Both Clementine and I have talked about that."

"Talking about it is not the same as understanding."

"Are you saying that we love each other too much? Is that what you're afraid of? That we love each other too much?"

"Yes. I think so. Yes. I am afraid for both of you."

"Mom. Okay," I said. "I hear what you're saying. And yes, I know I can't really understand what you mean the way you can. You loved that way. You lost that love. But I can't turn back now. I can't pull back or love less or give less of myself."

"I know. I know that."

"Then I don't know what else I can do. Clementine is as much a part of my life as I am. I believe the same is true for her. Look at the photographs she gave me. The two of us. Together. We are . . . dancing, mom. Dancing. Our life together is a dance.
A . . . tango. A dance. We can't not dance together now. We can't hold back from dancing. Dance with each other less or mean less when we dance."

"I understand . . . ."

"Then what . . . ."

"I just don't want the music to ever stop for you. That's all. I just don't want the music to ever stop for you."

"And it won't. Or I hope it won't. But if it does stop. If it does. Even with the pain that would follow, mom. At least we had as much of the dance as we did. That's all we can do. Dance as long as we can. We can't stop today or hold back today just because someday something may make us stop. We can't control what may happen. We can't protect ourselves from the kind of danger you're talking about. Because if we did, God, we'd be giving up so much. Too much. Holding back would be worse . . . less brave . . . than losing. Worse than having the music just stop."

"I know you can't hold back."

"Then what are you saying? If you could, would you have loved my father less? If you'd known he was going to die, would you have held back? Or would knowing you were going to lose him make you love him even more?"

It was my mother's turn to wait, to not reply.

"The only moment I can know, mom, is the moment now. The only way I know how to love is to love now. You taught me that by loving me. Grandpa taught me that by loving you and loving me. So I've grown up loving. And I know one day that you and I will lose grandpa. And I know that someday I will lose you. That's what happens in life. But I can't love you less or love him less just because some day I might lose you or lose him. Because I don't think you ever lose someone. Not even if the person you love dies. The love is always there. The hurt is always there. But the love is always there too."

"I know. I know," my mother said, tears welling up in her eyes.

"So I love Clementine each day as if there won't be another day to follow. I learned that when I was in the hospital. When she told me to not go away. To not die. When I wasn't sure I was strong enough to hold on. Her love. Her holding my hand. It kept me alive. That's all I know. So I hold on. Every day. I love and hold on and hope that there will be a tomorrow. But if there isn't then there will have been that day. That moment. And there isn't anything I can do to change that. I love Clementine because I love Clementine. That's all I know. That's all I can ever know."

"I know you do. And I understand. I have understood from the beginning. I just want you to know about the pain that might come some day. I don't want it to ever happen for you. But it might. And I wanted to be the one to say the words to you if it happens so you will know what you know."

I stood up and embraced my mother. I felt her tremble for a moment. I knew she was embracing my father as she embraced me. But that was all I could do, and that was all she could do. And we'd both said all we could say. With that our conversation ended. We have never spoken of the subject again.

33

The conversation between Clementine and her mother, which I didn't know about until Clementine and I were driving and she tried to tell me exactly what had been said, ironically—or maybe not so ironically—took place at the same time I was talking with my mother. I am not suggesting that the two women conspired to approach us simultaneously; rather, I believe that decisions and pending events prompted both of them to broach the subject of Clementine's and my relationship, each of them expressing her own profound concern. In any case, Clementine told me about her conversation with her mother after I told her what my mother had said when we were making our way across Florida on our way to St. Augustine and the first stop in our golf trip.

I was driving. Clementine was drinking her second cup of coffee. As we passed through Lakeland, she said she needed to tell me about the conversation she'd had with her mother two nights after we told my mother and grandfather and Ruth Ann about us going on a golf trip to the Atlantic coast together. She said her mother had come into her room as she lay in bed and had sat down on Clementine's bed and said she wanted to have a talk. Like me, Clementine assumed it was going to be about us going away together. Like me, she found out it was about more than just our traveling together when her mother said, "Clementine, I need to talk with you."

"All right."

"There's something on my mind," Ruth Ann continued.

"Is it about Tyler and me traveling together?"

"Yes. No." She hesitated.

"Are you going to object?"

"No."

"We've traveled together before. To Miami to meet the Raymonds. After the senior prom."

"I know."

"Are you going to ask about us having sex?"

"Clementine!"

"Are you? Because I'll tell you the truth. I won't lie."

Ruth Ann sighed. "I know you wouldn't lie."

"We didn't make love in New York. You knew that already."

"Clementine, that's not what I want to talk about."

"But we did in Miami. For the first time. Because it was the only way I could think of to love Tyler when he'd been so hurt."

"I know. I mean, I assumed," Ruth Ann said.

"And we did after the senior prom. Not the first night. We both just fell asleep. It was almost funny. But we did later. The next day. But we've never skulked around."

"Skulked around?"

"Yes. That's Tyler's word. He said we were never going to skulk around. Sneak around. We don't get in the back seat of our car the way some of our friends do."

"Clementine, you don't need to tell me those things."

"I just want you to know. Yes, we've been alone in our house when you were gone. But we studied. Or read books. Or watched television. The same is true when we've been in his house and Elizabeth and Professor Thomas were gone. We've never had sex in either of our homes. We thought that would be wrong."

"Clementine, please. I want to talk about something more important than that. I know you and Tyler love each other. I assumed that at some point you would become lovers."

Clementine looked at her mother. "Then what do you want to talk about?"

"About . . . you and Tyler. About black and white. About your father."

"My father?"

"Yes. I learned something during the time we were married. I learned about how hard it can be to find one's identity."

"Do you mean because he was both black and white?" Clementine said.

"Yes. But even more than that."

"I've met him, mother. Even I could see he was in conflict with himself."

"That's right. He's in conflict with himself. But it was your grandfather . . . his father . . . who filled him up with anger. Of course, I didn't know that when I met your father. He was a handsome man. He was charming and intelligent. But after we were married, I'd feel him looking at me. He was so confused."

"Because you're black?"

"Yes. Which he loved. And hated. Both," Ruth Ann said.

"Both? How can it be both?" Clementine asked.

"Clementine, your grandfather . . . your father's father . . . he was very badly treated by white people when he first opened his grocery store. It was a small store, but the suppliers charged him more than they charged white owners of stores like his. And truckers delayed bringing produce and meats. And then they charged him more than they charged white owners."

Like me, Clementine was willing to wait.

"When he found out, he tried to fight back. He tried to find other suppliers. But the other suppliers weren't interested. Then his store burned. He knew who'd done it. But the police didn't investigate. Not really. Not seriously. So he opened another store farther away. He found new suppliers who treated him fairly. It was hard, but he did it. Your father said that your grandfather didn't even have an apartment or a room. He slept in the back of the store. He was fighting for his life. He truly lived his work. And of course, it paid off. The second store was a success. He hired a man to help. He moved to a larger building. Not a big building, but a larger building. Then he hired another man. But here's what's important: he only hired white men."

"Really?"

"Yes. He hated black people."

"Why'd he hate Black people?"

"Not for anything they'd done. He hated them for being black. Because he was black. And he knew that if he'd been white his life would have been different. So he really hated himself."

"That's awful."

"Yes. But it's even more confusing than that. Because he also hated white people," Ruth Ann went on.

"He hated them too? But he hired white people."

"Yes. But that was to protect himself. It was white people who had made him miserable when he'd been in school. He'd hated segregated schools. Not because they were segregated but because they were horrible buildings. And the students had second hand books. He knew why. He knew who'd done it to him. So he hated white people. But then after his store was burned down and he opened a new store, he knew he had to play the game."

"That must have been terrible."

"Yes, it must have been. Who was he supposed to be? A black business man? Who only hired whites? Then civil rights came along. And he knew he had to hire black people. When he opened a second and then third store, he began to hire women. White women first. Then black women. And all of a sudden, he was being honored by black business organizations as a pioneer. He was honored by white business organizations as an example of a black man who could help bridge the racial gap between blacks and whites. Then he married a white woman. He was forty, which was late, but he married a white woman. The first white woman that he'd hired five years earlier. And she gave birth to your father, who was raised in both worlds. But what did that mean? Who was your father supposed to be? Because he got stuck being a black boy in a school of predominately white students, some of whom hated him, some of whom patronized him."

Clementine was quiet for a moment. Then she went on. "Why did he marry you?" she said.

"To make amends, I suppose. To salve his guilt. His anger at being black. At being mixed."

"But you're a black woman. I mean, there's no hiding that."

"Clementine, I'm uppity. You know that's what a whole lot of white people think about me. I'm uppity. At least, that's what they thought about me at New York University."

Clementine smiled. "Yes, I guess you are pretty uppity."

Ruth Ann smiled in return. "Damn straight, I am. And I'm proud of it. It took me a long time to get up the courage to be uppity. But here's the real kicker. Your grandfather . . . your father's father . . . as uppity as he'd been . . . as uppity as he'd had to be . . . he didn't like me one bit."

"Really? Why?"

"Because to him, I was getting educated beyond my station."

"Your station?"

"Yes. I was determined to become educated. More than he thought a black woman needed. To be a good black woman, that is. To stay at home and have babies and take care of his son."

"But my father went to college. That's what you said. He went to college."

"Yes. And he went into his father's business. And he was good at it. He probably still is. He's smart and charming, and his workers thought he was a super boss. But when he came home he was a whole different man."

Clementine felt the pain coming. "What did he do? How was he different?"

"He'd stand in front of the mirror and look at himself and become so angry."

"Angry? At what?"

"At his complexion."

"Really?"

"You saw him. Now look at me. Because that's what he did."

Clementine was quiet for a very long time. Then she nodded and said very quietly, "Identity."

"Yes. Identity. What was he supposed to be? He looked like a black man, but he wasn't colored like a black man. So he raged inside. He was fierce. He held onto my black skin like he was dying. He made love like he was in a war. I didn't understand. I thought he would be tender. I thought he would be gentle. A charming man. A caring man. But he was at war with me, with himself, with his father, with his mother. It was horrible, Clementine. I watched him disintegrate a little more every night. I watched him gather up the pieces the next day and dress up and go to work where I knew he was professional and charming and made everyone love him."

Clementine was quiet. She looked at Ruth Ann. "Oh, mom, how . . . I don't know what to call it. Horrible? Terrible?"

"Bitter," Ruth Ann said.

"Bitter?"

"Yes. Bitter. He was bitter. Like his father. But it was worse for him. Because he couldn't identify the enemy. His father had. His father learned how to win the game. But your father . . . who was he supposed to hate? Who was he supposed to beat? Himself? Was that it? He was supposed to defeat himself? But what part? His black blood? His white blood?"

"So you left him?"

"He hit me so I took you and left. Because I didn't want to be his enemy. And I didn't want you to be his enemy."

"So now he's married Hispanic."

"Yes. Now he's married Hispanic. Now his children can be one half Hispanic, one quarter black, one quarter white. And maybe that means he can love his wife because she's not black so she's not part of his war, and his children will be as much her as him, so they maybe they won't have to be part of his war. Which is why I want to talk to you."

"What?"

"Which is why I want to talk to you."

"I don't understand what you mean," Clementine said.

"I want to talk about you and Tyler."

"Mother, don't. Tyler and I aren't about black and white."

"Yes you are. You can't avoid it. It's all around you."

"Mother, the world has changed. We don't have to fight any wars. We can just be who we are."

"Clementine, the world may have changed some, but that doesn't mean you and Tyler won't always have to deal with the fact you are black and he is white."

Clementine's voice pitched. "What do you want me to do? Give him up? Not love him?"

"No. I can't think of anyone better for you to love."

"Well then what is this all about? Why are you telling me these things?"

"This is about your children."

"Our children?"

"Yes. Because one day, you two are going to have children."

"That's a long way off, mother."

"I don't care if it's ten years from now. You will have to face it. Your children are going to be racially mixed."

"Our children . . . since you've got us having more than one apparently . . . our children are going to be loved by us because they are our children."

"Who will have to live in a world that will regard them as racially mixed," Ruth Ann said with temper.

"What do you want us to do? Not have children?"

"I'm not saying that, Clementine. I'm trying to talk about something that is going to happen if you remain lovers and if you get married. You will have to take stock of your children's grandparents. Of your children's great-grandparents. I mean, do the math, Clementine," Ruth Ann said.

"Do the math?"

"Yes. Do the math. You're good with math. Do it as fractions."

"Mother, people are not fractions."

"Yes they are. For my purpose, that is exactly what they are. Do the math."

"All right, Clementine said, relenting. "I'll do the math. I've got a tablet. What do you want me to write down?"

"Write Tyler."

Clementine did as her mother asked.

"And like everyone, Tyler has four grandparents," Ruth Ann went on.

"Yes."

"And all four are white. Am I right?"

"Yes. As far as I know. He's never said any different," Clementine said.

"Fine. So Tyler is 4/4th white. Right?"

"I don't like where you're going with this, mother."

Ruth Ann smiled her don't-try-to-stop-me-smile and said, "I'm not concerned whether or not you like where I'm going with this. I'm just telling you to go with me."

"All right," Clementine said in a whisper.

"Now write Clementine," Ruth Ann said.

"In a separate column?"

"Yes. In a separate column. But next to Tyler."

Clementine wrote.

"Now, Clementine has four grandparents. One is a black couple. That makes two black. The other couple is mixed. One black. One white. Right?"

"If you say so."

"So Clementine is 3/4th black and 1/4th white. Right?"

"Yes," Clementine said quietly.

"Now, add your fractions together, my darling."

"Add Tyler's and my fractions together?"

"Yes. Add them together.

Clementine added the fractions.

"So what do you get?" Ruth Ann asked when she saw Clementine adding the fractions.

"You mean racially?"

"Yes."

"I'll have to change it to 8ths to have it make any sense."

"Fine. Change it to 8ths."

"All right. If I do that, then Tyler's and my children will be 3/8ths black and 5/8ths white. Is that what you want me to see?"

"Yes. That is exactly what I want you to see."

"Which is supposed to mean what?" Clementine said.

"Love, Clementine."

"Love? Will we love them, do you mean?"

"No. That's not what I mean. I know you will love them."

"Will you love them? Will Elizabeth love them?"

"You know the answer to that too.

"All right. You will both love them. Edward will love them. Whoever they are and how ever many there are, since you seem to be planning our lives," Clementine said.

"I'm not planning your lives or their lives. I'm just asking the question."

"Which is?"

"Will they love themselves?"

"Will they love themselves?" Clementine asked.

"Yes. Will they look in the mirror and love themselves . . . your 5/8ths white babies and 3/8ths black babies."

Clementine spoke after a very long hesitation. "You taught me to love me."

"Yes, I did."

"And when I look in the mirror—if I use your fractions—when I look in the mirror I see a 3/4ths black person and 1/4th white person. But that isn't what matters. Because when I look in the mirror what I really see is you standing behind me, and I know you love me, and I see Tyler standing beside me, and I know he loves me. And for me that's all that finally matters."

"Good. That's good. All right," Ruth Ann said.

"All right . . . what?"

"All right. That's all I wanted to say."

"But what did you say?"

"You did the math. That's all I wanted to say. I just want you to know what you know."

"Mom . . . " Clementine began.

"I just want you to know that you know what you know. That way you can go live your life. And by the way, even if it's a long time from now, you need to have two children."

"Two children?

"Yes. Elizabeth and I have talked. You will need to have two. That way, when all of us are together, she will get to hold one, and I will get to hold one. We don't mind switching them back and forth. In fact, we plan on doing that. We just don't want to have to compete with each other if you only have one. So you will have to have at least two children."

34

By the time we reached Orlando, Clementine had finished her story. I didn't say anything after she stopped talking. I'm sure she expected me to respond, but at that point I wanted to think about what Ruth Ann and she had discussed before I said anything. In any case, I surprised her by turning off Interstate 4 and into the Sea World parking lot. We'd been to Sea World once before with a group of our friends early in our junior year at Tampa Coast. Several times since, Clementine had said she wanted to go back, but she hadn't known it was going to be that day. I suppose this was more of my grandfather's influence—the fun of surprising people, especially Clementine.

Even though it was a very warm day, we walked through the park, enjoying all of the shows, especially the dolphins. Then, as we sat at a restaurant overlooking the largest lake on the property, I told her I wanted to return the favor by trying to summarize the conversation I'd had with my mother at the same time she'd been talking to hers. When I finished doing so, I added that it seemed obvious each of our mothers had informed the other that she was going to have a serious talk with each of us. I said it sounded as if they even may well have agreed that each one of them should talk to each of us about their individual concerns. Clementine agreed that, yes, they probably had conspired to express their personal concerns about our continuing relationship while, at the same time, affirming how much they loved each of us.

"They're amazing women," I said to Clementine.

"Yes. They are," she agreed.

"For two people being raised by single mothers, I'd say we were very fortunate."

Clementine said she thought that was true. "It's also helped to have your grandfather be part of all of our lives, Tyler," Clementine said.

I said that she was right. Then we finished our meals and went back to see the rest of the shows. As we left, I told her I wanted to stop at the gift shop for a moment because there was something I wanted to buy. Urging Clementine to look at things on her own, I went directly to the jewelry counter where I found exactly what I wanted. With the help of a salesclerk, I had Clementine come try on a dolphin ring. Clementine looked somewhat skeptical as I asked her to hold out her hands. She was even more skeptical when I told her to close her eyes. When the clerk slipped the ring on the ring finger of her left hand, she started to open her eyes, but I told her to keep them shut. It took two tries to find a ring that fit perfectly, but at last we did. After the clerk slipped the ring off of her finger and put it behind the counter, I told Clementine to turn away and open her eyes and go back to looking elsewhere.

"Tyler, are you buying me a ring of some sort?" she asked.

"Clementine, please, just go away and leave me alone," I said.

Putting on her I-am-really-pleased-but-I-think-I-need-to-act-like-I'm-irritated-frown, she turned and did as I had asked. Then I had the clerk fit me for a matching ring: two dolphins, each touching the tail fins of the other to form a very delicate, very subtle circle, as if each was chasing the other or was a part of the other. With that, we left the park, Clementine looking at me as women sometimes look at men when they know something is coming, me walking with the rings tucked away in my pocket, trying to look as innocent as I could but certainly not fooling my wise Clementine.

35

It was almost 7 P.M. by the time we turned off Interstate 95 onto the road that would take us to St. Augustine and the Holiday Inn where we were going to stay. But rather than go directly to the hotel, I drove east until I came to a small ocean-side park. Before Clementine could ask what we were doing, I got out and came around and opened the door for her and said, "C'mon. There's something I need to do."

So we walked across the narrow stretch of grass to the water's edge where we stood together for some time looking at the ocean. Then I turned to Clementine and held out the small box in which I had the two rings. As she looked at me, I said, "Clementine, I love you. You know that. And we are going to be together for the rest of our lives. But here, among people, who don't know us, I want us to do something that will make our lives easier."

Clementine waited.

Then I opened the box and took out the ring I'd bought for her. Taking her left hand in mine, I slipped the ring on her finger. "Clementine, some day we'll do this in front of our mothers and my grandfather and anyone else you want to have there, and we'll do it with a Unitarian minister if you want and with rings that you and I pick out together, but right here, right now, I declare that with this ring, I thee wed." Then I slipped the ring on her finger.

Clementine was quiet for a moment. Then she took the other ring out of the small box and took my left hand in her left and said in a whisper, "Tyler, you are right. Some day we will do this with our mothers there and your grandfather there and with a Unitarian minister and with rings that you and I pick out together, but right here, right now, with this ring, Tyler, with this dolphin ring," she said, smiling, "I thee wed." And she slipped the dolphin ring on my hand. And we stood and looked at each other. Then she stepped close to me and kissed me and said, "And I know exactly why you've done this, Tyler. And as always, it's to take care of me, and I love you for it." Then we stood and looked at the water. Then she said, "Let's go play golf." So we turned and went back to our car and drove to the Holiday Inn where we checked in and unpacked and got ready for five days of playing golf on five different courses.

36

I have always found it interesting that for two people who worked as hard as we did at learning how to play sports in which scores are kept and winners and losers declared, neither Clementine nor I are particularly competitive. We've talked about it a number of times. What we finally determined was that Clementine simply loved to run. She was never focused on beating other runners, even though that's what she did most of the time. Instead, she said she tried to focus on the challenge of the moment.

I approached football in much the same way. I don't think I was ever trying to defeat an opponent. I was just trying to play the game as well as I could. When it was all over, other people totaled up the score and declared a winner and a loser. It may sound strange, but there were times when I honestly turned to a receiver who had beaten me or a running back who got past me and told him he'd made a good move or even congratulated him for scoring. I know my teammates thought that was odd. I know some of my coaches weren't particularly pleased by my occasional comments, but I meant it. Some of the players against whom I competed were simply exceptional athletes, better than me, for sure. I didn't see any harm in telling an opponent that I admired his skills, not just after the games but sometimes during the games.

It was very much the same with Clementine. She admired runners who worked hard at their skills. I know she's congratulated people who've beaten her just as she's congratulated runners she's defeated. I think that's why we enjoyed playing golf together. I was always as excited for her when she made a good shot as I was pleased with myself when I did the same. I know that's how Clementine felt as well. For us, it was always the pleasure of not just playing golf but of playing together that mattered most. That's why I don't have a problem telling you that Clementine was and is a better golfer than me. Yes, she uses the women's tees, which means the holes are a little shorter for her. I'm not talking about that. I'm talking about the fact that she hits a more true tee shot than me, that her short irons are beautiful to see, and that her putting, especially from inside twenty feet, is always wonderfully true.

At the same time, I know that she admires the way I can get into and then out of trouble, which I do far too often . . . getting into trouble, that is. So for us, playing courses along the Atlantic Ocean, some of which over looked the water, was simply an absorbing, rewarding experience.

Of the five courses we played that week, the short course north of St. Augustine was challenging because it had so many quick turns; the longer course near Vero Beach was challenging because of the wind: the front nine faced into the wind; the back nine faced away. Making the adjustment was what kept us focused that day.

Clementine had a particularly good day on the course when we stayed in Daytona Beach. She must have been particularly relaxed, because her tee drives were the best she'd ever struck up to that day. In fact, on more than one hole, she out-drove me by at least twenty yards.

Of course, the five days weren't just about golf. We ate dinner each night at a different seafood restaurant facing the ocean. We made love with our balcony doors open and the ocean wind blowing into the room. The second night we stayed in a Holiday Inn I told her that lying next to her as the light dimmed and the evening came on was as close to Heaven as I ever imaged myself wanting to be. On the third night, when it began to rain, which we could hear on the roof of our room on the top floor of the building, was even better. "I could spend the rest of my life just like this," I said. "Lying next to you. Listening to the rain."

Clementine did not speak in response. Instead, she pressed her face closer to mine, and wrapped her right arm over my left shoulder, and began to sing very softly, "When you're down and troubled, and you need some loving care, and nothing, nothing is going right," which are the first lines of the Carole King song that by then we had made *our* song. The song then goes on, "Close your eyes and think of me, and soon I will be there, to brighten up even your darkest night."

I joined her for the chorus: "You just call out my name, and you know wherever I am, I'll come running, to see you again. Winter, spring, summer, or fall, all you have to do is call, and I'll be there, yes, I will, you've got a friend."

Having finished the song, we lay listening to the rain before we closed our eyes and fell asleep.

37

At the end of the week, we drove back to Tampa and met my mother at the airport. We asked her about the conference, which she described in detail that evening. She asked us about our golf, which we said had been wonderful, going on to describe the hotels and the courses and the restaurants over dinner in as much detail as we felt was appropriate.

Three weeks later, my grandfather and Ruth Ann returned, both of them filled with stories about driving west, about my grandfather's friends. My grandfather told us that everyone had enjoyed meeting Ruth Ann, that she had been the center of attention on more than one occasion.

Of course, none of the three of us asked any questions about my grandfather's and Ruth's relationship. That was their business. We assumed they would tell us what they wanted us to know when they wanted us to know it.

Then it was time for both Clementine and me to begin sorting out what we were going to take with us to our universities. I had to report to the University of Georgia at the beginning of the second week of August to begin football practice so I was beginning to become more and more nervous. Clementine calmed my nerves by talking about other things: where I would live, what courses I would take.

Three days before I was scheduled to leave, Clementine and I bought a newer used car with Raymond money. Even though she wanted me to take it to Athens, I insisted that I keep the station wagon she and I had driven all through high school and that she take the newer car. Finally she gave in. Then, because I had to go to Athens before Clementine went to Atlanta, my mother and grandfather and Clementine and Ruth Ann all took me to the University of Georgia where I reported to the Athletic Department and was given my room assignment in the Athletic Dormitory. So the five of us trooped in, carrying my suitcase and two footlockers of clothes and personal items and the few special books I wanted to have with me. I can tell you that the first thing I did, after meeting my roommate, Barry Slayman, and his parents, was to arrange the photos that I'd brought on the shelf over my bed: Clementine and me at the senior prom, Clementine's graduation portrait, the two pictures she'd given me as a gift when we'd vacationed in North Carolina with the family, and a photo I'd taken of the four of them: my mother, my grandfather, Clementine, and Ruth Ann, sitting in the snow on the porch of our winter vacation house in North Carolina. It was my favorite because all four of them were smiling.

As might be expected, although I had hoped it would not happen, Barry's parents were very polite but at the same time demonstrated in the way they looked at each other their surprise that their white son's white roommate was dating a young black woman. I hoped it was not a harbinger of things to come. I wanted Clementine to come to Athens as often as she could, especially during football season. As nice as Barry seemed when we first met, I hoped I hadn't been saddled with a roommate who was prejudiced. As it turned out, he was not, although I was never sure that his parents got over their surprise at meeting Clementine and Ruth Ann.

When everything was settled, the five of us went out for dinner. And even though I had by then turned nineteen and thought of myself as grown up, when it came time for the four of them to leave for Tampa, it was a very hard experience. I embraced my mother and told her I loved her. I did the same for my grandfather. In fact, when my grandfather told me how proud he was of me, I put my head on his shoulder and cried very quietly. After all, my grandfather had not been just a provider for my mother and me; he was my mentor and my hero. I told him I loved him very much. He said, "You have to write to me about your classes, especially your history classes, Tyler." I said I would.

I am proud to say that Ruth Ann embraced me and said she would miss me. I said the same to her, which I meant. She had been a greater influence on my life during my high school years than either of us understood at the time.

Then the three of them walked to the car so Clementine and I could kiss each other goodbye. And while we knew that Clementine would be going to Georgia Tech in just two weeks, and that we would figure out how to see each other regularly, after all we had shared, after all we had become for each other, the idea that I would not see her for two weeks was just beyond my comprehension. So we held on to each other for some time, so long that it was obvious my mother and grandfather and Ruth Ann were eager to leave. Finally, we told each other that we'd talk on the telephone three times a week, and we'd write every other day, and we'd be seeing each other in two weeks anyway, because I was planning on driving to Atlanta when she moved into her dormitory.

As affectionate as Clementine and I were and still are, except for holding hands sometimes, we've never been particularly demonstrative in public. We both felt that our expressions of affection were a private matter. But on that occasion, we kissed for a very long time. When we held each other afterwards, I said I wanted to memorize the smell of her skin, which made her laugh and say, "It's smelled the same for four years, Tyler."

"I know," I said. "But right here. Right now. I want to memorize it so I can lie in bed and night and imagine you are with me."

With that we embraced, and then she turned and walked away from me toward the car where my mother and grandfather and Ruth Ann waited. As they left, I stood in the driveway in front of my dormitory and waved goodbye for as long as I could see them. I was not the only young man doing that, by the way. There were at least five others scattered along the curbing doing exactly the same thing. In fact, when the last of us had waved the last goodbye to our departing families, we walked into the dormitory together. As we did, I felt an arm around my shoulder. When I turned, I was looking at the biggest football player I'd ever seen in my life, a young black man who smiled rather wistfully and said, "Damn, that was a hard thing to do."

I smiled through my own tears and said it was a whole lot harder than I'd thought it would be. A tall young man walking in front of us turned around and said, "You've got that right." And in that moment I realized I was now among new friends.

38

It is not my intention to detail either my academic or football career at the University of Georgia. Certainly there were important experiences in both spheres that further shaped who I am, what I believe, what I have done with my life since. However, what is more important to this memoir is the role Clementine played in my education. For her role may have changed, but it was not diminished.

I was introduced to collegiate football the day after my mother and grandfather and Clementine and Ruth left. And as much as I knew it would not be high school football, it was still a major adjustment as not only I but all of the first year players quickly learned. I had thought I was in good physical shape when I reported for practice. I learned in the first two days that what I considered good physical shape was not going to be nearly enough. Everything happened in drills and in practice faster than I had thought possible, even if I'd watched college football on television and in person. As everyone who has ever played at the university level can attest, the game comes at you faster than you could have imagined. I cannot even conceive how fast the professional game must be.

Be that as it may, first year players worked together for three days, during which time the coaches evaluated not only what skills we were lacking. They also tried to decide where each of us might fit into the larger scheme of things. Yes, there were some tense moments, and yes, sometimes the coaches let us know that we had to work both faster and smarter, but overall we were also made to feel welcome. By the time we joined the varsity team, which was itself an intimidating morning, we were made to feel even more welcome. It may be true at many other universities as well, but for sure at Georgia when you are invited to become a Bulldog, you become a part of a family. Even the seniors made it clear that as far as they were concerned, every freshman was still expected to contribute in some way or other.

As for me, my first impression was that some of the players were the biggest, strongest human beings I had ever seen. That some of those very large people were also among the quickest was even more amazing. Then they topped that off by also being a very nice group of young men. Certainly I fouled up in drills on many occasions, but I never heard about that from any of the players. The coaches, yes, sometimes, but never my fellow players. After all, if I was going to pull my weight, they knew I had to learn how to play Georgia football. I wasn't going to learn to do that, or even more important, I wasn't going to want to do that if more experienced players were critical of my errors. So I was able to learn not just from the coaches but from the older players as well.

After the first morning when he welcomed us to the University, Coach Dooley didn't have much daily contact with us. It was the assistant coaches who worked with the various position players. But he was always there, and all of us knew he was taking in everything that we did. Obviously, all of us were trying to impress him every day. How much we did that showed up in our playing time. As a first year member of the team, who was not nearly as fast or as strong as most of the others, I had to impress him with my smarts. So I listened and studied and tried to anticipate what I should be doing rather than figure out what I was expected to do after it was too late.

What mattered even more to me were Clementine's and my telephone conversations and her letters. The first one arrived two days after I had first reported for football practice. It is among the things I have kept over my lifetime. I share it with you now not so you can learn anything about me but so you can hear Clementine for yourself.

August 22, 1984
Dear Tyler:

I don't ever want to do that again. I don't ever want to have to say goodbye like that again. I know we have to now. You have to follow your own notions about how you want to be educated, and I have to do the same. I know in the long run it will probably be best for both of us. Each of us needs to learn more about who we are. Each of us needs to test who we are individually. Sometimes I don't know where my opinion ends and yours begins or where your insights into things end and mine begin. That's how close we've been for the past four years. So it will probably do us good to find out more about ourselves by not being together so much. Of course, even if that is true, it doesn't make it any easier. Certainly it didn't make it any easier when I got into the car, and the four of us drove away. Yes, my mother and your mother and your grandfather were very kind to me, and my mother let me sit close to her and lean my head on her shoulder like I lean on yours when we've driven with them. I know your mother was having a hard time after saying goodbye to you, but she was even more concerned about me. Once, just before we got to Atlanta, she reached over from the front seat and took my hand, and even though she didn't say anything, it helped.

By the time we reached the motel in Macon, I had stopped crying. No, I didn't cry out loud. I cried silently. I leaned my head against the window and tried to tell myself that this wasn't going to be forever. I reminded myself that I would be going to Georgia Tech very soon, and that I'd be coming to see you for the first football game.

Don't worry about playing, either, Tyler. I know you're good. The coaches will learn that very soon. I know you always said you were showing off for me when you played at Tampa Coast, and I know I said I was showing off for you when I ran, but you don't need to try to show off for me any more. You are my whole life. You help me think. You help me see and feel. You make me laugh. That's what I missed the most on the way home. I know that you would have seen things as we drove back to Tampa and then said something to make me laugh. I think that's what your grandfather misses too, Tyler. He said as much after we were almost all the way home. You are sensitive and kind and strong, and you make all of us laugh. What could be better than that? That's one of the reasons why I want to spend the rest of my life with you.

It's late now, and I want to mail this letter early in the morning. I will see you very soon. I know it would be very hard for you to come to Atlanta when my mother and your mother and your grandfather take me to Georgia Tech. (Yes, your mother and your grandfather are both coming, which is very nice of them It will help my mother.) So I will call as soon as I'm settled and give you a telephone number where you can reach me.

Until we get to see each other again, stay focused on what you are doing. I know that's what you would say to me so I'm saying it to you first.

I love you, Tyler.

Your Very Own Clementine

39

Before I tell you how I responded to Clementine's letter in writing and then how I surprised her by being in the parking lot in front of her dormitory when she arrived at Georgia Tech, I need to tell you about two things that happened during the first two weeks of football practice.

The first took place at the evening training table meal four days into the practice sessions. Barry Slayman and I had gotten our food and were sitting at a table with two other players when to my surprise Joe Norwalk sat down next to me and started arranging his food so he could eat.

Joe Norwalk is black. He was recruited as a defensive end. He was big and fast and strong, and even in those early days of practice I knew he was going to become an important player at Georgia. After a moment, he turned to me and smiled and asked how I was doing. I said I was fine. I was sore, but I was fine. He said he understood because he felt the same way. Then he said, "I hear you're dating a sister."

I turned to him. "A sister?"

"Yeah. You know. A black girl. I hear you're dating a sister."

My first instinct was to fear that he was going to be critical. That he didn't approve. I was instantly prepared to defend myself and to tell him it was none of his business when he said, "She's the new runner at Georgia Tech? Right?"

I hesitated. "Yes. But how did you know that?"

"My cousin runs for Tech. He told me the coach said they got this real good middle distance runner out of Tampa. None of the runners have met her yet, but the coaches said she's a real nice person. Then someone at Tech told my cousin that she dated a new Georgia football player. My cousin said he heard the guy's name is Tyler, which I figure would make it you."

I waited for a moment before answering. I wasn't sure where the conversation was going. Finally I said, "Well, your cousin's right. I am the guy. We do date," adding, "Since we were freshmen in high school."

Joe nodded and said, "Since you were freshmen in high school? Damn. That's a long time," he said, nodding. Then he smiled and said, "So you must be all right, then."

"I must be all right?" I said,

"Yeah. You must be all right. Cool. To be dating a sister." He smiled. "You must be a good guy. If she's kept you for four years. That's serious."

I smiled. "I hope."

"You hope which?" he said, smiling but obviously not joking. "That you're a good guy, or that it's serious."

"Both. I hope I'm a good guy. And it is serious."

"Good. I'd hate to see a sister get hurt. Especially a nice one."

I glanced at Barry then turned to Joe. "She'll never be hurt by me. We take care of each other," I said.

Joe finished a mouth full of food. "Good," he said. "That's good. That's cool." Then the three of us took up talking about practice and about the assistant coaches and about Georgia football with two other players who joined us at the table.

40

The other incident took place on Monday evening of the second week of practice. I was in my room sitting at my desk studying the play book. Suddenly Vince Dooley was standing in the doorway. In my surprise, I stood up. "Coach Dooley," I said.

"Tyler," he replied.

I fumbled for words. "Come in, sir. Please."

He was already in the room.

"Please, sit down if you'd like," I said, hurrying to pull Barry's chair out so he could sit.

"That's okay, Tyler. I just stopped in to see how you were adjusting."

"I'm fine, sir. I'm fine."

"I try to get around to visit the new players early in the practice session," he said, moving to the bookshelf where I'd arranged my grandfather's books and the pictures of my mother and grandfather and Clementine and Ruth Ann and me.

"This your grandfather?" he said.

"Yes, sir. And my mother."

"I've read two of his books."

"Really. I didn't know that," I said, stumbling over my words.

"I read history," he said.

"Yes, sir. I heard one of the players . . . one of the juniors . . . say that you earned a master's degree in history."

"That's right. I do have a master's in history."

"And that's how you read my grandfather's books?"

"Yes. I enjoyed them. He tells a hard truth. But it's a truth that needs to be told."

"He does do that."

"You must be proud of him."

"I am, sir. Very proud."

He looked at the photos again. "Is this your girlfriend?"

I moved closer to where he was standing. "Yes, sir. And her mother. Ruth Ann Brown."

"She's an historian too, isn't she?"

"Yes, sir. She is."

"She wrote a book with Professor Thomas."

"Yes, sir."

"I'm reading it right now. At home at night. Their lectures. The ones they gave in Edinburgh."

"Yes, sir," I said. "I got to go with them to Edinburgh. Ruth Ann's daughter, Clementine. She and I got to go with them."

"Clementine? That's her name. Your girl friend's name?"

"Yes, sir. Clementine Brown," I said.

He looked again. "Very pretty. Very intelligent looking." Then he turned to me. "Is she in school?"

"Yes, sir. Georgia Tech. She's a runner. The 440 and 880."

"Hard races," he said. "How come she didn't come with you to Georgia?"

"She wants to study biology. So she can go to medical school," I said.

"Ah. She could have come here. Georgia has a good pre-med program. But as long as she's happy. That's what counts the most."

"Yes, sir. I agree, sir," I said.

"Do you remember the letter I wrote to you, Tyler. When you were at Tampa Coast High School?"

"Yes, sir. I still have it. It's framed and hanging on my wall at home."

"Really? Framed?"

"Yes, sir." Then I added, "Would you like to sit down?" I pulled Barry's chair out from his desk and turned it toward the middle of the room.

"Fine. Thank you." He sat.

"I competed against your father, you know."

"Yes, sir. I did know that."

"When Auburn played Maryland. In 1952."

"Yes, sir. Maryland won, 13-7."

Coach Dooley smiled. "Yes, Maryland won. Although you didn't have to say that."

"Sorry, sir."

He smiled. "I'm only joking. It was a very good game. Close all the way."

"That's what I read. After you wrote me the letter, I looked it up."

"Then you know your father had a very good day running the ball."

"Yes, sir. I saw that."

"In fact, late in the fourth quarter, he ran right over me."

"Really? Sorry, sir," I said.

Vince Dooley looked at me for a moment and smiled. I tried to smile in return.

"Don't be sorry," he said. "That was his job. I tackled him early in the quarter. Which was about as hard as anyone had ever hit me. Then in the fourth quarter he ran right over me. Very embarrassing."

"Yes, sir," I said, aware that I shouldn't say I was sorry again.

"What I remember is that two plays later, I came up again and tackled him as hard as I could. When we got up, he turned to me and said, 'Good play, Dooley.'"

"Really?"

"Yes. 'Good play, Dooley.' No other opponent had ever said that to me before, and none ever said it after that day."

"I've been told he was like that, sir."

"Yes, he was. A very decent man. A tough player, but a very decent man."

"Thank you, sir."

"It was very sad about what happened to him later."

"In Viet Nam?"

"Yes. That was too bad. It was tragic. He shouldn't have died like that. But that's also true of a lot of other good men. None of them should have died."

"I agree, sir."

Coach Dooley was quiet for a moment. Then he looked at me. "He'd be a good man to model yourself after, Tyler."

"Yes, sir. That's what my grandfather says."

"Your grandfather would be a good man to model yourself after, as well."

I nodded. "I'm trying to do that, sir. After both of them."

"Good," he said, standing. "Well, I just wanted to come by and say hello. If you need anything, let me know. But from what I know about you, I'd say you'll do very well here at Georgia."

I stood up quickly. "I will certainly try to, Coach Dooley. I wouldn't want to let you down."

He smiled and extended his hand, which I shook in return. "See you in the morning. Bright and early," he said.

"Yes, sir. Bright and early."

Then he was gone. Coach Vince Dooley. Coach Dooley. Nationally famous. Respected. Smart. I sat down again and tried to picture what had just happened. The man who had played against my father. The man who was the reason I'd wanted to play at Georgia. He'd read my grandfather's books and was reading my grandfather's and Ruth Ann's book of lectures. Then I thought about my father. I wanted to make him proud. I wanted to make him . . . . I needed to get a picture of him from my mother and put it on my shelf. I looked at the picture of Clementine. I wanted to make her proud. I wanted to make my mother proud and my grandfather proud. Most of all, I wanted to make Clementine proud of me so she would love me and want to be with me for the rest of my life. I wanted to make her proud.

41

Later that night, after Barry had come in and gone to bed, I lay awake for some time thinking about all that had unfolded in my life, all that was happening at once in my life. Reaching over to my desk, I found a pad of paper. Then, in the dim light from the campus street coming in through the drawn blinds, I wrote:

In my dream of satin
you are sweet smelling and
smile and are dancing
to a long, sonorous violin solo,
double-bowed, Slavic,
crossing borders between
here and there and every
shade of color in between.
In my blue dream of black satin
your skin is sweet smelling and

Then I stopped. There were no more words. I tried to read what I'd written. Slavic? What was I thinking of? Russian, maybe. Or Polish. Tchaikovsky? Dvorak? Why Slavic? Why a violin solo? I tried to hear what I'd written. But nothing more came. It was silent. I could hear Barry sleeping. I could hear a door opening in the hallway and closing quietly. I could hear someone passing by our room on his way to the restroom, I assumed. But I could hear no more words. I could hear the music. I could hear "In my blue dream of black satin/your skin is sweet smelling/and . . . ," but that was the end.

I put the pad of paper and pen on the floor next to my bed and rolled over and went to sleep. My plan was to drive to Atlanta in two days to surprise Clementine when she arrived at Georgia Tech. Maybe that's why I'd run out of words. I would see Clementine and Ruth Ann my mother and grandfather in two days, and they didn't know I was coming. I wanted to see the look on Clementine's face when she arrived and found me waiting. I wanted to see her smile. "Your black skin heals everything you touch." I heard those words as I fell asleep. "Your black skin heals everything you touch."

42

So there I was in the parking lot, my car lined up among other cars that had brought new students and siblings and parents to Georgia Tech, waiting in front of Allison Fisher Dormitory, my heart pounding, my memory racing back over four years, waiting and waiting and waiting, counting down the minutes, the seconds, until they would arrive. I had gotten up early, shaved and showered and left Athens, eating a quick meal at a Burger King on Interstate 20, following the directions Clementine had sent, knowing that they all expected me at noon, but how, in God's name, was I supposed to wait until noon?

So there I was, trying to look as inconspicuous as I could while all around me the earliest arrivals moved back and forth, unloading suitcases and boxes and stereo sets and portable television sets into rooms on the first floor, the second floor, the third floor. I drank my second cup of coffee slowly. Then I saw them. I looked at my watch. It was exactly 9 A.M. I wanted to remember the time. It was exactly 9 A.M. Ruth Ann was driving the van my grandfather had rented. Clementine was in the front passenger's side seat. My mother and my grandfather were in the back seat. The rest of the van was loaded with Clementine's personal things. I could see that as they pulled into the parking lot. Once I saw where they were going I moved between cars so I would be standing behind them as Clementine opened the door and got out.

I could feel my heart beating. Ruth Ann nosed the van into a parking place. I saw her glance into the rear view mirror. I know she saw me. Then the passenger's side door opened, and Clementine got out slowly. She turned to close the door. Then she saw me over her left shoulder. I didn't move. I just stood with my arms stretched as wide as I could make them stretch. I was the lover waiting in the airport. I was the lover waiting on shore. I was the lover waiting in the parking lot of the Allison Fisher Dormitory on the campus of the Georgia Institute of Technology. I was Clementine's . . . .

She turned and ran straight at me. I braced myself. Then she leaped into my arms, kissing me and holding her face against mine, her legs wrapped around my waist. I could feel her body shaking. I could feel the tears on my cheek. I could feel her lips pressing against mine, speaking my name even as she kissed me. Holding on as tightly as she had ever held on. And so we were together again. "Tyler, Tyler, Tyler," she kept saying. And I laughed. I laughed and laughed and laughed. And then Ruth Ann was there and my mother was there and my grandfather was there. And all of us were hugging and talking at once. But Clementine, by then standing, did not let go. She just kept saying, "I thought you were coming at noon" and "You said you would get here at noon." And I said, "Did you think I could wait?" and "Did you really think I could wait?"

Then we were all calm again, and the unloading began. In two hours it was over. Clementine was settled into room 207. And we all stopped and looked at each other. And Ruth Ann said, "Tyler, I am so glad to see you. My daughter has put on a brave front in the last two weeks, but I must tell you, she is not much of an actress when it comes to her feelings about you."

I smiled and said, "I'm not much of an actor either."

Then we went to lunch, and they wanted to know about Georgia and football. And I told them it was hard, but I liked the coaches, and I liked my teammates, and I liked my roommate. And then I told them that Coach Vince Dooley had come to my room, and we had talked. And I said, "He's read two of your books, Grandpa." Then I turned to Ruth Ann. "And now he's reading the lectures you and Grandpa gave in Edinburgh."

"Really?" Ruth Ann said.

"He has a master's degree in history," I said

"Really?" Ruth Ann said again.

And all the time we talked, under the table, I pressed my right leg against Clementine's left leg, and she pressed her shoulder against my shoulder, and I could feel her warmth, and she could feel my warmth. And for a moment it was as if we were back in ninth grade in Mrs. Justine's biology class, back on that first day when I knew I was so much in love with Clementine that I couldn't even speak. So she had been the one to speak first when she asked me, "Should we be lab partners?" And I had wanted to say, "I'll be your partner for the rest of your life," but I hadn't, of course. I had just said, "Yes." But I knew it was true, nonetheless. I wanted to be her partner for the rest of her life and the rest of my life. So here we were, four years later, Clementine and me and her mother and my mother and my grandfather eating lunch together in a small restaurant to which we had walked, two blocks from the Georgia Tech campus. And Clementine and I were still partners. Clementine Camille Brown and Tyler Thomas Raymond were still partners.

43

There is a long tradition in both Judaism and Christianity of what is sometimes termed ecstatic literature. The tradition is part of other religious disciplines as well: literature expressed by prophets or seers or visionaries who are driven into spells of ecstasy by their pursuit of the divine. The whirling dervishes come to mind as well as a number of the prophets of the Torah and the Christian mystics. The same sense of ecstasy also shows up in Western world literature, especially in Romantic poetry. So if it seems at times as if this memoir borders on ecstatic, even poetic portrayals of the profound and often times overwhelming emotions that Clementine and I experienced individually and shared in our partnership, I defend my narration by arguing that I am doing nothing more than trying to tell what I remember as our truth. It is possible, after all, for two people to be so deeply in love, so much at-one, so atoned, that their lives become their shared affection.

At the same time, I am aware that it is not unusual for high school students who swear they are in love while they are in their teens to find that they grow in different directions, so to speak, once they begin their college studies, especially if they are not on the same campus. The fact that did not happen to Clementine and me warrants examination.

First, both of us were fully aware that it was race that brought us together. That is, we know we live in a racist nation. Prejudices by whites against blacks and blacks against whites can be traced even farther back in time than the advent of chattel slavery. But for my purposes, I will begin with that abomination.

When African chattel slavery was transported to the colonies, it created a two fold relationship between the races. Obviously, it created a body of hatred. Africans forced onto slave ships and brought in chains to the New World quickly learned to hate their captors. Whites learned to fear reprisal by their captives. At the same time, once that institution was created, it brought the races into unavoidably close if antagonistic relationship. Yet within that antagonism other complex relationships also formed. Very often, black women were forced to become the sexual subjects of white men. From those unions often times came children. In nearly all cases, the children were then raised within the slave worker community, which had, apparently, the capacity to love the mixed race children in equal proportion to the white community's cruel rejection of their offspring. When those mixed race children then very often married within the mothers' community, a new psychological dynamic was introduced into the black culture that varies from a claim of an elevated status on the part of the mixed race children, as being more white than their siblings or cousins, to a rejection of their claim by some blacks who argued that their mixed race heritage made them less pure.

Clementine grew up aware that her mother was a black woman and her father was a mixed race man. She became aware of the reasons he became as prejudiced against blacks as he was angry at whites. In short, she became aware that her father was in conflict with himself, a conflict that injured him in ways even he did not fully understand.

At the same time, Clementine did not inherit any of his self-directed anger, which is a credit to both her mother's wisdom and her mother's parents' unconditional love. And while all of that was positive, there was also no way that Clementine or her mother or any other black person, for that matter, can ever escape the fact that blacks are a minority racial group within a majority white society. Her mother's struggles to establish herself in the academic community, a struggle at which she succeeded, were evidence enough.

At the same time Clementine was growing up with her mother, who was battling the odds on both her own behalf and on behalf of her beloved daughter, I was being raised by a mother and, even more, by a grandfather whose sense of moral justice required that they do more than just reject racial prejudice; it required that they speak out in their work against all forms of disenfranchisement. My grandfather's career is testimony to his commitment. Small wonder then that I grew up believing that the wrongs blacks had suffered in America were crimes against their humanity. Small wonder then that given the apparent willingness of blacks, when allowed to do so, to live side by side with whites rendered them more than just morally admirable, it made them morally superior. After all, I asked myself many times as I grew up, would I have had the capacity to try to befriend whites if I'd been black? Or would I have responded to injustice with hatred and violence? As much as I wanted to believe that I would have followed the example of Martin Luther

King, I suspected that I might not be that large minded or good hearted. I suspected I would have been far more inclined to become a Black Muslim and reject white society entirely.

What does all of that have to do with Clementine's and my relationship? The answer: everything.

Clementine did not and does not hate being black. She did not and does not hate whites. She has inherited an inordinate capacity for loyalty and love. Frankly, I came closer to disavowing whites than she ever did. At the same time, my admiration of black culture was both sincere and profound. So the question Clementine and I have addressed many times is not what most people think: how could two people, one black and one white, manage to love each other in a world that would seem determined to drive them apart? Rather, the question we considered during more than one discussion was could we have avoided falling in love? Yes, each of us professed we were in love with the other's person, but at the same time, we could not deny that we were in love with each other's race just as much. For Clementine, white men seemed to be the movers and shakers of society. For me, black women were particularly powerful expressions of the Gaia, the mythological Earth Mother deity who birthed, nurtured, and sustained all of humanity.

Does that mean our affection was not sincere? Does it mean Clementine fell in love with me *because* I was white? Does it mean I fell in love with her *because* she was black? Could she have loved a black man in the same way she loved me? Could I have loved a white woman in the same way I loved her? Did she stay with me because, having fallen in love with a white man, she did not wish to prove herself prejudiced by eventually rejecting him in favor of a black man? Did I stay with her because, having fallen in love with a black woman, I did not want to prove myself prejudiced by eventually rejecting her in favor of a white woman? Or did it mean that unlike so many high school students of the same race who fall in love and who then go away to college and fall *out* of love, Clementine and I were bonded together in a way that transcended our relative immaturity because our differing races required we confront and understand complexities in our personal natures and in our society in ways that same race couples did not. Thus, ironically, the American racism that could/should have driven us apart instead knitted us together in a way that disallowed our relationship from ever coming undone. In short, having become who we wanted to believe we were worthy of becoming in the process of falling in love with each other, would we risk becoming less worthy if we ever fell out of love with each other? It is a question we asked each other on more than one occasion. It is also a question we never tried to answer, at least, not in words. Instead, we let the question be the answer. We let the answer be our love. Fortunately, we never questioned our love of one another because, in the final analysis, we simply liked being together. We were not just lovers and companions; we were best friends. We decided that we would be fools to ask for more than that.

44

The first football game of the 1984 season for the Georgia Bulldogs was against Southern Mississippi. Southern Mississippi is not the same caliber football program as Georgia, but the Golden Eagles are still a very well organized and well coached team. Certainly they were in 1984. We managed to beat them 26-19, but it was a very competitive game from start to finish.

What I remember most clearly about the game are two things: sitting in the locker room before the game with the other players after we'd come in from warm-ups, everyone was tense. I tried to manage my emotions, but it was very difficult. Of all the things that happen in preparation for a football game and during a football game, it is the final twenty minutes in the locker room before the game that most players dread. Certainly I did.

The second thing I most clearly remember is coming down the tunnel from under the stands and going onto the field. University of Georgia fans are the most loyal fans in college football. They come in droves. And they all wear red. When the players come out through the tunnel and are suddenly in the sunlight and on the field, the sound of the fans cheering and the band playing and the sea of red are almost overwhelming. For me, even with all of that emotion—seeing Vince Dooley leading us onto the field and to our sidelines, wondering how my father must have felt when he'd gone on the field for the University of Maryland the first time—I still looked for Clementine and my mother and grandfather and Ruth Ann, because they were all there. Of course, even though I knew where they were going to be sitting, I couldn't locate them. Part of that was because of the surge of the crowd moving all through the stands. Part of it was my vision was blurred by the sunlight. Part of it was simply emotions. What was Clementine feeling? What was she thinking? As I got to the sidelines and looked around at my teammates and looked up into the stands, I remembered what it felt like after my first game on the junior varsity team when I was in ninth grade at Tampa Coast when I was leaving the field and Clementine surprised me when suddenly she was walking beside me. I remember her saying, "You played very well, Tyler." I remember how proud that made me feel. So here I was, on the playing field of the stadium at the University of Georgia, and all I wanted to do was not do anything that would disappoint Clementine. And as odd as that may sound to some of you, I assure you it is exactly what any number of players were feeling that day about their own families. Barry Slayman, my roommate that first year, who was a quarterback, told me once that he played football from junior high school all the way through the University of Georgia in the hope he would make his father proud.

I'd love to tell you that I played an important part in Georgia's victory that first game, but that would be an exaggeration. I knew I wouldn't be playing the safety position that day. I wasn't experienced enough. Yes, there were other first year players who got into the game. Three even started. But they were top quality players. I was the kind of athlete who shows up, works hard, is dependable, but certainly not gifted. I would play a role on the team. For me, that was enough.

In any case, I did get into the game on the kick off team three times. The first time, I was blocked out of the play. I remember that it hurt. Any player who tells you that being blind-side blocked doesn't hurt isn't telling you the truth. I saw stars for a moment as I trotted off the field. The second time, I closed in on the ball carrier, but seeing I would not get to him, instead I took out two of his blockers, which allowed the outside contain man to make the tackle. As I came off the field two players patted me on the back and told me that was a smart play. Finally, the third and last time I was on the field that day, I made the tackle, but I paid a price, because the Southern Mississippi runner saw me coming so he turned up field to make sure that when we collided, he could deliver the blow. Since I was trying to do the same thing, it was the hardest hit I'd ever experienced in football up to that point. It wouldn't be the last time I got hit hard while making a tackle, but it was hard enough to serve as an introduction.

I remember getting up off the Southern Mississippi player and looking into his eyes. I'd hoped he would be intimidated, but I certainly didn't see anything like that in his face. As I came to the sidelines I finally saw Clementine standing up and cheering. Then I saw my grandfather and mother and Ruth Ann. That made it all worthwhile. Seeing Clementine cheering didn't make it hurt less, but it did make the pain worth it. The fact Coach Dooley walked past me on the sidelines and said a hurried "Good tackle, Raymond," as he continued talking to an assistant coach through his headset microphone was as much reward as I needed that day.

Of course, after the game, once I'd showered and dressed, I found my faithful family waiting for me outside the locker room. I don't know if any of you have ever gone on a long cruise on a ship or a long trip on an airplane and come home to find the person you love the most in the whole world waiting for you. And when you arrive in the waiting area, that person leaps into your arms with excitement, but if you have then you know what it felt like for me to walk out of the University of Georgia football locker room after a first game victory and have Clementine run toward me and throw her arms around my shoulders and tell me she loved me at the same time she was kissing my lips. I'm not sure how she did that, of course—kissing me while at the same time telling me she loved me—but she did. And right then and there, all of the hurt in my left shoulder magically disappeared. It came back later, when we were eating dinner together, but for the moment, when she kissed me and said, "I love you, Tyler," it was gone.

45

I don't want this part of my memoir of Clementine to turn into the story of my football exploits, first, because my career isn't worth talking about in detail, second, because the only reason I bring up the games at all is to demonstrate the importance to me of Clementine's continuing support. Yes, Georgia lost to Georgia Tech that year, 36-18. And yes, Clementine came and sat with my family, but I had told her before the game to not feel badly if she cheered for Tech. After all, it was her university. She said afterwards that she hadn't cheered for either team. She had just sat quietly and tried to watch without being emotional except to hope that I would get into the game. When I did, she said she then hoped I wouldn't get hurt. For Clementine, that must have been very challenging.

It was easier for her when we played the University of Florida. Not only is the game played in Jacksonville, Florida, which for all practical purposes is neutral turf, I actually played almost one full quarter at safety. Georgia lost the game 27-0 because at that point Florida was beginning to become a national power. Florida threw a touchdown over me early in the fourth quarter. Fortunately it was called back because the receiver had used his hands to push off as we ran stride for stride into the end zone. Later in the game, I got caught going the wrong direction by a running back who went on to score. The fact none of the Bulldogs played well that day didn't help how I felt after the game. I'd over thought the touchdown run and gone the wrong way into coverage when my instincts had that told me the right thing to do. It was a lesson I tried to keep in mind in the future.

It was some consolation that we beat both Clemson and South Carolina that year, and that we were invited to play in the Citrus Bowl, in Orlando, against Florida State. But before that happened, an issue arose that for a few days made things very difficult for Clementine at Georgia Tech, and because of that, it made things difficult for me.

Let me explain first that the dormitories at Georgia Tech are very much like the dormitories at Georgia. Students come and go, visiting for all sorts of reasons. Because Barry Slayman was a handsome guy as well as very good in math, a number of our football player friends used to come to our room to get help from him with their class assignments. In fact, our room was sometimes so crowded just before tests with friends trying to review with Barry that I couldn't even lie down in my own bed. The fact he was a quarterback on the team brought girls to our room as well. No, he wasn't a starter yet, but everyone said he would be in a year or two. So I think a couple of the girls were trying to get a head start on being his girlfriend.

As for me, I spent some time reading essays that my friends had to write for English and history class. I didn't have as many people looking for help as Barry, but I did have some, especially when a history test was coming up, because I took very good notes in class, and I knew how to review. What is important to the story I'm going to tell you about Clementine and me is the fact that when people came into Barry's and my room, both males and females, they saw the pictures of Clementine and Ruth Ann and my mother and grandfather and me. When anyone asked me who Clementine was, I always said she was my girlfriend and that she went to Georgia Tech. If I was not in our room but Barry was, he always said the same. The guys usually had very little to say about the pictures except that Clementine was pretty. The girls always said she was very pretty and that she looked like a very nice person and that we looked as if we meant a lot to each other.

Much the same thing happened in Clementine's dormitory, except that males were not allowed in females' rooms. So Clementine's visitors were both her friends from the dormitory and her friends from her classes. Because she was superior in everything, especially in biology, you can imagine how many young women came looking for help. And just as happened in Barry's and my room, when her girl friends did come, they saw the pictures she had on her bookshelf of me as well as the pictures she kept framed of her and me together and of Ruth Ann and of all five of us together. Unfortunately, the comments made by one young woman about me were not at all what Clementine had expected they would be or what her other friends said about how we looked happy together.

What does all of that have to do with Clementine and me? A great deal. You see, one weekend when Georgia did not have a football game and Georgia Tech did, I drove to Atlanta and went to the Tech game with Clementine. I'm sure I wasn't the only Georgia player who went to the game, just as I'm sure that Tech players came to Athens if they weren't playing a game and Georgia was. It's an in-state rivalry, after all, but at the same time many of the players had grown up together playing on the same high school teams or against each other.

What matters is that when Clementine and I went to the game, she introduced a number of her friends, both females and males, all of whom seemed very nice. And while I took some good natured kidding about going to Georgia, the fact I was sitting in the Tech student cheering section and that I cheered for Tech during the game kept everything friendly, or so I thought.

After the game, because Clementine had checked herself out of her dormitory for an overnight, she and I drove north of Atlanta to Altoona Lake where I'd arranged for us to stay in a cabin on the water. It was the first time we'd been together as a couple since before we had started school, and both of us needed time to talk and laugh and think about what we were doing and about how much we loved one another. Because the Tech game had gone until almost 4 P.M., it was nearly dark when we got to the cabin, which meant we'd have to put off walking along the lake shore until the morning. So that night we ate the food we'd bought in town. Then we sat by the fireplace and talked. What I noticed, however, was that as we curled up in front of the fire, Clementine seemed somewhat distant.

Now, I fully understand that Clementine is sometimes rather quiet because she is also a very sensitive and introspective person. She's told me many times that if it hadn't been for me, she probably wouldn't have ever learned how to talk to many people at Tampa Coast. "You can talk to anyone," she used to say. "Everyone loves talking to you," she said on more than one occasion. But this night, even as we undressed and went to bed and lay in each other's arms and then were lovers again, she remained even more quiet than ever before.

I will admit that I became concerned. Were her feelings for me beginning to change? That was the first thing I wondered. Had I done something wrong? That was the second thing I wondered. Had I acted as if I expected her to make love that night without any regard for how she might really have felt or what she really might have wanted?

I refused to believe that her feelings for me had changed. I couldn't think of anything that I might have done that was wrong. I wasn't so sure about us being lovers that night. By 2 A.M., I was awake listening to her sleep. But even that sounded different. I knew what Clementine sounded like when she was sleeping deeply and peacefully. The sound she was making that morning was not the same. Finally, I got up and went out into the cabin living room and sat down in front of the last embers as they were flickering away. Then I heard her behind be. That's when it started.

"You're up," Clementine said.

"So are you," I said without looking over my shoulder at her.

Clementine moved to the couch and sat down next to me, pressing her shoulder against mine. "Is something wrong?" she asked.

"You tell me," I said.

She was quiet for a moment. "What does that mean?" she said.

"It means, 'You tell me' if anything is wrong."

"Have I said something is wrong?"

"No. Not in words."

"I don't know what you mean, Tyler."

I waited before I replied. Clementine did not speak. I tried to find the words. She was listening, but she looked uneasy.

"It means, you've been uneasy since we got here. I thought you'd like getting away from the dorm. I thought you wanted to spend time with me," I said.

"I do want to spend time with you. And time away from the dorm."

I looked at the fire. It couldn't last much longer. I could see that. "All evening, before we went to bed, you acted as if something was on your mind."

"Did I?"

"Yes, Clementine, you did."

Clementine was quiet. Not quiet as in she had nothing to say. But quiet as in she was mulling over what she wanted to say. I knew her well enough to know the difference.

"It's something Shawna said."

"Shawna?"

"Yes. Shawna Williams. She lives in the room across the hall from me."

"All right. What did Shawna Williams say?"

"It was about you."

"About me?"

"Yes."

"Have I met Shawna Williams? Did I meet her at the game today?"

"No. She was there. But you didn't meet her."

"Then I don't understand."

"It's something that she said last week."

I sighed. "All right, Clementine, what did Shawna Williams say last week?"

Clementine was quiet for some time. I waited because at that point my job was to wait.

"You're very handsome, Tyler," Clementine said.

I turned and looked at Clementine. "Shawna Williams said I was very handsome?"

"Yes."

"And that has you upset?"

"No."

"Then what has you . . . upset or whatever it is that you're feeling?"

"Tyler, you are a very handsome man. You were a handsome boy in school. You are a handsome man now."

"Clementine?"

"Let me finish."

"All right. Finish."

"You are a very handsome man. You are what most girls want."

"Oh, for pity's sake, Clementine."

"Let me finish," she snapped.

"You have long blonde hair. And you have very blue eyes. And you have a very fair complexion."

"What in God's name are you talking about?"

"Tyler, please. Let me say what I have to say."

That made me afraid. I didn't know why, but it made me afraid.

"Your picture is on the bookshelf in my room. Several pictures. Some of the same ones you have."

I wasn't about to respond. This was her conversation. I just knew that I was more and more uneasy.

"You are tall and handsome and very intelligent and very friendly. And you have a wonderful smile. And people like you from the moment they meet you."

"Clementine, why are you saying these things?"

"Because . . . I am not tall and blonde and blue eyed."

"What?"

"I am not any of the things that you are."

"Clementine, you are the most beautiful woman in the world to me."

"Yes. To you. But not to anyone else."

"What?"

"Not to anyone else."

"That's crazy. You are slim and lovely and graceful and . . . beautiful. God, Clementine, you are so beautiful sometimes I don't understand why you ever got interested in me."

"Tyler, I am beautiful to you. I am beautiful to *you*."

"So. That's a good thing, isn't it?"

"It's wonderful. And terrible."

"What?"

"It's both. And that makes me afraid."

"Afraid of what? We've been together for four years. Now five. What are you saying to me? I don't even think I want you to answer that question. But you have to answer that question."

By now I was on my feet and standing in front of the fire place.

"I don't want to be your black nookie, Tyler."

I was stunned. She'd never used that term before. Neither of us had ever used that term before. I tried to re-gather my wits. "Clementine, what are you talking about?"

"About you and me."

"Clementine. 'Black nookie?' What in hell does that mean? Why would you say that to me?"

"That's what Shawna said."

"That's what Shawna said?"

"Yes. When she saw your picture. She looked at your picture and then she looked at me and she said, 'He must like black nookie, honey.'"

"Clementine, that's horrible. That's terrible."

"'Because you ain't much to look at, baby doll,' is what she said to me."

I stood still. I looked at Clementine. My own darling Clementine, curled up under her long flannel nightgown against the back and armrest of the couch like a child looking for a place to hide. "Clementine, first, you are very much to look at. Second, you are intelligent . . . even if you don't sound like it right now."

"Tyler . . . " she began.

"Let me finish."

She was quiet.

"You are intelligent . . . even if right now you act as if you've forgotten most of what you've learned."

She started to speak, but I held up a hand to stop her.

"You are sensitive and sensible . . . usually."

She was quiet.

"You love the same things I love: the arts. Opera. Music. Jazz. Paintings. Plays."

She looked at me. I'd never seen her look that afraid.

"You are the only woman I will ever love."

"But Tyler, you are so handsome . . . "

"Clementine, I don't look at myself. I look at you. My world is about you, not about me."

She was quiet for a moment, but I could hear a comment coming. "Shawna says she's known white men like you."

"White men? Since when I did become a white man?"

"But you are a white man."

"And you're a black woman."

"Which is the point."

"What's the point?"

"That some white men like black women."

"What?"

"That some white men like black woman in bed."

I moved to the end of the couch and sat down.

"Haven't we had this conversation before?"

"No."

"I think we have. I think we had it in high school. And I think that was enough."

"It made me afraid."

"What made you afraid?"

"What Shawna said."

"Clementine, damn it to hell, this Shawna whatever her name is doesn't know me. She doesn't know you. Not really. And she sure doesn't know us."

Clementine was quiet.

"So if some . . . girl in your dorm . . . some black girl . . . . Are you going to listen every time some black person says something about us? Aren't we past that? Didn't we get past that in Tampa?" I moved away from her. Then I turned back, my body rigid with anger. "So what did you say?"

"What?"

"What did you say? When this Shawna . . . when she said I wanted some black nookie?"

"I was stunned."

"Fine. You were stunned. But when you got over being stunned. What did you say then?"

"I left the room."

"You what?"

"I left the room."

"But it was your room. You said she came into your room."

"I left the room."

"Didn't you say something? Didn't you get angry? My God, she called you a whore. She called me . . . I don't even know what word to use. A john. A . . . ." I was nearly choking. "God, Clementine, didn't you say anything?"

"I don't remember."

"You don't remember? How can you not remember? You remember what she said. You remember she said I liked black nookie."

"Tyler, I'm sorry. I was afraid."

"Afraid of what? Of her? Why would you be afraid of her?"

"Tyler, it's hard. I'm there without you."

"And I'm at Georgia without you. So what? Why didn't you say something? Why didn't you defend us? Defend me?"

"She wouldn't have listened. She thinks she knows everything."

"Well, if that's an example of how she thinks, she doesn't know anything. I've fought fights for you. I've . . . done everything for you."

"Am I supposed to reward you for that? For fighting for me?"

"No. That's not what I mean."

"Then what do you mean?"

"I mean, you and me . . . we've been through things together. Hard things together. Your father. The Raymonds. And we've . . . we've loved each other. Doesn't that count for something?"

"It counts for everything."

"Then why didn't you tell her to go to hell?"

"Because I was afraid it's true."

"What?"

"Someplace. Deep down. I mean, someplace you don't even know about. Maybe it's true."

I stood silent. I could not believe what I was hearing. True? I moved to the window. Outside the night was black. Stars glistened in the sky. The wind was moving. I turned back to Clementine. "Clementine . . . ." Then I stopped. I looked at her. "I don't know what to say. How could you ever think any thing like that?"

"I don't want to think like that."

"Then don't. Marry me right now."

"You don't have to prove anything, Tyler."

"Marry me."

"We've talked about that, Tyler. We will. But not yet. We have too many years of school left."

I walked back to where she was sitting. "Clementine," I said, "I want to tell you something very interesting. Something I think you need to know. Something you need to think about."

She waited.

"People come into my room, too, you know. Into Barry's and my room. Men and women. To study."

"Women come into your room?"

"To see Barry. They're starting to line up. He's a quarterback."

"But they see you?"

"Clementine, let me finish."

"All right."

"They come into our room. Black and white. Men and women. And they see your picture. And the men say you are very pretty. And the women say you are beautiful and that you look intelligent and that we . . . that you and me . . . that we look very happy together."

"Which means?"

"Which means . . . isn't it interesting that at the University of Georgia, so far at least, every person who has seen the picture of us together . . . every one has said we look very happy together. Even Vince Dooley said it. The head football coach at Georgia said we looked very happy. And not one person . . . no one has ever said anything about the fact that you are black and I am white. No one has ever even mentioned race."

She waited.

"Clementine. Don't you hear me? Blacks and whites at the University of Georgia . . . none of them have ever said anything negative. But a black girl at Georgia Tech . . . one black girl, from what you've said . . . one black know-it-all-bitch of a woman . . . she said something." I waited for a moment. "Damn it! A black woman said something to you. And you didn't stop her."

Clementine was silent.

"If the white people at the University of Georgia . . . all that I know, at least, don't care that you are black and I am white . . . then who in hell does this black woman think she is that she has the right to say something that stupid?"

Clementine was very close to tears.

"God, Clementine, I don't care what anyone says. If someone says a nice thing about us—good. But that isn't why I love you. If someone says something bad—tough. Because I don't care. I love you because I love *you*. That's all. I love you because I love you."

Clementine did not respond. I went to her and knelt down in front of her and took her hands and put them on my face and held them there. Then I reached for her and brought her face next to mine.

"Clementine, remember me? The boy who got into a fight in ninth grade with Timmy O'Brien. The guy who ran Blessed Billy off the beach. Remember me? The guy you ran to at the end of your state championship races. Remember me? You jumped up into the stands and hugged him right there in front of the whole world. Remember me? I'm the guy who slept on the floor in New York so you could sleep on the couch when the sirens made you afraid."

"Yes," she whispered.

"Well, keep on remembering him. Because he's still here. Five years after you asked him to be your lab partner. And he's going to be here for the rest of your life unless you send him away. And he doesn't care what some Shawna whatever says or what some dumb check out girl says in North Carolina. He doesn't even care that some well meaning couple in the restaurant after the homecoming dance said they thought we looked nice together. All he cares about is you. All he cares about is you, Clementine."

Clementine's tears were running down my face. My tears were running down my face. "I love you, Tyler. Please. I love you," she whispered.

I didn't speak.

"She made me afraid. I'm sorry. She made me afraid," Clementine said.

"You don't ever have to be afraid, Clementine. Not about me loving you. Never about me loving you."

We stayed there for some time, with her sitting on the couch and leaning against me, with me kneeling on the floor in front of her. Which was fitting. Because she was my princess. One day she was going to be my queen. Then I stood and picked her up and carried her back into the bedroom where I lay her down on the bed, and then I lay down next to her and gathered the sheet and blanket up around us, and I held her against her fears, and she held me against my fears, and we lay like that in the quiet listening to the cabin beams creaking in the wind and the night birds outside calling to one another in the stand of trees that ringed the lake until at last we finally fell asleep.

46

The fall semester ended with both Clementine and me doing very well on our examinations. As quickly as the semester seemed to pass in terms of our studies, the football season had gone even faster than I ever would have believed when football practice began. It all ended with Georgia playing in the Citrus Bowl against Florida State University.

Florida State had one of the best football programs in the country. It was exciting to play them to a 17-17 tie and to know that I'd played a part in our success when, late in the game, I was able to deflect away a pass that would have let the Seminoles score a touchdown and take the lead and probably win the game.

When the game was over, I didn't have to go back to Athens. Barry was going to close our room for winter vacation. Instead, I went with my mother and grandfather and Clementine and Ruth Ann to a hotel at Disney World where my mother and grandfather and Ruth Ann spent two days touring the park while Clementine and I played golf on two of the courses. Then we all drove home to Tampa for the rest of our winter vacation. Our second day home, I took Clementine to a travel agent and began having a serious talk about a trip to West Africa. Clementine couldn't believe what I was doing. And even though I explained that I wasn't prepared to commit to any time period or make any final arrangements, I did say it was wise for us to start looking at where we would need to go and where we would have to stay.

As part of our preparation, Clementine and I went to the public library in downtown Tampa and began examining books about the regions in Africa from which Black slaves had been brought to the Caribbean Islands and then to the North American Continent. It was complex material because very few reliable records had been preserved. Of course, with both my grandfather and Ruth Ann as resources, we were able to begin to make sense out of what we learned. What seemed obvious to us was that it was most logical to assume that Clementine's ancestors had been brought from the Ivory Coast, which meant more reading about the history of that nation. As you would expect, none of the reading was pleasant. In fact, most of it was very painful. Clementine and I spent a great deal of our time sitting silently and looking away from what we were reading or going for walks along the Hillsborough River after we'd finished reading and taking notes for the day.

What came home to us were the lectures Ruth Ann and my grandfather delivered at the University of Edinburgh. We assumed that it was going to be impossible to locate the specific region and the specific village from which any of Clementine's ancestors had come. In the end, that did not prove to be the case, although we could not have known it in December, 1984.

The rest of the vacation itself was wonderful. Ruth Ann and Clementine took two days just for themselves so they could shop and talk through all of the things they had wished to talk about while Clementine was away. I did the same with my mother. If I had ever had any doubts up to that point in time that my mother was a wise woman, they disappeared during those two days when we went out together and talked. More and more she understood the nature of my love for Clementine and Clementine's for me. More and more our relationship was becoming a part of the way she envisioned our futures.

I also had a chance to play my grandfather a chess match that lasted one whole day. What I noticed, however, was how tired my grandfather was beginning to look. When I expressed my concern to my mother, she simply said he hadn't been sleeping well. I wasn't satisfied with that answer, but it was all I could get out of her at that time. I would learn more later, and it would not be good, but for the time being, all she would say was that he complained almost every morning of not sleeping well the night before. "That's all he'll tell me, Tyler," she said. "I can't get him to go to a doctor, although I talk to him about it two or three times every week."

As we had before, the five of us attended the Winter Solstice service at the Tampa Unitarian Church, after which we drove to our house and ate our celebratory meal and exchanged gifts. After our dinner was over, I helped Ruth Ann clear away the dishes because I wanted to know if my grandfather had said anything to her about his health. So when the two of us were out of ear shot of the others, I approached the subject. Ruth Ann responded by saying, "I know he's becoming very tired, Tyler. I can see it when he comes to the University and we go to lunch. Or when we go to a movie. I've started dropping him off in front of the theatre and parking the car so he won't have to walk so far."

"And he lets you do that for him?"

"Not at first. You know him. He balked like a mule. But finally I insisted. I think that's what he was waiting for. For me to take charge."

I was quiet for a moment. "Has he gone to a doctor?" I asked.

"I've tried to get him to go," she said. "But so far all I've gotten is a promise that he will once it's the new year."

"I don't like the way he moves his hands, Ruth Ann," I said. "He's being deliberate. Cautious. As if he doesn't want to make a mistake. I can see it."

"You're right. I've watched him. And he knows I'm watching him. That's when he gets irritated with me."

"Irritated with you?"

"Yes. He doesn't say anything, of course. He never would. Too much the gentleman. But I can see he's having some problems, and both things bother him."

"Both things? What do you mean 'both things'?"

"Both. That he's having problems. And that I'm watching him."

I understood. I had seen and felt the same thing when we were playing chess. He was becoming self-conscious. He had never ever been self-conscious before. And I could tell he didn't like the way I was watching him.

Then Clementine came into the kitchen, and Ruth Ann and I changed the subject. When the evening was over, I wasn't sure if I was glad I'd gotten the information or not. What I did know was that I wanted him to see a doctor. I didn't know what kind. But I wanted him to go see someone. At least that would be a start. And yes, I know I should have been more assertive. I should have insisted he talk to me, that he tell me more about how he was feeling. But that's hindsight. All of us are great at hindsight. But at the time . . . given how much I loved him and respected him and honored his sense of self, what was I supposed to do? What should I have done? All I could do was return to the vacation. To being with my family, to being with Ruth Ann, which was why Clementine and I decided not to travel during the rest of the vacation. Besides, most of all we wanted to sleep in our own beds in our own homes. Anyone who has gone away to school will understand the feeling.

So the five of us celebrated New Year's Eve by going to a movie and then coming home and watching the celebration in Times Square on television and kissing each other and going out onto the porch and listening to the neighbors shouting "Happy New Year" up and down the street.

Of course, by the time the vacation was over, Clementine and I were ready to go back to our universities, not only because we looked forward to continuing our studies but because with football season over and track season not yet begun, Clementine and I would have one month of weekends together. On our way back to Athens in Clementine's car, where she would drop me off since I'd left my car on the University campus when I'd traveled with the football team to Orlando, we agreed that she would plan our second and fourth weekends away from campus, and I would plan the first and third. We agreed to not tell each other about our plans: all four would be surprises.

As you would expect, saying goodbye to one another was hard. But this time we knew it was only going to be for one week. Then we would be off on another adventure. What I had to do, of course, was come up with something that would make it worth while for Clementine to tear herself away from her books. I decided that what she and I needed was music because by then she had become a rather accomplished guitarist, and I had managed to learn a number of songs in the Welsh language. What I wanted to do most of all was hear some folks singing in the Celtic tradition who really knew what they were doing. During the fall semester when I'd asked people who I thought might know where I might go to find that kind of music, several of them agreed the best place in the Southeast was North Carolina. So I picked Clementine up after classes on Friday. By 3 P.M. we were on Interstate 85. By 8 P.M. we stopped at a motel on the outskirts of Asheville. As we checked in and went to our room, Clementine finally insisted that I tell her what we were up to. When I said, "Music, my dear. Celtic music," she smiled as broadly as I have ever seen her smile. That told me everything was going to be good. Very, very good.

47

At this point, I have to be candid and warn you that if you're reading this memoir in the hopes you will find yet another story of angry young people denouncing their parents and raging at the injustices of the world, you have come to the wrong place. That does not mean that Clementine and I were not aware of the injustices that permeate society. Given who Clementine's mother is and who my mother is and who my grandfather was, how could it have been otherwise? We are very much aware and have done what we could to respond to those things about which we care deeply. And it does not mean that we did not go through trying times or that we did not ever experience insecurities, because we did. But the truth is, we were both raised well, loved deeply and unconditionally, allowed time and opportunities for our relationship to develop and mature, supported in our educational and career aspirations, and attended generously when we decided to marry.

At the same time, yes, there were losses and challenges and times when we needed to rely on our mothers and my grandfather and on each other to sustain our lives. It is very likely true many of you have had to do similar things when you faced similar challenges. The point is, I am fully aware that given the way life can some times sneak up on a person and do very great harm, Clementine and I have been blessed in many ways. So what

I'm trying to achieve in this memoir is much more than just a catalogue of the hard times in our individual lives and our shared life in the hope you might admire how we have conducted ourselves; rather, I am trying to tell the story of what was from the beginning and continues to be today an affirming relationship and affirmed lives. In other words, given all that we experienced together, our lives have been happy. I trust that won't disappoint you. But it's the truth. And at this point in my life, with a wife and twin daughters I love and a teaching position I enjoy, I'm not going to fudge the truth just to make the story of Clementine Camille Brown more dramatic. That wouldn't be honest. It wouldn't be fair. It certainly would not be the tribute to her person that I believe she deserves.

48

The Grey Eagle Tavern and Music Hall in Asheville is a gathering place for Celtic musicians and a center for Celtic music. Clementine and I managed to hear the last two hours of music that Friday night. I don't know if you've ever had the opportunity to listen to a really good Scots or Irish or Welsh or even Breton Celtic band, but if you have then you know what I mean when I tell you that there is no way you can sit still and listen. It is music that demands you move. The Scots Runners was a particularly good band. So was Welsh Knights and Pipes. They used the Welsh bag pipe, which is different from the Scots bag pipe. It's a more harsh yet more touching sound. More melancholy. More sorrowful.

What was as interesting to me as the music was that after we got back to our motel and had showered and were sitting side by side on the bed, Clementine turned to me and said she wanted to contact her father's parents. When I said, "Really? You've never said that before," her explanation made perfectly good sense.

"My psychology professor is a Jungian," she said, referring to Carl Jung, the pioneer psychoanalyst. "Jung believed in archetypes. He believed that archetypal wisdom comes to us in dreams. That the dreams are genetically driven."

I waited.

"So I want to know something about my paternal grandmother. My father's father is a black man. I know that. And with my mother and her family being black, it was only natural that I identified with my African ancestors as I grew up. But being with you . . . especially when we were in Scotland and then in Wales . . . knowing how important your Celtic heritage is to you . . . I'm beginning to wonder about my white heritage."

"That makes sense," I said, not sure how much I should elaborate on what Clementine was saying or how much I should leave it to her to go ahead and define her objective.

"I find myself responding to Celtic music as much as you do," she said. "So I wonder if it's just that I like music because Celtic music is irresistible, or if there's more to it."

"Are you saying you wonder if your father's white mother might be Celtic? Irish or Scots or Welsh."

"Yes. I think that's what I'm saying. The music you used to play for me when we had time together in Tampa. The Irish music. The music from Brittany. I can remember some of it almost note for note. I think I must hear it in my dreams sometimes. I don't know if it's because I dream of you and because I associate you with the music or if the music itself resonates in my imagination for some genetic reason."

I waited for a moment. "That's a profound question, Clementine."

"Tyler . . . " she started to say, as if she thought I was making fun of her.

"No. I mean it. It's a profound question. It's important. Because I think you're right. I don't mean about your grandmother," I said quickly. "I don't know anything about your grandmother. I mean that I grew up knowing that my heritage spoke to me in my dreams. Ever since I was a child. I've just always assumed the same thing happens to everyone."

Clementine looked away for a moment. Then she turned to me and said, "I don't know," she said. "But at least I want to try to find out."

I reached over and took her hand and said in a mock-whisper, "And so you shall, my dear. And so you shall," as she leaned her head against my shoulder.

Then we were both quiet. "Turn out the light, Tyler," she said after a moment. "Let's go to bed."

The next morning when I woke up, Clementine was already up and dressed. "It snowed last night," she said. "Get up and get dressed so we can go outside.

I moaned a little, although I didn't mean it. When Clementine smiled, the whole world was filled with joy as far as I was concerned. When she came over to the bed and climbed up on my chest and started putting her cold hands against my face because she had already been out, I shouted for her to stop, which was not only what I didn't want her to do, it was what caused her to put her cold cheek against mine and start laughing as I howled my mock protest. Only when I told her that I couldn't get up and go outside with her as long as she sat on top of me did she relent and get down off my chest and off the bed and start sorting through my clothes for what she thought I should wear.

Twenty minutes later I was shaved and showered and dressed and following her across the parking lot to the Denny's Restaurant that adjoined the motel. Once inside, we ordered coffee and omelettes and opened the highway map to see which road we should take to get higher up into the mountains, charting our route with the aid of the waitress while we ate. Twenty more minutes and we were on the road, climbing slowly up out of Asheville until we came to a hill on the edge of town where a number of parents and children were sliding down a steep hill into a flat valley below on three toboggans. Stopping my car, I got out and stood watching. Clementine joined me. After a few minutes, one of the little girls in the group came running over to us and asked if we wanted to make a run down the hill. I wasn't sure what to do until her father waved and called out, "C'mon. It's great. Make a run."

So we crossed the crest to where he and the other parents were standing. Along with a number of children who piled on the other two toboggans, we sat down and got ready. Then before we knew what was happening, two of the mothers gave us a push, and laughing along with everyone else we went plunging down the slope, Clementine behind me clinging for dear life, the snow flying up into our faces, until we came to a slow stop beyond where the children had come to the end of their run.

Rolling over, Clementine fell with me into the snow, laughing all the while. Then we stood and brushed off as much snow as we could from our coats and pants and stocking caps and started the long climb back up the hill. We spent another hour with the families, meeting them, returning their introductions, answering questions about where we went to school and what we were studying. Then it was time for the families to pack up their gear and start back to their houses, so we shook hands all around again and left them, returning to my car and starting up the mountain road toward the summit from which, as the waitress that morning in Denny's assured us, we could see for more than fifty miles. "All the way to Tennessee," one of the men said. "We'll do that with the twins when they're old enough," I said as we negotiated the curves in the road.

"Tyler . . . " Clementine started.

"Don't say it," I responded quickly. "I've already told you what I dreamed. That's all I'm going to say on the subject."

"Tyler," Clementine said quickly before I could stop her. "How can you know we're going to have twins?"

"Clementine," I said smiling, "there are more things in heaven and earth than are dreamt of in your philosophy."

Clementine smiled and turned away. "God, now he's quoting from *Hamlet*," she said.

"No better source of wisdom, my darling Clementine. No better source of wisdom than William Shakespeare."

We spent that Saturday evening at the Jack of the Wood Pub and Brewery listening to two traditional Irish bands, one of which brought along a troop of dancers. Over our Killian Red beers, we laughed and joined in the chorus of a number of songs with the rest of the audience. At the end of the evening, we drove back to our motel room and sat next to each other on the bed and talked about both the courses we were taking at that point and the sequence of courses that lay ahead in each of our disciplines. I told her I was concerned about my grandfather. She said she understood. Then we were lovers. Then we slept.

The next morning we left and drove back to Atlanta where I said goodbye to Clementine in the parking lot of the Allison Fisher Dormitory. Clementine said that for the next week, she wasn't going to take off the dolphin ring that she wore when we traveled together. I said I would do the same. Then I walked her to the dormitory entrance, and we said goodbye again.

By the time I got back to my dormitory in Athens, it was late enough that I wasn't sure if I should telephone my mother or not. When I got to my room, I found a note from Barry that said my mother had called and that I should call her no matter what time I came in. When I reached her in Tampa, my mother said that my grandfather had been to a doctor, who then made an appointment for him with a cardiologist. "We don't know anything yet, Tyler. And the doctor said there isn't any cause for alarm. I'm telling you what I know so you won't wonder if he's actually seen a doctor or not."

I told her I appreciated her telephone call, and I appreciated being kept up to date.

"Ruth Ann is going with him on Tuesday to see the cardiologist. She has time in the morning. I think maybe it's better that she go than me. He seems to take orders from her better than he takes them from me."

"That's because he wants to protect you," I said. "But Ruth Ann can bully him. I've watched them together. It lets him give up authority to someone he trusts."

My mother said she understood.

Then I asked how she was doing. She said she was okay. School was going well. She was concerned about her father. I told her he was too strong a man to give in to anything easily. Certainly he wasn't going to give in to his age without a fight. That made her laugh.

She asked about Clementine, and I told her we'd gone to Asheville for the weekend to listen to Irish and Scots and Welsh musicians. Then it was time for her to hang up and go to bed. We said goodnight.

But after the receiver went dead, I stayed on listening for some time. I don't know why. After all, all I could hear was the dial tone. I think I was trying to not let go. I think I was trying to hang on to both my mother and my grandfather.

Finally, after several minutes, the line began to beep to tell me my telephone was still off the hook. Conceding to the inevitable, I hung up the receiver and went back to my room, where I found Barry asleep.

The next two days seemed to go very slowly as I waited for either my mother or Ruth Ann to telephone and tell me what was going on with my grandfather. I tried to concentrate on the lectures in both history and philosophy, but it was hard, as I'm sure you can understand.

Talking to Clementine Monday evening helped. She knew her mother even better than I did. "If anyone is going to help your mother see him through whatever is wrong, it's my mother, I promise," she said.

I said I agreed he was in good hands.

49

Tuesday was a very long day. I tried to stay as focused as I could during my Spanish II language laboratory, but couldn't keep my mind from wandering. After an hour and a half of what should have been a two hour session, I picked up my books and signed out and left and went for a walk. After a while, I sat down on a bench along one of the many walkways that knit the campus together. When I looked up, I was face to face with Jack McAndrew, my history professor. It didn't take him very long to see I was a troubled young man. "Can I sit with you for a moment, Tyler?" he said.

"Yes, sir. Please," I said, motioning for him to join me.

Professor McAndrew looked out across the campus. "It's cold," he said. "Too cold for you to be sitting here unless there's something on your mind."

"Yes, sir. You're right. It is too cold. And there is something on my mind."

"Do you want to talk about it?"

I was quiet for some time. I watched several students walk past us.

"If I'm intruding, you don't have to say anything, Tyler," Professor McAndrew said.

"You're not intruding. It's just hard finding the right words."

"The dilemma all of us face sometimes."

I nodded. "It's my grandfather."

"Professor Thomas? That grandfather?"

"Yes, sir."

"Is he all right? Is there a problem?"

"I don't know. I mean, yes, there's something wrong, but we don't know what it is."

"Ah. The hard part," Professor McAndrew said. "Dreaded anticipation."

I was quiet again for several minutes. "He's having a test today," I said. "A cardiologist."

"His heart?"

"That's what it might be. We don't know. That's why he's having the test."

"And you're worried?"

"Yes, sir. He's getting older, of course. So things happen. My mother and I know that."

"One of the perils of life, Tyler," Professor McAndrew said. "Especially a full life. And if anyone has ever had a full life, it's your grandfather, young man."

"I know that. But that doesn't make it any easier."

Professor McAndrew was quiet.

"I'm trying not to worry. It might not be anything specific. Or it might not be anything that's going to show up on a test. It might just be his age."

Professor McAndrew nodded. "You know, I read his first book when I was in undergraduate school. I was very impressed. He's a fine writer. He's a great thinker, but what makes his work so wonderful is how well he writes. He keeps you wanting to read the next sentence, hear the next idea."

"Yes, sir. That's certainly the way I feel about his work."

"And his lectures in Edinburgh with Professor Brown. They're really very special."

"Yes, sir. They are. I got to hear them."

"You got to hear them? In Edinburgh?"

"Yes, sir. With Professor Brown and her daughter."

"I didn't know Professor Brown had a daughter. Of course, I didn't know her work until the lecture series was published."

"Yes, sir. She's very close to my grandfather and my mother. And her daughter, Clementine, she and I are very much in love."

"Really?"

"Yes, sir. Since ninth grade."

"Since ninth grade? That's impressive, I must say."

"Yes, sir. She goes to Georgia Tech."

"Really? Well, that's an unfortunate decision," Professor McAndrew said, smiling. "But I guess we all can't be bulldogs."

"No, sir. But Tech is right for her. She's majoring in biology. She wants to attend medical school."

"I see. And what about you? Are your plans that certain?"

"I want to be an historian, sir. I don't think I've ever wanted to be anything else."

"Yes. That follows."

"My grandfather has really been my father since my father was killed in Viet Nam."

Professor McAndrew was quiet.

"I haven't talked to anyone here at Georgia about these things, sir."

"I will respect your confidence, Tyler. And we can talk if you wish in the future. Just come by my office. I'd be glad to help you in any way I can," he said, standing.

I stood. "Thank you, sir. I very much appreciate your stopping to talk with me."

"I don't know if I've done anything that merits thanks, but if my stopping has opened up a dialogue between us, then I am very pleased."

"It has, sir. Thank you."

Then he smiled again and turned and left, and I sat back down for a moment. Professor McAndrew was right. It was too cold to stay there much longer, so I got up and walked to the library and went back to my studies, struggling to focus on the issues at hand rather than what I could not affect.

50

When I went back to my room at 2 P.M. I found a message from Barry that I was to telephone Clementine. Barry and I had a telephone in our room by then. We divided the cost each month. I sat down and dialed and listened as Clementine's telephone rang once, twice, then three times. Then I heard her come on the line.

"Clementine. It's me."

"Have you heard anything yet?" she asked.

"No. I thought you might have news."

"I don't. I tried to call my mother ten minutes ago because I know it was a 10 A.M. appointment, but she didn't answer at home or at her office."

"I'll call home. If he's there, he'll answer. Or your mother will answer."

"He's going to be all right, Tyler. You know that, don't you?"

I hesitated. "I want to know that, Clementine. I want to know that he's okay. But I don't. I'm worried. He's getting older. You can see it just as well as I can. Maybe better."

"Tyler, he's going to be okay. He's strong. My mother says he's a very strong man."

I sighed and said I would telephone her with any news I could get. Then I heard her say goodbye and hang up. I sat back and waited. I wanted to dial my home phone number, but I couldn't make myself do so. Instead, I sat staring at the telephone. Should I call? Should I try? Or should I wait and do nothing? I dialed. Doing nothing was worse than doing the wrong thing. At least, that's what seemed to me to make sense. I heard the telephone ringing in the dining room of my house. After five rings, I heard the receiver being lifted and Ruth Ann saying, "Hello."

"Ruth Ann. It's me. Tyler. You're back from the doctor's office?"

"Yes, Tyler. We are."

"And?"

"And he had tests. On his heart. And blood work. And a treadmill test."

"And?" I said again.

"I'm afraid it's serious. He's been holding out on us. Not telling us how he's been feeling."

"I thought as much," I said.

"I think he's been like this for some time. Maybe even back to when we drove to California. He just didn't want any of us to be distracted. He wanted you to be enrolled at Georgia before he did anything about the pain."

I swore under my breath. "He's a whole lot more important than my being enrolled at Georgia or us being distracted."

"I know that. I agree."

"So what's going to happen?"

"He has to have a heart by-pass operation."

"A heart by-pass?" I said, interrupting.

"Yes. Two of his heart arteries are blocked. One about fifty per cent. The other maybe eighty. He's been walking around acting like everything was just fine when all of the time he's been risking a heart attack."

"My God, Ruth. Oh, my God," I said, slumping back in my desk chair.

"The doctors are concerned about his being under for so long. They have to evaluate his lungs and liver. He'll have to be under anesthetic for what could be two hours. Maybe more. That's a long time for anyone. But for someone Edward's age . . . that's a very long time."

"What did they say? Is he strong enough?" I said.

"So far all of the tests say he is."

"I don't know if I'm glad or sad about that."

"I guess . . . given what needs to be done . . . we should be glad."

"When is this going to happen, Ruth Ann?"

"Friday."

"Friday? This Friday?"

"Yes."

"So soon?"

"It has to be soon. It should've happened months ago. But who knew? Certainly he didn't say anything. According to your mother, he's always been a high energy person, as if he expects to be vigorous forever. I suppose everyone in his life started expecting him to stay the same. To keep on keeping on. But he can't do that. Not any more."

"Is a by-pass going to cure the problem?" I asked.

"It's supposed to. The doctor says it should."

"It should? Doesn't he know for sure?"

"He says he's done the operations hundreds of times. He says it almost always works. He's only performed three that didn't," Ruth Ann said.

I was quiet for some time.

"Tyler?" Ruth Ann said softly.

"I'm going to drive to Tampa. I have to be with him."

"I think that's wise, Tyler. It's a very complicated procedure. Your mother will be with him. And I'll be with him."

"I know. And that's wonderful. I know it means everything to him having both of you there." I hesitated, trying to think clearly when all I wanted to do was swear my anger. "I can leave Thursday after my morning lab. I can miss my Friday classes. It's all right," I finally said.

"I certainly understand. I'd want to do the same thing if I was you."

"I'll call Clementine. She's wants to know what's going to happen. You know she's going to want to come with me."

Ruth Ann was quiet for a moment. "I know she's been worried about Edward. We've talked about it. And if you drove by yourself, she'd worry about you as well."

I was quiet for a moment.

"Tyler?"

"I'm still here. Can I talk to him now?"

"I got him to go to bed. He went through a lot this morning. None of it was painful. Not really. But he went through a lot. And he was more worried than he wanted me to know."

"All right. Let him rest. Tell him I love him. Tell my mother I'll call this evening. And Clementine and I will be home Thursday night. And thank you, Ruth Ann, for all that you're doing."

"I want to help, Tyler. You know that."

"I do know that. And it means everything to me, Ruth Ann. It truly does."

Then we said goodbye, and I telephoned Clementine, and she insisted that she needed to drive with me, for which I was thankful. She said her plans for our weekend would wait. This was more important, she said. And I agreed. Then I started to cry. I hadn't thought I would. I'd thought I was under control. That's what I wanted to do—be under control. But the fear I welled up in my chest so much that I felt as if my chest was going to burst. I could hear Clementine trying to calm me, reassure me. What I wanted most was for her to be with me. For her to hold me in her arms. But I also knew this was not the time for me to worry about my own pain. I had to be strong for my grandfather. I had to be with my mother. I had to support Ruth Ann. It was important. But all I could feel was my fear. "I'm not ready for this, Clementine," I said in a whisper. "I'm not strong enough," I said.

"You're strong enough, Tyler," she said in reply.

"I'm not so sure."

"I am. You've been well trained. You've been raised to the task, Tyler. You've been very well trained. I've watched you for five years. You've been very well trained."

51

I was in Atlanta and on the Georgia Tech campus by noon Thursday. Clementine was ready when I pulled into the parking lot. She came to me and kissed me tenderly and got into the car, and we started driving. Both of us were very quiet. None of the usual rush to express our affection. None of the urgency to share events since we had last been together. By the time we got to Interstate 75, I was struggling with my emotions. What could I say to her? What could she say to me? Yes, we had shared hard experiences before: when I went with her to meet her father at Disney World, when she had come with me to meet my Raymond grandparents in Miami. We had been able to predict, at least to some degree, the tension that would prevail, the animosity that would be expressed. But this was my grandfather, Edward Thomas. What lay ahead? What should we expect?

"It's going to be okay," Clementine said after we'd driven twenty-five miles. "I talked to my mother. She's talked to the doctors. They know what they're doing, Tyler. It's going to be okay."

"Clementine, he's seventy four years old."

"And he's strong. He's taken care of himself. He's a good candidate. That's what the doctors told mother."

I was quiet. "He's a great man," I said.

"Yes, he is."

"Not just because he's my grandfather. His life. His whole life. He's been a great man."

"Yes, Tyler. I agree. My mother agrees."

I was quiet again for some time. Then I glanced at Clementine. "Your mother loves him, doesn't she," I said.

"Yes. She does," Clementine said.

"How ironic," I said.

"Ironic?"

I didn't answer. I knew Clementine understood.

"I can drive some when you get tired," Clementine said. "You don't need to wear yourself out."

I smiled rather weakly. "I need for you to be with me, Clementine."

"I know."

"More than ever. You're the only one."

"I know," she said again. "I'm here, Tyler. I'll always be here."

"I've known something would happen someday."

I could feel Clementine looking at me, but she didn't speak.

"I've always known that he wouldn't . . . ." I was quiet for a moment. "I don't know what my mother will do."

"Tyler, he's strong. Don't anticipate the worst. My mother said he was resting comfortably. That he's relaxed. He's ready to get this over with."

I glanced at Clementine but didn't reply.

"But it's major surgery, Clementine."

"I know it's major surgery. That's why the doctors are taking every precaution, Tyler."

"They have to . . . what? Open his heart? Stop his heart?"

"Yes and no. They open his heart. They keep it going. They cut out the clogged arteries. Then they sew in the by-pass arteries."

I sighed and tried to control my emotions.

"They know what they're doing, Tyler. They've done this before."

"Not to my grandfather," I said quickly, an edge in my voice.

"No, Tyler. Not to your grandfather," Clementine said. Then she waited for some time before speaking. "What you're feeling . . . it's what people feel when someone they love goes through surgery like this, Tyler. It's okay to be concerned."

"Concerned?" I said, almost mocking her.

"Afraid. It's all right to be afraid. Just don't give in. Your mother needs for you to not give in, Tyler."

I knew she was right. I was quiet.

"I talked to my mother this morning. She's already at the hospital. So is your mother. I talked to both of them. The doctors are very confident."

I nodded and took a deep breath and then exhaled slowly. "I need a cup of coffee," I said. "And something to eat. I didn't eat any breakfast. Did you eat anything this morning?"

"Not much. Not enough. So let's stop." When I didn't reply, she went on. "We have time, Tyler. We'll be in Tampa by 6. The surgery isn't until tomorrow morning. We have time to stop and eat."

I was glad Clementine had said that. I needed for her to guide me. If I was going to try to take care of my mother, I knew I needed Clementine to take care of me.

"I'll take care of you, Tyler," she said, as if she'd read my mind. "Just like you've always taken care of me. Now it's my turn to take care of you."

I turned and saw her smiling. Her smile, her expression, her goodness and strength, they made me want to weep with joy, with hope. They made me want to smile and weep both at once. But I did neither. I just nodded and said, "Yes. Please." And I started turning my car off the interstate onto an exit ramp so we could stop to eat.

"Up ahead," she said quietly, her voice expressing her humor. "Your favorite. A Waffle House."

I laughed quietly for the first time since I'd talked to Ruth Ann. And we turned toward the Waffle House Restaurant.

52

Five hours later, by the time we left Interstate 75 and turned toward the University Community Hospital, near USF, I felt as if I was being overwhelmed by conflicting emotions. I was going to remain calm come hell or high water, but at the same time, the flood was churning in my chest: my grandfather needed me to do more than just act grown up. He needed me to be prepared to assume my role in the family. Clementine understood. As we walked across the parking lot, she took my hand, letting me lead as if I knew where I was going, but at the same time leaning toward me and brushing against my shoulder as if guiding me into what we both knew was going to be a new kind of unknown place in our lives.

We found Ruth Ann in the surgical Waiting Room on the fourth floor in expectation of our arrival. After a moment of embracing and kissing and quiet words of concern and reassurance, she and Clementine pointed me down the hallway to the room where I found my mother sitting quietly in a chair beside my grandfather's bed.

When I stepped into the room, my mother looked for a moment as if she did not recognize me. Then she stood and I came to her, accepting her into my arms as she tried to both not cry for my sake yet release her tears at the same time. After a moment of confusion, she finally gave way and let herself be consoled. Then she directed me to my grandfather's bed, where I stood looking at the man who only two and a half years before had stood over me when I'd lain in my own hospital bed. After a moment, his eyes opened and he whispered, "Tyler."

I reached for his hand with one hand and touched his face with the other. "Grandfather," I whispered in reply.

"Sorry you had to come so far," he rasped.

"We wanted to, Grandpa," I said. "Clementine and I wanted to."

"Clementine's here?" he tried to say.

Clementine was at my side. "Right here, Grandpa," she said.

My grandfather smiled. "At last," he said.

We waited.

"You finally called me Grandpa," he rasped, smiling.

Clementine smiled and touched his hand.

"You're going to be fine, Grandpa," I said.

"I know," he said slowly. "It doesn't feel like it now. But that's what they tell me."

I waited for a moment. "I wish you'd said something months ago, Grandpa," I said quietly.

"He and I have had this conversation," my mother said in a whisper, stepping close to me.

"He's stubborn," Ruth Ann said, moving next to my mother.

I sighed and shook my head. "He's that for sure," I said.

"You're all ganging up on me," my grandfather said quietly.

"Only because we love you, Edward," Ruth Ann said.

My grandfather smiled. Then he licked his lips. I turned to the table next to his bed and bought the cup of ice to his lips. He opened his mouth and took in chips of ice. Then he smiled and whispered thank you.

I turned to my mother. "The surgery?" I said.

"8 A.M."

"Why don't you go home and get some sleep," I said to her. "I can wait here."

"Why don't all of us go get some sleep," Ruth Ann said.

"I want to stay with Tyler," Clementine said in a whisper.

"But Elizabeth will want him to come with her," Ruth Ann said.

"I need to stay with Tyler," Clementine said.

Both Ruth Ann and my mother heard the difference.

"Then you go with them," Ruth Ann said. "If that's okay with you, Elizabeth?"

My mother said it was fine. "Do you want to come stay with us too? You know we've got three bedrooms."

Ruth Ann looked at Clementine. She knew her daughter well enough to know when Clementine was resolved. "Fine. I'll go home and then come stay with you. I think that'd be better for me in any case."

My grandfather coughed, and we all turned to him. "I just want to sleep. All of you go away." His mock irritation was not convincing.

My mother went to the door. When she returned, a nurse was with her. She introduced Clementine and me to the nurse. Then she told the nurse the four of us were going home to sleep but that we would be back in the morning.

"We'll start preparations at 7," the nurse said. "If you come by then, you'll be able to talk to him before he goes into surgery."

"We'll be here," I said.

After the nurse left, assuring us that she would be in the room watching how he was sleeping, each of the four of us went to his bedside and kissed him goodnight. Each of us had something to say.

I don't know what the others said, but when it was my turn, I bent down to him and whispered, "I love you, Grandpa."

"I know that," he whispered in return.

"You're my hero. I want you to know that. All of my life, you've been my hero," I said, trying very hard to get the words said through my tears.

Clementine was standing by my side holding on. My grandfather looked at her. Then he looked at me.

"And you're my son, Tyler. You've always been my son," he said. Then he closed his eyes, and because I was the last of the four to speak to him and kiss him good-bye, I stepped away, and we let him drift away.

Twenty-five minutes later, my mother and Clementine and I were in my house. Ruth Ann arrived fifteen minutes later and joined us for tea. We sat together for some time trying to talk and say encouraging things and trying to not say what we most feared to say.

Then my mother said she was going to bed. She said she would change the sheets in my grandfather's room so Ruth Ann and Clementine could sleep in his bed. But Ruth Ann said she didn't need to bother. "Edward and I have slept in the same bed before," which was the first time she had ever said that even though the three of us had known for some time that it was true.

Then Clementine stood and said, "I'm staying with Tyler."

A silence followed. Then my mother said, "Whatever you wish to do." And Ruth Ann said, "All right," without any further comment, and so the four of us went off to our beds, Clementine following me into my bedroom and, after showering, following me into my bed where she rolled over and lay next to me and held me against my fears, consoling as only she can console, her voice soft and gentle and tender and wise, assuring me, preparing me for the next day. And I accepted her whispered affection. I accepted her sweet breath on my face. I accepted her warmth, all the while knowing that none of us were going to sleep very well that night. But we had to try. We had no other choice but to try.

53

Six hours later, all four of us were back at the hospital standing in my grandfather's room, watching as two nurses readied him for transportation to the surgical unit where he would be prepared for surgery. We watched without comments, the four of us linked by hands and arms and shoulders touching one another as if we were a barrier against his pain, against the danger. None of us spoke. None of us had to speak. Our love for Edward Thomas was beyond words, beyond expressing save for what we could do: stand shoulder to shoulder, stepping back when it was time for him to go. My mother moved to his side and touched his hand. I moved to his head and touched his face. Clementine did the same. Ruth Ann reached out as his bed passed and touched his left foot under the blanket. He turned as well as he could and smiled at her whispered, "You come back here to me, Edward. Don't you forget to come back to me. We have work to do together." Then he was in the hallway. Then he was gone.

For a moment we stood watching, not speaking, just watching. Then it was my mantle to assume. "C'mon. The three of you go to the Waiting Room. I'll go get coffee from the cafeteria."

My mother and Ruth Ann started to walk in the correct direction. Clementine took my hand and whispered, "I want to go with you."

Twenty minutes later all four of us sat in the Waiting Room along with two other women and one other man, all of us enveloped in silence. My mother and Ruth Ann and Clementine and I ate the donuts Clementine had picked out. We drank the coffee I'd promised. And slowly, very, very slowly, time passed, and fate unfolded the way fate always unfolds. An hour passed. Two hours passed.

Then I understood what I had to do. So I stood up and without speaking walked away from my mother and Clementine and Ruth Ann until I found a window overlooking Tampa where I stationed myself. For it fell to me to remember. To recall. To hang on. To stand at the window and remember every moment of my life that I had shared with my grandfather, every walk, every time we threw a baseball or a football in the park, every book he ever read to me, every story he ever told, every treat he ever shared, every surprise he ever organized. And I cried. Not loudly. But I cried—deeply and truly and sincerely. And another hour passed. And I felt Clementine behind me, wrapping her arms around me, pressing her head against my back, not speaking but leaning for support, offering support, the steady rhythm of her breathing the love I needed most, the steady rhythm of her pulse my connection back to life. So I held on to my grandfather while Clementine clung to me so together we could hang on to Edward Clayton Thomas.

54

After four hours, one of my grandfather's doctors came out into the waiting room. His message was that my grandfather was doing well. It had taken more time to do some of the work because he had lost more blood than they had originally anticipated, but his pulse was still strong, his breathing was still steady. The assumption was that he would be out of surgery and in the recovery room in less than an hour.

Almost two hours later, the door to the surgical unit opened, and the doctor who had performed the surgery came out and told us my grandfather was in the recovery room, but he would be groggy for at least another two hours. We were advised to go get something to eat if we hadn't done so already and then return to the intensive care unit by 5 P.M.

After standing and embracing one another for several minutes, the four of us went to the elevator so we could descend to the hospital cafeteria. Only then did any of us realize we'd had nothing to eat that day. "How much coffee did I drink?" my mother asked.

"I dunno," I said. "I lost count myself."

Clementine and Ruth Ann agreed. "None of us will be able to sleep tonight," Ruth Ann said as we got off the elevator and turned toward the smell of food in the hallway.

Thirty minutes later we were all standing along the wall of my grandfather's intensive care room as the nurses finished their work and left us with what was by then a very pale man who looked older than I remembered and more frail than I could have imagined. When he opened his eyes, and all four of us released a collective sign of relief. He turned and motioned for me to come to him and to bring a paper cup of ice to wet his lips, and I did. He gripped my wrist to steady my hand. My mother joined me at his bed side. Clementine stood next to me. Ruth Ann stood next to his left foot, her hand on his leg. "It's good to see you, Edward," Ruth Ann said.

My grandfather smiled. My mother leaned down and kissed his forehead. I kissed his cheek. Ruth Ann pressed her face against his. Then Clementine moved to him. As she did, he reached up and touched her cheek with his left hand. Clementine did not move away but allowed him to touch her that way for some time before he slowly lowered his hand and closed his eyes and drifted off to sleep. When she turned back to me, I could see tears in her eyes. I could see tears in all of our eyes.

55

Clementine and I returned to Georgia Tech and Georgia Sunday afternoon, which meant she and then I arrived in our dormitories very late. However, we agreed it was worth it. The next two weekends we did the same. Then in February, Clementine started indoor track practice, and I made the trip by myself for three weekends before she was able to travel with me. During those weeks, my grandfather recovered slowly but steadily, so much so that by March he was not just sitting up at home and beating me at chess, he was ready for walks around the neighborhood. On one of those walks he started talking to me about how much he had loved my grandmother, Ethel, and how hard it had been for him when she died. He'd never spoken of her in that way before. In the past, his comments had simply been that she was a good humored woman who had stood with him when their first born child, a boy, had died at birth, and then as they battled to keep my mother alive when she was four and contracted scarlet fever. "The fact Elizabeth not only survived but grew up to be a strong young woman is to Ethel's credit. She was the one who was always there while I was off traveling from campus to campus giving lectures. Sometimes I think I might as well have been a traveling salesman. But she said she wouldn't have it any other way. She said she was proud of my work, even when some damn fools burned a cross in our yard during the Civil Rights upheavals in Cleveland."

As we sat on a park bench, he continued telling me stories of how much she loved it when Elizabeth married my father. "Ethel died before your father died, Tyler, which was probably a blessing in disguise. She thought your father was a splendid young man, which he was. I don't know how well she would have taken it when your father died, leaving your mother alone to raise you on her own."

He paused for a moment. "Of course, by then, I was alone myself, so it was only natural that I'd ask the two of you to move into my house. I certainly didn't want to be alone, and there wasn't any reason for your mother to have to struggle even more than she did so she could go back to school."

I waited.

"It's funny how life works out, isn't it?" he said, going on. "Here you are, studying social and racial history at the University of Georgia, when during the time I was at Cleveland State, I had to fight against my inclination to think that every white person who lived in Georgia was a bigot. I guess it either proves how wrong I was or how much times have changed." Then he almost laughed. "And Clementine. There's no way you could ever fall in love with a young woman more wonderful than Clementine. But when I was on the picket lines in Cleveland or giving lectures that made the University administration uncomfortable—and more than once I was advised it would be better if my rhetoric wasn't quite so blunt—I could never have imagined that my grandson would grow up to love a young black woman because I didn't have faith the world would let that happen. For sure I could never have imagined that she'd be going to Georgia Tech and running track and that she'd want to be a doctor. I swear, Tyler, sometimes the world is a mighty interesting place after all. I guess what a person has to do is live long enough and keep the faith that sometimes good things happen even if bad things happen at the same time and wait and hope everything works out for the best." He smiled and turned away for a moment. Then he turned back to look at me.

I told my grandfather I agreed. "I would have loved to have known my father, Grandpa. And I would have loved to have been with you in Cleveland when you were fighting for civil rights and voting rights. Because I've always counted it a privilege that I was raised by you."

My grandfather reached over and put a hand on my knee. "Well, raising you has been a privilege for me too, Tyler." Then we got up and started back towards the house.

The next morning, Sunday, I had to drive back to Athens, stopping at Georgia Tech to have dinner with Clementine on the way. The next week, on Thursday afternoon, I returned to Atlanta for Clementine's first indoor track meet, and as we always had done before, she had me take her to the field house where she kissed me goodbye, telling me to watch her, as if I watched anyone else.

56

I'm not going to chronicle every track meet in which Clementine participated and every race she ran for Georgia Tech. That's not what I'm trying to accomplish in writing this memoir. And that would be too many details. What I want to do with this narration is to portray who Clementine was and is and how much she has influenced my life not because my life is particularly important but because how she influenced me is further evidence of the quality of her person.

However, even with that said, let me emphasize that Clementine's first year of running for Georgia Tech was very successful. Because she was a first year runner, Coach Davidsen believed it would be best if she only ran the 440 during the indoor season. The 880 would wait until the outdoor season began, a decision that paid dividends because Clementine won a number of both 440 and 880 yard races in outdoor dual meets against more experienced runners so convincingly that it was obvious to people who follow track closely that she was going to be an important member of the Georgia Tech team. In the races she did not win, she pushed the eventual winners into running their best times. Just as had happened at Tampa Coast, her lithe physique did not tell the tale of her strength of body or of her character. More muscular and more accomplished runners glanced at her and wrote her off even after their coaches had warned them that her times were improving steadily. That was particularly evident in the season opening dual meet against the University of Virginia, when the two best runners for Virginia, in what proved to be a foolish gesture, ignored Clementine when she tried to make polite conversation with them before the 440 race. From where I was sitting, it was obvious that Clementine was nervous, for good reason. There were two very strong 440 runners on the Virginia squad. But that is getting ahead of my story. Let me tell you what happened.

Three Tech runners were participating along with three from Virginia. Because dual meets mean one school is hosting one other school, and there are fewer participants, dual meets tend to be rather relaxed affairs, which allows the runners to very often talk more freely before and after races. But that is not what happened at the Tech-Virginia meet held on the Georgia Tech campus, which I, of course, attended. The Virginia runners, at least the two best runners, made the mistake of snubbing Clementine when all of the runners were waiting together before their race was called, both of them turning their backs on Clementine when she tried to say something cordial. From the look on her face, and as always I was watching her through binoculars, Clementine was surprised. This was not what she had expected. Then I saw her face cloud up, something I'd seen before. I knew at that point that the Virginia runners were in for a very big surprise. When one of them even shouldered her way past Clementine as she started moving toward the starting line, I knew she in particular had made a very big mistake.

On more than one occasion while she was in high school, and on more than one occasion after she became a university runner, I watched Clementine go out fast in the 440, drawing the field along with her, then let runners pass her as if she were fading, only to have her put on a closing sprint that allowed her to win the races going away. That is not what Clementine did against Virginia. Instead, when the race began and the Virginia runner who had snubbed Clementine pushed her way to the front, her expression suggesting she thought this was going to be easy competition, Clementine moved up to the Virginia runner's shoulder, not allowing her to build a lead. As they went into the final turn, I saw the Virginia runner glance over her shoulder where Clementine was running. She must have been surprised because for an instant it looked as if she broke her stride. That cost her the race, because by the time they came out of the turn and she had returned to form, she and Clementine were running side by side, which was when I knew Clementine was going to win. With forty yards to go, Clementine simply shifted gears, bursting past the Virginia runner, leaving her behind, pulling away until the Virginia runner was even passed by one of Clementine's Tech teammates.

When the race was over, and Clementine was accepting the congratulations of both her Tech teammates and the other two Virginia runners, it was her turn to turn her back on the Virginia runner who had been favored, leaving her to try to sort out how she had managed to lose a race to a runner who looked like someone's little sister. Then, as Clementine left the track, as was always her practice, she turned to where I was sitting and waved and mouthed the words "I love you," pointing to herself on the word I and to me on the word you. As you would expect, I returned the gesture.

The other race I want to detail is the Atlantic Coast Conference championship race at the end of Clementine's first season, which was held on the campus of the University of Maryland. But before I do that, because I also want to maintain the chronology of events, I need to talk about spring vacation and the time Clementine and I spent with my grandfather.

59

My grandfather's health improved steadily, so much so that he and Ruth Ann spent four week days on the Gulf of Mexico at a small resort on Long Boat Key, just south of Sarasota. My mother said that by the time they got back, my grandfather had actually begun to tan again. Apparently Ruth Ann had led him on walks along the beach every morning and every evening. They had even gone on a deep sea fishing charter boat one afternoon, which Ruth Ann reported both of them had enjoyed.

I came home almost every weekend to visit with him during the spring, except for those times when Clementine had track meets. Clementine came with me three times. My grandfather said he was very sorry that he had not been able to attend Clementine's meets, which he had intended to do. Clementine said she certainly understood. What I have tried to recall for this memoir is the conversation Clementine and my grandfather and I had on what proved to be Clementine's third and last visit with him that semester. For he said things to us on that occasion that he had never said in quite the same way before.

I assume that by now you recognize that my grandfather was a thinking man. Certainly he had the best mind I've ever known, and I don't just mean the best intellectual mind I've ever known: I mean the best, most profound, most sensitive mind I've ever known or engaged. For that reason, he said, he always enjoyed aquariums more than any other kind of public museum: "You have to slow down your mind when you sit in front of a large tide pool tank," he said more than once. "And when you do, you start sensing your connection to something much more grand than just yourself or your family or even the human species," he said as Clementine and I sat with him on a bench in front of a display in the Clearwater Aquarium.

"Do you mean 'meditation and water are forever wedded'?" I said, quoting one of my favorite lines from Herman Melville's novel *Moby-Dick.*

"Yes. That's exactly what I mean," he said. Then taking up my cue, he went on. "Do you remember how Melville introduces that idea?"

"I do," I said. "He wrote about how almost every footpath, no matter where it starts, finally leads to water. He wrote that if you go to the wharf at night, you will find people standing at the water's edge looking into the distance."

"That's right," my grandfather said. "And it's the footpath analogy that's most important."

"That everyone wanders somehow to the water?" Clementine said.

"Yes. Because everyone is trying to get back to the mother."

"The mother?" I said.

"Yes. Our human mothers. Our mythological mother. The Gaia. The mother of life. Water. The sea."

"Origins?" Clementine said.

"Yes. Origins," my grandfather said.

"Whitman's 'Out of the cradle endlessly rocking,'" I said.

"Yes. Whitman's poem."

Clementine and I let him go on.

"But look at the difference. It's the difference between a poet and a novelist. Whitman's personne goes to the seashore and floats in the waves. Melville's protagonist goes to sea and dives as deeply as he can into the mysteries of life."

Clementine and I waited.

Then my grandfather looked at Clementine and then at me. "You two are lovers," he said.

From his tone of voice I could not tell if he was asking a question or making a statement.

"We are," Clementine said quietly but without hesitation.

My grandfather nodded. "Good," he said.

I wasn't sure where he wanted the conversation to go or what he wanted to say.

"I've very much enjoyed watching the two of you grow up together," he said.

Once again, both Clementine and I waited.

"There is something very special about what you two share. And I don't mean just the race thing. Something much more important than that."

"What's that?" I said.

"I think it's the Gaia notion."

"The Gaia?" I said.

"Yes."

"Do you mean that Clementine is the Gaia that I'm trying to get back to?" I said.

"No. Well, yes. In a way. But no. That's not it. Not all of it, at any rate."

"I'm not sure what you mean," Clementine said.

My grandfather nodded. "Tyler is a very sensitive young man."

"Yes, he is" Clementine said.

"Not just unusually sensitive. Profoundly sensitive. Intuitive. That kind of sensitivity."

It was not my place to comment.

"He is," Clementine said. "I agree."

"Sensibility. He has remarkably well developed sensibilities," my grandfather said.

"Yes, he does," Clementine said.

My grandfather turned to Clementine. "I am not surprised that he fell in love with you, Clementine. I don't see how it could have been otherwise. And not just because you are beautiful and intelligent and sensitive. Although that's part of it. But there's more to it than just that," he said, turning back to the tide pool tank and watching as the cycle of water rushed in, flooding the rocks and raising the water level to the top of the display. "It's the two of you together. Two people. As one. How you atone. At- one-ment. You are both seeking the Gaia. Something greater than yourselves. Something even more profound than the idea of the African Gaia, the mother of life. The origin of origins."

I sat listening.

"Tyler is a dreamer," my grandfather said. "He's a Celt. He would have been a shaman two thousand years ago," he said, turning to Clementine. "And you would have been a shaman in Africa two thousand years ago. So you're both out of place here. This America place is too young for the two of you. Too new. But here you are. So you found each other. Not by accident. It was divined. Fated. You found each other. And together you become one journey. You atoned. You plunged into the ocean. Like Melville. Not like Whitman. Like Melville. You plunged into your affection. Your love of one another. That is how you enter. That is your corridor. Your sexual relationship," he said. "It's a sacrament. It's sacred. Not many people will ever understand that. But that won't matter. You two understand. Even if you've never said it to one another. Even if you've had to find other words. It's what you mean. And I've been privileged to watch. I've seen you hold hands and dress up and go to dances and win races and embrace for the world to see. And that's what I think you must do when you are alone together. You are plunging into Melville's ocean. You are swimming deeper than his ocean. You are swimming out beyond the origin of origins. You are discovering life. You are life. You two *are* life."

He stopped speaking. By then he was looking at the tide pool tank again. We sat on each side of him. He was holding Clementine's left hand and my right hand. Then he spoke in a whisper. "When I die . . . " he started to say, both of us interrupting, protesting even as he said, "Hush." So we were quiet again.

"When I die, I am leaving a special section in my will for the two of you. Some special money. Set aside." He turned to me. "Tyler, you and Clementine must go to Africa. Go to the Ivory Coast. Take this lovely woman. I don't care about when you marry her. You can do that when you both finish your studies. That's up to you. But when I die . . . the summer after I die . . . you two must take each other to Africa, and when you do, you must find a shaman. A real shaman. Not some tourist actor. A real shaman. A black shaman. And you must tell him or her . . . I don't care which. Maybe a her would be best. But you must find a shaman, and you must have the shaman marry the two of you using the old words. It won't matter if you two understand the words. You will understand the meaning. You must find a shaman who still knows the old words. And you must be married. Don't tell anyone. Don't tell your mothers. Tell them after you get married here. That's what I want you to do. That's what the special money is for. I want the two of you to go to Africa."

Then he was quiet. Clementine leaned forward slowly and looked past him at me. I leaned forward quietly and leaned past him. Neither of us spoke for a moment. Then I said, "Clementine, when the time comes . . . whenever the time comes . . . will you go with me to Africa and be married by a shaman?"

Clementine did not smile. Not with her lips. This was too important for a smile. But her eyes smiled. Her joy smiled. "Yes, Tyler," she said, "I will go with you to Africa and find a shaman and marry you if you will go with me to Africa and find a shaman and marry me."

I looked at her and nodded. Then I sat back and looked at the tide pool display, and Clementine sat back and looked at the tide pool display, and my grandfather sat and looked at the tide pool display. And all the while, he continued to hold our hands. And all the while, we continued to hold his. Then he said, "Good. And I will be with you. I promise. I will be there with you." Then he was silent, and we knew he had said all he wished to say. And we understood. And he understood that we understood. So we sat and watched the tide pool tank pass through its ebb and flood cycle three more times before we finally stood and, without speaking of the matter any further, returned slowly to my car and drove back to Tampa for dinner with my mother and with Ruth Ann.

60

Because Clementine was to travel to the University of Maryland for the Atlantic Coast Conference track and field championships on the Georgia Tech team bus, I left Athens for the University of Maryland on very early Friday morning, driving all day and into the evening, passing though Washington, D.C., in time to meet Ruth Ann and my mother and grandfather, all of whom flew from Tampa to Baltimore. From the International Airport we then drove to a hotel not far from the University campus.

I had never been on the University of Maryland campus, where my father had earned his Bachelor's and Master's degree, and my mother had not been back since she and my father had gone to his five year graduation reunion shortly after they had gotten married. Walking across the campus on Saturday morning, therefore, was an emotional experience for both of us, although for very different reasons. My mother was obviously cast back to those days when she had been rapturously in love with my father, which I am sure made her return both bitter and sweet. At the same time I was looking at her face for signs of her emotions, I found myself looking at every sidewalk and wondering had he used that particular pathway? Had he sat listening to lectures in the buildings I passed? Had he ever looked out across the campus lawns and sensed in some vague, unconscious, dreamlike way that one day the son he would not be allowed to raise would come to the campus to watch his lover run in the Atlantic Coast Conference track and field championships?

Yes, I was aware even as I walked that it was a silly notion, a metaphysical question that no one could answer, least of all me. But no matter. It animated my imagination and sent it off following three different streams of consciousness at once: what he must have felt about himself as he engaged life every day growing up on the Maryland campus, what it must have meant to him to share something of his life there with my mother when they visited years later, what it meant to me to be on the campus all of those complex years later when everything in my life was good but every good was tinged with a sense of loss. At the same time, walking, I also tried to keep my mind focused on the matter at hand: Clementine's first Atlantic Coast Conference Championship track meet. So I wondered how her bus ride had been. I wondered how she felt that morning getting ready. I wondered what she was feeling at that exact moment as my mother and grandfather and Ruth Ann and I walked in the crowd moving to the stadium for the morning events.

The day itself was bright and clear. It was not as humid as it would be in a month. With very little wind coming from any direction, it promised to be an exciting meet. Clementine had told me the previous Monday when we'd talked on the telephone that given the talent level of the runners from all of the universities in the conference, the expectation was that a number of records would be broken. She said that the 440 was going to be a wide open field, with at least five runners who could win the event. She went on to say that the favorite in the 880 yard sprint, a young woman from North Carolina State University, was being touted as a potential United States Olympian, so Clementine said that event in particular should be very exciting. Clementine had run against the North Carolina State runner in a dual meet and had only lost to her by four tenths of a second. Clementine said that even though she had improved her own time in the 880, she also assumed that the North Carolina State runner had improved her time as well.

For me, it was wonderful having my mother and grandfather and Ruth Ann all in tow. It harkened back to the times we'd attended Clementine's track meets in Tampa and in Gainesville and Orlando. My grandfather was in an especially good humor since it was the first time he'd been well enough to watch Clementine compete at the university level.

As we took our seats and settled down for what proved to be both a long and an exciting day and evening of events, I asked Ruth Ann if Clementine had ever said she felt the same kind of butterflies I was feeling in my stomach when she had come to Georgia to watch me play football. Ruth Ann smiled in response and said, "Tyler, when you go on the field, Clementine usually grabs my hands and hangs on for dear life. All she wants is for you to never get hurt again."

I nodded and said I understood. "That's all I care about too," I said. "I just don't want her to get hurt." Ironically, that was exactly what was going to happen before the day was over: Clementine was going to be injured.

61

I don't remember all of the preliminary events that took place that day. I confess I don't even remember all of the preliminary races that Clementine ran. What I do remember is as the evening began to settle over the stadium, Clementine took her place in the starting blocks for the 440. This was the event that she had told me was wide open, which was her way of telling me to not expect too much from her. Understanding her code, I had told her all I wanted her to do was run a good race and have fun. With that as a prelude, all of us were surprised not just that Clementine won the race, which she had not expected to do, but how easy she had made it appear. From the starting gun through the first turn, four of the runners had looked to be dead even. Then Clementine had simply sped away from the rest of the runners, as if she were not even running on the track, reminiscent of how she had run at the state championships in Florida during her senior year at Tampa Coast. By the time she crossed the finish line, there was a good three yards between her and the second place runner, who was challenged for that place by three other runners, including one from Georgia Tech.

Up in the stands, the four of us shouted and cheered as Clementine took a short warm down run and waved to us and threw her usual kisses our way. Then she disappeared among her teammates, and my mother and grandfather and Ruth Ann and I filed down out of our seats and went to the concession stands where we bought our evening meals.

Once that was accomplished, we returned to our seats and watched as slowly but surely the events moved toward the finals of the 880 yard run, the race about which I was most nervous and which I knew, for Clementine, had become the event on which she was focusing most of her energy. As I've tried to remember the race and tried to remember what I was feeling, I am not certain if my trepidations were as strong before the race as I think they were or if I simply have the advantage of hindsight, given what actually happened and how I remember that unfolding. It is a question I cannot answer, of course, which finally doesn't matter. All that matters is what happened.

Sitting in the stands with my binoculars trained on Clementine, her body language told me she was nervous in a way I had never seen before. To this day she says she cannot explain why she felt so unsettled, but she admits that she was feeling more insecure as she lined up for that race than she had ever felt before or after. I have told her that what happened justified her sense of insecurity; she says perhaps her sense of insecurity caused what happened. It's a question we never expect to resolve.

62

The race began as I had expected. Clementine did not want to be trapped in a pack of runners, all but one of whom was more muscular than she. Yet that is exactly what happened as the runners broke out of their lanes along the back stretch. She was trapped along the inside lane by two runners in front of her, one on her right shoulder, and three running side by side behind her. I wasn't watching the others, of course, as much as I was watching her. What frightened me the most was that except for two of the runners behind her, she was the smallest runner on the track. Certainly she was lighter and more lithe than the runners by whom she was surrounded. I could see her looking for a place to get out. She turned her head once to her right. From where I was sitting, I couldn't see anyplace she could go. But she must have. For she tried to move away from the inside trap and more to her right. The runner on her shoulder gave way slightly, as if she didn't want to get in a tangle. Then Clementine made her move. Taking two very quick strides forward and to her right, she tried to spring free. For an instant I thought she had done it. I started to say "She's out" when it happened. Just as she moved to the outside shoulder of the runner who was on the outside of the two runners ahead of her, an elbow came up and caught her upper arm. I saw Clementine start to stagger, fight to stay upright, take one leaping stride to get free, then start to stagger again. Then I saw the runner who had been on her right side and who was now behind her start to stumble, her left leg catching Clementine's right leg, the touch sending Clementine falling away, staggering then falling again. Then the pack was in my way, and I could not see her. I was standing and starting to say something when I heard Ruth Ann cry out. I stumbled forward against the person sitting ahead of me. I felt him resist. Then I was looking through my binoculars again. The runners were well into the top of the final turn. Clementine was on the ground. I had seen her fall. It registered in my brain. I had seen her go down, her legs up over her head, her arms flailing as she fell. I had seen her head strike the track. I was down out of my seat and into the aisle, desperately looking for a clear path. My binoculars were still in my hand. I looked again across the track. Two officials were moving toward Clementine.

I found an avenue through the stands and started running, leaping from row to row until I was near the end of the horseshoe stands. The runners on the track were in the home stretch. Coach Davidsen was running across the infield with two Georgia Tech athletic trainers. I vaulted over the front rail of the stands and ran as fast as I could along the curve in the track. I could see one of the officials standing over Clementine. I could see her trying to sit up. My heart was in my mouth. I could see blood on her face and on her right hand and right elbow. Coach Davidsen got to her first. The trainers were on her heels. I was next. Breathless, I arrived and threw myself down on the track next to her on my knees. Clementine was crying. Blood was running down over her right brow and into her eyes. She was trying to wipe the blood away with her left hand. One of the track officials was trying to wipe the blood off her face. A trainer reached and pushed the man's hand away and took charge of putting a compress on her face. I bent down and took her right forearm and held it for the other trainer. "It's not broken," I heard the young woman say. Then I saw her lift up Clementine's right arm and start cleaning away the blood on her elbow. The skin was not cut, but the abrasion was bleeding. Clementine saw me through the maze of arms and hands trying to tend to her. "Tyler," she whispered. "Tyler . . . ," and I said, "I'm here, Clementine. I'm here."

Clementine started to lean back against the official who was behind her. "I thought I could get out," she whispered. "I thought I could win."

I moved behind her, pushing the official away. "I've got her," I said to him. "I've got her."

The man moved and let me catch her as she leaned back. Coach Davidsen was saying, "I want to check her eyes. Check her eyes, Amy," she said to the second trainer."

I reached under Clementine's arms and held her against me and then steadied her head so the trainer could look into her eyes. "Move your eyes to the right," she said.

I could not see from where I was kneeling, but Clementine must have done so. Then the trainer had her move her eyes to the left, then up, then down. "She's okay," the trainer said.

"Let's get her up," Coach Davidsen said quietly, her voice calm and reassuring.

I lifted Clementine slowly until she was on her feet.

"I'm okay," Clementine started to say just as her knees started to buckle under her.

I caught her and lifted her up, my arms under her thighs, Clementine instinctively reaching her right arm up around my left shoulder, her head slipping back against my chest.

"We'll get a stretcher," Coach Davidsen said.

"I've got her," I said, interrupting.

"Are you sure?" Coach Davidsen said.

"I've got her," I said, my voice sharp. "I've got her," I said, turning and starting to follow Amy the trainer as she started back across the infield toward the Georgia Tech team that had clustered with their assistant coaches on the other side of the infield.

So I carried Clementine Camille across the grassy infield, listening to her trying not to cry, listening to her saying, "I'm bleeding on you, Tyler," as the trainers walked with me, trying to attend to her injured right knee and injured right elbow as I did.

"It doesn't matter," I said, lifting her higher so I could steady myself as I walked. "You know that doesn't matter," I said.

Then I felt her head pressing against my chest. And people in the stands starting applauding. "They're clapping for you, Clementine," Coach Davidsen was saying as we continued across the infield. "Can you hear them?" she said. "Can you hear them?"

But Clementine did not lift her head off my chest. And I did not respond. Instead, we continued making our way across the infield. The applause grew louder as we neared the Georgia Tech team. But I couldn't hear any of it. All I could hear was Clementine's heart beating and my heart beating. All I could feel was Clementine's head pressed against my chest. All I could feel was how much I loved her. How very, very much I loved her.

Part Three

. . . possibly their roads had been mapped out from the beginning, and they had no choice but to follow them.

Isabel Allende

Of Love and Shadows

1

Accompanied by Coach Davidsen and one of the Georgia Tech trainers, I carried Clementine under the stadium stands and into the locker room the Georgia Tech women's team was using where we were met by the doctor who had been called to examine Clementine's injuries. Because the track meet was not over, I was able to wait until he completed his examination. His concern was not the abrasions on her face and elbow and knee. He said that while they would scab and be uncomfortable for several days, if they were dressed properly they would heal. There might be some scaring on the knee, which could be problematic, but he did not think any of the abrasions were serious. He was concerned, however, about the blow she suffered to the head when her face hit the track. He spent almost twenty minutes looking into her eyes and asking her questions about the headache that she said she felt coming on. He asked Coach Davidsen if Clementine was scheduled to stay with the team overnight before they all rode the bus back to Atlanta. When he was told that yes, that was the plan, he asked if there was any way she might have supervision during the night. When I asked him what he meant, he said that it was important someone monitor her sleep for the next twenty-four hours to be sure that no signs of a concussion showed up. He said that someone would have to wake her up every thirty minutes to be sure she was all right.

"I can do that," I said to both the doctor and Coach Davidsen. "I drove here from Athens. I had planned to stay overnight in a hotel with Clementine's mother and my mother and my grandfather. I can take care of her."

Coach Davidsen explained that under normal circumstances, athletes who came on the bus to a meet and had stayed with the team in a hotel had to return the same way. I protested that this was not a normal circumstance and that I was sure Clementine's mother would sign any release necessary so we could take care of her. When Coach Davidsen asked Clementine what she preferred to do, Clementine said, "I'd rather stay with Tyler."

So the matter was settled. Clementine would leave the team and stay with her family. The two of us would then drive Ruth Ann and my mother and grandfather to the airport on Sunday morning, and then I would drive Clementine back to Atlanta. Because Clementine was not scheduled to begin her final examinations until Tuesday, I told her that when we got tired, we would stop for the night along the way. The doctor thought that was a wise decision. "Most of all, I don't want her getting too tired. Certainly she shouldn't do any driving." I told the doctor I would take care of her.

When I left the locker room and found Ruth Ann and my mother and my grandfather waiting, I explained what had been decided. Ruth Ann said she was very grateful.

When we had arrived at the hotel on Friday evening, my mother and Ruth Ann had stayed in a room together, and I had stayed with my grandfather. When we arrived at our hotel this time, Ruth Ann said she would get a room and stay with Clementine. Clementine said no. She wanted me to stay with her. So I booked us into a room. That is when the comedy began.

I don't know if any of you have ever tried to sleep sitting up, but it is no easy feat. I don't know if you've ever tried to monitor another person's sleep on a regular basis over night, but that's not easy, either. Following the doctor's advice, we had to devise a way for

Clementine to sleep sitting up, and we had to set an alarm clock so I would wake up every thirty minutes to check her breathing.

First, Clementine tried sitting in a comfortable chair, but she couldn't get enough support for her neck, and even if she could have, I would have had to either sleep in the chair next to her so I would be close enough to hear any change in her breathing, or I would have to get up out of bed and come to her to check on how she was sleeping. When that didn't seem reasonable, she tried sitting up in bed, propping herself up with pillows against the bed head board, but the pillows were too soft and wouldn't stay in place.

Then I tried sleeping against the headboard myself, with Clementine sitting between my legs and leaning back, but when I fell asleep her head wouldn't stay upright, which was what the doctor wanted, and I couldn't see her face when the alarm went off. By 1 A.M., we finally figured out that if we used the cushions from the chair as supports, and then padded them with pillows, and I slept on the bed next to her, she could sleep upright, and I could check on her without waking her up. Of course, that meant that my sleep was interrupted every half hour from 2:30 A.M. to 6:30 A.M., because we were scheduled to meet Ruth Ann and my mother and grandfather in the dining room at 7:30 for breakfast before we drove them back to Baltimore International Airport for their 10 A.M. flight. As you might imagine, when I awoke Clementine and said we had to get ready to meet the others, she was not enthusiastic. When she realized that I had slept even less, she was more sympathetic. By the time we met them, both of us confessed that all we really wanted to do was sleep. But no matter. It was time to get on with our day. What neither of us realized as we ate breakfast with Ruth Ann and my mother and grandfather was that we had more to do that day than just drive our family to the airport and then start our own drive back to Atlanta. We had a stop to make in Washington, D.C. That is, I had a stop to make. And if Clementine was thankful that I was with her all night, I am thankful that Clementine was with me that day.

2

The Vietnam Memorial Wall opened to the public in 1982. My mother had not attended the opening; she did not explain why. She did not need to. At Tampa Coast High School, both of my history teachers made reference to the Wall during my sophomore and junior years. When they did, I did not respond even when the both classes had animated discussions about the war and about the memorial. When my junior history teacher, Helen Berg, asked me if I wanted to contribute to the conversation, I said I didn't. When she asked me why, I said, "Because I assume my father's name is on the Wall." No one pressed me on the issue after that.

As Clementine and I drove through Washington on our way to the freeway that would then take us into Virginia and points south, I found myself caught in a conflict of emotions. I remembered how seeing "Miss Saigon" had affected me when Clementine and I had been in New York. I didn't want to go through that experience again, and I didn't think it was necessary to ask Clementine to go through it with me. At the same time, that morning before we checked out of our Baltimore hotel, I'd found a map of the center of Washington, D.C., on which the Vietnam Memorial Wall was marked. After Clementine and I said goodbye to Ruth Ann and my mother and grandfather, and we returned to my car, Clementine found the map on the front seat. As she looked at it, she found the Wall just as easily as I had. What I remember to this day is that she did not ask me if I planned to go to the Wall or ask if I wanted to go to the Wall. Instead, she looked at the map and then looked at the highway ahead of us and said very quietly, "Get off at the next exit. 17th Avenue. It will take us there."

For a moment I didn't know what she meant. I glanced at her and saw she was looking at me. As I turned back to the highway, she did the same. "I'll be with you," is all she said.

"My mother doesn't want to go," I said in a whisper.

For a moment Clementine did not respond. Then she said, "I'll be with you, Tyler."

"I'm not sure she ever will."

"I'll be with you, Tyler," Clementine said again.

Twenty minutes later we were standing at the corner of 17th and Constitution Avenue. "I'm not sure we should do this, Clementine," I said.

"We're here, Tyler."

"I know we're here. But I'm not sure we should be. Remember New York. Remember how hard that was for me. How hard I made it for you."

"You didn't make it hard for me."

"Well, then remember how hard it was for me."

"Tyler, this is important. If it wasn't, you wouldn't have picked up a map this morning. You wouldn't have understood what I meant when I said 'Get off here.'"

I was silent for a moment. We started walking west along Constitution Avenue. "This is a terrible place, Clementine," I said.

"No, Tyler. It's not a terrible place. It's an important place. You know that," Clementine said.

I sighed and took her hand, and we crossed Constitution to the south side of the street. As we walked west, I said, "We should go there, instead," gesturing toward the Lincoln Memorial

"We'll go there, Tyler. We can go there first, if you want. But we're also going to the Viet Nam Wall. Then we can start back to Atlanta."

I wasn't going to argue with her. There was no point. She was right, and I knew she was right, and she knew I knew she was right. So we walked west until we came to Henry Bacon Drive, which leads from Constitution to the circular drive that surrounds the Lincoln Memorial. Five minutes later we were among a crowd of Sunday visitors climbing the steps so we could view the great statute of Abraham Lincoln. And as moving as it was—and it was a moving experience—I am not making less of it than it was, I found my hands shaking as we turned and looked back northeast toward the Reflecting Pool and the Vietnam Veterans Memorial Wall. Clementine sensed my trepidations. So she took my hand and said, "Let's sit for a moment."

"Are we just putting it off?" I said, sitting down on the Lincoln Memorial steps just as hundreds of other tourists were doing.

"No. We are resting for a moment," Clementine said.

"All right."

We sat quietly for some time looking out across the expanse that extended all the way to the Washington Memorial. "It's really lovely, isn't it?" she said. "I was here with my mother when I was ten. Something like that. Ten or eleven. During the summer. It's exactly what I remember," she said.

I did not speak.

"It's even more important now," she said. "With you."

I nodded that I appreciated her comment.

"And you were wonderful yesterday. When I fell. When I was lying on the track. I could see you coming."

"Really?"

"Yes. I could see you coming. I knew you would."

"I was really frightened."

"I know. For a moment, so was I. Then I saw you coming."

We sat quietly for a few more moments. There were families all around us. Fathers and mothers and children of all ages and races and descriptions. "This is really something, isn't it?" Clementine said.

"Yes, it is," I replied.

We sat for a few moments longer. Then she said, "All right. Let's go. I think it's time that we go."

I said I agreed. So we stood and walked slowly down the stairs and turned toward the Vietnam Wall. As we came closer, we passed four canopies under which men stood behind small tables on which they had arranged pamphlets. Some of the men were wearing black POW MIA tee shirts. Some were wearing parts of what must have been their service uniforms. All of them looked tired. Some had short gray hair. Others wore ponytails drawn back over their shoulders. They greeted the strangers who stopped to look at the literature, some of them smiling, some of them not, all of them looking as if they wished they could be some place else other than there even while they also looked as if they knew there was no other place for them to be. When we stopped for a moment so I could get my bearings, a gaunt man in a black tee shirt said, "You can find names in the books."

I turned and looked at him. "What?" I said.

"In the notebook. Over there," he said, pointing at lecture style stands on which notebooks stood open. "If you're looking for a specific name. You can find it in one of the notebooks."

"I'm looking for my father," I said, although I did not know why I did so.

"Yeah. Well, sorry. But you'll find his name in the notebooks."

I thanked him, and Clementine and I walked to the notebooks. We found my father's name. Next to his name was the year of his death and the block of the wall on which his name appeared. "I don't want to do this, Clementine," I said in a whisper.

Before Clementine could respond, a voice from behind me spoke. "None of us want to do this, but all of us have to, young man."

I turned and looked at the speaker, a slightly stout man with gray hair, maybe 55 years old or so.

"You'll be all right," the man said. "But you have to do this. All of us have to do this."

I wanted to speak in response, but I could not. Instead, I looked at him for a moment. Then I turned to Clementine, gesturing with my head toward the Wall. She turned and led me down the sloping walkway until we joined the slow moving crowd of people walking the length of the Memorial Wall. As we did, like everyone else, we turned and saw ourselves reflected in the marble. At first the names were a blur, not because we were moving quickly but because there were tears gathering in my eyes. So the names became a chronicle, a blurred chronicle, a succession of letters that seemed to blend and fold into one another. I could feel Clementine's hand holding mine tightly. I could feel her looking at me. There were small American flags standing upright in the grass at the base of the Wall. People of all ages were passing in review. Some had stopped to make rubbings of the names. A man was sitting in a wheel chair crying. Two others stood at attention, their hands held in formal military salutes, their faces rigid with emotion. Beyond them, a woman older than my mother was helping a child press his fingers into the letters of a name while a young woman, perhaps my age, perhaps somewhat older, stood next to her, the younger woman's eyes, like the older woman's, filled with tears. Then we came on a couple, a man and a woman, older than my mother, the man gaunt and bent with age, leaning their faces against one another as they leaned against the wall, the man reaching his left hand up over his head and touching the letters of a name, whispering each letter until he said the full name.

I felt Clementine stop, her body pressing against mine as she did. And I knew why. I turned and saw the block number. I saw the list of names. I saw the capital letter R. The series of names that began with R. I let myself look slowly down the list until I came to my father's name. Raymond. Robert. Captain.

I felt my knees give. I felt my chest constrict. I felt my heart break. Because there was nothing I could do. Clementine turned and pressed her body against mine. I wrapped my arms around her shoulders as she wrapped her arms around my back. "I want to make a rubbing. I want to have his name."

I took the rubbing paper I'd been given by the veteran who'd talked to me when we first arrived and the pencil he'd offered and reached up to my father's name and rubbed the pencil the way the veteran had told me I should. My father's name appeared. "Oh, God," I whispered. "Oh, my God," I whispered. I stepped back and looked at the piece of paper . . . at the name on the paper: Captain Robert Raymond. I felt Clementine embrace me against my pain, against the bitter loss that should not have happened. The loss that need not have happened. I could not speak. I could not move.

"It's time to go, Tyler." I felt her moving me away. I gave over and let her have her way. She was right, of course, just as she had been right that I had to come. It was time for us to go. There was nothing we could do to change anything that had happened. It was time to go.

We walked across the lawn to a bench sitting on the other side of the Reflecting Pool where we sat and looked back across the water at the Wall. We did not speak for some time. Neither of us had any more words. Neither of us had anything to say. So we sat and watched what by then had become a parade of visitors moving along the walkway. Then I turned to Clementine. "I wonder if I'm going crazy," I said.

"What?"

"I wonder if I'm going crazy. Or losing my grip. Or something."

"Why do you say that?" Clementine asked.

I took a deep breath. "When I came on the campus . . . the University of Maryland. Today. When I walked across the campus, I thought about my father."

"Why is that strange?" Clementine said, interrupting. "It's where he went to school. Where he played football."

"That's not what I mean. I mean, it's what I mean. But it was more than that."

"Tyler, what are you trying to say?"

"I thought about him. About . . . . I had questions about him. When I crossed the campus with my mother and your mother and my grandfather. Did he walk the same sidewalk? And we passed buildings. Did he ever sit in those buildings? In the classrooms I could see? Did he ever dream about me? About the son he would not raise."

Clementine looked away.

"And now here. Today. The end of it all. A name carved into a marble slab. A name. The end of something." I hesitated. "I had to see it. I didn't want to see it. But I had to see it. To make a rubbing. A record."

"Tyler, that's not you being crazy. That's you being who you are? Sensitive. Thinking. Trying to sort out what life means. Who we are. That's not crazy or strange. It's just that you are so open."

"Open? Me, open?"

"Yes. You think you're closed. That you don't tell people who you are or what you think. But you do. In a hundred ways."

I frowned as if I did not believe her . . . because I didn't believe her.

"You don't even know it, Tyler. But you do. People who know you—they can feel what you're feeling because you're feeling it, and it's obvious you're feeling whatever it is you're feeling."

I smiled. "I thought I was disguising how I felt."

"You can't disguise anything, Tyler. You are honest and open, and the more you try to be quiet, be private, the more open you are. You don't even know it. But I do. I could see that the first day I met you. It's one of the things I love about you."

I was quiet again. Then I said, "Whatever I've learned, I swear I've learned from you. I feel sometimes as if I didn't know a damned thing until I met you. I measure my life from that date. The biology class." I smiled. "My life is BC and SC."

"What?"

"Before Clementine and since Clementine."

Clementine laughed softly. That was enough. That was more than enough. All the while, Clementine held my hand.

Thirty minutes later, we were back on the highway driving south. Clementine leaned her head back against the seat and closed her eyes. "Be careful," I said. "It hasn't been twenty-four hours yet. I have to keep watching you."

Clementine smiled even while she kept her eyes closed. "I know you will," she said. "I know you will."

By the time we cleared the Washington, D.C., region, it was too late in the afternoon to drive all the way to Atlanta. So that night we stayed in Durham, North Carolina. Because Clementine showed no signs of distress due to her fall, both of us slept soundly. The next morning we left early, driving through South Carolina. When we stopped in Greenville and bought a newspaper to read over lunch, we were greeted by a quarter page color picture in the sports section of the Charlotte Sunday newspaper of me carrying Clementine across the infield at the University of Maryland, taken by a photographer using a very powerful zoom lens. What was as interesting as the photograph was the fact that the photographer not only got Clementine's name right, which was not surprising since she was a Georgia Tech track star—that's how she was described: "Georgia Tech track star Clementine Brown, who fell while running the 880 at the ACC championships Saturday, . . . "—that the rest of the caption was also correct—" . . . is carried from the infield by her boyfriend, Tyler Raymond, who plays strong safety for the University of Georgia."

For a moment neither of us knew exactly what to say. I looked at the photograph again and said, "It's a good picture." I looked at the photo credit under the picture. "This Bryan Haywood, the photographer. He's sure got a good zoom lens."

Clementine grimaced. "It figures I'd get my picture in the newspaper when I fell."

I smiled. "It's a nice picture, though. You gotta admit."

"It's a nice picture of you, Sir Galahad."

I smiled again. "Well, if I do say so myself . . . ."

"Eat your lunch," Clementine said, trying hard not to smile.

"Yes, Miss Clementine," I said, mumbling and putting my head down like a school boy who's just been scolded by his teacher.

Clementine looked at the picture again. "My hair looks horrible," she said.

"Yes, Miss Clementine," I said softly.

Clementine looked at me, her face mocking her anger. "You don't always have to agree with me, Tyler."

"Yes, Miss Clementine," I said.

Then Clementine was serious. "I wanted to win," she said looking at the picture again. "I thought I could win."

"You will," I said, equally serious. "Next year. You will."

4

By the time Clementine got back to the Georgia Tech and I got back to Georgia, the photograph of the two of us had created a ripple of interest, albeit brief. Nevertheless, it created enough interest, both positive and, unfortunately, negative, that both of us heard about it on our respective campuses.

First, Ruth Ann called Clementine and said the photo was on the front page of the *Tampa Tribune* sports page, the caption mentioning that both Clementine and I had graduated from Tampa Coast High School where Clementine had been a track stand out and I had played football. My grandfather called me and said the photograph was the best picture he'd ever seen of us together. "Even better'n your senior prom picture, Tyler. In fact, I'm gonna try to get a copy from the Associated Press."

On the Georgia Tech campus, Coach Davidsen said when she saw the photograph she thought it was charming. She had known me, of course, since she had come to Tampa to recruit Clementine. She said she thought it was splendid the way I carried Clementine off the track to the locker room.

In the next three days, the Georgia Tech Athletic Department received twenty letters, most of the expressing some surprise that the Georgia Tech Yellow Jacket was being courted by a Georgia Bulldog, but in the main they had been impressed by what was obviously my affection for Clementine. Unfortunately, Clementine received two letters, one unsigned from Mississippi and one signed by a Grand Dragon of a Ku Klux Klan chapter in Riverside, California, both of which said it was just that kind of relationship that was going to pollute the blood of the white race. Neither of the letters threatened either Clementine or me, so Clementine turned the letters over to Coach Davidsen. Three days later Clementine received another letter from a woman who identified herself as a seventy year old graduate of Georgia Tech, who went on to say she thought it was simply wonderful the way Clementine's boyfriend had come to her rescue. The woman said that even if I was a Georgia Bulldog, she thought I must be a very nice young man. Clementine's friends at Georgia Tech echoed the woman's sentiment.

On the Georgia campus the reaction was much the same. Two letters asked if I couldn't have found a University of Georgia girlfriend rather than have to take up with a Yellow Jacket. Three others said they thought it was wonderful the way I had helped Clementine. I was told later that when the letters were turned over to Vince Dooley, who said he thought the picture was terrific, he wrote a letter that was sent to everyone who wrote the University, both positive and negative, that he was proud the University of Georgia football team was producing not only athletics and scholars but "young gentlemen for whom chivalry is obviously not dead."

Unfortunately, I also received three nasty letters, one of which was from the same Riverside chapter of the Ku Klux Klan, which both Vince Dooley and I dismissed, the other of which came from Texas in which the writer said I should be ashamed of myself for consorting—that was the word that was used—"consorting"—with a negro athlete who was obviously only interested in me because I could help her escape the *immoral curse* of her race. The letter went on to say that Clementine and I should never, ever come to Texas as a couple because "we know how to deal with race polluters like the two of you." Coach Dooley called the F.B.I and had them take charge of the Texas letter. I never heard what came of the matter.

As you would expect, before the week was over, the matter was forgotten, although my grandfather made good on his promise, and when Clementine and I arrived back in Tampa for our summer vacations once our final exams were finished, he had a framed 11 x 17 inch reprint of the photo for each of us. Today, Clementine keeps her copy on the wall of her medical office in Augusta, and I keep my copy on the wall in my office on the Augusta State University campus.

Clementine took her final examinations the week she got back to Atlanta. I took mine a week later. She earned her usual straight A grades. Mine were a mixture of both A and B grades. Then we went home for the summer and worked for the University of South Florida as arranged by Ruth Ann in a program that brought students from disadvantaged schools to the campus where they enrolled in both remedial study programs as well as courses designed to enrich their educations. In the mornings, Clementine taught the students a basic how to study science class; I taught an American history projects course. Then in the afternoons both of us helped the students build sets for the drama program. While we enjoyed the morning sessions, I think because we were doing something we'd never done before, our afternoons working with high school and middle school students who'd never had a chance to build a set or perform in a talent show were the most fun.

Before the summer was over, however, and before I had to report back to Athens for fall football practice, Clementine and I took a trip to Kiawah Island, South Carolina, where we played golf every day on what is still one of the most beautiful golf courses in the world. The resort where we stayed was so picturesque that for a while we forgot that we had to be separated again when we returned to our schools. In addition to the course, what made the ten days particularly wonderful was meeting a number of very nice people, all of whom proved to be good golf partners when we played in foursomes.

Then it was time to return to Tampa in preparation for our return to Atlanta and Athens. While the drive back to Tampa was a mixture of pleasure at having been together for ten uninterrupted days, it was also tinged with melancholy. I remember that as we passed through Orlando, Clementine, who was driving, turned to me for a moment and said, "You still want to marry me, don't you, Tyler?"

I hesitated for a moment, not because I was unsure of what I wanted to say in response but because I was surprised by the question. After a moment I turned to her and said, "First, keep your eyes on the road."

Clementine laughed.

"Second, Clementine Camille Brown, if I can't marry you, then I won't marry anyone . . . ever."

"Really? Ever? Not ever?"

"Clementine, my fate was settled—and I mean settled in the most joyful way possible—that day when you asked me to be your biology lab partner. If you ever have any doubts about that, I can tell you it was absolutely and forever settled when we went to the homecoming dance that same year—when we were in ninth grade—and you said I was the only man you would ever love."

Clementine nodded and watched the road. "And you're going to hold me to that statement? Made when I was only fifteen."

"You're damned right I'm going to hold you to it."

Clementine was quiet for a moment. Then she said, "Good. Because I'm going to hold you to your statement that I'm the only woman you'd ever love."

I smiled but did not respond, because there was no need to speak.

5

As I think back on the 1985-1986 academic year, Clementine's and my lives seem to slip into a blur. Not that wonderful and interesting things didn't happen, because they did. It's just that my grandfather's health became a concern again. That coupled with both the redundancy and the intensity of both Clementine's and my studies tends to lessen the clarity of my memories. Yes, Clementine and I wrote to one another three times a week, and yes, both of us saved the other's letters. But I'm trying to write this memoir from memory. That is more true to its purpose.

Two events during the 1985 football season stand out, neither of which has to do with games. Not directly, at least. The first took place after a Georgia home game. Clementine and I were walking across the campus in Athens at about 8 P.M. on our way to a restaurant when we were suddenly confronted by three men about our age. I don't know if they were students or not. They didn't look like students to me. It was the first and only time anything like it happened to me on the University of Georgia campus in four years, but that wasn't much comfort at the time, because it was happening then, and I knew it was serious.

Standing in front of Clementine and me, one of them said, "Well, well, what do we have here?" looking at me and then looking at Clementine. I thought, here we go. I can see it in their eyes.

Then the second one said, "I'll bet she's a good one." That's when I knew what was going to come next. So did Clementine. I could feel her hand holding mine hard then letting go. I could feel her other hand on my back.

"You three are making a big mistake," I said, preparing myself for what I knew was coming. "You'd better leave now. Because you aren't going to touch her," I said, my voice turned to a snarl.

Then a third one appeared. "Yeah, you're a real killer, faggot," he said, laughing. Then he said, "Of course, maybe she'd like to go with three real men instead of a faggot."

That was it. I wasn't going to let anything happen to Clementine.

"Tyler, let's go," Clementine whispered.

Then the first one spoke again. "You didn't answer my question, Tyler . . . faggot," the first one said, his voice dripping his prejudice. "'What do we have here?'" he said, gesturing toward Clementine.

That's when I heard Ricky behind me say, "What we have here, cracker, is the strong safety on the Bulldogs football team."

Everything went silent. I knew the voice. Ricky Marston, defensive end on the Georgia football team and my friend.

The three crackers went pale.

Then I heard Sam's voice. Sam was the starting defensive right tackle on the Bulldogs that year. "You heard him, cracker. You're talking to Ricky Marston. Two hundred and fifty pounds of pure mean black man. And I'm even bigger. And my friend here, Philly Jones, he's just about as big as Ricky."

Philly Jones, the other starting defensive tackle, weighed at least 250 pounds. Maybe more. So all of a sudden, it wasn't three skinny white men against one strong safety: it was three skinny white men against four members of the varsity football team, three of whom were black, all of whom were bigger than me and a whole lot bigger than any of them.

"Maybe you'd better get your skinny white asses off our campus, cracker," Philly Jones said very slowly.

"Yeah, cracker," Ricky said. "Maybe you'd better get your skinny white asses off our campus and don't be botherin' our man, here," he said, putting a big hand on my shoulder. "Especially when he's with a sister."

"And especially since he'd could whip your sad asses even without our help," Sam said.

The white men looked at the three of them for a moment.

"We're just going to stand here and watch him take you three apart," Philly said, laughing in his most menacing voice.

Without a word the three white guys took several steps back then turned and started running. Sam and Ricky and Philly started laughing.

Clementine released a breath.

"You could'a taken them, Tyler. We just wanted to make sure it was a fair fight," Ricky said.

"I was afraid you were gonna hurt them," Philly said.

Then Ricky had a hand on my shoulder again. "C'mon. You two best come with us."

"Come with you where?" I said.

"To a party, man," Philly said. "C'mon. We'd love to have you come with us. It's right here," he said, pointing across the street to the Alpha fraternity house.

I was about to resist and tell the three of them that I appreciated them coming along at just the right time when Ricky put his hand on my shoulder and said, "You haven't introduced us, Tyler," smiling and looking Clementine. "You've got to be Clementine."

"I am," Clementine said.

"You have to be, sister," Philly said. "Cause all Tyler will tell any of us is that you're beautiful and smart and you can run like the wind. And you certainly look like all of those things and more."

"C'mon, Clementine," Sam said. "We've been trying to get Tyler to come to one of our parties all season. You two gotta come along now. If you don't, and those three crackers come back, Tyler'll get himself in trouble with Coach Dooley when he whips them all."

"Coach hates us getting into trouble," Philly said.

"All right, all right," I said, more relieved than I've ever been in my life. So laughing, Clementine and I turned went with them across the street to the Alpha House.

Once we were inside, we were greeted by maybe twenty men and even more women from the Georgia campus, all of whom were black, all of whom were smiling and laughing and dancing.

I heard a voice shout, "Tyler!" but I couldn't tell who it was. Another shouted, "Tyler, my man!" Then a young black woman I recognized but didn't know well was standing in front of us. "You have to be Clementine," she said.

"That's me," Clementine said, smiling.

"I'm Roxanne," the young woman said, putting a hand on Clementine's shoulder.

"Hi, Roxanne," I said.

Roxanne leaned toward Clementine. "Hear that? 'Hi, Roxanne.' That's all I can ever get out of Tyler."

"Really?" Clementine said.

"Really. He'll stand up when one of the sisters come to the table in the student union or the cafeteria. And he'll even push in our chairs when we sit down. But he doesn't say anything more than that." She laughed. "He's a real shy one, honey," Roxanne said.

Then a second young woman was standing with Roxanne. I knew her name from an English class. Tracy.

"You must be Clementine," Tracy said.

Clementine laughed. Before she could say anything in response, Tracy went on. "You're the Tech runner, aren't you?"

"I am," Clementine said.

"I wish you were running for us," Tracy said. "You ran me right off the track last spring."

"I thought I recognized you," Clementine said.

"How could you recognize her?" Deena Wilson said, stepping into the circle. "You never saw Tracy. But she sure saw your fine ass," Deena said, laughing.

"Yeah, yeah. That's true. That's about all I did see of you, Clementine," Tracy said. "You were gone before I even knew which direction I was running."

All three of them laughed. Clementine did too. I felt like an outsider, mostly because at that moment I was.

Then Clementine leaned toward Roxy and said, "So he behaves himself when I'm not around?"

Roxy smiled broadly. "Honey, I don't know what you've done to this man, but I can tell you, a whole lot of women . . . and I mean both black and white women . . . they'd love to get him to pay some attention, but he just goes off and studies."

"And writes you letters," Tracy said, moving closer to Clementine. "I know that because I've seen him in the library writing those long love letters that you get."

"Really?" Clementine said.

I knew Clementine was enjoying all of this. When she turned to me she could see I was embarrassed.

"Look at his face," Deena said. "Now that man is embarrassed," she said.

I smiled meekly. "Yes, Deena. I am."

All four of them laughed. "Don't worry," Tracy said to Clementine. "He's yours through and through."

"Thank you, Tracy," I said quietly.

Then Philly was standing next to us. "C'mon, Clementine, let's dance." With that, he took her hand and pulled her toward the center of the room where a big group was dancing. Clementine glanced at me as she went with Philly, although truth be told she didn't have much choice.

Roxy smiled. "Well, if Philly is gonna dance with Clementine, then I'm going to dance with you, Tyler," she said, taking me by the hand an leading me into the group, Tracy and Deena laughing behind me as I followed her. However, it didn't take Roxy long to realize that I was about as uncomfortable as a person could be. "Don't you dance, Tyler?" she said when I moved clumsily with her.

"Yes, I dance," I said. "It's just that I've never danced with anyone but Clementine."

"What?" Roxy said as well as she could over the music.

"I've never danced with anyone but Clementine."

Roxy stopped and looked at me. "You've got to be kidding."

"No. We love to dance. But we always dance together."

Roxy smiled. "Tyler, you're a lovely guy," she said, "But this is ridiculous," turning me toward Clementine who was trying without much success to dance with Philly. "And I know the sister can dance better than that," she said, pointing at Clementine. "C'mon."

So Roxy pushed me toward Clementine and Philly. Then she shouted, "Philly, let her dance with Tyler."

"What?" Philly said over the music.

"Philly, let her dance with Tyler. They don't dance with other people. They only dance together."

Philly raised a hand and gave me a high five. "I thought something had to be wrong. I know the sister must be able to dance." Then he turned Clementine toward me, and we were back together again. From behind me I heard Roxy say, "There you go, Tyler."

Clementine and I danced together the rest of the night. Later, after we'd driven back toward Atlanta and checked in to the small country inn style hotel Clementine had rented for us, we danced together again, this time to very slow music, before we went to bed.

6

The other thing that happened that year that I remember clearly was Thanksgiving. Because of football, I couldn't go home for vacation. At the same time, because Ruth Ann's parents were flying to Tampa to be with Ruth Ann and Clementine, my mother and grandfather flew to Atlanta on Wednesday, where I picked them up, and we drove back to Athens where they checked into a hotel so we could eat our Thanksgiving meal together. We weren't alone, of course. Four other football players and their families checked in to the same hotel so we all had a meal together, which turned into a very nice occasion. Later the next afternoon, as I drove them back to the Atlanta airport, my mother and grandfather and I had talked. Most interesting to me, my grandfather shared ideas he had about a new book about baseball. "Did you know, Tyler, that there were black men in the baseball major leagues in the late 1890s, but they were so good that the white players demanded they not be allowed to play anymore."

I told him I didn't know that.

"Most people think that Jackie Robinson was the first black to play in the major leagues. And he was, of course. The first in the modern era. And what he did was very important. But he wasn't the first. So I think I should write a book about how prejudice drove blacks out of the game in the 1890s."

I told him I thought it was a fascinating topic and that he should definitely write a book about the subject.

My mother talked about her plans to become a school administrator and about her studies at the University of South Florida. That, of course, made me think of Ruth Ann, which made me think about Clementine, which made me miss her more than I could say. However, even then my major concern was my grandfather's health. He said he was feeling fine, and he tried hard to seem like his old self, but I could see it in his eyes: he was becoming very tired. I knew it was not a good sign.

As the three of us were walking through the Atlanta airport, I told them it looked like Georgia was going to be in another football bowl game so I couldn't say when I'd be home for winter vacation. My grandfather said he felt horrible that he'd not gotten to any of my games that year. I told him I understood. He had to take care of himself. He said he had a big surprise for all of us when Clementine and I did get home to Tampa in December no matter what the date might be. Then I kissed them both goodbye, and they boarded their plane and left.

As I turned away from the airline gate and started back through the airport toward the parking garage, I realized I was about as lonely as I had been in years. On Monday, the team would resume preparations for the November 30th game against Georgia Tech, and I knew Clementine would be back in Atlanta for that, but my Thanksgiving Saturday and Sunday were going to be horrible. What in God's name was I going to do with myself on what would be an almost deserted campus.

Then I saw her. Standing at the end of the corridor leading to the central terminal area, where everyone who uses the Atlanta airport crosses, Clementine Camille Brown was waiting. She didn't gesture to me. She didn't have to. She just smiled, and I melted. I walked toward her and held out my arms, and she came to me and embraced me and held on. And she said, "Did you really think I'd leave you all alone?"

"I thought you'd be in Tampa."

"I was," she said. "And it was nice seeing my grandparents."

"I thought I was going to be without you for the whole vacation."

"Tyler, did you really think I'd leave you all alone?"

7

The 1985 season was only slightly better than the 1984 season. The Bulldogs finished with a 7-3-2 record overall and 4-2-1 in the Southeast Conference. We were able to beat South Carolina at home and Florida at Jacksonville, both of which were big wins. Losing to Auburn at home after having lost to Auburn at Auburn the year before was a big disappointment. Losing to Georgia Tech at home, the second year in a row that we lost to the Yellow Jackets, was even more painful. My only personal consolation was that because of injuries in our defensive backfield, I became a starter when Georgia traveled to Oxford, Mississippi, to play Ole Miss, a game that we won. I was even able to make a contribution by intercepting two passes in the second half, one of which I returned to the Old Miss twenty yard line, after which we scored in one play. Yet even with the disappointments, our 7-3-2 record earned Georgia a second bowl bid, this time to play Arizona in the 1985 Sun Bowl in El Paso, Texas.

Because El Paso is a very long way away from Tampa, and because my grandfather seemed increasingly frail, I urged my mother and grandfather and Ruth Ann and Clementine to not try to make the trip. I knew the game would be televised so I knew my family could watch. However, Clementine was not about to be denied. Without telling me she was going to do so, and with the help of Roxanne and Tracy, with whom she had become friends, Clementine bought a Georgia Bulldogs sweatshirt and scheduled herself on the student charter plane from Atlanta to El Paso. I didn't know anything was going on until Philly came over to me and kept telling me what a super crowd had come from Athens. I turned and looked and agreed. Then Barry stood next to me on one offensive series and asked me if I'd ever written the poem about the Georgia fans that he and I had discussed when we'd taken the field for our first game as Bulldogs. When I said no, I hadn't, and then asked why he asked, his answer was so obviously evasive that I knew something was going on. When Randy came over a few minutes later and asked me if I'd checked out the crowd, I knew for sure my friends were trying to pull off some kind of trick. Then I heard her voice: "C'mon, Galahad! Get in there and do something!"

I turned around and there she was, standing with Roxanne and Tracy, all three of them pointing at me and shouting together: "Gal-a-had! Gal-a-had! Gal-a-had!"

Randy was standing next to me. "Gal-a-who?" he said.

"Nothing," I said.

"No, c'mon, man. Who's this Gal-a-whatever?"

Then he looked at the three young women who were laughing and pointing at me. He turned to me and nodded. "Oh, it's you. Galahad. I get it. Prince Galahad."

I looked at him and smiled.

"Wow! Pretty cool, Tyler," he said.

Then the crowd roared, and we turned back to the game, which finally ended in a tie, 13-13. And even though we would have liked to have given Coach Dooley a win, a tie was sure a lot better than a loss.

After the game, which took place on the 28th of December, the team stayed in a hotel. The fans stayed in the same hotel, so several parties took up the evening. The next morning, every one boarded our planes and flew back to Atlanta. Because I'd left my car parked in the security lot on the Athens campus, I left the team in the Atlanta airport, and Clementine and I started our drive back to Tampa, stopping that night very late just south of the Florida border at an Interstate motel. As we lay down next to each other that night, which was the first time we'd been alone since she'd come to stay with me over the Thanksgiving Saturday and Sunday, I finally had a chance to ask how she'd arranged to fly to the Sun Bowl.

"I had good help, Tyler," she said. "Roxanne invited me. And Tracy got all of the players who figured out something was up to keep it a secret."

"Well, it worked. I really didn't have a clue," I said.

"You know, they all respect you, don't you?"

"Do they?"

"Yes, Tyler. They respect you."

"Why? I'm certainly not a star football player."

"But you're a player, Tyler. That's what Randy said to Tracy. You're a *team* player. They respect that. And you're a scholar. They respect that too."

I rolled over and looked at her as she lay looking at me. "They're great guys, Clementine. I really mean that. They're great guys. But I still didn't think you'd be there. I didn't have any reason to think you would. And you didn't say anything."

"You didn't think I let you be alone, did you?" said, kissing me on my eye lids as she spoke, which is the last thing I remember before I fell asleep.

When I told my two teaching compatriots at Augusta State, Leah Strigler, who teaches Jewish and Middle Eastern history, and Al Ventini, who teaches social philosophy, that I was going to write a memoir of my life with Clementine, Leah asked if Clementine and I had ever gone through any kind of conflict in our relationship. "Do you mean, have we ever had a lover's quarrel or ever doubted our love for one another?" I asked.

"Yes," she said. "Most couples do, even if they get married and have a good life together. You know, differences of opinions."

"Those are two different things," I said.

"What do you mean?" Leah asked.

"Doubts about our relationship. No. Never. Differences of opinion. Certainly," I said.

"No doubts ever. Not even when you were in college on different campuses?" Al asked.

We were sitting in the Augusta State University student union. Al and I were drinking coffee. Leah was drinking tea.

"No," I said. "We figured the world had enough doubts about us. We didn't need to help it along. As for differences of opinions: certainly. But we respected each other. So neither of us ever staked out ego territory. When we differed, and we did many times, we talked. Then we came to an agreement. Then we went on."

"That's pretty exceptional, don't you think?" Leah said.

"I suppose. But you have to remember that we grew up together. We matured together. And each of us valued the other so much we didn't want to damage our relationship. We still respect each other. I know I'm not right about everything. Clementine says she knows she isn't always right. So we talk to each other. We figure the odds are that we'll sort out the right thing to do if we really talk and listen to each other."

Al shook his head.

"You disagree?" I said to him.

"No. I just think it's very rare."

"Clementine's a rare person," I said.

Leah smiled and poured another cup of tea. "I still think it's unusual," she said.

"Clementine's an unusual person," I said.

Which brings me to Clementine's and my winter vacation in 1985. Frankly, there was nothing we wanted to do more than just be at home. Just as we had in 1984, we really just wanted to sleep in our own beds and go for walks and read and not think about school or football or track. But we also knew my grandfather wanted to spring another surprise on all of us. So without a word to one another, but with glances that said all that needed to be said, we helped him load both his car and Ruth Ann's with food and clothes and presents. Then we drove south of Tampa and Sarasota to Fort Myers Beach, where he'd rented a fourth floor, three bedroom condominium facing the Gulf of Mexico. As Clementine and I drove Ruth Ann's car behind my mother, who was driving my grandfather and Ruth Ann in his car, we agreed that making my mother and her mother and especially my grandfather happy was more important than our sleeping in our own beds. All three of them wanted to have some vacation time away from Tampa.

Of course, we weren't sure what to expect when we got to the condominium, but we shouldn't have been. Because after we started unloading our suitcases, Ruth Ann said, "You two take that room," pointing at the third bedroom.

When Clementine hesitated as she picked up her suitcase, Ruth Ann went on. "Elizabeth and I agree. We can't stand hypocrisy."

"You've never sneaked around," my mother said. "You have always been very honest about your relationship. We both appreciate that," she said.

My grandfather was too busy putting food in the refrigerator to comment. So Clementine and I moved into the third bedroom. We let the three others settle who would sleep where. We didn't want to know.

That evening we celebrated our Winter Solstice dinner and exchanged presents. Then we sat on the balcony and enjoyed the soft wind off the Gulf. When we finally went to bed that night, Clementine and I lay together, wrapped in each other's arms talking very quietly about what we wanted our life to be in the future. The interesting thing is that what we envisioned then is what we've done. That does not mean there have not been losses and difficulties and stresses. And it doesn't mean there have not been spontaneous moments of great creative joy. It simply means that we have let our love for one another always be what mattered most.

9

Then we were back in school. Classes were interesting if at times also challenging. Clementine started training for the track season. The expectation was that she would win both the 440 and 880 yard Atlantic Coast Conference championships. I faced spring football practice, this time as the starting strong safety. So both of us had to deal with other people's expectations. I didn't complain about that. Neither did Clementine. After all, that's why we wanted to play at the collegiate level: to test ourselves against the best in our sports. But when you face public scrutiny every time you step into a competition, you have to work very hard to get past a self-conscious awareness of other people's expectations and try to focus on the task at hand. That's what I learned from Coach Dooley. You play the game for the sake of the game and the sake of your teammates. You don't play so you can be a hero for the public.

Clementine learned the same thing from Coach Davidsen at Georgia Tech. She ran because she loved to run. She ran to help her teammates run better. The crowd could cheer all it wanted or not cheer all it wanted. What mattered was the race. What mattered was running the best race you could run when it was your turn, which must be true, or at least, which must have worked, because that spring Clementine only lost one dual and triple meet 440 yard sprint. And she won every one of her dual and triple meet 880 yard races. What's more, she broke Atlantic Coast Conference records in both events at the University of Virginia Conference championship track meet. She was, in short, now a name on the national scene. I couldn't have been more proud. My darling Clementine was rapidly becoming the darling of the track world. It was only spring, 1985, but already her name was being mentioned as a potential 1988 American Olympic runner. But there was something wrong. Even when she won both races, I sensed—I felt—there was something wrong.

Then, to compound my sense of anxiety, no matter how any of us insisted that it would be best if he did not travel to the University of Virginia, in Charlottesville, where the Conference championships were being held, my grandfather said he was coming if he had to fly there all by himself. Obviously, we weren't going to let that happen. So just as we had the year before when the ACC championships were run at the University of Maryland, in Baltimore, and I had met Ruth Ann and my mother and grandfather at the Baltimore International Airport and then transported them to the hotel and to the track, I drove from

Athens to Richmond, Virginia, where I met all three at the Richmond airport, and then drove them to Charlottesville on Friday night for the preliminary events.

Clementine had arrived with the Georgia Tech track team Thursday night and had gone with them to the stadium to begin preparations. When we got to the stadium, she was able to come up into the grandstand for a few minutes and talk to us. What I noticed was how nervous she seemed, which was unusual. Always before, no matter the event, Clementine had been able to detach herself from the tension that so many athletes feel before competition, a feat of mind that had always let her perform wonderfully well. This time she seemed tense. Yes, she sat next to me as she always had, and she joked with me in the same way, but I got an uneasy feeling that she was playing a part, as if she were saying words she'd said before. When I tried to hold her hand for a few minutes she kept taking it away and drinking water. When I asked her how she was feeling, she protested she was fine, but I didn't like the tone of her voice. It was sharp and edgy. It was not her.

Then that night she won her heats in both the 440 and the 880 going away. When she joined us later for dinner, she seemed fine. But she was not fine the next morning when we saw her preparing for the finals. What I detected was a nervousness in her warm up that I'd not seen before. By then, I knew her warm up routine by heart. I could have gone down on the track and imitated her. I put my binoculars on her as usual and watched. There was something in her stride that was different. Of course, I wasn't about to say anything to Ruth Ann or my mother or grandfather. That would have worried them. And after all, Clementine knew what she was doing, I told myself. Coach Davidsen knew what Clementine was doing. So I sat back to watch the finals.

The 440 finals were over before the runners made the first turn. Clementine went out with two other runners from the University of North Carolina, drawing them to her, then left them and the other three runners in her wake, winning the event in Conference record time. Watching her through my binoculars, what I saw concerned me more than ever. She may have won, and she may have set a new Conference record, but I didn't like the look on her face. It was more strained than joyous, more anxious than happy. She drank water as she came to the rail of the stadium where I met her. "See, I'm fine," is all she said as I reached over to embrace her. "I told you, I was fine."

I climbed back up to my seat high up in the stadium where Ruth Ann and my mother and grandfather waited. I agreed with Ruth Ann and my mother that she'd run wonderfully well. Then I sat next to my grandfather. He was happy for Clementine, naturally. But he's no fool. "What's up, Tyler?" he said as he looked at my face.

"I don't know, Grandpa," I said.

"Something about Clementine?"

"I don't know. But yes. Something about Clementine." I was just about to say more when Ruth Ann asked me what we were talking about. I told her we were just saying how super Clementine looked when she won the race.

I felt my grandfather nudge my shoulder with his. I could feel him looking at me. I nodded and glanced at him, and I could see that he understood I was concerned, but I could also see that he understood we couldn't talk about it there. So nothing more was said.

Later in the evening, Clementine lined up with the other runners for the finals of the 880 yard run. As she did very often, she went out quickly, drawing other runners with her, then on the first back stretch she let a number of them pass her, slipping into the pack but not letting herself get caught on the inside as she had the year before. By the time the runners completed the first lap, she was sitting comfortably in third place, with the first and second place runners in easy striking range.

What concerned me as the race entered the first turn of the second lap was that Clementine seemed to be straining. It looked as if she wanted to run shorter strides but was forcing herself not to. Down the back stretch she moved up on the shoulder of the second place runner. As the crowd began to shout, I watched intently. This is where she fell the year before. But she wasn't going to fall this time. She certainly wasn't going to let herself be pushed as she had the year before. Instead, she entered the final turn in a burst of speed, passing the second place runner. By the time she caught the leader, she was entering the home stretch.

Then I could see it. She was hurting. Her stride had opened up again, but I could see pain in her face. But it didn't seem to matter. She kicked into a running gear I'd never seen before, sprinting the last forty yards as if she were running a 100 yard race, leaving the pack of runners behind, bolting across the finish line so far ahead that she didn't just break the Conference record, she shattered it by three seconds, an unheard of accomplishment at this level of competition. Raising her arms, she turned to the crowd and to the four of us in the stadium who were shouting her name and waved. Then she turned into the infield and ran another fifteen yards on the grass then collapsed to the grass where other women runners on the Georgia Tech team swarmed all over her. By the time she was back up on her feet, I was at the railing of the stadium again. She ran across the track and reached up and pulled me over the rail so I could lean down and kiss her. She was shouting and crying all at once. And I heard her say in a whisper in my ear, "I hurt, Tyler. I hurt so much. I hurt. I hurt."

I stood up straight and tried to look at her face and tried to respond, but by then Coach Davidsen was there hugging Clementine, the two of them crying with excitement. Then she was swallowed up by other runners, and I turned and walked back up to my seat in the stadium where Ruth Ann was waiting to hug me and my mother was waiting to hug me and my grandfather was waiting to hug me. Only he didn't. He held my face against his, and I said, "She says it hurts, Grandpa. She says it hurts."

I felt one of his strong hands on my shoulder. "You'll have to find out what it is, Tyler. She isn't going to tell anyone else."

I knew he was right. I just didn't know what to do. I was worried that she wouldn't tell me until maybe it was too late.

Then it was summer, and we were back in Tampa teaching in the school camp at the University of South Florida again, which is when, without any warning, life interfered with life, if you know what I mean. Life just jumped up and interfered with life.

The cliché that everyone has 20/20 vision in hindsight has become a cliché because it's correct. Once something has happened, almost everyone can look back and see the warning signs. That summer, I saw the warning signs before the crisis unfolded, but when I tried to ask Clementine how she felt, why was she drinking so much water, why were her muscles sore after we ran together every evening, she did what she so often does:

she deflected my concern by saying she was fine, just fine, which I should have known at the time was her code for "I'm concerned, Tyler, but I don't want to alarm you." It is an endearing characteristic in Clementine—her desire to not be the center of attention. At the same, it is irritating in the extreme, because that summer she should have let herself be the center of attention; certainly she should have been more forthcoming. Perhaps if she had the tragedy that almost engulfed her and all of us who loved her might not have happened. Unfortunately, it did.

It started in July. Both of us were looking forward to our junior years at Georgia Tech and the University of Georgia. We started counting down the days before football practice was scheduled to begin. We had gotten to ten when it happened. Clementine and I were running the track at the University of South Florida, as we did every evening, when she suddenly stopped and stood still. I ran on another twenty yards before I realized what had happened. When I turned back to her, I could see her standing stiff. I could see her arms were rigid and her fists were closed. She looked at me as I walked back to her and asked if she was all right.

"I can't feel my legs, Tyler."

"You can't what?" I said.

"I can't feel my legs."

"What are you talking about? What do you mean you can't feel your legs?"

"Running. Standing here right now. I can't feel my legs."

"My God, Clementine," I said, moving to her side. "Sit down."

"Right here?"

"Yes. Sit down."

She sat. She was in pain. I could see it in her face. I could feel it in her hands as she grasped mine.

"Tyler," she said. "Tyler," she said again. Then she rolled toward me.

"Clementine," I said. "Clementine," I said again as I caught her in my arms, laying her down so I could look at her.

There were other college runners on the track. Men and women. Two women stopped. "Is she all right?" one of them asked.

"Get an ambulance." I said.

"What?" the girl said.

I was holding Clementine's wrist feeling for her pulse. Something was wrong. "Get an ambulance. Just get an ambulance."

The girl turned and began running back toward the closest building. I picked up Clementine and started moving as fast as I could toward the parking lot where I'd parked my car. The other girl was trying to help me. "There isn't time to wait. Help me get her into my car. How do I get to the University hospital?"

"At the main road. Turn right. It's on the other side of the campus," the young woman said.

We arrived at my car. "My keys," I said. "Damn. They're in the bag on the track. The Georgia Bulldog bag."

The young woman ran as fast as she could back to the track where she retrieved the bag Clementine and I had brought.

"In the side pocket," I yelled as the young woman came running towards me.

She fumbled in the bag but found my keys.

"Open the door," I said as she arrived at my car. She tried one key. It didn't work. "The other," I said.

She tried that key. It worked. "Open the door," I said, which she did. Then I put Clementine in the car in the passenger's side seat.

"Can I help?" the young woman said twice.

"Get in the back seat. Hold her up. Don't let her head fall to the side."

The young woman got in the back seat. I pulled the safety belt around Clementine's body. Her eyes were open, but just slightly. "I can't feel my legs," she said in a whisper.

"We're going to the hospital, Clementine."

Then the first young woman was running towards us. "The ambulance is coming," she shouted.

"Tell them we couldn't wait. We're on the way to the hospital."

"Judy!"' the young woman shouted to her companion.

"I'm going with him. Follow us," Judy shouted to her friend.

Then we were driving as fast as I could. I raced through a campus stop sign, turned right, drove as fast as I could across the campus. I could see the hospital ahead of me. I turned into the emergency room entrance and jumped out of the car and starting shouting: "I need help! We need help here!"

I ran around to the passenger's side door and opened it and unbuckled Clementine's seat belt. Judy was out of the car running into the emergency room. "We need help!" I heard her shout.

I lifted Clementine out of the passenger's seat and turned and started toward the emergency room when two attendants and Judy came running out pushing a stretcher. The two attendants helped me lay Clementine on the stretcher. Then they took charge and pushed her inside. I followed. Judy stood inside the door and waited.

A doctor and two nurses came running. "She just collapsed on the track," I said quickly. "She said she couldn't feel her legs."

The three of them rolled her away toward a closed off section of the emergency room. I followed. Judy said she'd park my car. I turned and shouted to her, "Thanks! Thanks!" Then I turned the corner and followed the doctor and the nurses and Clementine lying on the stretcher.

Twenty minutes later Ruth Ann and I were standing in the hallway outside of the emergency room partitioned area where Clementine lay connected to a maze of tubes. "She's a very sick young woman," the doctor said. "This is serious."

Ruth Ann was shaking. I put my arm around her and tried to hold her against her fears. "But she's a runner, doctor," Ruth Ann said. "A nationally known runner. At Georgia Tech. She's never been sick in her life."

"That may well be, Mrs. Brown. But right now, she's a dangerously ill young woman." Then he turned to me and asked me to describe what happened. I did so as clearly as I could.

The doctor nodded. "We're going to run a whole battery of tests. But I'm as sure as I can be that what I've told you is the right diagnosis." Then he turned to me. "Have you noticed any problems lately?"

I hesitated. "Yes," I said. "But she kept shrugging them off. I kept insisting, but she kept saying she was fine."

The doctor said that was not unusual. "Lots of people don't want to talk about what they're feeling. But in her case . . . in Clementine's case . . . what did you notice?"

"It started at the Conference championships last May. The Atlantic Coast Conference. At the University of Virginia. I knew something was wrong. She wasn't running the way she had."

"But she won both races, Tyler," Ruth Ann said.

"That may be," I said. "But she also told me she was hurting. That she was in pain. When I tried to get her to talk about it later, all she would say was it was the stress of the day. Of trying so hard to win."

"What else?" the doctor said.

"What else?"

"What else? Since you've come home for the summer."

"She wasn't running as well everyday when she went to the USF track. She was hurting. She said she was just stiff. But I said she needed to see a doctor. And she was drinking water. She's always drunk a lot of water. Runners do that. But since we've been home she's been drinking a whole lot more. And going to the bathroom, of course."

The doctor looked at Clementine's chart. "All of those are worrisome signs. I have to be honest," he said. Then he turned to Ruth Ann. "Now, you're her mother. Right?"

"Yes," Ruth Ann said.

"And you. Tyler. You're what? Her boyfriend?"

I hesitated. "Only family can be with her. Right?"

"Yes."

"I'm her husband."

The doctor looked slightly surprised.

"Tyler?" Ruth Ann started to say. Then she saw my face and stopped.

"She's wearing her wedding ring," I said quickly. "So am I."

Neither the doctor nor the nurse looked as if they believed me, but I could also tell neither one was going to argue. Clementine's condition was too serious to waste any more time.

"We're going to move her in a few minutes. There's a whole lot more that we have to do. I've called for another doctor to come help. She works with insulin shock all of the time. But I have to warn you the danger now is that she could lapse into a coma."

"A coma?" Ruth Ann said, her voice on the edge of breaking.

"Yes. I'm afraid it can happen that way."

"But she hasn't been sick. Not since she was a child."

"She's been ill for some time now, but she's been covering up. Or she really didn't know. Or she didn't understand what her body was telling her," the doctor said.

"But she's a pre-med student," I said.

The doctor almost nodded. "Oh, well, pre-med students are the worst."

"The worst what?" Ruth Ann said.

"The worst at taking care of themselves. They're either hypochondriacs who imagine they've got whatever illness they're studying or they think they're invincible. I suspect if Clementine is the runner you say she is she's the latter. She probably just didn't want to bother either of you."

"God, that sounds just like Clementine. She never wants to bother anyone with any of her problems," I said quietly.

"Look, this is going to be a very long night," the doctor said. "For her and for the two of you. So if you're going to stay with her, you may want to either go change your clothes, Tyler, or you may want to ask someone to bring a change of clothes here to the hospital."

"Can we see her?" Ruth Ann said.

"I can take you where she is now. But she's not going to have much to say. She may even be asleep. We're worrying about shock at this point. The danger of coma could come later. Or shock could trigger a coma. I don't know. Her body's been fighting this off for some time. But finally it just couldn't hold out any longer."

I wanted to cry. "I should have said something. I should have insisted," I said.

"It probably wouldn't have helped," the doctor said. "I've seen people like Clementine before. They're awfully hard to convince.

Ruth Ann looked as if she was about to faint. I turned to her and said, "Ruth Ann, you've got to sit down. Please."

"I'm all right," she said.

"Mrs. Brown, you aren't all right," the doctor said. "You need to sit down. You can wait in the hallway. There's a place. I'll come get you as soon as you can see Clementine. I promise."

"C'mon, Ruth Ann. Let's go out in the hallway. I'll call my mother. She and Grandpa will want to know what's going on. Clementine and I were going to have dinner with them tonight. They'll be worried."

Ruth Ann accepted, and we went out into the hallway, following the doctor's directions. Ruth Ann sat down on a couch. Four other people were in the area. I went to a pay phone and called my mother and told here where I was and what had happened. I asked her to gather up some of my clothes. "I may be here for some time, mom," I said. "Maybe for days. I'm going to need clothes and a razor and all of that sort of stuff. And books. Bring me some books or I'll go crazy." Then I said, "And the ring. The silver ring on my chest of drawers. Bring that. I'm going to need that too."

My mother said she would do what I asked. She said she and my grandfather would come to the hospital to be with Ruth Ann and me.

12

A half hour later my mother and grandfather found us in the hospital waiting area. My mother gave me a suitcase in which she'd packed clothes. My grandfather gave me three books and the most recent copy of "Opera News Magazine." Both of them embraced Ruth Ann and me. Then my mother sat down next to Ruth Ann and took her hands in hers. Ruth Ann leaned over and put her head on my mother's shoulder and let herself cry softly. I sat next to my grandfather.

"Is it what you thought when we were in Virginia?" he said.

"I don't know. But what she was feeling then . . . I think it was a first sign."

"You can't blame yourself, Tyler."

"Grandpa . . . ."

"No, listen. I know you. I know how much you love Clementine. But you can't blame yourself. She kept telling you she was all right. And you're not a doctor."

"I know. I hear what you're saying. But it's hard not to think that I should have been more insistent. I wanted her to go see a doctor. She just kept putting it off."

"Clementine's quiet, Tyler, but you know she's got a mind of her own."

"I know."

Then a nurse came into the waiting room and asked for the family of Clementine Brown. All four of us stood up. "I just need her immediate family," the nurse said.

"That's us," my grandfather said.

"I'm her mother," Ruth Ann said. "He's her husband," she said, gesturing toward me.

God bless them, my mother and grandfather never missed a beat. "I'm her mother in law," my mother said.

"I'm the grandfather," my grandfather said.

The nurse nodded as if she understood what was going on. "All of that may be, but right now I need her mother and you," she said, turning to me. "Her husband," she added as if she didn't believe it but at that point wasn't going to argue.

Ruth Ann and I followed the nurse through double doors and into a hallway where we were led to a hospital room. Entering, Ruth Ann almost cried out. Clementine was lying in a bed, her eyes closed, an IV in each arm, a breathing tube in her nose, a monitor connected to her chest showing her heart beat.

A young woman dressed in a white medical coat introduced herself as Doctor Lata Bansal. She said she was a neurologist. "I'm not a diabetes specialist. But I work with patients when there's some neurological risk involved. At this point, we're concerned that Clementine may be lapsing into a coma even as she's fighting her way out of the initial diabetic shock that she suffered earlier this afternoon."

Ruth Ann looked as terrified as a person can look. I was fighting back a combination of anger and tears. What was happening? Clementine. What was happening to her? Somewhere she was fighting back. I just knew it. Somewhere deep in her brain, in her mind, somewhere deep in her body, she was fighting a terrible battle against things I didn't understand but about which I would learn a great deal in the days and weeks and finally months ahead. Which is what I meant when I said that sometimes, just when everything in your life looks like it is right and true and going exactly the way you'd dreamed it life jumps up and gets in the way and suddenly you're clinging to the hope that the person you love more than anyone else in the whole world will not die right there in front of you in a hospital bed as you stand next to her and know you can't do a damned thing but hold on. Just hold on for dear life. For her dear life.

13

By that evening, the monitors told the story. Clementine Camille Brown, straight A scholar graduate at Tampa Coast High School, straight A scholar in microbiology at Georgia Tech University, Atlantic Coast Conference women's track champion and new record holder in the 440 and 880 yard runs, mentioned as a promising American Olympic prospect, lay in a bed, the sheets tucked in on three sides tightly to protect her from any spasm that might occur, hooked up to tubes, her heart beating steadily, but unable to respond to any spoken word, in danger of lapsing into a coma, caused by a ruptured cerebral aneurysm that showed up on her MRI, and never fully regaining consciousness.

And that evening, Tyler Thomas Raymond, a fellow graduate of Tampa Coast High School, her high school boyfriend, her college lover, majoring in history at the University of Georgia, listed by nationally regarded Georgia Bulldogs Coach Vince Dooley as the starting strong safety for the University of Georgia football team, sat by her bed, then later lay down on a cot brought into the hospital room where he would sleep not just that night but for every single night for the next sixty two days, fighting as hard as he could against his despair, against his fear, against a brand of sorrow that he knew would overwhelm him if Clementine Camille Brown were to die. A doctor came in after ten days to say that I really didn't belong there. When I asked him if he was going to throw me out by force, my question obviously more a threat than an inquiry, he looked at me for some time before saying, "No. As a matter of fact, what you're doing is exactly what needs to be done." Of course, even if the doctor had told me I had to go, I wouldn't have done so. Because what he could not understand, and what I did not expect him to understand, was that the relationship that had started six years before as a ninth grade romance between two youngsters, both of whom were new to a big school in a big city, a relationship that had deepened and matured and blossomed into a deep and mature love . . . now hung in the balance, now hung precariously in the balance between life and death, between joy and sorrow. Now hung in the balance between what might be and what might have been.

So I took up residence. The days passed. The days did not matter. The nights did not matter. Georgia Tech was informed about Clementine's illness. Coach Davidsen was informed. I did not report to the University of Georgia fall football practice. I did not register at the University of Georgia for classes. The University of Georgia Registrar's office was informed. The director of housing was informed. Coach Vince Dooley was informed. August passed. September passed. I sat every day by Clementine's bed from the time I woke up in the morning and shaved and showered in the bathroom in her room and ate my breakfast sitting by her bed and then started my daily ritual of reading to her from books of all sorts, books I knew she loved, books she knew I loved: *True Grit* and *To Kill a Mockingbird* and *A Woman Named Solitude* and *I Know Why the Caged Bird Sings* and *Pride and Prejudice* and *Little Big Man* and *The Old Man and the Sea* and *The Man Who Killed the Deer* and *A Room with a View*. I read poems by William Butler Yeats and William Carlos Williams and Maya Angelou and Elizabeth Bishop. I read three full length plays: *A Mid-Summer Night's Dream* and *Much Ado About Nothing* and *The Tempest*. And we listened to the news. I had Ruth Ann bring Clementine's short wave radio so I could play the British Broadcasting Corporation programs directly from London and the Canadian

Broadcasting Corporation from Toronto. So every morning at 6 A.M. and every midnight I turned on Clementine's shortwave radio and listened to the BBC and hoped against hope that she was listening as well. And every morning at 10 A.M. and every evening at 7 P.M. I turned on her shortwave radio and listened to CBC and hoped against hope that she was listening as well. And I sat next to her bed and told her everything I remembered about our life together. When the doctors came in after three weeks and told me to go home because I was growing pale, I told them that when I was injured in a football game and there was a danger I might die, Clementine stayed with me and held on so I would come back to her. "I will do the same," I said.

When they argued that my motives were very noble, but it wasn't going to do Clementine any good if she came out of her coma only to find that I had become ill while staying with her, I began working out right there on the floor of her room doing hundreds of sit ups and push ups. I had my mother bring running shoes and running shorts and tee shirts so I could run up and down the back entrance stairs, from the first floor to the fourth floor where Clementine lay in her bed. When I returned to her room I would shower and sit next to her bed and tell her about the every chapter in our time together: meeting one another in ninth grade and the homecoming dance and tenth grade and our trip with Ruth Ann and my grandfather to Scotland and eleventh grade and her track victories and New York City and "Chorus Line" and "Miss Saigon" and our senior year at Tampa Coast and our winter vacation together with her mother and my mother and my grandfather and Clementine's and my golf trip and then us enrolling at Georgia Tech and Georgia and my games and her races and where we were going next, because some day very soon we were going to Africa to find a hill for her just as we'd gone to Wales and stood on my hill. And all the while she lay still and silent, I wanted to cry. I wanted to shout. I wanted to grab her hand and pull her up and hold her in my arms and kiss her lips and say, "You've got to hear me, Clementine. You've got to hear me." But I didn't. I couldn't. All I could do was read and talk and comb her hair and stand next to her when Ruth Ann came and stood with me and stand next to her when my mother came and my grandfather came and stood next to me. All I could do was stand by her bed in the circle we made when Marni Harmony, a Unitarian minister from Orlando whom we'd met a year before when she'd spoken in the Tampa Unitarian Church, came every ten days and held my hand and Ruth Ann's hand as Ruth Ann held my mother's hand and my mother held my grandfather's hand and he held Marni's hand, and we all spoke words Marni taught us about the universe and words about the energy of time and space and belief and faith that asked courage to come cloak her bed and cloak her and touch her and reach deep into her mind and tell her to come back to us.

Then it was cooler outside. And I watched Georgia football games on television. But I didn't care. That's not where I wanted to be. That's not who I was. I was Tyler Thomas Raymond, and I was in love with Clementine Camille Brown, and I was there, right there, next to her bed, reading and remembering and talking and touching her hands and touching her face. And then one day a new person came into the room. At first, I didn't know who she was. Then I did. It was Barbara Dooley, Coach Dooley's wife.

I had just gotten down off the bar stool chair that my mother had brought me so I could sit but still be at bed level next to Clementine and started to comb Clementine's hair when I looked up and saw her standing in the doorway. It took a moment to register who she was.

"Tyler," she said very softly.

"Mrs. Dooley?"

"Yes. It's me."

I was stunned. "Mrs. Dooley. Please, come in. Come in." I moved to shake the hand she extended to me. "It's so kind of you to come here," I said.

"I asked Vince how Clementine was doing. He tries to keep up through the letters you send to Barry Slayman. When he told me she was still in a coma, I said one of us needed to fly to Tampa to tell you that the whole Bulldog nation was praying for her."

"That is very kind of you, Mrs. Dooley. Very kind of Coach Dooley."

"He cares about his players, Tyler. He cares about you. And I remember meeting Clementine last year at the Sun Bowl. She's a lovely young woman. Very poised and intelligent."

"Yes, ma'am. She's all of those things."

"And I could certainly tell you two are in love."

I smiled. I hadn't smiled much for some time, but I smiled then. "Yes, ma'am, we are very much in love."

"Vince misses you. The whole team misses you. But he understands. This is more important than football. You will be welcome to come back to Georgia when you are ready. Certainly he wants you to come back and play for the Bulldogs."

I was overwhelmed. "Did you have other business in Tampa today, Mrs. Dooley."

She smiled. "No. I just wanted to come see Clementine and you."

"Really?"

"I told Vince yesterday at breakfast that since he couldn't leave the team right now during the season, I should come to Tampa on his behalf. So I flew in this morning and took a cab. From your letters I knew I'd find you here. I'll take a cab back in a few minutes and fly back to Atlanta."

"I don't know what to say, Mrs. Dooley. I can't thank you enough."

"That's all right. And listen, I've got notes here from so many of the players. When I told Vince what I was going to do, he told the assistant coaches. They told the players. We had players bringing notes for you to our house until almost midnight last night."

I took the bundle of envelopes from Barbara Dooley. "I don't know what to say."

"Don't try to answer them all. But if you could write a letter to everyone and send it to Vince, he'll make sure it gets posted in the team room."

I said I would do that. Then I turned back to Clementine and explained to her who had come to see her. It was hard for Barbara Dooley to come to the bedside. I could see that. But she is a brave woman and sensitive woman. So she stood with me as I combed Clementine's hair and retied the blue ribbon that I had put in her hair that morning. "I change ribbons every day," I said. "Then I tell her how pretty she looks. And I tell her about the ribbon. Sometimes I change her earrings and then tell her which ones she's wearing. But mostly I read to her or just sit and talk to her or we listen to the news from the BBC or the CBC."

I could see tears in Barbara Dooley's eyes. Then I asked her about Coach Dooley and the team. I said I watched the games on television and read about them in the newspaper. I knew they had beaten Duke but lost to Clemson. I knew they had won at South Carolina and that in three days they would play Ole Miss in Athens. I told her I was confident the Bulldogs would win that game.

She told me about the team and about things Vince Dooley had said and about the way the fans were supporting the team as they always did. Then her time was up, and she stood and told me that she would have to leave. I stood and told her I could never thank her enough for her kindness. Then she went to Clementine's bedside and leaned down and kissed her on the forehead. "You are very much loved, Clementine. So you need to come back to be with all of us very soon."

Then Mrs. Dooley turned and with a soft smile to me prepared to leave the room. But just before she stepped through the door, I said, "Mrs. Dooley, will you do me a favor?"

She stopped and looked at me. "Of course, Tyler. Whatever you want."

I hesitated. "Will you please tell Coach Dooley that I am very proud he knew my father and that my father would be proud that he is my coach."

Barbara Dooley was silent for a moment. I could see tears in her eyes even though I hadn't wanted that to happen. I'd just wanted her to tell her husband how much he meant to me.

"Tyler, I will be honored to tell Vince what you said." Then she was gone. And I didn't know what to do or what to say. I leaned down very close to Clementine and whispered, "Clementine. That was Vince Dooley's wife. Can you imagine? That was Barbara Dooley. She came all the way from Athens just to tell you how much everyone loves you and how you need to come back to us very soon because . . . ." My voice broke. I leaned forward and cried. I had not cried much up to that moment. I hadn't allowed myself any self-indulgence. Besides, I didn't think my crying would help. But now I couldn't help it. I couldn't not cry. "Oh, God, Clementine. Oh, please, my darling Clementine. Please." Then I put my head down on the bed next to her arm and went ahead and let it happen. It was a flood gate. A silent flood gate. I cried until I just could not cry anymore. Then it was dark outside, and I could hear voices in the hallway. I looked up, and my mother and grandfather were in the doorway. "You're going to need more clothes, Tyler," my mother said.

"Yes, ma'am. I am afraid I am."

14

The University of Georgia Bulldogs football team played the University of Mississippi Rebels football team in Athens, Georgia, on October 4, 1986. The game was broadcast on television. I turned on the game and sat on the bar stood chair next to Clementine's bed watching. The game was close, much closer that it should have been, in my opinion. At the eight minutes to go mark in the third quarter, I felt Clementine's hand twitch and grasp mine more tightly. That was not the first time she had done that. I turned to her and looked for a moment. But she didn't move. Her breathing was regular, but it had been regular for several days. So I turned back to the game. I had turned the sound down so it would not disturb anyone, but I could still hear it.

There was a lull in the action when Ole Miss took a time out. Then I heard a very faint, hoarse voice say, "Is that a football game?"

I froze. I turned. Clementine's eyes were squinting, but they were open. "Yes," I said.

"Oh."

A very long silence passed. I turned on my stool until I was leaning out over her.

"Is it Georgia?" she whispered.

My heart was pounding so hard I thought I was going to pass out. "Yes. Versus Ole Miss," I said very softly, trying to retain my composure.

"Oh," she whispered, and then she closed her eyes.

Several very long moments passed. I did not move a muscle.

"Shouldn't you be there?" she whispered, opening her eyes wider than before.

I looked at her. I was crying. "No, I need to be here with you."

"Oh," she said very softly.

"Did you think I was going to leave you alone?" I said, leaning down and touching her right cheek with my left cheek.

"That's my line," she said.

I stood up again. I reached for her face and touched her left cheek and touched her lips.

"I'm hungry, Tyler," she said.

"You're what?" I whispered.

"I'm hungry," she said again.

"Oh, God. Clementine. Oh, Clementine."

"Tyler, I'm hungry."

I stepped back from the bed. I started to cry. I turned and stumbled to the hallway. "Someone," I shouted. "Nurse! Someone! She's hungry. My God, Clementine Brown is hungry!"

I heard voices from the nurses' station and then the sound of feet running toward me. I turned back to Clementine. She was looking at me. "You aren't supposed to shout in a hospital, Tyler," she said even though I could tell it hurt her voice to speak.

I stood in the doorway and started to laugh. "Sorry," I tried to say though my joy. "Sorry. I'll try to keep that in mind. I'll try to remember. I swear. I'll try to remember not to shout in the hospital."

Then a nurse was in the doorway. "The doctor is on his way, Tyler. The doctor is on his way."

15

Clementine's return to consciousness required three levels of explanation, for she had only a vague memory of what happened that fateful day on the track at the University of South Florida. First, the doctors tried to sort out why she had fallen victim to diabetes mellitus. While there are a number of kinds of people who are susceptible to diabetes, Clementine fell into two categories: persons who have a family history and persons of African descent.

In Clementine's case, her African heritage was a general contributing factor. More specifically, Ruth Ann's mother had dealt with diabetes all of her adult life. Of course, when the doctors connected Ruth Ann's mother's diabetes to Clementine's attack, Ruth Ann felt horrible. The doctors did a very fine job of explaining to Ruth Ann and all of us—my mother and grandfather and me, all of whom were present when the discussion took place—that it was not appropriate for her to feel any sense of guilt. Diabetes is diabetes; it shows up or it does not show up. The human gene system is complicated. Clementine would now have to learn how to deal with her condition, but having survived shock and then a very unusual coma, she needed to start the second phase of her circumstance: medical and physical therapy.

When Clementine was first admitted to the hospital, the emergency room doctors and nurses worked to save her from her diabetes attack. By the time she was coming out of that phase, she went into a coma. Ironically while she was in her coma, the doctors then regulated her insulin injections. At the same time, they knew they were fighting a serious battle against the possible ramifications of an ongoing coma that could have, in fact, become so deep that she either did not return to normal conscious life or died while in the coma. While they did not think she was going to die, they were concerned about the possible loss of brain function. Her brain activity had remained fully active while she was in her coma, but they could not have promised that normal activity would last indefinitely if she did not wake up.

The doctors then explained to Clementine how long she was in her coma and how precarious her physical health was during that time. She had been on a battery of monitors to make certain she was going to be in as good health as possible when she returned to consciousness—and they did not ever give up hope that she would return—but because she had been in a mid range coma for sixty days, her physical recovery would now take a very long time. Muscle atrophy, after all. Clementine, who had been a superbly conditioned athlete, could feel immediately how weak she was when she tried to move her arms and raise her head. The doctors said that she would not only need to learn how to deal with monitoring her insulin levels and then administering herself or having some one else administer insulin injections perhaps as few as twice and as many as four times a day, she would have to enter into a regular and demanding program of physical therapy before she could return to normal activities.

Clementine asked questions, of course, not only because she is an intelligent young woman but because her ambition was to become a pediatric physician. After her medical questions were answered, Ruth Ann asked the doctors to explain to Clementine and to her and the three of us what it had meant that I had stayed with her twenty-four hours a day reading and talking and touching her and combing her hair. I had not wanted Ruth Ann to ask the question, not because I was not aware that I had made a difference, but because I did not consider what I'd done heroic. I did what I did because I loved Clementine. I assumed she would have done the same for me if the circumstances had been reversed. In fact, I could point out that it was Clementine's voice that I had heard when I went into the second of my surgeries when I'd been so seriously injured playing football for Tampa Coast during my junior year. As Ruth Ann and the doctors then told Clementine how I had conducted myself, how I had insisted that I be allowed to stay with her, what I had done, what books I had read to her and what poets and what plays I had read to her, Clementine started to cry, which was exactly what I didn't want her to do. Moving to her side, she held my hands with as more ferocity than she ever had before. Then she turned to me and said, "I could hear you, Tyler."

All of us stopped short.

"I could hear you. I know that I could hear you."

"Clementine . . . ," I started to say. Then I couldn't speak. I just lay my head on her stomach and cried my own tears.

I felt Clementine's hand on the back of my head and neck. "It was as if Tyler was in another room. I could hear him. It was as if the door was partly closed and partly open. I could hear him. But I couldn't say anything back to him."

I remained where I was, my head pressed against her stomach.

"I wanted to, Tyler. I wanted to tell you how much I love you," she whispered.

I could not speak.

Then she turned to her mother and the doctors. "Tyler saved my life, mother," she whispered.

"I know," Ruth Ann said. "I know he did."

"I would have gone away," she said quietly. "That's what it felt like. I was going to go away, but he kept calling me back."

I felt her hand stroking my hair. I have never felt anything that was as comforting or wonderful before or since. Clementine's hand stroking my hair. I would ask nothing more of the world for the rest of my life. Clementine's hand stroking my hair. She was alive again. I was alive again. We were alive again.

16

The next three months were a great test for all five of us. Ruth Ann continued her teaching at the University of South Florida. My mother had just become the new Principal at Carrollwood Elementary School. My grandfather was beginning serious research into the history of black players in the baseball major leagues during the late 19th century before white players drove them out of the game. Because Clementine would need around-the-clock supervision as well as a start on her physical therapy, which was going to be very slow going for a very long time, she was moved into my family's home. Ruth Ann would have preferred that she be brought to her house, but she understood that it would make it easier for me to take care of Clementine if she not only lived with me but that she lived in a three bedroom home. So I moved into my grandfather's bedroom, although most nights I slept on a cot in what had been my bedroom but which had now become Clementine's. My grandfather moved most of his clothes and the books he needed into Clementine's bedroom, taking up residence with Ruth Ann. While the shuffle was taking place, Clementine kept saying she was sorry she was being so much bother. My grandfather told her to stop worrying and just start getting well. My silence told her to stop apologizing.

The routine for the rest of the fall and into December was that I got up early in the morning and prepared breakfast for my mother and Clementine and me. Then I helped her shower and dress in clothes suitable for her therapy. Part of the time was given over to both of us learning how to monitor her insulin levels and how to administer her insulin shots. The monitoring part was reasonably simple. Administering shots was harder; not for Clementine, who was by disposition prepared to do that kind of thing, but for me. I was an historian, after all, or at least, I fancied myself becoming an historian. Giving another person injections was never on the list of skills I wanted to acquire. However, necessity always or nearly always overrides hesitation. So I learned. In fact, Clementine began to say that it hurt less when I gave her the insulin injections than when she did. I told her that was only because she got to look away when I gave her the injections. It was a subject we would discuss for several years.

Harder for her was the physical therapy, not because she was not brave and eager to get on with it, but because, frankly, it hurt at first. She was very weak for weeks. When she tried to get out of bed in the hospital, she could not do so on her own for almost ten days. When she finally could, her steps were as insecure as they could be without her falling down. So once more we were constant companions, both in the hospital and then when we moved her to my family's home. We weren't married yet, but for all practical purposes, Ruth Ann said, we had certainly become man and wife. She said many times that I was now her son. My mother said the same thing about Clementine: "You are my darling, Clementine, just as much as Tyler."

For weeks Clementine was helped into our living room where, lying on a mat next to me, we went through the exercise routine that had been prescribed. At first, it hurt so much she wanted to cry. When she did, as much as I wanted to hold her in my arms and free of her pain, that was not my task. So I waited until she finished. Then we started again. Yes, there were times when she wanted to swear at me. I could certainly see that in her face. But she didn't. So we worked together.

During the afternoons, we read together. At first, she had some difficulty concentrating, so I read to her. But finally, after about three weeks of that, I told her it was time she started reading to herself. She seemed startled that I was so abrupt, but then she looked at me and said, "I know what you're doing. And you're right. It's time."

Four days a week we went to the hospital and worked with a physical therapist. Clementine later would say that every time she wanted to complain to me that I was being too hard on her, she just contrasted my more gentle touch to the physical therapist, who didn't seem to have any sympathy at all when she grew tired and wanted to stop her exercises. Of course, she was also smart enough to understand that was what the physical therapist was supposed to do. One day, she complained that it wasn't fair. When I asked her what wasn't fair, she said, "Being smart enough to know what you two are doing when what I really want to do is feel sorry for myself."

I laughed and told her that yes, it was a problem being too smart by half, but she would just have to deal with it for the rest of her life.

Finally, one day when we were driving back to the house from the hospital, where she met with her doctor who checked both her urine and blood sugar and found them within normal limits—she asked the next big question: "What about school, Tyler?"

"What about school?" I said.

"What are we going to do about school?"

"What do you want to do about school?" I said in response.

"I want to go back to school as soon as I can."

"When should that be?" I said.

"I don't know. Could we go back in January?"

I hesitated. "Maybe. We could ask the doctors."

"Should I go back to Georgia Tech?" she said.

"What?"

"Should I go back to Georgia Tech? Or should I transfer?"

I was startled she had raised the subject, although I must admit that I had given thought to the matter myself. "Where would you transfer? To Georgia?"

"Should I?"

"I can't answer that question, Clementine. That has to be your decision."

"But what's your opinion?" Clementine asked.

"Clementine, you're putting me in a very difficult place with that question. Yes, I'd love to be with you every day. But you went to Georgia Tech for very specific reasons."

"I know that. But things have changed, haven't they?"

"Yes."

"Then I think I need to consider transferring."

"To Georgia?"

"Yes."

"Should we consult with someone, or do you want to make the decision on your own?"

"Who would we consult with?"

"I don't know. The people at Georgia Tech. The people at Georgia."

Both Clementine and I were quiet for some time. This was a very important decision, as important as our original decisions to go to Georgia Tech and the Georgia had been. I turned into her neighborhood. "Aren't we going home?" she said.

I smiled. "I thought we should go see my grandfather."

"Ah," Clementine said.

"Yes. Ah," I said.

"Good choice," Clementine said.

17

What has always intrigued me about Clementine—what continues to intrigue me about Clementine—is how when we come to a major decision of some sort, and she suggests that we consult with someone else, or else I suggest we consult with someone else, and she agrees, is the fact that in most cases she's already made up her mind. The question of us returning to our university studies is a case in point.

My grandfather was delighted to see us, of course. As always he loved sitting with the two of us and talking over anything that we had on our minds. But it didn't take very long for him to decide that Clementine had already made her decision. When he said so she replied, "Yes, I have. But I want to make sure that Tyler and I agree."

I waited because I knew there was more to come.

"I'm not going to run track anymore," Clementine said.

"You're sure about that?" my grandfather said.

"Yes. Perhaps I could. I don't know. But I'm not convinced dealing with insulin injections and training for track are compatible. It's also a psychological decision," she said.

"A psychological decision?" I said.

"I'm not sure I could get myself back on a track with the kind of focus that running for Georgia Tech requires."

I nodded but waited.

"I would like to drive to Georgia first, Tyler, to see about transferring. I know the pre-med program is excellent. I went to Tech to study micro-biology and to run. Now I don't want to run anymore. I want to be with you."

I wanted to respond very carefully. This was new territory. Not our love of one another. Not how much I missed Clementine every day when she was at Tech and I was at Georgia. But I wanted to understand fully what she was thinking. "We can do that," I said. "We'll talk to your doctor and your physical therapist. But certainly we can drive there if that would be comfortable for you. Or we could fly," I said.

"We can drive. I can sit up. Or I can lie down if I have to. I want to start driving again anyway," she said.

My grandfather smiled. "I get the feeling I'm not needed in this conversation," he said.

"No. You are. Because there's another issue," Clementine said quickly.

"And what's that?" my grandfather said.

Clementine was quiet for a moment. She looked at me. Then she looked at my grandfather. "If I went to Georgia, I would not want to live in a dormitory. I've lived with Tyler now. In the same house, at least, ever since I got out of the hospital. And I meant it when I said I could hear him when I was in a coma. I've tried to remember things he said to me, but I can't do that. But I do remember hearing him. I could almost see him. I know that's just my imagination because my eyes weren't open. So it must have been like a dream. But what I know now for sure is that I want to be with him for the rest of my life."

I sat silent for a moment.

"Tyler?" my grandfather said.

I turned to my grandfather. "I cannot imagine living another day without Clementine in the same house. When she was in the hospital, and I stayed with her, I knew I could never go back to not being with her," I said. "I'm just not sure how to do that if we go back to school."

"You aren't?" my grandfather said.

I smiled. "Okay. I do know. I just haven't had a chance to talk to Clementine about it."

"You can talk to me now," Clementine said. "That's why we came here. To talk."

"To talk to my grandfather," I said.

"And to talk to one another," Clementine said.

I sat back and reached over and took her hand. "All right. I will talk to you right now. Right here and right now."

Clementine and my grandfather both waited.

"Clementine Camille Brown . . . if you were to transfer to the University of Georgia in January, and I were to go back to Georgia in January, I know I could not do it unless I lived with you."

Clementine started to speak, but I interrupted.

"But I would not ask you to live with me if we were both single," I said.

She smiled.

"Yes, I know, given what we've been through, that sounds a tad strange. We live together in my mother's house right now."

She waited.

"So if you decide to transfer to Georgia in January, and I decide to go back to Georgia in January, I would want us to be married." That was it. I had said it.

Clementine looked at me. Her expression was very serious. "Are you asking me to marry you, Tyler Raymond?"

"I am. Yes, I am. I am asking you to marry me, Clementine."

My grandfather let out a sigh and turned to Clementine.

"If that is what you are asking, then my answer is yes," Clementine said.

My grandfather laughed. "Wonderful," he said.

So it was decided. We would marry. But first we had to drive to Athens and talk to people at Georgia.

"Of course, we're assuming I can get into Georgia," Clementine said.

I laughed with my grandfather. "I think that's a safe assumption," I said, with which my grandfather agreed.

18

That evening, Clementine and I took Ruth Ann and my mother and grandfather out to dinner. And while it was Clementine's first time out to a restaurant since she came home from the hospital, we viewed it as our opportunity to explain to Ruth Ann and my mother what Clementine and I had decided.

Both Ruth Ann and my mother were silent at first. Nothing in their expressions suggested they disapproved. They were simply silent until finally my mother turned to Ruth Ann and said, "Ruth Ann and I have been expecting this for some time now." Then she turned to Clementine and me and said, "I couldn't be more happy."

Ruth Ann echoed my mother's sentiment. "I know you two have been through a lot together, the last four months especially. And if you can do that, you can do anything."

With that my grandfather stood and said, "I propose we raise our wine glasses to the two finest young people I have ever had the privilege to know." He hesitated for a moment. His emotions were obvious. Then he said, "The fact I have had the joy of being grandfather to one and surrogate grandfather to the other is simply more than I ever expected out of life." He turned to both of us. "I love you both. And you love each other. And your mothers love both of you. There is nothing better than that." With that he raised his class, as did Ruth Ann and my mother, and together they said, "To Clementine Camille and Tyler Thomas."

Clementine held my hand very firmly. I turned to her to see her looking at me. "You are the only man I will ever love, Tyler," she said.

I nodded and smiled at her. "And you are the only woman I will ever love, Clementine."

"Which is why," Clementine said, turning to her mother and then to mine, "that we want to get married in December. And rather than have other people stand up with us, we want the three of you to stand by our sides. If that's okay with you."

Ruth Ann and my mother and my grandfather were all silent for a moment. "By God, that sounds like a fine idea," my grandfather said, smiling broadly in joy.

My mother agreed. "I would be honored to stand up next to you, Tyler," she said.

"No, Mom. That's not what we want," I said quickly.

"What?"

"I want Ruth Ann to stand with me. Clementine wants you to stand with her. And we want Grandpa to stand with Marni Harmony, the minister we know from Orlando."

Ruth Ann laughed. "Isn't it just like the two of you to do something out of the ordinary . . . and wonderful at the same time."

My grandfather laughed. My mother smiled her approval. So it was decided. Something out of the ordinary and wonderful at the same time.

19

The following Monday, Clementine and I drove to Athens where she interviewed with the admissions officers of the University of Georgia. She was given forms to fill out, but she was assured that she would have no difficulty transferring her credits. Then we visited with the Director of Housing and arranged to get a one bedroom apartment in one of the married students' apartment buildings. Then I said I wanted to visit with my advisor, Professor McAndrew, and with Coach Dooley.

I had telephoned ahead and made appointments with both. Both men were eager to see me and to talk about my return to the University. Professor McAndrew agreed that in addition to the spring semester, I would have to attend summer school if I wanted to try to catch up with my graduating class. He emphasized that it was not necessary that I do so. I could delay graduation if I chose to do so. But I said I wanted to move along as rapidly as possible since I was also intent on attending graduate school.

Coach Dooley was wonderful about my return as I had expected. We had exchanged letters during the football season, in which I had told him how much I wanted to return to the University, and he told me how much he wanted me to do so. He said he was happy to see Clementine up and around. When I told him that we were getting married and that Clementine was transferring to Georgia so we could be together, he said he was very proud of the way both of us had responded to what might well have become a tragedy. "Your teammates respect you, Tyler. For all sorts of good reasons. They will be pleased that you're back."

"I am too, sir. I'm looking forward to spring practice. But as soon as we are settled here on campus, I'm going to need to get back into the weight room and start running."

Coach Dooley said he was sorry that Clementine's running career was over. "You were a splendid athlete," he said. "But you are also probably wise to make the decision you've made."

With that he extended an invitation. "When I told Barbara you were coming today to meet with me, and that you were bringing Clementine, she said you had to come to our house for dinner."

Both Clementine and I were delighted to accept. With that, we left and made our way back to my car and then drove to our motel so we could rest and then dress for dinner. As we walked across the campus holding hands, I could not help but think about how our relationship had started. I could not help but think about all that we'd been through. Just as I was about to say something to Clementine, she stopped and looked at me as I stopped and turned back to her.

"This is where I want to be, Tyler. With you. This is the life I want to live," Clementine said.

I walked back to her and then carefully and tenderly lifted her face to mine and kissed her very slowly, letting her relax into my arms, letting myself feel her warmth, letting the wind blow around us, letting students who were passing from class to class walk around us as we stood on the sidewalk holding each other for some time before we let go and walked to my car holding hands.

20

The next day before we left Athens, Clementine and I made final arrangements to rent housing from the University. Although we did not get to walk through the specific apartment we rented, we did walk through one that had the same floor plan. From there we went to a furniture store close to the campus and bought what we would need, specifying a move in date in January.

Then we drove to Georgia Tech where Clementine made arrangements for her transcript to be sent to the University of Georgia. The Dean of the School of Science expressed his regret that Clementine was leaving, but he also said he understood the circumstances that led to her decision. His parting offer was that he would be pleased to write her any kind of letter of recommendation she might need in the future. He was confident that she would do well in the Georgia pre-med program and, if she chose to apply to the Medical College of Georgia, in Augusta, he would be happy to do everything in his power to support her application.

When we got to the Allison Fisher Dormitory, I waited in the lobby while Clementine went upstairs and said goodbye to her friends. It took longer than she had said it would, but I had expected as much. When she came back down to the lobby, there were traces of tears in her eyes. Sensing my unease, she quickly assured me that she did not regret her decision to move to the University of Georgia to be with me. "Saying goodbye is hard, Tyler. It would be hard for you. But that doesn't change my decision. My life is with you."

I admit that her statement kept me from feeling guilty. After all, she had invested two years of her life at Georgia Tech, two very successful years at several levels. It was an unfortunate medical change in her life that made the change in her schooling logical. I tried to keep that in mind during the weeks and months that unfolded for us at Georgia when I saw she was reading the sports page for news about her Yellow Jacket friends, especially during track season. At the same time, she never once expressed any bitterness that she had not been able to continue her academic and running career at Tech. It is one of the remarkable things about Clementine that I have always admired: while I tend to linger in the past, even as I try to climb into the present, Clementine has always had the ability to decide to decide. Once she does that, she moves on to the next chapter in her life. I have always believed she is a healthier person as a result. Certainly she is much more grounded in the reality of life than I am, for all of my efforts to be reasoned and reasonable.

The hardest departure for Clementine, as you can imagine, was saying goodbye to Coach Davidsen. Coach Davidsen had come to Tampa to recruit Clementine. She had demonstrated in many different ways her sincere interest in Clementine as a person as much as an athlete. When Clementine was in the hospital, among the many people who inquired about her condition, no one's telephone calls were more regular than Coach Davidsen's. By the third week when I stayed with Clementine, I found I could set my watch by Coach Davidsen's Wednesday afternoon telephone call. As a result, when Clementine came out of her coma, the first person I telephoned was Coach Davidsen. Then I telephoned Barbara Dooley. Then I telephoned Marni Harmony. After that, the telephone began ringing off the hook as the news spread, spurred on to a large degree by television sports reporters in both Atlanta and Tampa who had monitored Clementine's condition as well as my vigil.

When we left Coach Davidsen's office, Clementine asked if we might go to the stadium where she had run so many races. I didn't know what kind of impact that sort of visitation might have on her, but I certainly wasn't going to resist. So we walked to the track stadium together. Once we were there I let Clementine climb into the bleachers so she might say goodbye in her own way. It took some time for her to do so, but in the end, when she came down onto the track where I was waiting and we walked out of the stadium and back across the parking lot to my car, she didn't say anything. Finally, as she got into the passenger's side seat and buckled her safety belt, she looked at me and said, "Thank you. Now that's over. Let's go home."

I leaned over to her and kissed her cheek. "You are a remarkable woman, Clementine."

She started to speak, so I put a finger on her lips to keep her from protesting. "Clementine, you are a remarkable woman, and I love you."

Clementine leaned forward and accepted my kiss. Then she smiled and said, "Let's go home" a second time.

"Yes, ma'am," I said, smiling. "As you so desire."

21

Once we were back in Tampa, Clementine and Ruth Ann and my grandfather made the arrangements for our wedding, which we wanted to be a private, family occasion. The five of us drove to a very nice family run resort my grandfather knew about south of Sarasota where, on December 15, 1986, we were married by the Rev. Marni Harmony and my grandfather, who shared in reading the words of the ceremony Clementine and I designed. True to our request, my mother stood next to Clementine, and Ruth Ann stood next to me.

What I remember very keenly about the preparations was that five days before the ceremony was to take place, when I was wondering what I should wear, my mother came to me in the morning and said, "I have something for you, Tyler."

With that she led me into her bedroom where lying on the bed was a double breasted pin stripped suit. When she held it up for me to see, it was obvious that it was an expensive suit, undoubtedly custom tailor, certainly nothing like I'd ever seen or ever worn before.

"It was your father's," my mother said. "He wore it when we got married."

"And you've kept it ever since?" I said.

"Yes."

I was quiet for a moment.

"When your father died, I thought about giving it to the Good Will people. I gave most of his other things to them. But when it came to this suit, I couldn't do it."

Now both of us were quiet for a moment.

"It meant everything to me that day . . . that I was marrying him. So when I got to this suit, I decided that I would keep it. Because I thought that maybe, one day, my son—you, Tyler—I thought that maybe my son would want to wear his father's wedding suit on the day he got married."

There wasn't anything I could say at that point. Sometimes words just don't work. So I went to her and put my arms around her. We stood like that for some time. Then I stepped back and went to the suit and picked it up and looked at it. It was beautiful. Yes, it had been tailored years before, but that didn't matter. It was classic. And classic is timeless.

"I would be honored, mother, to wear this suit," I said.

"Then try it on. You're almost as tall as your father was, but he was heavier. He was older, of course, which is why. But he was heavier. So we'll take it to the woman who alters my clothes. She does men's suits as well."

I took the suit to what was now Clementine's and my bedroom and put it on. Clementine came into the room and saw me. "What're you doing?" she said.

"You aren't supposed to see me. Get out of here," I said, laughing.

After she left, I hitched up the pants and put on the jacket and went back to my mother. I knew that for her it was going to be a mixed blessing, but the suit was very close to fitting.

"Yes, you're almost as tall. The length can be fixed. You'll need a little taken in around the chest, but not much. As for the waist, that will take maybe two inches. But I know it can be made right."

So it was settled. I would wear my father's wedding suit. I was honored.

As for Clementine: she wouldn't tell me what she and her mother were planning, but I knew, as always, she would be beautiful. Of course, Clementine is one of those rare women who looks good in anything. I used to tell her when we were in school that if she wore a gunny sack to school one day, she'd start a fad. What she did that day, however, outdid even her.

The night before we got married, Clementine stayed in her mother's room at the resort so none of us would see her before the ceremony. As planned, my mother and grandfather and I met Marni Harmony in the lobby of the hotel and then walked together to the small room overlooking the Gulf where we waited. When Ruth Ann came in, followed by Clementine, I was breathless. There she was in a pearl gray sweater material dress that started with a tight collar around her neck and extended, form fitting, all the way to the floor. Over the dress she wore a long sleeved sweater of the same material. The sweater was open exposing a single strand of pearls around her neck. The strand of pearls were matched by her earrings. Her hair was combed out. It framed her face softly, falling all the way to her shoulders. As usual, she wore very little make up. She didn't need make up. She never has.

I didn't know what to think. Why was this beautiful woman marrying me? What could I have possibly done to deserve this day? I am not being sentimental. I really did think those questions. And to be honest, not only do I continue to ask myself those same two questions even today, I still have not come up with any good answers.

The language of the ceremony itself was exactly what Clementine and I wished to express. It began with Rev. Marni Harmony saying, "Clementine Camille Brown and Tyler Thomas Raymond have come this day to this place in this company to marry one another. Clementine and Tyler passed through adolescence together."

Then my grandfather began what was his refrain: "And in so doing they learned how to love."

I looked at Clementine, who was looking at me. She was smiling her lovely, gentle smile. I was smiling my is-this-really-true? smile of joy.

Marni Harmony continued: "Clementine and Tyler passed through their young adulthood together." Followed once again by my grandfather's refrain: "And in so doing they learned how to love."

Marni then said, "As their relationship matured, Clementine and Tyler faced the outrages of racial prejudice together," which was followed by my grandfather saying, "And in so doing they learned how to love."

The ceremony began to change when Marni said, "Tyler passed through the shadow of death with Clementine at his side." My grandfather said, "And in so doing they learned how to love."

Marni continued the theme of danger by saying, "Clementine passed through the shadow of death with Tyler at her side," echoed by my grandfather's refrain, "And in so doing they learned how to love."

Marni then concluded her part of the ceremony by saying, "So on this day and in this place and in the company of those whom they love and who love them in return, they now marry one another."

Then Clementine and I removed the rings I had purchased for us in the gift shop at Sea World years before and moved them to the ring finger of our right hands. My grandfather then gave each of us the matching flat white gold rings we had chosen, which we each put on the other's hand as Clementine said, "Tyler, I have known from the first day that I met you that you are the only man I will ever love."

I then said, "Clementine, I have known from the first day that I met you that you are the only woman I will ever love."

We then ended the ceremony by saying together, "And so on this day in this place and in the company of those we love and who love us in return, we pledge our lives to each other in the full confidence that when each of us ends our life in this world, it will truly be said of us, 'And in so doing they learned how to love.'"

Then, directed by Marni, we kissed each other very tenderly, and then my mother kissed Clementine, and Ruth Ann kissed me, and my grandfather kissed us both, and Marni kissed us both.

Then Marni said, as must always be said at the end of a marriage ceremony, "By the power vested in me by both your pledge to marry, in the full and certain knowledge of the obligations and joys and possible sorrows that attend that promise, and by the powers granted to me by the State of Florida, I pronounce that you two are today married."

So that was it. What started with, "Should we be partners?" in a ninth grade biology class made a full circle, ending with "you two are today married." I could not have been more happy. Clementine's eyes told me she felt the same.

Once the ceremony was over, the six of us walked to a second small room where we sat at a table from which we could still see the Gulf of Mexico. After we were seated and a waitress had brought us a bottle of champagne, and after my grandfather stood and went around the table and poured each of us a glass, he toasted Clementine and me by saying, "Your love speaks clearly to the possibility of life. I am honored that you have shared your lives with me."

Then Ruth Ann stood and toasted us by saying: "Today I affirm what I have known from the first day I met you, Tyler, that you are the man with whom I wish my daughter to spend the rest of her life."

Then my mother stood and toasted us by saying: "Today, I too affirm that I have known from the first day I met you, Clementine, that you are the woman with whom I wish my son to spend the rest of his life."

Both of them were crying, of course.

Then Clementine stood and said, "With all of my heart, I thank the three of you for teaching me to love, so I can now spend the rest of my life loving Tyler."

Then it was my turn. Echoing Clementine's words, I said in not much more than a whisper, because that was all the volume my emotions would allow, "With all of my heart, I thank the three of you for teaching me to love, so I can now spend the rest of my life loving Clementine."

What now occurs to me, having recalled and written as much as I have thus far about my life with Clementine—the question that I sometimes ponder late at night when I am in my study writing—is who I might have become had I not grown up with such a remarkably strong and positive mother and grandfather? Clementine has said the same thing about her mother: "Who might I have turned into had my mother not been such a force for good in my life?" And sometimes when we are talking of such things—which usually happens at night when we are lying in bed sharing our most intimate thoughts—we think about the countless number of people who were denied those kinds of bonds and that kind of unqualified affection, and whose lives too often come crashing down around them—we ask ourselves: what was it in the daily mix of life that didn't happen for them that did happen for us? Of course, I never have to think very hard to find the answer, because it is so obvious that it was my mother and grandfather who made the difference, in the same way that I cannot imagine who I might have become had I not met Clementine. I am certain I would not have accomplished what I have accomplished in my life had I not met and courted and then married her. Fortunately for me, she very often says the same thing about her relationship with me, although I have never figured out with any certainly what it is I have given to Clementine save for my undying love and respect. She says that's what she means when I sometimes question her assertion about her life being shaped by knowing me. Then at that point, I am smart enough to let the subject rest for fear that one day she might have second thoughts about loving me. That is a nightmare scenario that I know I could not face.

22

When the meal was finished, Clementine and I said goodbye to Ruth Ann and my mother and grandfather and started our short trip south to Miami for our honeymoon, during which we met briefly with the Raymonds' lawyer, who had written me and asked back in the fall if I intended to continue my schooling, since he had not received notification of my registration at the University of Georgia. When I told him that he would receive notification in January when I returned to my studies, he said that I would then find the money the Raymonds were providing for me in my account. When I told him that I had married Clementine, he offered his congratulations, although he added that he did not think it his place to inform the Raymonds of my change in circumstance. I told him I understood but that I would take care of the matter sometime in the future when I decided the time was right.

Then Clementine and I left his office, certain in our own minds that we probably were not out of the building before he was on the telephone talking to one if not both of my Raymond grandparents about what I had done. However, as the trust fund was dependent only on my continuing my studies, for however long I chose to pursue degrees, I was confident nothing would disturb the funding arrangement. That fact, coupled with my own academic and athletic scholarships to Georgia and the academic scholarship that Georgia had agreed to offer Clementine when she transferred assured us that we could continue our plan for Clementine to attend medical school, and I could go to graduate school in history.

When we returned to Tampa and to our mothers and my grandfather, we all observed the Winter Solstice at our annual dinner. Then we exchanged gifts.

Four days later, we celebrated New Year's Eve together, after which, on January 2nd, Clementine and I drove my car to Athens. The next morning the furniture we had bought arrived at our apartment, and we started the process of setting up our first home together.

23

If it now sounds as if Clementine and I entered into an idyllic period of time in our life together, you are right. It was idyllic. I relished my return to the University of Georgia not only because I had missed the academics but because I had missed the friends I'd made through my classes and the football team. Because Clementine was now on the same campus with me, I know I was much more open to meeting new people.

At the same time, as much as she had enjoyed her two years at Georgia Tech, Clementine very quickly started making her own friends. She is, after all, a warm and winning personality. So as much as we were and still are private people, our apartment became a sanctuary for a number of people who trusted our companionship. Barry Slayman, who was by then the starting quarterback on the football team, and his fiancé, Marilyn, came for dinner so regularly that some people thought the four of us were living in the apartment together. Many evenings we sat with two or three or four other friends playing board games or talking or watching sports on television. As a consequence, the spring semester of the 1986-1987 academic year was as wonderful a time as I had ever had or would have in college. Much of that has to do with the fact Clementine's and my relationship had survived so many challenges. Another reason was that within weeks of her arriving on the Georgia campus, Clementine's quiet, poised person won many new friends who simply wanted to be around her even if she never tried to assert herself in any social situation. I can't tell you how many times I'd make a suggestion to one of my football teammates—usually some guy who weighed two hundred fifty pounds or more, because we had a number like that—who would hesitate before he'd accept my invitation and say, "Gee, Tyler, I'd love to come for dinner, but is it okay with Clementine?" I even told her more than once that it seemed to me that the affection my teammates felt for her seemed to be in proportion to their sizes. The bigger they got the more clumsy they felt around her. It was so true that some of them even started calling themselves "Clementine's Famous Trained Bears." When someone one evening said the name should be "Clementine's Famous Trained Black Bears," I remember Harold Miller, a white guy, objecting because, as he said, "She's got as many white guys who think she's super as she does black guys." When the black players agreed—that unless you called them "Clementine's Famous Trained Black and Polar Bears" the name wouldn't be fitting, everyone there on that occasion agreed that the name should just stay what it was: "Clementine's Famous Trained Bears." What I should add, though, is that her sometimes clumsy, always affectionate, almost boyish "Trained Bears" were a fearsome lot when they were tuned loose on Saturday afternoons on the football field.

One Athens sports writer, Mike Bandstra, wrote a story about Clementine's illness and how I had stayed with her and as a consequence missed the 1986 season, going on to detail how we had married and she had transferred from Georgia Tech to Georgia but would not be running track any more, ending the story with the tag lines: "Strong safety Tyler Raymond's lithe and lovely wife seems to have become the beloved sister of every member of the defensive team at Georgia. So the word around the Bulldogs' training facility is that opposing teams best beware when Clementine Brown brings her big brothers out to play."

Of course, we are also quick to add that our families had been extraordinarily supportive and broadminded about our love for one another, but that support had not always been mirrored in the larger society around us. We knew full well we had weathered a number of storms. We did not talk about those incidents in order to congratulate ourselves; self-congratulation was never our style. Neither was being self-satisfied. We both had very long academic roads ahead of us. The fact we could share each other's road was what made our married life so wonderful. I watched Clementine study for hours on end. She watched me do the same. I watched as she wrote treatise after treatise on any number of medical subjects. She watched as I wrote critical essays for both my English and my history classes. Because both of us were eager to have the other read our papers and ask questions and offer suggestions, both of us were increasingly successful as we moved closer and closer to the most advanced courses in our undergraduate curriculums.

I had also returned to the athletic training room where I not only found myself welcomed by teammates from my first two years of football who had not yet graduated, I found myself making friends with players who had been with the team during the season when I was at Clementine's bedside. Coach Dooley helped me design a system of workouts that would not only increase my strength but would help with my endurance. Clementine even came with me to the track and gave me advice on increasing my speed, which was always my weakest point as a player. I was reluctant to ask for her help at first, fearing that it might open the wound of her having been forced to stop running, but she said that was not the case. She liked being around the track, especially working with me. And I had much to learn. In her own kind way, she made that very clear. In the end, despite the fact that I'd played football for four years at Tampa Coast High School and two years at the

University of Georgia, it wasn't until Clementine began coming down onto the track and giving me advice about my stride that I began to understand what running was all about. It was just one more instance of Clementine's wisdom shaping what I was able to achieve.

I suppose it goes without saying that our personal life together was joyous beyond my powers to describe. More than one morning, when I woke up before Clementine, I lay next to her and just looked at her sleeping. Other mornings when I awoke after she had awakened, I found her doing the same. And lest you think that sense of wonder and awe was only because we had been married for a short period of time, let me tell you that it still happens. I still wake up and lie next to Clementine when she is sleeping and wonder the stars aligned themselves so perfectly that Clementine Camille Brown came into my life. She must feel the same, because very often when I am reading, I will look up and see her looking at me. When I ask if there's something she wants, she always replies, "No. I just like looking at you."

After spring football practice ended, and both Clementine and I finished our final exams and most of the Georgia students began packing up and going home for the summer, Clementine and I stayed on. We couldn't make up completely for the semester we'd missed in the fall of 1986, but she managed to complete two major courses, both of which included meeting her first patients in the University medical clinic, and I managed to complete three courses, two of which were in the history department. What that meant was that as the fall of 1987 approached, we were not quite back on track, but we were very close.

When summer school ended, we went back to Tampa and stayed with Ruth Ann for two weeks, visiting every day with my mother and grandfather. I found my visits with my grandfather very rewarding, because by then he had put together most of the notes he was going to use for his new book, *Blacks, Baseball, and American Prejudice: A History of Racial Fear*. The fact he spent four days with me going over all of his thinking was flattering in the extreme.

Then it was time for me to go back to Athens and start fall football practice. Clementine stayed with her mother for an extra week. Then she rejoined me, and we settled down for what we most sincerely hoped would be very good senior years. What we didn't know was our idyllic life was about to come to an abrupt and awful end, for fate had yet another cruel surprise coming our way. And when the tragedy struck—and *struck* is the only appropriate word—it would require all of the strength we could muster to survive the pain.

24

Medically, Clementine was making excellent progress. She had learned how to monitor her insulin level and administer insulin injections so well that neither ever interfered with her academic or our personal life. As for me, I could monitor her insulin levels as well as she could because reading the scale was easy. Giving her injections was another matter. That I found very hard to do. When she said I didn't need to take a turn each day because she hated to see me in more pain that she was feeling, I told her that I had to keep on being a part of the process. "Some day there may be an emergency when I have to give you your shot. I don't want to not be able to do that," I said.

"But you always look like you want to close your eyes just when you insert the needle," she said. "You look like you're aiming in the dark."

"That's because I want to close my eyes when I insert the needle," I said, a comment that made her laugh for several minutes. "But I still have to learn how to do it," I said.

"Do you realize that I hate seeing your face all contorted in agony so much that just before you inject me I turn away?" she said.

I laughed. "That makes two of us," I said.

"What do you mean?" she asked.

"Well, I look away too," I said. Before she could howl her frustration, I added. "That is, I did until last week. Now I'm looking all the way."

She smiled with relief. At least, I think it was relief. Perhaps it was something else.

25

It is widely held that college football is a religion in the American South. I have to tell you that it's true. College football in the American South *is* a religion. Or if it's not a religion, it certainly is an all-consuming way of life. And nowhere is that more true than at the University of Georgia. Perhaps, at some unconscious level of mind, that's why I wanted to attend Georgia in the first place. Besides my profound respect for Coach Vince Dooley, I wanted to be a member of the Bulldog Nation. And believe me, it is a nation, with all of the attending attributes that attend nationhood. At least, that was certainly true as the team entered the 1987 season.

Viewed from the outside, the 1984 University of Georgia football season would appear to have been a success. The team record was 7-4-1, with a 4-3 South East Conference record. Viewed from the inside, the season was less than satisfying: a loss to the University of South Carolina was followed by a loss to the University of Florida, 27-0, which was followed by a loss to instate rival, George Tech, 35-18. The fact Georgia went on to tie Florida State, 17-17, in the Citrus Bowl, in Orlando, was some but not much consolation.

The 1984 season was followed, in 1985, by another 7-3-2 record overall and 4-2-1 in the South East Conference. What made the year even better for the Bulldog Nation than the record appeared was the win over South Carolina, 35-21, and the win over the University of Florida, 24-3. What left a bitter taste in the teams' mouth, however, was another loss to Georgia Tech, 20-16. The taste didn't get better when we tied Arizona, 13-13, in the Sun Bowl.

The 1986 year, in which I did not participate, was again a mixture of success and frustration. Yes, the Bulldogs beat state border rivals South Carolina 31-26, but then they turned around and lost to Florida, 31-19. The win against Georgia Tech, 31-24, was then dampened to some degree by the loss to Boston College in the Hall of Fame Bowl 27-24.

With all of that behind them, Coach Dooley prepared the team for the 1987 season. And while I was technically somewhere between my junior and senior years, and had another year of eligibility left, because I knew I wanted to graduate at least by the end of the summer and begin my graduate studies, I knew that this was going to be my last year of football. As a consequence, I resolved that it was going to be my best year of my life, focusing every day when I was on the practice field not just on being sure I was in game playing condition but that I was mentally prepared for the challenges. I worked harder than ever at reading quarterback tendencies. I worked harder than ever with the Georgia receivers, tying to anticipate routes, getting a number of them to stay late after practice to run routes against me so I could improve my covering ability. And if that was not enough, I always ended practice with Philly Jones on the tackle dummies, because both of us resolved that any receiver coming in to our areas of coverage were going to pay a dear price for catching passes. Many evenings after practice I came back to Clementine's and my apartment so tired I could barely sit up to eat. More than once I feel asleep at the table, only to awaken at 10 P.M. knowing that I had to study at least three or four hours to be ready for the next day's classes. Had it not been for Clementine taking care of my diet and forcing me to sleep whenever I could, I'm not sure I would have gotten through the regime successfully. That I did is a tribute to her discipline not my energy.

With Clementine and Ruth Ann and my mother and grandfather back in the stands among the Bulldog Nation, the team began with a win over Virginia, followed by a big win over Oregon State. That was followed by a disappointing loss to Clemson. We beat South Carolina in the border war in Athens 13-6. Then we traveled to Oxford, Mississippi, and defeated the Rebels 31-14. Unfortunately, our two game winning streak was all we could put together, for we let LSU beat us on our home field 26-23, a defeat that rankled as much as any that year, or so we thought at the time. Of course, as always, Vanderbilt was no problem. We ran up 52 points that day, the most we'd scored in all of my time at Georgia. I even scored my first collegiate touchdown in the third quarter off an interception when we took charge of the game. That was followed by two more wins in a row: 17-14 against Kentucky, which should not have been that close, and the big one against Florida, 23-10. It was probably natural that we would then suffer a let down against our next opponent. Unfortunately, it turned out to be a very sound Auburn squad, who brought us back to reality when they took us to task, 27-11. And as sorry as the team was about the loss, the feeling of disappointment a number of our player friends expressed that night when they came by our apartment to eat pizza was only the beginning for Clementine and me, because at 11 P.M. we received a telephone call from Ruth Ann saying my grandfather had suffered a massive heart attack when she and my mother and he were driving to Atlanta, where they planned to stay for the night before flying home to Tampa on Sunday.

Leaving our friends to clean up the kitchen and close our apartment, within fifteen minutes Clementine and I had packed clothes and were in her car driving to Atlanta Baptist Hospital, on the south side of the city. An hour and ten minutes later, we joined Ruth Ann and my mother in his room as he lay helpless, hooked up to tubes and monitors. Shaken more than I had ever been shaken before by his appearance, I stood at the foot of my grandfather's bed, unable to speak. How could such a fine man, such a noble man, such a wise and kind and strong and moral man be reduced to such a state? How could such a vital and courageous heart give out?

"He shouldn't have come," I said to my mother. "He shouldn't . . . ."

"He wanted to come, Tyler," Ruth Ann said.

"But he shouldn't have," I said again.

"Tyler, nothing gave your grandfather more pleasure than seeing you play football for Georgia," my mother said.

Clementine was behind me, her left hand on my left shoulder, her right hand on my right arm. "You were his pride and joy," she said in a whisper.

My body was rigid. I looked at my mother. What will she do if he dies? What will I do? Most of all, what will she do? I thought, unable to articulate the words, unable to make any sound except the sound of bitter tension running from my skull to my feet.

A nurse was in the doorway. Then she was at his side. She touched his brow for a moment. Then she did the kinds of things nurses do: tested the monitors, checked his IV, took his temperature. She turned to my mother as if she was about to say something, but then she did not. She moved to his other side, going around the four of us who was pressed against his bed. She looked at another monitor then turned to my mother. "He's not improving. The doctor will be here in a moment. He may want to change the medication." Then she was gone.

The four of us looked at each other. Had we expected this moment? Certainly. Had he fooled us over the years because of his physical vigor? Yes, he had. Because all of the time he was being strong—appearing to be strong—his heart was slowly but surely giving out. Only his determination to get on with life and participate had kept us from seeing the truth. He was worn out. His long and productive and creative and brave life had worn him out. I thought of the metaphor in Shakespeare's sonnet, "That Time of Year in Me Thou Mayest Behold," the metaphor of the fire: the ashes of the fire are the history of the fire; the fire is consumed by its own life. And my grandfather had lived life. Truly *lived* life. *Experienced* his life. His passions had taught others to be passionate. His morality taught others to be moral. His steadfast opposition to any and all forms of prejudice had taught others to be steadfast. What more could anyone of us ask of him? I knew him well enough, loved him deeply enough, respected him profoundly enough to know that he was satisfied—not with his achievements, for he never put much store in achievements—but satisfied with the opportunities he had forged for himself. "He once told me all he wanted to do in life was matter," I said in a whisper. "He just wanted to matter."

Ruth Ann and Clementine and my mother were silent.

"And by God, he mattered," I said. "By God, he mattered."

I heard Ruth Ann whisper "Amen to that" under her breath. I saw my mother take her father's hand in both of hers. I felt Clementine's face against my shoulder. I heard the wind blowing outside. I felt the twinge in my legs as pains left over from the game moved down my body. Then I reached out and touched his ankles through the sheets. Then I heard it: the long, whining, level sound of the monitor telling us that his heart had stopped.

I started to move around to the side of the bed where Ruth Ann was standing, but before I could even reach his side two nurses were in the room followed by a doctor. Pushing us aside, they started trying to resuscitate his heart by pressing on his chest. As one nurse was doing that, another came into the room with a long-needled syringe.

Taking the syringe from the nurse, the doctor plunged it into his chest, which sent me reeling backwards as I saw my grandfather's body stiffen from the pain. Then another nurse was in the doorway with a rolling cart. After moving the cart to the bed so they could prepare the defibrillators, the nurse pushed us even further back from the bed until all four of us were lined up against the wall. After the nurses stripped away my grandfather's gown from his chest, the doctor applied the defibrillators. "Now," he said sharply. A nurse pressed a monitor. My grandfather's body jerked. The level heart monitor sound did not change. "Now," the doctor said again. Again nothing changed.

Clementine turned and buried her face in my chest. I stood rigid. My mother stood rigid. I could feel her body next to mine. I could taste her fear.

"Again," the doctor said. Again my grandfather's body jerked. "Again," the doctor snapped. The defibrillators jumped again.

The doctor listened with his stethoscope. When he started to apply the defibrillators again, the nurse across my grandfather's body said, "Enough, doctor." The doctor stopped and looked at her. "Enough," she said again. The doctor looked at her for a very long minute. Then he picked up the defibrillators and slowly turned and slowly gave them back to the nurse standing behind him.

For a very long moment—for what seemed like several moments—the two nurses and the doctor stood silent. Then the doctor turned to the four of us. "I'm very sorry," he said. "I'm so very sorry." Then he turned back to my grandfather and very tenderly gathered my grandfather's torn gown around his chest. As he did, one of the nurses began to remove the monitors from my grandfather's face and chest and body.

The other nurse turned and came to the four of us. "You should go outside now," she said very softly. "Wait for me at the end of the hallway. I'll be with you in just a moment."

Without replying, all four of us turned and started toward the door. But just as she was ready to step outside, my mother, who had been in the lead, stopped and turned back to my grandfather. Then she walked back to his bedside and standing next to an orderly who was gathering up the paddles, she touched her father's left hand and said in a whisper, "I love you, dad."

Then Ruth Ann was at her side guiding her back toward the door. I let them pass through before I turned back to look at him lying still in the bed. I started to speak, but I could say nothing. I simply stepped back into the room and let my body slide down the wall very slowly until I was sitting on the floor at Clementine's feet. After a moment, I felt her sit down next to me. I felt her press her head against my shoulder. Then it was silent.

The cart on which the orderly had brought the defibrillator moved past us silently. A nurse followed him. The other orderly was assisting the second nurse in gathering up the monitors. Then they were silent. I felt the nurse looking at me, waiting.

Then Clementine made herself stand up. Once she had, I felt her hand pulling me up to my feet. I resisted for a moment. I did not know if I could stand or not. But she lifted me harder, and so I stood, sliding up the wall in the same way I had slid down the wall, until I was standing.

Then guided by my darling Clementine, I went into the hallway and turned right and walked to the end where we found Ruth Ann and my mother in each other's arms, waiting, crying softly, both of them trying to be brave, both of them trying to do what people do when the center of their lives disappears and the joy they experienced because of his presence in their lives suddenly becomes the great hollow place that opens up in their hearts, leaving them lost in a world that no longer seems to make any sense.

26

There are occasions in life when it would be best if time would slow down. Obviously, when we are involved in some sort of joyful experience, it would be enriching if we could more deeply engage the moment. Perhaps if we could do that our lives would seem more meaningful or more rewarding or more worth living. Conversely, there are times—painful times—when we need time to slow down so we can comprehend what is happening, what we feel, what we must do. If we could do that—face the pain at a more deliberate pace, confront the anguish at a more reasonable rate—then perhaps we might manage our loss with more sensitivity, more sensibility, more intelligence. Yes, there have been many times in my life when I have undergone the former; I treasure those experiences more than I can say. There have also been times in my life when I have undergone the latter. It was those occasions during which I needed for time to slow down most of all. The pain—the overwhelming pain of losing my grandfather—seemed to swirl around me like a silent storm as I walked with Clementine to the end of the hall where Ruth Ann and my mother waited. And in the storm I heard the questions: What must I do now? How can I save my mother from despair? What do Clementine and I do to consol Ruth Ann? What do we tell the world? Because the world—at least a part of the world—would want to know Edward Thomas had died. Most of all I wanted to know how much of the responsibility for dealing with the aftermath of his death fell to me? I was not his child, after all. My mother was. It was, at least in large part, her place to make the decisions that I now felt pressing in on me. I was only his grandson. Yet, I knew that was not the whole truth. I was more than his grandson. I was the son he did not ever have. He was the father I lost. He was my mentor. I was his mentee. He was my teacher. I was his student. He was my hero. He thought of me as his apprentice. He expected me to take up the reins, to assume the mantle, to put on the garb, to fulfill my obligation to be Tyler *Thomas* Raymond. I did not wish to do anything that would dishonor his name. I did not wish to fail him.

Neither Ruth Ann nor my mother spoke as we approached. For a moment, all four of us hesitated. Then stirred by what we had lost, we melted into each other's arms, crying, pressing our faces against each other, gathering our arms around each other, Ruth Ann's strength rippling around us, my mother's sensitivity centering us, Clementine's steadfast love holding us all together. What I contributed to the circle I cannot say. Later, weeks later as we lay next to one another in bed one night, Clementine would turn to me and say, "None of us could have survived without you there, Tyler." When I told her that I did not understand what she meant, she said, "Every day in every way, we looked to you."

"But each of you made decisions, Clementine. It wasn't just me," I replied.

"Yes. We did. But each time we did, we turned to you for your approval. You may not have seen it at the time, but we did. We could not have survived had you not been there."

But that came later. As we stood in the circle, I only knew three things for sure. First, Ruth Ann and my mother had to go back to their hotel to sleep. Clementine and I needed to do the same. Second, we would return to the hospital so my mother and I could make arrangements to have my grandfather cremated, because that was what he wanted. Third, the next day, Ruth Ann and my mother would fly back Tampa with his remains and wait for Clementine and me to join them. Clementine and I would drive back to Athens and the University so we could make arrangements to not be in our classes and so I could make arrangements to not be at football practice. That way we could then return to Atlanta and fly to Tampa to continue doing what needed to be done.

Fortunately, Georgia did not have a football game the following Saturday, so in essence I had a week to accomplish all of the immediate things that my grandfather's death required and deserved.

With those obligations pushing me forward, having spoken to the hospital staff to tell them that my mother and I would return early in the morning to make the necessary decisions, I guided Ruth Ann and my mother to Ruth Ann's rental car and Clementine to ours. Then we followed them to the hotel were they were staying, and all four of us tried to sleep in preparation for the demanding days that we knew lay ahead. And it was only then, only after Clementine and I had showered and gone to bed, that lying next to my beloved wife, having endured the first wave of shock and grief in the hospital room and in the hallway, I let myself feel the second. So I let myself cry. Clementine did the same. Which is how we fell asleep. Crying softly in each other's arms.

27

The next morning, all four of us returned to the hospital. The night before, in keeping with my grandfather's wishes, my mother had signed the necessary papers that allowed his vital organs to enter the organ-donor bank. "If something of mine can help someone, so be it" he had said many times. My mother and I arranged for his body to be cremated, which was what he had specified. "Take me out onto the Gulf of Mexico," he had written in his Living Will, "and scatter my ashes. Say a few words," he'd gone on to say. "Something that you think I might approve. Martin Luther King, for instance, or Roy Wilkins or Paul Robeson. And a Negro spiritual."

Ironically, with all of the pain the four of us suffered as we went through the motions of finalizing my grandfather's death, what began to haunt me that day and the next and continued to wake me up at night for weeks was the notion that my grandfather had died after seeing the Georgia Bulldogs lose late in the game when an Auburn receiver found the seam between the weak side safety and me, at strong safety, did nothing to restore my spirit. As always, my mother's wisdom brought me around, for she told me that while my grandfather had been sorry Georgia did not win that game, he was not discouraged. "In fact, Tyler," she said, "he was confident Georgia would beat Georgia Tech on November 28th."

With all of that taking place, it was very hard for both Clementine and me to drive back to Athens, knowing my grandfather would never make the trip again. It was hard going first to her advisor, Laura Ross, to explain that my grandfather had died and that Clementine would have to go fly home to Tampa to take part in his memorial service. As I had assured Clementine would be the case, Professor Ross was very understanding. She promised to contact all of Clementine's professors and let them know what had happened.

The same thing happened when I went to my advisor, Professor McAndrew. He expressed his profound regret at my grandfather's death, whom he called "one of the most important civil historians of the century." When that conversation was over, we left and drove to Coach Dooley's home.

Standing on the front porch, I could hear music from inside. Both Barbara and Coach Dooley like big band music. I recognized the sound of the Les Brown band. When we rang the doorbell, it did not take long for Barbara Dooley to answer. Seeing both Clementine and me, and seeing the expressions on our faces, she had us come inside, voicing her concern even before we'd said anything about what had happened.

When Coach Dooley came into the room, both Clementine and I were still standing. He shook both of our hands and then asked what was on our minds.

"I have to go to Tampa, sir," I said. "My grandfather has died."

Before I could finish my sentence, Coach Dooley interrupted: "Do you mean Edward Thomas, Tyler?"

"Yes, sir. Edward Thomas."

Vince Dooley was quiet for a moment. "I can't tell you how sorry I am, Tyler. I know he and you were close."

"Yes, sir. Very close. He was really my father."

Barbara Dooley put an arm around Clementine's shoulder. "This must be very hard, Clementine. For both of you."

"Yes, ma'am. It is. Professor Thomas was a grandfather to me, too," Clementine said.

"Is there anything I can do?" Vince Dooley said.

"No, sir," I replied. "I'm going to help my mother write an obituary. We're going to send it to all of the major newspapers in the country because his friends and former students are scattered all over the place."

"That's good," Barbara Dooley said. "People will want to know what's happened."

"When do you think the memorial service will be, Tyler," Vince Dooley asked.

"I'm not sure, sir. I hope by the end of the week. Maybe Saturday."

Vince Dooley nodded. "Please telephone when the arrangements are finalized, Tyler. I want to know when it's going to be."

"Thank you, sir. That's very kind of you," I said.

"Would either of you like something to drink?" Barbara Dooley asked. "Coffee or tea maybe?"

"No, ma'am," Clementine said. "We have to drive back to Atlanta and then fly to Tampa."

Barbara Dooley took Clementine by both hands. "If there's anything we can do, please tell us. Now. Or later this week. Or when you come back."

"Thank you, ma'am," I said.

Then she turned to Clementine. "Tyler is going to need you at his side, Clementine. I know he's strong, but you're going to have to be strong for him as well."

"Yes, Mrs. Dooley. I agree. And I'll try," Clementine said.

Then Vince Dooley embraced first me and then Clementine, which he had never done before, but which we both appreciated. "Take the time you need, Tyler. The Georgia family will rally around you. I promise," he said.

"Yes. We'll all be praying for both of you," Mrs. Dooley said.

With that we said our goodbyes, and Clementine and I left, driving first to our apartment to gather the additional clothes we would need, telephoning Barry Slayman to tell him what had happened and that we would be gone until next Sunday or Monday.

28

On the flight back to Tampa, following my mother's advice and Ruth Ann's input, I wrote the obituary that we emailed across the country to major newspapers.

By late in the day Tuesday, we had received ten responses from professors and former students who wanted instructions as to how they might attend the memorial service, which we planned for the following Saturday at 2 P.M.

By Thursday afternoon, we realized that perhaps a hundred people were planning to come from out of town, so we made two further arrangements. First, after the memorial service was over, the four of us were prepared to take my grandfather's ashes out into the Gulf of Mexico, which had been his desire. Second, with so many people responding, and we expected more to arrive unannounced, we knew we would have to arrange for a very large buffet meal after the service.

Working with Rev. Janet Newman, the minister of the Tampa Unitarian Church, and Rev. Marni Harmony, from First Unitarian Church, Orlando, our good friend and trusted cleric, we designed the service around both Rev. Newman's and Rev. Harmony's commentaries on life and death and the transcending spirit of moral courage that characterized my grandfather's life, providing a number of places in the service where those who would come to pay their respects to Edward Thomas might have moments for brief comments. But in keeping with my grandfather's wishes, both ministers agreed that the service would finally conclude with four statements: the first by Ruth Ann, the second by Clementine, the third by my mother, and the fourth by me.

I said I would prefer if my mother might be the final speaker, but she insisted that I end the service. "It's what my father said he wanted," my mother explained.

"But you were his daughter, mom," I said more than once to her. But she would not be moved.

"No, Tyler. He wanted you to end the service. He trusted you. He trusted what you would say."

I sat that evening with Clementine and tried to say that I didn't think I would be strong enough to offer a concluding eulogy. Clementine's uncharacteristically sharp response, "Are you going to let down the man who loved you more than he loved anyone else in the whole world" brought me up short. "Modesty is not what we need right now, Tyler. Strength is what we need."

"But that's just it. I don't know that I'm strong enough, Clementine. I don't know if I can hold myself together."

After a moment an agitated Clementine faced me down. "Tyler, you have been strong enough to face down everything life has thrown at us since the day I met you. And sometimes it's been pretty awful stuff. So you are strong enough to do anything. Why do you think I fell in love with you? Why do you think I married you? Because I knew I would be safe with you. Because I believed I could be a human being with you. I knew that with you I'd never have to be a dumb woman or a dumb black. And I know better than anyone that I'm still alive because you would not let me die."

I was silent. I knew it was best that I be silent.

"You are as strong as your grandfather, Tyler. And loving you has made me strong. You are as brave as your grandfather. And loving you has made me brave. Your mother wants you to be the final speaker. I want you to be the final speaker. You are not going to let her down. I won't let you. So you will be the final speaker, Tyler. You will be the final speaker."

With that Clementine stood and looked at me. I'd seen that body language before. It was her *no one expects me to win this race, but damn it, I'm going to* body language.

I was not going to challenge her declaration. The task fell to me. I would be the final speaker.

29

I know that all four of us, Ruth Ann and Clementine and my mother and I, spent a good deal of the week writing our eulogies as well as finalizing all of the arrangements necessary for my grandfather's memorial service.

When Saturday morning came, the four of us gathered for a late breakfast and then drove to the Tampa Unitarian Church together. Our plan was that after the service and after the reception, we would drive to Tampa Bay where a boat would be waiting for us to take my grandfather's ashes out onto the Gulf so they could be scattered on the water.

When we arrived at the church two hours before the service was to begin, we already found perhaps fifty people gathered. Several of them explained that they had flown into Tampa that morning from out of town. "I just came directly to the church," one man said who had studied with my grandfather twenty five years before. "I'll go right back to the airport when the service is finished. From what others have said, some of them are doing the same thing."

All four of us tried to meet and greet those who had come so early. Rev. Newman opened the church earlier than she had planned so at least those who had arrived early would have a place to sit. Then she and Rev. Harmony and the four of us walked through the ceremony very briefly.

By the time the service began, the church was filled to overflowing. My mother said that my grandfather would have been very pleased. "To know that he was remembered would have moved him deeply," she said. Ruth Ann added quickly that "It's no more than he deserves, of course, but people don't always get what they deserve in this life."

While I was supposed to wait until the service was over to meet people I did not know, with the crowd coming the way it was, it was impossible to not go ahead and move among them, introducing myself, shaking hands, accepting the embraces that many men and women both offered as gestures of sympathy. As you would expect in such a circumstance, their comments were all very gracious, from "He was simply the best teacher I've ever had" to "His thinking changed my life" to "He was a model of both intellectual and moral courage for everyone to follow."

Later, many of those same people whom I met before the service as well as many I did not meet until the reception said similar things during that part of the service designated for them to speak. In all, fifteen people said at least something during the service. Many others said they wished to do the same, but as one woman said, "A number of people said what I wanted to say, and they said it better than I could have." Another man said, "If all of us had said what we wanted to say, the service would have gone on for ten hours. Besides, when Julian Bond spoke, what more needed to be said?" And while both my mother and I knew that my grandfather had known Julian Bond, of Georgia, for years, and that Julian was one of those people in the Civil Rights struggle for whom my grandfather had the deepest respect, neither of us knew that during the last ten years of his life, my grandfather had corresponded with Shirley Chisholm, the former member of the United States House of Representatives. Her comments about my grandfather's work on behalf of women generally and black women specifically were very moving. Of course, very few people could move a crowd as could Shirley Chisholm.

What meant the most to me was that both Barbara and Vince Dooley came to the memorial service for my grandfather. I had not expected them to do so. That would have been presumptuous on my part. But they came, nevertheless, even if it meant, as was true of so many others, that they had to leave the service and then fly back to Atlanta and then drive to Athens that same day.

What meant the most to Clementine was that every one of the members of "Clementine's Famous Trained Bears" also attended. They had driven together in three cars almost all night to get to Tampa, arriving at the service after they had gotten less than four hours of sleep in a motel. When the service was over, they would have to turn right around and drive back all night so they would be in Athens by Sunday evening.

Parenthetically, while it was true that the memorial service prompted many people to share their sense of loss at my grandfather's death, the reception, as is frequently the case, turned into a sharing of the joys folks had experienced at knowing him. However, nothing that afternoon brought more smiles and more pleasure to more people than seeing Clementine surrounded by fourteen young men, both black and white, the smallest of whom weighed two hundred twenty pounds, four of whom weighed at least two hundred sixty pounds, and three of whom weighed two hundred eighty pounds, each of whom gave her a very public hug when Ruth Ann and Clementine and my mother and I stood in the reception line. When each of them put his arms around Clementine, she was swallowed her up in their genuine affection. Standing among the academic community members, they truly did stand out but in the best way possible. The Bulldog Nation would have been proud.

In any case, since that day—a day of so many cross-current emotions—love and loss and pride and honor—I have preserved the written texts from which Ruth Ann and Clementine and my mother and I read that day. Given the objective of this memoir, I believe it is also appropriate that I include them here. For even though they were focused on each author's sense of personal loss at my grandfather's death, if you read Ruth Ann's and my mother's and mine carefully, I maintain you will hear the role Clementine played and continues to play in our lives.

30

Ruth Ann Brown

Dignity is not a disguise. Dignity is *not* a disguise. You cannot put on dignity like a coat. Putting on a coat does not change who you are. Putting on a coat is a presentation. But dignity—how one conducts oneself, which is a manifestation of what one believes about oneself—is not a disguise. One must never try to hide behind a show of dignity. Dignity is not dignity if it is not the truth.

I learned that from Professor Edward Thomas. He did not lecture me on the subject. He did not tell me what to do. He showed me. And as he did—in his everyday kindness, in his ironic sense of humor, in his steadfast generosity—we began to talk. As we talked, I began to learn.

My struggle for dignity began when I was a very young girl. It continued all through my academic training. It continued through a painful divorce. It continued as I made my way into an academic career. But my struggle for dignity was really my struggle to find a disguise behind which I could hide my fear I might never achieve anything of worth. My hope was that if I played the role of the dignified black woman long enough, I would one day become a dignified black woman. Through his respect for my mind, for my teaching, for my person, Edward Thomas taught me that I did not need to hide behind the mask of the dignified black woman. I could simply be a black woman who comported herself with dignity because that is who I am.

I first came to know Edward Thomas when my daughter, Clementine Camille Brown, became friends with Edward's grandson, Tyler Thomas Raymond. As my daughter's and Tyler's relationship developed, as it matured, as it blossomed, so did my relationship with Edward Thomas. When Professor Thomas was invited to lecture during the summer of 1981 at the University of Edinburgh on the history of slavery in the New World, he said he would only accept the invitation if I was invited to come with him to deliver what he said would be alternating and complimentary lectures tracing the origin, the practice, and the ramifications of that profound and painful chapter in American life. Working with him, I crystallized my own thinking and focused on his objective: to tell the truth, the whole truth, and nothing but the truth. That we were able to do that—and I believe the text of our lectures is evidence we did—is much more a tribute to his guidance than my expertise. For even as I wrote my lectures, his questions led me more and more deeply into the psychological agony I wanted to define, the sociological consequences I wanted to portray.

For those of you who knew him well, you will understand when I say it was difficult to get him to accept credit for influencing my work. Always and to the end, he protested that knowing me had influenced him. And he meant what he said. He was, in short, the most honest thinker I have ever known. He was never driven by ego; he did not seek praise; he did not want to win accolades. All he wanted to do was tell the story of the continuing struggle to sort out what the term racial justice means, what the practice of racial justice requires.

During one of the last years of his life, he and I traveled together all the way to California and back, which was for me a great privilege, for on that trip, I met many of the people with whom he had been associated for years in his teaching, people for whom he continued to have respect until his dying day. That I now count many of them who are gathered here today among my friends is an honor that enriches my life.

For me, then, this day marks a four fold loss. I have not only lost a mentor, a compatriot in thought, a travel companion, I have lost the one man to whom I truly offered my heart, the one man I trusted with my love. That our relationship came so late in his and my life is a great sorrow. That our relationship happened at all is my great joy.

Edward, I shall miss you more than words can ever hope to express.

Clementine Camille Brown

Dr. Edward Thomas is dead: the world has lost a noble crusader for racial justice. Professor Edward Thomas is dead: the academic world has lost a forthright and honest intellectual. Edward Thomas is dead: my mother has lost a kind and loving friend. Edward is dead: my mother-in-law has lost her gentle and adoring father. And *Sir* is dead: I have lost my surrogate grandfather; my husband has lost the only father he has ever known.

Words will not suffice, but words are all we have. We cling to words. We curse words. I harbor the hope that somewhere, buried in what I will say, you will hear what I mean.

Edward Thomas loved history. Edward Thomas loved stories. Here is a story that I believe would have made him smile:

Once upon a time, a young black girl fell in love with a young white boy. The first time that young black girl did anything to show the young white boy how she felt was when she went to the young white boy's first high school junior varsity football game. When the game was over, and the young black girl saw the young white boy walking with an older man, she boldly went to the field and began walking with the boy, who, being well mannered, introduced the young black girl to the older man. "This is my grandfather," the young white boy said. Then he turned to the older man and said, "Grandpa, this is Clementine." And then the young black girl, as nervous as she had ever been in her life, held out her hand, as her mother had taught her was what she must always do when meeting an elder, and the older white man accepted her gesture with equal good grace—which is how I first met Edward Thomas.

I went home that afternoon and explained I had gone to the Tampa Coast High School junior varsity football team game because my biology lab partner, Tyler Raymond, played on the team, and that after the game I had met Tyler's grandfather, and that Edward Thomas, the grandfather, had seemed a very nice man. And that was the beginning. That was how my life changed.

Yes, I would learn that Edward Thomas was a famous historian, whose books my mother had studied in graduate school, and yes, I would learn that Edward Thomas was more than just a grandfather for Tyler—that he was really Tyler's father because Tyler's father had died in Viet Nam. And oh, my, that summer, in what felt like a dream, yes, I traveled to Scotland with my mother and Edward Thomas and sat in a lecture hall with Tyler at the University of Edinburgh and listened as my mother and Edward Thomas delivered a series of lectures on the subject of chattel slavery in America to brilliant men and women, who stood and applauded my mother and Edward Thomas when they finished because they had been brave enough to tell the truth.

Later, on vacations with my mother and Tyler and his mother and his grandfather, Edward Thomas did his best to teach me how to play chess. He arranged for us to go on winter sleigh rides in the mountains. Most important, he watched while Tyler and I fell in love and our mothers became best friends.

When Tyler was injured in football and could have died, and I stayed with him while he was in the hospital, I spent hours with Grandpa Thomas standing next to the bed of his beloved Tyler. Later, when Grandpa Thomas had a first heart attack, I stayed with Tyler when Tyler stayed with his grandfather, watching as Grandpa Edward held his grandson's hand. And in doing those things—in being there with both of them—I learned about a kind of love that is so profound it requires no words, a kind of love so true it needs no ceremony, a kind of love so powerful that it changes people's lives. Later, when I became ill and was in a coma, and Tyler stayed with me day and night for two months, Grandpa Edward came every day and stood as part of the circle that surrounded my bed. And even though the doctors do not think I knew they were there with me, I believe I did know they were there. I believe I knew my Grandfather Edward was there. Because through everything . . . through moments when the black girl and the white boy faced people who hated the fact she was black and he was white . . . through the pain and emotional confusion that comes with growing up . . . through everything that happened to me since that day when I first met him on the football field at Tampa Coast High School . . . Grandfather Edward was there—kind and funny and generous and understanding and wise. For he was a man who loved giving other people surprises; who loved taking his beloved family on trips, a man who understood before others understood that Tyler and I were not children. That we had fallen in love, really and truly in love. He was the seer, the visionary who understood that his grandson is the only man I will ever love. He understood Tyler meant it when he said I was the only woman he would ever love. Grandpa Edward was the man who shaped and guided and affirmed the young white boy I first met and loved, the young white man I would continue to love, the grown up white man with whom I now share my life.

But what will hurt now—what will hurt my mother and my husband and his mother and me now—is that on those quiet Sunday mornings when we walk together in the park, or on those cold winter afternoons when we walk in the mountains, or on those gentle evenings when we walk by the Gulf of Mexico, Grandpa Edward will not be there with us. I mean, he will be with us. He will be with all of us—all four of us—in our memories for the rest of our lives. And that is some consolation. But he won't be there—*really be there*—no matter what tricks we try to play on ourselves, to do what he loved doing the most: smell the aroma of tree leaves changing colors or feel the chill of snow coming on the wind or see salt spray rising as the sun goes down on the Gulf. And that is going to hurt: not hearing his voice or feeling his hand taking mine when he wants to say something important or hearing his laughter when he sees one more irony in life or seeing him touch Tyler's face in the loving way he always touched Tyler's face—especially after Tampa Coast High School or the University of Georgia lost a football game—that is going to hurt. For what you must understand, ladies and gentlemen, what you must understand, all of you who were his academic peers, all of you who were his students, is that more than anything else—more than a world spokesman for racial justice, more than a teacher taking those in his charge on journeys through the confusions of history—more than anything else, Edward Thomas was a father and grandfather and a friend. He was my best friend. And I shall miss him and miss him and miss him until the day I die.

Elizabeth Thomas Raymond

I am the only child born to Ethel Jane Rees and Edward Clayton Thomas. But that neither turned me into the doted upon child or the lonely little girl. Instead, from the beginning, my parents balanced my need to be affirmed in my person with my need to be held responsible for my actions. By the time I was in junior high school and witness to the rebellious students around me who complained either that their parents did not love them or that their parents' rules were too strict, I felt none of those resentments because my parents talked to me. It will undoubtedly come as no surprise to those of you who were my father's students that, first, he never raised his voice in anger at me; second, that he was always prepared to discuss anything I wished to discuss, even if he and my mother maintained it was their responsibility to make the final decision if there was a difference of opinion. You will not be surprised when I tell you that on my fifteenth birthday, my father sat me down and said, "You are a young woman now. From now on we are not going to tell you what to do or what is right or what is wrong. You will have to decide. However, please know that we will always be here for you. You may come talk to us about anything you wish. All we expect is that conduct yourself in a way that you believe is your best possible course of action." Those may not be his exact words, but they are very close.

With that as background, let me now praise my father's many qualities. First, he was a man of humor. No, he did not tell jokes. His humor was more situational. He saw ironies in almost every part of life. He never tired of pointing them out for both my mother and me to enjoy. Second, he hated hypocrisy. You can imagine, therefore, what he had to say about many politicians. I will not on this occasion repeat what he had to say about television evangelists. Third, he was passionately truthful about history, particularly American history. When I was in high school, and he read my American history text, I knew I was in for a treat, because no one I have ever met knew more about the silly and fraudulent pap that is found in the watered down history texts most American students are required to read. At the same time, rather than just rail at what was wrong, he would sit me down and talk about the many things the texts did not say. When he did that, I always took notes, which armed me wonderfully for the next day's class discussion. It pleased him no end that many times, after a spirited disagreement in class with either one of my fellow students or with the instructor, that I could support my statements chapter and verse from historical texts while all they could do was offer popular generalizations, almost none of which held up under scrutiny.

By the time I began my university studies, my interest in probing beyond the so called prevailing wisdom became the mantra by which I conducted myself, an attitude I owe to my extraordinary teacher father.

Of course, many of you know that about him. What else you might not know is his love of surprises. He would plan elaborate trips but not tell us where we were going. His tactic was to listen to our comments while we were in casual conversation; then he would put together a plan to fulfill our desires. One time, for instance, after having my mother and me pack clothes for a week, he even went so far as to take us to the airport and then blindfold us once we flew from Cleveland to New York. Then he enlisted the help of a flight attendant in getting us on board our plane without us knowing where we were going. Once we were airborne, under the pretext that my mother and I were nervous about flying, which was not true, he asked that the pilot come back into the cabin and summarize the flight plan, which is how we learned our destination. That surprise, by the way, took us to Paris for six days of art galleries, one opera, two ballets, and one international soccer game, which just happened to be France versus Wales.

That was the other subject on which my father could both wax poetic and express his political passions: the country of Wales, specifically the coal mining culture of South Wales, his ancestral home. As a consequence, I may well know more about the two Rhondda Valleys than almost anyone in this room, not because I read much on the subject but because I simply listened when my father talked with my mother, whose heritage was also Welsh.

However, even with all of those interesting and endearing qualities—his integrity, his humor, his steadfast love of my mother and me and then my husband, Robert Raymond, and our son, Tyler, and Tyler's wife, Clementine, and during the later years of his life, Ruth Ann, Clementine's mother—it was his passion for justice that means the most to me. Despite the fact that gathered here today there are many very intelligent and accomplished people whom my father respected and admired and loved, I reserve the right to believe that I shall never meet his like again. For in the end, my loving, kind, funny father was a man of singular passion: he hated prejudice; he hated injustice. And he did not care which fools were offended by his indignation. It is a legacy to which I aspire. It is the legacy to which I know my son aspires. For it is the legacy of a man whose capacity for love was only equaled by his capacity for moral courage.

Tyler Thomas Raymond

I am Tyler Thomas Raymond, Edward Thomas's grandson. It falls to me today to articulate the final eulogy of this ceremony. Please know that I take my task very seriously.

My grandfather was a reader. You who knew him know that. He was a story teller. As part of this ceremony, I wish to call on another story teller to both begin and end my tribute.

In the middle of Harper Lee's novel *To Kill a Mockingbird*, which is set in a small fictional Alabama town, the white lawyer, Atticus Finch, accepts the challenge of defending an innocent black man who has been charged with rape by a troubled, psychologically wounded, and unstable young white woman. When the jury of white men find the defendant guilty, which does not come as a surprise despite the miscarriage of justice that the verdict represents, the specific scene I wish to recall takes place.

After the defendant is taken away to jail to await sentencing—and Atticus Finch has promised that he will appeal the verdict—the white audience clears courtroom. At that point, Atticus begins to gather up his papers and put them in his brief case in preparation for leaving. As he does, the blacks of the town, who have been seated in the upstairs gallery, the court being segregated, do not leave, but wait as a gesture of respect for Atticus for him to depart, led in doing so by a black minister, Reverend Sykes.

Seated among the blacks are Atticus's two young white children, a son named Jem and a daughter named Jean Louise, later called Scout, who serves as the narrator of the story. What matters in the moment is that as Atticus begins to leave the courtroom, following the center aisle to the exit, the blacks in the balcony above him all stand. As they do, Scout relates the scene this way:

> Someone was punching me, but I was reluctant to take my eyes . . . from the image of Atticus's lonely walk down the aisle.
>
> "Miss Jean Louise?"
>
> I looked around. They were all standing. All around us and in the balcony on the opposite wall, the Negroes were getting to their feet. Reverend Sykes's voice was as distant as Judge Taylor's:
>
> "Miss Jean Louise, stand up. Your father's passin'."

And that is the reason we have gathered here today. A man of noble, honorable conduct, a man of noble, honorable passion, a man of noble, honorable beliefs has passed. A man who has shared his mind with many, who has shared his wisdom with many, who has taught you and, in his words, learned from you, has passed. But we, who now stand in his wake, what must we do? How shall we remember him? How shall we cope with his loss? Who will step forward and take up his mantle?

From what he said to me as I grew up by his side, from what my mother has taught me as I grew up in her care, it must be me. But please know that I harbor no illusions. I cannot be Edward Thomas. I cannot hope to replicate or duplicate his strength or his wisdom. I can, however, do what he has trained me to do: I can try to be the man he asked me to be, the scholar he challenged me to be, the teacher he encouraged me to be. Whether I succeed in those tasks, of course, must be judged by others in years to come. But on this day, in this place, in this company, I pledge I will try.

At the same time I am trying to be the public thinking man that my grandfather's legacy inspires me to be, I must also try to be the private man my life with him requires. For in the end, at the end of each day, he was a private man who loved good food and good company, who loved opera and baroque music, who loved modern jazz. Yes, he read history, but he also read novels and poetry. Yet as much as he was a man who loved being indoors reading, he was also a man who loved being outdoors in the sun, in the rain, in the cold, and in the snow. He was a kind and mirthful man. He was a man who radiated joy. During those years when he suffered from the loss of his beloved wife, my grandmother, Ethel Jane, he took up the task of raising his grandson in the company of his widowed daughter. What more could the world ask of him but that demonstration of sincere and steadfast loyalty? Thus, for me, he did not become the scholar, the crusader for Civil Rights, until I was older and in school. For me, the boy on his lap when he read stories, he was simply Grandpa, the man who never ran out of answers for the boy who never ran out of questions.

What more could I have asked of life? Yes, I would have loved to have been raised by my father, a teacher and scholar who fell under the spell of both Professor Edward Thomas and under the spell of Elizabeth Thomas, Edward's daughter, whom Robert would marry. That would have made a more just world for me. But the world is not always just. And when my father died in a war he did not support while doing his faithful duty to a country he believed was headed in the wrong direction, my grandfather became my father, my mentor, my advisor, my hero. For I have not only known him as the man who was willing to throw a football to me until I could run no more, he was the man whom I saw stand in the middle of a lecture hall stage at Edinburgh University and say truths that no one has ever said in that way before, define crimes against a race that no one has ever confessed in that way before, face up to facts to which no one has given witness in that way before.

Thus, on this occasion and in this place, in his name but most assuredly without his permission, I say to you who have gathered and graced this ceremony by your presence, we must all "' . . . stand up. [For Edward Thomas] is passing.'" Edward Thomas has passed. Long live Edward Clayton Thomas.

31

After the memorial reception ended, at which I made it my duty to greet and thank every one of the two hundred twenty two persons who attended, some from as far away as California and New Hampshire, Ruth Ann and Clementine and my mother and I, in the company of Rev. Janet Newman and Rev. Marni Harmony, drove to the pier on

Tampa Bay where we had arranged to meet the boat that would take us out into the Gulf so my grandfather's ashes could be loosed to the wind. It was, as you would expect, a melancholy journey for the four of us. We had said all of the words we could muster during the service, and we had responded with as much grace as we could to each of the people who had wanted to express their feelings of loss to each one of us. But when they all left, leaving us behind to try to refocus our energies and obligations, the adrenaline let down was palpable. As I drove Ruth Ann and Clementine and my mother to the pier, I felt as if I was being swallowed up by a black hole. I am sure, given the silence in the car, that the others felt the same. Only Clementine's hand resting on my right thigh as she sat next to me kept me from breaking down again. I knew then that I was entering the third stage of grieving: the moment of dread anticipation when the finale to the ceremony of parting must come to an end.

Once the six of us were on the boat and had gone out the required distance, the pilot slowed down so Janet and Marni could say the words they had prepared. I will always remember the sense of sympathetic elegance that their words conveyed and Marni's last words, "Now let Edward Thomas be at peace." Then, as my mother wished, I followed with words that paraphrased Walt Whitman's poem: "And so we return you, honored grandfather, to the cradle endlessly rocking." Then my mother opened the top of the cremation vase and, taking up handfuls of ash, let her father slip through her fingers just as he had slipped out of our lives. Then she passed the vase to Ruth Ann, who did the same, who passed the vase to Clementine, who did the same. Then it came to me. I looked down and took the last ash remaining in my right hand and held up my fist, opening it slowly, feeling the ash flow away between my fingers until it was all gone. As I stood at the rail watching the last of the dust cloud disappear on the wind, Clementine came and stood behind me, wrapping her arms around me from behind as she had when I had kept my vigil during my grandfather's heart by-pass operation. Then we all felt the boat engine shudder and roar back to life. Turning around, we left the Gulf behind us, returning to shore after dark. Embracing both Janet and Marni, my mother said, "It is over." Then the two ministers went their ways, and the four of us returned to my mother's house where we would all sleep as well as could be expected given the circumstances.

The next morning, Ruth Ann and my mother took Clementine and me to the Tampa airport where we flew back to Atlanta. In Atlanta, we retrieved our car and drove back to Athens. By 6 P.M. that evening, I stood in front of the long, narrow table that Clementine had placed against a wall in our apartment, looking at the last photograph taken of my grandfather: the picture was of me in my University of Georgia football uniform, dirty and tired after a game, standing next to my grandfather, whose right arm is around my waist. We were both smiling. He could not have looked more proud. It was a moment and is a photograph that I treasured then and still treasure to this day. It did not seem possible to me that he would not be at the next game. That he would not telephone sometime during the upcoming week and talk to Clementine and talk to me. It did not seem possible that he was gone.

By 8 P.M., exhausted physically and emotionally, Clementine and I were in bed, asleep in each other's arms, the steady rhythm of her breathing connecting me to the life we had lived together, the touch of her hand on my side connecting me to the life we were living, the sweet smell of her skin connecting me to the life we would live in the years to come.

32

Then it was Monday morning. Sitting quietly over breakfast before we went to class, Clementine once again demonstrated both her wisdom and her strength. "I'm going to see my advisor this morning, Tyler. She collected notes from all of my instructors. The notes will help me catch up."

I was quiet over my English muffin and coffee.

"I'll go see Dr. McAndrew. I'll get your notes. That way you can just worry about classes and football practice."

"Thank you," I said quietly.

Clementine waited for a moment before going on. "Tyler, you will have to be in this place now," she said.

"What?"

"You will have to be in this place now. Here. With me. At school."

I understood what she meant even if I didn't want to.

"It will be hard, Tyler. For both of us. We will need to help each other. I can't do it alone."

"I'll try," I said.

"Tyler, you have to do more than try."

"How can I do more than try?" I asked.

Clementine looked at me for a very long time before speaking again. Then she said, "Tyler, it's what Grandpa Edward would have wanted. You've got to be here. Right here."

"I'll try," I said.

"Tyler, I need you to be here," she said more sharply. "With me. I need for you to be here with me."

I said I understood. I said I would. I promised I would.

Both of us finished our meals and finished preparing for the day. As we left, I wanted to stop at the photograph table and look at the picture of my grandfather and me together. But I did not. Looking at the picture wasn't going to change anything. Besides, I carried his picture in my memory. In any case, Clementine wasn't going to let me stop because, as I passed by the table, she pushed me from behind so I had to keep moving.

Thirty minutes later I was back in class. I assumed Clementine was doing the same thing. That afternoon I returned to the football team. When I went into the locker room and began changing into my practice uniform, none of the players said anything to me. Even the ones who had come to the funeral were silent. But I understood that was their gesture of respect for my grandfather and for me because usually the locker room is noisy with music and conversations. As we walked to the practice field, Ricky walked next to me. Just before we got all the way to the field, he put an arm around my shoulder and said very quietly, "We think you and Clementine are incredible people, Tyler."

I must have mumbled my thanks because he went on.

"We don't know how you did it. Saying what you said. Then talking to everyone afterwards. None of us think we could have done what you and Clementine did," he said.

Then he took his arm off my shoulder and turned away toward his practice group, and I turned away toward mine.

The rest of practice that day felt like a dream. Sitting in the film room and looking at Georgia Tech's most recent game felt like a dream. Everything was far away, hazy around the edges. People's voices sounded as if they were coming from a different room or from down a hallway. That night, when I lay next to Clementine and I told her I felt as if I were moving in a fog, she said she felt the same way.

"It's going to be hard, Tyler, getting back to where we were. Or where we need to be. But we have to. We don't have a choice."

I whispered, "I know. I know."

"No, Tyler. You can't just know. You have to do it. Both of us. We have to do it."

Then it was Tuesday and I was walking across the campus. Suddenly, without any warning, I realized either we'd missed Thanksgiving or Thanksgiving was coming. Good grief. Which was what Clementine said when I told her: "Good grief. Really?" Then she said, "That explains my mother's phone call."

"What phone call?"

"Just before you got home. She and your mother are flying to Atlanta tomorrow morning. Then they're renting a car and coming here."

"Why? I mean, that's wonderful. But why?"

"To make dinner."

"To make dinner?"

"Yes. For us. And for as many friends as we want to invite."

"For Thanksgiving?"

"Yes. They want to come together and make dinner for as many of our friends as we want to invite."

Before I could ask any questions, she went on. "They've rented a room at the Howard Johnson's across from the campus. They're going to shop as soon as they get here. They want to cook dinner for us, Tyler."

I was stunned. I was pleased, but I was stunned.

"They need to come make the meal, Tyler. Just like we need them to make the meal," Clementine said.

I replied that I understood, which was true. I had spoken to my mother on Monday evening just as Clementine has spoken to Ruth Ann. Then Clementine had spoken to my mother just as I spoke to Ruth Ann. None of us had much to say. Each of the four of us had asked the question, "How are you?" to which the other person had said, "I'm fine. It's hard, but I'm fine."

But that wasn't enough. All of us understood that wasn't enough. We also understood that was all we could ask and all we could say. So I understood why our mothers would go to the trouble of flying to Atlanta and renting a car and staying in a hotel together and then shopping for as many of our friends as we wanted to invite to our house. Because it wasn't trouble. It was therapy. It was part of our very complex and very real process of recovery. And Clementine and I needed to go through it, which is why, on Thursday at noon, six of our football player friends, three of their girlfriends, two of Clementine's friends from pre-med, and two of my friends from one of my history classes, all came tumbling into our small apartment, each trying to help, each trying to hold up their end of the unstated agreement that it was going to be a joyous occasion. Ruth Ann and my mother, by the by, were marvels, which did not surprise either Clementine or me. But truly, they were marvels. So there we all were on Thanksgiving, 1987, a gaggle of very nice people sitting on top of each other balancing plates of food, talking quietly but all talking at once, making a family when making a family was exactly what was needed. The only person missing, of course, was my grandfather. But we all knew that as well. No one had to say it. We all just knew it. And that was enough.

33

I knew that the Georgia Tech game, which was played in Atlanta, was going to be my last regular season game ever. I also assumed that Georgia would be invited to yet another post-season bowl game. So on one hand I approached the Georgia Tech game with both a sense of finality, which was warranted, and a sense that even when that game was over, there was going to be one more "final game" to play.

For Clementine, driving to Atlanta with her mother and with my mother must have provoked many mixed feelings. After all, she had enjoyed going to Georgia Tech. Yet the only Tech football games she'd ever gone to had been when Tech played Georgia, at which she obviously felt very mixed emotions. The season finale in 1987 wasn't going to be any different for her. In fact, it was going to be even more complex. She'd only left Georgia Tech to enroll at Georgia after she went through a very long process of recovering from her coma. But the return to the Tech campus would mean she would see not only places she had enjoyed, it was likely she would see the friends who had meant much to her. At the same time, she would be surrounded by her new friends who were part of the University of Georgia community. All of which may explain why I didn't try to draw her into a conversation about how she felt. It was best to just leave her alone to either sort out her feelings or to simply let them play out as they would.

In the end, Georgia beat Tech 30-16. What I remember even more clearly is that I had a very good game. I was determined that I was not going to get beaten on any long pass plays, and that if I had to come up and tackle either receivers who had caught passes or ball carriers who had gotten into the secondary, I was going to make the tackles count for something. In the end, I know I played better than I had ever played before, because Coach Dooley said so after the game as we were celebrating on the field and then as we walked back up the tunnel to our dressing room. My only comment, and I meant it, was that I felt as if both my father and my grandfather had been watching me. "You played that way, Tyler. That's exactly the way you played," he said. What I didn't expect was what happened in the locker room after the game.

Usually Coach Dooley and the assistant coaches give out "Game Ball" awards right after a victory, especially a well played victory in an important game. Georgia had lost to Georgia Tech in my first two years on the Georgia team, so the coaches certainly weren't going to give out game balls on those occasions. When Georgia beat Tech in 1986, I'd watched the game on television with Clementine because at that time we were still in Tampa. So this was the first experience I'd had and the only experience I would ever have being a part of a Georgia team to win the Tech game. But when it came time to give out the defensive player of the game award, Ricky said the defensive players needed to get dressed first and then meet him out by the bus that would take us back to Athens. All of the other players on the team seemed to understand except me. It was the second time my teammates had managed to keep a secret.

So when all of us were dressed, and the defensive players had gotten themselves organized, we went out to where our bus was waiting. Naturally, we were greeted by Bulldog fans. But when most of them had cheered themselves out, Ricky gathered the defensive players in a circle. Then in the biggest surprise that I'd ever had at Georgia, the circle opened up and Clementine came into the center. Then Ricky moved to her side. This is what he said:

"All of us know that Clementine used to go to Georgia Tech. And all of us know that she only became a Bulldog because her track career at Tech ended. But we want her to know that we all love her. And we're glad she's one of us now. So the members of 'Clementine's Famous Trained Bears' want her to have the defensive game ball, because it has been hers and Tyler's courage that have shown us how to meet a challenge."

Then Ricky gave the ball to Clementine, who by then had tears in her eyes. Then each member of the defensive team lined up and walked past her. The members of the Trained Bears group gave her a hug just as they had at the memorial service reception. The ones who didn't know her as well shook her hand. When Ricky signaled that I should come up and join her, the rest of the players then gave us a round of applause. I remember Clementine turning to me and trying to give me the ball, but I refused to take it. "They're honoring you, Clementine," I said. "The game ball belongs to you."

What I couldn't have known that day was that just a month later, after the 1987 Liberty Bowl, played in Memphis, Tennessee, in which Georgia defeated Arkansas, 20-17, Frank Long, the defensive coach with whom I worked the most, awarded me the game ball because, he said, "Not only did Tyler make two interceptions today, the last one ensuring our win, just the fact he came back and played football during his senior year, with all that he's been through, means he deserves the award." Since that year, Clementine and I have proudly displayed our matching Game Ball Awards side by side on our bookshelves at home. Clementine has always maintained they are the best awards that either of us has ever received, a sentiment with which I agree.

34

As wonderful as those two moments were for Clementine and me, an even more lasting scene took place on December 25, 1987, in the hotel room where my mother and Ruth Ann were staying so they could attend the Liberty Bowl.

Our mothers had flown from Tampa to Memphis on the 23rd so they could join Clementine. I had traveled to Memphis with the team several days before not only so we could practice but so we could take part in a number of activities that surround the bowl game. Clementine arrived the same day as our mothers. All three then stayed together in the same hotel as the Georgia football team boosters club. On December 25th, after a team breakfast, I joined Clementine and Ruth Ann and my mother in their room so we might have a chance to talk privately about a number of very important decisions that each and all of us had made.

Ruth and my mother said they had decided it was foolish financially for them to try to maintain separate homes. Ruth Ann said they had found a very nice house half way between the University of South Florida and my mother's school. "The house had four bedrooms," Ruth Ann said.

"Four bedrooms?" Clementine said. "Why so many?"

My mother smiled. "Because each of us wants her own bedroom, naturally. Second, we want to have a guest room for anyone who might come to visit." Before I could comment, my mother went on: "And we're making a bedroom for the two of you."

"For the two of us?" I said. "But we're not moving to Tampa."

"We know that," Ruth Ann said. "But we want to have a bedroom just for the two of you so you'll feel free to come for vacations any time you can."

Clementine smiled. "All right. I guess that makes sense. But doesn't that mean the house costs more than a three bedroom house?"

"Not much," my mother said. "Not enough to offset both the fact you two will always know you're not upsetting any plans if you come to visit, and not enough to keep us from making the investment."

"Besides," Ruth Ann said, "it's our way of trying to heal. We all suffered a very difficult loss when Edward died. It's going to better for us to have someone to be with at the end of the day."

"And it's time both of us starting doing things," my mother said.

"Things? What things?" I asked.

"Things. Fun things. We've worked too hard for too many years. It's time we started taking care of ourselves by having fun," Ruth Ann said.

"That's great, mom," Clementine said. "But what things do you have in mind?"

"Things at the Unitarian Church," Ruth Ann said. "And travel. We both love to travel. Now we can travel together."

I couldn't argue with anything they'd said.

"And golf," my mother added.

"Golf?"

"Yes, Tyler. Golf," my mother said.

"All right. That's good," I said.

"You sound like you have doubts," Ruth Ann said.

"No, no," Clementine said quickly. "Golf is fine. It's great. Tyler and I love playing golf."

"Which means we can all play together when you come to Tampa," my mother said.

"Okay. We can all play golf together when we come to Tampa," I said, glancing at Clementine who didn't know what to think.

"Which will be fun. But enough about us. What about you two?" Ruth Ann said. "Clementine said both of you can graduate in the summer, Tyler. So is this is your last football game?"

"That's right. Coach Dooley says I could petition the NCAA for another season of eligibility since I didn't play during what would have been my junior year. But I told him I didn't want to do that. I want to go to graduate school," I said. "So does Clementine."

"Good," Ruth Ann said. "We assumed you would. But that doesn't explain what's going to happen next? What your plans are. Or if you've made plans."

Ruth Ann and my mother were sitting in two easy chairs separated by a small table facing the couch, on which Clementine was sitting. I was sitting on the floor in front of Clementine, who was straddling me. I felt her hands press down on my shoulders for a moment.

"It's complicated, mother, but it's also going to work out very well," Clementine said. "Assuming that we both get into the schools to which we've applied."

"And we've been assured by people at Georgia that we will. It's just that we won't know for sure until March 1st for Clemetine and March 12th for me," I said.

Our mothers waited. "All right," my mother finally said. "And your plans are . . . what?"

"I've applied to the Medical College of Georgia," Clementine said. "In Augusta."

"Augusta, Georgia?" Ruth Ann said.

"Yes, mother. Augusta, Georgia," Clementine said, tightening her grip on my shoulders.

Ruth Ann looked dubious. "You aren't going to apply anywhere else?" she said.

"Like where?" Clementine said.

Ruth Ann looked away. "Oh, I don't know. Harvard. Duke. The University of Chicago."

Clementine waited for a moment before responding. "Mom, we've been through all of this before. I went to Georgia Tech so I could eventually go to the Medical College of Georgia. The fact I transferred to the University of Georgia hasn't changed my plans. In fact, the longer I've lived in this state the more I'm convinced that I came here for the right reasons."

"And what reasons are those?" Ruth Ann said.

I could tell Clementine was not happy her mother's questions because she tightened her legs around my shoulders. "Mom, when I was getting ready to go to college, I told you I didn't want to apply to an Eastern university because I didn't want to be just one more liberal black woman among a whole lot of other liberal black women."

"I know you said that, Clementine. But I didn't agree with you then. And I don't agree with you now," Ruth Ann said.

Clementine took a deep breath. "First, I don't know how you can say that since you teach in a Florida university. Second, the longer I've lived here the more I am convinced that I can make a difference."

"Medically or politically?" Ruth Ann said.

"Both," Clementine said.

"Both?"

"Yes, mom. Both." A silence passed between them. Then Clementine went on. "I want to be a doctor. A pediatrician. That hasn't changed. That's why I majored in microbiology at Tech. I want to know how to diagnose children's illnesses. That didn't change when I came to Georgia. Even if the pre-med program in Athens is a little different from the program at Tech, it will still take me to the same place. And that's the Medical College of Georgia. And before you say anything more, just ask yourself this question. How can I have more impact: by being a northern liberal black woman who is a good doctor or by being a southern liberal black woman who is a good doctor?"

"You could have an impact anywhere you go, Clementine," Ruth Ann said.

"Yes, mom, I can. And I hope I will. But I think I might end up being more of a role model for young black girls living in the South than I could on black girls living in the North. For me, it's as simple as that. I want to have the kind of role model influence on black girls . . . on all girls for that matter . . . that you had on me. I think that's a worthy ambition, don't you?"

Clementine's last sentence did what it had to do. Ruth Ann had no choice but to agree. But then Clementine added, "Besides, my plan works out perfectly with what Tyler and his advisor, Jack McAndrew, have laid out for him."

My mother and I had stayed out of Ruth Ann's and Clementine's brief discussion. But now it was my mother's turn.

"And what plans are those, Tyler?" my mother asked.

I waited for a moment before answering. There were several factors that attended my plans. I wanted to be sure I explained them clearly. "I know I want to come back to Georgia to earn my Ph.D.," I said. "I want to be able to work with Professor McAndrew. He understands the focus of my interests. But he recommends that I go somewhere else and work with other people to study for my master's degree. So I've applied to Augusta College."

"Ah," Ruth Ann said.

"Yes, mother, 'Ah.'" Clementine said, laughing.

"You two are schemers," Ruth Ann said.

"No," Clementine replied. "We just talk everything through very carefully."

"What I want to do eventually is take up Grandpa's project about black men and major league baseball. But I want to go beyond that. His notes indicate he was going to focus on the way black men during the 1890's were excluded from baseball by white players and white owners as an example of racial prejudice. I see it as even more than that. I see the exclusion as a reaction to the progress in race relations and education for blacks that took place after the Civil War ended. I see it as part of a pattern of fear of black achievement by whites, that ended up with President Harding being sworn in as a member of the Ku Klux Klan in a ceremony that took place in the White House."

"Good God," my mother whispered.

"Yes, good *something*," I said.

"Augusta College," my mother said, pursing her question.

"Yes. Augusta College. Because there are two people there with whom Prof. McAndrew wants me to study. The first is Lynne Hull in the Social Science Department. The second is Lori Howe in the English Department."

"The English Department?" my mother said.

"Not history?" Ruth Ann said.

"Augusta doesn't award a master's in history. But it does in social science. Which is fine. Because the background I'm going to need to write the Ph.D. dissertation I want to write—which I envision as a book not just an academic work—extends beyond just history."

"How so?" my mother asked.

"Lynne Hull's discipline is environmental sociology. Her specialty is the relationship of land use and the economy that resulted to racial policies in the South. She's written a number of excellent articles that detail the way blacks were shut out of the economic system so they couldn't gather up a capital base, which meant that they never had enough political clout to challenge the Jim Crow laws that were instituted by whites."

"Blacks were kept 'in their place,'" my mother said.

"Right. What I want to study with Professor Hull are the details of how that system worked. Because both Professor McAndrew and I think that her evidence will help me make my larger case about white fear that blacks would out achieve them if they were given a chance."

Ruth Ann nodded.

"What about English? Why study English?" my mother asked.

"There are four types of writing with which I need to become familiar. Black and White," I said.

"That's two kinds," my mother said.

"Each subdivides."

"Into what?" she asked.

"The white writers subdivide between those who were trying to portray Southern life honestly, with all of its complexities, with an eye toward improving race relations."

"And the others?"

"The others are white racists who had a disproportionately important impact on white social thought. The ones that preached the racist doctrine that later showed up in things like minstrel shows and D. W. Griffith's film "The Birth of a Nation."

"And this Lori Howe can help you read that kind of material?"

"From what Jack McAndrew says, she can help me read both that and black writers."

"Which you said are subdivided into two groups," Ruth Ann said.

"Yes."

"Which are?"

"First the blacks who tried to tell the story of the South with an eye toward changing the situation for the better. The second were the 'Back to Africa' blacks who rejected America on the premise that whites were never going to give blacks a real chance to develop a racial identity in this country other than the one the whites wanted to force on them. So they wanted to return to what they thought of as their Motherland. Their homeland."

"That sounds like a very ambitious undertaking, Tyler," my mother said.

"It will be. And whatever kind of master's thesis that I write won't encompass all of my studies. I'll have to write a rather narrow study of one part of my reading. It's the change to do the reading that's most important. And to get started teaching."

"Teaching?" my mother said.

"Part of the deal at Augusta will be to teach two sections of history while taking four classes. Tutition free, I might add."

My mother looked pleased. She turned to Ruth Ann. "It's just as we suspected," she said.

"Yes," Ruth Ann replied. "You two are almost too smart by half." Then she smiled. "Sometimes when I think back about how all of this started . . . your relationship. Our relationship," she said, gesturing toward my mother, "I wonder what might have happened had Tyler not agreed to be your ninth grade biology lab partner, Clementine?"

Clementine smiled. "It wouldn't have mattered."

"Really?" Ruth Ann said. "How can you say that?"

"Because even if he hadn't been my lab partner in that class, I wasn't going to let him out of my sight."

I laughed. "And the funny thing is, Ruth Ann, even if she hadn't asked me to be her lab partner, I wasn't going to let her out of my sight either."

"So you two . . . your relationship . . . it was . . . what?" my mother said. "Preordained or something?"

"I don't know if it was preordained, Elizabeth," Clementine said. "But it was going to happen. Tyler and I have talked about it over the years, and we've decided that somehow it was definitely going to happen."

35

That evening we joined other team families in the dining room of the hotel for a very nice meal. The next day the team practiced as well as joined in charitable activities organized by the Liberty Bowl committee, the most moving of which was visiting children in hospitals. The fact they wanted all of us to autograph footballs and jerseys and pictures was a profound experience. The team had done the same when we'd played in earlier bowls, but because I knew this was going to be my last made it even more memorable.

The four of us agreed that we'd celebrate our Winter Solstice meal when Clementine and I came to Tampa for the rest of our winter vacation from school. So after the game, Ruth Ann and my mother flew back to Tampa. I returned to Athens with the team. Clementine traveled with the Georgia boosters back to Atlanta and then back to the Athens campus. The next day, after packing and organizing the books we wanted to bring with us, she and I drove to Tampa for our time with our mothers.

Knowing that in the future it might well become more and more difficult to spend time in Tampa, Clementine and I took advantage of both the days we had at our disposal as well as the warm weather and the facilities the Bay area affords. We went to both the Tampa and the St. Petersburg art museums. We attended a classical music concert at the Tampa Performing Arts Center and saw two local theatre productions. Most important in the long term for us, however, was organizing the trip to Africa that my grandfather had wanted us to take. Although we knew he had made the provision, when his will was read, both Ruth Ann and my mother were surprised that he had set aside $5000 for Clementine and me to visit the Ivory Coast. When we explained that my Grandfather's wish was that Clementine find her own hill, they both said they understood. Armed with the money he had provided, we spent time with Dorothy Kopp, a travel agent, who arranged for our flights from Atlanta to Paris and then on to Cairo, from which we would fly to Lagos, Nigeria. From Lagos we would take a train following the Slave Coast to Abidjan, Ivory Coast, where we would try to fulfill both my grandfather's hopes for Clementine and her expectations.

Dorothy said she had never arranged for anyone to make that kind of trip before. "I'm a little apprehensive about your arrangements only because I have so little frame of reference. But given what you want to accomplish, I think these arrangements are the best I can make."

"We do have a contact in Lagos," I said. "A professor who knew my grandfather. If he's still teaching at the University of Nigeria, then we should be able to get help."

Clementine had said almost nothing as we made the arrangements. My assumption was that it was because she did not have any specific comments to make. Later, sitting with her on the front porch of my mother's house where we were staying, she said, "I know exactly what kind of experiences I want to have. I'm just having a difficult time convincing myself that our trip is actually going to happen."

I smiled and put and arm around her shoulder. "It's going to happen, Clementine. Just look at our life together. Just look at what's happened since we first met."

She smiled and put her head on my shoulder.

"I promise you, Clementine, it's going to happen."

Of course, as I made my promise, I thought of my grandfather, for it had been his promise to Clementine as well.

36

By the time we returned to Athens for what would be our last full length semester in undergraduate school, it felt as if time was speeding up. We had both done such a good job of catching up courses that we'd missed when Clementine had gone through her illness and I'd stayed with her, that it now appeared we could go through the first of two short summer school sessions rather than one longer session. That would give us time to move to Augusta before our trip to Africa so we would already be settled when we returned to the states for the beginning of Clementine's medical school and my graduate studies. When that news was topped off in March by Clementine being formally accepted to the Medical College of Georgia and me being both accepted into the master's degree program at Augusta College and being offered a teaching assistantship in the history department, we celebrated with a number of our friends who had also received letters of acceptance into graduate schools, some of which were out of state. That meant that for all of our shared joy, there was an element of sadness. How often we would see each other in the future was uncertain. Nevertheless, even with the mixed feelings, it was a celebratory occasion.

As for Clementine and me, we knew we were in good order financially. Our undergraduate studies had cost very little due to a combination of athletic and academic scholarships. In addition, I'd received the Raymond trust each semester that I'd been in school, and that would continue without any conditions except that I do passing work. Because the acceptance to Augusta College graduate school also involved teaching, I would have no tuition to pay. We reasoned that even if Clementine didn't win a substantial scholarship to the Medical College, and we were assured she would certainly win something given the quality of her undergraduate work at Georgia Tech and at the University of Georgia, our finances would still be sound. Of course, as both expected and deserved, in the end Clementine did receive a half tuition scholarship.

As all of that was unfolding and falling into place for us, what amused both of us—perhaps bemused would have been a better word—is that Raymond money would pay for me to continue studies that I hoped would lead to a book that challenged the very social and economic system from which the family had benefited all the way back to the days when slaves were being imported into the Americas. "Sounds like poetic justice," Clementine said.

"Or karma," I said, "catching up to them."

Then the biggest surprise of all happened. Clementine and I graduated from Georgia at the end of the summer semester. That meant the graduation ceremony was large enough to be interesting but small enough so we could actually wander some afterwards among our fellow graduates and their families and have conversations. After we had done that for a few minutes and had returned to our mothers, who were as proud as you can imagine, we were suddenly found ourselves being greeted by Mildred Raymond, who held out her hand and said, "Congratulations, Tyler."

I have never been so surprised in my life. Of all of the people in the whole world, she was the last I ever expected . . . .

"Thank you," I said after a moment, returning her gesture.

It took another moment to recover. Mildred was overdressed, of course. But she was there.

Before I could ask, she quickly said, "Your grandfather is in Canada playing golf with friends." She didn't say, "Or he would have been here," because I knew that certainly wasn't the case. In fact, the only reason she was there was because he was out of the country. That was so obvious she didn't have to say anything more.

Then she turned and greeted my mother. The two women exchanged greetings that were so polite they bordered on open contempt. I quickly interceded and introduced Clementine, whom Mildred said she remembered from having met her in Miami. Then I introduced Ruth Ann. It gave me a moment of great pleasure to see the way Ruth Ann's expression cut Mildred down to size, although had anyone been standing by and observing the scene he would never have thought an untoward moment had passed: that was the power of Ruth Ann to speak with her eyes. Mannerly contempt are the words that leap to mind.

Then I did something that I must now confess—with great embarrassment—was something that I was arrogantly proud to do: "Mildred, Clementine and I are married," I said, waiting for her to finally crack and give voice to her distain for my black-mixed-race-companion-lover-wife. But I underestimated Mildred. She didn't even shudder as I had hoped and expected. She just said, "Congratulations, my child. I sincerely hope that you and Tyler will be very happy together." But that was it. Ah, I thought. It isn't in her expression. No sign of shock or anger. And it isn't in her words. They were correct enough. But it's in what she doesn't say, because most folks would have at least one more comment, one more question: "And when did you marry?" or "What are your plans?"

or, to Clementine, "Are you still planning to be a medical doctor?" But damn, she didn't budge.

"Congratulations, my child. I sincerely hope that you and Tyler will be very happy together," was all she said. It wasn't until later, when Clementine said she thought "my child" was her way of saying "boy" and that "I sincerely hope you will be very happy together" was her way of saying, "Well, Tyler, now you've really done it. I hope you're proud of mixing the races like that."

So I guess in our own way Clementine and I won the day. Because when I then said, "Ruth Ann and my mother and Clementine and I are going to join some of our friends and their families at a restaurant nearby for dinner, Mildred. You are welcome to join us," the look of fear that took charge of her face was priceless. Because for just a moment she fumbled for the perfect response. When she found it, to no one's surprise, she said, "Thank you very much. That's very kind of you. But I do have to get back to my hotel so I can make my flight out of Atlanta. I just wanted to come attend the ceremony so I could tell you how proud your grandfather and I are of all that you have achieved, Tyler."

When she then spoke Ruth Ann's and my mother's names as gestures of goodbye bordering on dismissal and then Clementine's as a gesture of whatever she was feeling—probably disapproval—and then mine in a similar way, I assumed her intent was to end all further obligations on her part toward me as well as put a stop to any silly notion I might entertain that the Raymonds owned me anything more than money. So with that, she turned and was gone, and my mother said, for the first time I had ever heard her say such a thing in my life, "I hate that bitch," which said it all, producing smiles at first and then sympathetic if somewhat uncomfortable laughter as we watched my mother's consternation at the language she had used and emotion she had expressed.

37

Five days later, I leaned my head back against the tall seat and looked at the perfectly ordinary gathering of passengers on our plane heading for New York. I closed my eyes for a moment, breathing slowly, trying to relax. Clementine sat next to me reading a small paper back book, *A Pocket History of West Africa.* As she always did when she was reading something that she believed she needed to remember, she underlined passages with a pen. In between reading and underlining sentences and paragraphs, she looked out of the window at the landscape passing below us. Watching her for a moment, tracing her profile with my eyes, I wondered what she was wondering. Was she excited? Looking forward to new experiences? Was she afraid? Hesitant? What did she expect was going to happen? What could I do to help her fulfill her expectations? What could I do to protect her from disappointment? But all I had were questions. I had no answers. I suspected she didn't have any answers either.

Clementine put aside her book when one of the flight attendants served us coffee. As she drank slowly, looking out of the window all the while, she leaned her right shoulder against my left shoulder, giving her usual signal: Tyler, I am glad I am with you. Tyler, I want to talk. Tyler, I don't know where to begin. I felt her shoulder pull away. I understood what was next.

"What part are we playing, Tyler?" she said, turning to me as she spoke.

"What part in what?" I said.

"In the triangle?"

"The slavery triangle?"

"Yes. What part are we playing?"

I looked at her for a very long time. "Which part do you want to play?" I said.

She shook her head and looked at me again. "I don't know. You and me, we aren't European kings sending goods to West Africa so our traders can buy slaves from black African kings."

"No. We aren't doing that."

"And we aren't slaves being transported to the New World."

"No. We aren't."

"Even though I'm related to ancestors who were."

"Even though you're related to ancestors who were."

"And we aren't transporting raw materials from the New World back to Europe, which completed the triangle."

"Right. We aren't transporting raw materials back to Europe," I said.

Clementine turned and looked at me very intently. "Then what are we doing? What part are we playing on this trip? What part am I supposed to play?"

"What part do you want to play?"

Clementine breathed deeply. I recognized the sound. It was her Tyler-I-don't-expect-you-to-have-an-answer-but-I-wish-you-had-an-answer tone of voice. "You sound like a rabbi," she said quietly.

I smiled.

"What is the meaning of life, rabbi?" Clementine said, mimicking my favorite philosophical scenario, throwing her voice so she could play both roles: "What would you have it be, my dear?"

She took another sip of coffee. "Which isn't an answer, is it?" she said, not looking at me.

"No. But maybe it's the only answer he could give," I said. "Or maybe it's the best answer anyone can give."

Clementine smiled. "I hate it sometimes when you are poetic, Tyler," she said.

"I thought you liked it when I was poetic," I replied.

"Not when I'm looking for an answer to a question," she said.

"But the answers are in the question," I said quietly. "Or the answers are the question," I said.

"I know. I know. God is not the answer. God is the question."

"Right."

"But that still doesn't tell me what I need to know," she said.

"And what is it that you need to know?"

"I need to know what part I'm supposed to play on this trip. Why did Edward want me to go? Us to go."

I leaned back and was quiet for some time. "He wanted you to have what I had when he took me to Wales," I said.

Clementine looked away. She took another sip of coffee. "I don't see how that's possible," she said.

"Why not."

"Because your Welsh ancestors weren't hauled out of Wales as slaves," she said.

"No, but they were forced out by economics. By politics. By violence."

"Is that the same?" Clementine said, turning back to me.

"I don't know. Probably not. But it must have been hard."

"But they decided to go. They weren't sold to slave traders by their own kings."

"They didn't have any kings of their own. They didn't have any princes of their own."

"The Prince of Wales," she said quickly.

"Clementine, the Prince of Wales is a title and a role forced on the Welsh by the English. The Prince of Wales has nothing to do with the princes that once ruled Wales. The Prince of Wales is an Englishman."

Clementine was quiet. Then she turned and looked at me. "But what part am I supposed to play on this trip, Tyler? Find a hill of my own? That's what you said we would do. I would find a hill of my own. But if I do that . . . or when I do that, what I am supposed to feel?"

"Clementine, I can't answer that. You will feel what you feel. You can't make something happen that isn't real. You can't decide before hand what you are going to feel."

"But didn't you do that in Wales? Didn't Edward know what he wanted you to feel?'

I was quiet again for a moment. "I think he must have hoped that standing on the mountain side above the village from which my most important ancestor came would tell me something about me."

Clementine nodded. "Did it?" she asked.

"Some," I said.

"Some? What does that mean? Some?"

"It means that it resonates in my imagination. It means it animates my imagination."

"Is that all?" Clementine said.

"Clementine," I said, my voice suggesting my momentary irritation, "that is a great deal. That's a lot."

Clementine turned away and was quiet for several moments. Then she turned back to me. "Sorry. I'm not belittling what happened for you in Wales. Or even what happened in Scotland," she said. "It's just that I don't know if anything like that will happen for me in Africa when we get to the Ivory Coast."

"I know you don't know," I said in a whisper. "You can't know. We just have to go there. And you have to let it happen. That's the best we can do."

"But what part am I playing?" she said again. "In the triangle?" she said. "I don't want to be a dilettante. I've seen magazine articles about black people who go back to Africa and who come away saying they've discovered their roots. But I don't believe them. I don't think you put on your roots, so to speak, like a coat. I don't think a person can 'Do Africa' they way you can 'Do Disney' or some place like that. Africa isn't a theme park. The people in Africa aren't performers waiting for their American cousins to come spend their money. Because the ancestors of all of us American cousins got sold down the river. We're the ones who really and truly got sold down the river. So what part am I supposed to play in the triangle, Tyler?"

"Clementine, the triangle is gone. It was destroyed long ago. The world changed," I said, which wasn't much of an answer, but it was the best I could do in the moment.

She quickly smiled in what appeared to be a sneer. "You think the world is a better place, Tyler? Today? Right now?"

"I didn't say that, Clementine. I said it had changed. It's still a very hard place to live."

"And it's the only place we have. I know. I know what you're going to say," she said quickly, her reply almost overlapping my response.

"Well, if you know what I'm going to say," I said after a moment, "why do you ask me questions?" I said in reply.

"Because I need to ask the questions, Tyler. And I need to hear your answers."

"Even if my answers aren't really answers?" I said.

"Yes. Even if they aren't really answers. Which they are, of course."

"Which they are, of course . . . what?"

"Answers. Good answers. The best answers."

I put my head back. "You should have majored in philosophy, Clementine," I said, my affection betrayed in my mock irritation. "That's your true calling."

"I didn't need to," Clementine said, the humor returning to her voice. "I've got you."

I laughed for myself as much as for her. "Yes, you've got me," I said. "You definitely have me," I said.

"Then I'm fine," Clementine said. "That's all I need. Except maybe a few direct answers to my direct questions. That would be nice, too," she said, leaning her head against my shoulder.

"Don't hold your breath, my love," I said in a whisper. "Not on a trip like this one."

Her left hand reached over and took a firm grip on my left arm. Her head pressed against my shoulder more firmly as she closed her eyes. "I won't," she whispered. "I promise," she whispered.

Then I felt her slipping away to sleep. As she did, I knew that the next time Clementine raised the subject our conversation would have to be more focused because the next time she would be more demanding, speaking both for and to her sensitivities and sensibilities in a much more profound and therefore much more painful way. I wasn't afraid she wouldn't be up to the task for I knew she had a reservoir of strength on which she could rely. I was not as confident about myself.

38

We had a three hour layover in New York at Kennedy Airport, during which we telephoned our mothers to reassure them that both of us were fine and that Clementine was fully prepared to take her injections as we traveled. At 8 P.M., we boarded our flight for Paris. What became obvious to me shortly after we took off was that Clementine's trepidations about what she would experience in Africa were overwhelmed by her joy at flying with me over the Atlantic again. We could have flown directly to Cairo from New York and then gone from there to Africa, but Dorothy Kopp, our travel agent in Tampa, agreed with Clementine's doctors that it would be better for her to fly to Paris and stay in a hotel near the airport for twenty-four hours before going on to Cairo. Our plan was to stay in

Cairo for another twenty-four hours before going on to our final destination. The concern was that even as much as Clementine and I enjoyed flying—and we do—it would be better if we took the trip in stages that would allow her to have full nights of sleep in a bed rather than try to count on sleeping on the plane to Paris and the plane to Cairo.

After we arrived in Paris, we went directly to our airport hotel. When I suggested that we eat breakfast and then stay awake until at least the middle of the afternoon to insure that we would then sleep all night through, Clementine said that would give us time to take a bus to Paris and at least see one of the sights before we returned to the hotel and went to bed. "We're going to have three days in Paris when we come back, Clementine. Are you sure you're up to going into the city right now? So early in the morning."

She said she was, which is why, after changing clothes, we took a bus from the hotel to the one place Clementine most wanted to see: the Eiffel Tower. "I want to sit with you and have coffee in the restaurant at the top of the Tower," she said as we rode toward the city.

"You're sure there's a restaurant at the top of the Tower?"

"Yes," she said. "I read about it. I've seen photographs. We don't need to do anything else today. But that's the one thing I've looked forward to most of all."

One of the continuing joys of my life with Clementine has been to watch her when she is happy. Yes, we've gone many places that both of us have wanted to visit, and yes, on those occasions, I derived some of my pleasure from my own experience. But in the end at least half if not more of my happiness has always come with watching Clementine be happy. It is part of being in love, I suppose. At least, that's what Clementine says.

So there we were on a bus into the city. Then we took a cab to the Eiffel Tower. After paying our tourist fares, we rode the elevator to the observation deck. Of course, like everyone else that morning, which happened to be very clear and mild, we took photographs of each other. Then we asked an older man if he would take a picture of us together, which he did. He looked disappointed when we told him that we were only going to be in Paris for one day. He was happier when we told him we were coming back after our trip to Ivory Coast, Africa. "It is a city for people who are in love," he said. Clementine told him that meant it was a city for us.

As we sat at a small table drinking coffee and eating pastries, I could not keep from looking at Clementine as she sat and looked at the people sitting around. Both of us are people watchers, for lack of a better term. But on that morning, I only glanced at the other visitors to the Tower. My interest was in my darling Clementine. It seemed to me that more than anyone else or anything else that morning, she lit up the room. What I remember most clearly is the way she turned and looked at me and then reached across the table and took my hand and said, "Here we are, Tyler. Just think. Here we are at the top of the Eiffel Tower."

I knew what she meant: that we had shared and were still sharing an extraordinary journey. I smiled and paraphrased Robert Frost: "Yes, Clementine, and we have miles to go before we sleep."

On the ride back down the elevator, Clementine pressed herself against me, hanging on as if only I could protect her from what ever dangers might present themselves. As she did, I kissed her temple and held her as tightly as I dared. Then I felt her shiver once, which told me it was time for an insulin injection as soon as we got back to our hotel.

The next morning, after eating in the hotel dining room, we returned to the airport and boarded our flight for Cairo, the second stop in our trip.

39

Planes do not fly over Paris. Therefore, our flight did not let us see the city from the air. However, that did not keep the trip from being beautiful, for the route we followed from Paris to Cairo took us over Southern France and along the Southern coast of Italy and then Greece. Together, Clementine and I spent the flight trying to identify which region and which city we were looking at as we strained at the small window to see the mountains and then the countryside and the coast line below. Fortunately, we were seated on the left hand side of the plane. Even more fortunate, it was a crystal clear day. Once we passed over Crete, which meant that Cairo was not far away, Clementine sat back and asked me what I knew about Egypt. I told her I knew very little. Yes, I had read two short accounts of Egyptian history as preparation for our trip, and yes, I had read a short summary of the history of Cairo, itself. But no, I had not ever had any courses that took up the Middle East generally let alone Egypt specifically.

Clementine smiled. I knew what was coming: her I've-been-studying- something-you-haven't smile. I was right.

"Did you know that Cairo was once ruled by former slaves?" she said.

"I didn't know that," I replied.

She sat back and looked out of the window. Then she turned back to me. "When Saladin ruled Cairo, his army was mostly slaves and former slaves who had been given a chance to prove themselves."

"Really?"

"Yes. Mostly they were Caucasians. From the Caucasus region of Europe. But yes, they were slaves or former slaves. There was even a woman ruler at one time."

"A woman? Who?"

"Shagaret-el-Dorr."

"And who was Shagaret-el-Dorr?" I said.

"She was a slave who became the wife of Al-Salch. I think I'm saying that right. Al-Salch."

"Who was . . . "

"Who was the last Ayyubid Sultan. He was a Mamelouk. That was an important house in Egyptian history."

"Like the Lancasters or the Yorks in England?"

"Yes. Like that. And when he died in 1249 . . . I think it was 1249, because there was no strong male to take his place, Shagaret-el-Dorr took the throne. She was the last woman to rule Egypt."

I was impressed. "You've been reading," I said.

"Yes, I have," she said.

I waited for her to go on.

"Shagaret-el-Dorr was the last of three women who ruled Egypt."

"The other two being . . . ," I said, letting my question hang in the air.

"The first was a woman named Hatshepsut. I don't know anything about her. The second was Cleopatra."

"I've heard of Cleopatra," I said.

"Everyone's heard of Cleopatra. Mostly because of her love affairs with Roman rulers. But the fact is, she was a very good queen."

"I'm sure she was."

"What is interesting about Shagaret is that after her husband died . . . "

"Al-Salech."

"Yes. Al-Salech. After he died, she was persuaded to marry the chief Mamelouk officer, a man named Aybeck."

"That sounds like trouble."

"It was trouble. For Aybeck at least. Because when he decided he wanted to marry another woman, Shagaret had him assassinated."

"Assissinated?" I said. "That's serious. So then what happened?"

"The Mamelouks decided she had gone too far, so they assassinated her."

"That sounds about right."

"In what way does that sound about right?" Clementine said quickly.

"I don't mean that it sounds right that she was killed. I mean it sounds about right historically. Women rulers have very often been murdered or deposed."

"Because they are women?" she said sharply.

I waited for a moment. "Yes, because they are women. Which was wrong," I said quickly before she could object or misinterpret my comment.

Clementine looked out of the window. Then she turned back to me again. "There were other slaves who became rulers. Men slaves who became rulers."

I did not need to ask a question for her to go on.

"One was a former Russian slave. Qalaun. And his son, Al-Naser. They get credit for many of the Islamic monuments in present day Cairo."

I sat back and closed my eyes. "Egyptian history must be interesting," I said quietly.

"It is. All of the Middle East is interesting," Clementine said. "And I think it's particularly interesting that slaves rose to positions of power. There was even a group called the Tower Slaves who ruled Egypt for hundreds of years after Qualaun."

"History is tricky," I said quietly.

"History is what?"

"History is tricky," I said.

"What does that mean?"

I replied without opening my eyes: "Because it is easy for events and important people to be forgotten," I said quietly.

Clementine did not reply immediately. After a moment she said, "Yes. And if it's easy for important people . . . public people . . . to be forgotten, think how easy it is for ordinary people to be forgotten."

"If anyone ever knew about them in the first place," I said.

Clementine was very quiet. "And even if ordinary people might not be forgotten . . . at least not by their own people . . . they certainly get forgotten when their own people are captured and then ruled by other people."

I smiled without opening my eyes. "Now you've discovered the problem of history," I said in a whisper.

"Which is?" Clementine said.

"That the winners get to write the story. Which means the losers get themselves forgotten."

"Empires?" she said, implying a sweeping generality.

"Yes. Empires. Running over other empires. Groups running over other groups."

"Races running over other races?" Clementine said.

"Particularly races running over other races," I said, opening my eyes. "Then rewriting history for their own purposes," to which I am sure Clementine would have had a specific and pointed response had not one of the attendants come on the public address system to say that all passengers needed to prepare for our landing in Cairo.

40

Despite the fact that Clementine and I had grown up in Florida and attended universities in Georgia and were used to the idea of wearing light weight and light colored clothes during the summer and never going outdoors without hats, we were not ready for the heat that struck us like rolling waves when we descended from the airplane and crossed the tarmac to the terminal. I actually saw Clementine's knees almost buckle for an instant, and that from a young woman who had run middle distance races for Georgia Tech. When I took her elbow and tried to offer her support without making it obvious, she did not resist, which told me a great deal about what we might expect when we got to the Ivory Coast the next day.

Once we were inside the terminal and going through customs, it did not feel much cooler. The building was crowded with people speaking several languages, only two of which we could understand: English and Spanish, neither of which helped us very much. However, when I explained that we were only staying over for one night so my wife could sleep in a hotel and that it was a matter of her health, the Egyptian officials were very helpful. One even escorted us to where we could catch a taxi cab to our hotel.

By the time we got to the hotel, the sun was beginning its descent toward the desert. We knew that once that happened, it would be cooler. So after unpacking the clothes we would need for the next day, we changed into casual clothes and, in keeping with Clementine's one adamant wish, took a taxi to the outskirts of Cairo to the Giza plateau so we could view both the Great Sphinx and the Pyramids of Khaufu, Khafue, and Menkaura.

Because the city has spread all the way to Giza, we let our taxi cab go, knowing that we would find another without difficulty. Then we walked the short distance necessary until we could stop and stand and look at truly one of the most marvelous and most haunting sites in the world.

As many photographs as we both had looked at growing up in school, and as many guide books as we had read in preparation for even our overnight stay in Cairo, nothing truly prepared us for what we saw. I could perfectly well understand why words might describe the facts of the monuments but never capture the power and beauty and majesty of either the Sphinx or the Pyramids. Both of us were stunned. Both of us stood silent. Clementine grasped my hand tightly, but neither of us tried to explain our feelings. Then because we had come at exactly the right time, when twilight still shows in the sky but shadows on the ground are lengthening, the lights that illuminate the Pyramids began to take hold, both heightening the sensation of size and capturing the night sky at the same time.

I don't know how long most tourists stand looking at the sites, especially people who do not intend to enter the Pyramids or take a more extensive tour of the Sphinx, but whatever length it might be, we felt as if we must be raising the average. In brief, we stood and looked and tried to memorize what we were seeing until I felt Clementine shiver with the rising cool air. So I broke the mood and said very quietly, "We need to go back to the hotel so you can get your sleep, Clementine."

She did not resist but grasped my hand more tightly and said, "You're right. But I'm glad we did this."

"So am I," I said.

With that we turned very slowly and looking back over our shoulders, returned to the row of taxi cabs waiting to take people back to the city. Thirty minutes later we were in the hotel dining room eating a light meal. Then we went to our room where Clementine showered first. Then I showered. Then we went to bed.

Two hours later, perhaps more, I awoke to find Clementine sitting in the straight back chair that had been pushed up next to the hotel room desk. Sitting up, I waited for a moment before speaking, because I was not sure she was aware I was awake. Then I slowly brought my legs out from under the sheet so I could sit on the edge of the bed. After a moment, seeing her in the dim light coming through the window from the city beyond, I said, "Clementine. Are you all right?"

She did not respond immediately. So I waited. Then I spoke again. "Clementine, are you all right? Do you feel all right?"

Clementine turned toward me very slowly. I could see her silhouette even if I could not make out her facial features clearly.

"Is it your diabetes? Do you need an injection?" I said.

"I don't think so," she said.

"You don't think so . . . what? That it's not your diabetes? That you don't need an injection?"

"Both," Clementine said.

I waited. I knew enough at times like this to wait. Clementine would tell me what she wanted me to know when she wanted me to know it.

"It's me," she said.

I stayed silent.

"It's this trip. It's me. It's both."

"Do you want to talk about it?"

"Yes," she said quickly. "No," she added in a moment.

I watched as she stood and moved to the window. She was wearing boxer shorts and no top. I could see her body against the curtain. She stood for some time before speaking. Then she said, "I don't know what I'm supposed to do?" she said. "I don't know what I'm supposed to feel."

"I understand," I said in a whisper.

She turned on me. "Do you? Do you really understand, Tyler?"

"I think so," I said.

"How can you understand? How can anyone understand?" she said, her voice sharp, agitated, tense.

"Clementine, I think I understand . . ." I started to say before she cut me off.

"They were slaves, Tyler. Slaves! They didn't want to leave. They didn't want to have their lives destroyed. They didn't go to the New World because they wanted some sort of opportunity for whatever it is people go to the New World to find."

"What do you want me to say, Clementine?"

"I don't know. I don't know. Just not that you understand. You can't understand. I don't understand so you certainly can't understand."

I felt the hurt in her voice. I felt my own hurt at what she had said. "I am trying, Clementine."

"Well, you can't," she snapped.

"I have been trying all of my life."

"You've been trying ever since you met me."

"What's that supposed to mean?"

"It means you've been trying since you took up with a black girl, that's what it means."

I waited for a moment. "Now you're being cruel, Clementine."

"Cruel? How is that being cruel? You are white. You can't understand what it means to be black. In America. In Africa. Anywhere."

She was facing me. I could not see her clearly, but she was facing me.

"Any more, I suppose, than you could understand how I felt in Wales looking at Maerdy," I said, my voice sharp although not as sharp as hers.

"Maerdy? How you felt in Maerdy? It isn't the same, Tyler, and you know it."

"No, I don't know it. I mean, yes, it was different, because people are different in different places at different times. But it still must have been hard. To be driven out of your home. To not be able to feed your children and have to go all the way across the Atlantic to a whole new place. Without money. Without friends."

"Tyler, they left Wales to make a better life. Black Africans did not leave Africa to make better lives."

"They were still required by the economics of the times or the politics of the times to leave."

"It's isn't the same."

"I didn't say it was the same. I said it was what they had to do. Are we going to argue about misery? About whose misery was the worst? Is that what this trip is about? So you can justify your anger. Or get mad at me because I'm not black? Or what . . . get mad at the world because you are black?"

"Tyler, that's terrible. You've never said anything like that before."

"Because you've never acted this way before."

"Because I've never been on a trip like this before," she said, almost shouting.

"And neither have I," I said just as sharply.

"Do you want to go home?"

"What?"

"Do you want to go home? Do you want to desert me?"

I moved away from her. Then I turned on her. I tried to hold on to my hurt, my rising frustration. "Clementine, I am here because I love you and because this trip is important to you and because I want to be with you when you experience whatever it is you are going to experience."

She was quiet for a moment. I could hear her voice. It sounded deep in her chest, but she did not make any words. "You are here because . . . Tyler . . . because . . . I cannot do this without you," she said very slowly.

I counted to ten before I spoke. Then I said in a whisper, "I am here, Clementine . . . because I love you . . . and because I think you need to make this trip and because I believe I need to be with you when you do."

"To take care of me?" she said, although her question was a much a statement of agreement as anything else.

"To do whatever you need for me to do, Clementine," I said, moving to her in the darkness.

"Thank you," she whispered, her voice barely audible above the sound of the traffic below us in the streets.

"You are welcome," I said.

She shivered again. And I knew from her expression that it was time. So I gestured that she should sit back down in the desk chair, which she did. Then I walked into the bathroom and brought back her insulin kit. Without saying anything more, I bent down until I was on both of my knees so I could give her the injection in her left thigh. As I did, she rested her right hand on my left shoulder and her left hand on my right shoulder. When I was finished, I remained where I was until I had put the syringe back in its case. Then I stood and looked at her as she stood and faced me. Then without speaking Clementine was in my arms. At first, I could feel her body shudder. Then I could feel her warmth. I could feel her face against my neck. I could feel her breath on my chin and cheek. I could feel her heart beating. We stood that way for some time before she whispered, "I want to go back to bed, Tyler. Will you come back to bed with me?"

"Yes, Clementine," I said, "I will go back to bed with you."

41

The next morning, after our morning plane made a stop in Monrovia, Liberia, we arrived in Abidjan, the capital of Ivory Coast. When we first boarded the airplane in Cairo, I was one of several white people among the majority blacks. By the time we arrived in and then departed from Monrovia, I was the only white person left on the plane, which was the first time I had ever been in that situation. As I sat on the plane trying not to be concerned about the sudden turbulence, which I credited to both the size of the twenty-five seat aircraft and the fact we were then flying at no more than five thousand feet along the South Atlantic Ocean coast line, I found myself aware of both the circumstance and, even more, alert to my feelings, which were a mixture of curiosity about the people around me and about my own feelings, which were, I must confess, a sense of unease. No, I did not expect anyone to say anything untoward, and indeed, they did not. Yet I could not help but be aware of how very white my skin appeared among the very dark skinned Africans. I wondered if that was how Clementine and all of the black people I had known in my life felt every day? Or had the blacks I knew in America become so accustomed to being in the minority that they put aside any feelings of discomfort. I knew I could not answer the question for them just as, at that moment, I could not answer the question for myself.

At the same time, I wondered what Clementine must have been feeling. Yes, I knew that her mother's parents lived in a majority black neighborhood, and I knew that Clementine had visited with her mother's family, both immediate and extended, very often when she had been a child and that she and Ruth Ann had visited with them after the two of them had moved to Florida. But when that happened, I wondered, did they feel a sense of racial ease, or did they know that Ruth Ann's parents' black neighborhood was an island in a much larger sea of white people.

Clementine and I did not talk very much on the flight from Cairo to Monrovia, and we spoke even less on the second leg of the flight to Abidjan. I am not sure why. Perhaps both of us were confronting feelings that were so new we neither understood them nor knew how to articulate them to the other. I know that without being too obvious I watched Clementine as much as possible. What I saw in her expression was a combination of wonderment and anxiety.

I interpreted her expression as saying that even though she had identified with her mother and her mother's black heritage all of her life, she acknowledged that her complexion, which was much lighter than the majority of black people around us on the plane, juxtaposed two feelings: yes, she was among black Africans now, from which her black ancestors had come, albeit painfully. However, her lighter complexion clearly marked her as not one of them. I sensed that everyone on the plane who bothered to look at us knew full well we were Americans even before we spoke.

Second, I sensed that her anxiety was also a juxtaposing of two contrasting feelings: yes, she was now in Africa, but could she—dare she—try to identify with people whose continental culture and regional experiences were so very different from her own? Would she find any sense of identity among the people of Ivory Coast? Or would she feel as much an alien here in Africa as she did in America? In fact, would she, ironically, feel more an alien in Africa than she did in America? I knew I could not ever hope to answer those questions either for her for me. I wondered if she would ever be able to answer them for herself.

When we arrived in Abidjan, we found the customs officials both curious about the two of us, evidenced not by anything they said but by their glances, although I must admit that I could not decide if their glances were because we were a mixed race couple or because Clementine was beautiful if light complexioned or if because we were Americans. Perhaps it was all three combined. Later, Clementine said she thought it was our mixed races that mattered most because that was what they saw first. She said that the fact we were Americans was second. The fact she was she was lighter complexioned than any of them was the least of their interests.

In any case, after we landed on what was a very hot and humid day, we took a taxi to our hotel, Sofitel Abidjan, where the staff had our room waiting. We also found a message waiting for us from Paulist Manes, a professor of history at the University of Liberia, who had agreed, in honor of my grandfather, to be our guide into the interior of Ivory Coast, for both he and I were now responsible for telling Clementine a story that Ruth Ann had told my grandfather and then, later, told me, but which she had never fully explained to Clementine. In fact, it was that story that had prompted my grandfather to urge Clementine to make the trip to Africa, and it was that story that, in the end, I believe, changed Clementine's psychological life. I know it certainly changed mine.

42

Professor Paulist Manes was born in Monrovia. His mother had been born in the interior of Ivory Coast but had won a scholarship when she'd been a student at a school run by the Paulist Catholic priests, who served as missionaries in several West African countries, to travel to Monrovia to study. That was where she met Professor Manes's father, who was also a scholarship student at the University of Liberia. After they married, they settled down to careers as school teachers in Monrovia. When their only child, a son, was born, they named him Paulist in honor of the Catholic order that had brought them together.

Paulist Manes grew up in a household where books abounded and intellectual achievement was the norm. He earned his own undergraduate degree in African history at the University of Monrovia. Then he earned a master's degree in African studies at the University of Madrid. While in Madrid, his advisor suggested he try for a scholarship for a second master's degree at Cleveland State University, which had begun to enjoy a reputation among African intellectuals as a school with much promise, largely due to the work of a white man, Professor Edward Thomas, whose essays had begun showing up in European scholarly journals. Four weeks after he was informed he had won the Cleveland scholarship competition, Paulist Manes found himself in my grandfather's office. That evening he found himself in my grandparents' home, where he would meet both my grandmother and my mother, Elizabeth, who was a grade school student at the time.

When Paulist Manes left Cleveland, he traveled to Oxford, where he earned his doctorate in Slave Coast African social history at Christ College. From there he returned to Monrovia where he took up the teaching position he held for the rest of his career. It was, therefore, Paulist Manes's continuing relationship through letters with my grandfather, acting in concert with Ruth Ann's family story, that prompted my grandfather to fund Clementine's and my travel to Ivory Coast. When I told Clementine that story as we sat in the hotel lobby waiting for Professor Manes to arrive, she said she was amazed. "I didn't know any of this, Tyler," she said.

"I think that's the way my grandfather and your mother wanted it. They didn't want you to build up an expectation that might not be fulfilled. But after my grandfather died, your mother took up making arrangements. That's why we've come here. You and I finalized the details in Tampa, but it was your mother's plan that we were following."

Clementine looked at me for some time. "Do you have any more surprises for me, Tyler? Things you and my mother know that I don't," she said.

I smiled and took a sip of my lemon drink. "As a matter of fact, the biggest surprise is still coming."

"And this Professor Manes—he knows what the surprise is?" she said.

"Yes, Clementine. He knows what the surprise is."

"And do you?"

"I know some of it. I don't know all of the details, but I know the story outline."

"And the story 'outline' as you call it—it has to do with me?"

"The story has everything to do with you."

Clementine was quiet for a moment. "Are you going to be like your grandfather, Tyler? Springing surprises on me all of the time."

"I'm not sure if I'll be able to spring very many surprises on you, Clementine, because sometimes you're too smart by half. But yes, every time I can, I'm going to spring some sort of surprise on you."

She shook her head and looked at me as if she didn't know what to do—be irritated or be delighted. I think she opted for delighted, because the next thing she said was, "Well, I guess I haven't got much choice but to trust you, do I?"

I smiled and nodded and was saying, "It looks that way," when I saw a short but very distinguished looking man with gray hair and wearing a tan suit with an open collar shirt come through the front double doors of the hotel. When he stopped for a moment and then looked our way and smiled, I knew Professor Manes had arrived.

43

I had taken extensive notes when Ruth Ann told me the story she wanted Clementine to know. I took more notes when Professor Manes sat with Clementine and me over dinner at a small restaurant within walking distance of our hotel where we went so we could both begin to experience Ivory Coast society and be able to talk with Paulist Manes at length.

Ruth Ann was born in 1946, which meant that in 1988, which is when Clementine and I went to Ivory Coast on what we very quickly came to understand was both Clementine's pilgrimage and a ritual that closed a profoundly important circle for Ruth Ann's family, Ruth Ann was 42.

When Ruth Ann grew up, she had known her Great-Grandmother, Ida, who died at 94 in 1948, which meant Ida had been born in 1854, in South Carolina, to a slave woman, Arway, which in the Kru tribal language meant beautiful, as in beautiful girl child. Arway's name was changed to Fonsiba by the wife of her owner for reasons that no one could ever explain.

Fonsiba or Arway was born in 1816 on a South Carolina rice plantation near the Atlantic Ocean. She died in 1887, having gone through emancipation after the War Between the States.

Fonsiba's mother was named Donyen, which in the Kru tribal language also means beautiful girl child. The family story that has been passed down from generation to generation is about Donyen.

Donyen was fifteen when she was bought by a South Carolina plantation owner at the slave auction in Charleston in 1789. She died in 1834 on the same plantation at age 60. What is important is how and why she was brought to South Carolina from Ivory Coast when she was fourteen.

Tragically, it is very rare that a black family living into the twentieth and now the twenty-first century knows very much with any certainty about the history of their slave ancestors let alone their African ancestors. However, Ruth Ann's family, through the women, had managed to hold on to what they believed was a very important true story.

Donyen was the daughter of an important Kru tribal chief. The Kru people were coastal traders. The Kru peoples had come from what is now Liberia as early as the sixteenth century by sea, which both distinguished them from some inland tribes and sets the stage for the story.

Donyen's father was an important chieftain trader, who with his men rowed out into the ocean where they met with European ships come to the Slave Coast to trade goods and, eventually, to purchase slaves from the tribal leaders who made their people available. Of the European nations who worked the slave trade, the Portuguese were the earliest to establish relations with African tribal leaders.

Donyen's father did not trade in slaves. His goods were raw fruits and vegetables and some meat and fresh water. Over time, he became friendly with one of the Portuguese captains, who more than once invited him aboard his ship as it was loading food stuffs trade in preparation for sailing after having made his necessary purchase of inland blacks for the slave markets in the New World.

On one of those occasions, Donyen's father let her ride in his canoe to the ship where the captain saw her. As she was a beautiful child on the verge of becoming a woman, the captain decided that he would try to negotiate a trade and take her with him. He did not intend to put her into the hold with the other slaves. Rather, he would enjoy her sexually himself as the ship sailed for the Americas. He knew that if he took very good care of her, he would be able to get an exceptionally good price from white slave owners in the New World who were similarly inclined. When Donyen's father refused to trade his daughter, who was destined to become the Queen of his tribe, the captain had his men take her by force, throwing Donyen's father into the water then fighting to keep his followers from coming aboard to recapture their Princess and punish the Portuguese for their treachery. Tragically, the Kru men were not able to rescue Donyen, and she sailed away never to return to Africa.

By the time the ship reached South Carolina, the Portuguese captain had wearied of her favors, for she had fought him as hard as she could for weeks when he kept her in his cabin. So he released her for sale in Charleston, where she was purchased by a family who tried to train her in domestic labor. The father of the family found her particularly promising, but when her temper did not improve, he released her to one of his overseers who mated her with a native born American-born slave black man. Only then did she settle down to the life routine on the plantation. Yet all through the years, no matter that she labored with the other blacks in the fields, she always held herself apart from the others, and they, believing the stories told about her, treated her with great deference, for by the time she was a mature woman who had given birth to four children, one of whom was Arway, her fellow slaves very much enjoyed the notion that they had among them the Stolen Princess of the Kru. When Donyen died in 1834, the story then focused on Arway, who did not ever speak of the story herself but who certainly enjoyed the fact that the elder story tellers on the plantation repeated the tale countless times for both the adults and the children who lived on slave row.

The story of Arway was then transmitted to her children, one of whom was Ida. From Ida the story passed through the generations to Ruth Ann, who by the time she began her university studies was determined to conduct research to confirm the story. Unfortunately, as much as she believed the story, or wanted to believe the story, beyond fragments of information, she could not with any certainty say that the events had taken place as they had been told to her by her Great-Grandmother Ida. Yet she did not ever give up her ambition. Some how, some day, some way, she vowed in secret, she would find out if the story of the Stolen Sacred Princess was true. It was, therefore, an extraordinary godsend when she met my grandfather, for when she told him the story and then asked if he might be able to help her, he said he would contact his former student, Professor Paulist Manes, who taught at the University of Monrovia.

When Paulist Manes wrote back that he had come across the story years before, told from the African point of view—the story of treachery that led to the Kru people losing their Sacred Princess—my grandfather and Ruth Ann vowed that even if they were never able to go to Africa themselves to try to locate an African story teller who might be able to narrate the African version, they would one day send Clementine and me. If you joined that to my grandfather's preoccupation with his and my Welsh background and his affection for Clementine, you will understand why he funded our trip in his Last Will and Testament.

Clementine had not been told for fear the African version might suggest it was about some other young woman stolen by a Portuguese trader, about some other tribe. When the letter arrived from Professor Manes expressing his sympathy at my grandfather's death, he also vowed he would carry on his research. Months later, he wrote and said he believed he could confirm the accuracy of the New World version.

So there the three of us sat over a meal of chicken and rice and coffee, with Professor Manes telling Clementine that he believed he could take her to a Kru village inland in which an elder woman would confirm the tale: that Clementine Camille was the great-great-great-great grandchild of Donyen, six generations of direct descendent women removed from the Stolen Princess of the Kru People.

When I finished summarizing the story Ruth Ann had told me, and Professor Manes told her the story as he had found it still being told by a Kru elder woman, Clementine sat silent for some time. I thought that by then I knew all of her expressions, but that day I saw a new one: something very profound was moving in her. Something profound and serious. She was connecting back across time in a way that would reconstitute, reshape, restore her identity in a way that very few black Americans will ever experience. For the morass of slavery, the tragedy of chattel slavery, was so complete—is so complete—that any attempt to verify a specific genetic lineage is virtually impossible. Yet here was my darling Clementine with a story just waiting to be confirmed. No wonder that night she did not fall asleep until well after midnight, for it was our intention to join Professor Manes early the next morning so we might begin our trip north into an Ivory Coast region where the Kru people still lived and where he believed we would find confirmation of Clementine's heritage. No wonder she rolled over twice, awaking me each time she did when she touched my face and whispered, "Tyler. Is this real? Am I dreaming? Are we really going to find the truth?" To which I replied both times, "We'll find the truth, Clementine. Whatever it is. I promise we'll find the truth."

44

Of the many characteristics I have always admired about Clementine, the one that has always meant the most to me is her steadfast courage. Like most people, she has faced challenges and losses; unlike many people she usually does front on, never trying to avoid the facts, never trying to shirk her responsibilities. But that evening in our room, as we prepared to go to bed, I could both feel her nervousness and see her anxiety, not by what she said but by what she did not say. For every time I raised the issue of Professor Manes making arrangements for us to visit a village he had located where the story of the Stolen Princess was still told, she changed the subject. "You said we would have time to look at African art," she said in response to almost every comment I made as I sat over a map of Ivory Coast looking at where Professor Manes said he wished to take us. Finally, when her voice had risen in pitch and intensity to a point that I had never heard before, I turned to her and said, "What do you want me to do, Clementine?"

"I don't know what you mean?" she said sharply.

I waited for a moment. Then I went on. "Clementine, a number of people who care about you very much have arranged for you to have this trip. Professor Manes has spent a great deal of his time making arrangements for us to go in land for what he believes will be an important experience."

"And," she snapped.

"And so why are you being so difficult?"

"How am I being difficult?" she said.

"Because every time I try to talk about us going with Professor Manes to where he wants to take us, you change the subject."

"No, I don't."

"Yes you do."

"No, I don't."

"Clementine, stop. I've never seen you this way before. What are you afraid of?'

"I'm not afraid of anything, Tyler. What are you talking about?"

I sat quietly for some time looking at her.

"Why are you doing that, Tyler?"

"Doing what, Clementine."

"Sitting and looking at me that way."

"And what way am I looking at you, Clementine?"

"You are accusing me of something."

"Or you are feeling guilty."

"I'm not feeling guilty. Why would I feel guilty?"

I shook my head and turned back to the map. "And what would you like to do tomorrow, Clementine?" I said without looking at her.

"I want to shop for art," she said.

"Shop for art?" I said, turning to her slowly.

"Yes. I want to buy sculpture. I want to buy paintings. For my mother. For your mother. And for us," she said.

"All right. We will shop for art. I will talk with Professor Manes and see if he can help us."

"Why do you have to ask him? Can't we just go places and look at art?"

"Yes, Clementine, we can just go places and look at art. But what kind of art do you want? Art for tourists or art for Africans?"

"Now you're insulting me, Tyler. You've never insulted me before."

"I am not insulting you. I am trying to make sure that when this trip is over and you look at the art you've bought you will know that you have pieces that mean something."

"You don't think I'll know the difference?" she said.

"Clementine, I don't think either of us is trained in African art. I don't think we're trained in any kind of art. Not enough to be collectors. So if you want to buy things on our budget then we will have to be very selective." Before she could interrupt I went on: "And if you're going to buy something for your mother and my mother, then I think we will need help."

Clementine turned away from me and went to the window.

"Besides, I don't think this has anything to do with art," I said. "I just think that you are afraid."

"Afraid of what?" Clementine said, turning back to face me.

"Afraid of where Professor Manes's research might lead. Afraid of what it might mean."

"What are you talking about?" she said, moving back to the window and sitting down on the sill and looking out toward the harbor.

"I think you are afraid of who you might be," I said.

Clementine did not respond.

"I think, Clementine," I said, "I think that you know something about yourself. That you've always known something about you. Sensed something about yourself. But you didn't know what to call it. And now," I said quickly as she turned to me, preparing to interrupt again, "and now, we are getting very close to finding out whatever it is, and you are afraid."

Clementine looked at me and muttered something under her breath that I could not understand.

"I couldn't hear you," I said.

"I didn't say anything, Tyler," said.

I waited. Clementine dislikes it most of all when I refuse to take the bait and disagree but instead just wait for her to go ahead and say what she really wants to say but doesn't want to say.

"I said, 'Now who's too smart by half?'" she said quietly, looking at me, trying very hard to repress her smile, trying very hard to keep her hands from shaking, trying very hard to keep the tears that were welling up in her eyes from spilling over.

I laughed quietly with her not at her. "I don't know, Clementine, who is too smart by half?"

The next morning, we met Professor Manes and told him Clementine wanted to shop for art. He said he knew several young artists who had said they would be honored if we would visit their studios. So that is what we did for the rest of the day, purchasing three paintings and four sculptures, Clementine once again her charming and winning self, asking question after question when we talked with the three artists we met.

When we stopped in a small restaurant Professor Manes knew and ate lunch together, Clementine talked about the food we were ordering with the waiter, asking so many questions that the waiter finally took her back into the kitchen where she not only met the chef, she talked with every other member of the service staff, thanking them personally. That afternoon, when we bought five beautiful floor length dashiki—two for Clementine and two for Ruth Ann and one for my mother—Clementine struck up such a personable conversation with the young woman who helped her that I was sure she was on the verge of inviting the girl to come to America and live with us and go to Augusta State University before Professor Manes kept her from making too many promises. And as much as everything Clementine said with all of the people she'd met was said sincerely, for she is a woman of a singularly good and steadfast heart and generous and giving nature, I could see she was still cloaking her trepidations, still working a tad too hard at working too hard, if you know what I mean, which I add I do not mean as a criticism. It is simply an observation. At the same time, had I known what was going to unfold for her the next day, I would have been a little more sympathetic.

45

Although Professor Manes and I had not discussed Clementine's disguised anxiety, it was obvious to me that he was moving her with sensitive delicacy toward what would prove to be her most important experiences in Africa. To that end the next morning, having told us to pack clothes for an over night stay, he drove us west along the Ivory Coast seaside highway through several villages where we stopped to sample local foods. As we did, he explained that Ivory Coast had been spared most of the horrors of the European slave trade because the ports were not deep enough to moor the sailing ships the slave raiders used. He explained that "Yes, there were occasional raids, and certainly those brought devastation to some villages and families, but it was not as serious as many other places along the Slave Coast."

When we reached the border and crossed into Liberia, he said that he wanted to show us several stations to which slaves had been brought and from which they had been transported. With that we stopped at two remnant buildings which had served as holds for the Africans who were destined for the New World.

As you would expect, it was a very hard experience for Clementine, as it would be for any sensitive American black person. After all, the cruelty of the African Disapora cannot ever hope to be explained in words. The chattel slavery system simply disregarded African humanity, reducing human beings to property to be sold or stolen and then transported to a world that used them as labor without any regard for their persons. After years of study I have concluded that it was the most immoral practice ever perpetrated by one race on another, rivaled only by what the Nazi Reich did to the Jews and Romano peoples of Europe in what has since then been termed the Holocaust. The most widely accepted estimates are that in excess of fifteen million men, women, and children were stolen from Africa and taken by force to the Americas. It is a scar that runs so deeply in the consciousness of people of color that I, for one, have never understood how or from where African North Americans, as well as Africans transported to what became Central and South America, have found the strength to reconstitute both their race and their varied cultures after such a horrifying crime. So while Clementine was undergoing the kind of cathartic experience that, on one hand, I had hoped she would have, with all of its complex ramifications, I was also undergoing my own epiphany, an experience that would, in the end, give focus to both my writing about African Americans and the consequences of racism and my subsequent teaching, for I knew full well that Clementine was not the only one who would be changed by our trip.

That night, Professor Manes and Clementine and I stayed in a small seaside hotel in Greenville, Liberia, where we sat together after dinner for several hours facing the ocean while Professor Manes and Clementine carried on the conversation that I believe both my grandfather and Ruth Ann had wanted for Clementine. For in Professor Manes she found not only a wise historian, she found a sensitive man who was able to guide her thinking in a way that helped her avoid the trap of bitter anger that could well have attended her experience, helping her to understand the struggle the African Slave Coast peoples were waging to revitalize their cultures. As for me, sitting in silence as they spoke but listening to every word, I found myself examining my own consciousness and conscience in ways I had never attempted before.

When the evening ended, and Professor Manes went to his room and Clementine and I went to ours, Clementine was very quiet, undressing and lying next to me in my arms, saying almost nothing. For a moment I feared that she might wish to pull away from me and not allow me to touch her. But she did not. Instead, we lay side by side, her right arm resting on my chest, my right arm under her shoulders, which was when I truly realized not just how much I loved her but how much she loved me. I could only trust that all of her experiences in Africa would leave her feeling the same. For I must admit that if she felt anxiety about facing the bitter truth of African history, I feared that she might one day allow that history to invade our relationship. It was that thought, a persistent undercurrent running through my emotions, that I struggled to hold in check. For most of all, this trip was not for me; this journey was for Clementine. I had to always keep that uppermost in my mind. This journey was for Clementine.

The next day, we arrived in Monrovia where we spent the day visiting the campus of the University of Monrovia, meeting two of Professor Manes's teaching peers, Professor Tibesti and Professor Niamey, lunching with them at a restaurant near the campus where all three were greeted by students coming for their own meals. What I found particularly gracious on their parts was their questions about both my own history studies at the University of Georgia and my plans to pursue a teaching career. Professor Tibesti had read three of my grandfather's books; Professor Niamey had read Ruth Ann's and my grandfather's book of University of Edinburgh lectures.

That evening, Clementine and I were guests in Professor Manes's home, where we met his wife, Sierra, who could not have been more kind, even though she spoke very little English and we, unfortunately did not speak her language at all. Sitting with the two of them in their modest but clean and well appointed apartment, I could not help but feel a sense of camaraderie during our dinner as I sat facing two walls of books. In that moment, I was reminded that those of us who teach form what amounts to an international fraternity of people committed to transmitting history and ideas and, we hope, some wisdom to the next generation just as history and ideas and wisdom have been transmitted to ours. That most teachers are not known outside of a relatively small community is not important. We all don't need to be famous. But we all need to continue our efforts. After all, without our energies, the world would fall even more hopelessly into a mire of ignorance and misunderstanding and violence. Professor Manes's kind sympathies and penetrating intelligence gave me courage to think that perhaps what he and my grandfather and Ruth Ann were doing and what I wanted to do really did matter.

Then it was morning, and Professor Manes and Sierra Manes drove us back to Ivory Coast where we all stayed in our hotel for another night. It would have been better for Clementine had she been able to sleep more soundly, but at the same time I understood why she did not. After all, the next morning we were to venture deep into central Ivory Coast where Clementine was to meet the elder woman Professor Manes had located, the woman who had become, over her life time, the keeper and teller of the story of the Sacred Stolen Princess of the Kru people.

All fictional literature asks readers to suspend disbelief. Otherwise, the world the writer wishes to explore and portray cannot be experienced. If that world cannot be experienced, then the literature being related cannot inform the readers' lives. If that connection cannot be made, then the function of literature is lost. Very often historical narrations require the same thing: readers must suspend disbelief even if the history writer, by contrast to the author of fiction, who only claims that the events might well have happened or could have happened or *should* have happened, argues that the events really did take place.

Admittedly, memoirs such as this one can be even more tricky. After all, I am not trying to write fiction that might or could or should have happened, just as I am not trying to write history, in the broad stoke manner. Rather, I am trying to tell a story that I lived about the only woman I have ever loved, and I am doing so in the first person voice; i.e., I was there; I saw what happened; I experienced what happened with her; I have tried to understand what it all meant to her just as I have tried to understand what it meant to me. For those reasons, the story I am now going to tell asks you to do more than just suspend disbelief. It asks that you believe what I am going to tell you so profoundly that you participate in the event, hear the implications of the words rather than just the definitions of the words, try to feel what Clementine was feeling, what she felt, what mattered to her when it was all said and done. For I promise I will recreate the scene as accurately as my memory allows. I promise my mind will be faithful to the moment as my heart was and is and will always be faithful to Clementine.

The old woman was in her seventies, perhaps in her eighties. It was hard to tell for she had lived a hard life. The standards of care that apply to the Western World do not apply to her world. Which is not to say she did not eat regularly or live fully or love deeply, for she did all of those things. It is simply to say that having come more than half way around the world, I had to leave the standards and practices of the world I knew behind and accept that for all of my sincerity, I could not possibly hope to really know and understand the standards and practices of her world. At the same time, when I stood and looked at her, when she touched my hand in greeting, when I let her eyes record my face, I also understood that something so human and humane were unfolding that it transcended the limitations of culture and society. In short, she was the essence of Woman. Even more important, once Professor Manes introduced Sierra and Clementine and me to Oume Touba, explaining that Sierra was his wife but that Clementine and I had come from the New World of America to meet her, I could tell that it was her silence that meant the most. For her silence was not the silence of ignorance or distain. It was the silence that accompanies the penetrating observation, the detailed examination, the sensitive evaluation. When she spoke in her native tribal Kru tongue, Professor Manes translated. Obviously, it is his translation into English that I have tried to recall.

"You are the child who has come far?" Oume asked.

Clementine replied, "Yes, I am Clementine."

"Let me touch your face, child," the old woman said as she closed her eyes, beginning to hum a rasping, tuneless chant. After a moment, she opened her eyes and whispered, "I have waited all of my life for you to return."

Clementine did not respond, but I could see her body was tense, alert, from the way she shivered perhaps even tingling.

"There was a child like you once among our people," Oume continued. "A Sacred Princess."

"I have told her the story," Professor Manes said to the old woman.

"Did the story go with the Princess?" Oume asked.

"When she was stolen?" Professor Manes said.

"Yes. Did the story go with the Princess?"

"Yes. It was not lost. It was told by others. But yes, it went with her."

"Through how many generations?" Oume wanted to know, which caused Professor Manes to turn to Clementine and me and say he had to remember how to answer her question. Sounding out the words silently at first, he finally turned back to Oume and said, "She is the sixth. I believe the Sacred Princess was her Great-Great-Great-Great Grandmother. For the story passed to her even through her own grandmother and her mother. Both of whom also heard the tale."

Then Oume turned to Clementine. "And do you believe the story, child?"

"I do not know what to believe," Clementine said.

Oume smiled. "You need to believe, young one," she said. Then she took Clementine's hands in hers and said, "I can feel it in my fingers. I can feel it in the blood."

"But there have been other daughters in my family," Clementine replied. "Women born of women."

"That may be true. But that does not matter. For the blood passes in one line only. I can feel it in your hands."

Clementine was silent, her eyes fixed on the old woman's face.

Then Oume turned to Professor Manes. "Do you believe it, too?" she asked.

Professor Manes smiled then did not smile. "I do not know if I should believe or not believe. I only know I have brought her to you."

Oume turned back to Clementine. "We were never the same people after Donyan was stolen. The slavers took away our hope."

Clementine continued to be silent.

"But we women of the Kru, we have spoken in secret for all of the generations. Some had visions. Some heard voices. I only know what I have been told and what I feel in your hands, child."

"What do you feel in my hands?" Clementine said in a whisper.

"That you carry the blood. That your heart is good. That you will make peace for us with the Great Mother."

"How can I do that? What must I do?"

Oume released Clementine's hands and stepped closer to her, reaching out and touching Clementine's belly. "You will grow large one day with a girl child." Then she hesitated. "You will not birth a boy child. That is not your task. You will birth a girl child." For a moment Oume stopped moving her hands over Clementine's belly and looked into Clementine's dark eyes. Then she slowly touched Clementine's loins, holding her hands in place for several moments, her eyes closed, as if she was listening. Clementine did not flinch or move or stop looking at the old woman. Then Oume opened her eyes and said, "There will be two."

"Two daughters?" Clementine said.

"Yes. Twins. Two daughters. Two at once, child." Then Oume's expression showed her concern. "It will be difficult for you, dear one." Then she looked at Clementine and then at me. "He will care for you," she said. "He understands who you are. He will take care of you." Then Oume looked at Clementine again and stepped back so she could see her whole body. "That is all I can say to you. You need nothing more from me. You have brought me joy. I will weep now this night like an old woman. But do not be afraid. I weep for all of the women who have come and gone without knowing you." She looked at Clementine again. "Your beauty is her beauty. Your beauty is your own. Your beauty is in your heart."

Clementine was silent. I was silent. Professor Manes rested for a moment. Then the old woman began speaking again, and he resumed translating in his quiet voice so as not to distract Oume.

"Your daughters will be joyful," Oume said. "They will carry the blood. They will be happy and be mothers of daughters. You must care for them. They will look to you. I look to you. You have closed the circle that was broken when our hearts were broken. You are very brave." Then she stopped speaking for a moment and looked at me and then looked back at Clementine. "What else do you wish of me?" she said in a whisper.

Clementine did not answer. I did not think it was my place to answer.

"She wishes to know what else you wish of her," Professor Manes said to Clementine and then to me.

Clementine hesitated. She looked at me. I did not speak, but she understood what I was thinking. She turned back to Professor Manes. "We have come to have her or someone like her say marriage words to us. We have come so I might stand on a hill and see into the distance of a place like this."

Professor Manes nodded. He understood. He turned to Oume and explained what we wished. The old woman smiled and said something in response. Professor Manes turned back to us. "We are to go to the trees," he said, gesturing toward the edge of the village. "We are to wait there. She says she understands. She says that what you wish is good. That it will heal many wounds. So we should do what she says."

With that Professor Manes and Sierra and Clementine and I walked across the village to the stand of trees that edged the village to the north. From among the trees on the rise of land that marked the edge of the trees, we could see the land fall away and then rise again to the mountains. Professor urged us to drink water, which all of us did.

"Do we need to do anything?" Clementine said.

"I don't think so," Professor Manes said.

"I think we just need to wait," Sierra said, her husband translating for us. "These old women . . . women like Oume . . . they know what they know. There is nothing any of us can do or tell them."

By then Clementine had moved away from the three of us and was standing just beyond the trees looking north across the landscape. I was unsure as to what I should do.

Should I leave her to her own thoughts? Should I move to her side and simply reassure her that I was there? Should I say something to her?

Clementine turned back to me and held out her hands. I moved to her and took her hands and let her turn back again to the distance. "This is why your grandfather wished for me to come, isn't it, Tyler?" she said quietly.

"I think it was."

"And my mother. Do you think she knew too?"

I waited for a moment. "If anyone knew, it was your mother."

"She should have been here with me, Tyler," Clementine said.

"Maybe," I said. "Or maybe not. It's your role, Clementine, not your mother's. It's you who need to be here."

Clementine did not respond so after a moment I left her to continue her vigil as I returned to Professor Manes and Sierra Manes where I waited. We did not have to wait long. For in a moment, we saw five old women moving towards us, led by Oume. All of them were garbed in long dashiki. All of them were smiling. One of the women was carrying a jug of what proved to be water. Two of the women were carrying a long cloth sash. All of them were carrying small decorated hand fans.

The woman with the water jug came to the two of us and after pouring water into her hands washed our faces, wiping away the dust of the day. Then the women all moved to us and touched our faces. Then they stood us side by side and formed a circle around us. Professor Manes and Sierra stood outside the circle.

Then Oume began a chant that Professor Manes did not try to translate. He did not need to. Neither Clementine nor I understood the words, but we did not need to understand them to understand their intent. For in the chant, in her low throated sing song voice, Oume spoke words that were so slowly said and so rich in their sound that I felt as if it was the words not just the wind through the trees that was caressing our faces, caressing our bodies. Then one of the other women stepped forward and said something more. Then another woman did the same. Then one by one, each of them came and touched Clementine's face and touched my face. Then the two women who had carried the long sash moved to us and bound our hands together and wrapped the sash around our waists and tied a knot. Then Oume said more words to us, and the women all stood in the circle and said words to us. Then they all smiled, and the sash was untied, and each one of the women came to each of us and kissed us on our cheeks. Professor Manes signaled to me from where he stood that we should kiss the women's hands. So both Clementine and I kissed each woman's hands. Then it was over. It was as simple and complex and profound as that. It was over. We had been married by Kru Wise Women in a small African village simultaneously removed from our world in America by miles and generations yet connected to our world in America by centuries of pain and joy and endurance and hope. And so everything my grandfather and Ruth Ann had wanted for us had happened. Everything Clementine had wanted to happen had happened. And I stood side by side with my darling Clementine in the wind moving through the trees, wondering, as I still find myself wondering many times when I look at Clementine when she is not looking at me or looking at Clementine when she is asleep, who is this woman and how did I ever end up with this woman and why have I been so blessed to be loved by this woman? And although I would most sincerely like to have the answers to those questions, I am also wise enough to know that I will never know the answers to those questions, so I do not push my luck or worry my mind. It is pointless. It is futile and pointless. Life is what life is. And I knew then and know now that I came to that conclusion while standing side by side with Clementine in the wind among the trees in the village in Africa—that it would be best to simply let be what would be and be glad. I decided to simply and forever be very, very glad.

48

Two days later, Clementine and I said our goodbyes to Professor and Sierra Manes at the airport in Abidjan. Hours later we were in our hotel in Cairo. Although she had been sincerely cordial with both Paulist and Sierra Manes during our final hours with them and had expressed her appreciation for all that they had done for us when we said goodbye at the airport, she said very little on the airplane, a silence that I ascribed to what must have been complex and possibly conflicted feelings as she sat at the window looking down at the African landscape as we made our way north.

In Cairo, she was much the same. We attended to travel duties, made our way to our hotel, unpacked enough for our overnight stay, ate a light meal, and then went to sleep. I did not want to press her to explain her feelings for I knew her well enough to know that she would start to talk when she was ready. However, on our flight to Paris, where we were scheduled to stay for three days, while she did not offer what might be interpreted as decisions about her individual reflections or conclusions about our shared experiences, she did turn to me three times and start to say something before she cut herself off and went back to looking at the marvelous Mediterranean and then Italian vistas out of the window. Once, she did turn to me and say, "Do you understand what it meant?" To which I said, "Do I understand what you mean by 'what it meant?'" But she did not explain further, so I could not respond to her question. Five minutes later, she turned back to me and said, "The slave holds. Where they were kept before they were put on ships."

I said I still didn't know what she was asking me. I said I could certainly understand it was a painful experience for her, but I did not know what she was asking me to say. So she turned back to the window and did not say anything more about whatever it was she was thinking.

When we landed in Paris, I could tell she had lost interest in touring the art museums, even though she had expressed regret when we'd passed through Paris earlier that we only had one day. That was when I had to make a decision about how best to respond. Yes, I certainly understood that what she had experienced was a combination of pain and revulsion and wonderment and reward. I even understood that it had turned into much more than my grandfather or Ruth Ann or I had ever envisioned for Clementine. At the same time, watching her, loving her as I did, I was unwilling to let her silence keep us from doing what I knew she had wanted to do when we'd made our original plans. So without consulting her further on the matter, but sensitive to her moment by moment responses, I went ahead and took her to places we had agreed on the flight over to Paris that we wanted to see. As I look back now on those individual yet connected experiences, I believe that her responses in Paris were as telling as her responses in Africa.

When I took her to the Rodin Museum, because he is our favorite sculptor, I watched Clementine as much as I looked at the work. What was most interesting and, I have come to believe, most telling, is the way in which she moved close to each piece and stood with her hands extended, moving them over the works without touching the art, as if she was feeling an invisible energy that Rodin had invested. I tried to not let her see me watching her, but as she moved among the sculptures, I felt as if I was watching a child who had been blind all of her life who suddenly one day wakes up and can see so she has to go into the world and feel without touching all of the things she had not been able to see before. When we went to the Musee d'Orsay, her reaction was equally telling.

The Musee d'Orsay was once a great, rectangular railway station. When it was turned into a museum so works that had not been displayed at the Louvre could be shown, the architect retained the great arcing windows at each end of the rectangle and the extraordinarily high vaulted ceiling. In doing so, a balcony area was created from which one can see the crowds down in the galleries as they move from painting to painting and sculpture to sculpture. When we arrived at the museum, Clementine said she wanted to stay on the balcony. When I started to protest that doing so would mean she would not see the paintings, she said, "I don't want to see them. I want to watch you looking at them." When I expressed my concern that for me to look at the works in even a cursory manner might take two hours, she said that was fine. "I want to wait. I want to watch you." So I left her on the balcony, although as I moved through the partitioned sections of the gallery I could see her at the same time she was seeing me.

The second day in the morning we went to the Louvre, which Clementine had always said she wanted very much to tour. But when we got there, she said all she wanted to see was the Mona Lisa.

I will admit that before I saw the Mona Lisa in person, I had always assumed that actually seeing the painting might end up being a less moving experience than the anticipation promised. But I was wrong. We stood together and looked at what may well be the most moving portrait ever painted. I'm not sure I can really make that claim with any certainty, but I can at least argue sincerely that it is a penetrating experience. What was even more interesting to me was Clementine's comment as we left when she said, "I know what she's thinking." When I asked her what that might be, she said, "I'll tell you someday." Then she said, "I don't want to see anything else, Tyler." Before I could ask her why, she said, "Anything else will be artificial." Then she said, "I want to walk along Des Champs Elysees with you." So that is what we did.

That afternoon, following a lunch of crepes bought from a street vender, we went to the Musee de l'Orangerie to see the two oval Monet water lily mural rooms, which for me remains the most profound experience any one who loves art can have any where in the world. As we stood in the middle of the first room, Clementine put a hand on my back and said, "Go ahead." When I turned to her and asked her what she meant, she said, "Go ahead and move closer. You know you want to look at the brush strokes. Go ahead and move closer." So I did. And all the while, Clementine stood in the middle of the room and watched me. When I moved along the length of the paintings, glancing over my shoulder at her as I did, she was watching me. When we went into the second room, she did the same thing: watch me as I inspected the paintings as closely as I dared go and then from farther away. What I remember most clearly is that as we left the museum and started walking back toward our hotel, Clementine took my hand and said, "For a moment I thought I'd lost you."

Without looking at her I replied, "You will never lose me, Clementine."

She did not say anything in reply, but I felt her hand grip mine even more firmly as if she did not want me to get lost in the crowd or as if she did not want to get lost as we continued walking.

On our last day in Paris, we started by going to Notre Dame, and while I must confess I was more interested in the ancient Celtic ruins that were being excavated under the cathedral, we joined other tourists in climbing to the top of the cathedral from which we had a wonderful view of parts of the city, so wonderful, in fact, that she said it made her want to go back to the Eiffel Tower one more time, which I was glad to do since her request was the first she had made during those three days. In fact, she had been so quiet that I had begun to fear her trip to Africa had done her more harm than good, my fear underscored when we arrived at the Eiffel Tower early in the evening as the lights of the city were beginning to rise against the descending dusk. For after we had ridden as far as we could on the elevator and then walked on up to the observation platform and stood in the evening breeze, where she had pressed herself into my arms just days before when we had come to the Tower the first time, this time she stood away from me, looking into the distance, pulling farther and farther away I feared. But I should not have been so quick to judge or feel insecure. What she was doing, I now know, was carefully and deliberately finding her way back to me. I know that because, after we had left the observation platform and gone inside the restaurant where we sat drinking coffee, without any prelude, she reached across the table and took my hand and said very quietly, "Thank you for marrying me, Tyler."

I had been looking out at the city when she spoke because I had been afraid to look at her. Hearing her voice, hearing the animation that I had so feared she might have lost somewhere in the pain that Africa could not help but represent, I turned to her and said in the best Georgia accent I could muster, "Clementine Camille Brown, I will marry you over and over again as long as you are willing."

She smiled her I am delighted smile and said, "I don't think we'll have to do it again since we've now gotten married three times."

"I know," I said, lapsing back into my own more normal voice, "But I just want you to know that I'll say whatever words you want me to say any time and any place you want me to say them. Just as long as it ends up with us being together."

Clementine smiled and started to turn away. Then she turned back to me and said, "But what does it mean, Tyler? What's it supposed to mean?"

"What is what supposed to mean?" I said.

"That Oume . . . that the other Kru women . . . that they think I'm the long lost granddaughter of their Stolen Princess," she said. "What's that supposed to mean to me, Tyler?"

I smiled. "I don't know what it's supposed to mean to them or to you. All I know is that you're not lost, Clementine. You're the most found person I've ever known."

She looked at me for a moment. "I don't understand what you mean, Tyler. How in the world am I the most found person you've ever known?" she asked.

"Because I found you, Clementine, and you found me. And I love you, and you love me," I said. "You can't get more found than that."

Clementine's expression said she was not sure I was right, but she wasn't prepared to argue. She took a sip of her coffee. After a moment, she looked at me and smiled and said, "Tyler, let's go home. It's time. I want to go home."

Part Four

"Nothing can be as astounding as life," Saim said exultantly, "except writing."

Orham Pamuk
The Black Book

1

By November, Clementine and I were settled into our separate studies. She continued her interest in microbiology, focusing on childhood diseases and pediatrics at the Georgia Medical College. Her ambition was to join a private children's medical practice as well as give time to children's community health clinics.

At the same time, I had started my teaching at Augusta College, which at first was rather intimidating. It is one thing to be a student; it is quite another to be the teacher responsible for both designing and guiding students through a body of material. In my case, the task was made somewhat easier because the course was the required Western Civilizations class that most incoming first year college students have to fulfill. In addition, my departmental mentor, Briggs Dyer, a man of considerable experience and even more expertise, proved to be an invaluable aid. For instance, as he reviewed my syllabus and plans for essays and examinations, he helped me avoid the mistake of over teaching, which almost every first year teacher at any level makes if left unadvised. In the end then, what I really did was offer Professor Dyer's course, with my added insights and ambitions worked in as gracefully as possible.

Because I was contracted to teach two sections and to enroll in four graduate courses, I was able to plunge into the program of study that I had designed with Professor Jack McAndrew, at the University of Georgia, calling on Lynne Hull to guide me through a number of pitfalls. My focus was then and remains today the social history of African Black American culture in the south. From the first day, the courses were both interesting and enlightening. I felt as if new levels of understanding were unfolding every week. While I discussed some of my reading with Clementine, because she had still to define in more detail her feelings about everything she had experienced in going to Africa the summer before, I did not press the materials on her, but let her draw me into conversations about my reading.

That first Thanksgiving, our mothers both came to Augusta to celebrate with us. That proved to be a wonderfully rich occasion for all four of us. Clementine and I had thought about inviting other people to our apartment because we had done so much of that in Athens, but we decided against it. After all, both Ruth Ann and Elizabeth only had Wednesday through Sunday for their vacations, and Wednesday was largely consumed by flying from Tampa to Atlanta and Atlanta to Augusta. Because we didn't want them to feel obligated to spend all of their time cooking, Clementine and I prepared as much of the food as we could during the week before they arrived.

Although I don't think either Clementine or I expected it to be so emotional, as much as we looked forward to seeing them, when Ruth Ann and my mother came through the doorway into the airport waiting room in Augusta, both of us found tears welling up in our eyes. For a moment, I didn't understand what I was feeling. When I looked at Clementine, who by then had put a hand on my right arm, I did. Here we were, married, living in a city a long way away from Tampa, at the start of the next phase of our life together, and there they were, our beloved mothers, now constant companions and best friends . . . the two women who had steadfastly stood by us as we grew up individually, as we grew up together . . . who had loved us and taught us to love . . . laughing as they came toward us not just because they were happy to see us, but because, we would learn later, Ruth Ann, as usual, had been telling my mother a funny story. When that laughter became part of their obvious joy at seeing us, two adults doing with our lives exactly what we had said we wanted to do, the moment was almost overwhelming. So as each of us embraced each of them, the hurt that my grandfather was not there to share in the joy was evident but only momentary. For I could see the same emotion in their eyes as well. And as if those expressions served as a warning, we all turned away from our shared anguish and focused, instead, on the rush of happiness that we all felt.

As we gathered up their suitcases and walked to my car, Clementine and Ruth Ann were arm in arm. My mother did the same with me. Settling into the car, with Clementine and Ruth Ann in the back seat, and my mother in the passenger's seat while I drove, the first thing both mothers said was that they wanted to see our apartment. When I told them that would have to wait, they wanted to know why.

"It's time for dinner. So we're taking you to the Boll Weevil, our favorite restaurant, which is downtown near the Savannah River walk," I said. "We're not going to let you just sit around our apartment," I said.

"We've got a whole new city to show you," Clementine added.

"And two new schools to show you," I said.

Both Ruth Ann and Elizabeth said that would be fine. They looked forward to anything we wanted to share.

Twenty minutes later, after having ordered, we were sitting over glasses of red wine. Ruth Ann took the initiative and raised her glass in salute to Clementine and me. "To the continued health and happiness of my two favorite people in the whole world," she said.

We raised our glasses. "We cannot possibly tell the two of you how proud we are of everything you are doing," my mother said. "And who you are together."

Then Clementine did something I think she had been waiting all of her life to do. Raising her own glass, she turned first to Ruth Ann and then to my mother and said, "And to the two women who have been with us every step of the way. And who we love," she said, looking at me as I joined her in her toast.

"Here, here," I said, for there was nothing more I needed to say. The three most important women in my life had said it all.

2

The conversation that first evening was directed discreetly by Ruth Ann toward the issue of race when she quietly asked how we felt we had been received in Augusta.

"By white people, do you mean?" I said.

"Yes," she replied.

I took a deep breath, looking at Clementine as I did. "I can only speak for my own perceptions, Ruth Ann. I certainly can't speak for Clementine," I said.

"I know. But I want to know what you think," she said.

"Frankly, I haven't felt any hostility so far," I said. "I'm not saying some folks haven't looked at us when we've gone to movies, which we try to do so we won't end up studying all of the time. Maybe someone in the audience around us looked at us and wondered about us or maybe didn't like it that we were together. But certainly no one's said anything."

"What about at college?" she said.

"I don't know. Clementine was with me when I interviewed. No one seemed at all concerned. And there are African American students on campus. I have a racially mixed class. Maybe not as much as it should be, but I've been told the numbers are going up every year just like they are everywhere else. And with what I teach, Western Civilization, with the focus on European society, there isn't much space in the text about the slave trade, although my advisor, Briggs Dyer, has provided me with materials to use, because he includes it himself, and he knows it's my focus. We aren't far enough yet, but we will be soon. I'll just have to see how that goes."

Ruth Ann turned to Clementine. "What about you?" she said.

"Do you mean, am I aware of anything at the Medical College?"

"Yes."

"I'm not sure. I try not to pay attention. Are there professors in the college who don't want me there? I don't know. I've never heard anything. Are there students who wonder if I'm qualified? Maybe. There are three black men in my class. I heard one of them say something about it during the first week. But we haven't talked about it since. We're too busy trying to keep up, mother. So I just go to school and try to do the work and try to be nice to everyone. So far everyone's been nice to me."

"I'm not sure what you want us to say, Ruth Ann. We go to school and do our studies and come home at night and are together," I said.

"I'm not trying to get you to say anything in particular, Tyler. I just want to know what you've perceived."

I waited for a moment. "I know Augusta, like all of Georgia, has a difficult race history. I know it's gone through difficult periods of time even recently. It will undoubtedly go through more. Racism is deeply ingrained in the American psyche, after all. I don't have to tell you that. But at least so far, I don't think Clementine and I have faced any overt prejudice."

"Is that because you're educated?" my mother said.

I turned to her. "Do you mean, is it easier for whites to be prejudiced against uneducated blacks than against educated blacks?"

"Yes. That's exactly what I mean," she said.

"What do you think?" I said, turning to Clementine.

"You're probably right," Clementine said to my mother. "At least socially. The people we're around—both of us—they're educated, so they tend to accept anyone else who's educated. As for poor black people—I don't know how they feel about them. So maybe what we're seeing is another kind of prejudice. Class prejudice. It's just since we're not part of the uneducated class, we can't speak for what they experience."

"And that would apply to whites as well as blacks," I said quickly.

Ruth Ann nodded. "You're probably right. That's what I sense on the campus at South Florida. But when I go into Tampa, even in the best department stores, I feel something else."

"But you're dressed well, mother," Clementine said. "I can't imagine anyone thinking you were a poor black woman."

"Well, if they do, then they don't know anything about style," Ruth Ann said, smiling.

"But we've seen it when we were together, Tyler," my mother said. "When Ruth Ann and I go into a department store. I can see clerks looking at her but not at me. And when we go into a restaurant . . . not all restaurants . . . but some. The waiter or waitress will turn to me first. I've even had them give me the check rather than Ruth Ann. So it may be 1988, and things may have changed . . . at least in big ways. But that doesn't mean it isn't still there."

"I'm sure it's still there, mother," I said. "I don't think Clementine or I are saying it isn't there. I'm just saying . . . and I think she's saying . . . that so far, at least, in Augusta—on the College campus and the Medical College campus—we haven't run into anything that was obvious."

"But that doesn't mean we won't," Clementine said. "Because we assume that one day we will."

"And what then?" Ruth Ann said.

I smiled. "Well, we've gotten pretty good at deflecting the hurt when it shows up, Ruth Ann."

"We got pretty good at it in Africa, mother," Clementine said. "Because there were people we saw around us in Ivory Coast and in Liberia who looked as if they didn't like the idea of a black woman with a white man, that was for sure."

"Really?" Ruth Ann said.

"Mother, why would it be different there? C'mon. People are people. The Africans have their own history of racial prejudice."

"But isn't that justified, Clementine?" Ruth Ann said. "Just look at their history."

"I'm not saying their history doesn't justify it," Clementine said. "Maybe it does. I'm just saying that in more than one public place, after the people looked at me and wondered where I'd come from, they looked at Tyler, and they didn't like that he was with me."

"But we didn't feel it in Paris," I said. "That was the interesting part. In fact, the sense I got from a number of French men as they looked at Clementine and then looked at me was that they were envious." I said.

"Ah, yes. The black vixen," Ruth Ann said.

"I don't think it was that," I said. "I don't think it was as much that Clementine is black as it is that she's beautiful. French men like men everywhere love looking at beautiful women. And like men everywhere, they admire and maybe even envy other men who are with beautiful women. So I don't think it was race, Ruth Ann. I think it was beauty."

"But you can't know that for sure, can you," Ruth Ann said.

"No, I can't know that for sure just like I can't know for sure what anyone who looks at us is thinking," I said.

"Which is why Tyler and I have made a pact, mother," Clementine said.

"A pact? What kind of pact?" Ruth Ann asked.

"We've decided that because we can't know what someone else is thinking, unless that person says something to us, we've decided that we just won't worry about it," Clementine said.

"Really?" Ruth Ann replied.

"Because there isn't any point," I said quietly. "What someone else thinks has nothing to do with us," I said.

Ruth Ann was quiet for a moment. Then she nodded and looked at my mother. "They're pretty smart, wouldn't you agree, Elizabeth?"

All four of us laughed. "Yes, I would," my mother said. "Pretty *and* smart." But neither of them looked convinced. And as had happened before, they would be correct. It would not be as easy as we had hoped.

The next day, we all got up early and after a light breakfast began preparing the meal together. As we did, Ruth Ann asked what it had been like for us to go to Athens for football games when I wasn't a member of the team. I admitted that it felt odd at first watching other people, many of whom I still knew, playing a game that I'd played for so many years. At the same time, I said, it was a whole lot less painful. "No aches and pains the day after," I said. "Or the rest of the week."

I told Ruth Ann and my mother that I was still in contact with Barbara and Vince Dooley. "When I told them both of you were coming for Thanksgiving, they asked me to extend their greetings."

"Does Coach Dooley still wish you'd stayed on to play a fourth year?" my mother asked.

"We don't talk about it," I said. "He's focused on what he's doing now. So am I. He respects that."

The rest of our conversation dealt with what our mothers were doing in Tampa. They assumed that we were coming there for the Winter Holiday from our schools.

"This is the only year I'll have a real winter vacation," Clementine said. "After this, I'll be too far into my studies to leave for very long."

"So the answer is, yes, we are coming to Tampa for two weeks in December," I said, finishing Clementine's explanation.

By 1 P.M., I'd turned on a professional football game, which we watched without much interest. By 3 P.M., we were all gathered around the table eating. The conversation for the rest of the day and into the evening had to do with other members of Clementine's New Jersey family: who was living where; who was doing what.

We then told our mothers that we'd been invited to a small gathering of Augusta College faculty and friends at a home in the city. When they started to protest they probably shouldn't go with us, we assured them that they were personally invited by Briggs Dyer, who very much wanted to meet both of them. "He's read Grandpa's books," I told them. "And he's read your lectures with Grandpa, Ruth Ann. So he wants to meet you in particular."

As I look back on the rest of the academic year, it feels as if it passed very quickly. Our only real break was our trip to Tampa in December. What both Clementine and I found was that had we not been married and living together, we would have had very little time shared. If we weren't on the campuses of our respective schools, we were home buried in books. The only time we really had together—and we made a promise that we would some how or other fix time to be together—was Sunday mornings when we lay together in bed as long as we could before hunger drove us to the kitchen. After showering and eating, we would then sit together some place away from our books and away from any reminders we needed to clean the apartment, and we would drink coffee and talk. Later in the year, we found a nice neighborhood coffee shop that also served bagels. After that, we always went there every Sunday morning, walking the five blocks each way no matter the weather. We called it our private time. For us, it was sacred.

Then all of a sudden, the year was over. Clementine had excelled in all of her course and laboratory work, as I had said she would. I had plunged head first into reading both the history of the South in the broadest sense, and the history of chattel slavery as it both threatened to destroy Black African culture and begin warping white social psychology. For from the beginning, I could see that the violence affected both races. It might not seem that would be true, but as much as the slave suffers the most in any system of repression, it can also be argued with authority, I believe, that the slave master suffers another kind of lasting corruption. I am not arguing that the slave master society needs anyone's sympathy. Certainly not in the way slaves deserve compassion for what they endure, but there is no denying that the full humanity that might have developed in the slave master society had it not engaged in such a reprehensible practice is warped in ways it does not understand at the time and may not understand for centuries.

My reading of both black and white writers asked me to visit the conflict from obviously widely differing points of view. Ironically and sadly, I concluded, on many occasions the writers representing the two races were much closer in their definitions of the pain each was suffering than either probably understood.

What was most difficult for me, of course, was researching primary source journals describing the chattel slave system as set down by white men. The insensitive, callous, and matter-of-fact tone of voice in which their accounts are narrated brought me to tears sometimes, to profanity on other occasions, for just like Nazi writers detailing the capture, deporting, and murder of Jews and Roma peoples during the Holocaust about which I would read in later years, white slave owners never once questioned their moral authority to enslave members of the black race for the purpose of their own economic gain. When I sat at night reading materials of that sort and Clementine asked me what I was studying, I found myself evading her questions, saying things like, "Just some old journals" or "statistical stuff" or "just routine background." Interestingly enough, even though her eyes told me she knew I was not telling the whole truth, she took my inexact answer as a signal that I didn't want to discuss the material with her. It was the first time that I found myself bringing a racial self-consciousness into our relationship. Given where my studies would lead me in the future, it is a wonder that we managed to keep the issue at bay. And as much as I would like to take some credit for our having avoided any intrusion of that sort into our love for one another, in all honesty I really have to credit Clementine. She was sensitive to my discomfort. When she saw it, she did not press the matter. Rather, she let me walk around it and then return to her in some other way by starting a conversation about some entirely unrelated topic. Most often, I did so by asking her questions about what she was doing, because to me it was all fascinating. I was going to spend my life teaching ideas; she was going to spend her life healing children who had become ill. I didn't have to think very hard to see which one I thought mattered most.

The two weeks we spent in Tampa were about as relaxed as Clementine and I were going to be for the next three and a half years. I remember one day when I lay in bed awake and then back asleep again and then awake and then back asleep again until noon. I'd never done anything like that since my surgery. I've never done it since. But I must admit that it brought me a very interesting sense of peace and security to hear my mother's voice and Clementine's voice and then even Ruth Ann's voice from the kitchen talking as they went about what ever they were doing. It may have been one of the most wonderful centering experiences I've ever had, at least until our daughters were born and I heard them and Clementine in the kitchen, although as you also might expect, those times in bed did not last very long before one or both of the girls were in the room jumping on the bed and laughing and crawling all over me until I got up.

In any case, with no appointments or obligations, except some reading that I wanted to do in preparation for our return to Augusta, the two weeks were sweet and easy. At the same time, when they were over, and Clementine and I were driving back to Augusta, we had an interesting conversation about wanting to get back to work.

"It was an odd feeling, Tyler," Clementine said as we crossed the Florida border into Georgia. "But yesterday, I was ready to go. I was ready to get back to our apartment and our life together."

"I understand," I said quietly, looking out of the window as Clementine drove. "I love them both. And the house is wonderful. Which both of them deserve. And playing golf with them was a trip. I really didn't think they'd be so good. But I know what you mean. I remember what you said in Paris on our last day. 'Tyler, let's go home. It's time. I want to go home.'"

"You remember that?" Clementine asked.

"I always remember what you say."

"Then I'd better be more careful about what I say."

I laughed. "Don't be. I love what you say."

"Really?"

"Really. That's why I remember."

5

As you might well have figured out by now, Clementine and I were being naïve if we thought that the issue of race was not going to intrude on our lives. We were living in Georgia, after all. That should have be enough warning.

It started one Saturday morning when Clementine was not in class and I had no reading to do that couldn't wait. We decided to steal some time together by having breakfast at the International House of Pancakes on Washington Avenue, which by then was our favorite early morning and sometimes late evening restaurant.

On Friday, the day before, Clementine had by accident listened to part of a discussion on a local radio station about the Georgia state flag, which was reminiscent of the Confederate Flag when Southern States tried to leave the union, which in turn started the Civil War. Apparently a white man was arguing that the Confederate Flag was a symbol of a long standing and broadly social heritage that deserved to be honored. By contrast, and for good reason, a black man called into the radio station and said that, as far as he was concerned, the so called heritage the Confederate Flag symbolized was in fact the enslavement of his people by the white people. He said he saw it as a vile reminder of a criminal act perpetrated by one economic class so they might stay in power, and that only a truly ignorant man would be willing to argue otherwise.

Needless to say, that comment triggered an angry outburst by the first caller, the white man, which then erupted into a name calling contest that very quickly evidenced the radio host's sympathy for the people who wanted to defend retaining the Confederate Flag as a Georgia symbol. At that point, Clementine had arrived at the Medical College and couldn't listen to any more, although she said there probably wouldn't have been anything else worth hearing. "It was going to be a name calling contest from that point on, I assumed. Probably the only word that wouldn't get on the air was nigger. But all the coded words probably did."

I agreed with her that since it was now 1989, nigger may not have made the cut. But she was also right in thinking every other code word for nigger and nigger hater and nigger lover probably would have. At the same time, that radio argument should have been a warning to us.

With that, as we crossed the parking lot and went into the restaurant, where we were greeted by the wonderfully friendly black waitresses who take care of us, which always allows us to relax into both our meal and our conversation. But those women and their good intentions also allowed us on that occasion to do what we had been doing since that night on the Georgia campus when we'd been confronted by three young white men bent on doing us no good who had fled when three of my black teammates had shown up and taken charge of the situation: walk around the mine field by acting like it was not there even if both of us suspected that it was a romantic but naïve notion and a very poor defense.

As I look back on that first year in Augusta, for all of the wonderful experiences we both had then and still continue to have today, it is clear we should have been more honest with ourselves and with each other. It is clear we should have been more prepared. My only explanation is that it took some time for the matter to make itself evident—it took more than a year, in fact—but when it did, neither of us should have been surprised. That we were shows how hard we had unconsciously worked, without realizing we were, at avoiding the complex social reality in which we had chosen to live. So I will start with what happened to me, because it was only when I confided in Clementine about the incident that she then confided in me.

6

I make no claims about my appeal to the young women whom I taught at Augusta College. I am not the first nor will I be the last young instructor to find himself in an awkward conversation with a female student who, for her own reasons, expresses an interest in him that is inappropriate to their professional relationship. With that said, what turned what I assumed was an academic meeting with one specific young woman into a difficult situation was not just that she hinted at an interest in me that was not just personal, she came at it from the point of view of race.

It began one morning during my second year at Augusta College. I had, by then, become comfortable with the classes I taught and comfortable in the campus surroundings, particularly in my office in one of the older and rather charming buildings. In any case, I was sitting in my office when a young woman knocked on my open door and asked if she might come in and talk to me about the essay she was due to write and submit the next week. I said yes, she could. With that, she came in and sat down and we had what seemed like a perfectly normal discussion of how she wished to approach the assignment and how many critical sources she needed to use to support her thesis. When that discussion ended, and I assumed it had ended well, for she seemed to know what she wished to achieve, she stood and thanked me and started to leave. However, as she did, she turned to the one of the ceiling-high built-in bookshelves that stood on either side of my door and paused. When I looked up to see if she had more questions, I found her looking at the pictures of Clementine and me that I had once had on display in my room at the University of Georgia. She glanced at me for a moment then moved to the other bookshelf, which while it was primarily crowded with books, also had two pictures of Clementine and one of us together standing on an eye level shelf. After a moment, she turned and said, "This is your wife, isn't it, Mr. Raymond."

I replied that it was. I said that her name was Clementine.

"I heard she's a student at the Georgia Medical College," the young women went on.

I said, "Yes. That's right. We graduated from Georgia together. Now we're here in Augusta."

She nodded for a moment and then stood looking at me as if she had more to say. I waited because I did not know if my assumption was correct or not.

"She's a black woman, isn't she, Mr. Raymond?"

I did not like the question. I did not like the look in her eyes. She was a very blonde young woman. Her accent was very definitely southern Georgia or perhaps Alabama. "Yes, Clementine is African-American," I said very quietly, using the racial term that was by then becoming more and more used, at least in intelligent and polite society.

"But you're not African-American," the young woman said, her voice just slightly but very definitely mocking the term *African-American*.

"No, I am not," said, my voice growing more grim, certainly more unsettled.

"I was just curious," she said softly.

I did not know if I should respond in some way that would tell her to get out of my office and leave me alone or not respond at all, which I hoped would be signal enough. She apparently took my silence for interest in what she had to say.

"So you're a mixed-race couple," she said in what sounded to me like a mock and overly polite Southern woman's attempt at genteel coyness.

I was not about to respond to that. I should have told her that my private life was none of her business, but I also did not want to extend this conversation any further. Then she dropped the bomb. "The reason I ask is that two of my other white female friends and I were talking about you just yesterday."

The tone of voice she used in saying *white female friends* was the most arrogantly and racially charged expression I had heard since I didn't know when. But by now I was very nervous. This conversation was going no where good very quickly. I wanted to say,

"Well, frankly my dear, I don't give a damn about what you and your white female friends may have been saying about my wife," but I didn't. I knew there were two possible dangers in this conversation, and I didn't want to confront either of them. But she was not about to leave yet. She had come to say something, and she was obviously going to get it done no matter how embarrassed it made me.

"We were just wondering if you've ever been with a white woman, Mr. Raymond."

I could not believe what she had just said. I came out of my seat as quickly as I could and stood looking at her for a moment. I responded by saying that her question was inappropriate in the extreme. When she started to move her mouth into what looked to me more like a snarl than a smile, I moved past her as quickly as I could and stepped into the outer hallway. I'm not sure what I had in mind, but I knew I needed help. Fortunately, I saw one of the history Department female instructors coming toward her own office, which was opposite mine. I asked her to come into my office. My tone of voice must have alarmed her, because she did so without questioning what I wanted. As she entered, I stepped back so she could see the female student, who by then was standing in the middle of the room between my desk and the bookshelves.

I am stuck here in telling the story, because as much as I would like to use the names of both of the women, I don't think that is a wise course of action. What I did do however was say, "Miss _______ and I have been talking, and I fear her comments have become too personal. I believe she should leave my office. I would appreciate it if you would tell her that she should do so."

For a moment, my teaching peer did not know what to do. There I was, a man in my middle twenties, standing in my office with a very attractive female student who could not have been more than twenty, asking her, a teaching friend in her middle thirties, to join me in asking a student to leave my office. I don't blame her, but her question, "Do you want me to call security?" didn't help at all.

"No. That isn't necessary. I would simply prefer that this conversation end," I said.

My teaching peer then turned to the student and said very politely, "I don't know what's been said here, but apparently, Mr. Raymond is not comfortable with you in his office. So I would suggest that you leave."

The young woman looked at me and then looked at her. "Am I going to be in trouble?" she said, her tone of voice both a plea and a threat. "Are you going to report me to someone?" she said, turning to me.

"No," I said. "There is nothing to report," I said. "I would simply prefer that our conversation end," I said with as much composure as I could muster.

The young woman looked at me for a moment. I could not tell if she was relieved or angry. I looked away. My teaching friend waited. Then the young woman left as quietly as she had come.

I stood with my friend for a moment before I turned and thanked her for her help. "My God, what did she say, Tyler?" she asked.

I moved to the window of my office, from which I could see part of the campus lawn. "She looked at the pictures of Clementine and me," I said. "Not at first. At first, we talked about the essay she has to write. Then she looked at the pictures of Clementine and me," I said.

My friend acted as if she did not understand.

"She wanted to know if Clementine was black, which she obviously is. So the question was a set up."

"A set up for what?" my friend said, moving to the bookshelves and looking at the pictures as I moved back behind my desk.

"For her to ask questions about us. About Clementine and me."

She turned to me. "What kind of question did she ask you, Tyler?"

"A racial question."

After a moment she said, "What did she say?"

"She wanted to know," I started to say. Then I hesitated. "She wanted to know if I've ever been with a white woman."

My friend was quiet for a moment. "Oh," she said. "Well, that certainly explains why you'd want someone to come in and hear you ask her to leave."

I nodded and started to sit down, but she was still standing, so I did not. "I certainly wasn't going to answer a question like that," I said.

"Certainly. I understand. It must have been very embarrassing."

"It wasn't just embarrassing," I said. "It was inappropriate. I don't want to know what she and her 'white female friends' wonder about."

"Her white female friends?"

"That's the term she used. She and two of her 'white female friends' wondered if I've ever been with a white woman."

My friend stood next to the door for a moment. "I can certainly understand why you wouldn't want a student to ask a thing like that, Tyler. I can certainly understand why you wouldn't want a conversation like that to go on."

I agreed with her, but I did not say anything.

"Of course, I have to confess, Tyler, that I've wondered the same thing myself."

I could not believe I had heard her correctly.

"It's a question, Tyler, that a white woman would ask, you know."

"What?"

"Tyler, please. Don't be naïve. You're an attractive man, after all. And there are adult women on this campus who wonder the same thing."

"What are you talking about?" I whispered.

"Of course, if you don't want to talk about it, then that is certainly your right. It's a very personal matter, I agree. So I'm not going to ask you about it, that's for sure. But others have wondered, Tyler. Others have wondered why you would . . . "

"She's my wife! Clementine is my wife. I love her!" I said, raising my voice in frustration and anger and confusion. "She's my wife!"

"Of course. And she's a lovely woman, Tyler. And I am sure you love one another," she said, turning toward the door. "And I'm sorry your student embarrassed you." Then without any reference to what she'd just said that was just as offensive, she left my office, with me still standing behind my desk, my hands shaking, my body rigid, trying to understand what in God's name had just happened, trying to understand what I should have done, what I might have said, what in God's name people were saying. I turned to the wall behind my desk, which was also a window that looked across the street from the campus at the commercial shops that lined the road opposite. I was shaken, I have to admit. What kind of place was this? Who were these women? What possessed them to think they could . . . .

I turned back to my desk and picked up my coffee mug and held it up as if I was going to throw it as hard as I could across the room toward the door. But then my better wisdom prevailed. After all, as angry as I was it would have been just my luck to hit some innocent person walking past my door. That wasn't going to answer my questions or salve my wound. So I put the mug down on my desk more carefully than necessary and walked to the easy chair in my room and picked up my corduroy jacket and, closing the door behind me, went for a walk on the campus until I was more calm. Sadly, it was not the last time I would have to walk off my anger that year.

7

The next day, I went to Briggs Dyer and explained what had taken place. I said that I wasn't trying to make the matter into a serious issue. I just wanted him to know. "I suppose I'm trying to insure that I'm covered in case anything more comes up."

Briggs responded by saying he thought I had handled the situation as well as it could have been handled. Having another teacher, especially a woman teacher, come in and be there when you sent the young woman on her way was very wise. "Have you said anything to Clementine about what happened?" he asked.

I said I had not.

"Are you going to?" he asked.

My hesitation suggested I was not going to.

"You might want to, Tyler. Pick your time carefully, but it's exactly the kind of thing that I can imagine would bother her if she heard about it later from someone else."

I said I would think about it. With that our conversation ended, and because I wasn't going to go say anything about what my teaching peer had said, I left and went on to one of my courses.

Three more days passed. I didn't say anything to Clementine about what took place in my office, and I didn't say anything to her about my discussion with Briggs Dyer, because I didn't have the slightest idea of how to raise the subject. As it turned out, I didn't have to.

Clementine is a remarkably intelligent person. I assume that the stories I've told about her up to this point have made that clear. I also assume that this memoir makes clear the fact that she is even more remarkably intuitive. In brief, she has been able to read me like a large print book from the first day we met. You can imagine then that it was not difficult for her to sense that something was on my mind, not by what I said, because I did one of those classic if silly male things of claming up about so many things that shouldn't have caused me any discomfort that it was obvious something more serious was wrong. In her own way, Clementine knew exactly what to do: she told me a story.

We were sitting in our living room on our love seat. It was Sunday afternoon. Each of us was reading the newspaper, which by then was scattered all over the floor. It is one of our rituals. Something she read must have triggered her sense that it was time because she turned to me and asked me a question about some sort of feature story in the *New York Times* about husbands and wives who love one another not being able to keep secrets very long.

When I turned to ask her what she meant, she said, "For instance, I've never told you about Bernard, have I?"

"Bernard who?" I said.

"Bernard Wilson. At Georgia Tech."

"Bernard Wilson at Georgia Tech?"

"Yes. I knew him. When I was a sophomore."

I put down my newspaper. Damn, was she now going to tell me that there'd been a boyfriend or something at Georgia Tech? I tried very hard to remain calm. I realized this was the second time in just one week that I'd had to be calm. I found that ironic. I also found it unpleasant.

"I didn't know him very well. We had a class together. And one of his girlfriends lived next door in the dorm," she said.

"Did I ever meet him?" I asked.

"No. I don't think so. There'd be no reason for you to meet him."

I hesitated. Was I now going to find our more than I wanted to know?

"And he never talked to me. Not outside of class at least," she said.

I felt relieved. I also felt confused. "Then what is the story you want to tell me about Bernard what's-his-name?" I said.

"Bernard Wilson."

"Okay. Bernard Wilson. What's the story you want to tell me about Bernard Wilson . . . which since you've brought it up now sounds like you think it's a secret or something?"

"It's about something he asked his girlfriend. Or least, she said he asked her. I sometimes wonder if it wasn't her question."

"You have me at an advantage, Clementine, since I don't know the question that he supposedly asked his girlfriend."

"It had to do with you, Tyler."

"With me?"

"Yes. With you."

"All right. So. What was the question?"

"Promise you won't be offended."

"Oh, no. You aren't going to trap me. How can I promise I won't be offended if I don't know what the story is? Maybe I will be offended. Maybe I should be offended. Maybe I won't be."

"Promise you will try to not be offended?"

I looked at my darling Clementine for a moment. I didn't know where she was going with her story. At the same time, I had a sneaking suspicion I knew where she was going. I didn't like either feeling.

"Apparently, according to Shelia . . . his girlfriend . . . according to Shelia, he wondered why I would be with a white man when there were so many black brothers on the campus who thought I was pretty and . . . he even said . . . sexy?"

I waited. I had learned a very long time ago to wait until I had heard all of the words rather than start planning my response when the person talking to me was only half way into the sentence.

"And you are telling me this story . . . why, Clementine?"

She sort of smiled. Not exactly smiled. Just sort of smiled. "Well, I guess it's because I've thought of it as a secret."

"You have?"

"Yes."

"You call that a secret? That some black guy wondered why you . . . a very pretty black woman—and I would have said beautiful black woman—but that's just me, Clementine. You think I shouldn't be offended because some black guy wondered if I was good enough for you? Sexually good enough for you?"

My voice had become tense. I was as aware of that as was Clementine.

"You said you wouldn't be angry."

"I said I would try."

"Well, keep on trying, Tyler. I'm not trying to upset you."

"Really?"

"Tyler, you are good enough for me. Okay? You have always been good enough for me."

"Sexually?"

"Yes, sexually. You know I've never been with another man. I've never wanted to be with another man."

"But you've thought about it? At least, you thought about it after Bernard the black guy brought it up."

"No."

"No what? That you haven't ever thought about it? Or that you haven't thought about it since Bernard brought it up?"

"No . . . both. Neither. I'm not concerned. I'm happy."

"With me?" I said, starting to stand up.

Clementine put a hand on my arm and kept me in place. "We aren't going to have an argument about sex are we?" she said.

"I don't know. Is there anything to argue about?"

"Tyler, I think it was amusing."

"Amusing?"

"Maybe that's the wrong word to use."

"Do you think?"

"All right. I thought it was silly. I can't imagine anyone being a better lover than you, Tyler. I can't imagine ever being with any other lover. That's all. I said you were the only man I would ever love. I said that when I was fifteen. And I meant it."

"So why did you bring up this secret story of yours right now? Today. While we were sitting here on the couch reading the newspaper."

"Because . . . I read an article that I thought was interesting. And that made me think of the story. And I wanted to share it with you."

"Clementine, you do not simply drop a story like that into our Sunday afternoon newspaper quiet time . . . no matter that you just read a feature article about secrets . . . you do not drop a story like that into our quiet Sunday afternoon for no reason. I know you better than that."

Clementine looked at me for a very long several moments. "And I know you well enough, Tyler Thomas Raymond, the man with three first names . . . "

"You haven't said that in a very long time," I said, interrupting.

She repeated herself, her tone of voice telling me that I should let her finish her sentence this time: "And I know you well enough, Tyler Thomas Raymond . . . to know that something is on your mind . . . and that it has to do with me . . . and with us, because when things have to do with me and with us you act just like you've been acting the past three days . . . which is okay, because I am ready to hear what you wish to tell me. But I wish you would just get on with it and tell me what has happened because . . . "—she put a finger on my lips so I would not interrupt again—"because I would rather you just went ahead and got it said instead of going around the apartment acting like there was nothing on your mind."

Then she was quiet. I knew she was done. So now it was my turn. I sighed a very deep breath. "Okay. You're right. Which I don't need to tell you because you are always right . . . which I have gotten used to . . . "

"You're doing it again," she said.

"All right. All right. I will tell you what happened." Which I did. Slowly. In as much detail as I could remember. Including the fact that Briggs Dyer told me I should tell her. Which she particularly enjoyed, although I could tell from her expression that she had not enjoyed the other part of the story. Or stories, I should say.

"So. That's it," I said when I finished.

"That's it?"

"That's it."

"Do you think the student is going to say anything more?"

"What would she say?"

"I don't know."

"To who would she say it . . .whatever it might be?"

"I don't know," Clementine said.

"Then I guess I can't answer your question. Except to say that I hope she's embarrassed enough by what she said to never bring it up again."

Clementine smiled her "I doubt that very much" smile and said, "I doubt very much that she was embarrassed by what she said. In fact, I'd bet she rather enjoyed the fact you were offended."

"Really? Why?"

"Because it will confirm what she wants to think."

"And what is it that she wants to think?"

"Wants to think and is afraid of thinking . . . at the same time."

"And what is it, Clementine, that she wants to think but is afraid to think . . . at the same time?"

"That black women are sexually alluring to white men."

"Really?"

"Really what?"

"Not really . . . that black women are alluring to white men," I said, "although truth be told, they probably are . . . which is another subject for another day. But *really*, that's what she wants to think, but she's afraid to think it," I said.

Clementine shook her head slowly. "Tyler, sometimes . . . for all that you have studied, you amaze me."

"Why do I amaze you . . . even with all that I've studied?"

"Because you have told me before that it's all about sex."

"What's all about sex?"

"Racism. Race. Black and white. Or white and black, if you prefer."

"Well, it is all about sex. Sex as territory. Physical territory and psychological territory."

"Black men and white women? And white men and black women?"

"It's anthropological," I said.

"Anthropological? I thought it was social. Cultural."

"It's more ancient than society. Much more ancient than society. Each warrior tribe wants to protect its territory. Its tribe. To protect its tribe, it must protect its women. The mothers of the tribe. If the mothers of the tribe are attracted to the warriors from the tribe over the hill, then there goes their territory."

"And the women? What do they feel?"

"I don't know. Maybe it's the same thing. The mothers of the tribe don't want their warriors to start going over the hill to have sex with the mothers of another tribe . . . or else there will be another third tribe to worry about."

"And your young woman?"

"Don't call her my young woman!" I snapped.

"And the young woman *student*," Clementine said, correcting herself. "She sounds very Southern, Tyler?"

"Yes, she is very Southern," I said. "And very white."

"And your *unnamed* teaching peer, as you so delicately put it?"

"I was most surprised by her. But yes, she is also white. She may not be *as Southern* but she's Southern enough, apparently."

"And for both of them, Tyler, I am black."

"Yes. You are black. And you are Southern."

"Just like you, Tyler. Except you are white and Southern."

"I suppose. For Bernard, at least. I am white. And I am Southern. At least, he thought so. And you are black."

"Which means?"

"Which means I have come over the hill to get you. And he doesn't like the idea that you would let me do that."

"And the young woman . . . she can't figure out why you would want to go over the hill and be with me?"

"Yes. I think that's probably right. Or more likely she is afraid of you. Which of course is all right at one level, isn't it. Because it means she now has a really good reason to resent you."

"And if she has a really good reason to resent me?"

"Then she has a really good reason to try to convince herself that you are not as good as she is or else you wouldn't have to come over the hill to find a white man when there are lots of black men you could be with."

"That's complicated, isn't it?" Clementine said after a moment.

"Yes. It is. And your Bernard must have felt the same way. Or at least he wondered about the same things."

Clementine shook her head and then leaned over and put her head on my shoulder. "Well, no matter what Bernard thought or what your student thought or even the other teacher thought, Tyler, right here, right now, this is me . . . coming over the hill to get me a white man," she said, smiling.

"Good. And this is me, Clementine, putting my hand on your breasts because more than anything else, I want to get me a black woman," I said.

With that, Clementine did what she does when she is trying to be loving and affectionate: she hit me in the ribs, which was my signal, because in less than three seconds, we were on the floor laughing and wrestling, which always ends up with us kissing and then hugging and then doing whatever else seems appropriate in the moment.

8

The second incident also took place later in the second semester of the 1989-1990 academic year, although it began innocently enough in one of the two sections of Western Civilization history that I was teaching when a student asked if I would tell the class about my master's degree thesis. I was hesitant to do so not because I was reluctant to delineate my thinking. I had, after all, spent two years at Georgia and now two years at Augusta College bringing together several lines of thinking in an attempt to explain a very complex racial issue in as clear a manner as possible. My reluctance was born of a concern that if I talked about my thinking too much before I was deep into the writing that by the time I was composing my thesis it would begin to feel redundant to me. It was a concern that more than one member of the English Department with whom I had studied said attended their work. "Talk too much about it and it starts becoming stale before you've had a chance to really plunge into the words," Lori Howe had said.

My other concern was the subject matter itself and where my research and thinking had led me. I knew full well that what I was finally going to write ran the danger of being controversial. I wasn't afraid of controversy, but I was concerned that trying to explain the many facets of my research in what was going to be ten minutes at the end of a class session was not only not going to do my subject justice, it might well lead to a gross misunderstanding of my analysis and, as a result, create a controversy that was not, in fact, justified by the work I was trying to achieve. In the end, though, I did give in and try to summarize what I explained was four years of research and reading and compiling and assessing. What apparently made the most impression with my students was my hypothesis that the concerted legal and extra-legal and illegal effort of white society to prevent and then thwart and finally to undermine the education of free black people after the War Between the States was not because the whites feared the lowering of social standards or even the so called mongrelizing of the white race through the intermarriage of whites and blacks, but because after two hundred years of contact with blacks, whites feared that a politically freed and intellectually educated black population might well prove to be not only the full equals of whites in all endeavors, it would prove to be superior in so many areas of activity that white supremacy would be displaced by a more egalitarian society in which the only thing that would finally matter in the body politic and the economic marketplace would be individual skills.

I justified my hypothesis, for I had to admit that my thinking was moving quickly beyond the hypothesis stage into the thesis stage, based on what I termed the two messages of white legislation against black participation in Southern society. First, the laws that were passed in the aftermath of the Reconstruction era once whites regained the seats of power were done so ostensibly to prevent the lowering of broad social standards by intellectually uneducated and morally ill-equipped blacks. However, the real objective of the power grab was to prevent fair competition from becoming the practice of the land. "It was a turf war masquerading as a moral crusade," I said. "But in the final analysis, it was simply an immoral extension of chattel slavery of which white Americans should be ashamed." I then added that "The fact black American culture has managed to survive at all is a tribute to the righteousness of their humane cause as much as it is defiance of the ill-conceived and ill-practiced white social system."

For a moment, the class was quiet. As I look back on the moment, despite the fact most of the class members knew that my subject had something to do with the history of slavery, I don't think any of the white students ever expected what seemed to them to be a stinging condemnation of white society in the same way I do not think any of the black students—and perhaps one third of my class were African-Americans—ever expected my argument would so stridently affirm of the worth and dignity of black society. It took a moment, therefore, before one young black man sitting near the front of the room started applauding, which was something I neither expected nor wished to have happen.

When I held up my hands to signal that he should not respond in that manner, that it was not necessary, he not only did not stop, he was joined by several of the other black students as well as a few but certainly not all of the white students. However, before any of the students could ask me any questions, which I sensed would only lead to more misunderstanding rather than clarification of my proposition, I said that class was over, moving as quickly as I could to gather up my texts and notes so I could usher the group out of the room.

What happened next was a surprise, even if looking back I should have known better, especially after I discussed the matter with Clementine that evening, who was wary about what might happen. For as has been true in most complicated instances in my life since I first met Clementine, she understood better that me that there would undoubtedly be two reactions to my statement. However, even Clementine could not have known how the two would converge and in so doing put me smack in the middle of a confrontation of points of view. Ironically, the conflict proved to be my first real moral test, enough so that in the end I got at least an inkling of what my grandfather must have withstood decades before at Cleveland State University when his outspoken support of civil rights for black Americans stirred up the academic pot, so to speak, as it had never been stirred on that campus before or since.

In my case, it began the following Monday when Jefferson Cleland, the young black man in my class who had started the applause, came to my office before my first class to ask if I would deliver an address in the Student Union Thursday evening lecture series. I told him I was aware of the ambition of the Forum, which was to not only bring scholars from off campus to Augusta College to address a wide range of topics, but to invite select members of the faculty to the Forum to speak on subjects relating to their fields of academic expertise. I told him I was flattered to be asked but I was concerned that, since I was only a teaching assistant and a master's degree candidate, if I accepted and gave an address it might well offend some of the fully tenured professors who had never been asked to speak.

"Maybe they haven't been asked, Mr. Raymond, because they don't have very interesting things to say."

I found his remark both telling and embarrassing. I could well see why some of the faculty in some disciplines might not have anything to say to a general audience. However, by contrast, it was also embarrassing because it suggested I might have something to say that would be of interest to the students and the community while other faculty members might not. In the end, I said I would like to speak to my thesis advisor and mentor before I committed myself to speak. Jefferson said he understood, although I detected in his voice a suggestion that he was disappointed. I think he had assumed I would be more bold. Perhaps I should have been.

As it turned out, I didn't have to wait until I could go to Briggs's office to discuss the invitation, for by 11 that morning he found me.

"I hear you've been invited to speak at the Forum," he said.

I replied that I had. When he wanted to know what had prompted the invitation, I said that I had responded reluctantly to a question from one of my students about my thesis, and that my response had apparently provoked the invitation.

"That's pretty much the way I heard it, Tyler, which isn't surprising. After all, you're plowing some dangerous ground."

"Do you think I should refuse?" I asked, willing at that point to take his advice. "I'm new here. I don't want to offend anyone. At least, not until I'm more ready to," I said. "Do you think I should refuse the invitation?" I said again.

"No. I didn't say that. I just think it may well prove to be a more interesting occasion than either the forum committee or you or even I imagine."

"That sounds ominous," I said.

"Ominous may be a good word. After all, this is still Georgia, for all of the changes that have happened in this state in the last thirty years. And it is still Augusta. Those two factors alone should offer pause. But on the other hand, if this college is going to live up to its intellectual and moral obligations, it's about time we had a speech at the Forum that did a little poking and prodding. I just don't want you to be the one who gets poked or prodded."

I told Briggs that I had not yet accepted. That I had told Jefferson Cleland that I would give him my answer tomorrow. I then explained to Professor Dyer that as much as he was concerned about the subject in general I was concerned about being able to condense my thinking down to a thirty minute presentation.

"I can understand your concern, Tyler. I know how many pages you envision your thesis being when it's all finished. But think of this as a summary or an abstract. Maybe you can get most of the gist of what you plan to write condensed down to twenty pages or so."

"Do you think it will have to be that short?" I said.

Briggs laughed because he understood my confusion. "Thirty minutes is about fifteen to twenty double spaced pages, Tyler. Depending on how fast you talk. But yes, if you're only going to talk for thirty minutes, you'll have to hold it down to no more than twenty pages, tops."

I told him that not only had he not clarified what I should decide about the invitation, he hadn't reassured me at all that I could write what I wanted to say in such a short lecture.

"That's what I'm here for, Tyler. To help you in any way I can," he said, laughing and then saying goodbye and going on his way. As he did, I decided that before I decided anything, I had to talk with Clementine.

9

The cliché when it rains it pours is a cliché because very often it is true. That night I fully intended to ask Clementine what she thought about the invitation to speak at the Forum. I even mulled over how I might word my analysis so she would fully understand my reluctance. However, before I had a chance to start, I could see that something was troubling her. As that didn't happen very often, I determined that it would be best if I waited. I wanted to hear what she had to say, and she obviously wanted me to hear.

"It's something at the College," she said. "Something that's happened."

I thought, now that's ironic, but I didn't say anything. It was her turn.

"You remember how we talked about my informing my supervisors that if and when a special seminar or study program in pediatrics came up that I'd like to be considered?"

"I remember."

"Well, one has come up. And it's been offered to me."

"Clementine, that's wonderful. What is it?"

"It's in Charleston."

"South Carolina?"

"Yes. At the South Carolina Medical University. In two weeks."

"So what's the problem?"

"It's in orthopedics."

"Orthopedics?"

"Yes. Pediatric orthopedics."

"I still don't see what's the problem. It's pediatrics. So go. I'll drive you there if you want. When is it?"

"Tyler, please. Listen."

I listened.

"I'm interested in the seminar. But I'm not that interested."

I vowed to continue listening.

"If it was pediatric diagnosis or pediatric infectious diseases, I'd jump at the chance."

"So it's not quite your area of interest. I still don't see the problem."

"Because Taylor really wants to go."

"Taylor Rogers? The guy I met at the Christmas party?"

"Yes. He really wants to go. He wants to specialize in pediatric orthopedics. He wants to become a surgeon. It's all he ever talks about."

"Okay. But the supervisiors . . . who ever they are in this case . . . they didn't pick him. They picked you."

"I don't want to take his place."

"Wait. How did it become his place?"

"Because he wants to go. I don't."

"Clementine, is this going to be racial?"

"Maybe. I think so."

"But Taylor is black. You're black. So how can it be racial?"

"That's not what I mean. I mean, it is what I mean. But that's not what I mean."

I sat down at the kitchen table. "Well that clears up my confusion, at least."

"Tyler . . . " Clementine began.

I interrupted. "Clementine, you need to be a bit more obtuse. I don't see the problem."

"If I turn down the seminar, I might not get another one."

"Ah."

"And if I go in and say I think Taylor should go, they might not give it to him either."

"Because he's black."

"Yes."

"And they don't want to appear to be handing out seminars only to black medical students."

"Yes."

"I see the problem."

"Good," Clementine said. "I knew you would." She waited for a moment. "So what should I do?" she said.

"I don't know how to answer that question."

"Please, Tyler. I'm coming to you."

"Clementine, I can't answer that question. I don't know what the atmosphere is like at the Medical College. I'm not even sure I understand my own College let alone yours."

"What?"

"Never mind."

Clementine looked at me as if she knew there was something on my mind. But she also knew there was something on her mind, and at that moment hers was more immediate.

"If I go in and say don't think I should be sent to the seminar, the supervisior, Dr. Bannister, he's going to want to know why. And even if he decides he's never going to send anything my way again, there isn't any reason to think he'll send Taylor in my place. For the reason you named. I mean, there are only seven black people in the whole second year class. There a lot more white students. And some of them are just as qualified as either Taylor or me."

"Yes, but if you let this chance go by, and it's given to a white student, then the next time something comes up like this, the doctors may decide that since a black student turned them down before, which would probably be embarrassing since I'll bet a whole lot of folks know you were offered the seminar, then they won't bother to even consider a black student. Am I right?"

"Yes. That's it."

"Clementine, do you really think that race is that big a factor? Have you seen any evidence that it's that important?"

"I'm not sure. Sometimes I think it is. Sometimes I think the black students are given favors, as if the supervisors are bending over backwards to make sure we succeed . . . or at least make it we look like we're succeeding . . . or it looks like they aren't doing anything to keep us from succeeding."

"Those are two different things, Clementine."

"I know. But I think both are there. At least, unconsciously. I might be wrong, but I think they're there."

I waited. Clementine was going to have to reason this out herself. I could ask questions, but that's all I could do.

"I could go in and let Dr. Bannister know how much Taylor is interested in going," Clementine said. "I could say it's because he wants to specialize in pediatric orthopedics."

"You could. But how would Taylor feel? Does he want to go so badly that he's willing to let you speak for him?"

"I don't know. He certainly hasn't asked me to speak for him."

"That's not the same thing. Does he want to go so badly that he's willing to let you speak for him?"

"I saw him in the cafeteria just after it was announced. He could hardly look at me. I don't know what he'd feel if he found out I turned down the seminar so he could go," Clementine said.

I nodded as if I had some sort of insight.

"You're thinking something, aren't you, Tyler?"

"I'm just wondering about the male pride thing as well as the black thing."

Clementine looked both surprised, but not so surprised to suggest that she hadn't thought of it herself. "That could be a factor," she said.

"Then you've got a very complicated situation on your hands, don't you," I said.

"It appears that I do."

"Which only you can sort out, my love."

"I know."

"Do you want to go across the street for soup and a sandwich?" I said.

"I will if you'll tell me what's on your mind."

"Is there something on my mind?"

"Tyler . . . " she began.

"Mine can keep," I said.

"Tyler, it will not keep. I've shared with you. Now you share with me."

"Over soup and a sandwich," I said.

"Fine. Over soup and a sandwich."

10

After we ordered our potato soup and hot Reuben sandwiches, Clementine's expression said it was my turn. So I explained how one of my Western Civilization sections had wanted me to describe the focus of my master's thesis. I told Clementine what I had said—as much as I could remember—and about what happened when my student, Jefferson Cleland, came to my office and invited me to speak at the Student Union Forum. I explained to Clementine that while I was flattered that students would want me to expand on my remarks, I was also concerned about both the reaction among full time faculty that I would get an invitation to speak and my ability to summarize the complex thinking that had gone into what I was at that point writing.

"Why would you worry about full-time faculty?" Clementine asked.

"Because I'm only a teaching assistant. I can't believe any number of them aren't going to resent that I was asked in only my second year at the College and some of them have not been asked no matter that they've been on the faculty for years."

"But maybe their subjects don't lend themselves to a public speech," Clementine said.

"That's what Jefferson said, in so many words," I said.

"So maybe it's true. That doesn't mean they aren't good teachers. And it certainly doesn't mean that their subjects or their work isn't important."

"I know that," I said. "I agree with what you're saying. I just don't want to have any bad feelings on campus, that's all," I said.

Clementine ate her soup. Then she looked at me. "You know, if you pursue the subject of racism in America the way your studies are taking you now . . . and I know your ambitions are not just for a master's degree and for a doctorate . . . I know from what you've said that you want to meld your studies with the book Edward was planning to write . . . then you are going to end up speaking in public. And your work is going to create controversy. There isn't going to be any way around it. You know that as well as I do." She smiled. "In fact, it's supposed to, Tyler. That's the point, isn't it?"

"Yes," I said. "That's fine. When the time comes. But I'm not sure the time is now. I haven't finished my own research. I've only got a good start on the thesis. This isn't the same thing as speaking after a book has been published . . . if it's ever published. A whole book gives an author time to define the perimeters and define the details. The students are asking me to summarize in thirty minutes at least three very complex lines of history and analysis that I'm trying to synthesize into one treatise. That's a whole different thing, Clementine, the feelings of full time faculty notwithstanding."

Clementine was quiet for some time. She does that when she's thinking, especially when she knows I wish she'd respond immediately. "What does Briggs say?"

I smiled. "He said it was up to me. He said that was his role. To help me all he could by leaving it up to me."

Clementine nodded and spread mustard on her Reuben sandwich. "What do you think Edward would have done?" she said without looking at me.

"Clementine . . . " I started to protest.

"What would he have done, Tyler?"

"That isn't fair."

"Why isn't it fair? I'm just asking you what you think your grandfather would have done in this situation."

"I don't care how you explain it, that's not a fair question."

"All right. Is this a fair question? What would he want you to do in this situation?"

"Clementine, that's even more unfair."

"Why? Because it asks you to let your conscience be your guide," she said, quoting the one moral cliché that I didn't want to hear.

I scowled and turned to my food. "I still don't think you're being fair," I mumbled under my breath.

Clementine leaned forward and held the salt shaker in my face. "I'm sorry, sir," she said. "My listeners couldn't hear your response. You said something about my not being fair. Just for the record, would you please say it again, but this time speak into the microphone."

I looked at Clementine. I wanted to be mad. I wanted to be upset. I wanted to feel as if my feelings had been hurt. But I couldn't. First, because she made me laugh with her salt shaker microphone routine. Second, with her terrible radio announcer's voice. Third, because I knew exactly what she was doing, and I suppose it was what I wanted her to do. I sat back and looked away. "I didn't do this to you," I said in a whisper, still trying to be mad at her but not succeeding.

"I know. And I do appreciate that, Tyler,"

I turned back to her. "Then why are you doing . . . what you're doing to me?"

"Because you were trying to be fair and noble and show respect for my maturity and my ability to make up my own mind."

"Yes, I was," I said, feigning injury.

"But I'm not trying to do that. Because I'm a woman and your wife."

"What does that mean? What does that have to do with anything?"

"It doesn't have anything to do with anything Tyler. Because I'm not trying to be fair. I'm just challenging you to do the right thing."

"Clementine . . . " I started to say in frustration.

"There's no use protesting, Tyler. I'm not bound by the same rules as you."

"What?"

"That's just the way it is, mister. And you might just as well get used to it."

I sat back and shook my head. "If I didn't love you so much, Clementine . . . " I said.

"I know," she replied. "And if I didn't love you so much . . ."

"Life would be a whole lot easier sometimes," I said.

"Yes. It would. But it wouldn't be as sweet, either, would it?" she said.

I looked away again. "No, it wouldn't," I mumbled.

"What's that, sir?" she said, holding the salt shaker up again in front of my face. "My listeners didn't hear your last comment, sir."

I turned to her and smiled and leaned forward and said very slowly and quietly into the salt shaker, "I want to have sex with you, miss."

Clementine pulled the salt shaker away from my face and put her other hand in front of her mouth and said in a hushed voice, "Please, sir, you must not talk like that on the radio. There may be children listening."

I leaned back and laughed. "Well, let them," I said, pointing at her. "Because you are one hot honey, Miss Radio Announcer. And I don't care who knows I think that."

Clementine joined me in laughing.

Ironically, I didn't have to make the decision myself. Enough was said to Briggs Dyer and then to me that the two of us didn't even have to discuss what I should do. It was obvious.

11

The following Tuesday morning I did what I always did on Tuesday mornings: I went to the library and buried myself in the reading room, which made it easy for Briggs Dyer to find me.

"We need to take a walk," he said without any preamble.

"A walk?"

"I am going to a meeting. You need to come with me."

"You look upset."

"I am. But not with you."

"Where are we going?"

"To the Temple Café."

"Should I ask why?"

"Don't bother," Briggs said. "Just come with me. You'll see soon enough."

"It's about the Forum, isn't it?" I said.

"Just come with me. But let me do the talking."

So I gathered up my books and notes, stuffed them into my backpack, and we walked across campus to the Temple Café. When we entered, I saw a large white man I'd never met before sitting in the half circle corner booth. Briggs looked at the man, who looked at Briggs and at me. Without any gesture of recognition, the man slid more deeply into the center of the booth as Briggs and I walked to him.

When we arrived, the man held out a hand and shook Briggs's hand and introduced himself as Louis Samson. Briggs returned the gesture as well as introduced me.

"I hadn't realized Mr. Raymond would be with you, Professor Dyer," Louis Samson said. "I assumed that as you are his advisor, what you and I decide today will be all that needs to be said."

Briggs was tense. I could feel it even more than see it. "As what you and I decide today concerns Mr. Raymond, I felt it appropriate that he should at least be privy to our conversation."

Louis Samson did not agree, but he was not going to argue at this point. He had other more important things to say. "I'm a man of few words, Professor Dyer. So I will speak plainly."

"Fine," Briggs replied.

"It has been brought to my attention that Mr. Raymond has been extended an invitation to speak at what is known at Augusta College as the Student Union Forum."

"That's correct," Briggs said quickly before Louis Samson could go on.

"And that Mr. Raymond, here," Louis Samson continued, nodding toward me but certainly paying me no mind, "is your master's degree advisee." Before Briggs could say that was correct, Louis Samson went on. "And that his subject has to do with the history of black slavery in the American South."

"As that is the region black chattel slavery served, then yes, it will be about the South."

Louis Samson was not used to anyone commenting on his pronouncements; that much was obvious by his facial expression and his large fists, which were coiled but not tightly on the table top near his cup of coffee. When Briggs glanced at Louis's hands, Louis smiled his very gracious but insincere smile and said, "Where are my manners. Would either of you gentlemen like to have a cup of coffee?"

"Yes, I would," Briggs said, turning to me as he did. "Tyler?" he asked.

"Yes, sir. I would," I said, mostly because I could see our responses to the question had broken Louis Samson's rhythm, and even at that point in our conversation I wanted to break his rhythm. I had other thoughts for a moment as well, but I let them pass unacknowledged.

Louis Samson raised his very large right hand and snapped his fingers at the waitress who was some distance away. That'll sure win friends, I thought to myself.

The waitress came hurrying to our table, which is not the same as saying she came happily. It is simply to say that she came in a hurry. Within minutes, both Briggs and I had cups of coffee served, which allowed Louis Samson to return to the subject at hand.

"I have also been given to understand, Professor Dyer, that Mr. Raymond here . . . that he apparently contends that black people are superior to white people, a notion that I would suggest is not only factually untrue, it smacks of a kind of distortion of the historical truth that both I and a number of my friends are shocked is being articulated by an Augusta College faculty member."

Before I could speak in defense of my work, Briggs Dyer glanced at me to signal that he would do the speaking. I took a sip of coffee and waited.

"First, Mr. Samson, your information about Mr. Raymond's work is, itself, a distortion of the truth." Before Louis Samson could object, Briggs went on. "He has never at any time ever contended that black people are superior to white people in the same way his work does not contend that whites are superior to blacks."

Louis Samson started to speak, but before he did, Briggs continued. "His studies, in fact, do not take up the issue of racial superiority or racial inferiority. I know, because I have worked with him for almost two years now, and during that time I have been in constant communication with his advisor at the University of Georgia, where Mr. Raymond intends to pursue his doctorate once his degree work at Augusta is completed."

I thought Briggs had said his piece very well. Louis Samson apparently disagreed.

"But he has been asked to speak at the Student Union Forum? Isn't that correct?"

"It is," Briggs said.

"And he intends to talk about what . . . since my reports seem to be in error."

Briggs turned to me. Then he turned back to Louis Samson. "Tyler intends to summarize his research into the racist literature white men promulgated during the last 19th and early 20th centuries. He intends to suggest that the fear expressed in that literature of black equality, presented under the guise that the innate inferiority of blacks in all walks of life would lower the standards of educational and professional institutions in the South, is, in fact, really a fear that blacks, if given an equal opportunity, might well prove to be the equal of whites in all endeavors."

Louis Samson was not a happy man.

"At this point in his studies, Mr. Raymond is only interested in unmasking the themes that fear mongering white racist authors used in promoting segregation, which therefore disallowed blacks social and economic and educational opportunities."

"Are you saying that Mr. Raymond here intends to disprove the writing of respected white men who have demonstrated on countless occasions that blacks, even if they are perfectly nice people to meet, are not intellectually equal to whites?" Louis Samson said.

Briggs was growing more tense by the moment. I was having a hard time, but I was trying my best to remain silent as Briggs had requested. "Mr. Samson, please try to understand. Mr. Raymond is a scholar. His intention is to look beyond what he considers propagandist logic encoded in racist writing and then ask the question, what did the whites really fear?"

Louis Samson's hands were shaking with rage. It was obvious from his expression that he was used to people giving him what he wanted when he was angry. "And what will come of Mr. Raymond's academic evaluation, as you call it, Professor Dyer?" he said.

"I would hope, like Mr. Raymond, that perhaps it might lead to a new kind of relationship between the races in the South and in America, which I will allow is a lofty ambition, but I, for one, applaud his willingness to make a contribution to that effort."

Louis Samson was quiet for a moment, but only for a moment. "And you realize that no matter what he says or how carefully he says it, he is bound to be misunderstood by all sorts of young people at the College?"

"That, Mr. Samson, is a risk we take at the College every day. It is a risk everyone takes when statements designed to challenge a community's or a region's thinking is presented. But that does not mean a person should not try."

Louis Samson was silent. Then he smiled. "Well, I certainly join you, Professor Dyer, in encouraging Mr. Raymond to speak his mind, as you call it. And I certainly understand that it must be hard day in and day out to get young people to listen closely enough so they understand what a body is really trying to say. But you know how young people are these days. They only hear what they want to hear. So my concern, I suppose, is that some people might think Mr. Raymond's thinking goes beyond the College's responsibility to teach history. For instance, I for one don't see that it is the College's obligation to try to stir up the pot, so to speak. Don't you agree?"

"No, I do not."

"You do not?"

"No, sir. I do not. Quite the opposite, in fact."

"Really?"

"I would argue that the College's obligation is to both stir up the pot and, at the same time, to equip students to sort out what is correct and what is incorrect when they engage challenges to widely accepted notions."

"You do?"

"I do, sir. If a College is only going to mouth that which has been accepted as truth, then it fails its duty to evaluate and re-evaluate and re-evaluate again and again."

"Then does the College never arrive at a proven truth, sir?"

"It arrives at stepping stones, Mr. Samson. But it cannot rest there. Today's accepted truth frequently becomes tomorrow's laughable fallacy."

Louis Samson looked out of the window. Then he turned back to Briggs. "I am to take it, then, that I should tell my friends who find the idea of Mr. Raymond's speech objectionable that you intend to support him in his ambition?"

"First, Mr. Samson, Mr. Raymond has not yet accepted the invitation. He is, himself, concerned that he might not be able to summarize his research in thirty minutes, for like me, he does not want his studies to be misinterpreted. Second, although I personally wish he would accept the students' invitation, since it did come from them, it is for him to decide, but his reason must have to do with the academic issues involved, not what it appears to me to be pressure from you and whoever your friends are who do not wish the subject of race relations and race prejudice to be addressed in any manner."

Louis Samson raised his hand in protest. "Professor Dyer, you have apparently misunderstood my concerns. I am not a racist. I run a very large construction company in

North Augusta. Only yesterday I gave orders that from now on thirty percent of all of our subcontracts should be let to black owned firms."

Briggs smiled and said that was very commendable. He was sure I would agree.

Mr. Samson went on. "In addition, my company is right now preparing to make a substantial cash contribution to the College, of which the President is aware, to further the good work you folks are doing."

There was a long pause as Briggs and I waited for the other shoe to drop.

"However, if Mr. Raymond were to give his speech, and it happened to be misunderstood, I can assure you that, in what might prove to be an unpleasant aftermath, my own company would then have to reconsider our contact letting policy, and I almost certainly assure you that my company's gift to the College would be re-evaluated."

Briggs nodded slowly. Then he smiled. "And I also suppose if your friends were to hear that Mr. Raymond intended to give his speech, not only would your company re-evaluate its policies and charitable intentions, some of those friends might even wish to attend to see that Mr. Raymond was not able to speak at all."

Louis Samson smiled a very hard smile. "Professor Dyer, I did not come here to threaten either you or Mr. Raymond. It is not my place to dictate what the College should do. It is also not my place to tell my friends what events they should attend or not attend. You misunderstand the lengths and limitations of my influence in matters such as this."

Briggs smiled broadly. "Oh, no, Mr. Samson, I do understand the lengths and limitations of your influence just as you must understand the lengths and limitations of mine."

"And what does that mean, Professor?" Louis Samson said in a whisper. "Are you inferring some sort of threat against me?"

"Not at all, sir," Briggs said, smiling what appeared to me to be a cutting smile. "However, I should explain several factors of which you may not be aware." Before Louis Samson could interrupt, Briggs went on. "First, you apparently do not know it, but Mr. Raymond, here, is *Tyler* Raymond. He is the grandson of the late Professor Edward Thomas, a very important historian whose work focused on racism in America."

"I did not know that. No, sir, I did not," Louis Samson said. "But may I ask how that factors into this circumstance?"

"Well, as your friends might well prefer that Tyler not give a speech that might, as you said, be misunderstood by students if they did not listen carefully, because of his relationship to Edward Thomas, Tyler is known to a great many important people in the black community across the country, who . . . and I could name names if you wish . . . "—Briggs raised his right hand to keep Louis Samson from interrupting –"who if they knew about his speech, would undoubtedly want to be assured that he could go forward in and accept the invitation of the Student Union Forum and deliver his address."

Louis Samson was quiet for a moment. "Professor Dyer, I know a threat when I hear one, and that, sir, is a threat."

"No, sir, it is not. No more than your concerns are a threat," Briggs said. Then he turned to me. "And if you gave the speech, Tyler, isn't it possible that people from the University of Georgia . . . Vince Dooley for instance . . . might wish to attend?"

It was my turn. "I haven't invited him to come. Of course, that's because I haven't made up my mind about speaking or not speaking. But yes, if I were to contact Coach Dooley and tell him about the invitation and about my subject, and if I were to tell him about our conversation with Mr. Samson, here," I said, nodding toward Louis Samson but not looking at him in the same way he had earlier nodded at me but not looked at me, "it is possible he might attend."

Louis Samson looked very surprised. "Now wait a moment, Professor Dyer. Why in the world would Coach Vince Dooley come to Augusta to attend Mr. Raymond's speech?" he said.

Briggs smiled. "You apparently don't follow Georgia Bulldog football, sir."

"No. I'm a Clemson man, myself," Louis Samson said.

Briggs smiled. "Then I guess that you don't know that Tyler here is the same Tyler Raymond who was Vince Dooley's starting strong safety for two years and that Coach Dooley recruited Tyler to come to Georgia from Tampa, Florida, where he played football, because Vince Dooley had great respect for Tyler's late father, who played football at the University of Maryland when Vince Dooley played at Auburn, and that Tyler's father, Captain Raymond, died a hero in the Viet Nam war."

Louis Samson was finished. There was no way he could oppose my giving an even tempered and reasoned address to whatever students wish to attend on a Thursday night in the Student Union building if the word got out that not only was I the grandson of an important American historian who had been an early leader in the Civil Rights movement, I was the son of a Viet Nam war hero. If both of those things weren't enough, I had also played football for Vince Dooley. What Louis Samson could not have known, of course, was that I would never have presumed on my relationship with and respect for Vince Dooley. Samson was simply so used to manipulating people with his financial power that he assumed I would use whatever connections I might have to anyone who might be able to help me in the face of his opposition. So the conversation ended with such an obvious and resounding thud of resignation on Louis Samson's part that, after the three of us parted company and Briggs Dyer and I walked back across the street towards the campus buildings, Briggs turned to me and said very quietly, "I've wanted to do something like that to someone like that all of my life, Tyler. Thank you for providing the opportunity."

I replied that I considered it a privilege have done so. When I got back to our apartment that evening, Clementine agreed. Her only regret was that she had not been there to witness the conversation. When she said that I laughed and said, "If you'd shown up with us, my love, that probably would have done the poor man in." She understood what I meant.

Then I asked her what she had decided to do about the medical seminar in Charleston. She said that as she had driven to school that morning, she asked herself what her mother might do in a similar circumstance. "By the time I got into the building, I concluded that she would have faced the issue straight on and tell everyone involved the truth."

"Which means you did what?" I asked.

"Which means I went to Dr. Bannister's office and told him that as much as the seminar would be interesting for me, it might well be vitally important for some other student more interested in orthopedics. When he asked me if I had any suggestions, I said I wasn't sure it was my place to give my opinion, but if he really wanted to know what I thought . . . ."

"You're so cool, Clementine," I said, interrupting.

Clementine smiled. "I told him that I thought Taylor would benefit a great deal from the experience."

"And he accepted your suggestion?"

"Apparently, because Taylor came to me and thanked me later in the afternoon."

"And he isn't bothered about the woman-man thing?"

"I guess not. At least he didn't act like it."

I smiled and held her in my arms. "My darling Clementine strikes again."

She rested her head against my shoulder.

"You are one very fine person. Do you know that?"

"That's sweet, Tyler. But what have you decided about the Forum?" she said.

To answer her question, I told her that I was going to speak partly because I thought Briggs Dyer had handled Louis Samson with such finality and partly because I felt as if Briggs had extended himself so much that I felt an obligation to him. However, mostly, as she had suggested would be the case, I was going to give the speech because I decided that's what my grandfather would have done, controversy or no controversy. Of course, as might have been expected, the ultimate irony is that while upwards of three hundred faculty and students attended, no controversy resulted. I should have had more faith in the Augusta College community. As Briggs Dyer said afterwards when he said that I had done a very good job of summarizing very complicated research, "If a man gives a speech about controversial ideas but no one who attends thinks of them as controversial can we still call the event controversial?"

Standing with a smiling and proud Clementine, who had come to hear me speak but who had remained toward the back of the hall so she would not distract me when I delivered my address, I replied, "Briggs, I didn't know you were a Zen philosopher."

Briggs Dyer smiled. "I'm not, Tyler. Far from it. But I am a damn good poker player."

12

A month later, I was offered a position as Instructor of History at Augusta College, beginning with in the fall of the 1990-1991 academic year, on the proviso that I completed my master's degree in good order. Three months later, in May, 1990, I received my Master's Degree in Social Science from Augusta College, which finalized the offer from the College. Of course, Clementine and Ruth Ann and my mother attended the graduation ceremony, which the four of us celebrated by playing golf together the next day.

Two weeks later, Clementine and I drove to New Jersey to visit her maternal grandparents, John and Emily Nelson, and her aunts and uncles and cousins. I was aware it was the first time in my life that I was the only white person in a household, even if no one in the family gave me any reason to feel uncomfortable. Apparently, Ruth Ann's letters had been telling them about me and about Clementine and me for years. All they wanted to do, both of her grandparents said, was finally meet the smart young man who had captured their beloved granddaughter's heart. The only even remotely embarrassing moment came when one of Clementine's high school age female cousins, Clarisse, said in front of the whole family when she and I first met, "Clementine, where in the world did you get yourself a man like this? Because wherever it is and however you did it, I want to go there and do the same thing myself."

When the week was over, and Clementine stood hugging and kissing her grandparents, they would not let us go until we promised that we would come back very soon.

I promised that we would. That earned me a grandmother's hug and kiss of my own. But later, when we were driving back to Georgia, I asked Clementine why she hadn't taken me to meet her family earlier in our life together since they were so nice and so much fun to be with and seemed so happy to meet me?

She said she wasn't sure how I would feel being the minority person in the group. I responded that given my moral sentiments I was surprised to hear her say such a thing. Her reply was that, "It's one thing to play football with black guys at Georgia, Tyler. And it's one thing to marry a black woman like me. Because in those situations, you know you still live in what amounts to a predominately white world. It's a very different thing to know that you are staying in a house with a family, even though they are prepared to accept you . . . it's a very different thing to know that you are staying in a house with a black family when you are the only white person in the group." She hesitated for a moment. "I didn't know what it would be like for you. And I didn't want you to be uncomfortable."

"Clementine, I went with you to Africa," I said.

"Yes, and you were uncomfortable. I could see it. You didn't say anything, because you were thinking about me. But I could see you were uncomfortable."

I didn't know what to say next. I knew what I felt. I knew what I wanted to say, but I wasn't sure I could explain myself very well. But when we stopped at a restaurant on Interstate 95 just south of Washington, D.C., I went ahead and tried when, over lunch I said, "Clementine, have you ever considered the possibility that maybe you are more uncomfortable being around other black people than I am or that you are self-conscious enough about being married to a white man that you worry about what other black people might think about you?"

I knew I had said a mouthful, no pun intended, not because Clementine responded immediately or because she acted as if she were hurt, but because she was quiet for a very long time before she said, "Yes. I have thought about those things, Tyler. I have thought about both of them."

The silence that followed her comment told me that the matter was not closed, that it would come up again later when she was ready. But that day was not the day it was going to happen. So we paid for our coffee and sandwiches and left the restaurant and continued driving back to Augusta and to our apartment and to our life together.

13

The next year was interesting in two ways. Clementine was a third year student at Georgia Medical College; she was doing more and more work in children's clinics in the Augusta area. At the same time, I was both teaching a full load of four classes, each of which met three times a week, which also required office hours so I could meet with students who needed to talk with me about their work, and I was working with Dr. McAndrew at the University of Georgia in the preliminary stages of my doctorate. With Briggs Dyer serving as an informal supervisor, I began outlining where I believed my master's thesis analysis of white racist writing in the late nineteenth and early twentieth centuries melded into the studies my grandfather had completed prior to his death, in which he had taken up the subject of black professional baseball players in the major leagues in the 1880s and 1890s before a boycott by white players forced them out. And while it was not my intention to write as extensively about the exclusion of black players as my grandfather had intended, I found their story both morally moving and useful as a metaphor for what then transpired in America, epitomized by the racist portrayal of blacks in D. W. Griffith's epic film, "The Birth of America," which even educated people such as President Woodrow Wilson claimed was gospel truth.

What all of that meant was that except for stealing away on three Saturday afternoons so we could drive to Athens for Georgia football games, Clementine and I saw very little of each other except when we each arrived back at night in our apartment, which we had taken to calling Base Camp. We did manage to attend Augusta Symphony concerts twice, all four of the Augusta Ballet productions—because I surprised Clementine with season tickets—and one Augusta Opera production. I got to a second opera with Briggs and his wife Miranda, who were rapidly becoming what Barbara and Vince Dooley had been for me at Georgia—mentors and friends and family. I think it was harder for Clementine in that she had even less social time than I did. My clearest memory that fall was of her sitting hunched over her desk with two or three or even four text books open at once, taking notes, drinking coffee, which I brought to her when I was in the apartment at the same time. Even our Sunday newspaper reading sessions were abbreviated two or three Sundays a month. In short, if we had not maintained our time lying in bed talking before we fell asleep, I'm not sure what kind of communication we might have had.

What all of the work told me was that I loved her more every day that I wasn't with her. Yes, I was focusing on work I wanted to achieve, and yes, I was thoroughly enjoying my teaching, and yes, I was tremendously proud of Clementine's work, but like other couples our same ages in countless graduate school programs, we had a hard time not feeling very much alone too often for our own goods.

Finally, in December, I realized that something had to change, even if it was only temporary. Clementine was losing weight, and that was not good for her in any way I could think of. I assumed that two or three more months of the same kind of intellectual academic stress combined with her long hours in laboratory classes and at the two clinics she was by then serving would do all sorts of bad things to her diabetes. As a result, I went to Dr. Bannister and asked if I might take her out of town for ten days during my winter break from Augusta College. Fortunately, he was also concerned about Clementine's loss of weight. So without telling her anything, just after Thanksgiving weekend—and we ate our celebratory meal at a Denny's Restaurant rather than with our mothers—I started making plans.

First, since Clementine and I had already spent time in North Carolina more than once, I asked among my fellow teachers if any of them knew of a cabin hideaway somewhere in Tennessee that I could rent for ten days in December. Three couldn't help. As I should have known, Briggs Dyer could.

Briggs and Miranda had spent more than one summer in cabins outside the town of Grandview facing Walden Ridge. With their help, I rented a cabin for ten days so we could be there together for Winter Solstice and then for nine days afterwards. Then I set out to pack Clementine's winter clothes without her realizing what I was doing. I stored away food that we would need in our utility room behind boxes that we'd used when we'd moved to Augusta.

The night before we were to leave, although I still hadn't told her my plans, she came home and said Dr. Bannister had come to her and told her to take a long weekend. I said that was great. Maybe she could get some sleep. She agreed that would be wonderful.

But she had reading to do. So even if she had four days, she also knew she would be busy. I said that wasn't why Dr. Bannister had wanted her to have a four day weekend. "He didn't send you home so you'd have more time to read, Clementine. He sent you home so you would take better care of yourself."

Clementine looked at me very warily. "What do you know, Tyler? What's going on?"

"Why do you think something's going on?"

"Tyler Raymond, what have you done?"

I held up my hands as if to show her there was nothing up my sleeves. "Clementine, I have reading to do too. But first, you have to help me with something."

"What?"

I started to walk away, talking to her over my shoulder as I did. "First, go ahead and take a shower. Then put on your jeans and a sweatshirt."

"Tyler, I want to take a shower. I am tired. A hot shower will be wonderful. But why do you want me to put on my jeans and a sweatshirt?"

"And your old flannel shirt. The one you wear like a jacket sometimes."

"Tyler, what's going on? I can see it in your eyes. Something's going on."

"Clementine Brown, do me a favor."

"What?"

"Go take a shower. Then put on the clothes I've asked you to put on. Then come with me."

"Come with you where?"

"Come with me to . . . paradise."

"Paradise?"

"Clementine, just do it," I said, my voice sharp but not seriously sharp.

Clementine looked at me for a very long time. "All right. I will take a shower. I will dress in my jeans and a sweatshirt and my old flannel shirt. But if you've planned some sort of surprise . . . let me tell you . . . "

"Clementine, please. Just do it."

She looked at me again for a moment. Then scowling she turned and went into our bedroom. After a moment, I could hear her going into the bathroom. As soon as I heard the shower water start running, I turned and ran into the utility room and made two trips down to our car where I packed the last of what we were going to need in among the things I had been packing for two days. Once I was finished, I ran back up the stairs to our apartment just as she was coming out of the bedroom dressed as I had asked her to dress.

"Fine," I said. "You look just fine. You're dressed just like me," I said.

She looked at me. "Tyler, that's the corduroy shirt you always wear when we travel."

"Is it?" I said, looking at my shirt as if I were surprised.

"Yes, it is. So what's going on?"

"Go back in the bedroom and see if I've put everything in your toilet kit that you'll need."

"Do what?"

"I could take care of everything else. But you'll have to check if I put everything in your toilet kit that you will need."

She stood and looked at me for a very long time without speaking. Then she turned and went back into the bedroom. After a few minutes, she came out with her toilet kit in hand.

"Good. Now we can go."

"Go where?"

"Go away."

"Go away . . . where?"

"Where I am taking you, my love. Now no more questions. Everything is arranged. Everything will be just fine. If you will stop complaining and just come with me."

"I only have four days, Tyler. So where are we going?"

I smiled. "No, Clementine. You have ten days. I have ten days. Which means *we* have ten days."

She started to protest.

"Not another word, woman. Come with me right now. We are leaving."

Clementine was not happy only because she didn't know where we were going. But I could see in her mock-scowl that she was happy to be going somewhere. So she followed me to the car where, once she saw how much I had packed, including three of the text books I knew she would need, she sat back and looked out of the window and said, "Grandpa Edward would be proud of you, Tyler. Because I didn't have a clue you were up to something."

"Good," I said, and started the engine. "Pour me some coffee, will you, as long as you're sitting there not doing anything."

Clementine smiled and started pouring coffee as I turned onto Interstate 20 and turned west toward Atlanta, from which we turned north, driving until found a motel south of Chattanooga, where we stayed for the night. The next morning, we crossed the border into Tennessee. By noon, after stopping in Dayton for the fresh groceries we would need, we were unpacking our clothes and storing the foods we would use for the next nine days. By 3 P.M. Clementine and I were walking along a winding road, her left arm around my waist, my right around her shoulders, looking west at the clouds which were beginning to gather over the mountains for the night.

14

To this day when I think back about our ten day trip to Tennessee, I am still not sure what I expected to happen. But I did know something needed to be expressed. Only this time it wasn't me. It was Clementine.

If you love someone the way I love Clementine, and she's been a part of your life for as many years as Clementine had been a part of mine, even then in the fall of 1990—and you are paying attention—you begin to sense or intuit changes in that person's demeanor that signal something more important is going on. That was the case with Clementine.

Yes, she was studying hard, but she had always been a serious student. And yes, her progress in medical school was even more important to her future plans than had been her progress in undergraduate school. And yes, she was working too many hours: medical school classes, two clinics, and then trying to come home and share time with me. But lots of people have too many things to do. Yes, she was a diabetic, which certainly exacerbated the stresses she was feeling. But I know other people who study hard and work hard and are diabetics. And they cope as well as they can. Which is not to say that Clementine was not coping. For she was. And that is my point: for Clementine, study had always been joyful; working in the clinics had originally been exciting for her. Coming home to me, she said countless times, was her great relief, her great passion. So I'm not talking about those kinds of things. I am talking about something else . . . something I did not understand, that I could not define, that I could not remediate. It took the mountain to do that, which is why I took her there. It took the mountain, and it took two days. But it did come. On the third night. It rose up as if it had been buried at sea for centuries. It rose up and Clementine rose up in her sleep and thrashed out with both of her hands and cried out, "She died! She died! She died!" Then she was crying.

I awoke quickly enough to hear her cries. I sat up in time to have her right hand smash into my face. Recoiling, I fell back and grabbed my nose. It was bleeding. The room was dark, but even in the darkness, I could feel the blood running down my face.

I rolled away to she wouldn't hit me again in her dreaming. I ducked as well as I could under her agony, only to receive another glancing blow across the top of my head. Then she was in my arms crying, whispering, choking on the words, "She died! She died! She died!"

I held her against me awkwardly, for she was sitting up and I was leaning towards her. I fumbled for a light. Finding a bed side lamp in an unfamiliar house means knocking things over, which I did. Then I rolled over to the side of the bed and found the lamp and turned it on.

Clementine was up on her knees, her nightgown down around her waist, as if she'd been struggling against someone trying to undress her, which I had not been doing. She turned and looked at me. Her eyes were wide open. She was terrified. I couldn't tell if she was really awake or not. Her eyes didn't tell me that. But she was looking at me, her mouth working, whispering words, as if she was trying to explain, as if she was trying to understand.

I moved back to the bed and go on my knees so I could match her position. I reached out and touched her face. "Clementine," I said as urgently but softly as I could. "Clementine. You're dreaming. You're dreaming."

She looked at me. "Am I?" she said in a whisper.

"Yes. You're dreaming. Are you all right? Can I help you?"

She looked at me again as if she'd never seen me before. Then she closed her eyes hard then opened them again. "You're bleeding," she said.

I touched my face. She was right. I had known that. I was bleeding. I looked at her. "I'm bleeding on the sheets," I said.

I got up out of bed and went into the bathroom and looked in the mirror above the sink. There was blood on my face. She had not broken my nose, but she had caused a nosebleed. I washed myself off as well as I could. I was still bleeding. I washed the blood off my chest. Then I wet a washcloth with cold water and pressed it against my nose.

I heard Clementine from the other room. "I'm sorry," she was saying. "I'm sorry. I was dreaming. Of Fonsiba," she said after a moment.

I returned to the bedroom. There was blood on the sheets. I didn't care because they were the ones we'd brought from home. Then Clementine looked at her hands and her nightgown. My blood had smeared on her as well as splattered on the sheets.

"Fonsiba," she whispered. Then she slumped back down into the sheets and onto her pillow. "She died," she said quietly.

I moved to her side. "Fonsiba died decades ago, Clementine. More than a hundred years ago," I said as quietly as I could manage.

"She died in my arms," Clementine said quietly.

"Clementine. No. Fonsiba died more than a hundred years ago. She was your grandmother. Your great-great-great-great grandmother. She died more than a hundred years ago."

Clementine turned and looked at me. I still could not tell if she was asleep or awake or somewhere in between. "Fonsiba died in Augusta," she said in a hoarse whisper.

"Clementine, we don't know where she died. Most likely it was South Carolina."

"Fonsiba died in Augusta," she said again. "Last week."

I sat on the edge of the bed and looked at her as she turned away from me and fell back to sleep without saying another word. What in the world was she talking about? Who died in Augusta last week? What could she possibly mean?

I waited for a moment. Clementine's breathing changed. It was no longer hard and short. She was no longer struggling. She was deep asleep again.

I stood and looked at her. Very carefully, I moved around to the other side of the bed and pulled the sheet up over her until she was covered up to her shoulders. Then I went back around to my side. I pushed the bloody spots into a crease as well as I could before I lay down on as much clean space as I could organize. I did not move for several moments but listened to Clementine's breathing. She was fully asleep. So I reached over and turned off the light, dropping the cold wash cloth on the floor beside the bed as I did. I had no idea what had awakened Clementine. It obviously sounded as if she had juxtaposed two things in her dream. I had no idea what that meant. I could only hope the next day would bring some clarity, more for her than me. But for me as well. After all, I was the one who was going to have to explain to her why my nose was swollen and there was blood on the sheets when she woke up in the morning. I was the one who was going to have to tell her what she had said and what she had done. She would have to do the rest.

15

The next morning, I let Clementine sleep. Given what she had been through the night before, I decided it was best to let her sleep as long as she could. So I got up, shaved, showered, and dressed in warm clothes and went out into the living room-kitchen combination and started making preparations to cook breakfast for the two of us. Once everything was in order, I sat down with a cup of coffee and started reading the previous Sunday's edition of the *New York Times*. At the same time, I tuned in our short wave radio to the BBC World Service, keeping the radio volume turned down low enough so it would not disturb Clementine. Sitting at the small kitchen table next to a large double window, I watched as the sun came over the mountain from behind the cabin, throwing spears of light out across the rolling landscape. While I was sorry Clementine was not awake to enjoy the slow unfolding changes, I knew there would be other mornings just like this one. It was better she be able to stay in bed.

Shortly after 9 A.M., Clementine appeared in the doorway to the bedroom, dressed and smiling her I'm-still-sleepy-but-I'm-glad-to-see-you smile. I held up the coffee mug I gotten out of the cupboard for her. "Yes," she said. So I got up and poured her morning coffee, which she accepted, kissing me on the cheek as she did as she sat down opposite where I had been sitting.

"I'm ready to cook bacon and make omelettes whenever you wish," I said quietly.

"It's nice just sitting here, Tyler," she said. Then she turned to the window. "It's pretty here. I'm glad we came."

"Good," I said. Then I sat down at the table and looked at her. "Do you want to talk about last night?" she said.

"Did I dream?" she asked.

"Yes. You were dreaming. That's how I got this nose."

She turned and looked at me. "Your nose is swollen," she said. Then it occurred to her what I had said. "Did I do that?"

"Yes. You were dreaming. I woke up and tried to hold you. You were flailing around. It was an accident."

"Oh, Tyler. I'm so sorry," she whispered. She looked at me more carefully. "Are you okay? Is it broken?"

"No. I'm okay. It's sore, that all. That's why there's blood on the sheets. I got a nose bleed, but I'm okay now."

Clementine looked very embarrassed. "What did I do? What did I say?" she wanted to know.

I hesitated for a moment. Everything that had happened when she was dreaming told me this was going to be hard for Clementine. Something was going on. She needed to deal with it. But it was still going to be hard. "I'll start making breakfast," I said, getting up and moving to the kitchen counter.

"Tyler, what did I say?" Clementine asked, her voice more insistent.

I turned to the sink as I cracked open five eggs one at a time and put the contents in a bowl. "At first you said, 'She died. She died.' When I tried to wake you up and tell you that you were dreaming, you said, 'Am I?'"

Sitting at the table over her cup of coffee, Clementine turned away, looking out of the window again. "Did I wake up?"

"I don't know. You talked to me. But I don't think you were really awake."

"What did I say?"

"You started talking about Fonsiba. You said you had been dreaming of Fonsiba. You said she died in Augusta. I tried to tell you that Fonsiba had died more than a hundred years ago. But you said she died in your arms." Then I was quiet. I had said enough. I could see Clementine was shaken by what I said she had said. She sat for some time looking out of the window.

She turned back to me. "Are you making cheese omelettes?"

"I am."

"Nice," she said. "And did you say bacon?"

"I did. I'll put it on now before I start the omelettes."

Clementine nodded and picked up her mug of coffee and took a long drink. I was putting the bacon in the oven to broil. When I stood up I could see she had turned and was looking at me. "She did die in my arms, Tyler."

I waited. "Then we are obviously not talking about the same Fonsiba," I said.

"No. We aren't," Clementine replied.

"Then you need to help me, Clementine, because I don't know about any other Fonsiba."

"I know you don't. But I do."

I waited. The bacon was broiling. I turned back to the stove and poured the beaten eggs into the frying pan. I turned to Clementine, but she did not appear to be ready to explain what she meant. So I began to grate the block of cheese that we'd bought in town. When I had enough, I went to the refrigerator and got a green pepper, which I cut into small pieces for the omelettes. For a moment, I watched the eggs begin to cook. Then I glanced at Clementine again. "Who is the Fonsiba who died, Clementine?"

She did not look at me. But she spoke: "A patient at the south side clinic."

I nodded. "You never said anything about a patient dying."

"She wasn't my patient. She was. But she wasn't."

I knew she would explain what she meant so I did not ask.

"She'd come in twice before I ever saw her. She had a respiratory infection. One of the doctors gave the mother a prescription. The mother got it filled. Then she forgot to keep on giving it to the girl."

"How old was she?"

"The girl?"

"Yes."

"She was nine."

I turned back to the omelettes, putting in the cheese and the green peppers. Then with the spatula I found in a kitchen drawer, I folded the omlettes in half. I looked at Clementine for a moment. Then I turned back to the stove. I cut the omelet into two halves and put them on the plates that I had ready. Then I opened the oven door and took out the broiler pan of bacon. After I let the bacon cool for a moment, I carefully put three pieces on Clementine's plate and three on mine, leaving the other pieces for another morning. Then I brought the two plates to the table and gave one to Clementine. She looked up and smiled. "It looks wonderful, Tyler. It really does," she said.

I thanked her and then sat down. I had already put salt and pepper and ketchup on the table. After a moment, Clementine got up and went to the refrigerator and got out the carton of orange juice we had bought in town and poured two glasses full and brought them back to the table.

"Sorry," I said.

She did not reply. So we sat for a few minutes, beginning to eat, the silence hanging over us like a curse. For I knew even as I was going about all of the small tasks of making the meal that each thing I did was part of her approach avoidance, which was something I had never seen in Clementine before. She had always been a face-on person. But this was different.

"What happened?" I finally said.

Clementine hesitated over her meal. "The mother brought her back to the clinic a third time because she wasn't getting any better. That was when I happened to be there. So I talked to her. I asked her if she had been giving her daughter her medicine. She said she had forgotten. I tried to explain that if she didn't give her the medicines, the girl's condition would only get worse. She said she understood. But I didn't believe her. I knew she wasn't going to do what the doctors had said. I could see it in her eyes. She wasn't hearing me. She hadn't heard them, and she wasn't hearing me."

Clementine stopped speaking for a moment. "The child's name was Fonsiba. It's a coincidence, I know. But it's true. The girl's name was Fonsiba. Which resonated for me, of course. And I knew as the mother took the girl away that they would be back and that when they were we would need to take the girl to the hospital if it wasn't too late by then."

A very quiet moment passed. "And they came back," I said in a whisper.

"Yes. Four days later. When I was there again. She brought the girl in. The girl was burning up. I kept asking the mother if she'd given the child her medicine. She said she had, but when she gave me the bottle I could see far too few had been used. I wanted to send the girl to the hospital immediately, but before I could do anything, she began to spasm. As if her whole body was turning inside out. I got help, and a nurse called the hospital for an ambulance. Then the girl went quiet. I could feel her face was burning up but her body was getting colder and colder."

Clementine stopped again. Then she went on: "I knew her name was Fonsiba. I knew that by then. So I tried to talk to the girl. I tried to tell her that I would take care of her. I stroked her brow and held her hand and bent over her and tried to whisper that I liked her name. I told her that one of my great-grandmothers had been named Fonsiba. But then I could hear the girl's breathing grow shallow. Then I heard her rasp. A nurse heard it too. We had monitors on her by then. Then she went flat line. God, it was awful. Awful. So the nurse and I tried to revive her heart. We did CPR. We didn't have anything else. The clinic isn't equipped for emergencies like that. We breathed into her mouth and worked her chest. But the flat line didn't change. We couldn't get a pulse. And all the while the mother just stood and watched as if she didn't understand what was happening. By the time the ambulance arrived, it was over. Fonsiba had died. She died right there. And her face, her expression, her eyes when we closed them . . . she was asking me why it had happened. What had gone wrong? What had she done that she had to die at nine years of age?"

I had stopped eating when Clementine had started to explain.

"I wanted to turn to the mother and scream at her. 'This is your fault' I wanted to say. I wanted to swear and call her names. 'You stupid woman!' I wanted to scream. 'You killed your daughter! You killed your daughter!' But I didn't. The nurse and I just did what we had to do so the ambulance could take her to the hospital so the doctors there could formalize the girl's death."

I waited.

"And it didn't have to happen. That's the ugly part, Tyler. That girl did not have to die. But she was black. Her mother is black. And the mother is to blame. And being black is to blame." Clementine was almost choking on her words. "God, I hate black people some times. I hate them! I hate what they do! I hate what they don't do! I hate what's been done to them!"

I had never heard Clementine speak like that before. I didn't know what to say or how to respond.

"The brain, Tyler. The human brain. The mind. If it isn't used. If it isn't stimulated it atrophies. It dies! It just dies right there up in someone's head. In that black woman's skull. And who's to blame for that? Her? That stupid mother? I don't know. Racism? The way black people have been denied? The way they have been treated generation after generation? I think it's that. I think so many black people have been denied for so many generations . . . their imaginations have been warped. Corrupted. Destroyed. Not allowed to develop. I don't know," she said, her voice hard and rasping as she got up from the table. "The whole history of being black. Of slaves. Of good brains . . . of good minds left to rot. To eat and sleep and have sex. Minds left to rot."

Clementine moved away into the living room. She stood at the window. "Look at us, Tyler. Look at you and me. Our minds. We were always stimulated. Our mothers saw to that. Art museums. Music. Good music. And books and plays and ideas. They talked to us. They asked us to use our minds. We developed horizons. Imaginations. We could see and wonder and try to find answers. So our brains were alive. They weren't left to rot. So we ended up smart. Stimulated and smart. But that woman. Fonsiba's mother. No one ever cared about her mind. She was just one more black woman. One more black girl growing up poor and uneducated and stupid who ended up having babies. She was just one more nigger in whole world of niggers who've had their lives stolen. Who have died and never even lived. And no one will ever know if they were smart or not. No one will ever know because no one ever cared enough to find out."

She turned on me. "What if that woman was smart, Tyler? What if when she'd been a child someone had read to her? What if someone had read to her mother or her father? Maybe she wasn't born stupid. Maybe she had the makings of a good mind. But what happened? I don't know what happened. But there she stood across the room from us as the nurse and I—two black women whose minds had been stimulated . . . who'd gotten educations . . . she just stood there and looked at us as if we were from Mars or somewhere. She didn't live among people like us. You could smell it. And she'd never had any reason to think she could have been like us." Clementine's body was shaking. "It was as if we weren't the same race. Or the same species. And I hated her, Tyler. She had watched her daughter die right there in my arms, and I didn't feel sorry for her one bit. I hated her. I was embarrassed to be black. I was angry that she had to be black. I was humiliated. But when she left . . . when she left with the ambulance . . . the nurse and I went to the small back room where we can drink coffee and eat and without even saying anything to each other we just started crying in each other's arms. But we weren't just crying for Fonsiba. And we weren't just crying for Fonsiba's mother. We were crying for black people everywhere. People who never got a chance to find out if they knew anything. Who never got a chance to learn anything."

Clementine turned away. "And then that night I came home and there you were with a meal prepared and wine for me to drink and two really funny stories to tell me about funny things that had happened that day on campus, and I listened and laughed with you and ate the good meal and drank the wine with you. And then when we went to bed and made love and you were tender and sweet and you told me over and over again how much you loved me, and I melted into your arms because that is the place I wanted to be most in the whole world, and it began to rain, and we lay together naked under a sheet and fell asleep together, and I wondered . . . I kept wondering . . . what did it mean that little Fonsiba was dead and would never know anyone like you or be in love with anyone like you the way I am in love with you?. I kept wondering why me? Why was my mother my mother? Why was I so lucky? Why had I been blessed? But I couldn't answer any of those questions because I don't think there are any answers to those questions because I don't think anyone or any God is in charge of the universe because if someone or some God was in charge of the universe, little Fonsiba of Augusta, who had never hurt anyone, would have had a chance to find out if she had a mind and a chance to fall in love instead of die in the south side clinic in my arms because she was black in a world that doesn't give a good God damn about people who are born black."

With that, Clementine stopped speaking and stood motionless in front of the window. I could hear her breathing. I could feel the anger in her body from across the room. I could feel the hurt in her arms and legs. And when she turned to me I could see the anguish in her eyes. So I stood and did the only thing I could possibly do: I went to her and put my arms around her and let her lean against my shoulder and let her cry as she had never cried before and as she has not cried since because there are times in life when the only thing that is real are tears that come welling up from the bottom of a person's person, and when the only thing one can offer in return is silence. And even that is too little. Even that is too little and too late.

16

After a few moments, we returned to the kitchen table where we finished our meal, which by then had grown cold. Drinking a second mug of coffee, I looked at Clementine and said, "You are a healer, Clementine. You will heal the world one child at a time. That's worth doing. Don't ever doubt that. Please, don't ever question what you're doing."

Clementine sat looking at her mug of coffee. Then she looked at me. "I know. And you're right. But you have an even bigger task, Tyler."

I waited for a moment. "What's that?" I said after a moment.

"You're an educator." Before I could interrupt, she went on: "I will treat one patient at a time. I will talk with one family at a time. But you stand in front of classes of twenty students at a time. Twenty-five at a time. Sometimes more. Sometimes many more. And each one of them matters. And each one of them might talk to one other person about what you've said."

I understood what she meant. But I felt as if she was underestimating what she was doing and overestimating what I might be able to do.

"But I never know if they're listening, Clementine. I don't know if any of them are listening," I said in a whisper.

"But they do listen. They listened to your grandfather. They listen to my mother. Maybe not every one. But some. Most. And so things change. And things have changed, Tyler, despite my angry outburst. Things have changed. There weren't any black people in unions until people started to say there should be. Or in schools. How many black people were in law schools fifty years ago? Or medical schools? Or the military academies. How many blacks were at West Point or Annapolis in the 1920s or the 1930s? How many black men were officers in the army before World War II? Someone was talking, Tyler. And someone was listening. Or the Civil Rights Movement. Think about how long it took before black people could even register to vote in the South. Someone was talking. Really talking. And someone was listening. And that's what you have to do, Tyler. You've got to keep reading and thinking and writing and talking, because that's the only way things will ever get changed. If you and people like you and Briggs Dyer and Professor McAndrew at Georgia will keep on talking about what matters things will keep on changing. You know that's true. History tells you it's true. If you don't, then nothing will change."

I sat quietly for a moment looking out the window at the distance. "I know," I said. "But it isn't easy. And it certainly isn't exact. What gets heard and what gets dismissed. What happens and what should happen and what doesn't happen. It's a crap shoot. Every day. It's a crap shoot."

"No. It isn't. It's more certain than that. The people who fought the good fight were joined by others because the fighters didn't give up. And that's you, Tyler. You were raised to the task. Your grandfather raised you to the task." Clementine looked at me. "And I love who you are, Tyler. I love your passion. I loved you so much that night when you stood in front of the Forum at the College and very quietly and very exactly explained what your reading has taught you. I was proud because there you were, trying to get folks to think. And they did. They were. I could see the faces around me. They'd heard all of the racist messages. And parts of those messages have stuck. Maybe they didn't even know they'd stuck. But they had. And there you were, Tyler Raymond, one man, one teacher, standing in front of them and telling them that the racist message was not the truth. There was a better truth. A more humane truth. A truth that's fair. Just plain fair. And that the only way the South will ever get free of the racist legacy is to face its past and then start over." She hesitated for a moment. "They were listening, Tyler. And some of them were thinking, 'Hey, this guy's got a point. He's got a point.' I could see it. That's why they applauded at the end. Some of them got it. Some of them really got it."

I sat for a long time over my coffee as it grew cold. Clementine did the same. Then I said, "Let's go for a walk."

With that we got up and put our dishes in the sink in water and rinsed out our coffee mugs and then gathered up our scarves and our parkas and caps and went for a very long walk, holding hands all the way to the crest two miles away where we sat for an hour. We sat and talked as we looked at the distance. We leaned against each other and talked about music and a poem I'd read and a story a nurse friend told Clementine about her daughter who was moving to Chicago. Then the cold drove us back to our cabin. When we arrived, we took off our scarves and gloves and coats and then we lay down and stretched out on the couch in front of the fireplace and wrapped ourselves around each other as the wind outside began to moan through the trees, threatening snow before nightfall. Then just before I dozed off, I saw Clementine smile as she fell asleep, which told me she was going to dream a better dream than she had the night before.

17

Clementine and I observed the Winter Solstice in our rented cabin in the mountains together that year, but without either of our mothers. It felt strange, but we knew that it might well happen with some frequency in the future. We walked into Clearview on the morning of the 25th and telephoned Clementine's grandparents in New Jersey, where Ruth Ann had taken my mother for the holidays. Not only were her grandparents glad to see them, which they told Clementine when she talked to both of them, from the sound in the background of the family sharing presents, which Clementine could hear when she talked to her mother, apparently my mother was having a wonderful time. When we were walking back, a most wonderful thing happened as we passed the Ebenezer African Episcopal Methodist Church, which is on the main highway at the junction we needed to take. An older black man, perhaps in his late sixties, carrying what appeared to be a cardboard box, was following his wife into the church building when he turned and called out to us, "You two going to join us?"

We both stopped and turned and looked at the man.

"It's Christmas day. You should be with lots of people," he said.

"We're staying in a cabin up on the ridge road," I called out. "We were just talking to our mothers on the telephone."

"Have you got people up in your cabin?" the man said.

"No, we don't. We came here to get away from things for a while," Clementine said.

"That's fine. I understand how you might feel that way. Life can be mighty complicated sometimes. But this is Christmas day. It shouldn't be just the two of you up there all by yourselves," the man said.

"We don't know anyone around here," I said, starting to move Clementine back onto the roadway.

"That's what I'm talking about," the man called out. "That's what I mean. You two young people need to be with real folks. People who want you to come on and join them."

"Are you inviting us to join you?" Clementine said, hesitating as she did.

"You got that right," the man said.

"You two should join us," the woman said, coming back onto the steps. "Alvin here is real good at inviting people in. So are all of us. So why don't the two of you come in and have your Christmas meal with us?"

"We don't have anything to bring to the dinner," I said.

"You've got appetites, don't you? Cause that's all you need," Alvin said, smiling broadly.

"If you walked all the way down from the cabins up on the ridge road, you must be hungry," the woman said, starting to come down the steps as another woman appeared in the doorway.

"What're you two doing?" the woman called out from the door.

"We're trying to invite these two young people inside so they can eat with us, Ida May," he said, turning to the woman in the doorway.

"If Alvin's asking you to join us," Ida May said, "then you must be nice enough. So come on. Don't be shy. There aren't many of us for dinner today, but I know everyone would want you to come in."

I turned to Clementine, "Should we?" I said in a whisper.

"They want us to join them," she said.

"It does sound like that."

"Then I think we should accept."

And that is how Clementine and I spent our Christmas day, in 1990, eating with twenty-two of the most senior and most gracious members of the Ebenezer African Episcopal Methodist Church of Clearview, Tennessee, each of whom smiled and introduced him or herself when we came in as if we'd been expected. Then we sat down to a meal of turkey and ham and sweet potatoes and boiled cabbage and sweet peas and carrots, during which they all seemed determined to find out where we were from and what we did for our livings and how long we had been married, which I could tell two of the most senior of the women found a miraculous thing because they sat Clementine down between them during the meal and insisted she explain how she ever ended up with a fair skinned man like me. When Clementine told them that we had gone to school together since the ninth grade and that neither of us had ever even dated anyone else and that she had once run track for Georgia Tech and I had played football for the University of Georgia and that Clementine was going to be a doctor and I was going to be a history professor, they took turns saying, "Well, I'll be" and "Doesn't that just beat all" and "That's just the most wonderful thing."

When they started asking me what kind of woman Clementine was—and one was named Florence and the other was named Linda Ann, but afterwards Clementine and I disagreed about which was which—and I told them Clementine was the smartest and nicest person I had ever met and that she cared about people and that she was going to be a wonderful doctor, one of them said, "I can see that by just looking in her pretty eyes," and the other one said, "I think she's got herself the perfect man if that's what you really think about her, young fella."

When the men of the group heard Clementine say that I had played football for the University of Georgia, several wanted to know if Vince Dooley was as much a gentleman as he appeared to be when he talked on television. I told them he was. Then they wanted to know what it was like playing in those big stadiums that they saw on television. I told them it was an intimidating experience, that everything on the field happens real fast. They said that sounded about right.

Finally, at about 4 P.M., everyone in the group had finished eating, so the clean up started. And as much as the men told me not to worry, that I was a guest, that they would clear the tables and put them away with the chairs, I got up and helped them anyway. When the woman moved into the kitchen to clean the serving dishes before they all took their own and went home with them, Clementine went with them even when they tried to shoo her out by saying she was a guest.

In the end, when everything was back in order, they all started to file out, each of them coming to us and shaking our hands. Then Alvin and his wife offered us a ride up the hill, which we gladly accepted. As we crossed the church yard to his car, I heard one man say in a half-whisper, "You see, I told you some white folks are real nice," to which his wife replied, "Bertrum, the young woman is black. Couldn't you tell from lookin' at her, you fool?" to which he said, "I know she is. But you know what I mean."

Later, when I told her what the man had said, Clementine laughed and replied, "I know what he means."

After that we went to bed, both of us sleeping more soundly than we had in weeks.

18

The three days after the 25th were quiet. It snowed, which both kept us inside close to the fire and let us walk when we needed exercise, wrapped in our parkas and scarves and stocking caps and gloves. Twice we walked in the morning, twice at sunset.

I watched as Clementine sat for two days and drank tea and hot chocolate and read Isak Dinesen's novel *Babette's Feast* and W. Somerset Maugham's *Ashenden* while I banked pillows in front of the fireplace and read John leCarre's novel *A Perfect Spy* for the third time. Only on the morning of the third day did we allow ourselves to look at any study materials. So it was not until that afternoon that Clementine turned her attention back to the text books that I had brought with us for her to review. As for me, I refused to look at anything until the morning of the 29th.

When we sat at the kitchen table over lunch that day, we finally began thinking about going back to Augusta. Clementine had gained perhaps four pounds, which showed very nicely around her cheeks. Her hands were more steady. She seemed much less tense. As for me, because she was smiling more readily, I was happy. In short, the ten days away had done exactly what needed to be done: allowed both Clementine and me to unwind some, ratcheting down the pressure so we might well manage it better when we went back to our schools. Clementine was, after all, closing in on her medical degree, which would then mean more work in the hospital as she began her advanced study in pediatrics. As for me, even after that academic year was over, I still faced three more, but given the support I was receiving, not only from Briggs Dyer and Jack McAndrew but from the Raymond trust as well, I looked forward to what I might be able to achieve. As seriously as I had taken my study of racism in the past, my conversations with Clementine during our time in the cabin in Tennessee taught me that what I was doing was driven by more urgency than I had assumed in the past. "Because lives are at stake, Tyler," Clementine had said. "Real every day lives are at stake." She reminded me of one of my favorite stories, which for the first time I believe I truly understood: after World War I, a French Field Marshall was standing with his forester looking across the Marshall's family estate at a wonderful old stand of trees on a distant hill. When the Field Marshall asked his forester if they might plant a grove of the same kind of trees on the bare hill behind them, the forester replied, "But sir, those are very slow growing trees. It will take a hundred years to grow a forest like that one on that hill."

The Field Marshall replied, "Then we don't have a moment to lose, do we."

The legacy of slavery and segregation and racism, Clementine pointed out, had grown slowly. Reversing the legacy would take a very long time. "So you don't have a moment to lose, Tyler," she said.

With that in mind, we began packing everything we had brought with us that evening so we might begin our drive back to Augusta on New Year's Day. But first, we had to celebrate New Year's Eve, which we began by driving down into town for dinner at a roadside café populated by local families.

When we returned to our cabin, we did as we had once done years before with Ruth Ann and my mother and grandfather: we bundled up and went out to the ridge and stood and looked at the town below and the mountains beyond and looked at the stars in the crystal black sky, and using a flashlight so we could read my wristwatch, we counted down until it was midnight so we could wish each other a very happy 1991: "Which is going to be wonderful, Tyler. I just know it. It's going to be a very good year," Clementine said. To which I replied, "Every year I spend with you, Clementine, is a very good year," making her laugh her shy, gleeful laugh, which is my favorite.

Then, as we had so many times in the past, we held each other against the wind without need of further conversation.

19

As Clementine and I drove down the mountain and then through Chattanooga and into Georgia, I found myself thinking that the two of us had become the people we had wanted to become. It was an odd sensation. Up to that point I had always had the unconscious feeling that somehow, given what we had experienced as individuals and as a couple, that we were still going towards an as yet undefined goal. Now I felt as if the shape of who we were was more clearly defined. I am not saying that I thought we would not learn more as we continued our work and our relationship; Clementine was then and remains today the most interesting person I have ever met. I assume I will never learn everything there is to learn about her, for that would suggest that she was not going to change any further, which I know is not true.

My point is, the girl had become a young woman; the young woman had become a fully formed adult. I assume she felt much the same about me, which is why we had become so comfortable with each other. I understood the perimeters of her person even if the depths remained to be explored. I believe that at that point, the same might have been said about me, even if, like Clementine, I was only twenty-five years old. Much of that feeling, I now sense, was the product of Clementine's and my long relationship. We had fallen in love at fifteen, after all, which is very unusual. At twenty-five we still were in love. Over the course of four years of high school and four years of undergraduate university study and Clementine's first two years in medical school and my two years master's degree study, nothing had ever wavered. What I concluded, although now when I look back I find it somewhat amusing—was that it was highly unlikely that anything would happen to us in the future that would have the impact that some of the past events had certainly had in turning us into the people we had become. I was, of course, very wrong. If I have learned nothing else since that day driving south from Tennessee it is that not only does tomorrow come, it comes in way that most of us could never predict. Certainly that was true for Clementine in March.

20

It was the middle of the month. For two weeks I had left Augusta on Thursday afternoon and driven to Athens where I stayed with Jack McAndrew so I might locate further research materials in the University of Georgia library. On what was supposed to be the second weekend of my work, I found that by late Saturday afternoon I had gotten my hands on more historical documents than I had assumed I might in such a short time. I decided that I missed Clementine far too much to stay over and work on Sunday in the research records when I could simply take what I had and go back home.

Knowing that Clementine was taking a rotation in the Augusta General Hospital emergency room and that her shift was scheduled to end at 9 P.M., I left Athens planning to show up at the hospital by 8:30 so I could take her out for a late dinner before we went home for the night. Driving on Interstate 20, I envisioned coming into the emergency room and surprising her and watching her delight that I had shown up. Of course, like many well laid plans, so to speak, this one went awry.

Emergency Room duty may well be the most taxing work any doctor or nurse can take on. Yes, there are times when nothing is happening. But usually when things start, it is not one problem or two or three but five or six or even more all at once. That's what happened that evening.

I know there is a saying among emergency room medical staffs that when it's a full moon and a weekend, all hell can break loose. Up to that point, Clementine had not yet been on duty on such an occasion so even she understood she had not yet been really baptized. She also knew—at least she used to joke with me and say—that she was overdue. So if you want drama in this memoir, I promise you what happened next in her life will be drama enough for anyone. It was certainly drama enough for me, because without intending to do so, I found myself unwittingly caught in the middle of what might well have turned out to be not just a serious medical emergency but a further disaster as well.

Clementine had been on the emergency room rotation twice before when emergencies had involved automobile accidents. The first time, a mother driving her two sons had been in an accident just south of Augusta. When the emergency medical technicians had brought the three of them to the hospital, Clementine had been part of a four doctor and four nurse team who attended their injuries, which while they were bloody did not end up being life threatening. When Clementine came home that night she said it was at first a frightening experience, for she'd dealt with the younger of the two five and nine year old boys. "He was about as afraid of what was happening as a person could be, Tyler. But I kept talking to him as calmly as I could while we got the glass out of his scalp. By the time we had his injuries dressed, his brother was having a broken leg set. Of all of them, the mother was the least seriously injured. She had a cut on her left arm that required a dozen stitches, but not much more. So while her older son was being attended by the orthopedist who had been called to the hospital, I sat with her and the younger son and tried to explain to them what the doctors had done to them and what they were doing to the other boy. It was a long four hours, but the hospital doctors and nurses did excellent work. She was a very grateful woman by the time her husband arrived to take all three of them home."

The second time was more trying. A drunken man had walked out into traffic along Bobby Jones highway and been struck by a car, which was bad enough, but when he was struck he was thrown down an embankment, where he ended up falling into a barrier fence. By the time a passing motorist notified police about the accident and the injured man, almost two hours had gone by on a cold night. So when the man was brought to the emergency room, he was not only weak from loss of blood and from his injuries, which included two broken legs, he was about as cold as he could get without lapsing into hypothermia. Of course, by the time he reached the hospital and was put on a medical table, he was sober, which in his case meant he was abusive. Clementine was one of two doctors who tried to calm him down before the surgeons could operate on his legs. All the time she and the other young doctor were trying to help, the man kept flailing his arms around and trying to get up. "In the end, he had to be strapped down and sedated," Clementine said. "So by the time he was wheeled into the operating room, he wasn't thanking any of us for what we'd done. In fact, I'm sure I'm going to have bruises on my arms from where he hit me more than once when he was swinging his arms around wildly."

I was none too pleased about that part, as you might expect. But I also knew that Clementine expected that sort of thing to happen. I resolved I would try to get used to whatever happened to her, come what may, as long as she was not in serious danger of injury. Of course, I was also perfectly well aware that if she were ever in danger of serious injury I would not be calm.

With that history, which was certainly limited, you can imagine how I felt that evening as I sat in the emergency room lobby waiting to surprise my darling Clementine when I suddenly heard what sounded like a troop of ambulances screaming outside the ER entrance. Like everyone else, I turned to the automatic double doors to see what was happening, when all of a sudden a number of paramedics burst in pushing two stretchers with what looked like school age children covered with blood strapped down. The first two stretchers were followed by two more. To everyone's horror, the third and fourth stretchers were followed by two more, all of which had school children strapped down, all of whom were bleeding and crying. Then the paramedics pushing the six stretchers were followed by three more paramedics, two of whom were half carrying, half leading an injured child each. They were followed by a paramedic leading a woman dressed as if she had been a van driver. The woman was crying hysterically and her face was bleeding. In less than five seconds, the dull quiet of the lobby erupted into shouting and medical doctors and nurses hurrying the patients inside as fast as they could, Clementine among them. When the woman driver started to pass out and fall to the floor, the paramedic woman who was helping her couldn't keep her on her feet. Because she was pushing past me as she started to fall, I reached out and grabbed her, catching her and the paramedic who was being pulled to the floor. Holding the woman up, I helped the woman paramedic get back to her feet. Then without thinking, I picked up the injured woman and followed the other paramedics and injured people through the doors into the ER treatment area. Instructed to take the woman driver into a partitioned area, I helped the paramedic woman lift the injured woman up onto the table. For a moment, I hesitated, unsure of what I could do to help. By then, I had blood on my hands and on my shirt. A nurse grabbed me and pulled my shirt off and pushed me toward a sink. "Wash then put on this gown," she said, which is how I ended up wearing a doctor's smock.

At that point, doctors and nurses were moving in all directions. A doctor came into the curtained area and saw me. "You're not a doctor. You shouldn't be here."

"He's helping me keep this woman on the table," the paramedic said.

"Jesus Christ!" the doctor swore. "This is madness." Then he turned and left.

The paramedic told me to hold the woman where she was as she stepped out into the corridor. "I need to clean this woman to find her wounds." No one answered so she came back to the curtained off area where I waited. "I know where some things are," she said, turning to the medical trays where she found what she needed to start cleaning the woman's face.

I could feel the injured woman's heart racing. Her body was starting to shake. "She's going into shock," I said.

"Hold her shoulders. I'll get something under her legs. She's got to be elevated," the paramedic said. With that, she found a blanket in a cabinet and folded it up and pushed it under the woman's legs. Then she pulled up the side bars on the medical table. "We've got to stop the bleeding," she said. She turned back into the hallway. "I need someone to help with stitches," she called out.

A nurse came in. "I'll get a tray," the nurse said as she looked at the woman and then left. "I'll be right back. Keep doing what you're doing. Both of you."

For a moment, the paramedic looked at me as I held the injured woman's hands. "Just keep her right there. You shouldn't be in here, but at this point I need your help."

The paramedic went out and called for one of her fellow workers. In a moment she was back with and another paramedic woman. As I held the injured woman, who by then was looking at me and saying, "The children. Oh God, the children. What happened to the children?" I tried to calm her as well as I could, saying, "Please lie still. Please lie still. Help is coming."

The woman looked at me and started crying. "The car came from nowhere," she said. "I didn't see him. He came through the light."

The two paramedics were cleaning her face and taking off her blouse so they could see if she had suffered any other injuries.

Just then another doctor came in. He looked at the paramedics and then at me. "Who's he?" the doctor said.

"He's helping. She's in shock. He's helping," the paramedic who I had helped originally said.

The doctor looked at me and then left.

A nurse came in. "I've got a tray. We can stitch up her wounds as soon as we're sure there's no glass in her cuts."

With that the nurse came to the table. The paramedics moved to give her room, one of them coming around on my side of the table. The nurse glanced at me as she started washing the woman's face and looking for glass shards. "Aren't you Clementine's husband?" she said as she worked.

"Yes. I am," I said.

"What are you doing here?"

"I was going to surprise Clementine. She didn't expect me," I said.

"Well, you're going to surprise her, that's for sure."

"Where is she?" I said.

"Taking care of the children. Trying to keep some of them from dying."

"It was awful," the second paramedic said. "When my partner and I got there, the children were all over the road crying and hurt and bleeding."

"There," the nurse said, holding up a long sliver of glass and dropping it into a surgical basin. Then she bent down over the woman again.

The woman's eyes were big and frightened. She looked at me. "What's going to happen?" she said to me.

"They're taking care of you," I said.

The cut below the woman's lower lip began to bleed more quickly. "Here," the paramedic on my side of the table said, taking my right hand and pressing it down on the gauze she had folded on the wound.

"Get him some gloves," the nurse said without looking at me.

The paramedic stepped back and got gloves out of a dispenser. "Here. I'll hold her. Wash your hands. Then put on these," she said, handing me a pair of gloves.

I went back to the sink and washed my hands and then slipped on the gloves. Then I went back to the table and did what I was told to do: apply pressure to the cut so it would stop bleeding at the same time the nurse finished removing all of the glass splinters that she could find. When she was finished, she stood up straight and looked at the paramedics. "She can stay here for a few minutes but not long. We've got children outside who are going to need attention." With that she turned and left, and the paramedics began trying to help the woman clean her hands and face and relax on the table. "It won't be long," the second paramedic said.

"What about the children?" the woman said in a choking voice.

"None of them were killed. Some had bad cuts. They'll have lots of stitches. There are some broken arms. But it could have been worse. You managed to keep the van from turning over. No one knows how you did that, but that was important."

The woman thanked the paramedic quietly. Then she closed her eyes. The first paramedic who had asked for my help stood and looked at me for a moment. "Maybe you should go now," she said. "You've been a great help. But the doctors are right. You shouldn't be here."

I thanked the paramedic for the compliment and said that I agreed. "This is not why I came here tonight," I said.

With that I removed my gloves and threw them into a waste basket. I just started to remove the gown when Clementine pushed back the curtains. "Tyler," she said.

I turned to her.

"One of the nurses told me you were here."

"I'm just leaving," I said.

"What are you doing?" she asked.

"I came to surprise you," I said, looking at her medical smock which was streaked with blood.

"I mean what are you doing here?" she said. "Back here with the paramedics."

"He was helping," the first paramedic said. "He helped me get the driver onto the table. Then he stayed when a nurse came and we took care of her facial cuts because there weren't any doctors available."

Clementine smiled her that may be true but he still needs to leave smile. "I'm going to be a while," she said. "Maybe you should go home. I'll join you when I'm finished."

"All right," I said, nodding and removing my gown and throwing it into a hamper.

"Obviously you two know each other," the first paramedic said.

Clementine smiled. "He's my husband. He's not a doctor."

"We know he's not a doctor," the second paramedic said.

"But we needed him. I needed his help with the bus driver. She couldn't walk when I brought her in," the first paramedic said. "So I didn't care at that point who he was. I needed his muscles."

Clementine motioned that I should leave. "I don't want anyone to get into trouble," she said in a half whisper.

"No one's going to get into trouble, doctor," the first paramedic said. "Or if someone does, it should be me. I'm the one who asked him to stay."

I thanked the paramedic for what she said. They insisted they should thank me. "You're the one who kept the bus driver calm when I thought she was going to go into shock," she said.

Then Clementine and I left the area, and I went back out into the lobby. "I thought you were going to be in Athens until Sunday," Clementine said.

"I finished early. I was going to surprise you and take you out to dinner."

"You certainly surprised me," Clementine said. "But I don't know how long it's going to be before we finish here. This was a terrible accident. There must be five or six children who are really seriously injured. So don't wait up for me." I hesitated. "It's okay. We're going to be busy. There's nothing more you can do here," she said. Then she kissed me on the cheek and stood watching as I walked back out though the double doors and into the lobby, waving goodbye to her as the doors closed behind me. When I turned around I saw upwards of ten or twelve terrified parents milling around trying to find out anyone who would tell them what had happened. When one woman saw me, she hurried to ask me if I knew anything. "I'm sorry," I said. "I'm not a doctor." I could tell that she was not satisfied with my answer. Before she could press me for more information, I said, "I know the doctors and nurses and staff are working as quickly as they can to take care of everyone." With that I left before anyone else asked me any more questions.

At this point in my narration, I know what you're thinking: that I didn't belong in the medical treatment area of the emergency room. And I agree. I didn't belong there. And I certainly wouldn't want to do what I did again. But I hadn't volunteered, after all. I just happened to be there when help was needed. Far more important to me as I left the hospital and walked to my car was remembering what Clementine had looked like in a medical coat covered in blood. I remember stopping for a moment and shivering even though it wasn't at all cold. After a moment, I went on to my car and drove home where I showered and changed clothes and sat down to wait. I was going to have a very tired wife on my hands when she got home. I would prepare chicken noodle soup, which is her favorite food when she is tired, and French bread, which she likes when she has to work late. And I would uncork a bottle of white wine. Then I would wait up. There was no way I was going to go to sleep until she got home that night. Clementine would need to talk. I was resolved to listen.

21

I was correct, of course. When Clementine came home at 1 A.M., she was as tired as I have ever seen her. After she undressed, I led her into the bathroom where she took a shower as I waited. When she was finished, I had her step out onto the bathmat where I dried her off and then led her to the bedroom where I helped her put on her robe. Then I led her to the kitchen where the soup was simmering. After she sat down, I brought the soup and French bread to the table and then poured her a glass of dry white wine. It took a moment for her to focus on what I wanted her to do. "Eat," I said in a whisper.

She picked up the glass of wine and took a sip. Then she bit into the French bread. After a moment, she turned to the soup.

"The nurses were talking about you, Tyler," she said between spoon fulls.

"Sorry," I said. "I hope it wasn't too embarrassing for you."

She stopped and looked at me. "Just the opposite. I got the whole story of how you were sitting in the lobby waiting for me when the ambulances arrived. The folks at the hospital want you to come volunteer to work in the emergency room."

I shook my head. "I don't think so, Clementine. Doctoring is your business not mine."

"That may be, but what you did helped even if it should never have happened."

"I hope no one is going to get into trouble," I said.

"I don't think so. Unless the bus driver complains, I think everyone will let the matter drop."

"Good," I said quietly. Then I looked at her. "You were heroic, Clementine."

She looked at me.

"I mean it. All of you. The nurses. The doctors. You. That must have been a terrible ordeal."

"It was serious. Twelve children have been admitted to the hospital plus the driver. It's a wonder no one was killed. At least, that's what the EMTs said. The driver who hit them . . . he ran a red light. And he was going way over the speed limit. What he did to those children is terrible. Not only were they injured, they were terrified. It must have been awful. The EMTs said when they got there, some of the children were out of the van wandering around as if they were in shock. That was as big a fear for them as the injuries."

I waited for her to say more. When she did not, I asked, "Did anyone talk to the parents? When I was leaving, there must have been a dozen of them trying to get information. It looked to me as if they were right on the edge of hysteria."

"They probably were," Clementine said. "But to answer your question. Yes. The chief of emergency medicine talked to them. I know he tried to explain to each parent what had happened."

"I'd certainly have been terrified if it'd been our child," I said.

Clementine was quiet for a moment. "I tried to keep them calm. The children, I mean. That was as important as tending to their injuries," she said.

We were both silent for a few minutes.

"Can you sleep late in the morning?" I asked.

"I want to. I need to," she said.

"If I wake up ahead of you, I'll be as quiet as I can," I said.

"I know you will," she replied.

"That was my last rotation in the emergency room," Clementine said.

"Good," I responded.

"I'm ready for pediatrics. Of course, I got a taste tonight since the patients were all so young."

I nodded and waited as she returned to her soup and bread. We sat together like that for some time, neither of us speaking. "I just hope I did all of the right things," she said after some time.

"I'm sure you did. I'm sure everyone did."

Clementine did not reply but turned back to her soup and her silence.

"I found the materials I needed," I said, looking at Clementine who was about to fall asleep in her food. "In Athens. In the library."

When she did not reply I got up and went around the table and moved the bowl and plate and wine glass. Then I reached down and picked her up and carried her into the bedroom where I put her into our bed. She was asleep before I could bring the comforter up to her chin. Then I went back to the kitchen and turned out the light and returned to our bedroom and lay down next to her, where I listened to her breathing for a moment before I too fell away into the darkness.

22

For the next several years, Clementine and I worked very hard at making a life for ourselves in Augusta. Clementine's studies at the Medical College of Georgia required four years, which meant she finished in June, 1992. Our mothers attended the graduation, of course.

During her fourth year, she began interviewing for residency programs in pediatrics. Her first choice, of course, was MCG. But to insure that she would be admitted to a residency program somewhere she also interviewed at Emory University and the Medical University of South Carolina, in Charleston. And while she was concerned she might not get into MCG, which was her first choice, I was more confident. So it came as no surprise to me when she was accepted and began three years of further study, which she completed in June, 1995.

At the same time, while I continued my teaching at Augusta College, I was also commuting back and forth on a regular schedule to Athens where I was a doctoral candidate in history. The fact I was enrolled at the University of Georgia meant that, in addition to my salary at Augusta College, I continued to receive Raymond trust fund money, although I had not heard from either my Raymond grandfather or grandmother since graduating from the University of Georgia in 1988. What that meant was that even though we had to budget our money carefully, with Clementine's partial scholarship to GMC and my salary at Augusta College, we were able to continue paying tuition at both schools. Of course, it also meant that we continued living in our two bedroom apartment, which, while it was small, was perfectly serviceable.

I would love to say that during those years, Clementine and I did not run into incidents of prejudice because of our differing races, but that would not be true. Not in Augusta, of course. For all of its racist past, Augusta seems to have come a long way. No, the first of two incidents happened in 1993 in Georgia when Clementine and I decided to drive to Tampa rather than fly. We had decided to not take the Interstate 20 to Atlanta and then Intestate 75 to Tampa for a change, which meant we followed highway 25 south though Georgia. After we'd eaten breakfast at the Huddle House Restaurant in Millen, where we had stopped twice before, and as Clementine paid the bill and I waited, a scrawny, rather unkempt white man hunched over his coffee and wearing a very greasy baseball cap and some sort of mechanic's jump suit looked at Clementine and then at me and muttered, "Interesting choice there, mister."

I waited for a moment before turning to him. "I didn't hear what you said," I said quietly.

"Me?" the man said.

"Yes. You. I didn't hear what you said," I said quietly.

By then Clementine had paid our check and was standing in the doorway ready to leave.

The man did not answer but looked at me with a smirk on his face.

"Tyler, are you coming?" Clementine said.

The man smiled again. "Better go, Tyler," he said quietly, the word *Tyler* said in a snotty, hateful way.

I could not resist. I was standing. He was sitting. I was bigger than him. So I leaned over toward him for a moment and looked him in the eyes. "You are a stupid little man, William," I said, reading the name stitched onto his mechanics uniform, "and she," I whispered, nodding my head in Clementine's direction, "is my wife and a medical doctor."

He looked at me as if he was going to speak.

Then I leaned my fists down on the table and then picked up his lit cigarette from the ashtray and said, "And I just know she would tell you that smoking is bad for your health." With that I pushed his lit cigarette down into his cup of coffee. For a moment, our eyes met, but he did not move. He apparently understood that it would be better if he did not. Then I stood up over him again. "Enjoy your breakfast, William," I said in a whisper, turning to Clementine as I did and leaving with her without further comment.

We have, by the by, been back to the Huddle House three times since then over the years, but we've never seen William again, which is just as well, because I'm not particularly proud of how I responded to him that day, but I would undoubtedly do the same thing again given half a chance.

The other incident happened in 1994 as we crossed into Florida. We stopped at a gas station outside Lake City, the kind that features trinkets and CDs and all sorts of gear for trucks. Clementine had used the women's restroom at the same time I used the men's. As I was coming out, a woman with bleached blonde hair who should not have been wearing tight clothing was waiting to get her turn in the women's toilet. As I passed her, we made momentary eye contact. "I suppose I'll have to wash the seat when I get in there," she said.

For an instant her comment did not register. Then it did. I stopped and turned back to her. "What did you say?" I asked.

She looked at me as if she was surprised I had spoken to her. "I didn't say anything to you," she muttered.

"You said something about having to wash the seat," I said, smiling as if I was going to make some sort of similar remark.

She nodded. "Because a black woman got in ahead of me," she said, emboldened by my response.

I drew myself up and looked at the woman very carefully. "A black woman with long wavy hair?" I said.

The woman scowled. "Yes."

I smiled. "You won't have to worry. She's exceptionally clean in her habits," I said.

"She's what?" the woman responded.

"She's my wife," I said. "And I can assure you she's exceptionally clean in her habits," I said again in a sarcastic, deliberately belittling tone of voice.

Then I stepped back as Clementine came out of the restroom and smiled and said, "I was just telling this white woman that you're clean in your habits." Clementine did not reply. She didn't need to. She understood what must have happened. So we turned and left together. And I did not look back over my shoulder because I didn't ever want to see the white woman's face again.

But other than those two incidents, neither of which brought out the best in me, we did not encounter any obvious racial hostility. Of course, it could have been that it was there but we didn't see it. Or it could have been that we just happened to be in places where things of that sort do not happen or in places where attitudes of that sort may be thought but are not said out loud. In any case, as far as we were concerned, we were just two people trying very hard to enjoy our marriage to one another while focusing on our studies, which at times each of us confessed we had begun to fear would never end.

Then it was June, 1995. Clementine finished her residency and began private practice, establishing hospital privileges in the process. I remember the morning she began her work with two other female pediatricians in their office. I went with her and helped her put her name plate on the door. Then, because it was her day not mine, I opened the door for her and said, "Have a nice day, Doctor Brown." As I held the door I could see the two doctors and the three nurses with whom she would now work gathered inside in the waiting room to greet her. Then I turned to leave so she could enjoy the moment with her new colleagues, but Clementine reached for me and grasped my arm. I stopped and turned back to her. "Thank you, Tyler Thomas Raymond, for being my lab partner."

I smiled and leaned toward her and kissed her more tenderly than ever. "Thank you, Clementine Camille Brown for asking me into your life." Then I watched as she turned and went into the office. As I started walking down the hallway, I could hear the women inside applauding as Clementine went in to begin her career.

At the same time, I also completed my Ph.D. dissertation at Georgia, which, under Jack McAndrew's direction and following Briggs Dyer's advice, I was able to turn into a book manuscript that was accepted for publication by the University of California at Berkeley Press and dedicated to my grandfather. As you would expect, our mothers attended both ceremonies.

It had always been my intention to enlarge on my grandfather's intention to chronicle the story of how black men were excluded from the major leagues of baseball in the late nineteenth century by white men who feared the blacks would prove to be superior athletes. That was why in my undergraduate studies with Professor McAndrew and then my master's degree studies with Briggs Dyer and then my doctoral research under Jack McAndrew, again, I had spent years looking at the two faces of racism in America: the openly hateful and public expressions of fear of the negative impact blacks would have on the so called superior white culture on one hand, and the equally hateful but repressed fear that given a chance for education and full participation in American social life, black people would prove to be, if not superior to whites at least their equals. Using both the logic of historical evaluation driven by the symbols inherent in Jungian psychoanalysis, I argued that what fair minded people termed the sickness of racism was not just a behavior, which then had a corrupting influence on the psyches of white society. Rather, it was a psychological distortion that had corrupting influence on social conduct. In other words, my position was that it was not external life that shaped internal life; it was internal life that shaped the external. My proposition stated that until American Caucasians rejected the morally untenable position they clung to, they would not only never cure their own illness, they should assume that eventually the Black people living in America would develop their own brand of racist resentment and accusation.

When I submitted the text to three university presses with which Jack McAndrew had connections, it was the University of California that responded not only first but most supportively. It was particularly encouraging to hear that one young female and one young male instructor who had been asked the read the manuscript after it was sent to the Berkeley editors not only supported its publication, they said that as soon as it was published they were going to include it as required reading in their history courses. And if all of that extraordinary activity was not enough, the general public and the faculty at Augusta College was informed that beginning in 1996, Augusta College would undergo a name change. Clementine and I decided that we would accept the coincidence she completed her medical studies and I completed my Ph.D. the same month it was announced that Augusta College would become Augusta State University as testimony we had made the right choice in centering our lives on both the city and our respective schools.

So there we were, a pediatrician just starting her private practice and an associate professor of history contracted by a university he had come very much to enjoy, living in Augusta, Georgia, finally starting the sanctioned and anointed and certified work lives for which we had striven for so long, still profoundly in love with one another, now free to travel as regularly to Tampa where we stayed with our mothers in the house they owned together. In fact, it was on our trip to Tampa in December, 1996, for our Winter Solstice holiday, that Clementine and I took our mothers out to dinner so we could tell them what they had both waited ever so patiently to hear.

23

The second night we were in Tampa on that trip, we took our mothers to a nearby Macaroni Grill Restaurant, which was one of their favorites. After we ordered our meals but before they came, Clementine very casually said she and I had just made two very important decisions.

"About what?" my mother said. "What's going on, Tyler?" she said, turning to me.

"About something very personal," I said, smiling and prolonging my mother's sense of expectation.

Ruth Ann reached over and touched Clementine's face and looked into her eyes. "Out with it, Dr. Brown," she said in her best Ruth Ann voice. "What are you keeping from us? What're the two decisions you have to make?"

"You aren't moving farther away, are you?" my mother said, a note of concern in her voice. "It's hard enough seeing you in Augusta and getting you to come here. If you moved farther away it would be even harder."

I smiled. "We aren't moving away, mother," I said quietly.

"We've picked two names," Clementine said.

"Actually, Clementine, it was four names. Two first names and two middle names," I said quietly, as if I was trying to speak to Clementine but not have our mothers hear.

Clementine smiled as if she understood my secret. "That's right," she whispered. "It was four names."

"Wait a minute," Ruth Ann said quickly. "What do you mean two names? Four names. Are you two talking about *baby* names?"

"Yes we are," Clementine said.

"Four names for two girls," I said smiling.

"For girls? Two girls?" my mother said.

"Yes," Clementine replied. "Twins. Just like Tyler said years and years ago when we were in school. Just like the Kru woman in Africa said when she touched my belly. I would one day give birth to twin girls."

Both of our mothers were silent for a moment as the news sunk in. "Clementine, is that going to be dangerous for you?" Ruth Ann could not keep herself from saying.

Clementine hesitated.

"We will have to be careful," I said patiently.

Ruth Ann looked at me and nodded. "Just as long as Clementine is going to be okay," she said.

"I'll take care of her," I said.

"I know you will, Tyler. I know that. But twins?" Ruth Ann said. "With your diabetes and all, Clementine . . . "

"We know, mother," Clementine said quickly. "My doctor will take every precaution. So will we. Both of us."

After a moment, Ruth Ann went on. "All right. So what are the names you've picked out?"

"Should we tell them?" Clementine said, turning to me.

"If you want to. They just have to promise to not make any editorial comments."

"Do you think they can keep from doing that?" Clementine said.

"I don't know," I said. Then I turned to Ruth Ann and my mother. "Are you two going to editorialize?" I said.

Ruth Ann smiled. "Tyler, if I've learned one thing about the two of you over the years it's that when you set your minds to something, whatever Elizabeth or I might say won't change anything."

"And whatever names you've picked out will be wonderful," my mother said.

"All right," Clementine said, smiling and turning to Ruth Ann. "One of the girls will be named Josephine Arway."

"Arway in Kru means beautiful," I said. Because Josephine is going to be beautiful."

Both mothers smiled broadly.

"The other girl will be named Abigail Donyen," Clementine said, adding quickly, "Donyen in the Kru language also means beautiful. Because Abigail is going to be just as beautiful as Josephine."

Ruth Ann sat back and looked at her daughter and then at me. "Well, well," she said quietly. "You two are really something. Individually and together. You two are really something."

"We are very proud, Tyler. Of both of you," my mother said, taking my hand in hers at the same time she also took Clementine's. "Of everything you've accomplished. And your grandfather would have been very proud as well."

"You'll have to get a bigger apartment, won't you?" Ruth Ann said after a moment.

"We're going to buy a house," I said quietly. "We've picked one out half way between Augusta State and Clementine's office."

"Really?" Ruth Ann said. "What's it like? What's the neighborhood like?"

We then set out to describe the house, which was a forty year old brick home lived in since it was built by a now elderly couple who had raised two sons. Now their sons were grown up with families, and the couple wanted to move to Florida to be near the younger of the two boys and three of their grandchildren. What appealed to us in particular was that the house had two bedrooms downstairs and two bedrooms upstairs.

"We'll put the nursery downstairs next to us," Clementine said. "Tyler can have an office on the second floor next to the guest bedroom. The couple who are selling the house made sure they had a bathroom for each of the bedrooms downstairs and a shared bathroom upstairs."

"And there's a big family room between the kitchen and the living room," I said. "And a small formal dining room and a nice screened in porch on the back of the house, which looks into a wooded area. So it's unlikely we'll ever have neighbors peering over the fence the couple had built ten years ago."

"What about the neighbors?" Ruth Ann asked.

"They seem nice," Clementine said. She did not elaborate. She understood what her mother was asking—the neighborhood was integrated and consisted mainly of teachers and professional people—but Clementine was not going to take the bait. "The people we've met seem very nice," she said again much to Ruth Ann's dissatisfaction.

With that, our mothers looked at each other and did what mothers having been doing for eons: they got up and came around the table and hugged each other. And Ruth Ann said, "Congratulations, Elizabeth." And my mother said, "Congratulations, Ruth Ann."

Then Clementine looked at them and said, "What about us?"

They both laughed and turned to us as we stood up, and each gave each of us a hug and said congratulations and how happy they were and that now, whenever we came to see them or they came to see us, they wouldn't have to worry about one of them not having a granddaughter to spoil. "We can each have one," my mother said, laughing.

"All of which calls for a toast," Ruth Ann said. So the four of us went back to our places at the table, and the two of them raised their glasses of wine to toast Clementine and me and the twins. "To the two of you," Ruth Ann said. "The four of you," my mother said laughing.

Picking up my own glass of wine, I said, "To Clementine, the love of my life," to which Clementine said, "To Tyler, the only man I will ever love," lifting her glass of iced tea because she would get no more wine until the babies were born.

24

So Clementine and I had arrived, so to speak. What had started out as two ninth graders in a biology lab falling in love and standing firm against the normal obstacles of life, coupled to the race prejudice they encountered over the years, had evolved into two adults, still deeply in love with each other, beginning their individual professional careers, all of which paled in contrast to their next adventure: becoming parents. For what mattered now was Clementine's health and the well being of our twin girls. Given Clementine's medical circumstance, the gestation period had to be monitored very closely. For that reason we met with her obstetrician every week. Fortunately, Clementine's medical practice partners, both of whom had children, understood Clementine's desire to give birth as early in her career as she could. They understood that her concern was not just about her age, although that was a factor, but her age coupled to her diabetes. Clementine's assumption was that every year she delayed in having children made her diabetes more of a threat. So even though it would have been more convenient to put off giving birth for three or four years until her medical practice was established, when everything was taken into consideration, it was judged best to give birth during the summer of 1997, when I could be at home with her, and then return to the practice as soon as she was able.

The task that fell to me then was to take very good care of Clementine's physical and emotional well being. Dr. Juliet Williams, her obstetrician, said that like many other women who live with diabetes, it would be best if Clementine only attempted to deliver a child once. The fact she was pregnant with twins was, therefore, a double-edged sword. On one hand, it meant she might well deliver two children, which would mean she would not have to risk another pregnancy if she and I decided we wanted to have more than one child. On the other hand, delivering twins is a risk for any woman even under the best of circumstances. Clementine's condition made carrying and delivering twins even more perilous.

At the same time, at least for the first four months of her pregnancy, Clementine wanted to go to the office every day and meet with what proved to be a rapidly increasing number of patients. What made it possible for her to do so was that every day she was in the company of her partners, Dr. Cynthia Roses and Dr. Nataly North, and the three nurses in the practice, Molly Wirt and Jennifer Koster and Andreea O'Kane, who protected her like the crown jewels while, at the same time, according her full and deserved professional respect. In brief, Clementine knew she was always in the company of people who cared about her as well as people who regarded her as a fully qualified medical equal. It is hard to think of another circumstance in which both of those needs could have been met simultaneously.

25

The next ten weeks unfolded as we had hoped. Clementine's medical practice and my teaching, for which we had prepared ourselves for so many years, were what we did individually. However, as important as they were, both paled by contrast to when we met, every evening, so to speak, at Clementine's pregnancy. I am sure I'm not the first husband who found himself looking at his wife from across a room as she sat and read or did something else equally absorbing as if she were a walking miracle while every day her body began to change more and more. I am sure I am not the first husband who sat next to his wife, his hand tenderly touching her growing belly, as her pregnancy began to show more and more. And I am as sure as sure can be that I am not the first husband who lay next to his wife at night, listening to her breathing, who pressed his ear against her belly and listened as more and more the cacophony of sounds that I heard became more than just her digestive system at work. For I knew that deep inside those sounds were the heart beats of two girl children beginning to become what they would be when they arrived. In short, Clementine's belly became the center of my world. Her womb became the miracle for which I had waited all of my life even if I had not known that's what I'd been doing.

Of course, the physical changes in Clementine were to be expected. When she was more and more tired at the end of the day, I tried to take on even more of the tasks that we had always shared.

When her ankles began to swell each evening and she started looking at herself in the mirror in wonder as the slim, lithe athlete became more and more what she said was dowdy, I tried to reassure her as much as a husband can reassure his wife under similar circumstances that she was not only just as beautiful as she had ever been, she was beautiful in a whole new way. And I meant it. Clementine lost none of her beauty. In fact, I argued with her more than once that she was more beautiful than ever. "You were a woman before, Clementine. Now you are *Woman*."

She looked at me as if she either did not understand—which I knew was not the case—or she did not believe me. When I tried to explain that for me, she had always been the Gaia woman, the earth mother, the center of my universe, now she was the earth-mother-center-of-the-universe for two brand new human beings. "Think of the Kru women who came before Fonsiba. Think of Fonsiba. Think of all of the women who link you to a past you cannot fully define. Think of how you are now them. All of them. Think of how you now link them to the future. My God, Clementine, you really are the center of the universe."

"Tyler, there are other women who have . . . " she stated to say.

"Clementine, I know there are other women who have done the same thing. I'm not a fool. You are not unique. Yet you are. Each one of us is ordinary. Each one of us is extra-ordinary. Yes, you are one more woman in the history of women more numerous than anyone could even guess who has given birth to children in the same way I am just one more man in the history of men more numerous than anyone could even guess who has fathered children. And that matters. But you are also you. You are Clementine Camille. You are unique. There has never been another you before, and there will never be another you again. At the same time, you are a link. You are the tie that binds. You are . . . "

"Are you going to start singing hymns now, Tyler" Clementine said, smiling.

I looked at her for a moment. "Only hymns of your praise, woman."

Clementine smiled her I-love-you-Tyler smile.

"You are the center of my world, Clementine. You are the center of those girls' world. That's all I'm trying to say."

"I know," she said quietly.

"And I am trying to tell you that you are beautiful. That's all. You are beautiful."

Clementine was quiet for some time. Then she looked away. I could see traces of tears in her eyes. But she did not speak. She did not have to. I knew just as well as she that what she was feeling, what I was feeling, was beyond words, beyond the need for words.

I reached over and touched her hand. Then I slid my hand down along her belly. And I felt movement; I swear, for the first time ever, I felt movement.

Clementine turned and looked at me. She had felt the same thing. So she smiled. And I smiled. She leaned toward me and kissed me.

I touched her face gently and kissed her in return. For we had felt the universe move. Not much, mind you. But that did not matter. We had both just felt the whole beautiful universe move.

If only my grandfather had not . . . . I did not complete the thought.

26

There were dangers, of course. There are dangers in every pregnancy. Everyone knows that. But for Clementine, the dangers were specific. She had managed her diabetes wonderfully well during her two years at the University of Georgia and her seven years at the Georgia Medical College. She had managed it very well once she began her medical practice. But now she was pregnant, and for her, that created a specific kind of danger that had to be monitored very, very carefully. For Clementine to lose the babies, less would have to go wrong than women who did not have diabetes. That was obvious. What it meant, of course, was that both of us had to take extra care that she ate properly, that she did not become overly tired at work, that she slept soundly and for sufficient time at night.

I relieved her of even more of the cooking that I had previously. I would not let her vacuum our house or do any heavy lifting. Because she was carrying twins, I would have done that anyway. Because she was a diabetic carrying twins meant she had to give in and let me do almost all of the physical tasks to make us comfortable. For me it was not inconvenient. I wanted to take care of her. For her, it was frustrating. When her frustration got the better of her, she sometimes started to complain about things that under normal circumstances she would never have even mentioned. I had talked with Ruth Ann about her pregnancy and with my mother about hers. So I had been warned. The gentle and calm and sensitive Clementine I had loved sometimes gave over to a more short tempered, more impatient, more demanding Clementine I had not met up to that time. I didn't have to be a clinical psychologist to understand what was happening. So whenever her mood became difficult, I responded by not responding to her directly. Instead, I started singing. I usually selected songs from Broadway musicals that I knew she liked, not because I am a very good singer but because the songs themselves reminded her of times when she had felt better.

The other issue was food. Very often what I prepared was not what she wanted even if she had said it was before I began cooking. So very often our menus changed in the middle of being prepared. I have to admit that I am rather proud of my cooking, so those times were a tad more difficult for me than when she didn't like the way I had changed the bed or the way I had cleaned the bathroom. Twice I told her that I was cooking exactly what she had said she wanted and that the best thing she could do was to go sit down in the living room and drink her orange juice and wait for me to finish preparing the meal. I'm not very proud of those moments, not because I was horribly impolite with her but because on those occasions I just simply forgot that her body was making all sorts of varying demands, some of which changed without warning. After she was more calm and I was more calm, she always said she was sorry, and I always said I was sorry, which then meant that I went out to the grocery store to buy something she wanted no matter what time it was or what it was she requested. I assume we weren't much different from most couples in that regard.

27

There were two incidents, however, that caused concern. The first took place in late May when Clementine became dizzy at work and had to be brought home from work, so I put her to bed for two days. She protested, of course, but I expected that, as did her partners. When Monday came around, she went back to the office, but for the rest of the month she came home by 2 P.M. every day. The second happened when I was home for the summer, which for all of our concern worked out as well as it could. By then it was agreed that with only three more weeks before her delivery date, Clementine should come home to stay. From that point on, I was able to monitor her activities; that is, I could make sure she got the proper amount of guarded exercise while, at the same time, insuring that she also both napped in the afternoon and slept all night as the doctor prescribed. Finally, Ruth Ann flew to Augusta from Tampa three days before Clementine was to go into the hospital to help with the final preparations. My mother came in the night before Clementine was to deliver. But even with all of the preparation and all of our precautions, Clementine was not out of danger. That became far too clear when she was wheeled into the delivery room for the Cesarean procedure.

The doctors said they would prefer if I was not in the delivery room for the operation. Had it been a more routine birth, they would have had no objections. I had gone to classes, after all, even though I knew it was not recommended that I be with Clementine. But then one of the nurses in the hospital came out and said Clementine was calling for me.

With my heart in my mouth, I was gowned and masked and followed the nurse. Clementine had coded. I wasn't sure what that meant. The nurse told me that the delivery had gone as planned, but then problems suddenly happened, the result of her being a diabetic despite all of the precautions that had been taken.

What I saw when I entered the delivery room was Clementine trying to remain conscious, the doctors bent over her working as quickly as they could to stabilize her heart, and two nurses, one each with a baby wrapped in white, moving away so they could care for the girls.

"Your daughters are fine," the nurse who brought me into the room said through her mask. "They're being taken care of right now. But your wife's heart rate suddenly went up. We're bringing it down right now."

I was directed to sit above Clementine's head. Her body was cloaked so I could not see what the doctors were doing. What I could see was Clementine's face. She was pale, and her lips looked dry and cracked. A nurse handed me a wet cloth and directed me to put it on Clementine's mouth, which I did. Clementine tried to look up to see me. "I'm here," I whispered.

"Tyler," I heard Clementine say in a rasping voice.

"I'm here," I said. "Hang on." I reached for her right hand and held it in mine. She clamped down hard. I could feel her body go rigid.

Then a nurse moved to her IV and changed the medication. "This will help," she said.

I felt Clementine relaxing. I could hear the heart monitor. It had been beating very fast. I was sure too fast. Now I could hear it slowing down. "I'm here," I said again.

"The girls?" I heard her whisper.

I turned to the nurse who had brought me into the room. "They're fine, Clementine," she said quietly. "Both of them are beautiful."

I was crying. I tried to wipe away my tears with my left hand so they would not fall into Clementine's face. I leaned down and pressed my right cheek against her left cheek.

"The girls?" I heard her say again.

"They're beautiful," I said. "The nurse says they're beautiful." I kissed her cheek again.

The nurse said she agreed.

"But then they'd have to be beautiful, wouldn't they," I said. "You're their mother."

I heard Clementine laugh quietly. "And you're their father, Tyler."

"Yes, Clementine. I am their father," I said. Then I pressed my face against hers again. I wanted to go to sleep right there. I wanted to roll over and hold her in my arms. I wanted to protect her from pain, from any pain, from every pain in the world.

"I want to see them," I heard her whisper in my ear.

I sat up slowly and looked at the nurse.

"As soon as the doctors are finished," the nurse said.

"As soon as the doctors are finished," I said to Clementine.

Clementine spoke without opening her eyes. "Which is going to be which, Tyler?"

"What?" I said.

"Which is going to be which? One came first. Then the other. Which is Josephine? Which is Abigail?"

I did not have an answer. We had not made that decision.

"I don't know," I said quietly. "Does it matter?"

"It matters to them," Clementine said in a whisper.

"Then you decide," I replied.

Clementine was quiet for a moment. The doctors stood up straight over her as if they had finished their work.

I turned to Dr. Williams. "Can Clementine see them now?" I asked.

"Yes," Dr. Williams said, stepping back so the nurses could bring the girls to Clementine.

The first nurse placed one of the baby girls in the crook of Clementine's right arm. The second nurse came to me and placed the second baby girl in my arms.

I moved around to Clementine's left side so I could see the baby she was holding. She turned to see the baby I was holding. "This is Josephine," she said, turning to look at the baby she was holding.

"And this is Abigail," I said quietly, holding her up for Clementine to see.

Clementine smiled and turned to the nurses. "Who came first?" she said.

The nurses smiled behind their masks. "The one you're holding, Clementine."

"Josephine," Clementine said.

"Okay, Josephine," the nurse said.

"Which is just as I thought," Clementine said.

"Just as you thought?" I said.

"Just as I thought," Clementine said quietly.

"So you knew?" I said. "Somehow you knew?"

"Yes," Clementine whispered. "I always knew. From the beginning. I always knew."

Shaking my head in wonder, I placed Abigail in Clementine's other arm and said very softly, "Girls, meet your wonderful mother."

Clementine laughed quietly. Then she said, "Girls, meet your wonderful father."

"Congratulations," Dr. Williams said, coming around and looking at the two baby girls. "My sincerest congratulations to all four of you."

With that, the two nurses who had brought the girls to us took them away as two other nurses came so they could begin preparing Clementine to be moved to a recovery room. At the same time, the nurse who had brought me into the room came to me and led me back out into the hallway where Ruth Ann and my mother were waiting to hear the news. What I remember about that was the way Ruth Ann's hands were shaking when she hugged me and how hard she held on when I told both of them that Clementine was weak, but Dr. Williams said she and Josephine and Abigail were all doing just fine. What I remember is the way she cried and smiled and laughed at the same time as she turned to my mother, who by then was crying and laughing in the same way. "Grandmothers," my mother whispered to Ruth Ann.

"Grandmothers," Ruth Ann said in return.

"My goodness," my mother said. "My goodness," she said again.

So that was that. Another chapter in Clementine's and my life together had closed; another chapter had opened. And oh, what a chapter it would be.

28

An hour later I was ushered into Clementine's room. Once it was apparent she was not only able but eager to see both of our mothers, they were brought into the room with us.

As you would expect, Ruth Ann headed straight for Clementine, with both of them hugging the other as tightly as Clementine could stand. Then it was my mother's turn. "We're so proud of you, Clementine. So proud."

Then two nurses brought the babies in for both of them to see. I knew that Ruth Ann and my mother were going to start clucking, which they did. And I knew they would start talking to the babies in adult words, which they also did. There would be no baby talk for these two girls. They would grow up hearing real words. The more the better, I thought.

Then for a moment it was silent. It was as if all four of us ran out of energy at exactly the same moment. Then Clementine started to laugh. She wasn't laughing at anything in particular. None of the three of us had said anything funny. She just began to laugh. I put my arms around her and let her laughter dissolve into tears. "They're so beautiful," she kept saying. "They're so beautiful."

"They are that," I whispered in her ear. "You do very fine work, Doctor Brown."

Clementine hung on hard for a moment. Then she whispered in my ear, "So do you, Doctor Raymond."

"We're grandmothers," Ruth Ann said.

"We're grandmothers," Elizabeth said.

Twenty minutes later the three of us were shown the door by the two nurses who came in to take the babies away. "Clementine needs to rest," one of them said. "She needs sleep."

It was 6 A.M. I kissed Clementine on her forehead and said I would be back during morning visiting hours. One of the nurses heard what I said and told me I should wait until at least 2 P.M. "She needs to rest. Cesarean sections are difficult," she said. "Twins make it even harder. Clementine needs to sleep."

I said I would be back at 2 P.M. Then Ruth Ann and my mother and I left. Once we got into the lobby I suggested that we eat breakfast since we'd been in the hospital since 5 P.M. the afternoon before, and none of us had eaten since then. With that we headed for the International House of Pancakes on Washington.

First, we were seated and we'd been served coffee and ordered our food. For a moment none of us said anything. Perhaps we were all weary. Perhaps we were coming down from our euphoria. In any case, all of a sudden, without any warning, sitting facing my mother and Ruth Ann, I turned to the window and looked out at the avenue, and I started to cry. To this day I cannot really explain what I was feeling. It was as if a surge of conflicting emotions jumbled together had suddenly surged to the surface. Part of it was relief because in all honesty I had been afraid ever since Clementine said she was pregnant. When the doctor told us she was carrying twins, I had to fight the panic that I felt in my chest. Since that day I had fought it off every morning and every evening when I was with Clementine. Another part was frustration. For I loved Clementine Camille Brown. I knew words could never say how much. Deeds would always fall short. It hurt that I could never show her how crucial she was to my life. It hurt that I knew I would die and never really have been able to demonstrate to her in any comprehensible way the fact that her person was responsible for who I had become, who I would be in the future. Another part was sheer, unmitigated joy. I now not only had Clementine Camille to love, I had Josephine Arway and Abigail Donyen to love and to protect. I realized for the first time that I was not just a lover and a husband. I was a father. Nothing . . . I swore to myself, nothing and no one would ever hurt those two little girls. All of that came tumbling up, and when it mixed with the fact I had not slept more than three hours in the last forty-eight, the result was tears. So there I sat with my mother and my mother-in-law at our table in the International House of Pancakes restaurant in Augusta, Georgia, miles and years removed from the ninth grade biology class at Tampa Coast High School, tracing back over the years, racing back over every emotion I had ever felt, every event that had unfolded . . . struck dumb in my wonderment at how it had all happened and how I had been so blessed and where I was now and what had just happened hours before.

I turned to my mother, who reached for my hand. "That is exactly what your father did the morning after you were born," she said. "My father told me that when the two of them went out for breakfast, he did exactly what you're doing now, Tyler."

I nodded but could not speak. Then Ruth Ann did a wonderfully Ruth Ann thing: she reached over and took my other hand and looked at me and said in a firm whisper, "Tyler Thomas Raymond, I am so very thankful that you fell in love with and married my daughter."

I turned to Ruth Ann. "Thank you," I said in a whisper. "Thank you very much," I said, after a moment adding, "That means everything to me."

The waitress was standing beside us with our food in hand. Faced with three people crying and smiling together, she did not know what to do.

"Twins," my mother said, looking at the young woman. "My very happy son and Ruth Ann's absolutely wonderful daughter," she said, nodding toward Ruth Ann.

"That's wonderful," the young woman said. "Congratulations to you," she said to me. "To all three of you," she said.

"Mother and daughters are all doing just fine," Ruth Ann added.

"That's just wonderful," the young woman said. "That's just wonderful." Then she began distributing our food. I used a napkin to wipe away my tears. And the three of us turned our attention to eating.

29

When Clementine had been in the hospital years before when her diabetes appeared, I stayed with her for nearly two months, sleeping in the same room so I could read to her around the clock. This time, there not only was no necessity for me to do the same, it would not have been allowed unless there had been an emergency. And for all of the potential danger of Clementine's delivery, nothing became truly life threatening, for which we were very thankful.

By that afternoon, the three of us were back in Clementine's room, all of us taking turns holding the twins, Clementine's maternal instincts showing more clearly than even I had imagined would be the case. By that I mean when she held the girls individually, her hands seemed to be magic, for each of them grew quiet. And even though neither could focus her eyes yet, both of them seemed to know their mother's voice. I sat back in wonder, not because I was seeing a side of Clementine that surprised me but because I was seeing yet another depth to her already extraordinary person. The same woman who had fought off pain as a runner, who had showed a steely side to her personality when it was necessary she do so, was now a gentle, hovering Gaia whose daughters drew in closer and closer to her the more her voice worked its magic. I didn't blame them, of course; I had fallen in love with that voice when I was fifteen. At the same time, I sensed that I was going to have to work very hard if I was going to be allowed to take a role in the circle the three of them seemed to be drawing around themselves.

I don't suppose my feelings are unusual. Most men must feel that way at some time or other in the experience of raising children. After all, no matter how hard we work or how sincerely we love, we are not mothers. The children we nurture as fathers were not carried by us for nine months, sustained by us for nine months. In short, we were not and can never be the carriers of the eggs, the protectors, the sustainers. All of which told me that I would never be anything remotely close to the Gaia for our daughters. I would have to define another role for myself. Sitting and looking at the three of them from across the room, allowing my mother and Ruth Ann their share of space and time with Clementine and Josephine and Abigail, I knew I would do everything in my power to prove myself worthy. For as much as I had loved my grandfather, as much as I loved my mother—seeing the three women who would from that moment on become the collective center of my life told me that I was going to learn how to love in a profoundly new way.

I know that some men may well end up by feeling pangs of jealousy. I not only hoped that would not be the case with me, I was confident it would not be. This was what I had dreamed of when I was sixteen even before I even knew it was my dream. That is what I felt as I watched Clementine and the twins: as if I was seeing something for real that I had already known was going to happen.

I remember turning to my mother when she came to sit by me and saying, "I'm home now, mother."

My mother touched my hand very gently. "Yes, you are, Tyler. Yes, you are."

Then Clementine looked up and called to me, "I think they want their father to hold them, Tyler," to which I replied as I moved to her side, "I think that's a wonderful idea."

30

In consideration of Clementine's diabetes and the fact Josephine and Abigail were delivered by Cesarean section, Clementine and the girls remained in the hospital for five days. Finally, on the sixth day, we brought all three of them home. Ruth Ann and my mother were waiting with a tray of hot tea and the kind of cheese bagels Clementine always bought when we'd shared late morning breakfasts. "You'll be eating early in the morning from now on," my mother said, with which Ruth Ann agreed.

What was most interesting was Clementine's reaction as she walked into our house and then into the girls' nursery, where we put them into their matching beds. "It feels like I've never seen this house before," she said. "Maybe it's because I'm seeing it in a new way."

I agreed that was probably it. Our world had changed since our daughters were born on July 4th. "How fitting," I said to Ruth Ann. "Because if ever two children are products of the American experience, it's those two."

Ruth Ann paused for a moment considering what I had said. Then she said she agreed. Looking at Clementine and then at me and then at our daughters, she said she understood what I meant. "The story of how all of us got to this place, to this moment . . . it's quite extraordinary."

"And ordinary at the same time," I added.

"You'll have a lot to write about, Tyler," my mother said.

I knew she was right.

Fortunately for both Clementine and me, the girls were good sleepers from the outset. Yes, they woke up in the middle of the night for their feedings, but no, they did not cry long after they were finished. In fact, for the first month, like most children, they spent most of their time either eating or sleeping.

By the second day she was home, Clementine wanted to go for a walk. I protested that she could come out into the back yard and walk there, but I wasn't convinced she should go much further. The next day, we began having guests stop by to see both her and the girls. Colleagues from both her work and mine came to pay their respects. As you would expect, all of them found the girls beautiful. I was most moved by Briggs Dyer.

He sat by their beds for some time talking to both of them. That was when I decided that I wanted him to be the male who stood with the girls when they were dedicated in the Augusta Unitarian Church. Clementine said she wanted her medical practice partners, Dr. Cynthia Roses and Dr. Nataly North, to be the women. Because she wanted to have two women stand with the girls, one for each of them, I said I also wanted to Jack McAndrew of the University of Georgia to be the second male sponsor. "Doctors and scholars," Clementine said. "Not much better than that." To our great joy, all four said they would be honored. The only question was who was going to sponsor whom. My mother said that since both girls were going to grow up to be lovely and accomplished women, and that both the two doctors and the two Ph.Ds were all wonderful people, we should have the four of them draw names out of a hat the morning of the ceremony. When we told Cynthia and Nataly and Briggs and Jack what we had decided, they all laughed and said that was fine.

Of course, before we had the ceremony, which would take place when the girls were two months old, Clementine insisted that she wanted to at least go to a shopping mall and eat in the food court. So I got out the double stroller we had bought, which put the girls side by side, and with our mothers still helping, we all set off for the North Side Mall.

Once we were inside, we began getting the kinds of reactions you would expect. First, people were struck by the fact the girls were twins even if it was somewhat hard to see the two of them sitting in their blanketed infant seats, which I had propped up and strapped into the stroller. Second, most of the people who saw them said they were beautiful. They were the kind who cooed and smiled and laughed with us. Third, a few—but only a few—took notice of the fact Clementine is a fair skinned black woman and I am a white man. They didn't say anything, of course, a reaction I credit mostly to Ruth Ann's presence. She isn't the kind of woman whose demeanor suggests she would brook any nonsense. But it was obvious they did not like what they saw. Most often, however, the people who stopped to talk to us about the girls did not seem a bit concerned about either Clementine's or my races or that the girls were racially mixed. All they saw was the two parents relishing the first flush of pride and joy. The fact it was obvious Ruth Ann was Clementine's mother and Elizabeth was my mother helped break the ice several times when women their ages struck up conversations about how beautiful the girls were and how they would just have to be seeing that their parents were both handsome people. Ruth Ann and my mother were quick to agree, naturally. Sitting over our food, Ruth Ann suggested that the varied reactions we'd gotten that morning would most likely be the reactions we would get for the rest of our lives. "It might change by the time the girls grow up," she said, "but I wouldn't hold my breath."

My mother agreed but added that she assumed we would always know what to do. "You two have done a good job up to now, so I assume you will continue to do the same in the future." Then she said, "But let's talk about something else. I want to know how Clementine feels."

Clementine smiled. "I'm fine. It feels good to sit down and eat. But I'm fine."

After we finished our meals and walked for another half an hour, during which time I persuaded Clementine to buy two new summer dresses and Ruth Ann and my mother bought more clothes for the girls than they needed at that point—but you know how grandmothers can be sometimes—we returned slowly to the car and drove home. By the time we arrived back at the house, I had decided it was time to buy a mini-van.

"Welcome to parenthood," my mother said, smiling. "I was wondering how long it would take for you to figure out you were going to need something besides your car."

Clementine agreed that the time had come.

And that was that. No dramas. No crises. Mostly just brief, friendly, passing conversations with other young couples who had their children with them on a Saturday morning in a shopping mall. Nothing could have been more normal or more satisfying or less threatening, which was exactly what we had hoped would happen. After all, Clementine's and my most serious ambition was that we could now just live normal personal and professional lives. Our most sincere ambition was that our daughters would grow up to be intelligent and generous women.

31

Because it was summer, I was home all day every day to be a part of taking care of the girls. By the time Ruth Ann and my mother went back to Tampa, Clementine was up and around and taking walks with me as I pushed the double stroller around the neighborhood. It was still too warm during the day to do much outside, but the evenings were beginning to cool down.

One evening while we were sitting in our screened in porch after eating dinner and Clementine had finished nursing Josephine and Abigail, I turned to Clementine and asked, "Do you miss running?"

Clementine turned to me. "What do you mean?"

"Do you miss running? In competitions? Are you sorry you didn't get to run for Georgia Tech your last two years in college?"

"Those are two different questions."

"Okay. Then are you sorry you didn't get to run for Georgia Tech your last two years in college?"

Clementine was quiet for a moment. She looked away at the shadows taking the woods behind our house. Without looking at me, she said, "I enjoyed running for Tech. I like my coaches. I liked my teammates."

"That doesn't answer the question."

"I suppose I'm sorry I didn't get to finish at Tech. I don't know. I really don't think about it."

I waited. I was right to have done so.

"What happened happened, Tyler," Clementine went on. "It could have been an injury. Athletes get hurt all of the time and can't compete anymore. You know that from football. What happened just happened. Diabetes isn't an injury, but it might just as well have been. So I moved on."

"But right afterwards. When you were told you wouldn't be running anymore," I said. "Were you sorry?"

Clementine looked at me. "I would have been if it hadn't been for you."

"What do you mean?"

"I mean that you were there, Tyler. You stood by me. You were strong for me. So I moved on because you showed me that I had to move on. Besides, when I couldn't run anymore, we got married. I certainly don't have any regrets about that."

I nodded and looked away and then looked back at her. "I don't either. I was just wondering about your running."

"I wish I could run now. Just to keep in shape. But I'm going to walk from now on. Maybe you'll join me on a regular basis. I hope so. But that's what I'm going to do. Take the girls and walk. Sometimes I'll even walk without them. But right now, I'm going to take the girls and start walking every day."

Clementine turned to me. "Are you sorry you didn't play football your junior year?"

I turned to Clementine. "Sometimes. I'm like you. I liked my coaches. There's no one I respect more than Vince Dooley. And I loved my teammates. Some of them, at least. The defensive players mostly. But that year . . . with what happened to you: being with you was all that mattered. I was afraid you were going to die. I was terrified," I said, turning away.

"Really?"

"Really," I replied turning back to face Clementine. "I can't conceive of what would have happened to me if you'd not come back to me. Sometimes I wake up in the night and the fear almost overwhelms me. And you aren't there next to me. And I want to scream."

"Tyler . . . "

"But I don't because I reach over and you are there. And so I listen to your breathing. I touch your skin and feel your warmth. I've even put a hand on you and felt your chest rising and falling as you breathed just so I could be reassured. I don't know what I'd do if anything happened to you, Clementine. My life would be over."

"But it couldn't be. Not now anyway. Not with the girls. You'd be all they had."

"Clementine, please. Don't say that."

"Don't say what?"

"Don't talk about me raising the girls without you."

"Tyler, I'm only thinking out loud."

"Well, don't," I said sharply. "Please." Then I was quiet.

After a moment Clementine spoke. "Are you all right, Tyler? I didn't mean to upset you."

I did not respond.

"Really. I'm sorry. I thought we were just talking. Seriously to be sure. But I thought we were just talking."

"I've lost too many people, Clementine."

"Tyler . . . "

"My father. My grandfather."

Clementine was quiet.

"And I know that someday I will lose my mother just like some day you'll lose Ruth Ann. But I couldn't face losing you. There's no way I could stay alive if I didn't have you."

Clementine was quiet for a long time. "I don't know if it's the way I was trained, or if it's a predisposition that made me choose medicine," she said.

"What?"

"You think about history. You think about what was and what it means that it was. You think about what might have been. I don't know if it's how you are trained to think or if it's a predisposition. More and more I believe it's a predisposition that is then trained in the art of thinking about history. But it's what you do. I see that more and more the longer I am with you. But I don't do that. Not the way you do, at least."

"What do you do instead?" I asked.

"I think . . . I want to think . . . that doctors look at what was only so we can understand what is. Then we look at what is only so we can think about what might be."

"A person's health you mean?"

"Yes. What was is instructive, but it's only instructive. What is matters more. Symptoms. Because symptoms tell me what I can do next. And that's what I need to do. Think about what I can do to help the patient get well."

"Ah," I said quietly.

"It's not the opposite of what you do, but it's certainly very different in its emphasis. It's focus. Maybe that's why historians are romantics and doctors are realists.

"Are historians romantics and doctors realists?" I said.

"I think so. You can't help it. You roam all over the past. Over what no longer is. Over what was lost. Over why something happened and why it won't ever happen again. You converse with people who are dead. In your imaginations, at least. Because to you they aren't dead. They're just beyond your reach, that's all."

"And doctors are . . . "

"Doctors have to get very quickly into the here and now."

I waited.

"Because the here and now is all I can deal with. Here and now in preparation for tomorrow."

"But historians are trying to get ready for the here and now. That's why we study history."

"Yes, it is. But if you had your druthers, you'd probably spend most of your time back there . . . wherever and whenever there is . . . or was."

"Is all of that supposed to answer my question about you missing running?"

"Yes."

"Does it?"

"I think so. Because what I'm saying to you is that it does not matter if I miss running or not. And I suppose it does not matter if you had to miss your junior year of football at Georgia. What matters is what we've done since then, Tyler, and I, for one, think we've done very good things since then."

I smiled. "I think we've done wonderful things. I know loving you is wonderful. And I know being married to you is wonderful. And as for these two girls . . . " I said. "What could be more wonderful than to be the father of Clementine Brown's twin daughters?"

32

On the last Sunday of September, two and a half months after Josephine and Abigail were born, each was dedicated in the Augusta Unitarian Church. The Rev. Dean Rhoads, the church minister, officiated, with the help of Rev. Marni Harmony, whom we invited to come from Tampa for the ceremony. Ruth Ann and my mother were present, of course. In fact, Ruth Ann held Josephine, and my mother held Abigail during the service. Clementine and I stood with them. Cynthia Roses and Jack McAndrew had drawn Josephine's name out of my grandfather's hat, which I kept in my closet. Nataly North and Briggs Dyer drew Abigail's name. Of course, we invited Clementine's maternal grandparents to come for the ceremony, but sadly John's health wouldn't permit him to travel, and Emily didn't want to come without him. We did not attempt to contact Clementine's father or the Raymonds.

What I remember is how profoundly moved I was by the vows that not only Clementine and I and Cynthia and Jack and Nataly and Briggs swore to take seriously—that all of us would participate in raising the two girls to bring honor to their families and honor to themselves by always conducting themselves forthrightly in their relations with others, by always aligning themselves with those who most needed their help, by never disparaging another person for race, ethnicity, or gender, by forswearing violence in preference for peace—I was pleased that the ceremony included a place for Ruth Ann and for my mother to pledge themselves to supporting Clementine and me as we raised our daughters to be intelligent and courageous and dignified women. There was no mention of a God to be worshiped or a devil to be feared, for Unitarians believe that we human beings make our own Heaven, so to speak, and our own Hell, so to speak, right here on earth during our lifetimes. What we must guard against most particularly is not making a Hell for others as we journey through our lives. We must always remember that we are part of families and communities that are more important than we are as individuals. The adults that day who stood with Josephine and Abigail pledged themselves to support the girls as they passed through infancy into childhood into adolescence into young adulthood into adulthood as much as the adults were able during their lifetimes. When Clementine and I were then asked to name our daughters so Dean Rhoads and Marni Harmony could introduce them to the congregation, I found myself crying unashamedly. And as I stood next to Clementine holding her hand while the girls were held up for the congregation to see, I very clearly understood how much I loved her and how much I loved Josephine Arway Raymond and how much I loved Abigail Donyen Raymond. Then something happened that confused me as much as anything had ever confused me in my life: for I saw Preston Raymond and Mildred Raymond stand up in the last row of the church pews and turn to leave, Mildred looking back over her shoulder at me and making momentary eye contact as they passed through the double doors and out into the lobby area. Then they were gone.

Clementine must have seen them as well, for just as I gasped under my breath and tightened my grip on her hand, she did the same, glancing at me as I watched them disappear. When I turned slowly to Clementine, she looked at me for an instant before she turned back to the ceremony, which was continuing. Then I heard her whisper, "Tyler, was that . . . ." She let the words hang in the air unspoken.

"Yes. I think so," I said under my breath in return.

"Really?" she said turning to me for a moment.

"How did they know?" I mouthed, making no sound but forming the words with my lips clearly enough that she understood.

Then Marni Harmony was asking the congregation if they would join Josephine's and Abilgail's parents and grandmothers and the four sponsors in standing by the girls as they grew up. The congregation responded that they would.

"Then in the name of this gathering I greet Josephine Arway Raymond and Abigail Donyen Raymond and welcome them into this beloved community," Dean Rhoads said, which ended the ceremony. With that all of we eight adults and two infant girls returned to our seats in the church, and the rest of the service continued.

Afterwards, the eight of us joined the congregation in Peace Hall for coffee and cake brought especially for the occasion. An hour later, Marni Harmony joined Ruth Ann and my mother and Cynthia Roses and Nataly North and Jack McAndrew and Briggs Dyer and Clementine and me for dinner at Clementine's and my house, which on that day I had arranged to have catered. I thought the highlight of the dinner was that amid the joy and the laughter and all of the good wishes, each of the adults present stood and toasted Josephine and Abigail and Clementine and me and each other, but I was wrong. Because then it was Clementine's turn.

What I will remember for the rest of my life was how graceful she looked as she stood, how elegant she looked as she turned and held her wine glass, how gentle she sounded when she said, "I have dreamed of this day since I met Tyler Thomas Raymond—the man with three first names—in ninth grade biology class. For I fell in love with him the first time he turned and spoke to me. And I have loved him every day since." Then she paused for a moment before going on to say, "And I will love him every day for the rest of my life just as these two little girls will love him. For I say to all of you without any hesitation or qualification, he is the finest man I have ever known, the finest man I will ever know." Then she lifted her glass and said, "So here is to our two daughters, Josephine and Abigail, and here is to you, Tyler Thomas Raymond, the King of my Heart, who even when I was deep in a coma from which I know some doctors did not believe I would ever return, you sat by my side and loved me back so you and I could share this joyous and singular day." Then turning to me she leaned down and kissed me on the cheek.

You will understand if I tell you that it took me some time to recover from Clementine's words. You will understand if I tell you that I have clung to them every day since she said them. You will also understand, I hope, why it was hard for me to stand and offer my toast to those who had come to be with us and to Clementine. But I did. I gathered my wits and said, as best as I can recall:

"I thank each of you for joining us this singular and joyous day. I thank you for being a part of our life. I thank you for all that you have done and all that I know you will do for Josephine and Abigail as they grow up." Then I turned to Clementine and looked at her. "And I thank you, Clementine Camille Brown, for asking me to be your lab partner in ninth grade biology. For that was the moment my life began. That was the moment that led directly to this day. You were the Princess of my Heart the moment I saw you and heard your voice. You have been the Queen of my Heart since the day we married. So on this occasion, I declare to you and to all who have assembled here to be with us that all I truly need and desire for the rest of my life is to have the honor of looking into your eyes and seeing your smile and hearing your voice, for that is where my joy resides, Clementine, that is where my dreams are fulfilled." And as she had kissed me, I kissed her.

Then our meals were served, and everyone was happy.

33

By the time Josephine and Abigail were dedicated, I was back at Augusta State University teaching. My assignment that fall was two sections of Western Civilization, one section of Southern Ante-Bellum history, with a focus on the central Southern States—South Carolina, Georgia, and Alabama—and one tutorial with three master's degree students, two of whom proved to be very interesting experiences by the second semester.

Clementine went back to her medical practice on a part time basis in the middle of September although her physical energy was monitored very closely by both Dr. Roses and Dr. North. By then, we had hired two young women from the University, Shannon Bandstra and Terry Cleveland, to come be with the girls when both of us were out of the house. Because both of them were very conscientious, the arrangement worked out very well. Then another unexpected event took place.

I was in my office one mid morning when the telephone rang. When I answered, I found myself talking to Mitchell Barrows, the Raymonds' Miami lawyer. He said he was prepared to fly to Atlanta to meet with me to discuss a financial settlement the Raymonds wished to make on Josephine and Abigail. When I asked him what he meant, he said, "They want to do something very much like what they did for you, Tyler."

I waited for a moment before speaking. "Why?" I finally asked.

"Why do they want to make a financial settlement in favor of your daughters?"

"Yes. I've had no contact with them except when Mildred came to my graduation from the University of Georgia. And I don't know who told her I was graduating or why she came. She didn't seem very interested in staying after and going with us to lunch."

"I believe she felt as if she would be intruding."

I hesitated again. "Then I saw both of them at the back of the church when Josephine and Abigail were dedicated. But they didn't tell me they were coming, and they didn't stay afterwards. So I repeat my question. Why do they want to make what you call a 'financial settlement' on my daughters?"

Mitchell Burrows was quiet for a moment.

"Mr. Burrows?"

"You're an intelligent young man, Tyler. I would have thought you could figure it out," he said.

I was quiet again. "Guilt?" I finally said.

"I'm not sure it's only guilt. It may be more than that, sir. But yes, that may be a part of it."

"And they think that making a financial settlement will make amends?"

"I'm not at liberty to discuss the whys of their wishes, Tyler. I only have the authority to give you the details and terms. So the question is, will you come to Atlanta to meet with me?"

"When do you wish to make the trip?" I said.

"I am free from Tuesday through Thursday of next week to fly to Atlanta. We can meet at a hotel. We can have dinner if you wish."

"I want to talk to Clementine before I make a decision."

"Is that necessary?" Mitchell Burrows asked.

"She's my wife, Mr. Burrows. They are her children as well as mine."

"But why would she object? The settlement has nothing to do with further contact, unless you would want it. It only has to do with future money."

"I think Clementine and I need to discuss the matter. From their point of view, I suppose, they believe they are being generous. And they certainly were with me during the years I was enrolled in school. But from my point of view, given what happened with my father—given their reaction to first my relationship with Clementine and then my marriage to her and now the fact we have children—I think there are things Clementine and I will need to discuss."

"You make it sound as if there is a racial bias matter intruding in this matter, Tyler."

"I don't know what else to call it. Certainly that was the message both Clementine and I got in Miami. It was the same in Athens when Mildred came to my graduation."

"You may be misinterpreting Mildred's feelings, Tyler. You may be misinterpreting her authority in this matter. And you may not appreciate fully her role in securing the trust fund for you or in the proposed trust fund for your daughters."

I hesitated for a very long time. It was Mitchell Burrows's turn to wonder if our conversation had come to an end. "Tyler?" he said.

"I will talk with Clementine tonight. If you telephone me tomorrow between 2 and 3 P.M., I will give you my answer. We can then go from there."

Mitchell Burrows thanked me for my time and for my candor. "As difficult as it is sometimes for me to sort out exactly what to say to you, Tyler, the fact you are not willing to give way to the money just for the money's sake . . . well, I find that interesting." Then he said he would telephone the next day. "I looked up two of your grandfather's books, Tyler. An early one and the one he wrote with Ruth Ann Brown, who I assume is Clementine's mother. The Edinburgh lectures. I suspect Professor Thomas would have approved of the way you have conducted yourself up to this point in your life."

I replied that I appreciated his comment, which I meant, and that I looked forward to hearing from him, which was both true and not true, for obvious reasons. I was conflicted, as you might expect. I assumed Clementine would be the same. I both did and did not look forward to our conversation that night, but I knew it had to happen. So it did.

34

With the twins fast asleep, Clementine and I lingered over dinner. After several moments of quiet, Clementine finally said, "Okay, Tyler. Out with it."

"Out with . . . "

"With whatever it is."

I took a deep breath. "I received a telephone call today from Mitchell Burrows."

"Mitchell Burrows?" she said.

"The Raymonds' lawyer. We met him in Miami."

She nodded but did not respond.

"He wants to meet me in Atlanta next week."

Clementine pursed her lips and narrowed her eyes slightly. "And why would Mitchell Burrows want to meet you in Atlanta next week, Doctor Raymond?"

"It's about the girls."

"And what about the girls?" she said very slowly.

"It's about a trust fund for each of the girls," I said.

I hesitated. "I said I'd talk to you, Clementine, about coming with me," I said. "If we go at all," I added quickly.

"You sound conflicted, Tyler," she said.

"I am."

"Why?"

"Because I don't know what to think about what the Raymonds apparently want to do."

"And what is it that they want to do for the girls?"

"From what Mitchell Burrows said, they want to insure their university educations."

Clementine was quiet. I knew she wanted me to say more. "I don't know any of the details, Clementine," I said.

"And you think . . . what? That we should go talk to him? That we shouldn't go talk to him?"

"I think . . . we should at least go hear what he has to say . . . even though I was offended before when we met them. And even though their money paid for part of both your and my educations. I am conflicted . . . for all of the reasons you can imagine."

The virtue of Clementine's temperament is that, most of the time, she listens carefully and thinks precisely before she responds, which is what she did on this occasion. She waited. Then she said, "I believe I understand why you would be conflicted. But I can also understand why you think we should go listen to what he has to say."

"When could you go?" I said.

"When could you go?"

"I'm good on Tuesday."

"I can arrange to go with you on Tuesday afternoon. Did he say when he would want to meet us?"

"He said he could meet anytime that will work for us."

"But he didn't say anything about what kind of trust fund the Raymonds want to set up?"

"No. Although I told him I think it's at least partly guilt money."

"And what did he say to that?"

"He said he didn't disagree. He said there was more to it than just guilt. But he said that may well be part of it."

"And you think we should go talk to him . . . on behalf of the girls?"

"He wanted to talk with me. I said I wouldn't come without you."

"Ah," Clementine said.

"Yes. Ah," I said. "Which is another part of my conflict. But to his credit he said he understood why I would want you to come with me."

"So you'll talk to him . . . when?"

"He's going to call me at the University tomorrow."

"So the question is settled?"

"I suppose," I said. Then I said, "Yes. It's settled. Except . . . ." I let my next word trail away to silence.

"Except what?" Clementine said.

"Except . . . . Why do you think the Raymonds came to Josephine's and Abilgail's dedication?"

"I don't know."

"And if they were going to go to all of the trouble of coming why didn't they stay and at least talk to us?"

"I don't know the answer to that question, either."

I sighed and sat back and looked at my cup of tea for a moment.

"Looking for answers in your tea?" Clementine said.

I smiled. "Maybe if I swirl around my cup of tea the tea leaves will give me the answer," I said.

Clementine laughed. "But we use tea bags," she said.

I shrugged my shoulders. Then I guess that won't work, will it?" I said.

"I guess not."

"Maybe I could ask the Raymonds some day."

"Maybe you could do that. If you ever get the chance, that is."

"I don't think I'll hold my breath waiting," I whispered.

"That's probably a good idea," Clementine said quietly, standing and beginning to gather up the dinner dishes.

35

Our meeting on Tuesday in the dining room of the Peach Tree Hotel with Mitchell Burrows went exactly as we expected. The Raymonds wanted to set up a trust fund for each of the girls to insure that their university educations would be paid for. They specified that they were not requesting any contact with either us or with the girls unless we should wish to do so. There were no conditions attending the trust funds except that each girl would have to be admitted to a university of her choice. Like the trust fund they had established for me, once a record showing each girl was enrolled was received by the Bank of America branch we specified, the funds would be released. They did not ask for grade reports or any correspondence, unless the girls should wish to do so with our permission. It was, in effect, gratis money, guaranteed to be at least $40,000 a year for each girl as long as she remained a university student.

Mitchell Burrows said he thought it would be wise for us to sign the documents. "They're both getting older," he said. "If you sign now, the trust funds will be set up without regard to the lengths of either of the Raymonds' lives."

Clementine and I looked at each other. "Do you know why the Raymonds came to Augusta and attended our daughters' dedication at the Unitarian Church?' I said.

"I knew they planned to attend. I believe they were interested in seeing you and Clementine and the girls," Mitchell Burrows said.

"But they didn't stay to speak to us," I responded.

"They did not explain their motives to me for attending or for not staying after the ceremony, but from what little they said to me I got the impression that they assumed they would not be welcomed."

"How could we have welcomed them if we didn't know they were coming or if they didn't stay?" Clementine said quietly.

"I understand your confusion, Mrs. Raymond," Mitchell Burrows said.

"Dr. Brown," I said.

Mitchell Burrows looked at me.

"My wife's name is Dr. Brown. She is a medical doctor."

"Yes. Of course. I apologize."

Neither Clementine nor I responded.

"The Raymonds find themselves in a somewhat embarrassing situation," Mitchell Burrows went on, "even though I'm sure that is Mrs. Raymond's sentiment more than Mr. Raymond's."

"I'm sure," I said under my breath.

"I am not privy to their conversations in regard to their relationship with you, Mr. Raymond."

"Doctor Raymond," Clementine said, returning the favor.

Mitchell looked at Clementine.

"My husband holds a Ph.D. He is an associate professor. So he's Doctor Raymond," she said quietly.

"Yes. Again, I apologize. I did know that, Doctor Brown."

"You were saying," I said to Mitchell Burrows.

Mitchell Burrows took a deep breath. "I was saying that I am not privy to their conversations in regard to their relationship with you, Dr. Raymond."

"Perhaps that's because we have no relationship, Mr. Burrows," I said, interrupting. "Except for the trust fund they set up for my university expenses."

"Yes. I understand. And which you used, I believe," Mitchell Burrows said.

"Yes. I did. Just as I am prepared to accept the trust fund money on behalf of our daughters," I said quietly. "Even though the Raymonds apparently do not wish any other sort of contact with us."

Mitchell Burrows hesitated before going on. "I can understand your consternation, Dr. Raymond. But please, do not judge both of them by the fact they have not contacted you. I do not believe I am betraying a confidence when I say that their silence was more Mr. Raymond's choice than Mrs. Raymond's. Which is why she attended your graduation from the University of Georgia."

"So it's Mr. Raymond who does not wish to have contact with Tyler? Is that what you are saying?" Clementine said.

Mitchell Burrows hesitated again. He was a cautious man. It was a posture required by his position. I could both understand and be sympathetic. "I would assume that might be the case, Dr. Raymond, but I am not free to offer and unqualified comment. All I would ask," he said as he reached into his brief case and got out several sheets of paper, "is that you make all of our lives easier by signing the papers I have prepared in the name of the Raymonds."

I glanced at Clementine. "We should read them, Tyler," she said under her breath.

"And so we shall," I said, which is what we both did, after which we signed the places Mitchell Burrows specified. Then he gave us two copies of each trust fund, all of which had been signed by both of the Raymonds. "One for your records of each trust fund and one for each of your daughters," Mitchell Burrows said.

Then he stood and offered his hand to Clementine, which she accepted as he said, "May I offer my belated congratulations to both of you on your marriage and on your university graduations and the births of your daughters?" he said.

"Thank you," Clementine said in her own very special quiet but serious way. "That is very kind of you. Of course, it would be even more kind if congratulations also came from the Raymonds, but perhaps that is more than we should ask."

Mitchell Burrows was quiet for a moment. Then he said, "Not more than you should ask, Dr. Brown," he said, extending his hand to Clementine, who shook his in return. "Just more than you should necessarily expect."

"Thank you, Mr. Burrows," I said. "And you are undoubtedly correct. It is more than we should expect." With that I shook hands with Mitchell Burrows, put the trust fund papers in my brief case, and Clementine and I left the hotel to begin our drive home to Augusta.

36

Although I could tell Clementine had wanted to discuss what had unfolded with Mitchell Burrrows, she did not press the matter. After several miles, I finally said, "Every time the Raymonds show up in our lives I think about my father."

Clementine waited.

"I wish I knew more about why he turned his back on them. I wish I knew what he would want me to do now," I said.

"Maybe you should talk to your mother," Clementine said.

"Maybe. Or maybe that would just bring up painful memories for her," I muttered. Then I said more emphatically, "I wish my grandfather was alive. I could talk to him. He'd know what I should do."

"But he wouldn't tell you, Tyler. You know that."

I was silent again. "I know. He'd tell me I had to decide."

"And he'd be right. From what your mother had said about your father, he'd probably say the same thing."

"Neither of which helps."

"But it does."

"How does it help?"

"Because that's what you have to do, Tyler. You have to decide. That's what Edward would have said. That's what your father would have said."

"But if they were here, I could try to read their body language. Or hear their tones of voice."

"Yes. You could. But then you'd be doing what you think they wanted you to do. And I don't think that's what they would have wanted. They would have wanted you to decide to decide."

I was silent for another ten miles. "Tell me about the clinic," I said.

Clementine knew me well enough to know that I needed time to think. She knew me well enough to know that at that point, I really did want to hear about her work. I didn't want the conversation to be about me any more. So she told me about what she was doing at the clinic where she worked with people who otherwise could not have afforded health care. She talked about two young women, both of whom had become pregnant, both of whom were intelligent enough to have gone on to college but who, by the time they got to her, had been convinced by their families that any more education was out of the question.

"I spent almost an hour with one of them giving her a list of names of people she needed to contact. I told her there was financial assistance available if she would just pursue it. She promised she would. I hope she will. She seems determined to do more than just let her life slip away. The other acts like she is afraid. As if someone had convinced her that she's not smart or not worthy. She acts like she should hang her head when she even talks to someone with an education. I cannot imagine what kind of life she's led to make her that way because at times, when I get her talking about books, she becomes so excited that I can't get her to answer my questions about her health. So something is going on there that I can't sort out."

I continued driving. Clementine was quiet. "That's why I'd like to have you talk to her," she said.

I glanced at Clementine. "Me?" I said. "Why me?"

"Because she's a very intelligent young woman. She says she writes poetry. But she never shows it to anyone. Maybe she'd show it to you. Maybe you could get her to talk to someone at the University."

"Clementine, are you working me?" I said even though I knew the answer.

"Yes," Clementine said.

"Clementine . . . " I started to say.

"So you might as well get used to it. Because every time I talk to someone who I think should talk to you, I'm going to send that person your way."

"Clementine, I teach history. I don't teach English. And I'm not a counselor."

"No, you aren't. But you know people who are. That's the point," she said.

I frowned my discontent.

"There's no use frowning like that, Tyler. Because I'm going to send people to see you even if you don't like it. Because it's about them, Tyler, not about you."

I knew there was no point in protesting. Clementine was going to do what she thought was best for her patients. If that meant she was going to volunteer my time, then she would volunteer my time. Since I loved her too much to seriously object, she knew just as I did that the matter was settled. Young people carrying Clementine's card would start showing up very soon.

37

I said from the outset that the objective of this memoir is to portray the way in which Clementine Camille Brown has shaped the lives of the people whom she loves. At this point therefore, I have to talk about three ways in which she continued my education. It started as we turned the corner a block away from our house. Clementine and I had both been rather quiet the last fifteen miles into town. But as the neared our house, Clementine said very softly, "Perhaps the Raymonds are making an overture, Tyler."

When I turned to ask what she meant, I could see she had turned away. By then I knew her body code: she didn't want me to respond. She just wanted me to think about what she said. It was her way of starting a conversation even if the conversation might not take place for another week or more. In the case of her comment about my Raymond grandparents, the conversation would not be resumed for another two months. By then the second experience had already taken place. Let me explain.

That fall I was scheduled to work with three master's degree candidates as their advisor. The first was a young man whose interest in American history was superficial at best. I won't go into detail, but what he wanted to do was something that could and should have been done as a college of education project. And while I had no choice but to work with him, I could see that before the year was over, he would want to find another advisor. For he was not as much interested in history as he was in getting a degree and moving on.

The second was Simon Milsap, a young African-American man with a first rate mind. Our relationship proved to be very important for me; I hope the same was true for him. Here is why.

Simon is probably six feet two. He is handsome and articulate and athletic. In fact, he had played basketball for the University during his undergraduate years. Because I was an athlete, I didn't make the mistake of putting him in the jock category. In fact, I hope I have never done that with any of the athletes I've taught. In Simon's case, I was perfectly prepared to consider him a worthy master's degree candidate. He'd been a member of one of my Western Civilizations classes when he'd been a freshman and had earned a solid A grade. But even with all of that background, when he sat down to explain his interests, I was still surprised. After all, by that point in my teaching career, I had gained a reputation among Augusta students as the white history teacher most interested in the black American experience. That reputation in concert with Simon's own race and his exceptional intelligence signaled to me that he would want to pursue some aspect of black American history. I was very wrong.

"I want to study the politics of Europe during Beethoven's times, Professor Raymond," Simon said as he sat down and opened a notebook.

"I beg your pardon," I said trying to not show my surprise.

"I want to study the politics . . . I suppose you'd call it the social politics . . . of Beethoven's times," he said.

"Beethoven? As in Ludwig van Beethoven? That Beethoven?"

"Yes, sir. That Ludwig van Beethoven," Simon said, smiling broadly.

"May I ask why?" I said.

"Why do I want to study the politics of Beethoven's times?"

"Yes."

"Because I'm interested in Beethoven. Particularly his piano compositions."

I waited.

"I play the piano. I've been studying piano since I was four years old. I play Beethoven," Simon said obviously trying to respond to the question that my expression stated without words.

"Are you a music major, Simon?"

"No, sir. I just play Beethoven. I'm a very good pianist, but not that good, sir. But I love Beethoven."

Again, I waited.

"What I want to do is study the social politics of Beethoven's times, not necessarily to make a direct or even indirect connection between politics and his music—I'll leave that for some scholar to sort out—but to simply better understand the world in which he was living."

"But it sounds as if that's exactly what you want to do. Do enough research so you can understand how the social politics of Beethoven's times shaped or at least influenced his music."

"His piano music."

"His piano music," I said, correcting myself.

"I suppose I am. I mean, I suppose I do want to make that connection. But I'm really doing it for myself. I want to know more about what made him tick." With that, Simon smiled again.

"All right. I understand what you're saying. And it's a very interesting topic. It sounds like it to me, at least. But that leads to the question why have you come to me? I have no particular insights into the relationship of politics and music. I'm not even a European history specialist. There are people in the history department who could help you. There are probably people in the music department who could help you as well?"

"There probably are," Simon said. "But I remember enjoying your class when I was a freshman. I remember hearing you speak at the Student Union Forum. I just think you have a way of thinking that would help me."

"I thank you for the compliment, but I'm still not sure of what you mean," I said.

"Professor Raymond, can I be frank with you?"

I sat up straight. "Certainly. I hope you will."

Simon hesitated. "I've come to you because of your reputation, sir."

I looked at him very carefully. "And what reputation is that, Simon?"

Simon drew a deep breath. "I know that you are the grandson of Edward Thomas. And I knew his work. My parents had his books in our house. So I've read them as well."

Before I could interrupt, which I probably would have done at that point, Simon went on. "I read his Edinburgh lectures. The ones he wrote with your wife's mother."

I knew this time I needed to be quiet and to let him go on.

"Maybe you think that because I'm black, I should take up some subject about African-American people in the United States. But I don't want to do that. I just want to study the politics of Beethoven's times." Simon looked at me very intently. He was not smiling. "I want to be free to study whatever I want to study."

I understood. At least, I thought I understood. I wanted to reply, to respond, to signal that I understood what he was saying, but I was not sure I really did. Not in the profound way he seemed to be expressing his hope.

"But aren't you free to do that . . . at this university . . . aren't you free to do that with someone in the history department who might be better educated in the subject matter you wish to study?" I said.

Simon looked at me as if I had hurt his feelings, which I not only had not wanted to do, I didn't even know what I had said that might have made him feel badly. "No, sir. I don't feel that way."

"You don't feel free or you don't . . . "

"I don't feel free, sir. Not here. Not anywhere," he said. Then he added quickly, "Except with you, Professor Raymond."

I waited for a moment. I wanted to really hear what he was saying. Before I could respond, he went on.

"Everyone here has been good to me, sir. Everyone. But that doesn't mean I've felt . . . free as you put it. I've felt . . . ." He did not finish the sentence. Then he did. "I've felt on display," he said. Then he was silent.

"And you think . . . "

"I don't think you'd be that way with me, Professor. I think you would be demanding because you are demanding. I don't want any favors. I want to be taken seriously." Simon said.

I looked at Simon very carefully. This handsome young black man was asking for help to be something more than just a handsome young black man. He wanted to be a man. Plain and simple. He wanted . . . .

"I want to earn a Ph.D. in history, Professor Raymond. I knew that the night you spoke to the Student Union Forum. That's when I decided," Simon said.

I was speechless. Really and truly speechless. I wondered how many students had said that to my grandfather. How many students had said that to Ruth Ann? And now . . . . What was I supposed to do? What a silly question, I thought. There was only one thing to do. "I will be honored to be your advisor, Simon," I said. But before he could thank me, I added, "But you need to know that as you do your research, I'll be learning right along with you."

Simon smiled. "That will make it more fun, sir. I think that will make it even better."

I said I hoped he would feel that same way in six months.

Simon smiled again and stood and extended a hand, which I accepted as I stood.

"Now you can go home and talk to Dr. Brown about our conversation," he said, still smiling.

"Dr. Brown? My wife?" I said.

"Yes, sir. That's what all of your students say. That you talk over everything with your wife."

I was startled. It was true, of course. But I was still startled. I didn't know if I was being patronized or criticized or what.

"It's what the students respect about you, sir. You're not a big ego. You talk to other people. Like Professor Dyer. We see you two talking on campus. The women in your class love the idea that you really talk to your wife."

"Really?" I said, which was about as clever a remark as I could come up with.

"Yes, sir. We've all seen you on campus with her, too. And at games. I remember seeing the two of you sitting together at basketball games when I was playing. We could all see how much you two talked about things together. And how you laughed together."

I had no idea what to do next.

"That's why so many of us respect you, sir. That and your teaching."

I fumbled for a thank you.

"I hope I haven't spoken out of turn, sir. I just wanted you to know. I hope I haven't spoken out of turn," Simon said.

"No. Not at all. My wife will be pleased to hear what you've said." I hesitated. "So am I, of course," I added.

Then he was gone. And I knew he was right. I would go home that night and talk to Clementine. When I did, she smiled and said, "Well, then there you are. Do you understand what he was saying?"

"I think so. I'm not sure, but I think so."

Clementine smiled her I'm-waiting-for-you-to-catch-up, Tyler, smiles, which does not belittle me; it does, however, tell me I've got to think a little harder.

"Tyler, Simon Milsap is what you and Edward wanted to have happen."

I waited.

"Maybe not completely, because he still feels somewhat self-conscious. But think about it. A black man. A black American man basketball player. Whom we've watched play. And who's good. And who's handsome and well liked. And all he wants to do is be free to study his passion . . . which has nothing to do with being black or American or anything else like that. He wants to be free to study Beethoven because he loves Beethoven . . . and he wants to do it in the context of a history master's degree because he's already figured out that Beethoven like everyone else was at least influenced by if not a direct product of his political times."

"I think I understand that," I said.

"Which is exactly what Edward was fighting for. What the Civil Rights Movement was all about."

I let her go on because I knew she had more to say.

"Simon wants to be a person, Tyler. A person. That's all. Free to follow his great curiosity. Beethoven's piano music."

I looked at her.

"Wow," she said. "Wow."

I laughed.

"And he came to you because he trusts you will just let him go ahead and do that."

"That's what he said."

"Then . . . wow! Tyler. Hot damn! Get it? Hot damn! And wow!"

I laughed hard and then stood up and walked across the kitchen to where she was standing and put my arms around her and said, "Yes, Clementine. Hot damn and wow!"

38

The next day, Pilar Small told me that the third of my master's degree advisees had come for her appointment. When I asked who it was, she said the young woman had not given her name but it looked as if her paperwork was all in order. When I went to my office, I found Pam Page waiting by my door. I could not have been more surprised. Yes, I remembered that Pam Page had been a member of my Western Civilization class during my second year at Augusta. But it was also Pam Page who had come to my office and asked about Clementine and asked if I had ever been with a white woman.

"I know you may be surprised to see me again, Professor Raymond. But I really do want to talk to you," she said as I stood and looked at her.

"Are you asking that I be your master's degree advisor?" I said.

"I am."

I opened the door and ushered her in and motioned she should sit down. Then I moved to my desk. Standing for a moment longer, I turned to Pam and asked, "And why would you want me to be your advisor, Miss Page?"

She hesitated before speaking. "Because since that day . . . when I came to your office and was so horrible, I've done a lot of thinking."

"Thinking is good," I said. "Sometimes." I said, "depending on what you think about, of course."

Pam looked very nervous. "I've thought about how much I offended you that day, Professor. I've thought about that a lot."

I waited.

"And that got me thinking about a lot of other things: racism, the history of the South. The history of slavery in America. But mostly racism. How it shows up in everyday life."

"That's very promising, Miss Page. At least, from my point of view. But it still all depends on where you're thinking has taken you."

"It's taken me a lot of places. It took me to Alabama two summers ago where I worked as a summer teacher in a camp for African American elementary school students. And it took me to Louisiana last summer where I helped a small community organize a reading program in a church for all of the African American middle school students in the area."

"I am impressed," I said quietly, unsure of what else to say.

"And it's brought me here. Because I want you to be my advisor."

"And you think I would want to be your advisor?"

"I hope you would want to be my advisor."

"What is your area of research?"

"Miscegenation laws."

"Miscegenation laws? Really?"

"Yes, sir. Laws prohibiting interracial marriage."

"I know what the word means, Miss Page. I am just surprised you find it interesting."

"I find the laws offensive, Professor Raymond. Morally offensive."

"So your attitude has changed?"

"If you mean, have I changed from the snotty young woman who came to your office and who asked inappropriate questions . . . then yes, I've changed."

"And you think I might be willing to help you research the topic of miscegenation laws?" I said.

"Yes, sir. I hope you will. Because the reading I've been doing for the last two years . . . it tells me there's a whole lot more to the laws than just bias against interracial marriage. I think the laws express a much bigger and more profound bias."

I nodded. "And I would agree, Miss Page. The laws against interracial marriage were something akin to a metaphor."

"I agree. I've talked to a number of people about the subject since that time when I came to your office. I agree the laws are only indicators."

"What kind of research do you wish to do?" I asked.

"I want to start with a chronology of the laws: where they were passed, what each law stated. Then I want to go back and look at the social situation for each of the laws. The times. The legislatures. The arguments that were made so the laws would pass."

"All right. That will take some time. But this is supposed to take some time."

"Then I want to look at the social and political ramifications of the laws. How many times were they used against couples who wanted to get married and who couldn't or who got married despite the law and then faced prosecution and what happened in those cases."

"I don't know if anyone has ever tried to gather together all of that information."

"If someone has, I haven't found it, Professor. And I've looked. Because I assumed that if the question occurred to me, it must have occurred to someone in the past. But I don't find anything that is as comprehensive as what I want to write."

"I must say, Miss Page, I am impressed. But I'm even more curious."

"Sir?"

"About your apparent change of mind. Or heart."

"It started with that day in your office. But that was only the start. I was very upset by what you did when you asked me to leave. Then I was embarrassed. I kept waiting for some kind of trouble to happen. But nothing did. You were true to your word."

I waited.

"Then I started seeing you and your wife on campus at different events. And I found out she's a doctor. A pediatrician. Augusta's a pretty small town. Then I read the book your grandfather and your wife's mother wrote. The lectures they gave in Edinburgh. And when you lectured at the racism forum . . . during Black History Week the year I was a senior, I came to hear you. By then I was already working with black students whose parents wanted them to have more practice reading. So it all worked together."

"You have gone through a change, Miss Page."

"I have. Yes. I think I have. And so that's why I decided I want to be a civil rights lawyer."

I was stunned. "Really?" I said.

"Yes. My family isn't very happy. They want me to be a lawyer, like my father and like my grandfather, but they aren't very happy about the civil rights part."

"My, my," I said quietly. "You have become a most interesting person, Miss Page."

"Thank you, sir. But I owe to it all to you. I haven't told my father that. He might want to come here and blame you. But I owe it to you. And to your wife."

"Then maybe you need to meet my wife."

"I would like that very much, Professor."

"I will tell her about our conversation. I am sure she will want to meet you."

Miss Page was quiet.

"But before you start your research I want you to write two hundred words on an excerpt from a poem that I'm going to give you."

"A poem?"

"Yes," I said, standing and moving to the book case on the wall next to my desk. "It's by Gwendolyn Brooks, an African American poet. A very important poet, I might add."

Miss Page waited as I found the paperback volume and returned to my desk where I sat down. Opening the book, I found the passage quickly. Taking up a pencil, I bracketed the lines that mattered. "Here," I said, leaning forward and giving Miss Page the book, "read these lines out loud."

Pam Page looked at the book.

"The bottom of page 20, I said, and the top of page 21," I said.

Pam Page looked at the lines. "Read them out loud?" she said.

"Yes."

She hesitated for a moment. Then she read: "(In a southern city a white man said/ Indeed, I'd rather be dead;/ Indeed, I'd rather be shot in the head/ Or ridden to waste on the back of a flood/ Than be saved by the drop of a black man's blood.)"

I waited.

"How horrible," she said looking up at me.

"Yes. And sad. A pitiful sad commentary," I said.

"And you want me to write . . . how many words about the passage?"

"Two hundred."

Miss Page looked concerned. "Professor Raymond, I could write two thousand on a passage like this," she said, holding the book up as if she was trying to show it to me. "It depends on how far out into history you want me to go."

"I want you to go far enough to write two hundred words but not so far that you need two thousand. Take the book with you. Stay focused."

She smiled. It was the first time she had smiled since she'd come into my office. "How long to I have?" she said.

"Until tomorrow at this same time."

She did not look concerned or flustered. Rather, she looked focused. "When you come back to see me tomorrow morning, I will have a formal invitation for you to our house for dinner."

"Which I will accept, Professor," Miss Page said, standing and handing me the advisor forms for me to sign.

I smiled. "Leave the forms with me," I said. "When you come back tomorrow with your two hundred words, I will read them, and then you and I will decide if you want me to sign the forms or not."

With that, Pam Page thanked me and left, after which I sat for some time wondering if she was ever going to really tell me what had happened to her since that unpleasant day in my office when she had commented on Clementine's race and on Clementine's and my relationship. Because if she was telling the truth, something or some things of profound importance had certainly taken place. And I wanted very much to hear her tell the story

39

That evening, after we had eaten and after the twins were asleep, I told Clementine that Pam Page had come to see me that morning.

"Pam Page? You mean the girl from . . . I don't remember how many years ago. That Pam Page?"

"Yes."

"And she wants . . . what?"

"She wants me to be her master's degree advisor."

"And you said?"

"We talked. She explained how she had changed. At least, she explained a little. I think there must be more. But she explained that she wants to do a study of the history of miscegenation laws."

"Really?"

"Yes."

"Then you really are her provocateur, aren't you?"

"Provacateur?"

"Yes. Provacateur. Something about you . . . probably me, if I remember right. Something about you provokes her. Or provoked her. Which ever. Or both. You haven't explained."

"I haven't explained because I don't know. And I don't think I'm her provocateur. I think I was just there at the right time to make her start confronting something in her that she didn't like and wanted to change."

"Her racism?"

"Her fear of her racism."

"Ah," Clementine said.

"She talked about teaching black children in Alabama two summers ago to read. She talked about doing the same thing in Louisiana last summer."

"And . . . "

"And what *and*?" I asked.

"And what else. Because those decisions . . . what she did . . . as wonderful as they sound . . . come from someplace."

"She said she attended one of my lectures on racism. At the University. And she read my grandfather's and Ruth Ann's book of lectures."

"The puzzle pieces start to fit."

"She wants to earn a master's degree in history and then go to law school. That's what she said. Her father is a lawyer. And her grandfather. She wants to be a civil rights lawyer. Apparently the family is happy about the lawyer part. But not the civil rights part."

"So that explains that day in your office."

I looked at Clementine. "How does it explain that day in my office? She was offensive in my office."

"Yes. But that was because she was about to step across the line."

"What line?" I said.

"The line in her imagination. In what she had been taught."

I looked at Clementine.

"About blacks. About black women and white men. She was just about ready to step across the line. Her fear was her last stop on the other side of the line. We're the first stop on this side of the line."

"Clementine, sometimes I think you should have been a psychologist. Or a psychiatrist. Because you seem to see what makes everyone tick. Or at last you think you see what makes everyone tick."

"You know I'm right," Clementine said.

"I know . . . something changed in her life. I don't know that you're right. Maybe you are, but so far I don't know that for sure. I just know what I know: she came to my office and asked what I considered inappropriate and offensive questions about you and then about you and me. Now she has come back and wants me to be her advisor so she can write a chronological study of the history of miscegenation laws and how they have been applied over the decades. Certainly something happened in between our two meetings in my office that signals a profound change in her. I don't know what it was. I hope she will explain. Because if I take her on as an advisee, I want to invite her to dinner tomorrow night."

Clementine was quiet for a moment. "That sounds like a good idea," she said. "Then I can see for myself," she said. "But I still think I'm right. She found you attractive.

But you are married to a black woman. She asked her questions, but she really wanted to confront her racism. She went away when she saw she had offended you and started thinking. She listened to you lecture. She read Edward's and my mother's book of lectures. She went away to Alabama and then to Louisiana to teach black children to read, even if she also knew that in an earlier period of time in American history there were laws against teaching black children to read . . . on the premise that they couldn't be taught because they weren't smart enough." Clementine held up her hands to stop me from interrupting. "Of course, if blacks were not smart enough to learn how to read, then laws against teaching them would not have been necessary. So the contradiction is obvious. So obvious she saw it herself. That is why she has come back to you, Tyler."

I waited for a moment. Clementine had said a mouthful. It was my turn to let it all sink in. Afterwards we could discuss what it all meant or did not mean. Because that was and remains what Clementine does best: help me see that which I should have seen on my own but do not until she comes along and explains the evidence.

And of course, as Clementine predicted, Pam Page did come back the next day. And to Miss Page's credit, her two hundred words were not only insightful, they explained the moral issue that the poem expressed with just the right balance of analysis and outrage. After all, if a fictional but very plausible Southern white man was so overwhelmed by hatred of black people that he would rather die than think that he had been tainted by black blood, then indeed the society he represented was almost hopelessly psychologically distorted and intellectually corrupted. What that white society might then do as an extension of its fear of blacks might have been anyone's guess, save that history supplied the information. For it inflicted violence on an enslaved people that far exceeded the need to control their actions. It dehumanized the enslaved people while all the time convincing itself that its brand of paternalism was, in fact, the generosity of a superior race to an inferior race. It rejected all notions of any common bond of humanity to the point that it declared illegal as many points of social and political and economic intercourse as might occur between the two peoples living and working in the same region, and it did so while holding up the banner of Christianity as testimony to the worthiness of its civilization. That is what Pam Page found implied in the Gwendolyn Brooks lines; that is what she argued an intelligent reader was required to intuit if not reason from the lines. Thus those two hundred words coupled to the list of books she had already read on the subject of racism and miscegenation as well as her serious and gracious response to my dinner invitation to come to our house that night where, as I told her, she would not only meet my pediatrician African American wife, she would meet our mixed race twin daughters, caused me to agree that day to be her graduate school advisor. So after she left, promising to arrive at our house at 7 P.M., and I took a moment to reflect on the fact that I now had two serious advisees with whom I could work, I realized that if all things went as planned, I had a very promising year in the offing.

40

That evening, Pam Page proved to be a most engaging guest. For the story she told was full of conflicts and contradictions and change. She began over our meal by explaining that she had been raised in a small town fifty miles from Atlanta by parents who were both lawyers and who both assumed she would do the same. Because the town high school offered very few Advanced Placement courses, her parents sent her to Atlanta to live with her mother's older sister and her husband.

Coming from a town that was clearly divided socially and economically along racial lines, the racially diverse Atlanta high school she attended forced her to find new friends whose thinking was much more like her own: "Black people needed to stay with their own, and white people should stay with white people," she said, which she quickly realized was a sentiment she should not express except to a select number of new friends. So while she faced more rigorous courses in Atlanta, she went through the final two years of her high school education in the same way she would have had she stayed at home: her world was divided by skin color.

"I never once exchanged a mean word with any black student," she told us that evening. "Because I didn't exchange any words at all."

When it came time for college, she decided that so many of her friends back at home and so many of her new friends at the Atlanta High School were going to enroll at the University of Georgia that she should go somewhere else. Augusta seemed like a logical and reasonable choice, which is how she ended up on the University campus and how she ended up enrolled in my Western Civilization course.

"But I began to change once I was a student here in Augusta," Pam went on. "Not that I wanted to. I tried very hard to hang onto the way I had been raised. Not that my parents ever said critical things about black people. It was more as if blacks didn't exist. They were there, of course. In the stores in town. Driving from place to place visiting friends and family. But as far as my parents were concerned, they didn't factor in. That's what I tried to hold onto when I came to Augusta. I didn't want to admit I was a racist. I didn't let it matter to me."

She hesitated over her meal. "Then I was in your course, Professor Raymond. And I heard other students talking. Some of them said some pretty small minded things. Not many. But some. Most of them didn't like it when some of the girls in class said things about you being married to a black woman. So I kept quiet. But it was simmering, apparently. Some where down inside me . . . in my mind . . . something was simmering. That's why I came to your office that day."

I was quiet.

"It was horrible. What I said. What I asked. It was horrible. When I left your office I went for a walk. I even saw you across campus later. You looked like you were still upset. Which is why I asked myself what in the world had I done? Why had I said such an insulting thing? I even watched as you walked away. And I knew there was something very mixed up in my thinking. In my parents' thinking. Because you were so smart and so nice. And your wife . . . her picture . . . you looked like such a nice person," Pam said, turning to Clementine. "I was so angry at myself that I sat down and cried. I know medical school must be hard," she said, turning back to Clementine. "And you were a doctor. So what in the world had I been taught? Why was I so afraid? Then I listened to you, Professor Raymond, when you spoke at the Student Union Forum. And that made me see how mean I'd been all of my life. Not so much because of what I'd said in school, but because of what I'd not said. So I started reading. I read your grandfather's book, Professor Raymond. The one he wrote with your mother, Dr. Brown. And all of a sudden everything just made sense. History made sense."

"You've come a very long way," Clementine said to Pam Page.

"Yes, ma'am," she said very politely. "Thank you. But I have a whole lot farther to go."

"We all have farther to go," I said.

"Yes, sir. I think the whole country has a whole lot farther to go."

With that, Pam began telling us about her summer in Alabama and her summer in Louisiana. "I sure hope I taught those children something those two summers because they certainly taught me a lot," she said. Then she smiled.

I smiled in return. "That's how it usually works out, Miss Page," I said. "For all that I think I'm teaching my students, in the end it's my students who really teach me. That's hard for someone who's never been a teacher to understand. But it's true. I swear it's true."

By the time our conversation ended late that evening, I knew that just like Simon Milsap, Pam Page was a very promising advisee. I only hoped I would be up to the task of guiding them along their individual ways.

41

The rest of the school year was exactly what Clementine and I both expected and wanted. Her medical practice had found its daily rhythm. My teaching was as compelling as I had hoped. No, we did not hear from the Raymonds. We wrote them a note and thanked them for the trust funds they had established for the twins. We even sent them a photo of the girls taken at three months when they were beginning to be more and more expressive. But we got no reply. However, that did not in any way lessen the joy of our life together. For instance, on Sunday afternoon when we were taking the twins for a walk in the park, each of us pushing the tandem stroller in turn, I got an idea. So the next day I went to Sears and bought as colorful a blanket as I could find. When I brought it home and Clementine asked me why I'd bought another blanket when we had several in the house, I told her it was because all of those blankets were for beds. What I wanted was a play area, a blanket the girls would identify as their magic carpet. When she asked me what I meant, I said, "Just watch."

I spread the blanket out on the front room floor and then brought the girls into the room and lay down with them. Immediately, they started to laugh. When Clementine joined us, it became a family game. Clementine and I lay entwined in each other's arms; we put the twins on top of us. "This is where I want to be, Clementine. Right here, with you and with them," I said. "I will work all day only so I can come home and crawl around on this blanket with you and with Josephine and Abigail."

Clementine laughed. "It's so wonderful having a romantic husband."

"It's so wonderful, having a romantic wife," I said in response. And it was—for both of us. Because from that day on, if I got home after Clementine, I would find her on the blanket with the twins. If she got home after me, that's where she would find the three of us. And the blanket went with us everywhere: to Tampa when we flew to our mothers' home for Thanksgiving. Then when we drove to Edisto Island, South Carolina, where my mother and Ruth Ann met the four of us for a six day winter vacation over the holidays. We took the blanket out into the back yard when we lay together and looked at the clouds or watched the rain sweeping in from the south. We took it to the Savannah River. Yes, before long, it began to show signs of wear and start to fade, but that didn't matter. Not to us, at any rate. As for the girls: each of them found a place in relation to where we lay that became hers. That is what I remember about the rest of that school year and about the next four years: Clementine and me lying together at all sorts of odd angles with two girls crawling all over the two of us as if they were puppies, laughing or crying, as the mood took them. I remember them sleeping next to one another or sleeping curled up in Clementine's arms or my arms or both of our arms.

By spring, both Josephine and Abigail were starting to walk. That changed the world forever. And of course it wasn't just each of the two of them that we had to guard; it was that third girl, the one they conjured between the two of them, if you know what I mean. She's the one who came up with notions the other two individually could not have imagined. It was that third girl—the invisible partner girl—who wanted to go everywhere and see everything and touch everything. Which Clementine and I loved. That was the joy of it all: to be with Clementine and watch her being a mother. For she was gentle and secure and reassuring and warm.

I once told her it was an honor just to be her attendant. She smiled and said, "Tyler, you are not my attendant. You are my husband. The girls adore you. And why not. You are the father every little girl should have." When she said that, I leaned towards her—we were lying on our family blanket in the park close to our house—and kissed her very tenderly on the lips.

"That's exactly the way it felt the first time you kissed me, Tyler," she said.

I smiled more inwardly than outwardly. "That is exactly the way it felt the first time you kissed me, Clementine."

Clementine smiled and made a soft sound and gathered up the girls and crawled up next to me where she lay looking at the clouds moving overhead. "I see a bird," she said.

"Where?" I said.

"Not a real bird. I see a cloud bird," she said, pointing.

"I think it's a gazelle," I whispered.

"A gazelle?" she said. "How is it a gazelle?"

I waited for a moment. "It's a gazelle," I said.

Clementine turned to me and punched me in the ribs. I grunted. She laughed. The girls made little girl sounds of delight.

"No, I was wrong," I said. "It's a bird."

"Told you," Clementine said.

I laughed as the twins started crawling up onto my chest.

42

I do not mean to suggest that just because Clementine and I were now living the life we had dreamed of when we'd first fallen in love and talked of our most fond hopes while sitting in the park in Tampa that we were becoming complacent. Life was too full of things we had to learn for us to do that. Clementine not only continued her medical practice, she also continued to work two afternoons a week in the clinic with children whose parents might otherwise not have been able to provide medical care. In addition, she became a leader in the local chapter of the Congress of Racial Equality, focusing her time on helping to recruit promising young African American high school students from Georgia and South Carolina with the aim of helping them enroll in regional colleges and universities.

I continued teaching. My book was widely enough read in academic circles that I was asked to deliver guest lectures at a number of colleges and universities in Georgia, South Carolina, North Carolina, and Tennessee. On those occasions, I tried very hard to not present myself as an expert on the challenges faced by both African American and increasingly Hispanic families and students. I was keenly aware of my own race. No matter the dedication of my energies and my sympathies, it would have been both arrogant and presumptuous for me to suggest that I understood the conflicts and confusions that people of color experience every day.

Ironically, one of my activities intersected with Clementine's work with CORE when three Augusta State undergraduate students came to me to ask if I would be the faculty sponsor of an academic tutoring club dedicated to working with area African-American and Hispanic elementary and middle school students by bringing them to the University campus for lessons in reading and mathematics. The students said they were well aware that my teaching was very demanding and that my off campus lectures took me away from Augusta at least two days each month. "And we know you have twin daughters, Professor Raymond. So we don't want you to think we're asking you to put in a lot of time," one of the two young men said. "We just need someone to supervise what we want to do, which is to teach kids."

After a conversation with Briggs Dyer, who by then had become the History Department Chair, I was encouraged to accept the students' invitation, which is how my extra curricular activity joined with Clementine's work with CORE, for on several occassions, we ended up responding to the same local schools and the same local students.

By the time the twins were three and were in day care, Clementine and I began to find it harder and harder to keep up with our mothers' desire that we travel to Tampa four or five times a year. As the years passed, they had to come to us if they wanted to spend time with their granddaughters, which they did, of course. After all, both of them knew these were the only two grandchildren they would ever have. As a consequence, the bond that developed between the two generations was wonderful to see. I know Ruth Ann loved and was proud of Clementine, and I know my mother felt the same about me, but watching those two grandmothers with their twin granddaughters was a sight to behold. In fact, one of Clementine's and my favorite things to do was to go to the North Side Shopping Mall and sit in the food court and watch as Ruth Ann and my mother took the girls by their hands and went off to shop for the things which grandmothers seemed born to buy. By the time the four of them got back, loaded down with packages, all four of them were laughing, and the girls were jumping up and down with excitement. It was moments like that, I must confess, that I missed my grandfather most of all. Nothing would have given him greater pleasure than to see me with my daughters, to see his daughter with her granddaughters, and for him to share time with his great-granddaughters. But it was not to be, of course. So I tried very hard not to dwell on the sense of loss. All I could do when those moods came over me was hold Clementine's hand, because I knew she understood what I was feeling without my having to say anything, and to rededicate myself to pursuing those issues that had meant so much to him.

I remember very clearly the day Josephine and Abigail started kindergarten. Yes, they had gone to pre-school from the time they were four, so yes, they understood what going to school meant. But like every other parent that morning who brought a child to Paul Dunbar Elementary School, we also understood that our daughters were crossing a truly significant threshold. I remember Clementine holding my hard harder than she had held it in years as we watched our daughters, who were also holding hands, as they turned and started into the hallway behind the teacher who had come to greet them and take them into the school. I remember both Josephine and Abigail turning and looking at each other and then looking back at us, Josephine on the left, Abigail on the right, and both of them waving. As they then turned back to the students they were following, Clementine put her head on my shoulder and whispered, "How many years for each of them, Professor Raymond?"

"Until they are finished with school?" I said.

"Yes. How many years?"

"Can't say," I said. "It all depends on what they want to do."

"I know that. I'm looking for a prediction," Clementine said.

I smiled and kissed Clementine on the forehead. "Can't say, Doctor Brown. Depends on what they want to do."

Then we turned and walked back to the parking lot and drove back home, where Clementine got out of my car and into her own, waving goodbye as she backed out of the driveway and turned toward her medical offices, and I started toward Augusta State University, having already agreed that at least for that first day, we would meet back at our house and then both of us would go to Dunbar Elementary School to pick the girls up after their first day of class. As I drove to the University that day, I realized perhaps more fully than ever before that this was exactly the life I had wanted—the one I was living. Watching Clementine's car turn the corner, I also realized perhaps more fully than ever before how much I was in love with my wife and companion. Which is why I bought flowers that afternoon and brought them with me when Clementine and I met at our house before driving to Dunbar School. And from that day to this, I have bought Clementine a bouquet of flowers each and every Friday on the premise that no one ever gets tired of being told she is loved.

43

The letter came on June 4th, just one month short of the twins' sixth birthdays. When I saw the Raymond family Virginia return address, I told Clementine I didn't know if I wanted to open it or not. Clementine said, "You have to, Tyler. You know you have to read it." So I did.

It was an invitation which read,

Come Celebrate an Extraordinary Marriage

You are invited to attend
A celebration of the Fifty-Fifth Wedding Anniversary
Of Mildred Marie and Preston Paul Raymond II
July 20, 2002
2 P.M.
At the Ashworth Golf and Country Club
Ashworth Creek, Virginia
RSVP by July 1st

A hand written note attached to the printed invitation added:

Dear Tyler: It would mean a great deal to me if you and your wife and daughters would come join Preston and me on this very important day. You may telephone me if you wish.

The note was signed, Mildred. Her telephone number was written below her signature. I read the invitation twice and the note three times before I looked up to see Clementine watching me. "An invitation," I said, giving it to her so she could read it. Once she had, she gave it back to me. "So what do you want to do?" Clementine asked.

I looked at her for a long silent moment. Then I said, "I don't know."

"I'll do whatever you think is best, Tyler."

I did not reply. Instead, I turned and went through the kitchen and out into the backyard where I walked to the back fence where we'd arranged two Adirondack chairs and a small table. I sat down and leaned back and looked up at the clouds overhead. The trees leaning into our yard blocked out the sun, which was just as well because it was a hot day. I didn't understand. What did Mildred Raymond want? What was she doing? An apology? A change to make amends? Why now? Their anniversary? Was I supposed to care about their wedding anniversary? Why? What were they to me? What was I to them? And Clementine. That would be just great. I'd bring my black wife and my two mixed race daughters to the Ashworth Golf and Country Club to do what? Be an exhibit? Be on show? I'm sure the good folks at the Country Club would be thrilled to see Dr. Clementine Brown and Professor Tyler Raymond show up with their twin daughters in tow. Damn it! It was too late. The whole Raymond clan . . . all of them . . . it was too late. I had a life. I was happy in my life. There wasn't anything I wanted from them. They'd volunteered the trust fund for me. For the girls. I hadn't wanted it. I took it, but I hadn't wanted it. But now. What in the world was I supposed to do? Go and act as if everything was forgotten? Act as if they'd not treated my father and my mother the way they did? To hell with that. To hell with them. They could celebrate their wedding anniversary without me and Clementine and Josephine and Abigail. They didn't need us. And I sure didn't need them.

Then Clementine was standing in front of me holding out a glass of iced tea. "I'd like to buy a new dress," she said. "And I think we should buy new dresses for the girls."

"Clementine . . . " I started to say.

"She's holding out her hand, Tyler. She's getting older. He's getting older. She's reaching for you, Tyler."

"I don't care. I'm not reaching back."

Clementine looked at me. "But you will, Tyler, because you are a kind man."

"I'm not that kind," I said sharply.

"And you are a strong man," she said.

"Not that strong," I said.

Clementine smiled. "You can't lie to me, Tyler Raymond, because I've known you since you were fifteen. And I know you are that kind and that strong. So I will need a new dress. And the girls will need new dresses. I even think you need a new summer suit."

I frowned.

"If you aren't going to call Mildred, I will, because I need to know how the women are going to dress," she said.

"Damn it, Clementine, I don't want . . . " I started to say.

"Tyler," Clementine said sharply. "This isn't about what you want. It's about what that woman needs."

"I'm not going there to forgive her," I said.

"I'm not asking you to forgive her. Or him, either. I'm asking you to be polite. Edward Thomas raised you to be polite."

"Why should I be polite to the two people who . . . "

She cut me off again. "For that very reason."

"What?"

"For that very reason. Because they were not polite to your father or your mother. But now it's your turn. You will be more polite then they were. You will show them you are a proud and dignified man. You will be polite because it is the polite thing to do."

"Clementine, sometimes I don't understand you at all," I said.

"Tyler, I'm not asking you to understand me. I'm asking that you be polite."

I looked at Clementine for a very long time.

"I will need a new dress, Tyler," Clementine said.

I did not respond.

"Tyler," Clementine said very slowly, as if she knew she was about to resolve the issue, "I will need a new dress."

Part Five

Woman, in the . . .language of mythology, represents the totality of what can be known. The hero is the one who comes to know. As he progresses in the slow initiation which is life, the form of the goddess undergoes . . . a series of transfigurations . . . . She lures, she guides, she bids him burst his fetters. And if he can match her import, the two, the knower and the known, will be released from every limitation.

Joseph Campbell
The Hero With a Thousand Faces

1

Following Highway 360 northeast out of Richmond for almost an hour, as the desk clerk at our motel had said we should, I turned our family van into the long tree-lined lane leading to the three large and two smaller buildings that formed the Ashworth Golf and Country Club. As we drove toward the compound area, two young men in uniform vests stepped into the road and directed us to continue driving toward the buildings. Another hundred yards and we were met by another young man who using hand motions gestured we should pull off onto the grass next to the road and park in the same way other cars were parked.

I could feel Clementine watching me as I nosed our mini-van up close to a car already angled off the road. When I turned to glance over my shoulder to make certain I was in the proper place as another car pulled up next to us, Clementine smiled gently, as if to say, "I know you are tense, Tyler. But I am here with you. All three of us are here with you."

I smiled in return with as much enthusiasm as I could muster and turned to Josephine and Abigail. "This is it, girls," I said.

They both smiled. We had spent a week in a rented house on Virginia Beach playing every day in the water, which had thrilled them. The only thing Clementine and I had said about the Raymond wedding anniversary reception was that all four of us had been invited to a very big party in a very nice place by some people who very much wanted to meet them. The fact the girls had gone with Clementine to buy new white dresses and new shoes before we left Augusta and that Clementine was wearing a beautiful new pearl white dress and that even daddy was wearing a new light tan suit and a tie that all three of them had picked out had helped keep them focused on how special the day was going to be without requiring that we provide any more details.

Taking a very deep breath, I opened the driver's side door and walked around to the passengers' side where I helped Clementine out of the van. Then she and I got the girls out of their safety restraints. So there we were, joining in the caravan of walkers heading for the club house, Josephine walking hand in hand with Clementine in the lead with Abigail and me walking behind. It did not take long before we passed the fountain that marked the entrance where we were directed by a very attractive young woman to follow the hallway into the garden on the other side of the building. Other people were ahead of us, of course, just as other people were following.

Then we stepped out into a beautiful garden, three sides of which were formed by the horseshoe shaped building. The fourth side looked out onto a perfectly manicured golf course. As we turned to each other to make some comment about what a pleasure it would be to play a course like that, a voice said, "You must be Tyler."

I turned to face a man who looked remarkably like the pictures I had seen of my father. "I am," I said.

The man held out his hand. "I'm Preston," he said. "Preston the third. I'm your uncle."

I accepted his hand. He smiled what seemed like a very constrained smile and said, "It's a great pleasure to meet you at last. I know my parents are very happy that you've come." Then he turned to Clementine. "And you must be Clementine," he said.

"I am," Clementine said, accepting his hand.

"My mother has told me so much about you. That you're a pediatrician in Augusta. Which she thinks is wonderful." He smiled again, but he did not seem any more comfortable with Clementine than he had with me.

"And you are . . . " he started to say. "You are . . . Josephine," he said, bending down.

"Yes," Josephine said, holding out her hand to be shaken.

"Wonderful. How wonderful," he said. Then he turned to Abigail. "And you are Abigail," he said, holding out his other hand and accepting Abigail's. "You two are so beautiful. You will be the most beautiful women here today." Then he stood, but still speaking to the girls he said, "Along with your mother, of course."

Then Preston turned to me. "I know we've just met, Tyler, but I feel as if I've known you for years. I know my father followed Georgia football so he could see you play. He was very proud."

"I didn't know he'd done that," I said.

"Oh, yes. When Georgia played on television he'd rearrange his whole day just to see you play."

"I'm very flattered," I said, which I knew wasn't much of a response, but it was the best I could do under the circumstances.

"And I know you ran for Georgia Tech for two years, Clementine," he said. "I got to see you run once."

"Really?" Clementine said, as startled by the news that the family had known about her running as I had been about my grandfather following my football career at Georgia.

"Yes. I went to the ACC championships. I think it was your first year. The year Tyler carried you off the track."

Clementine smiled. "I had better days after that," Clementine said.

Preston didn't know what to say next. So he resumed his role as host: "The four of you go ahead and join the others at the bottom of the terrace. The meal will be served in an hour or so. I'll go tell my mother that you're here. I know she wants to see you." Then he turned and was gone into the press of people.

Clementine turned to me. "He's nervous, Tyler. Be patient. He was very kind."

I did not reply.

"Did you know Preston watched Georgia football games on television?" she said.

"No," I said. "I didn't."

"That's rather interesting, wouldn't you say?" Clementine said.

I sighed very deeply. "I guess so."

"Tyler," Clementine said in her Tyler-you-know-that's-not-what-you-really-feel tone of voice.

"Yes," I said, correcting myself and pleasing her. "It's very interesting."

Then I felt my chest tighten. Mildred was coming towards us.

"Tyler, Tyler," she said as she approached. "I am so honored you've come. All four of you. I am so pleased," she said, extending a hand, which I accepted, but not gesturing for me to kiss her cheek although that's what the men and women were doing all around us as they greeted one another.

Mildred was dressed more elegantly this time. Not as over done as I remembered. More subtle. She looked very attractive. It was curious to me that I had not noticed that in Miami or at my graduation. What had I missed before? I wondered. Was it her? Was it me?

"Clementine, I am so very pleased all of you could come," Mildred said, extending her hand, which Clementine accepted. Then like Preston she leaned down and extended her hand to Abigail and then to Josephine, saying only, "My name is Mildred" to each of the girls although I sensed she wanted to say more and explain more. "And you are . . . " she went on, waiting for a response.

"I am Abigail," Abigail said.

"Yes, you are. And you are very pretty, Abigail," Mildred said. "And that means that you are Josephine," she said, holding out her hand for Josephine to shake.

"Yes, ma'am," Josephine said. "I'm Josephine Arway," she said.

"And I'm Abigail Donyen," Abigail said not to be out done.

"Our middle names mean *beautiful*," Josephine said. "Both of us," she said.

"And your names are very right," Mildred said, standing slowly, which appeared to be slightly hard for her. "You are both very beautiful," she said. "But of course, you have a beautiful mother and a very handsome father."

Both of the girls giggled. I think it was at the handsome father part that did it. Then simultaneously Josephine reached and took Clementine's hand and Abigail took mine.

"Well, I am so very happy that all of you could come to this party today. And do you know what the party is for?" Mildred went on.

"No," Josephine said.

"No," Abigail said.

"It's a party to celebrate that my husband and I have been married for a very long time," she said.

Her comment did not mean anything to the girls.

"So we are very glad that you could come celebrate with us," Mildred said. Then she turned and motioned for someone to come join us. "There's someone I want all of you to meet. She's a wonderful woman," Mildred said, leaning down to look at Josephine and Abigail. "And she knows all about all of you," Mildred said. "So she wants to meet you."

Then the young woman was standing at Mildred's side.

2

The young African American woman's name was Dr. Neema Johnson. Mildred told us Dr. Johnson was a psychiatrist who practiced in Richmond. After an awkward silence, Mildred excused herself, saying, "I know I'm leaving you in good hands." Then she was gone.

For a moment, none of the three of us said anything. Josephine and Abigail waited. They looked at Dr. Johnson, who was even more slim than Clementine, somewhat darker complexioned, and as tall me. Dr. Johnson looked at the twins. "I've heard about the two of you," she said. "One of you is Josephine, and the other is Abigail. Isn't that right?"

The girls said that was right. "I'm Josephine," Josephine said.

"I'm Abigail," Abigail said.

Another moment passed. "I know this must be awkward for you," Dr. Johnson went on. "I know a great deal about you. It's somewhat awkward for me as well," she said. "Since I'm Mildred's psychiatrist."

"We understand," Clementine said.

"But we don't know anything about you, Dr. Johnson," I said.

Dr. Johnson smiled. "First, you will have to call me Neema. Because I'd rather not have to spend the evening calling each of you by your titles."

"I'd like that too," Clementine said.

"But we still don't know much about you, Neema," I said.

For a moment, Neema Johnson acted as if she was not sure how to react. My voice had been too sharp. I knew that myself.

"I mean, we'd like to know how you know Mildred. That might make it easier for the three of us to talk," I said, trying to back track.

"Mildred came to our group practice three years ago," Neema said. "She wanted someone to talk with. She chose me."

I looked as if I didn't understand fully.

"I know it's interesting, her wanting an African American psychiatrist. It's been interesting for me as well. But her request was specific. There are two white men in our group and one white woman, but Mildred said she'd been sent to me by a mutual acquaintance to talk with me."

I nodded as if I understood although I really didn't.

"And so you've learned something about Tyler," Clementine said.

"I've learned a great deal," she said. "About both of you. All of it good, I must add."

"Really?" I said.

"Mildred thinks very highly of both of you," Neema went on. "I think you have to try to believe that. I can't talk about our conversations, of course, but you have to at least try to believe that. She thinks very highly of both of you. And of your mother, Tyler."

I frowned. "That's a tad hard to believe," I said.

"I'm sure it is. And I'm treading on very thin ice to say that to you, because of my relationship with Mildred. But I think you should give her some credit, Tyler. She is reaching out to you. To both of you. All four of you."

Clementine turned to me. "I think I should take the girls for a walk. They need to be able to look around."

I said I agreed. Then I turned to Dr. Johnson. "Can I get you something to drink?" I said.

"Yes. That would be nice. I believe there are drinks being served at the bar."

We turned and walked toward a long table where two bartenders were pouring wine for people who were standing and waiting. As we did, a man stepped into our path and said, "You must be Tyler Raymond."

I stopped and looked at him. He was smiling. A woman was standing with him. She looked like she must be his wife.

"I'm Billy Tyre," he said. "This is my wife Betty." He extended his hand for me to shake, which I did.

"And this must be your wife, Clementine," he said smiling broadly.

"No. It isn't," I said quickly.

"I'm Dr. Neema Johnson."

The man looked embarrassed.

"My wife is walking around with our twin daughters," I said.

"Twins? My word," Betty Tyre said. "Twin girls."

"Yes. It won't be hard to find them," I said. "They're wearing identical white dresses, even though we don't usually dress them alike," I said.

The man smiled one of those how-do-I-get-out-of-this smiles.

"It's very nice to meet you," I said.

"Likewise," Billy said. "And I hope you have a good time today. There's a whole lot of nice people here who want to meet you." Then he turned away, and he and Betty disappeared into the crowd of people he obviously knew.

"That says a lot," I said quietly.

"Yes, it does. But I wouldn't worry about it. He meant well," Neema said. I smiled, and we went on and got two glasses of wine.

"I'll get a glass for Clementine," I said. "For when she comes back."

Neema smiled. "Would you like to sit down?" she said, motioning toward a stone wall that divided the terrace from the grass that led to the golf course.

"Yes. Let's do that." So we worked our way past people until we were free to sit on the wall.

"I know this must be hard for you, Tyler," Neema said.

As usual, when I don't know what to say, I didn't reply.

"And I know that you know that I can't betray my professional relationship with Mildred when we talk."

I said I knew that.

"She's not trying to interfere with your life. I can say that as a friend."

"That may be true. It probably is true. The Raymonds haven't interfered with my life. In fact, it was the trust fund they set up for me that helped both Clementine and me complete our college studies. And I'm sure the same will be true for Josephine and Abigail. The trust fund they've established will support their college educations in the same way. But you have to understand there's a long history here. A legacy that goes back to my father and my mother. My father rejected the Raymonds for a lots of reasons. They rejected him and my mother in response. What am I supposed to do with that, Dr. Johnson?"

Neema was quiet for a moment.

"I can't tell you what you should feel," she said quietly. "That would be inappropriate. All I can do is urge you to be as patient with them as you can. Mildred is reaching out to you, Tyler. Try to keep in mind that Mildred lost everything when she lost your father."

"Is that what she thinks?" I said.

"Yes. I think she feels that she lost everything when she lost your father."

"When he wouldn't go to the University of Virginia or when he married my mother or when he died in Viet Nam?" I said, my voice sharp, hard.

Neema Johnson was quiet for a moment. Clementine approached us and sat down next to me. I gave her the glass of wine I'd gotten for her. "Thank you," she said.

"And where are the girls?" I asked.

"The Raymonds arranged for a tram to take all of the children for a ride around the golf course."

"And they're being supervised?" I said. "They'll be okay?"

"They'll be fine. I counted ten children. All of them were laughing when the tram train went over the hill following the golf cart path."

I smiled. "Dr. Johnson and I were just talking about the Raymonds," I said.

"I assumed you were," Clementine said. Then she leaned forward and looked at Neema Johnson. "But I thought she asked us to call her Neema, Tyler."

"I did," Neema said.

I did not comment.

"I think Tyler is feeling some tension," Neema said to Clementine.

"He certainly is," Clementine said. "And I've tried to tell him he shouldn't. It seems to me that Mildred at least is trying to reach out to him."

"I said the same thing," Neema replied.

I smiled. "This is great," I said. "This is poetry."

"What's poetry?" Clementine said.

"This. Us sitting here. Together. And sitting here . . . at this country club. A white guy and two beautiful black women. Two educated black women, I should add. At a club that both of you know good and well must have been restricted until not long ago."

Neema smiled. "That may be, Tyler. But it doesn't matter now, does it. About the history of the club being restricted or not. What matters is now."

"So we just forget the past?" I said.

"That's not what she means, Tyler," Clementine said.

"That's not what I mean, Tyler," Neema said.

"Okay. So what do you mean?" I said.

Neema looked away for a moment. "I mean," she began, not turning back to look at either Clementine or me, "that there is nothing any of us can do about the past. I mean that all we can do is deal with the present. All we can do is try to influence the future."

I turned to Neema. "With all of the psychiatrists in Richmond . . . and I assume there must be a number . . . why do you think Mildred came specifically to you?"

"Because I am a woman and because I am African American," Neema said in response.

I was startled, not by the truth of what Neema had said but by the fact she had said it so quickly.

"Well, that's an honest answer," I said.

"And it's the answer you expected, isn't it," Clementine said.

"It's the truth I expected. I'm not so sure it's the answer I expected," I said.

"Did you think I wouldn't tell the truth?" Neema asked.

"I'm not sure what I think. I don't know you well enough to make any assumptions," I said.

"And you don't know Mildred Raymond well enough to make any assumptions, either," Neema said quickly.

I did not reply.

"You are her only hope," Neema said.

I waited for a moment before replying. "Her only hope . . . for what?" I said.

"For posterity. For a legacy. For grandchildren," Neema said.

"And Preston, her son?" I asked.

Neema hesitated. Then she said, "Preston the third won't be fathering any children."

"Ah," Clementine said quietly.

"And Mildred's and Preston's daughter is dead," Neema added.

"Yes, and I know where she died and how she died and why she died," I said.

"That may be true. You may know where she died and how she died and why she died. But that doesn't alter the fact that she died. So you and Clementine . . . you are her only link to the future. Your daughters are her only grandchildren."

"And we won't have any others," Clementine said. "I can't have any more children," she said.

"I didn't know that," Neema said.

"Far too many dangers," I said. "There is no way I'd want Clementine to take the risk."

Neema was quiet. Then she said, "So for the Raymonds, their name will be . . . what? Carried on by your two daughters? Lost because there will be no possibility of a son?"

"For the Raymonds," I said quietly but firmly, my voice edged with a trace of bitterness at the Raymonds rather than at my daughters, "for the Raymonds, their blood, so to speak, will be carried into the future by two girls who are of mixed African American and European American blood, which is the most wonderful irony of all, wouldn't you say? Especially given the family's early history as part of the slave trade."

Neema was quiet. Clementine was quiet.

"Because their only grandson . . . and I am their only grandson . . . their only grandchild . . . fell in love when he was fifteen with the most beautiful, intelligent, caring woman he knew he would ever meet in his life. Who just happened to be a mixed blood herself, but who for the world was and is an African American woman . . . an African American princess, I might add. And I am serious about the princess part. Because if you were to go to the Ivory Coast in Africa, as we did, and meet any number of Kru African women, you'd hear the story of how Clementine Camille Brown . . . Raymond," I said, adding my name to Clementine's, "is the great-great-great-great granddaughter of a Kru tribal princess who was kidnapped and sold into slavery . . . which is how she ended up here, in America, meeting me and marrying me and birthing our two daughters, who also carry the same legacy, if the Kru women can be believed. Which means sitting here with you and me, Neema, is a Kru African Princess. And that is who," I said, "this Princess," I said, turning to Neema but touching Clementine's hand . . . "that is who the Raymonds can thank for having any grandchildren at all." I looked at Neema. "Now, if that isn't the most wonderful and most historically appropriate irony of all, then I don't know anything about history, and I don't know anything about irony."

"You've waited a long time to say that, haven't you, Tyler," Neema said.

I looked at her. "A very, very long time," I said.

Neema was quiet for a moment. Then she leaned forward and looked at Clementine. "Is he always like this?" she said, smiling.

"No," Clementine replied. "Sometimes he is rather passionate." Then the two of them laughed their most sincere affection as I sat in the middle.

As they did, Mildred approached, her expression saying something important was about to happen.

3

After a moment's hesitation, Mildred explained that food would be served in less than an hour but that in the meantime she hoped both Clementine and I would come with her because her husband, Preston, wished to speak to both of us. When Clementine asked about the children—when they might be coming back—Neema said she would bring them to us when they returned.

Following Mildred, we went back into the country club and down a hall to a private office. When we entered, we found Preston waiting to greet us. And while his words said he was pleased we had come, the tension in his face suggested something was on his mind.

"I cannot tell you how happy I am that both of you have come," he said, shaking Clementine's hand first and then mine, lingering for a moment before he released me. "And I'm very eager to meet both of your daughters once we finish here."

Clementine and I waited.

"There is something I need to explain to you, Tyler . . . and to you, too, Clementine, although I believe you will understand why I will address my comments mostly to Tyler since it concerns our son . . . his father."

Clementine said she understood.

"Mildred," Preston said, turning his wife. "You wanted to say something to Tyler first?"

"Yes. I do, Preston," Mildred answered. Then she turned to me. After a moment, because it was obvious whatever it was she was going to say was very difficult for her, she went on. "Tyler, please believe me when I say that I loved my son, Robert. Please believe me when I tell you that more than anything else in the world, I wanted to make peace with him. But then it was too late. And all I could do was mourn his death. So for years I lived with the horrible truth that my grief would never go away. That there was nothing I could do. Then Preston arranged for us to meet in Miami. And that is when I knew that someday, somehow, if you would accept my gesture, I might be able to begin to make peace with my sense of loss."

I did not know what to say.

"I am not asking for you to change anything about your life," Mildred went on. "You are a splendid man. You have made a very good life. Your mother and your grandfather Thomas raised you very well. And you are obviously wonderfully happy with Clementine and with your daughters." She hesitated for a moment. "But before it is too late . . . before any more times goes by . . . I wanted to ask if there was any way you could let me share in your life, Tyler? I want so very much to love you and Clementine and . . . I want so very much to love my great-granddaughters."

Mildred's hands were shaking. Tears brimmed over and ran down her cheeks. I stood still. I had no words. I did not know what to do. Then as always Clementine came to my rescue, teaching me in one gesture more than I ever could have reasoned out for myself when she stepped forward and put her arms around Mildred's shoulders and let the older woman press her face against hers as she said, "We would like nothing more than for you to love your great-granddaughters, Mildred. We would like nothing more than for you and Preston to be able to do that."

The two women stood with their arms around each other for some time. Then Clementine stepped back and turned to me. "Tyler," she said very quietly.

I knew exactly what Clementine expected of me. And I knew she was right. So I stepped toward Mildred and said, "There is nothing we would like more than to have you be a part of our lives, Mildred."

Mildred was shaking with grief and pleasure and hurt and joy. She did not say anything more. She simply enfolded me in her arms and pressed her face against mine. A moment passed. Then she stepped back and turned to Preston. "Now you have something to say, don't you, Preston?"

Preston hesitated for a moment. "Yes, I do, Mildred." Then he turned to Clementine and me. "When your father left us and went to the University of Maryland, I was very angry with him. I felt as if he was rejecting his family. I was a proud man at the time, Tyler. Too proud. Too arrogant. I know that now. Because what I couldn't see was the courage it took for your father to go his own way. I couldn't see how hard it was for him to call into question things about his family history that he found offensive. I should have but I didn't, which was my failure, not his."

Preston stopped for a moment and looked at me before going on. "When he married your mother, I thought it was more of the same. I only saw what he was rejecting, not what he stood for. That was my error. And it cost us . . . Mildred and me . . . it cost us our relationship with him. And with your mother and with you. And that was wrong as well."

I wanted to speak, but I had no words. Clementine moved to my side and took my right hand.

"When your father went to Viet Nam, I was very bitter. He did not have to go. He did not need to go. But that isn't the way he saw it. He told me in the one conversation we had before he left that even if he thought the war was wrong, he did not believe it was right that he should avoid going because he was educated and privileged and that other young men without those advantages had to go." Preston waited for a moment before going on. "I assume you know what happened as a consequence of his decision."

"I do, sir," I said. I felt Clementine's grip tighten on my hand.

"I don't know how to say this, Tyler. Because you may not know everything." Then he moved to the desk where he picked up a small leather case. Then the turned to me. "Your father was decorated because of his bravery, Tyler. Your mother may have known, but I was so bitter about everything . . . I was so blindly bitter that after Robert was buried I had no more contact with Elizabeth or with you. And so I have cheated both of you. And I cannot do that any longer."

With that, he held out the small leather case. "Open it, Tyler. Please," he said.

I opened the case very slowly. It was the Purple Heart Medal. I was stunned. I should not have been, but I was.

"I am giving this to you, Tyler. By rights it belongs to your mother, but she has every reason to not ever want to see us again. So I am giving it to you."

I stood looking at the medal for a moment. I did not want to take it out of the leather case. I felt Clementine's hand on my back even though she did not say anything.

"There's one more thing, Tyler. Equally important. Maybe even more important," Preston said.

"Sir?" I replied, turning to him.

"There is another medal that I want to give you. Like the Purple Heart, by rights it belongs to your mother, but for the same reason I'm giving it to you," Preston said. With that, he held out the second small case sitting on the desk.

I handed the Purple Heart case to Clementine as I accepted the second case from Preston. Then I opened the second case carefully. I immediately recognized what it was: the Bronze Star. I was speechless.

"What is it?" Clementine said.

"It's a Bronze Star," Preston said.

I turned to Clementine. "It's a Bronze Star," I said. "For Bravery."

Clementine said my name very softly.

"My father was a hero," I whispered.

"Yes, he was, Tyler. He didn't have to fly that last mission," Preston said.

"Grandfather Thomas told me," I said.

"I didn't pull any strings, Tyler. I promise. I could have. There were people in the administration who owed me favors. But your father was awarded this medal because that's who he was. That's what he did. And that's why he died." Preston was quiet for a moment. Then he looked at me very intently. "I didn't tell your mother about the medals when the army brought them to me. I kept these from her because I blamed her for our losing our son. But I was unfair. It was my hurt talking. It took over my heart. But I can't be angry any longer. I am too old. My anger has hurt too many people. Your mother has suffered. I am afraid I contributed to her loss when I should have tried to console her."

"I understand," I said quietly, although that probably wasn't true.

"I hope you do," Preston said. "And I hope you will forgive me," he said. "I don't know if your mother will ever forgive us. Forgive both Mildred and me. But I hope you will forgive me because the anger was more mine than Mildred's. She would have reached out many times, but I fought her. So it was my fault. When I watched you on television play football for Georgia, you looked so much like your father. I knew then that it was my fault that we didn't know you and that you didn't know us." With that Preston stopped talking. There was nothing more to be said. I turned to Preston and allowed him to come into my arms where we stood for some time without speaking. Then I heard Mildred say, "Preston, it's time we join our guests."

"Yes, Mildred. You're right. It is time we join our guests for lunch. And it is time I meet Josephine and Abigail. And it's time I introduce Clementine and Tyler and our great-granddaughters to all of our friends before we eat."

With that Clementine and I followed Mildred out of the room and back along the hallway out to the garden area. I brought the two medal cases with me. Preston followed. As we walked, I glanced at Clementine. "Jessica," I said under my breath.

I saw Clementine wince. She looked at Mildred, who was walking ahead of us with Preston hand in hand. Then she turned and whispered, "When they are ready, Tyler."

I started to reply, but she said in a hard whisper, "When they are ready. Not before."

I said nothing more but followed Preston and Mildred as they led us into a large dining room. As they did, the guests stood. Preston motioned they should all sit, which they began to do as he led us to a very large table set for seven people where Preston III waited. And true to his word, after we were joined by Josephine and Abigail, who had been brought back from their ride, Preston stood and announced that he and Mildred very much appreciated that so many of their friends had come that day to celebrate their wedding anniversary. Then he said, "We are so very pleased to not only to have our son, Preston III, with us today, but we had also been joined by our late son Robert's son, Tyler, and by Tyler's wife, Clementine, and by our two lovely twin great-granddaughters, Josephine and Abigail."

Before the gathering of family and friends could react to what Preston had said, Mildred stood and turning to the four of us said, "We cannot tell you how proud we are today that the four of you and our son Preston have come to help us celebrate this very special occasion."

At that point, it was obvious the gathering must have approved of what both Preston and Mildred said, because before Clementine and I knew what was happening, they were applauding, and we were being asked to join Preston II in standing. So Clementine and I did, Clementine picking up Josephine and standing her on her chair so the audience could see her at the same time I was doing the same thing for Abigail, which was when I leaned close to Clementine and whispered, "I'm going to write Jessica's biography."

"What?" Clementine whispered, trying to hear me as the applause began to die down and the four of us and Preston III took our seats.

"I said, I'm going to write Jessica Raymond's biography."

Clementine nodded and then turning to me so only I could hear, she said, "I assumed you would." And for a moment, I swear, for a moment the two of us were back on the Tampa Coast High School football field after my first junior varsity game when I was walking with my grandfather, and Clementine had surprised me by coming down out of the stands to walk next to me so she could say, "You played very well, Tyler," and my heart had swelled with joy. My heart had swelled with unspeakable joy.

Then it was August, and the four of us found ourselves riding out Hurricane Max in a school gymnasium where we met Arnold and his wife Marie in what I now contend was the second of the three events that both prompted and will end this narration. For after that restless night when Clementine and I lay huddled together with Josephine and Abigail, and Clementine said, "I did not marry you, Tyler, because you are a white man, and I did not marry you so our daughters could be more white than black," I found myself thinking back over my relationship with Clementine, thinking about her wisdom, her compassion, her strength, all of which she had shared with me in every possible way every day since we first met in ninth grade biology class, all of which has contributed in more ways than I can ever define to who I am and what I do. In short, Clementine has been and I know always will be not just the love of my life, the joy of my life, she will always be the *why* of my life.

So that night lying with her in the gymnasium, it hurt me very much that she would feel compelled to make her statement to me that she had not married me because I was a white man and because she wanted her children to be more white than black. After all, we had been through all manner of experiences together, some of which had to do with race and racism, but most of which had nothing to do with race. We had fallen in love, participated in our love, maintained our love, fought for our love, and then consummated our love. By the time we got back to Augusta after the hurricane passed, all either of us wanted was to simply get back to our routine, back to our perfectly normal life. The fact I spent six weeks researching the Australian government's racial and racist Aboriginal policy told me many things about racism in Australia, racism in America, racism in general. But it did not have anything to do with Clementine's and my relationship. In fact, I thought she had forgotten about the issue until one evening in December the question of our differing races came up again. Ironically, it seemed to me that it came up at a time when there was no obvious provocation, which is not the same as saying there was not a catalyst. For as has happened many times in the past and as will undoubtedly happen many times in the future, it was Clementine's intuitive intelligence that raised the issue and defined the issue just as it was Clementine who, in her usual wise but unapologetic way, dropped the issue without warning into my intellectual and moral lap, so to speak.

5

Although Augusta is a relatively small city, it has the advantage of being the home of the Augusta Ballet, a professional dance company that stages a season of dance performances each year downtown at the Imperial Theatre on Broad Street, to which Clementine and I have been buying season tickets each year since we moved to the city.

In addition, Augusta Ballet also runs a school of dance. That fall when they were six years old, Josephine and Abigail both said they wanted to take dance lessons just like a number of their school friends. So Clementine and I visited the ballet school, after which we enrolled them in dance classes. Impressed by the quality of both the company and the school, we were both pleased when the company announced it was time for their annual holiday production of "The Nutcracker," a ballet that has become the staple of most professional and school companies all over the country. We were even more pleased when the twins came home and announced they had been cast as party children and would appear on stage in the opening scene of the production. When we told Ruth Ann and my mother that the girls were going to appear on the stage with other dancers from the school and with the professional company, they said they were coming for opening night.

The news their grandmothers were coming to see them perform delighted Josephine and Abigail, of course. Then Clementine said we should also invite the Raymonds.

"You're sure about that?" I said.

"Tyler, you know you have to invite them. Maybe they can't come. But with all they've done for us over the years, and especially for the way they both reached out to us in July, it's the polite thing to do. You certainly wouldn't want them to learn their great-granddaughters had danced in 'The Nutcracker' but they hadn't been invited to attend."

She was right, of course.

"What do I do about my mother?" I said.

"You tell her about the wedding anniversary celebration. You tell her what both Mildred and Preston said. You tell her about the medals."

I said I would.

The next weekend, when Ruth Ann and my mother flew to Augusta, I went for a long walk with my mother in the morning and told her what the Raymonds had said and done at the country club.

My mother was quiet for a very long time. "What do you want me to do, Tyler?" she said. "Because if you think they felt bitter over the years then you need to know how I felt."

"All right. Tell me," I said.

"Right now?"

"Yes, because this is the time we have before the production opens tonight to which the Raymonds are coming as well."

"The Raymonds are what?"

"The Raymonds are coming."

"Tyler, why didn't you tell me that before I flew to Augusta?" she said sharply.

"How would I have done that? On the telephone? In a letter? And what would you have done if I'd done either one of those things?"

"I don't know."

"Yes you do."

My mother looked at me. I could see the conflict and confusion in her eyes, in her expression. "Yes, I do," she finally said.

"You'd have said, 'Why didn't you wait to tell me face to face?' Right?"

My mother smiled a thin but sincere smile. "You're probably right."

"I know I'm right," I said. So I tried to explain what both Mildred and Preston had done when we'd met privately before the wedding celebration dinner. I told her about the medals. She was as surprised as I had been. Not that my father had been brave, but that he had been awarded medals and that she had not known.

My mother looked as if she wanted to say something. Then she didn't.

"They not only wanted me to forgive them," I said. "They hope you will forgive them as well."

"Me forgive them? Tyler, do you know what you're asking?"

"I think so," I said. "I may not. But I think so."

"They rejected their son, Tyler. They rejected me."

"I know that. And they know that. And they know they were wrong when they did. They have been in pain ever since. Mildred lost her son, mother. Preston lost his son. They cannot undo what was done. They cannot go back and erase the fact they did not talk to him or receive his letters. And they have been grieving ever since. They may not have shown it to anyone else. But they have been grieving. Partly for their son. Partly for the way their relationship with him fractured. Now they hope you will forgive them. They can't go to my father. But they can come to you. They can come to you and to me."

My mother was silent for a very long time.

"What would Grandpa Edward have done, mother? What would he have wanted you to do?" I said.

"He would have said . . . . I don't know what he would have said."

"I think you do."

My mother turned away. "What would he have said?"

"He would have said that yes, it is hard to forgive. But if they are asking you to forgive them how can you withhold it? That's what I think he would have said."

My mother turned back to me. There were tears in her eyes. "My father was a noble man," she said. "More noble than me."

"Yes, mother, he was a noble man. But he was not more noble than you."

"It was so long ago," she said. "Maybe the bitterness has simply become a part of who I am."

"Mother, bitterness hardens people. You are not hard. You have carried your bitterness around for all of the years since they rejected my father. But that does not mean the bitterness is you."

My mother smiled. "How did you become so intelligent, Tyler?" she asked.

"I had very good teachers," I said. "All of my life. I had very special teachers. And now I have Clementine."

My mother turned and took my hand as we continued to walk. It was clouding over. It would be cooler by evening. That's what the *Augusta Chronicle* said that morning. It would be cooler, which meant all of us would have to dress in warm clothes.

6

Because the twins had to be at the stage door by 3 P.M. so they could begin preparing for the production, Clementine and I drove them downtown to the Imperial Theatre where we kissed them goodbye and said we'd meet them after the ballet, and we'd all go out for dinner. Then we drove back to our house where we and our mothers finished dressing for the evening. When we were all ready, the four of us drove back downtown, arriving with enough time to spare so we could stop for sandwiches and coffee at Tancred's Australian Grill across the street from the Imperial. After we finished our meals, we walked back to the theatre and went in.

The company was still in class on the stage, so the theatre was not open to the public yet. With twenty five minutes to spare, Clementine said she wanted to go for a walk with me, so we gave Ruth Ann and my mother their tickets and then stepped back out into the afternoon, both of us gathering the collars of our coats up around our ears.

"I've got a question for you, Tyler," Clementine said as we turned and started walking.

Somehow I had known she was going to have a question for me. I just hadn't known what it would be.

"I want to talk about how you're going to feel when the girls start to date," Clementine said.

"When they start to do what?"

"When they start to date."

"Clementine, they're six years old. We've got ten years or so before we have to think about them dating."

"Tyler, you and I were fifteen."

"All right. We have nine years before we have to think about them dating."

"Fine. Nine years. But what are you going to think in nine years?"

"Clementine, you have to be kidding. How do I know what I'll think in nine years? What in the world are you talking about?"

"You remember the Australian. You know what he was saying in so many words. You've been reading. I've seen you."

"Yes, Clementine, I have been reading. But when have you seen me not reading?"

"That's not the point."

"Then what is the point?"

"I want to know how you are going to react when the girls start dating."

"I don't know what you mean," I said.

"Tyler. You know good and well what I mean."

"All right. You're right. I do know what you mean. Or at least I think I know what you mean. But the truth is I don't want to know what you mean . . . if you know what I mean," I said, smiling my stop-it-Clementine smile.

"Tyler, we have to talk about race," Clementine said.

I stopped and looked at her for a moment. "Clementine, we are taking a nice walk before our daughters go on the stage in a ballet for the very first time. There will never be another night like this one. So why do you want to talk about race right now?"

"Because we are going to see them on the stage for the first time. And they will be beautiful. The audience will see them. The audience will think they are beautiful."

"And?"

"And someday before very long . . . and I mean before very long . . . one of them is going to come home and say she has been asked by a boy to go to a movie or a dance or a game at school because the boy thinks she is beautiful," Clementine said.

"Yes, I supposed that will happen, Clementine," I said. "So what do you want me to say? Tell me what you want me to say, and I'll tell you if I can say it or not."

"What do you mean?"

"I mean, it sounds like you've got some kind of bee in your bonnet, Miss Clementine Camille. Which means you've already got in mind what you want me to say. So what do you want me to say?"

"You could start by answering the question."

"And what is the question?"

"The question is . . . what are you going to do . . . if a black boy asks one of our daughters to go to a movie or to a dance or to a game?"

"Maybe she'll be asked on a date by a white boy," I said.

"Maybe. That's certainly possible. But that's not the question I'm asking. I'm asking what are you going to say . . . a white man married to a black woman . . . father of two lovely mixed race daughters . . . what are you going to say if the boy is black?"

I stopped walking. "Clementine, this is silly. We don't need to have this conversation tonight standing here on the sidewalk on Broad Street."

"No, we don't have to. But I've got you alone for a moment, so I want to know what you are going to say?"

"To the girls or to you or to the young man?"

"To the girls. That's the most important part. What are you going to say to the girls?"

I stopped walking and turned and looked at Clementine. I looked at my wrist watch. "We need to turn around and start back," I said.

"I don't want to turn around and go back right now. I want to know what you are going to say to them."

"Clementine, you have blind-sided me. And that's not fair. If we were at home alone and had been talking about other things and then you'd brought this up, maybe I'd be willing to give you an answer. But this isn't fair. This isn't a place where we can sit and think and talk about something as complicated as our daughters dating boys," I said.

Clementine was frustrated. I could see it in her eyes. When she is frustrated because I resist jumping with both feet into some subject she wants to discuss, there is a particular way she holds her lips. "Tyler, I hate it when you won't talk to me about serious things," she went on.

We had turned and were crossing the street toward the theatre when I stopped in the middle of the green space that divides the boulevard and said, "Clementine, that's not fair, and you know it. I'm prepared to talk about almost any serious subject if we can do so in the right setting. But tonight . . . we're going to the ballet with your mother and my mother. And from what Mildred said when she and I talked on the telephone, the Raymonds have flown all the way to Augusta and have tickets and will join us after the performance. So why have you chosen this particular night to bring the subject of our six year old daughters going out on dates?"

"That isn't the whole subject, Tyler. The whole subject is how are you going to react if the boy who wants to take one of our daughters to a movie or a dance or a game is African-American?"

Without replying, I crossed the second half of the street. Clementine followed. When we arrived in front of the theatre, I turned to her and said, "Clementine, we are right now almost inside the front door of the theatre. I can see your mother across the lobby. I can see my mother. So this is not where we should be having this conversation, no matter what you think or no matter how serious the issue is for you."

Clementine turned away. "We're not through with this conversation, Tyler. You know that, don't you?" she said without looking at me.

I sighed. "Yes, Clementine, I know you well enough to know this isn't the end of this conversation. But right now, since you've raised the subject . . . right now please give me time to think about an answer," I said.

"I don't want some cliché kind of response, Tyler. You know that don't you?" she said, turning back to me.

"Clementine, when have I ever tried to avoid a serious conversation with you by resorting to clichés?"

"Never. Not that I can remember, at least."

"Then have a little faith, will you? We'll talk about this very soon, even if I think you're jumping the gun," I said.

Then we entered the lobby and walked down the aisle to our seats. The hall was beginning to fill up. Our mothers were already seated. I stepped back to let Clementine go into the row first, which meant she could sit next to her mother. I followed. I could see Mildred and Preston Raymond four rows farther down the rows of seats and to our left. They apparently had not seen us yet.

All four of us opened our programs and were reading the history of the Augusta Ballet and the dancers' biographies. After a moment of impatiently turning several pages, I leaned over to Clementine and whispered, "When it happens . . . no matter who the boy is, Clementine . . . no matter his race . . . I will take the girl for a walk . . . or both girls if both have been asked . . . and I will tell her or them how we met and how we fell in love. And I will tell her a little at least what we went through to be together." I paused for a moment. Before Clementine could respond, I went on. "I will tell her how much I love you. And I will tell her that I am the most fortunate man in the world because I get to love the most wonderful woman in the world."

Clementine was quiet for a moment. The lights in the theatre were beginning to dim. I could feel her looking at me. Then she said, "And that's it? That's all you're going to say? You won't say anything more?" just as the music began to play.

"No," I said in a whisper as the curtain went up. "I won't, Clementine, because I think that will be enough."

After a moment, the first dancers appeared on the stage. As they did, Clementine leaned over and very gently put her head on my shoulder and pressed her lips against my ear and whispered, "Good answer, mister. That's a very good answer" at exactly the moment Josephine and Abigail came on stage, which told both Clementine and me that a brand new chapter in our life together was about to begin.

Author's Afterword

Clementine Camille: An American Romance is a work of fiction, the fact it is narrated in the first person by a young historian notwithstanding. Therefore, the characters that animate the story are fictional. However, in the process of writing the novel, on a number of occasions when I assigned names to characters who interacted with the heroine and hero or their family members, I used the names of members of my family or people I have known during my lifetime for whom I feel great regard. Call it my way of paying them respect and of expressing my affection. At the same time, the names given to those characters do not portray the real persons; i.e., the professions of the real people differ from the professions of the fictional characters. The exception is the case of a number of doctors, although in those instances the doctors' specialties have been changed to serve the needs of the story.

Interestingly enough, as the novel began to take shape and I told family members and friends what I was doing, those with whom I talked said they thought that was a nice gesture on my part. In particular, I trust the Rev. Dr. Marni Harmony, who really is a Unitarian minister, will also accept my placing her in the novel in her role as a cleric as my way of thanking her for the role she has in the past and continues to play in my life.

The role of Vince Dooley, the former head coach of the University of Georgia football team, requires special explanation. Unlike Tyler Raymond, I did not play football for the Georgia Bulldogs. However, I did have occasion in 1984 to meet Coach Dooley at the banquet honoring Orlando, Florida, area football players, one of whom was a young man I coached. When Vince Dooley spoke that evening, I was so impressed by his demeanor and his comments that I began following both his team and his own career with interest. Over the years, I found that my first impression was validated; he was a coach of uncommon skill and a man of personal integrity. When the story of Clementine Camille Brown and Tyler Thomas Raymond unfolded in my imagination, I discovered to my surprise that Tyler not only ended up playing football at the University of Georgia, he wished to play for Coach Dooley for both personal and worthy reasons. Thus, Coach Vince Dooley and his wife, Barbara, a woman I have also come to admire from afar, appear in a number of important scenes in the novel in both heroic and mentoring roles. I trust the real-life Dooleys will accept my use of their names for wonderfully admirable fictional characters as a gesture of sincere respect. Perhaps some time in the future I will get to meet and thank them for conducting themselves personally and professionally in ways that I continue to admire.

Ronald John Vierling

Born in Des Moines, Iowa, in 1938, Ronald was educated in the public schools before attending the Chicago Art Institute. After service in the army, he completed his B.F.A. Degree in art and English at Drake University in 1963. He then began what became a forty-year teaching career at five independent college preparatory schools in California, Missouri, and Florida, taking time out to earn his M.A. Degree in English from the University of Wyoming in 1973. In addition, he has also conducted further independent graduate research studies at the University of Wales, Swansea, focusing on the Rhondda Valley novels of labor-organizer Lewis Jones.

The father of five adult children, three of whom have been or are today English teachers, Ronald lives with his wife, Joyce Davidsen, a history teacher, in Orlando, Florida.

Ronald is the author of a volume of poetry, *The Prairie Rider Cantos*, a volume of stories, *[W]rites and Rituals*, and *The Kings Point Papers: The Maritime Court-Martial of Captain Ebenezer Ahab*. His Judaica drama, *Common Ground*, was the Florida New Play of the Year in 1999-2000. At present, he is writing *Clementine Camille: An American Memoir*, and plans to write a third and final volume, *Clementine Camille: An American Life*.

About Clementine Camille

Opening in Tampa, Florida, in the fall of 1980, *Clementine Camille* is the story of a young African-American girl who at age fifteen falls in love with a young Caucasian-American boy, Tyler Raymond. After Tyler grows up to become an accomplished historian, he decides to write a first-person account of his life with Clementine as his affectionate tribute to the girl and then woman and wife he continues to adore. Central to his portrayal is his account of the ways Clementine and Tyler must face the hard facts of American racism when it manifests itself in subtle aside comments made by strangers as well as emotional confrontations with angry individuals who would wish the young couple serious harm. As a part of his attempt to express Clementine's extraordinary person, Tyler's narration also demonstrates the profound and enduring significance of the wise and sensitive adult family members who stand by their children through every trial and tribulation as affectionately as they do every success and triumph. Thus, *Clementine Camille: An American Romance* is just that: a joyful and steadfast if at times difficult romance that very likely would not and could not happen anywhere else in the world except the United States.

www.ingramcontent.com/pod-product-compliance
Lightning Source LLC
LaVergne TN
LVHW050910080826
845145LV00001B/42

* 9 7 8 1 5 9 9 3 2 0 0 4 5 *